THE GHOSTS
OF
HAYWARD HALL

THE GHOSTS

OF

HAYWARD HALL

Lainie Jane Gray

LJG

A catalogue record for this book is available from the National Library of Australia

National Library of Australia Prepublication data service

Author: Lainie Jane Gray
Title: **THE GHOSTS OF HAYWARD HALL**
ISBN: 978-1-7643004-0-7

CONTENTS

1 AUTUMN LEAVES

Sunday 12 October 1975

There was no one to meet her.

A handful of leaves chased the disappearing train, falling back to earth in a flurry of autumn colours.

Jane stood on the platform, her suitcase beside her, while the last passengers hurried from the station, all of them confident they had somewhere to go. The sun had been shining earlier, but it was now behind a patch of grey cloud, and a chill breath of winter seeped past her scarf. She felt like crying, but she knew she had to stand up to the feeling; she couldn't stand here weeping on a train platform. She felt completely alone in the world. Everyone she loved was dead, and the new family who had promised her a haven had forgotten she was coming.

Perhaps the train was early. But a glance at the station clock dispelled that hope; it was exactly on time. Perhaps they were simply late and were even now hurrying to reach her, hoping she was okay. Or perhaps they were wraiths, coming from a strange other world to lure her to this place where she would be alone and lost, then disappearing from the face of the earth.

They had been rather strange in their way, or at least three of them had; the youngest man had seemed normal enough. She wished now that she had accepted the offer from the other young man to pick her up from Richmond.

Sarah had gone with her to the station, had hugged her before she got into the carriage, and waved goodbye as the train drew away, neither of them imagining there would be no one to collect her at the other end of her journey.

Two weeks ago life had been so different that Jane still wondered if this was all a bad dream. Soon she would wake up in her room in the house in Richmond, her great-aunt calling her to come down to breakfast so she would not be late for work. She had loved her job in the bank. She could walk there from home, and the other girls were all friendly,

1

although she knew they thought her a little apart from them because she had been to a posh school and didn't talk about boyfriends like they did. Not that she actually had a boyfriend to talk about. She loved the customers, old men who came in to withdraw a few pounds from their pension to spend on tobacco or beer, shopkeepers who came in with bags of coins that she put through a sorting box then carefully weighed or counted, children bringing in money boxes for her to empty and count, young men with pay cheques to bank, wanting cash to spend on cinema tickets and flowers for their girlfriends.

Now she no longer even had a job, and that was the fault of the man who had invited her to stay with him but was not here to meet her.

It had started when two policewomen had come into the bank and had spoken for a few minutes to the manager before he called her to his office.

Somehow she had known that this was bad news, some déjà vu feeling that this had all happened before. Her heart had lurched, for it brought back a memory she never wanted to face, her great-aunt and her father's friend Mr Allanstone in the office of the headmistress, scarcely three years ago when she was sixteen, there to tell her that her parents were dead in a train wreck in Switzerland, and she was now an orphan with no family left in the world except her great-aunt.

The manager was not an unkind man even though he was sometimes a bit free with his hands. You got used to it, sliding away if his arm slipped around your waist, or brushing off his hand when it touched your derrière. She knew that one of the girls was having an affair with him, but she had no idea how anyone could find him attractive enough for that. No girl could really be that desperate to sleep with a man. He was old, podgy, smelt of tobacco and stale sweat, and breathed like a sad old dog on a hot day.

He had stood aside as she entered his office, mumbling something about bad news, and had let the policewomen do the talking.

Jane's great-aunt was in hospital and was unlikely to survive more than a few hours. She had been found lying in the kitchen by Mrs Brennan when she came to clean the house at ten. She had been fine when Jane had left for work at ten to nine. A stroke, the policewomen had told her, but they were very kind, and she had gone with them to the hospital, held the hand of her great-aunt while she drew her last fragile breath. She was eighty and rather frail. Old people die, it was better than young people dying, but when the old person was your beloved Aunt Ellen, who had looked after you in the darkest moments of your life and was the only person left to care about you, it still seemed unfair.

A cold wind brushed her face as she stood on the bleak platform. An old man touched her sleeve. He was the porter, and he already had her case in his hand.

'Are you all right Miss? Do you need a taxi?'

He sounded kind. Could he see how upset she was? She would need to try harder to compose herself so she could answer him.

'Someone will be meeting me,' she said as confidently as she could manage, although it was quite obvious to both of them that so far no one had met her.

'Come inside, Miss. It's very cold out here today, like the first real nip of winter.'

She followed him to an empty waiting room. The trains were infrequent here it seemed, for there was no one else waiting.

'I am going to Hayward Hall. Do you know it? Could I walk from here?'

'Hayward? About three miles, Miss. It would take you best part of an hour.'

'I have a phone number,' she said, fumbling in her purse for the slip of paper her cousins had given her. 'Is there a phone box?'

The old man took the paper from her hand. 'The stationmaster will ring them for you,' he offered. 'Come with me.'

She followed him to the stationmaster's office.

'Young lady from first class for the Lindens' place,' he said. 'They're late meeting her. Can we give them a tinkle?'

The stationmaster rang the number.

'What name shall I give?' he asked.

'Jane Walters.'

'Are you Peter's girl?' the porter asked. 'I remember him well. He was a nice lad, and friends with my oldest boy Steve. He came here at the beginning of the War. There were a lot of children sent here from London, but Hayward Hall was his mother's old home, so naturally he went there. My Steve did the gardening at the Hall in the late fifties, after your father left to get married. They were a bed and breakfast then.'

The stationmaster had got through, and he relayed a message.

'Miss Linden says Pat left ten minutes ago and is on his way. It's not far to Hayward, so he will be here soon. Sometimes there are holdups with tractors or sheep on the road. There are farms between here and Hayward village. Lovely lady, Miss Linden. She gets the train here most Saturday mornings, first-class return to London to see a friend she was at school with.'

After the crowded impersonal train stations Jane was familiar with in London, it seemed odd to find that the people who worked here actually knew the people who caught the trains by name. Well at least the Lindens aren't wraiths, she thought, nor are they hermits, for Miss Linden visits a friend. And the porter had remembered her father. Jane had not known that he had once lived at Hayward Hall until Mary had told her only two days before.

She thought of him arriving here as a child, all those long years ago, to stay with his family as she was now doing. He would have been ten at the beginning of the War. He would have stepped from a train, stood where she had stood on the platform. It would have been a steam train in those days. Some trains had still been steam when Jane was very young, but now they all were diesel. Her father had always loved steam engines. Their favourite outings had been to heritage railways where steam trains still ran, and he would always chat to the engine driver and the fireman after the ride. Again she fought back tears. Perhaps he had arrived here by himself. And although his parents were still alive then, he may never have seen them again. Two years later they both were dead.

The social worker at the hospital had asked if she had any relatives, but Jane knew of no one related to her. There was a solicitor, she told them, Mr Allanstone, who had been a friend of her father and was her trustee, and when they asked about friends, she remembered Sarah who had been at school with her and was now married to Tony Ennis. Jane had been Sarah's bridesmaid only four months ago. Sarah now lived in the same street as Jane, and they sometimes shopped together in Knightsbridge.

The social worker had phoned Sarah, and for nearly two weeks Jane had stayed with her and Tony in their home. She couldn't stay by herself in her great-aunt's house; she just couldn't.

Sarah had been so kind, organising other friends for Jane to go to on the days that she worked, phoning the bank to explain that Jane would be away for a few days, helping Mr Allanstone with funeral arrangements, booking an appointment for her with the local doctor to get some diazepam tablets to calm her down. Jane had been given some three years ago when her parents had died, and she had remembered they had helped her.

At first the funeral had been awful. She had sat silently in the pew, dressed in unrelenting black, unable to compose herself even with her sedative, surrounded by old school friends who could do nothing to comfort her. They had put her into a car—Mr Allanstone with her as well as Sarah and Tony—to follow the hearse to the cemetery. But when the coffin had been lowered into the ground in the plot beside her parents, and she had been taken back to the church hall for sandwiches, she had recovered a little.

Mr Allanstone had been with her, Sarah had kept close to her, and there were four new cousins for her to meet. They had been together in another black funeral car.

She recalled they had been at her parents' funeral as well, and her great-aunt had clashed with them over where she was to live. Aunt Ellen was never angry, but Jane remembered her speaking very coldly to the older man. She had told him he was unfit to be in charge of a young girl, and they wanted nothing to do with him. Mr Allanstone had told her afterwards that her cousins had wanted her to go to live with them. However, her great-aunt was her legal guardian. That had been stated in her father's will.

Jane had loved her great-aunt. She had brought up Jane's mother Josie, and she had been part of Jane's family for all of her childhood. Jane had no desire to go to live with a family she knew nothing about and who had seemed to her at the time to be somewhat strange. The two men and the lady were dark haired, tall and thin to the point of seeming rather gaunt, and were obviously closely related. The boy was fair, about her own age, and he seemed like a changeling, for he bore little resemblance to any of the others. If he looked like anyone at all, it was the solicitor Mr Allanstone. The lady was the sister of the older man, the dark-haired young man his son, and the boy with the straight fair hair was the lady's son. That much she did remember, although she had scarcely thought of them since. However, she did know the older man was a writer of spy novels as she had once seen his name on a book in a bookshop and had asked her great-aunt if the writer was the same Daniel Linden who was her father's cousin.

Now here they were again, and they had spoken to her kindly enough, telling her she would be coming to live with them for a couple of months; Mr Allanstone had suggested it. They had stood beside her and Sarah as the mourners came to talk to her.

The oldest man was her father's cousin Daniel Linden, in his fifties she guessed, tall and slim and still strikingly handsome with hair only slightly touched with grey and worn in the old short-back-and-sides style of the fifties. His black suit was a little old fashioned, and he held a black trilby hat.

His sister Mary seemed much younger, no more than forty, elegant and beautiful, her hair in a perfect French twist. She was wearing an immaculate black suit, a small pillbox hat with a subtle wisp of black veil, and black pearl teardrop earrings. She was surrounded by the beautiful scent of old roses.

The dark-haired young man was Ryan, also strikingly good looking and slightly taller than his father, but his hair was longer and in rather unruly black curls.

The youngest man was Pat, no longer a boy, fair haired and not much older than Jane.

It appeared that Tony knew Ryan from school and Oxford. They had been chatting together a little apart from the others. That at least was comforting to Jane. This family were not all total strangers.

The bank manager had been there, coming up to tell her he had managed to get her compassionate leave approved although it was not in the rules.

'She was a great-aunt, you see,' he had explained to Daniel and Mr Allanstone. 'There is nothing in the book about that. You can have half-a-day's leave for an aunt's funeral, but there is nothing about great-aunts. I had to take it to the highest level to explain that she was Jane's guardian, but because the age is eighteen now, even that didn't apply. I managed to get Jane an extra three days' leave, and she has some annual leave, so she can have one more day before she needs to come back to us. That would be Tuesday. After that we can't pay her.'

His arm had crept around her in his usual fashion, and when she had squirmed away, he had patted her behind, his fingers straying further down still and touching her thigh beneath the short black skirt.

Tired beyond words, and wishing she had worn a longer skirt, she had managed to pull away from his touch. Surely, he could leave her alone at a time like this, and in front of her family and Mr Allanstone. She wondered if he would control his hands if he met the Queen.

'Jane is coming to stay with us for at least two months,' Daniel had told him. 'She won't be back at work before December.'

'Well, we certainly can't pay her for two months. I'm not sure we can even keep her job open that long. There are plenty of girls wanting jobs. Although Jane here is one of our best girls and not flighty like some of them. The customers all like her, and she is good with our new computer. I would be sorry to lose her.'

'Then if you can't give her back her job when she returns, I'm sure you'll be happy to give her a reference to find another one.'

'Well, I don't know about that. Employers do like girls to be reliable, not flitting off on flimsy excuses. We don't want to be replacing people on short notice. She should be over it by now. It was only a great-aunt. I will certainly ensure she is paid everything we owe her, but I can't promise anything more than that. How will she live without a job? Girls need to work until they find a husband. They can't be relying on distantly-related uncles to keep them. Doesn't look at all good, you know.'

Daniel had looked him up and down rather coldly. 'We are Jane's family, and we care about her welfare. When she has recovered, we will find her a job where she is treated with more respect. In any case she has money of her own, and has no need whatsoever to work for you or anyone else.'

That was when Jane had realised that she had now lost her job.

The manager had seemed a little disconcerted and had made a rather clumsy attempt to atone by saying he might be able to arrange a transfer for her if there was a branch of the bank near where she was going. Then he had hurried off with the excuse that he had to get back to work.

'Good riddance,' Sarah had said when he had disappeared from view.

'I did like working, and he is quite a nice man usually. It was good of him to come to the funeral.'

Sarah had nearly exploded. 'He's a slimy lecher, Jane, touching you like that. I would have slapped his face.'

'He means no harm. You get used to it,' Jane had assured her, unable to imagine herself slapping anyone's face, either there at the funeral or at the bank where she worked. Or rather had once worked.

At last Pat was there in the doorway of the waiting room, tall and fair, with the boyish smile she remembered and looking very cheerful for such a cold day. He looked more at home in his jeans and jumper than he had in the black suit at the funeral.

'I'm very sorry to be late, Jane. Jimmy had sheep in the lane. He was taking them across to John Phillips' farm to feed on the pasture there. He sends his apologies as well. He's dying to meet you; everyone here is. We don't have enough girls in Hayward. It's mostly boys. Jimmy's mum reckons it's something in the water.'

She wished he would hug her, she badly needed to be hugged, and she wanted to lean against his shoulder and cry.

He picked up her case, thanked the stationmaster, gave the old porter a smile and a tip, and she followed him down the steps to a green Rover.

'Daniel's car,' he explained as if to apologise for it not being the Jaguar that Ryan had driven to Richmond for the funeral. 'I don't have one yet. Ryan owns the Jaguar but he never lets me drive it, and I am desperately jealous of it. He wanted to pick you up, but for some reason Daniel wouldn't let him. He's been really nasty to Ryan these last couple of days. More so than usual.'

He opened the door for her, supported her elbow as she got in, put her case in the boot, then came around to the driver's seat and started the engine.

'Daniel gave Ryan the Jaguar for his birthday when he was twenty-five. He says young men under twenty-five should never be allowed to drive anything faster than a Mini, but we don't have a Mini, so he lets me drive this old thing of his. Not that this goes any faster than a Mini would. I am rather hoping he changes the age down to twenty-one. We are all grown up at eighteen now, so the sports car age should be reduced as well. I want an Aston Martin. I've been leaving motoring magazines on the coffee table, open at the picture of the one I want, but I don't think Daniel has got the hint yet.'

She couldn't help but laugh at this, and suddenly the day seemed brighter, even though it was late in the afternoon, and she forgot that she had felt like crying not a quarter of an hour before.

'He's my uncle Dan and Ryan's dad, but we both call him Daniel, so I think he will want you to as well, except that to his face Ryan and I usually call him Sir because he is a bit strict and we got used to calling people Sir at school. He gave me and Ryan a big lecture at dinner time yesterday on treating you like a sister, and not making passes at you, or he would throw us out of the house, so we will be on our best behaviour. He would sometimes clip us around the ear when we were younger, so we are used to doing as he says. Not that he really could throw us out. He needs Ryan to help him pay all the bills, and he needs me to do the garden.

'When you are feeling better, we can go out to the pictures, and there are occasionally dances at the village hall and in town. We do a lot of things with the McCann boys and their sister, who have the farm next door, and Reverend Colin runs a youth group here and takes us on walks and to see films in the winter, when we don't have cricket on the green. There are around twenty of us, and we have a lot of fun. It's supposed to be only teenagers, but he let me stay on. I was twenty in June.

'We don't have far to go. Hayward is less than three miles, so you can walk there from the station on a fine day.'

He chatted as they drove, but when she did not respond he fell silent, and she slipped back into thinking about the day of the funeral.

After the last sandwiches had been consumed, and the last of the mourners had left for the warmth of their homes, her cousins had gone back to her great-aunt's house with her for Mr Allanstone to read the will. Mrs Brennan had been asked to come back with them, and Sarah and Tony had as well, as Jane would still be staying with them at least for that night.

Mr Allanstone's black Mercedes had been parked in the driveway, with a green Jaguar parked behind it, which she assumed belonged to the Lindens.

Everyone had crowded into the dining room. There were nine people but only eight chairs, so Jane had fetched a stool from the kitchen for Tony.

Daniel had asked her if there was any whisky in the house, saying he desperately needed a drink, so she had found an unopened bottle in the cabinet in the dining room, and asked if anyone else would like some.

She had told him she didn't have any ginger ale to go with it—her father had always had it with dry ginger—but he had said that didn't matter. Tony had poured it for him and a glass for himself, as none of the other men wanted any. Jane had thought Tony was being polite so Daniel was not the only one drinking it. Tony had asked her for some ice from the fridge for his own, but Daniel had been happy to drink his straight. Jane had noticed his hand shook as he took the glass.

Her great-aunt's will was straightforward. There was a small legacy for Mrs Brennan, who had cleaned the house for Aunt Ellen for well over ten years, and the rest was to go to Jane. It was not a lot of money, Mr Allanstone had told her, but she had the inheritance from her father which would be hers in two years' time, when she reached twenty-one.

She knew that she already owned the house, at least in trust, as part of her mother's estate. It had been her grandfather's house, not her great-aunt's, and her mother had inherited it when he died. Her great-aunt had moved in with him in the nineteen thirties, when he was left a widower with a baby. The baby was Jane's mother Josie, and Jane's great-aunt had been left to bring up her niece alone after her brother had been killed in the Second World War.

Jane was to go to her cousins' house on Sunday afternoon and stay there for a few weeks until she was recovered enough to come back to live here. It was Friday, so she still had two nights with Sarah. The Lindens needed to get a room ready for her, and she needed to pack a suitcase. Ryan had offered to drive over and collect her, but Daniel had said he preferred her to come on the train.

'You will have your own bedroom, a sitting room and your own bathroom,' Mary had told her. 'We were a bed and breakfast once, through the thirties and the War and right up to the sixties, so we have a lot of spare rooms. That was how my mother managed to keep the house going.'

Jane was not sure she wanted to go with them, but she knew she had little choice. She didn't want to stay in this house by herself, and she couldn't stay with Sarah for too much longer. She and Tony were quite newly married, and it was not fair on them. There had been talk of Sarah, and another friend Rebecca, finding a couple of girls they all knew from school to share her house with her, but there had been no definite arrangements made before the funeral. Rebecca herself still lived at home with her mother and several younger brothers, and there was no spare bedroom there. Rebecca's mother owned a high-class boutique in Knightsbridge, and Sarah worked there for three days of the week while Rebecca worked the other three days.

Mary had asked if she could see over the house. It was semi-detached with a bay window and an arched front porch, built around the turn of the century. There were two good-size rooms on the ground floor as well as a kitchen and cloakroom at the rear. Upstairs there were three bedrooms and a bathroom on the first floor and three further small attic rooms above. Jane had shown Mary her aunt's room, her own room, and the spare bedroom where her father had stayed as a lodger before he married her mother. On the wall were the medals that his father had earned in both world wars, carefully framed. Jane knew that her grandfather had died in the last war and her father had cherished the medals. Aunt Ellen had taken them from their house in Kent when her parents had died and put them up in the room he had slept in here.

'We had those hanging in the hallway at home once,' Mary had told Jane. 'Their hook is still there. Your father Peter came to live with us at the start of the Second World War. Children were being sent to the country from London to keep them safe. He was ten then, and I was only four. Daniel was nineteen, but he was working for the War Office in London and was rarely at home with us. Peter's father was killed at Dunkirk. My father was killed much later, in nineteen forty-four. He was missing presumed dead, so we were never even able to bury him. Peter's mother was my father's sister, so Peter was my first cousin, and you and I are second cousins. She died in the Blitz, so he stayed living with us. She was a nurse, like your great-aunt. My mother put the medals together in a frame, and she hung them in the hallway so Peter knew we were all proud of his father. She hung my father's medals as well, of course, and they are still there.

'After Peter left us, he lodged here for a while before he married your mother. She and your great-aunt had come to stay with us for the summer, and your father fell in love with her the day she arrived. The last I ever saw him was the day he married; my mother and I came across to Richmond for the wedding. He did write to me though, and I still have every letter and the photos of you that he sent with them. You might like to read the letters, and if you have photos of him, I would love to see them. We were all very fond of him. He was like a brother to me and Daniel, although he was our cousin. Jane, I know that to you we are all strangers, but we have always known and cared about you.

'It seems strange now, but I saw your great-aunt not four weeks ago. Mr Allanstone's wife recently died, and your great-aunt was at the funeral. Before that I had only seen her again at your parents' wedding and their funeral, twice in twenty years. She said you had been unable to get time off work to come to the funeral, and she told us that you had a job at the bank and how proud she was of you. Ryan was with me, and she was very courteous to us both. He asked her if he and Pat could come and see you, perhaps take you both out for lunch, but she told him it was best to leave the past alone.'

Jane recalled Aunt Ellen going to the funeral of Mrs Allanstone, but her great-aunt had not mentioned afterwards that the Lindens had been there. She wondered what she had against them. They seemed nice enough.

'Jane, we have all lost people we love, and we do understand how you feel. Sometimes one loss brings back the grief of all the ones before. No one ever regrets that they loved someone just because it hurts so much to lose them. The pain never goes away completely, but it does get better with time. You can't let grief and loss define your life. After a while you remember that you loved them and they loved you, and remembering the love overcomes the sadness of losing them. You will feel a lot better when you have been with us for a month or two.'

So many people were dead, Jane thought. Her great-aunt had been born five years before the turn of the century, one of four children. Two of her brothers were army officers, both killed in the First World War. Her youngest brother, Jane's grandfather, had been too young to fight. Aunt Ellen had been engaged to a young man who had also died, and she had worn her engagement ring for the remainder of her life. She had been a nurse during the First World War and for several years after it. A photo of her standing with her three brothers, two of them in their uniforms, had pride of place on the mantelpiece, along with one of her with her fiancé, and wedding photos of Jane's grandparents and Jane's parents. Jane's grandmother had died when Jane's mother Josie was born in nineteen thirty-six, and her grandfather had been killed in the Second World War, leaving Jane's great-aunt to look after Josie.

And now the only one left was Jane herself. She was glad that she had found a new family even if they did seem a little strange. It was good to know she was not entirely alone and had someone to love and who could love her. Mr Allanstone was kind to her, but he wasn't family.

The Lindens had left to return to Oxfordshire in the Jaguar with Ryan driving, so she assumed it was his car. She had been given a slip of paper with their telephone number and the times of the trains she was to catch so she would arrive late on Sunday afternoon. It was a silent number, they had told her, and she was not to lose it, as she would not be able to look it up.

Ryan had spoken to her before they left, telling her he was looking forward to her staying at Hayward Hall. He and Pat had always known about her and had always wanted to meet her. They would look after her and try to cheer her up. He didn't live there all the time himself, but he came home every weekend. He had said it would be no trouble to drive over on Sunday and pick her up, but she had told him she was happy to take the train as Daniel had wanted, as she always enjoyed train rides.

Mr Allanstone had arranged for Mrs Brennan to come to the house every few days to keep it tidy and redirect any mail for Jane to Hayward Hall. He would look after her wages. He would increase the allowance for Jane, since she was no longer working. She had a bank account and a credit card, which she always paid in full when the statement arrived, and Mr Allanstone kept her bank account topped up if the amount was running low. Not that it ever did run low; she had her salary, she didn't spend a lot, and Mr Allanstone looked after the household bills. Once she reached twenty-one, he would hand the management of the money over to her if she wanted him to, but for the moment he was happy to give her any amount she wanted. Once the probate was sorted, he would transfer the remainder of her great-aunt's money to her bank account. She didn't need to wait until she was twenty-one for that, as the age was now eighteen.

He was always good to her, and he had always treated her like a favourite niece, although they were not blood relatives. He had no children of his own. He was her godfather—although that was all a bit old fashioned now—and her trustee, but not actually her guardian since she was now over eighteen. He had been good friends with her father, and had lived near them in Kent. After her parents had died, he had looked after winding up their estate, had come with her great-aunt to speech days at school, given her presents on her birthday and at Christmas, and he had looked after arranging her great-aunt's funeral.

At last Jane had been back at Sarah's house, feeling surprisingly better than she had for days.

'They did seem friendly,' she had said. 'It will be nice to see where my father lived when he was young, and they are my family, although I don't know why I was never told anything about them. I recall they were at my parents' funeral, but my great-aunt would not allow them to talk to me, so I assume there was some sort of rift. Apparently, my father used to write to Mary, so they knew quite a lot about me.'

'I found them all a bit strange,' Sarah had said, 'like a family from some vampire movie who turn into black bats when the sun sets.'

'Ryan Linden's okay,' Tony had offered. 'I knew him at school. I can assure you he doesn't turn into a bat. He told me he'll look after you. He'll cheer you up, too. When we were at school, he could always make us all laugh. He says the funniest things, and you are never quite sure whether they are true or he is just making them up. He was at Oxford with me as well but in a different college. He is into history and archaeology, and he did a lot of research into barrows and ancient history. For a few years after we all finished, he stayed on as a don, teaching the undergraduates, and now he is also doing research for a PhD, so he will soon be Dr Linden. He was head boy at school and perfect for it. He is very controlled and careful when he says anything. You get this slight pause before he replies while he considers very carefully what he will say, and it is always the right thing. He was a bit of a loner at school. Everyone liked him enormously, and he was our top all-round cricket player, but he was never friends with anyone in particular. You get chaps like that. We all enjoyed cricket at school. It is a relaxing game, everyone is part of a team, it is always played in summer, and there were usually strawberries for tea afterwards, so we both have fond memories of it. He said he still plays cricket but only on the village green. Usually the younger men play against the older men, but sometimes a team plays against the next village. The ladies watch the game and discuss knitting, and afterwards they all have lovely afternoon teas. I was quite jealous. I hope you know all about knitting, Jane.'

'Not very much. We did learn at school.'

'Sarah knitted a scarf for me once, when we were first engaged. But unfortunately, it started to unravel, and the end of the wool caught in the door of the car one afternoon when Sarah and I arrived at my father's country place, so by the time we reached the front door, half of the scarf was gone. Sarah was upset that I had been careless with the scarf, and the engagement was in jeopardy, but my stepmother fixed it all up. She is good when things go wrong. By the end of the weekend the scarf was as good as new, and Sarah and I were friends again.

'Ryan's father is a writer, and quite famous. He writes about spies mainly. The heroes are dashing young men with sports cars who bust international crime rings, or thwart nutcases who want to destroy the world, and they always sleep with beautiful and clever young women. But they never marry the women, as they have to be single for the next book, and the sex is sometimes a bit explicit. The stories are a bit violent at times, too. I'm not a fan of that sort of thing, but they have made a couple of his books into films, so he would make a bit from it.

'I gave Ryan my card and asked him to phone me so we could arrange to meet for lunch, but I somehow doubt that he will.'

'Mary seemed nice,' Jane had said. 'She was very kind to me.'

'She is very elegant and still quite beautiful,' Sarah had responded. 'With those cheekbones she will still be beautiful when she's ninety. And she was impeccably dressed. I couldn't put a name to her suit, but it wasn't bought off the peg in the high street. It was high end, probably bespoke. Her perfume was Joy. My mother wears Joy, although it seems a bit old fashioned now to smell of roses. She is a bit on the bony side—size eight I'd say—but she still looked good in her suit. If she came into the boutique, I could make her look quite modern and very chic. I would tell her how good she looked in the clothes, and what a pleasure it was to help dress someone with her slim figure. Then she would come back and buy from us again. She seemed very young to be the mother of the boy. They were all Lindens, so presumably she was a teenage single mum. She can't be anywhere near forty, but her son is about twenty. I asked him if he had known Tony at school, and he said he was six years younger than Ryan, so he didn't remember Tony.'

But later, while Jane had been helping Sarah rinse the dinner plates and stack them into the dishwasher, her friend had other things to say.

'Jane, I didn't want to say this in front of Tony, and please don't be offended at me talking about your cousin like this, but the oldest man was rather sleazy. He was one of those men who look you up and down slowly when they meet you as if they are assessing what you would look like without your clothes on. Then they give you a predator look that says *you and I both understand what I want*, and touch you as though accidentally, in the hope that you will respond. If they think you have got their meaning, they quietly ask you if you have a spare afternoon and would like to have lunch with them, except it would not just be lunch they had in mind.

'Your boss was like that as well, but nowhere near as subtle or as high class as your cousin. Jane, you need to learn a few things. A man putting his arm around your shoulders is usually okay. That is just a hug, and we all need the odd hug. A man putting his hand around your waist is sometimes okay too, particularly if you know him well, like a brother or a cousin or a really good friend, but definitely not a boss. Sometimes it is a pass at you, and you can deal with it according to whether it is welcome or not. But a man touching you on the behind is never acceptable unless you are already very intimate with him, and even then he shouldn't be doing it in public.

'If your cousin touches you like that, tell him off and talk to his sister about it. She won't expect you to put up with it. And don't allow it to escalate with the excuse that he always does that. Tony thinks he's an alcoholic, needing whisky in the afternoon, and he was shaky when Tony handed him the glass. So look out for him getting drunk and saying or doing things out of place. If you get out of your depth, call us, and we can drive over and fetch you back here. We can still arrange for some girls to share the house with you. We would work something out.'

They drove past farms and through a small but very pretty village with stone cottages. Pat pointed out a post office, a shop, a tearoom, a pub, an ancient church and a village hall. Continuing down a short leafy lane, they reached the gates of Hayward Hall. The gateposts were stone with gargoyles atop, and the dark green sign was a little battered but still legible. The gates were open and they continued along a neat gravel driveway, past a dilapidated lodge.

The clouds had drifted apart, leaving a weak late-afternoon sun to filter through the trees and touch the tired stones of the old house with an autumn glow. There were gables and mullioned windows, small diamond panes of glass glinting rosy in the last angled shafts of sunlight, chimneys and parapets, downpipes and gargoyles, all blurred and softened by time, and all set in a breathtakingly beautiful garden with late roses and beds of flowers. There was a pond with a fountain, walls and statues and seats, all in the same soft warm stone as the house.

Another day was closing, another year falling into the cold of winter, but for Jane it was the first day of a new life, and she had a strange thought that she had finally come home. She felt the house was reaching out to hug her, to absorb her into its warmth and comfort her, welcoming back one of its own. Her father had been brought up here, and for that reason alone she would have loved it. For a moment she imagined him standing at the doorway to welcome her in some magical warp in time. It now seemed so strange to her that she had never wondered about his life before she was born, had never seen this beautiful house where he had lived for so much of his life. He had met her mother here, and even Aunt Ellen had once walked in this garden and slept in this house. Why had her father never once spoken to her about his life here? What had prompted him to leave this quiet corner of heaven and never return?

When the car stopped on the forecourt, she realised just how large the house was, how different from anything she had expected. There were three gables across the front, the two outer ones each with two mullioned bay windows on three floors, then a round window at attic level in the point of the gable. The centre gable was narrower and not so high and was set back from the other two, with the front door and a window on either side of it, three high narrow windows above, and another round window near the top. Outside were some ferns and flowers in mossy stone pots.

Jane was reminded of a book she had loved as a child about an orphan who came to live with her uncle in a house with a hundred rooms, but she didn't think there would be a hundred rooms here.

Ryan was waiting to hand her out of the car, lead her up the two front steps and through the front door into the hallway. Ahead of her was an oak staircase, which reached a landing below a gothic window then split into two to continue its way up to the first floor. From there it disappeared into shadow, but there was a gallery around the first floor, and high above her was a bridge across the hallway on the next level.

There were pictures everywhere on the walls, the usual soldiers that every home had, and Victorian gentlemen and ladies, solid and prosperous, looking down in stern disapproval at their modern descendants. On the right side of the hallway, beside a doorway, was a large photograph of Daniel with a beautiful bride.

He had been married, Jane thought. But she knew that of course, as he had a son. Where was she now, that beautiful girl who was mother to Ryan?

Mary gave her a welcome hug, and Jane was glad that there was finally someone who would hug her. She took Jane straight upstairs to her rooms, Pat following with the suitcase. On the landing they passed another photo of Daniel with his wife, and one of a young man in an air force uniform.

The rooms were beautiful—large and surprisingly light for so late in the day. She had a sitting room with a bay window, a desk, several chests of drawers, a bookcase, a sofa and a small television. An oak mantel clock sat proudly above an old tiled fireplace, below a large oval mirror. Mary told Jane the clock had been a wedding present of her mother's and needed to be wound every Sunday morning.

The bedroom had a brass double bed with porcelain knobs with flowers on them, wardrobes and drawers, and a window seat in the bay window so she could sit and look out on the garden below. There was another window on the side of the bedroom, for it was in a front corner of the house. Behind the bedroom was a bathroom, a little old fashioned, but having her own bathroom was very welcome in a house with so many men.

There were photos on the walls in the sitting room, the same photo of Daniel and his bride but smaller and black and white, the young man in the air force uniform, her own parents' wedding photograph, photos of her father as a teenager and as a young man, a photo of Ryan with a dog, Ryan and Pat in a studio photo as children, Pat much younger than his cousin. She thought she had seen the photo of Ryan with the dog somewhere before. Perhaps it had been in her father's album. Rather surprisingly, there was also a photo of Jane, then aged three, in a blue liberty print dress with a panel of smocking across the front.

'These rooms were my mother's before she died,' Mary was telling her. 'I left some of her photos, so you had something on the walls.'

'Why is there a photo of me?' Jane asked.

'We have known about you all your life, and your father often sent us photos. My mother cherished them, although she was related to you only by marriage.'

Jane's mother had loved that photo of her in the blue dress. The original had been on the wall in the dining room in their house in Kent, and was now in the attic at her house in Richmond. Her great-aunt had made the dress for her all those years ago. It all added to the strangeness of her coming here. Her father had lived here, her parents had met here, and they even had photos of her on the walls. Yet she had never been here, and her father had never mentioned his old home or the Linden relatives who now claimed her as their own.

'My mother was Irish,' Mary told her. 'She was a Catholic when she first came here, but she converted to Church of England. She said if there was a division in heaven she would rather be with her husband.

But she still had some pictures of the Virgin with the Christ Child so we took those down, and also the photographs of my father.

'Towards the end of her life she could only walk with a frame, and she couldn't get down the stairs without a lot of help from Daniel or Ryan, so we set up a sitting room for her here so she only needed to go downstairs occasionally. Ryan suggested we could give you her rooms so you could be up here by yourself in the daytime as well if it took you a while to get used to living with us. Yesterday he helped me change some of the furniture and take down the pictures that he thought were the gloomy ones.'

Mary took Jane's coat and hung it in a wardrobe, offered to help her unpack her case, told her to come down the stairs when she was ready and find them in the kitchen, through the door at the back of the hallway to the right of the stairs as she came down, then across the dining room. They would have dinner ready shortly, and tomorrow in the daylight Mary would show her over the house. It was such a large house it would take some time.

Jane asked how many rooms, and Mary told her there were around thirty, more if you included bathrooms and cloakrooms and attics, but not all of them were used. There were twenty bedrooms, but they had always needed four for the family, so they could not all be let out. The boys had shared a room when the house was a bed and breakfast.

It all seemed very civilised, Jane thought, and the house seemed to wrap itself around her, as if it knew who she was, as if she belonged here and it wanted to welcome her home. Perhaps her mother had slept in this room. Certainly, she had walked through the hallway and up the stairs. And this family had known about her, cared about her even, for all those years when she had not even known of their existence. The only relatives she had ever known were her parents and Aunt Ellen. The rest were only photographs of uncles lost in the First World War, who, but for forces beyond their control, could have had families of their own, and she would now have second cousins on her mother's side as well. Of the three brothers and a sister, Jane was the only descendant left, the only one who cherished their memory and treasured their photographs.

She hung her dresses and skirts in the wardrobe on hangers that had *Hayward Hall* printed on the wood in black letters, put her jumpers and jeans and underclothes into the drawers, and placed her own photo of her parents' wedding on the dressing table in the bedroom along with her hairbrush and mirror.

The few books she had brought with her went on the bookshelf, her Jane Austen novels and the children's story of a girl who had come to live with her uncle in a house with a secret garden, always her favourite book. The uncle had been a sad man, stricken with grief over the loss of his beautiful wife. Had Daniel lost his wife? There she was looking young and beautiful in the photographs, but she was not here now. Was she dead? Or had she left this beautiful house and her beautiful son and made another life for herself?

Jane put on a cashmere jumper, for the house was rather cold even with the radiators on, and went back to the stairs.

Pat was sitting on the top stair, waiting to take her down to the kitchen below. It was now becoming dark outside, but the window on the landing was touched by the first soft glow of moonlight. There were lights in the corridor and a light in the hallway near the desk, but the lights for the stairwell were very high above them and quite dim.

The kitchen was warmed by a huge Aga stove in a vast old hearth. There were a couple of large dressers with a variety of plates and cups, some cupboards and a sink along the wall beneath the window, and the kitchen table, set for dinner.

Mary seemed more homely in a skirt and hand-knitted cardigan, with her hair in a bun rather than a French twist, but she still looked beautiful, and she had made Jane feel welcome. Jane was glad she had come here. It was good to have a family after she had felt she had no one left.

There was no sign yet of Daniel, but they indicated her place at the table, and she sat and waited. Pat was sent to fetch him. Ryan was putting food into a dish for a very soft and fluffy black cat. Her name was Jasmine because she was a Persian cat.

'Daniel gets a bit engrossed in what he does,' Mary apologised as Pat returned with him.

He greeted her, welcomed her to Hayward Hall, hoped she would be happy here with them, hoped Mary was looking after her, asked Pat to go to the cellar and bring up a bottle of Ryan's elderberry wine, they all liked that.

Mary found some glasses. Pat returned with the bottle, uncorked it, and put it down in front of his uncle. Daniel picked it up, but he was shaky, so Ryan reached across, took it from him without a word, and poured the wine.

Daniel continued unperturbed. 'Chanel, your perfume is Chanel; your mother wore it and so did my late wife. I first bought it for her during the War, when she worked with me at the War Office. It was difficult to get French perfume, but we had young men stationed in France, and they sometimes smuggled it back with them. I got Joy as well; that was my mother's perfume, and Mary still wears it.'

But then he suddenly turned to Ryan, who was sitting opposite Jane.

'Why are you still here? I thought Pat was taking you to the station when he collected Jane.'

For Jane it somehow jarred. Did they not get on?

'I thought it polite to stay tonight, Sir, with Jane expected. I'll go back to Oxford on the early train tomorrow.' He turned to Jane. 'I lead a double life. I have a room at Oxford where I live in the week, and I come back on Saturdays to help my father with the paperwork. Left to himself he forgets to pay the bills. I usually only stay here on Saturday nights. I think that is why my father asked you to come on the Sunday afternoon, when I would be back in Oxford, so you didn't have to cope with all of us at once.'

'I am hoping that Jane will help me with the accounting,' Daniel told his son. 'She worked in a bank. She can take over paying the bills. It will give her something to occupy her time here. Then you won't need to come home at all.'

'Don't forget you need me to sign the cheques, Sir. And you might want me to continue looking after the credit card statements. Do you really want Jane to know what you spend your money on?'

Oh, dear, Jane thought, this is getting rather spiteful. Clearly, they don't get on. But Ryan seemed amused rather than insolent.

'Transactions of that nature are always in cash,' was his father's rather smooth response. 'And I can easily go back to signing my own cheques. Or Jane can copy my signature and sign them.'

'I am happy to help,' Jane offered, unable to fathom what they were talking about, and not sure she wanted to be forging signatures. 'But perhaps I would need help from Ryan to start with.'

'Daniel needs Ryan to sign the cheques and letters, whatever he says,' said Mary. 'We are all very happy to have him whenever he can stay here. I really don't know why he doesn't just live here and drive into Oxford each day since it really isn't far. Did you enjoy working at the bank, Jane?'

Since Daniel had been responsible for her losing her job, this did not seem very tactful, but she knew that Mary was just trying to keep the peace and guide the conversation in another direction.

'Yes, I did. I met so many people, and it was always interesting. Banking is not just about numbers. It's about helping people look after their money. You have a very beautiful garden here. Do you have a gardener?' It was Jane's turn to change the subject.

'Pat works on it for two or three days a week and works the other days on Jack McCann's farm. Ryan helps as well, but these days he's rarely here. I do a bit of gardening but not as much as I would like. This is a large house to run, and it takes a lot of time. We have ten acres, but some of it is woodland. Pat will show you over it tomorrow if the weather stays fine. I know your garden at Richmond is quite small, but you lived for many years in Kent. I believe you had a beautiful garden there, as your father sometimes sent me photos of you in the garden.'

'Yes, it was beautiful, and my father was very proud of it. There was an old red brick wall all around it. The house was beautiful too. I wished it didn't have to be sold, but Mr Allanstone thought we would not be able to look after it as well as keeping the Richmond house where my mother grew up and my great-aunt lived. He said if I really wanted to keep it, we could rent it out, but in the end I let it go. We could have sold the house in Richmond and had my aunt live with me in Kent, but I knew she would not want to leave her friends. I was still at school then and only home on the weekends. And I would have been unhappy living there. It felt so empty and desolate when I was there on my own.'

The tears threatened again. She continued her dinner in silence, and after the meal everyone except Daniel helped Mary with the dishes. Jane dried them and stacked them on the table, and the young men put them away.

Mary was watching a film on television with Pat, but Jane had seen it before, so Ryan suggested she sit in the library with him, since he would be away in the week. The library was on the other side of the hallway and was accessed through the lounge.

'Have you read all these books,' she asked him, looking around at the shelves.

'I have read a lot of them. Some are out of date of course, but that doesn't lessen their value. We only go forward by building on the knowledge and experience of people before us. We have some fiction, all the Victorian novelists like Dickens, Trollope and Hardy, George Elliot, who was actually a lady, and Jane Austen. Most people like her books. I have some others up in my room, Oscar Wilde and Tolkien and Peake. And Mary will have some romance books you can read. Girls usually like romances.'

'There is nothing wrong with a bit of romance. It's the difference between lust and love, and if there was only lust, then men wouldn't stay with their wives, and the children would starve.'

He laughed, and pulled out one of the books.

'Here you are, Jane. Here is book by Thomas Hardy about a young lady named Bathsheba who has three men in love with her. You can't get much more romantic than that. Although the story hinges on a rather silly valentine card.'

'There's nothing wrong with valentine cards, either. My father sent my mother one every single year, and she kept every one of them.'

But then the memories flooded back. Aunt Ellen had found them, and she had packaged them up in tissue paper and ribbon, along with a lock of Jane's hair, cut when she was a small child, and given it all to the funeral director to put in her mother's coffin.

'They went back to Switzerland every year for their anniversary because they had honeymooned there. That was romantic as well.'

Except that they had died there in a train crash when the roof of a tunnel had collapsed, and Jane still had nightmares thinking about them lying there trapped in the darkness. How long had it taken them to die? And had they been conscious and worried about each other and about her?

He looked at her so kindly, sensing she was upset, perhaps even realising why, trying to steer her away from the memory.

'In this case it was the young lady who sent the card to the gentleman, and I have always felt that she should have known better than to lead a man on when she had no interest in marrying him. I always felt she did it purely for conquest, for vanity. But if you read the book, Jane, you can judge.'

She took the book and asked him why he signed the cheques for Daniel. Wasn't it Daniel's bank account?

'My father drinks too much, sadly, and by lunchtime he is too shaky to sign anything. Some years ago I learnt to copy his signature so I could help him, and now I just sign everything for him. If it's something that needs a witness, we get him to sign early in the morning when he is a bit steadier.'

She spent the rest of the evening sitting quietly in the library with him, curled up in an armchair, slipping off her shoes and hugging her knees, careful to keep her skirt wrapped around them so she stayed decent.

Daniel came into the library to join them, poured himself a whisky, offered one to Ryan who politely refused, and offered Jane a gin and tonic or a brandy. Jane thanked him but said no.

The black cat came in and jumped onto Ryan's lap.

Ryan told her some of the history of the house. His architect ancestor Charles Linden, who was her ancestor as well, had designed and built it in the eighteen sixties on the site of an earlier house of which only the vaulted cellar now remained. He had been a successful man, and he had bought the property from an old landed family who had fallen on hard times. The heir had apparently gambled away his family's fortune, and had no wife or children, so the previous house had fallen into dilapidation. Ryan was trying to piece together the details of the previous owners and by now had gathered quite a lot of information about them. Charles Linden had bought the estate, which had included several of the surrounding farms, and he had demolished the existing house, leaving only the cellar and the gothic-arched window behind the stairs, both of which were incorporated into the new building, as was much of the original stone. Neither of his sons was interested in becoming an architect, and they had instead both joined the army.

But gradually over the next two generations the fortune had been spent, and one by one the farms were sold. Ryan avoided talk of the

First World War because he didn't want to depress Jane, but he promised to fill that in at some future time. In the twenties there were two remaining Linden children, Ryan's grandfather James and his sister Grace, who was the mother of Jane's father Peter. Ryan's grandfather had married after the First World War ended, and Daniel had been born in nineteen twenty. By this time most of the farmland had been sold, his grandfather was still in the army, and his grandmother ran the house as a bed and breakfast to afford the school fees for Daniel. Mary arrived in nineteen thirty-five. She was fifteen years younger than Daniel.

He told Jane how his grandmother had kept the bed and breakfast going through the Second World War, with her husband away and Daniel working in London in the War Office, then through the fifties and beyond. After that they had gradually wound it down, taking fewer and fewer bookings, as Daniel was by then making money from the books. He didn't tell Jane about how and when his grandmother had died, what had happened to his grandfather, or anything about his mother, and Jane knew he didn't want to upset her by talking about people who had died.

Instead, he told her about the previous family, and how he was working on tracing their ancestors. He was going through the parish records with Reverend Colin and his wife Linda, and tracing the ancestry of all the local farmers so they could eventually draw up family trees for much of the village. A lot of the families had lived here for generations and were interrelated. He had found Hayward in the Doomsday Book as well. He was working on the Doomsday book for his thesis at Oxford, where he was doing research for a PhD so he would be Dr Linden when he finished, hopefully by June next year.

All the while Jane sensed the older man was watching her, and she remembered what Sarah had said about him looking at you as though he was imagining you without your clothes on. She understood exactly what Sarah meant. She tightened her hold on her skirt around her knees. She was comfortable sitting like this, in a thick tweed midi skirt, a soft cotton Liberty blouse and a warm cashmere jumper. There was nothing inelegant about the way she sat, and she was not going to be shamed into changing it. The skirt covered everything except her feet in her tights. At least Ryan didn't look at her like that. He only looked directly into her eyes.

He asked her if she was cold, then went into the lounge and returned with a tartan blanket, placing it over her so it covered her toes. Had he noticed she had adjusted the skirt around her knees, and seen the way his father looked at her? Or did he simply think her feet might be cold?

Eventually she said she wanted to go upstairs to bed, and Ryan suggested she let him make her a cocoa. He always had cocoa last thing at night, as it helped him sleep.

They sat in the kitchen, now the last two still up. He filled an electric kettle and switched it on, rather than using the kettle that was on the ledge next to the Aga. He told her it was an automatic kettle that he had bought after he accidentally left Mary's kettle on the hotplate of the Aga all night, and it had been wrecked.

Jane noticed he was left-handed. She always noticed if people were left-handed because Aunt Ellen had been left-handed. If her great-aunt put the kettle on, Jane would have to turn it around when it boiled so she could lift it with her right hand to put the water in the teapot. He wore his watch on his right wrist, too, as her great-aunt had always done.

He took out a biscuit tin and found there were two chocolate biscuits left in it. He told her he was not supposed to eat chocolate biscuits at night, a rule of Mary's left over from when he had nightmares as a child, and that left him in a bit of a quandary. If the tin had been full, two biscuits would have gone unnoticed.

But Jane had a solution. 'Easy. Tell Mary I ate both of them.'

The cat was rubbing against her legs, so she lifted it onto her lap and stroked it.

Ryan found her a leaflet that he had written when he was fourteen, with the history of Hayward Hall as he knew it then and some photographs of the house from the twenties to the sixties. His grandmother had sent it to be printed so she could give a leaflet to the guests if they asked about the house, and there were still some left even though there were no longer any paying guests. He thought Jane might like to look at it. He took a pen from his pocket, and on the back of the leaflet he wrote a phone number to contact him in Oxford if she ever needed to. It would not get directly to him but would reach his college, and someone would be sent to find him or to leave a note on his door to phone her back.

The nib of his pen was very fine, like a draughtsman might use for drawing, so his writing was very neat and rather spidery. She noticed he wrote with his right hand, but rather slowly and slightly awkwardly.

'You make the cocoa left-handed but write with you right hand,' she remarked, and he was clearly surprised she had noticed.

'My great-aunt was left-handed,' she explained. 'When she was young it was considered akin to witchcraft. I always notice left-handed people, so when you poured the water in the mugs, I thought you were left-handed.'

'I'm not really. I write with my right, but my left arm is stronger. When I was six, I broke my right arm rather badly so it had to be pinned, and the bone was never quite straight afterwards. I also broke two of my ribs and my collarbone, and damaged my right hand. I was in hospital for nearly a month, and I was very upset at the time. For years afterwards I had nightmares, and I still don't like to think about the day it happened. It took a long time to heal, so I learnt to do things with my left hand. I am still a left-handed cricket player. In the end it didn't stop me from doing anything I wanted to do, but I know I was very lucky to recover as well as I did. I damaged the nerves and tendons in my right hand and there are a few small fiddly things I have trouble with, but I manage.'

He held out his hand to show her that two of his fingers were not quite straight, but it was not something she would ever have noticed for herself.

'Was that when your mother died?' she asked him. Daniel had referred to her as his late wife, so Jane knew she was dead.

'No, she died when I was born, so I have no memories of her. I was only just saved. Sometime I will tell you the whole story, but for now I don't want to upset you. All families have their tragedies, and I think you have had more than your fair share.'

'Do you have a wife or a girlfriend in Oxford,' she asked him. 'You said you lead a double life.'

She thought it might be rather nice to be the girlfriend of this good-looking and very caring man. He didn't wear a wedding ring, but not all men did.

'No, I don't. I don't have a boyfriend either, if that's your next question. I'm just a lone wolf. I have a room in one of the colleges, and they cook all the meals and clean the rooms, so it's an easy life. I don't need anyone to look after me, and I like my own company. When I finish at the end of the year, I will stay on at the college and teach full time. I'll still come home at weekends, though. I love this house.'

He picked up the leaflet, took out his pen and drew a remarkably good picture of the head of a wolf beneath the phone number. 'That is so you remember the number is for me.'

He walked with her upstairs to her room, carrying her book and her leaflet, showing her where the light switches were located, telling her that the light by the desk in the hallway downstairs was left on all night. He said that when the moon was full, the hallway was very light at night because the moonlight shone through the window on the landing, but tonight's quarter moon would be set by now. In a week or so it would be full and last all night, and she would see it then. He thought his architect ancestor Charles Linden had designed the window to catch the moonlight, as it was always really beautiful when the moon was full.

Then he wished her goodnight and continued on up the stairs to his own room, somewhere in the shadowy heights of the floor above hers.

The lone wolf, she thought, back in his lair. He was interesting and rather good looking, and he had been very kind to her. It was a pity he would be away in Oxford for most of the time.

The room was rather cold—the radiator was scarcely lukewarm—but there was a thick duvet, and it was luxury to spread out in a double bed when she was used to a single.

Monday 13 October 1975

Jane always slept with her bedroom door ajar, as her aunt had thought it unhealthy to sleep in a closed room. At some time in the night the cat had wandered in and jumped onto her bed, for in the morning she found it curled up asleep near her feet.

It was nearly eight o'clock. She dressed and went downstairs to the kitchen, where Mary made toast and coffee for her. The cat had already come down and was busy eating breakfast. Ryan had returned to Oxford, Pat was at the farm, and Daniel was in his study, which everyone referred to as his den. Jane and Mary were left in peace to clean up the breakfast dishes and look over the house, the cat following them as they walked around the rooms, sometimes bounding ahead then returning to rub against their legs.

They started in the hallway as this was the showpiece of the house. It comprised the whole of the centre section and soared right up to the beamed and sloping ceiling of the top floor, connecting the two sides of the house into an H shape. The main staircase went up a flight at the rear of the hallway to a landing around two thirds of the way up to the first floor. A huge gothic-arched mullioned window reached from four feet above the landing almost to the ceiling, with the same diamond panes of glass as the windows at the front of the house. There were photographs on the wall below the window, which were at eye level when you were partly up the stairs. The staircase then split into two, with the next flights going up at right angles in both directions to the first floor. From there the landing continued back towards the front of the house with a gallery along each side of the hallway and across the front above the door, so you could walk right around the first floor from the top of one of the second flights to the top of the other.

The stairs then continued up on both sides, beyond the landing, to the second floor. There were two flights, the first straight up to a landing, the second reversing direction back towards the hallway, ending on a gallery at a higher level. The top galleries were then connected by a bridge spanning the hallway beneath the sloping beamed ceiling.

A desk near the front door, left over from the bed and breakfast days, housed the only telephone. At the back of the hallway were two glass doors, one on each side of the stairs, leading down a few steps into the conservatory, which occupied all of the outdoor space at the back between the two wings of the house. A cupboard below the stair landing was used to store Mary's polishes and a vacuum cleaner.

To the right of the hallway was a huge lounge, occupying the whole front on that side. Behind it on the far side was the library, leading through to Daniel's den—the door still with its *Private* sign from the bed-and-breakfast days—and on the near side a billiard room with a large billiard table and a smaller pool table. From there you could go back into the hallway, or out to the conservatory.

At the end of this wing, accessible from both the den and the billiard room, was a passage with a cloakroom and a small room that housed the hot water system for the radiators and bathrooms on the west side of the house. A door opened out to the garden, and a narrow metal staircase went right up to the top of the house, with a window behind it all the way up so you could look out into the garden as you climbed the stairs. The view from all the windows was sightly blurred by the irregularities in the diamond panes of glass, but if you stood close enough to a window you could generally see what was beyond quite well.

Mary told Jane the back staircases were originally for the servants to use, but were also for safety, in case there was a fire. Houses were built with such features in Victorian times because they had open fires and candles. Now the house was heated by radiators, which you could turn on or off individually so the hot water either bypassed the radiator or filled it to warm the room, but they only extended to the ground and first floors. The bedrooms on the top floor were heated with small electric convection heaters. There were fireplaces, but these were now only used at Christmas, and usually only one of the two in the lounge.

On the other side of the hallway was another large reception room that had been set up as the guests' dining room, with a dozen or so small tables, and dressers with pretty china. Behind that was the family dining room, with a vast table that could seat eighteen. At the back of this wing, beyond the dining room, was the kitchen, a small sitting room that had once been the housekeeper's room, a gun room, a boot room and a scullery, which now housed a washing machine and dryer. The hot water and the radiators for this side of the house were heated by the Aga in the kitchen. It had once burnt coal, but now it ran continuously on oil. It was not very efficient as the hotplates and ovens were always hot, but it did keep the kitchen beautifully warm.

This wing also had a cloakroom and a back staircase. A door opened onto some steps down to the cellar, and you could make your way out to the garden from here through the back door.

The conservatory had some cane armchairs with bright patchwork cushions, a table and chairs and a swing seat, as well as some plants in pots and a clothes airer. Mary told her it was a good place to dry clothes in the winter, but Jane was glad of the dryer, as she would not need to hang her underclothes on an airer or a washing line in view of the men. She knew she would need to take some care, living in a house with three men. She would never come downstairs in pyjamas, and it might be best to keep away from short skirts too, with all those galleries above the hallway. Sooner or later you would be standing close to the balustrade on the gallery, talking to someone in the hallway below, with your knickers in full view of them.

The gun room was always locked, and the key kept in Mary's bedroom, although the guns were now rarely used. Mary's mother had locked it when Daniel's wife had died, fearing that he would shoot himself. Mary still locked the room because she had two men in the house who were prone to depression. It was only unlocked when a shotgun was needed for Pat to shoot rabbits with Jimmy McCann, son of the neighbouring farmer, and then he had to ask her for the key. Ryan never shot anything, as he had a hatred of guns since an incident when he was a child, and it was many years since Daniel had gone shooting.

The old housekeeper's room, adjoining the kitchen, was set up with a sofa, an armchair and a television, and Mary used it as her own sitting room, as it was easy to heat if she was the only one at home in the evening. She had a bookcase with dozens of paperback romances, a small tiled Victorian fireplace, and an old treadle sewing machine. There were photographs on the walls of Pat, Ryan and Jane as children, and a graduation photo of Ryan, which Jane thought looked familiar.

The boot room had pegs for coats so they were close at hand if you wanted to go outdoors. There were spare pegs, so Jane's coat could be hung there next to a black duffle coat that Mary said belonged to Ryan, although Daniel sometimes borrowed it. Mary told her that Ryan always cleaned the boots, right from when he was a small child. When they had run the house as a bed and breakfast, the guests had usually been there for the walks in the surrounding countryside, and cleaning their boots was part of the service they had offered. When Ryan had been away at school, Daniel had cleaned them. There were no longer any paying guests, but Ryan still cleaned everyone's boots when he was at home at weekends.

The cellar had a very high window—it was not completely underground—but you still needed the lights on to make out anything in the gloom. It seemed to run for most of this side of the house. There were wine bottles on racks, and shelves with jars of raspberry jam, redcurrant jelly and brandied cherries, as well as bottled plums and pears. The jars were all labelled in Ryan's spidery writing, some of them with little pictures of plums or raspberries or cherries, all of them with the date. There was a crate of apples, carefully wrapped so they did not directly touch each other, another of potatoes, and some onions hanging in bunches. The ceiling was brick and vaulted, and there were pillars and dividing walls and a maze of small rooms along the sides, some with closed doors, others with no door at all, all of them dark and musty and secret. Jane felt she would not want to be lost down here if the lights went out in a power cut. She imagined going into one of the rooms then turning around to find the door had disappeared behind her, and she was left bricked up forever below the ground.

The cellar smelt a little of must and mice, although it seemed quite dry and was scarcely even dusty. But Jane was happy to leave its shadowy depths to their quiet ghosts and return to the warm bright kitchen.

Upstairs there were bedrooms—too many for Jane to keep count of—all with numbers still on the doors. Her own rooms had been Mary's mother's rooms for the last few years of her life, but before that they were guest rooms, the best in the house. There had been bathrooms right from the time the house was originally built, and after a few modifications to make them accessible directly from adjacent bedrooms as well as the passages, they could now be configured to be private to one room or public to several rooms just by locking or unlocking connecting doors. Mary's bedroom was above the housekeeper's room, and there were two smaller bedrooms above the kitchen.

On the other side of the stairs were five more bedrooms sharing three more bathrooms. All of those rooms were spare, as the three men slept on the second floor, the two young men above Jane and Mary, and Daniel in the front corner room on the other side.

Jane followed Mary up the stairs to the second floor, and they walked across the bridge. It looked a long way down to the tiled floor of the hallway.

'We would never let the boys play up here when they were small,' Mary told her. 'The balustrades up here are higher than normal, but it always seems a very dangerous feature to have in a house.'

Jane wondered how Mary reached to clean the dust and cobwebs from the windows and the ceilings up here, but there were no obvious cobwebs so there was clearly some way it was done.

Mary took Jane into Ryan's study to see the view from the front windows.

The room was very neat, and similar in size and aspect to Jane's sitting room directly below it, but with a better outlook, as it was higher. There was an armchair by the disused tiled fireplace and a desk with a portable typewriter. There were a lot of books. She noticed a shelf of children's books, with sets of *Biggles* and *Swallows and Amazons* and *Lone Pine Five,* all in height order, and a neat collection of small books about a steam engine called Thomas. She remembered her father reading those steam engine stories to her as a child. They had been his favourite books as well as hers. She felt she was intruding into Ryan's private space, so she looked at the view she was being shown and tried not to be too curious about the books or the room, or its interesting and attractive occupant.

'Daniel has asked that you don't go into the boys' rooms and they don't go into yours. That way you all keep your privacy and have your own space. He's asked them to treat you as if you are their sister. I trust them both, of course, but it can be difficult when young men and young women share the same house. Sometimes chemistry gets the better of common sense. I'm showing you Ryan's room this once so you can see the view. I asked him this morning, and he said he didn't mind as long as it was only his study.'

The view from this level over the garden and farmland and rolling hillside was breathtaking beautiful, perfect English countryside with autumn colours still adorning the trees and a weak October sun casting shadows over the lawns. From the front windows you could look down on the pond and see the slight ripple of orange and yellow koi in the depths of the water, on the roof of the little lodge by the gate, and the lane beyond the garden wall.

There were some empty bedrooms on this level too, with interesting ceilings that sloped above the point where the roof met the outer walls of the house.

From the window behind the back staircase, you could look down on a maze formed from clipped hedges and see the solution to it. Not that she would see the view from this level often, as all the front rooms belonged to one or other of the men, and she had only been allowed into Ryan's study to look at it that once. She would have no need to come up here.

Right at the top of the house was an attic space, accessed from a small stairway behind a door on the top landing near the back staircase, and lit by the round windows in the gables at each end of it. At the highest point the rafters were quite high above them, the walls sloping down from there to the floorboards. The dark brick chimneys came up through the space. There were metal tanks for hot water, old cabin trunks and suitcases, scattered cobwebby boxes, and a few broken chairs, patiently waiting to be mended.

The attic held a strange sense of timelessness, as though the room slept between the rare occasions anyone stood on the floorboards, watched the dust drift peacefully in the rays of the sun through the window or breathed the still air.

'My father, his two brothers and his sister—your grandmother—used to play up here when they were children,' Mary told her. 'Sometimes I think I hear their ghosts here, and Ryan hears them in the garden. They would have had a magical childhood, growing up in this house, and they were all quite close in age. Two of the brothers died in the First World War, and my father and your grandmother died in the Second. There is a similar attic on the other side, but we will look at that another day.'

They returned down the stairs, past the paintings and the photographs, the young man in uniform, the beautiful bride beside Daniel in a photo that had been lovingly coloured. They never look as good as genuine coloured photographs, Jane thought, but in nineteen forty-seven almost all wedding photos would have started life as black and white. She had been so beautiful, and she had died when Ryan was born, leaving Daniel to carry on living without her. It was all so tragic that it made Jane want to cry. She asked Mary about the young man in the air force uniform.

'He was Caroline's younger brother Nicholas, Ryan's uncle. He was a fighter pilot in the War, and he died when he was nineteen. Ryan's middle name is Nicholas. His mother had died, and his father was too upset to care, so my mother chose his names. She had two brothers who had died as babies. They were called Ryan and Patrick, so both Ryan and Pat were named after their great-uncles.'

Jane now knew that Daniel's wife's name was Caroline. This family had a lot of tragedy too, but for the moment she didn't want to think about it.

Outside was a coach house and stable block, now used as a garage for the two cars, and storage for lawnmowers, rakes and spades, the tennis net, and the racquets and balls. There were rooms above, once slept in by servants, but now empty. The tank for the oil was behind the coach house, and there was a shed with an ancient disused generator.

Mary made coffee at ten thirty, showing Jane how the percolator worked, as Jane had never used one, and they took a cup to Daniel in his den.

He said he wanted a break and would show Jane the garden when he had finished his coffee, so Jane sat with him, and Mary brought her coffee into the den for her.

There was a photograph on his desk of his wife, and another of Jane's mother in a blue suit and hat, which had been taken outside the front of Hayward Hall. You could tell that by the bay window in the background. Jane recognised the photograph, as it was a copy of one in her parents' photo album at home. All those years she had looked at that photo without knowing, or even wondering, where it had been taken.

They went out through the door beside the back staircase. Daniel offered her his arm to walk around the garden, then put his hand over hers where it lay on his sleeve, looking sideways at her. It made her feel uncomfortable, and she wished she had stayed further away from him.

But he was polite enough, asking her if she would help him with the paperwork, open the mail, see that the cheques were all banked, the bills all paid. He was not an organised man, and there were a lot of papers that needed sorting. Ryan did some of it, but he knew his son rather despised him for allowing things to get into such a mess. He would be so grateful to Jane if she could bring a bit of order to it all. Ryan would need to sign the cheques, as he himself was always too shaky to do it, but she could write out the amounts, make sure they went into the right envelopes, check the bank statements. Nobody at Hayward Hall was any good with figures. It would be so helpful to have someone who knew about banking, and it would give her something to do. He told her that her father had been good with numbers and had taught mathematics at the grammar school in Oxford before he had married her mother. Jane hadn't known that. She had only known him working as a statistician for the civil service.

Daniel took her into the centre of the maze, sat beside her on a stone bench, a pale October sun on their faces, the hedges sheltering them from a nippy little autumn wind that had teased them in the garden, telling them that winter was on its way, relentless winter that would soon see them to the end of another year of their lives, promising another spring but only at the cost of yet another winter and then another, the slow march of time that saw them all age and die, some before their time.

'You look so like your mother,' he said. 'I loved her, but she loved your father and I had to let her go. I thought she was sent by fate to console me for losing my wife, but fate doesn't always behave the way we would like it to. I'm not a saint, Jane, but life has never treated me well. She was nineteen, the same age as you are now, when she came here with her aunt—your great-aunt—to stay with us for the summer. Peter was twenty-six, but I was much older, and I can't blame her for preferring him to me. Now they are both dead, and it all seems so long ago.'

He fell silent for a while, and she stayed silent as well, not knowing what to say to him, but knowing he didn't expect her to say anything.

'Now you can try to find our way out of here. Can you do that?'

She wasn't sure. She had seen the maze from above and had easily seen the solution, but when you were inside the tall dark-green hedges the way seemed less clear. She knew a secret method for solving mazes that worked for most of them. You kept one of your hands on the hedge beside you as you went around the paths, and eventually you would go around all the twists and turns and reach freedom. Unless one of the dead ends landed you in trouble, a tiger lurking or a pit to fall into. But there were no tigers and no pits, although there were a couple of rather scary gargoyles that you came upon suddenly when you turned a corner into one of the dead ends. Her method worked and she eventually led him out into the garden.

Beyond the maze and the lawn and the tennis court, the garden merged into five acres of woodland, still within the stone wall that enclosed the whole garden. There were winding paths through the trees, timber benches to sit on, more stone gargoyles with soft green moss, which you came upon unexpectedly around a bend in the path, even a standing stone that Daniel said had been there for hundreds of years and had been incorporated into the garden.

Jane laid her hand on it, as she always liked to do with standing stones, feeling the power of the past flowing around her, one long continuum of living people and dead people, year on year, generation on generation, linking us with the people who came before us, the long-forgotten people who had first raised this stone in this place.

'Ryan will tell you how long it's been there, and how it came here. He knows about those things.'

They had passed two doors in the wall—one of them overgrown with brambles—that made Jane think of secret gardens, but Daniel told her they led out to Jack McCann's farm on one side and John Phillips' farm on the other. The garden was on the boundary between the two farms. There were raspberry canes growing against the garden wall, and he found a few late raspberries for her.

'Mary makes them into jam,' he told her. 'It's the best raspberry jam you ever tasted.'

They walked back past the coach house, a walled kitchen garden and an orchard, then along the drive to the front garden with the beautiful stone-edged pond with the koi, and a statue of two small children with an inscription on the plinth, *Charles and Eloise*. He didn't tell her who they were, and she didn't ask. She could only imagine they were children who had died. There were too many dead people, and she was not ready to cope with their story.

There were green timber garden seats on the lawn, stone seats by the pond where you could sit and look at the fish, yet more gargoyles, and stone mushrooms. There were flowers still, and late roses, walls to shelter them from the cold winds, ancient trees, and a glorious monkey puzzle right in the centre of a slightly unkempt lawn with meadow flowers. There were bulbs there in spring, he told her, daffodils and bluebells and snowflakes and in summer buttercups and daisies. He told her Pat loved the monkey puzzle but found it frustrating because it looked so interesting you wanted to climb it, but the leaves were like little daggers, so it would not be a pleasant experience. Jane knew what he meant, as there had been one in her parents' garden in Kent.

The lodge by the gate looked rather old and tired and in need of a paint, but everything else in the garden was perfect.

She was not sure what she had expected when she had left Richmond to come here, but it was not this grand house and beautiful garden. Yet she felt she had come home. Her grandmother had been brought up here, sister to Daniel's father. Her father was Daniel's cousin, although they had lived here together as brothers in the same way as Pat and Ryan lived here as brothers although they also were cousins. She felt that she belonged here just as much as they did, but for some reason she had been exiled.

'Why did you want Pat to pick me up and not Ryan?' she asked Daniel, for the question was nagging at her. The discord she had felt between Daniel and his son bothered her.

'Only because he's closer to you in age and much chattier than my son is. I thought you would be more at ease with him.'

'Pat told me he wants a sports car, but he has to wait until he is twenty-five. He said he leaves motor magazines around the house open at a picture of the one he wants. He is hoping you might relent and buy it for him when he reaches twenty-one.'

He laughed. 'I can't say I've actually noticed them, so it wasn't successful. He always has excuses why he can't get a proper job, then complains about not having enough money. When I was young, I earned money; it wasn't just given to me. You had a job, although you could easily afford not to work.'

'I don't have a job now,' she reminded him. 'You resigned me from it.'

But she was not sorry she was not returning to it. She could not have gone back to work any time soon, and they had expected her by tomorrow. She still felt like an emotional wreck, and she might have cried in front of the customers.

'Good thing too. That man was a predator and not fit to lick your boots. I saw where he had his hands, and he had the hide to question the propriety of you living here with me and Mary. And you do have a job. You're working for me. If you need more money, I can give you an allowance, the same as I do for the boys.'

'Thank you, but Mr Allanstone gives me whatever I need from my father's estate. Not that I needed any extra when I was working. What I need now is just a bit of time to get over it all, and I am grateful to you for offering that. I did feel very alone when Aunt Ellen died. I felt I had nobody left in the world I could care for, or who cared about me.'

'We all care about you—we always have—but your father would never bring you here, and your great-aunt was quite hostile to me. Your father sent photos of you to my mother and Mary. After your parents died, we only ever had one more photo that Allanstone sent to Mary. Your aunt had given him a print, and he thought Mary might like one as well. Your aunt relented and said he could send it to her. My son has a copy of it on his bedroom wall. It is a very pretty photo of you at a school dance in a blue dress, taken when you were seventeen. Ryan borrowed it from Mary and had it enlarged and framed, which was surprising for him because he never liked girls. Pat teased him about it, saying he wanted you for a girlfriend, and Ryan told him he thought you were one of us and should live here with us. I wanted a copy of it too, for my study, but Mary wouldn't lend it to me to have it copied. One time I stole Ryan's photo and put it up in my room, but he noticed it was missing and demanded I return it.'

Jane wasn't quite sure what to make of all that. They had been fighting over a photograph of her? It all seemed a bit weird, so she changed the subject.

'This is a very beautiful house and garden. It seems like paradise to me.'

'We only held on to it by the skin of our teeth. My mother ran it as a bed and breakfast through the thirties and forties, and right up to the late sixties we still had the odd guest in the summer. It is expensive to run. The heating oil alone costs more than some people earn. She worked like a slave to afford to keep us all fed and to keep me at school. My father was very grateful to her, as he had only his army pay apart from that. I used to give her most of what I earned and so did your father when he still lived here after the War. Ryan's all right, he doesn't spend much, but Pat thinks he's hard done by because I won't buy him a fancy sports car.

'Pat's not your brother. Peter lived here then, before he met your mother, and Mary didn't have a boyfriend that any of us knew about, but my mother knew Peter would never have touched her, and if he had, he would have married her, not left her in the lurch. They were cousins, so it would have been allowed. It turned out that Pat's father was married and couldn't get a divorce, or didn't want to. We never knew how or where she met him. She never went anywhere except to see a girl she was at school with. He paid for Pat's schooling, and he still sends money to Mary. It was arranged through Allanstone. That's all we know.

'Ryan's not your brother either, although I was once in love with your mother. I've told both of my young men that they are to treat you like a sister. It would be too easy for you to get romantically involved with one or the other of them, living here in the same house, or even worse, both of them at once. Then if it didn't work out you would want to leave here, and for now you have nowhere else to go. You are to do the same, and treat them like they are your brothers. I'll have no sneaking about at night.'

She laughed at this, and he said it was good to see her smile. 'We'd better go inside. Mary will be looking for us for lunch.'

'Why did my father leave here?' Jane asked Mary as they cleaned up the plates after lunch. 'He never once spoke to me about this house or his life before he was married.'

'Your mother came to stay with us for four weeks one summer, with her aunt, your great-aunt. My mother knew your great-aunt when they were both younger, and we did full board occasionally, instead of just bed and breakfast. Peter fell in love with her. It was love at first sight. I remember him telling my mother that he had been so fascinated with her that he had been watching her in the rear-view mirror after he had picked them up from the station—she was in the back seat—and he nearly ran into a sheep that was loose in the lane. But Daniel fell for her as well. He thought she looked like his late wife. She did look a bit like Caroline, with the same fair hair, though not so curly, and beautiful big eyes like yours. She even wore the same perfume that Caroline had worn. There was a row over her, and Peter left here with your mother and your great-aunt.'

Tuesday 14 October 1975

The following morning after breakfast, Jane helped Daniel by opening the day's letters. Each morning he spent an hour or so reading *The Times*, and then he would work either on his typewriter or hand correcting the current draft of the book he was writing. She could use the typewriter while he was reading the paper, or while he did the corrections. She was to write cheques for any bills that needed to be paid and type any letters and envelopes that needed to go with them. Ryan would sign the cheques and the letters when he came home on Saturday. For anything urgent and for cash for shopping, there were always a couple of signed blank cheques. It seemed easy enough.

The typewriter was an IBM Selectric golf ball and rather fun to use. Instead of the paper going from side to side, it stayed where it was, and the golf ball went along. There were spare golf balls in a drawer so you could type in italics or in a smaller size. The electric cord ran under a rug to reach the socket on the skirting board, but you still needed to be careful not to trip when you walked over it.

The den was frankly a mess, with newspapers in piles on top of the filing cabinet, on most of the chairs and in corners of the room. There were brochures and leaflets and letters piled on the desk, on the book-shelves and on every possible surface in the room, except for where the whisky decanter and glasses stood on a tray on a small side table. Even the lower shelf of the whisky table had a pile of papers.

He told her she could gradually go through them and sort out anything useful. He didn't really need any of the old newspapers, he just didn't get around to throwing them out, and he didn't like Mary to come in here except to bring his coffee and dust the room. It was his own space to mess up as he pleased.

There were photos of his wife all over the walls, dozens of them, some by herself, some with him, one with her brother, and yet another wedding photo. This one included Jane's father, who had been best man, and a very young Mary as a bridesmaid. She would have been about twelve then, Jane thought.

At ten thirty Daniel always had coffee brought in to him, and he would then continue to work until lunch time. In the afternoons he usually went out walking. It helped him to get his ideas together for the following morning's work, and he had been told he needed to get more exercise.

Jane could come with him if she wanted to, or help Pat in the garden, or Mary in the house, or walk by herself, or read a book or the newspaper. She could eventually sort the whole room if she felt like it, but there was no hurry for that. He just wanted her to have something to occupy her time so she didn't get depressed.

Later she could learn to drive. She could study something if she wanted to, get a qualification in accounting or office management. There were yoga classes at the village hall. In town there was a library, shops and a cinema. They all played cricket on Saturdays in the summer, and in the winter the local vicar ran activities for the young people. She needn't be bored.

Thursday 16 October 1975

It was Thursday afternoon when Jane met Jimmy McCann. She had gone for a walk through the garden, into the wood and along the path beneath the trees. She could hear a tractor on the other side of the wall, so when she reached the arched door in the stone wall that she knew led to the McCanns' farm, she decided to see if it was Pat driving it, as he was at the farm that day. The door had no lock, only a simple latch. She opened it and stepped through into a completely different world, pulling the door closed behind her, hearing the latch click into place. But she realised too late that on this side the latch was broken, so she was unable to open the door.

She found herself on the edge of a grassy field, with a muddy track running along the wall. She would need to walk through the mud along the outside of the wall, and back into the garden through the front gate.

There was a young man driving the tractor, pulling a trailer with several bales of hay, but he was not Pat. He was about her own age, with a shock of reddish-brown hair and a beautiful smile. He saw her and stopped, jumping down from the tractor. He was surprisingly tall and more heavily built than the Linden men.

'Miss Walters, I presume. I'm Jimmy McCann. We've all been dying to meet you. I won't shake your hand, as mine is rather dirty, and you look very clean.'

'Jane,' she said, 'please call me Jane. I seem to be locked out.'

He tried the door but he couldn't open it either.

'The latch is broken. You'll need to ask Pat to fix it. Then you can come across and see me any time without this happening.'

He looked down at her neat brown leather lace-up Oxford shoes with their medium-height heels and platform soles, then along the muddy lane that ran in both directions along the wall.

'You will have to climb back over the wall,' he teased. 'I could give you a leg up. Pity you're not in a miniskirt.'

'It's a very high wall,' she said doubtfully, thinking he really meant it. 'It would be a long way to jump down on the other side.'

'You could sit on the hay in the trailer, and I could drive you round to the front gate. I can't guarantee you won't be bumped off and land in a puddle though. Or I could carry you, although you might get a bit dirty off my jacket. We'll get it sorted out. Just stay where you are while I jump over the wall. We need you out of here before the bull sees you.'

She looked around the field in alarm, but she could see only sheep, and in the distance a pony, so she knew he was joking. He took a run at the wall and easily vaulted over it, although the top of it was higher than Jane's head. He landed on the other side and opened the door for her.

'Come and see my mum at the farm. My sister is at home because it's her half day off, and Pat's there helping Dad change the oil in the Land Rover. If you go out of your gate and along the lane to our gate, it's not too muddy. You'll need to get yourself some welly boots. Then none of this would be a problem. Just remember to always keep the door in the wall shut. You wouldn't want the bull to get into the garden. It might knock over a gargoyle.'

She returned to the house and told Mary she had spoken to Jimmy and he had asked her to go and see his mother. Mary couldn't find her any wellingtons that would fit—her own were too tight, and the men's were too large—but she said they could look for some in town tomorrow when they did the weekly shopping. She no longer had any from when the boys were younger, as they were always passed on to Anne McCann for her boys.

Jane walked to the farm gate, still in her brown lace-up shoes. The drive looked a little muddy, and there were several rather hissy geese, but she was able to dodge the puddles and the birds and reach the front door.

Anne McCann, Jimmy's mother, opened the door to her, instantly knowing who she was. There were five McCann children. Jimmy was the eldest, seven months older than Jane, as he would be twenty in

January. David was a year younger, but he wasn't there that afternoon, as he worked as a clerk in the town. Next was Claire who was seventeen and had long straight dark-brown hair and huge hazel eyes. She worked too, in a wool and haberdashery shop in town, but it was her half day off. The two youngest boys, Paul and Brian, would shortly come home from school on the bus. Then there was the farmer, Jack McCann, coming in from working on the Land Rover and washing his hands in the scullery, along with Pat who had been helping him.

They made Jane a cup of tea, and there were scones and cream, and stories about her father, who had been a friend of Jack McCann from when he had first come to live at Hayward at the start of the War.

The two youngest boys came in from the school bus. They asked if she was coming to the film on Saturday; Reverend Colin was taking their youth group into town to see *Gone With The Wind*. He always arranged things for them all to do on Saturdays, and Pat was going, of course. There was some question about whether there would be enough room in the Land Rover for Jane as well, but Pat said he could take Daniel's Rover if Jane wanted to come.

She asked whether Ryan would come with them, but it seemed he wouldn't. He wasn't a teenager, so he was not part of their group.

Claire told her about the ladies' yoga class that was held on Thursday evenings at the village hall from eight to nine, but you needed a mat. Jane said she would find a mat and start next week.

David arrived home from work on his motor scooter as she was leaving with Pat, so she was able to meet him as well. He told her he was saving to buy a car, as riding home on a scooter was miserable in winter, and there were no buses to Hayward, except for the school bus, because it was a dead end. If it was wet, Jimmy would take him and Claire to work—and collect them again—in the Land Rover, but most days they both went on the scooter.

Already Jane felt as if she had known the McCanns all her life, and she even thought she could remember all the names and which boy was which.

Friday 17 October 1975

On Friday morning Daniel took Jane and Mary into town to do the shopping. Jane went to the bank with Daniel and they deposited a dividend cheque and took out some cash. The manager came over to talk to them. Jane assumed it was because Daniel was one of their wealthier customers. When Daniel introduced her, she was surprised to find that the manager knew of her.

'Are you the young lady who worked in our Richmond branch? The manager there sent me a note to say he would give you a reference if you wanted to work here with us.'

Well, at least he had been decent enough to do that, she thought.

'Jane will be helping me while she is here,' Daniel told him before she had recovered from her surprise. 'But if she decides to work again, she will no doubt contact you. Meanwhile she will take over doing the banking for me.'

When they left the bank, he went to get his hair cut, and Jane was left to shop for herself, with instructions to be back at the car in an hour. She bought herself some green wellingtons, some black leather lace-up hiking boots and some sensible shoes with just a little bit of heel. She found a roll-up yoga mat at the sports shop. She also bought an account book so she could keep track of all the payments and the receipts and reconcile them with the bank statements.

In the afternoon Jane cut up some apples for Mary to put into a pie, before helping Daniel with the cheques and letters ready for Ryan to sign when he returned on Saturday.

But Ryan came home late on Friday afternoon, instead of his usual Saturday morning. He told Jane it was because Mary had promised to make an apple pie if he did, but Jane knew it was also on her account, and she felt rather flattered. He had bought chocolates for her and some for Mary.

After dinner she gave him the letters that were addressed to him, and they went through the list she had made of the inward cheque she had banked and the outward cheques that were waiting for him to sign for his father. She showed him how she was setting up a ledger so she could keep track of what came in and out.

She returned the book, which she had enjoyed, and they discussed the moral implications of the valentine card. Jane thought it just a rather silly thing the two young women had done, but Ryan thought the heroine had gone out of her way to make a conquest of the farmer because she was annoyed that he had not admired her as the other men had. Jane thought it was very sad that the farmer's life had been wrecked because he had loved Bathsheba too much, and they both agreed that fate was itself a character of the book, weaving through the story as if it had a mind and a life of its own.

He picked up another Thomas Hardy book for her, but decided against it.

'You might find *Tess* a bit sad as well until you recover a bit. Let's try *Middlemarch*, since most of the people who die in that are old. One of them is an old man we don't have much sympathy for, and that leaves the heroine free to marry his nephew, although there are some complications around an inheritance. She has to give up her fortune to marry him.'

He asked if she played chess, and she was happy enough sitting with him in companionable silence, planning her moves, remembering chess games with her father, now over three years ago. She felt that Ryan understood she still needed quiet relaxing things to do and simple unassuming friendship.

She asked if he was going with them to the film the following evening.

He thought for a moment, and she remembered Tony saying he always hesitated before he spoke. She found herself noticing that was true for everything he said. She could never imagine him being angry with anyone or saying anything he would later regret.

'I would happily take you out to a film if it was just you and me, or Pat as well,' he said. 'But a film night with a dozen noisy teenagers is not my idea of a fun night out. I don't like crowds, and they are all a lot younger than I am. Except Reverend Colin, of course. Have you met him yet? Have you walked to the village?'

'No, only in the garden here and to the McCanns' farm. I went through a door in the wall, but the latch was broken so I couldn't get back into the garden. Jimmy McCann had to climb over the wall and open the door for me so I didn't need to walk home through the muddy field. Pat is going to fix it. I walked down to the farm to meet them all. This morning Daniel took Mary and me into town to shop, and now I have some wellingtons.'

'Would you like to walk down to the village tomorrow morning? You don't need wellingtons for that, just sensible shoes. We can call on Reverend Colin, and I can show you the church. Even those of us who are atheists go to church on Sunday mornings, so I hope you will come with us. Mary will expect you to. Church is about community here, just as much as religion, and morality is a social responsibility. It doesn't rely on a belief in God.'

Saturday 18 October 1975

On Saturday morning, after an early breakfast, Mary went to London to visit her friend. She went there most Saturdays, but not all of them. Sometimes either she or her friend had something else on that they couldn't avoid. She would return by six o'clock, just in time for them all to have dinner before Jane and Pat went out to the film. Mary had set up a Crock-Pot, which cooked a casserole very slowly so it would be ready when she returned. Jane had never seen one before.

Pat drove his mother to the station in town while Ryan and Jane walked to the village.

She enjoyed being with him even though she didn't feel very glamorous in the low-heeled shoes. They walked around the village green, past the war memorial, the pub, the post office, the shop and the village hall, and went into the church. It was very old—Norman, he told her—and it was filled with timeless pensive silence and hazy dusty sunlight.

He showed her the plaque for his grandfather. He had been missing presumed dead near the end of the Second World War, so he had no grave at Hayward, and all that remained was his name etched on the brass plate and on the war memorial at the edge of the green. They would place a wreath there in November. Below the plaque for his grandfather were two others for his grandfather's brothers killed in their youth in the First World War. They were Ryan's great-uncles and Jane's as well, as his grandfather had been the brother of her grandmother.

They called at the vicarage—Ryan had phoned ahead to say they were coming—and she met Reverend Colin and his wife Linda. He looked a few years older than Ryan and had straight fair hair, which always seemed to be in his eyes. He and Linda had lived in the village for about six years. They had a small child of four years old, who had surprisingly long, and very curly, fair hair. Her name was Daisy, but Jane thought she should have been called Goldilocks.

Ryan picked her up and swung her around above his head. This appeared to be a ritual, as she had come running up to him as soon as she saw him come through the front gate.

Linda's next baby was well on its way. Colin's mother also lived with them, but this morning she was shopping in town. It was a very convenient arrangement, for it left Linda free to help Colin run his activities for the young people in the village while his mother looked after Daisy.

They were given coffee and biscuits, and Colin asked if Jane was coming to the film.

When she told him that Pat was taking her, Colin asked Ryan if he would like to come as well, but Ryan said there were too many people for him, and they were all too young. Pat would look after her.

In the afternoon Ryan took Jane to the farm on the other side of the Hall, advising her to wear wellingtons this time.

The farmer was an old man, over eighty, who walked with a limp from a shrapnel wound. He had fought in the First World War, and one of the bones in his shin had been destroyed, so he could still walk but could no longer turn his ankle, hence the limp. He told Jane it had probably saved his life, for he was wounded early in the War then sent home because he was no longer fit enough to fight. His name was John

Phillips and he was a widower, managing the farm with the help of his two grandsons, Winston and Adrian, who came on the weekends, and Pat and Jimmy, who sometimes helped him out in the week. He had two border collies, Felix and Casper, ran a few sheep, kept beehives and raised hens and turkeys.

The two boys boarded at a school near Oxford and stayed with their grandfather at weekends. Winston was just eighteen, Adrian two years younger. They took Jane outside to see the turkeys.

It was the first time she had seen a real live turkey, and there were a dozen of them in a large sheltered enclosure with a few ducks and some hens. In the spring John Phillips bought turkey eggs from a breeder, which he hatched in an incubator, and there were baby turkeys then which Jane might like to come and look at. The turkeys were given out to the local cottages and farms at Christmas, as thanks for the help his neighbours gave him during the year.

Jane enjoyed the film that evening, enjoyed going out with Pat, just the two of them in the Rover, enjoyed sitting between Pat and Jimmy in the cinema with Claire on the other side of Pat. She met the other teenagers in Colin's group, although she doubted if she would ever remember all the names. Most of them were boys. It was much easier to remember girls, as boys tended to all look the same. Pat had bought both her and Claire a box of Maltesers, and Jimmy bought her one as well, so she put Pat's box in her bag to take home to give to Ryan.

It was a long film, and it was rather late when they returned to the Hall. Pat put the car away in the garage then unlocked the back door.

'Do I get a kiss,' he asked before he opened it. 'When you go out with a guy in the country, he always gets a kiss.'

'I thought we had to be brother and sister,' Jane said rather doubtfully. 'We can't break the rules.'

'Yes, but we're not really all that closely related, so it's okay. Breaking rules only matters if you're found out. Daniel isn't likely to be watching.'

He pulled her against him and kissed her for a long time, and she liked being so close to him. At least he kept his hands to himself. Then he opened the door, and they went into the light of the kitchen where Ryan had already put the kettle on for cocoa. Jane assumed he had waited up and had heard the car drive in. She hoped he hadn't seen them kissing on the doorstep, but you couldn't see the doorstep through the kitchen window, as it looked out onto the conservatory.

She gave Ryan the Maltesers, and they all shared them for supper with the cocoa.

She had a message for him from Reverend Colin. The following Saturday afternoon he was taking the group on a cross-country walk to the next village, Peddleton, where they would all have tea at one of the farms before walking back. Normally Linda would come with them, but with a baby now only six weeks away, the five-mile distance would be too much for her. He had asked if Ryan would be good enough to come with them to help keep a watch over the group.

'I am happy to help if he needs me to,' he said. 'I'll talk to him tomorrow after church.'

Sunday 19 October 1975

On Sunday Mary cooked them all a classic English breakfast—a throwback to the bed and breakfast days—and they went to the ten o'clock service at the church.

Mary had picked flowers from the garden and arranged them in three neatly wrapped bunches in a flat basket. These were for the three most recent graves in the family plot in the churchyard. There was one for Mary's mother Kathleen Mary Linden, who had been born in eighteen ninety-five and had died in nineteen sixty-nine, one for two Linden children, Charles and Eloise, who had been born in the fifteen years between Daniel and Mary but had lived for only a day or two, and one for Daniel's wife Caroline Ann Linden, who had died on the fifth of March in nineteen forty-nine at twenty-six years old. There was a space below the inscription for Caroline, presumably for Daniel when he joined her, and at the bottom another line.

FINIS VITAE SED NON AMORIS

Jane guessed it meant *The end of life but not of love*, and Ryan confirmed that when she asked him. She knew what had happened to the beautiful wife in the photograph; she had died when Ryan was born. He had told her that on the first evening she had come here. Perhaps one day he would tell her more about his mother, but for now she felt so sad at any tragedy that she didn't want to know the story. She couldn't even begin to think how Daniel would have felt, and she didn't want to, lest she dissolved into tears during the service.

They shared a family pew at the front of the church, Jane between Pat and Ryan, and she felt the eyes of the rest of the congregation on her, for this was the first time she had been in church with the Lindens. She had worn her black suit, this time with a midi skirt, and a black felt floppy hat. It was good to be one of the Lindens, in their own front pew, all of them in black suits. Daniel had given them each a five-pound note for the collection.

After the service they chatted for a while with the local families, some of whom Jane had met at the cinema outing, before they walked back to the Hall in the sunshine.

In the afternoon she walked around the garden with Pat and Ryan, and they told her the names of the flowers and the trees, and explained what they did to keep the garden looking as good as it did. Ryan showed her a platform in one of the apple trees—all that was now left of a tree house that her father Peter had built for him when he was very small— and a white wooden cross with *Wolf* in black letters, marking the last resting place of Ryan's only pet dog.

Monday 20 October 1975

The weekend had gone all too fast.

Jane liked Ryan's company, but on Monday he was once again in Oxford. She was now spending her mornings sorting papers for Daniel and typing the cheques and letters.

He worked most mornings in his den, writing his latest book, completely engrossed in what he did. He told her that he once wrote the stories by hand, then edited them and typed up the final draft for the publisher, but he was too shaky to write for a lot of the time now, so he typed the first draft, corrected it by hand, and then typed the final one. He thought that she might do the final typing for him. While he worked on hand corrections, she could be typing. Better still, they could both type at once if he borrowed the typewriter that was up in Ryan's study. Ryan wouldn't miss it, as he was hardly ever here. He fetched it from upstairs for her to use.

They would give it a few weeks to see if the arrangement was working. Meanwhile she could also continue sorting the papers in the room. She had started organising them into separate piles on a table in the library. There were bank statements, bills, share certificates, dividend statements—some of them still with the cheques attached— contract notes for buying the shares, fan letters, newspapers, company reports and letters and cheques from the publisher. They didn't seem so formidable when they were sorted into categories, although she knew it would take her weeks to get through the backlog. She would then put each pile into date order and file them. The share certificates went straight into the safe—Daniel had told her the combination—the cheques were put aside to take to the bank on Friday, and the newspapers were taken to the kitchen for Mary to throw out.

He had previously cleared a small desk and a chair in his den so she could work near him, and he now placed Ryan's small typewriter there for her to use. The papers that had once been on the desk were still in a pile on the floor. He leaned over her to put a sheet of paper into the typewriter for her, his breath very close to her ear, and she shied away from him.

He told her he liked having her there, and at least she could oversee that he was not pouring himself a drink every time he paused to think. He said that he worked a lot better if he didn't drink in the mornings, but usually he did. He knew he was addicted.

Jane suggested he put the whisky decanter in the library so he was not constantly looking at it, and eventually he agreed to her putting it behind the desk so it was not in his view. Jane knew it was hopeless, that the only way he could give up drinking was if he gave it up completely, but she still hoped that if he reduced the absent-minded drinking, he might be able to reduce his dependence on it. She felt sad that somewhere along the line he had drifted from having the odd whisky to being a total addict. He was trying to have only two whiskies in the evening and none in the day, but short of locking up the bottle and the decanter Jane was not sure he would be able to. She suggested he try diluting it with lemon soda or dry ginger ale. At least that way it took longer to get through a glass, and after that perhaps he could put less whisky in the glass and more soda, so he was drinking the same amount, just less of it was alcohol.

Tuesday 21 October 1975

After morning coffee on Tuesday, she helped Mary change the sheets on her own bed and Mary's bed, but Pat helped Mary with the beds on the top floor. Mary's room was smaller than Jane's, but she must be content with it, as there were other rooms that she could have chosen now there were no paying guests.

Mary had a large black and white photo on her wall of a younger but very recognisable Daniel with another man that Jane thought was a younger Mr Allanstone. They were standing together in the garden near the pond with a beautiful child between them with dark curly hair, who looked about three.

Jane guessed it was Ryan, as Pat was fair. Mary had a lot of photos of the boys at various ages and also photos of her mother, Jane's father Peter, and even one of Jane as a small child in a striped multi-coloured cardigan with a hood, which Jane remembered because her father had called it her Joseph coat. They had the photo in the album at home. Mary told her that the cardigan had been knitted by Mary's mother and sent to Jane for her fourth birthday. There were so many strange things about this house and this family and how she was so connected with them.

She asked if it was Mr Allanstone in the picture with Daniel.

Mary told her he had been Daniel's best friend at school, and they had spent a year together at Oxford before the War. Daniel had joined the army, but Mr Allanstone had continued at Oxford. They had always kept in touch, and he had stayed with them for a few days in nineteen fifty-two when Ryan was three. Ryan had been a beautiful child, people would stop her in the street and say how lovely he was, and he was good natured as well, always hugging everyone he met. Jane's father had taken the photo.

The sheets and towels were placed in two large calico bags, which were picked up later in the day by a linen service, with clean sheets and towels left in exchange. The clean linen was neatly stacked in a cupboard behind the stairs to the second storey.

The days were passing quietly enough. She was glad to be useful, and she knew it was healing to be occupied with ordinary things. Every day the grief at losing her great-aunt seemed less raw. She had been here for a little over a week, but already she fitted in with the household routine, helping Daniel with the paperwork, Pat with the garden and Mary with the housework.

Most mornings she read *The Times* after Daniel had finished with it. She always read the engagements column, looking for the names of girls from school.

On Monday evening she had played chess with Daniel. She had enjoyed just sitting silently while they thought about the moves. She was not a fan of television except to watch the news, but there was a detective programme on Tuesday nights that she liked to watch, as it featured a very attractive young detective. On Thursday evening there was the ladies' yoga class at the village hall. Pat would walk her there and return to collect her when it finished at nine o' clock. On Friday Ryan would be home, and she was looking forward to spending the evening with him in the library.

In the afternoons she walked to the village or in the garden. Sometimes Daniel walked with her. He liked to think out in the fresh air, and at least there he wasn't drinking. He didn't say much and seemed lost in his own world. He always took a small bottle of pills with him from a high cupboard in the kitchen when they went out.

On Pat's gardening days she helped him, in her jeans and wellington boots. Mary found her an old hand-knitted jumper of Ryan's, as Jane's were all cashmere, and some gardening gloves so she didn't damage her nails. Pat was nice to talk to, not joking all the time like Jimmy, but still fun to be with.

They were pruning the older raspberry canes, and he showed her how to recognise the ones that had fruited. It wasn't the nicest job with the thorns, but it was good to be busy so there was less time to think about the past and the people she had loved and lost. Richmond and her great-aunt's funeral already seemed a long time ago.

She made herself a mug of cocoa last thing at night, even without Ryan there. She would sit by herself in the kitchen and think of things she would like to tell him when he returned on Friday. Everyone else seemed to go to bed much earlier than she did, but they all got up earlier too.

Friday 24 October 1975

On Friday morning they did the shopping again, and she bought some new jeans—more fashionable and tighter than anything she had already—a tunic-length jumper that was long enough to cover her derrière in the tight jeans, and a smart three-quarter length navy-blue duffle coat with a fur-lined hood.

When they returned to the Hall and had put away the groceries, she took the tags off the coat and hung it next to Ryan's black duffle coat in the boot room.

Ryan returned on Friday evening, as he had the week before. Mary had made an apple pie again. He had bought Jane a present, an electronic calculator for when she did the accounting. She didn't need one, since she added everything up in her head, but she thanked him, flattered that he had thought of her.

She had been helping Pat that afternoon, and she was still wearing her jeans and Ryan's old jumper. It was rather too large for her, and he laughed about it, so she changed before dinner and vowed she wouldn't let him see her wearing his jumper again.

Daniel and Ryan seemed a little more courteous to each other over dinner than they had been on the first day she had arrived, and Jane wondered if Mary had said something to them both. There was a slight tiff about Ryan's typewriter having disappeared from his room, but he said it was okay, as he rarely used it. If he needed to type something he would come down to the den to use it.

After dinner she went through the mail with Ryan in the library, giving him the letters that were addressed to him, and he signed the cheques. One of the cheques was to pay Daniel's credit card. She had been left wondering what he had spent that she was not to know about. There was a charge for a hotel in London, and train fares, but the remaining items were just purchases from a department store, and from a tailor in Savile Row.

When the paperwork was finished, Daniel and Ryan played snooker in the billiard room. Daniel was the more skilful player, but Ryan didn't seem to mind always losing. Pat joined them and played with Ryan.

There was the inevitable whisky decanter in the billiard room, and Daniel had a glass in his hand whenever he wasn't wielding a cue.

While the two young men were playing together, he set up a few balls on the smaller pool table and showed Jane how to hold the cue properly, standing behind her to guide her hands as she hit the ball, his breath warm on her neck, his body uncomfortably close to hers.

She was glad when Ryan asked if she would like to take his place and play with Pat, and he helped her choose which ball she should play and explained the rules.

Later Ryan remembered to swap her book, this time for *Silas Marner*, as he wanted her to read only happy books for the present, and they talked about *Middlemarch* while they drank their cocoa.

Saturday 25 October 1975

On Saturday Mary once again went to London, and they were left to fend for themselves until one o' clock when they met at the car park of the village hall to start the outing to Peddleton.

There were around twenty young people. Most of them were boys, so the half-dozen girls were treated especially well. All of the girls and most of the boys were younger than Jane. The oldest girls were Claire from the farm, Candy who was in her final year at the local grammar school, and Julie who was sixteen and worked during the week at the post office in the village.

Jane enjoyed the walk in her new jeans and duffle coat and her new hiking boots, although after a while they seemed to be rubbing a little. She walked mostly with Jimmy—who swung her off her feet to lift her down when they climbed over stiles—and sometimes with Pat or with Claire, Julie and Candy, but only occasionally with Ryan as he spent most of the time talking to Reverend Colin, both of them constantly counting heads so they all stayed together and no one was lost. She had wanted herself and Ryan to be the only ones with duffle coats, but nearly everyone had them.

The farmhouse providing the tea at Peddleton had tables set up in the garden, and they all washed their hands in the bathroom before they ate. Ryan had brought his camera with him, and he took dozens of photos before the afternoon was out.

She had worn ankle socks, as she had forgotten when she bought the hiking boots that you needed decent socks with them. However, the ankle socks were not high enough to protect her feet from the new leather, and they had slipped right down, so her ankles were badly blistered by the time they returned to Hayward Hall. She was limping slightly, trying not to let it show.

Ryan took her coat and hung it back on the peg beside his. He had a black cable knit pullover under his duffle coat, and black jeans. He looked different because he normally wore a jacket and a tie like Daniel did. When he came home from Oxford, and in church, he was always in a black suit, but for most of the weekend he wore a tweed jacket and a hand-knitted sleeveless Fair Isle pullover.

She sat on a bench in the boot room and let him pull off her muddy boots, but she couldn't suppress an *Ouch* and had to own up about the blisters. New boots, she explained.

'Holy socks! That looks painful,' he said when he looked at her ankles. She laughed, and he told her everyone at his college said that.

'Why didn't you say something, Jane? We could have phoned home from Peddleton, and Daniel would have picked you up in the car.'

She sat on the sofa in Mary's room with her feet on a small footstool and the cat on her lap while he carefully rolled up the cuffs of her jeans, pulled off her socks, put them on the radiator to keep them warm, and fetched antiseptic and plasters from the kitchen for her ankles. She rather liked the feel of his hands on her bare feet. When he had looked after the blisters, he pulled her warmed socks back on, straightened her jeans, and found her indoor shoes.

'You are very kind to me,' she said. 'Thank you.'

'I like looking after you. It makes me feel useful. I used to look after Pat when he was small and put his shoes on for him, but now he can put them on himself.'

She laughed; he could always make her laugh, and she felt so glad she had come here to stay.

After dinner, while Mary washed up and Jane dried the dishes, Ryan cleaned all the boots and returned hers polished and looking like new.

She played chess with Daniel in the library, Ryan sitting nearby watching the moves and occasionally helping her. Daniel was a better strategist than she was, and he easily won the game. But he did tell her she was a worthier opponent than Ryan. If he didn't constantly look at her as though he was undressing her in his mind, she thought, she might actually enjoy his company.

She sensed that he enjoyed hers, even when he was silent. He always seemed very self-sufficient, but she wondered if he was rather lonely. He and Mary spoke only of household matters and Pat and Ryan scarcely spoke to him at all. She knew that the antagonism between him and his son and nephew was his own doing, yet she thought he might have more in common with Ryan than he did with her, and it seemed sad that they were so curt with each other. She would try including both of them in conversation at meal times on the weekends, ask the opinion of both of them on things she had read in the newspaper, in the hope that they would interact a little more.

Sunday 26 October 1975

On Sunday there was the cooked breakfast, the bunches of flowers, the church service, the conversations with the other families and the walk home to the Hall for lunch.

In the afternoon Ryan drove her to look over a local ruined castle, but they didn't walk far when they arrived there because of the blisters. He seemed happy to sit with her on a seat, not too close to her, overlooking the ruin in the sunshine. He didn't say much, mostly telling her about the history of the place and a story about Pat climbing a wall there when he was small then being unable to get back down. Mary had been frantic, and Daniel had threatened to leave him there, to encourage him to come down. Eventually Ryan had managed to climb up and help Pat find the right footholds. He told Jane he had nearly become stuck himself and had wondered if they would need the fire brigade to rescue both of them.

She had only been at Hayward Hall for a fortnight, but sitting here beside him in the sunshine, her previous life seemed long ago and far away. She already felt so much better than she had on the day she arrived, when she had stood on the train platform and felt that everyone had deserted her.

They had tea at a nearby café, sitting out in the garden. The tea-room lady brought out their coffee and strawberry shortcake, and she lingered for a while to talk to them about the sunny weather and how good the tourist season had been that year. She seemed to know Ryan was from Hayward Hall. She remembered his grandmother Kathleen, and recalled the days when they had guests there, as they often came to see the castle and had tea at her café.

That evening was spent in the billiard room once more. This time Ryan and Daniel played billiards, which seemed to Jane to be very complex, as there were only three balls and it all relied on a complicated system of points. They did seem to get on a little better over the game, even if they scarcely spoke. Pat showed Jane how to play pool on the smaller table, and she got the hang of it quite quickly. Mary put a record on for them in the lounge and went to her room off the kitchen to watch television. Jane thought Mary deserved to sit down in the evening; she did a lot of housework and seemed to be on her feet all day.

Monday 27 October 1975

On Monday morning Ryan had gone again, back to Oxford, before Jane came down to breakfast.

Mary was making crocheted poppies to adorn a wreath of greenery for Remembrance Sunday. Pat had made a wire frame that she would decorate on the Saturday with foliage from the garden and the poppies. She showed Jane how to make them. It was easy enough when you knew how, and they were quick to produce. Jane sewed a button to the back of three of the poppies she had made, so the men could wear them in their buttonholes instead of paper ones.

Daniel went to London on the Wednesday morning and came back late on Thursday. Apart from that, the week passed in a similar way to the previous week, with Jane helping Daniel in the mornings when he was there, and Pat or Mary in the afternoons.

She ironed some shirts to help Mary—the men seemed to go through a lot of shirts between them—but as she had no idea whose shirt was whose, she left them on hangers on the clothes airer for Mary to distribute. Mary said the coloured shirts were all Pat's, as Daniel and Ryan only wore white shirts. Mary seemed to know which were Ryan's and which were Daniel's, but to Jane the white shirts all looked the same. In any case she was not allowed to take them up to their rooms.

Friday 31 October 1975

On Friday afternoon Jimmy called by at four o'clock with a fresh skinned rabbit for Mary. Jane didn't like to think of the rabbit being shot, but Mary seemed unfazed and told him she would turn it into a rabbit pie for dinner on Sunday. He asked Jane if she would walk with him in the garden.

She put on her coat and her outdoor shoes, and they walked along the wooded path. He growled at the gargoyles as he passed them, telling her he loved them really and wished they had some at the farm. They were much better than sheep, as they stayed where you put them, at least in the daylight. He knew they ran around the garden at night, but they never did any harm, and they helped scare off the foxes.

He wanted to go into the maze, but she told him she wasn't absolutely sure how to get them out, and it would be a shame for them to be stuck in there all night, especially as there were some gargoyles in the dead ends that would come alive and scare them. She walked with him back to the front gate and waited until he reached the farm. He turned and waved to her.

Pat had gone to pick up Ryan from the station, so she lingered at the gate, waiting for the car to return. She always felt close to her father in the garden. Would he mind that she had come to live here? Would he be glad that the rift with his cousin was now lost in the past? How could she judge that when no one would tell her what had happened to make him leave? Her father and Daniel had both loved the same woman for four weeks of a long-ago summer. Would that really have torn apart forever two men who had been brought up as brothers?

Dusk was already deepening, as daylight saving had ended last weekend. It was very still here. You could hear the soft splash of the fountain, the bleating of the sheep in the fields and a few restless birds. Perhaps her father had once stood here, listening to the same gentle sounds in the stillness of an evening. Perhaps their ancestor Charles Linden had stood here more than a hundred years ago. The sounds would have been the same even then.

When the car had returned and they were all indoors, Ryan gave her some thick blue socks, specially made for hiking, that he had bought for her in Oxford. He hoped the size was right. The girl in the shop had told him that most ladies' socks were the same standard size. She thanked him, surprised that he had thought of it. He was always very kind and caring.

She asked him if she could try out a poppy on his jacket, to check the button at the back would work to hold it in place. She didn't want to ask Daniel as she didn't like to get so personal with him, and Pat wore jumpers most days rather than a jacket.

He stood very still, looking down at his lapel as her fingers worked the button through the buttonhole, and she smoothed the red poppy against the black jacket, very conscious of how close she was to him. He seemed surprisingly tense, as if he didn't like to be touched, and she knew some men didn't. Perhaps he just didn't like her to be this close, so when she had tried out the poppy, she stepped away from him.

'Would you be good enough to make an extra one,' he asked her. 'I am going to see my grandfather on Sunday, and I would like to take him one. He was my mother's father, and he is the only grandparent I have left. He fought in the First World War and luckily survived to marry and have children, although his son was killed in the Second World War, and my mother died not long afterwards. I am all he has left. Would you like to come with me?'

'I would, but Linda is having a craft bee on Sunday afternoon to sew knitted squares into blankets for distributing in winter, and I have promised to help. I think she wants me to meet some of the ladies from the farms here. I will come with you next time. If you take this poppy for him, I will make another one for you.'

After dinner he swapped her book, this time choosing *Adam Bede*. He didn't want her to read *The Mill on The Floss* yet, as he thought she would find it too sad. They talked about her previous book, *Silas Marner*, over a game of chess.

2 GREY SKIES

Saturday 1 November 1975

On Saturday afternoon it was raining, so Reverend Colin had arranged table tennis in the village hall. There were five tables that were brought out from a back room and set up, and the mothers of the teenagers had sent a contribution to the tea after the game. Mary had made some jam tarts the evening before for Jane to take.

Ryan came to help Colin set up the tables, but he played beside Jane to make up the numbers on one of the tables. They played against David and Jimmy, while Pat was with Claire on another table. Colin had tried to space the girls so there was at least one on each table.

When the games were over, Jane and Linda made the tea and coffee, and served lemonade for any of the young people who preferred it, while the cakes and biscuits were rapidly demolished.

Jimmy asked Jane if she would like to go out to a film that evening. They wound up the table tennis at the hall at five, leaving plenty of time, but she enjoyed the evenings with Ryan at Hayward, and she didn't want to miss one. She arranged instead to go out with him on a Wednesday. Although not this coming one, as that was bonfire night. Reverend Colin was arranging a bonfire on the village green.

Sunday 2 November 1975

On Sunday Ryan left after lunch to see his grandfather, who lived near Bath, while Jane and Mary stitched squares into blankets in the village hall. Jane did wish she had been able to go with him. It would have been good to have had him to herself for an afternoon, away from Hayward, as she had the previous Sunday. However, she enjoyed meeting the wives and daughters of the farmers, and was surprised at how many of the older women remembered her father.

She showed two young girls of around ten how to stitch the squares together, and they asked her about London. Had she seen Buckingham Palace? Had she had tea there with the Queen? Had she fed the pigeons like in *Mary Poppins*? Although they looked rather alike, they were friends, not sisters. Their names were Jenny and Alice. Jane tried to remember that Alice was the one with the longer hair.

When they returned to the Hall, she asked Mary if Ryan was shy of girls. When she had buttoned a poppy into his lapel, she had felt that he disliked her being so close to him.

'He doesn't like to be touched—we hardly ever get a hug out of him—but he'll get used to you after a while, and then he won't mind so much. Just be careful not to get too close too soon. He really does care about his family, but he likes to be by himself. As far as we know he's never had a girlfriend, which is sad because he would make a wonderful caring husband for someone. When he finishes his next degree, he wants to stay on living at the college and teaching the students there. It's all men at his college, and I think he sees that as a safe way to live. He has been taking you out and looking after you, which is good to see, and since you came here, he has been at home a lot more often. I am grateful for that. I don't like him being by himself all the time, as he sometimes gets a bit depressed. Ryan was never a happy boy, but he was always very controlled and self-sufficient. When he was a teenager, he would go off walking by himself and stay out all day. He told my mother he walked and talked with the ghosts of the ancient people who had lived in the hills. My mother always worried about him, and she was always relieved when he returned home safely at the end of the day. Sometimes he took one of John Phillips' dogs with him. John didn't mind, and my grandmother was grateful, as she felt he was safer with the dog. John gave Ryan a puppy of his own, and it followed him everywhere when he was at home. Even Daniel enjoyed having the dog here. But they only last about ten years, and eventually it died. It was called Wolf. After that we got the cat, as Ryan was then rarely at home.'

Dinner that evening was rabbit pie. Jane wasn't sure she wanted to eat it, but Ryan told her to pretend it was chicken, it tasted similar, and she always ate chicken.

'It isn't the taste,' she explained. 'It's because I don't like to think of the rabbit running around free and then becoming rabbit pie. I once had a pet rabbit called Muffin.'

'This is wild rabbit,' he told her. 'We don't eat pets. And chickens run around as well. You just don't see them doing it. If Mary had bought the rabbit from the butcher, you wouldn't think twice, would you?'

She ate her slice of rabbit pie. She knew she had to get used to this sort of thing now she was living in the country with farms next door.

Wednesday 5 November 1975

Ryan came home for the evening on the fifth of November for the fire-works. He would stay overnight and return to Oxford the following morning.

Mary had asked Jane to try to keep Daniel from drinking during the day, so he was sober enough to come out for the evening with them, and she had managed fairly well, as he still seemed okay at dinner time. She had not been able to supervise him the whole time, however, as late that afternoon she had been helping Pat, Jimmy and Reverend Colin stack up the logs on the green for the bonfire.

That evening there were a lot of people on the green. Several guys, made by the children who lived at the surrounding farms, were thrown onto the fire, and Jack McCann and John Phillips were in charge of the fireworks.

It was difficult to find anyone in the dark, as there was no moon at all, although Ryan had found Jane a small torch. At first she had been with Ryan, but she somehow lost him in the darkness and found herself with Jimmy.

He took her hand, and they walked away from the crowd and sat for a while in the porch of the church, Jimmy joking about seeing a ghost in the churchyard and assuring her he was there to protect her. Jane was not sure she wanted to be alone with him like this, and she wished she had stayed with Ryan. But she didn't pull away when he kissed her. It felt good, and she knew she was safe with him. He kept his hands to himself and would do her no harm. For a while he sat with his arm around her, chatting about the farm and the fireworks and the table tennis.

Eventually she asked if they could go back. She didn't want Ryan or Mary to find them there, but she didn't tell Jimmy that; she just said it would be a shame to miss the last of the fireworks. He stayed with her until she finally found Ryan, who was still with Daniel and Mary, all of them merging into the darkness in their black clothes. Then he went to help his father and John Phillips tidy up from the fireworks.

She hadn't seen Pat the whole evening, but it was difficult to make out who was who in the darkness, especially as some children had sparklers, which dazzled your eyes, leaving coloured trails lingering in your vision.

The fireworks were over, the bonfire dying down to a pile of steadily burning logs, the guys consumed as though they had never been, the smell of gunpowder hanging over the green in the cold night air.

They walked back to the Hall, still without Pat. The kitchen was warm and welcoming after the cold of the outdoors. The coats were hung, and Ryan pulled off Jane's boots as he had when they had walked to Peddleton, promising to clean and polish them on Saturday, as they were too wet to polish tonight, and tomorrow he would be back in Oxford.

Her feet were cold from standing on the green, and his hands on her toes felt warm through the socks. He moved a chair so she could sit with her feet near the range in the kitchen. He had black sheepskin boots that he wore indoors in the winter, and he offered to buy some for her if she told him the size.

The cat, stressed by the fireworks and cowering on Mary's sofa in the darkness, was brought into the kitchen to sit on Jane's lap to be comforted. Mary found the cat brush so Jane could brush her. Both Jane and the cat enjoyed that.

Daniel had retreated to his den to catch up on today's whisky. Ryan made cocoa, but still Pat had not come home.

Thursday 6 November 1975

When Jane came down for breakfast, Ryan had already left for Oxford. Mary told her that Pat had eventually returned, but he had not been up early enough to drive Ryan to the station, so Ryan had parked the Jaguar in town. Daniel was walking there after breakfast to collect it. Jane was to go with him, so she went back upstairs to change into jeans.

He took Ryan's duffle coat and for once didn't wear his trilby hat. Jane told him it would look a little strange with the duffle coat, and he wouldn't need it because duffle coats had hoods. He wore Ryan's black beanie instead.

They followed the footpath through the fields, as it was safer than walking along the narrow roads. There were stiles of course, and men always held the hands of ladies over stiles, but apart from that he didn't touch her, and he was good company. Although he was often silent and lost in his own world, he always answered if she spoke to him, and he knew who owned the farms they walked through, who lived in each of the houses and when most of them dated from.

When they reached the town, he bought them coffee and a muffin each at a café, and pretended he had forgotten to bring the spare car key, so they would have to walk back home instead of driving the car back.

'You walk,' she said. 'I'll get a taxi. I always have two five-pound notes with me in case I need to get a taxi home. Aunt Ellen's rules.'

He didn't drive them straight home. Instead, he took the car for a drive along the main road southwards, sometimes driving at a speed rather higher than the limit.

'I enjoy driving this car. It goes much faster than mine. Mary would never allow me to do this when I take her shopping, but you'll be more lenient. I wanted to drive it on the motorway when we went to Richmond, but my son wouldn't let me. He said I would get caught for speeding, and he would get the fine because his name is on the car licence. He's never been fined for speeding in his life. He never sets a foot wrong. Sometimes I think this car is wasted on him.'

He turned the car around when they reached the next village, drove back to Hayward and stopped in front of the garage.

'There's an old airfield a few miles south of here. We could go for a spin there one day and see how fast we can go,' he said, putting his hand on her knee.

She removed his hand. 'That's not allowed, Mr Linden,' she told him, amazed at her own courage in dealing with him. 'And I don't think I want to break any speed limits. Mary would be upset if you killed us both, and Ryan would be upset if you damaged his car.'

She put her own and Daniel's boots by the radiator, next to Ryan's from the previous evening, and before dinner she cleaned all three pairs and polished them.

Friday 7 November 1975

When Ryan came home on Friday, he had bought her some dark-blue sheepskin boots to wear indoors when it was cold. They were not glamorous, but they were very warm, especially with jeans. Hayward Hall was rather a cold house in the winter. The radiators did their best, but the rooms were large, and the open hallway seemed to suck all the warmth from the rooms and send it up into the rafters.

Ryan noticed the polished boots and thanked her.

After dinner she sorted out the paperwork with him in the library, putting the cheques into their envelopes when he had signed them. There were always a surprising number of cheques and envelopes by the end of the week. There were accounts for the laundry, the dry cleaning, the garage where they bought the petrol, the whisky and wine that was delivered, the milk and the newspapers, as well as the electricity and the oil to run the Aga. She filled in her account book for each cheque that was written. Then there were cash cheques to be signed, which she would take to the bank the following Friday so Mary had money for the groceries and Pat and Ryan were paid their allowance for the fortnight. She was still using Ryan's typewriter in the den. He seemed to manage without it. He said he had another at the college.

He swapped her book for *The Warden* and *Barchester Towers*. He thought she could probably read both since she was indoors a lot more with the cold weather.

Saturday 8 November 1975

For once Mary didn't go to London on Saturday as her friend had something else on. Jane and Ryan walked to the post office with the letters. When they returned Jane helped Mary put the foliage on the wreath for Remembrance Day, and they stitched the poppies to it with thick button thread. It was finished by lunch time.

The weather was fine, so in the afternoon Colin's group played rounders on the village green. Ryan didn't join them. He didn't think he would be needed since Linda was able to help, and he wanted to catch up with some paperwork of his own. Jane rather missed having him there, and had trouble concentrating on the game, her thoughts wandering to where he was in the house, and what he was doing that required him to leave her alone all afternoon.

Sunday 9 November 1975

There was a service for Remembrance Sunday on the ninth of November. Jane tied one of the poppies to the plaque on the wall at the end of the pew for Daniel's father. You could just fit the thread between the wall and the plaque at the corners, and that was enough to tie on the poppy without damaging the plaque or the wall behind it. The men all had their poppies in their buttonholes, and Jane had put a pin on the back of two others so she and Mary could wear them as brooches.

The wreaths were left in the church after the service, and would be taken to the war memorial for a small outdoor service that they all attended on Tuesday morning, which was the eleventh and Remembrance Day. There were several Linden names on the war memorial as well as McCann names and Phillips names. Just names; all that now remained of the intricate complexity of their lives.

Ryan was at Oxford on the Tuesday, so he was not at the Hayward village memorial service.

Wednesday 12 November 1975

On most days Jane helped Daniel with the typing in the mornings, and she walked with him in the afternoons if she was not helping Pat in the garden. Sometimes he would touch her hair or her shoulder while she worked, leaning over her to check how she was progressing. At first she had thought nothing of it, her father had often stroked her hair, but this morning when she put something into the filing cabinet, he stood behind her to help her find the right slot, and his hand brushed against her derrière, as if by accident. She knew it was deliberate, and she didn't like it.

Afterwards he was a little bolder while she sat typing, slipping his fingers around her neck and beneath her collar at her throat. She brushed his hand away, telling him it tickled, but it felt rather creepy and she wished he wouldn't do it.

On Wednesday evening she went out with Jimmy. She had arranged that she would walk down to the farm after dinner, to avoid Daniel knowing where she was going. This was Mary's idea. He would be in bed by the time Jimmy dropped her home. Mary said it was all right for her to bring Jimmy into the kitchen afterwards and make cocoa for them, but she was not to take him up to her room. Mary found her a key and said she would leave the back porch light on, and the light in the kitchen.

The Land Rover was rather bumpy to ride in, but she enjoyed being out on a date. Jimmy held her hand at the cinema, bought chocolates for her, and behaved like a boyfriend should.

They had coffee afterwards in a little café, and he held her hand across the table.

'Jane, on bonfire night Claire didn't come home until after midnight. My father and I were out looking for her by that stage, and my mother was frantic. Pat was with her when she came back, and he said you had all been sitting in the kitchen at the Hall talking, and they hadn't realised the time. Was that true?'

Jane thought back, remembering they had missed Pat in the darkness, and he had still not been home when she and Ryan went to bed at nearly midnight. Pat had not been up early enough to drive Ryan to the station. She was not sure whether she should cover for them and say they had been at the Hall, or whether she should be honest, in which case Claire might be in trouble with her mother. She covered for them and said they had been there. But she did wonder where they actually had been that night.

When Jimmy dropped her back at Hayward Hall, he left the Land Rover at the gate, and they walked with a torch to the back door. He didn't want to drive in, he told her, in case he accidentally hit one of the gargoyles in the garden in the darkness. They ran around the garden at night, and they were stone, so they might dent the Land Rover.

She offered the cocoa, but he declined as they had only recently had coffee. He thanked her for going out with him and gave her a long and rather expert kiss. He waited until she was safely indoors before heading back to the Land Rover.

The kitchen light was on as promised. She almost expected Daniel to be sitting there waiting for her, but instead it was a Pat, and he seemed rather cross.

'Where have you been? The film finished an hour ago? What did you do afterwards?'

'We had coffee at a café.'

'Next week it's my turn to take you out.'

She didn't argue with him, as she was tired and just wanted to go up to bed. She didn't mention bonfire night.

Friday 14 November 1975

When they shopped in town on Friday morning, Jane's eye was caught by a calendar for next year in the window of the bookshop. It featured pictures of wolves. She immediately thought of Ryan, and she bought it for him.

He came home that evening with a portable electric Olivetti typewriter for her. He had one himself in his room at the college, and he said they were much easier to use because you didn't have to hit the keys so hard, which made typing faster. He set it up in the library. He said that was so everyone could use it, but in fact no one else was likely to use it.

Jane wondered if it was also because he wanted to be able to sit with her sometimes when she worked on it. He couldn't do that in Daniel's den. Or perhaps he was concerned at her spending so much time alone with his father. She was happy to have it in the library, as she felt more comfortable typing without Daniel constantly touching her.

He took his own typewriter from Daniel's den back to his study upstairs. Jane knew it belonged there, as she had seen it when Mary had shown her the view from the room.

She gave him the wolf calendar. He seemed surprised to be given anything, but he thanked her, and said he liked it.

'It's because you are a lone wolf,' she explained, in case he had forgotten what he had once said. 'Now every time I see a wolf, I think of you.'

'I hope you haven't seen too many in the garden,' he said. 'They worry the gargoyles. Gargoyles look ferocious, but they are actually quite scared of wolves.'

'Jimmy says they run around at night chasing away foxes,' she told him, and he laughed.

They talked about the two *Barchester* books. She didn't tell him that when Eleanor had married that nice Mr Arabin, she had imagined him looking a lot like Ryan.

He gave her *Tess* to read next; he thought she could cope with that now. It had become a game between them, and Jane enjoyed the books more when she could talk about them afterwards. It was also good discipline, as she had to finish the book by the weekend.

She now played chess with Daniel every Monday evening, watched a programme on Tuesdays, went out most Wednesdays and did the yoga class on Thursdays. But there was still plenty of time to read, either curled up on the sofa in the library, on the swing seat in the conservatory, or up in her own sitting room when everyone else had gone to bed.

Saturday 15 November 1975

On Saturday afternoon Colin's group walked along the footpath towards the town, stopping at a farm for tea and warm donuts, then walking back to Hayward. It was sunny but rather cold.

Ryan came with them, and he brought a book in the pocket of his duffle coat and read them the first part of *The Canterville Ghost* while they sat in the warm kitchen at the farm. He promised them the second part on the next walk. Jane hoped he would lend her the book so she could read the rest of the story ahead of time.

When they returned to the Hall, Daniel had already left to pick up Mary from the station. Ryan pulled off her hiking boots and found her sheepskin boots, and they sat for a while in Mary's room, as it was always warm there. She was by now used to the boots, and she had proper hiking socks, so they had not given her blisters since the first time she had worn them. The cat came to sit on his lap to be stroked and Jane stroked her as well, being very careful not to get too close to him or touch him.

After dinner he read the remainder of the story to her as they sat in the library.

Wednesday 19 November 1975

On the Wednesday evening Pat took her to a film in town, just the two of them. Daniel had gone to London that morning and would not be back until dinnertime on Thursday, so there was no one to stop them. Mary was quite happy for them to go out.

He held her hand through the film, just as Jimmy had, and they shared a box of Maltesers. When they returned home, he kissed her once again outside the back door, holding her close to him for a very long time. This time there was no Ryan waiting for them, as he was in Oxford. But once indoors he behaved impeccably, making them cocoa as Ryan did, and seeing her to the door of her room before disappearing up the next flight of stairs to his own.

When she lay in bed that night, she thought she might be falling in love with him. She imagined a life for them, away from Hayward Hall, just the two of them in a cottage somewhere, with her cooking the dinner, then both of them lying together, making love through the night.

Friday 21 November 1975

Jane liked to sit in the conservatory, even on wet days. There was a table with six cane chairs, two cane armchairs with a matching coffee table, and a swing seat that was just wide enough for two. A lovers' seat, Jane called it in her mind, for you were very close to the other person. There was a line of small potted citrus trees at the terrace end, and a gutter in the floor to drain away any excess when they were watered. In the summer they went out onto the stone-flagged terrace between the conservatory and the back garden. There were two fireplaces, one on each side. Jane doubted they would have given much warmth when they were in use, but perhaps they were just to help keep the frost at bay to protect the plants. Mary thought they were only there as they shared the chimney with the fireplaces in the bedrooms above them. If you needed to build a chimney, it might as well serve as many fires as practical. Most of the fireplaces in the house had not been used for years.

It was cold in the conservatory when the sun wasn't shining, but it was light and bright and interesting to be under the sky but still indoors, and it was cold in the house as well, except in the kitchen and Mary's sitting room.

On Friday afternoon Jane was sitting on the swing seat, finishing *Tess*, her book for the week. It was raining, a cold dreary incessant rain that made gardening impossible and walking miserable even with an umbrella. She had brought in a blanket from the lounge, as the conservatory had no heating apart from the sun, and today there was no sunshine at all. The cat sat on her lap, warm and comforting, audibly purring, although you could scarcely hear her above the patter of the rain and the gurgle of the water through the downpipes.

She had put down the book—it was getting too dark to read—and she was thinking about the past, near to tears again, lost in her thoughts, when Ryan came into the conservatory, back early from Oxford. She moved over so he could sit beside her.

He hesitated for a moment, and she remembered he didn't like being close to people, but he sat down next to her. She pulled the blanket over his knees as well as her own. The cat moved over to sit on Ryan, so Jane tucked up her feet and hugged her knees, leaving him to work the swing for them both.

'Jane, are you getting depressed? Was *Tess* a mistake?'

'No, the book is fine. It is rather sad, but I can cope with it. I'm not really depressed. Just sometimes I still feel very sad and alone, and I wish I could just go back to how it used to be, when we lived in the house in Kent and I helped my father in the garden. I used to wish I had been with them when they died in the train crash. When my great-aunt died, it all came back, but I am starting to get over it. I know my mother would have been glad I was still alive, and it would have been dreadful for Aunt Ellen to have lost me as well. I was all the family she had left.'

'That sounds like very depressed to me. I'm very glad you are here with us. We all are. You can't ever go back to the way things were when you were young, but you can treasure the memories of it. And you're not alone; we all care about you. You have brightened up this house so much that I actually want to come home at the weekends. During the week I think about which book you might like to read next and where we can go on the Sunday. Pat enjoys having company working in the garden. Mary loves having you here, and she told me that my father has been much easier to get on with since you came.

'When I was younger, I sometimes thought that people had the right to choose for themselves whether they wanted to be part of this life, but then I would think how glad my mother would have been to know they had saved me when she died, and how Mary gave up all her teenage years to look after me—she had to leave school—and how dreadfully upset my grandmother would have been to lose me. No one lives in a vacuum, and we all have responsibilities to other people.

'Once, when I was about sixteen, I found a length of rope hidden away in the stables, and it had a noose tied in one end. I was standing there with it, wondering how it got there and who had tied it, and looking up at the beams deciding which of them you would hang it from, when my grandmother came into the stables and went absolutely berserk at me.

'She told me that however bleak things looked there was always a way forward. Often you only had to talk to someone and things would seem better. But if you were dead, it was absolute, you couldn't change your mind, and then there was no way forward. You could always hang yourself tomorrow, but you couldn't unhang yourself today if you had hanged yourself yesterday. That made me laugh of course. She always knew how to make me laugh. She said the people who loved you would be the ones that suffered, and she told me that sometimes small things could overwhelm you, but if you talked about it to someone else, they could help you see it from a different perspective. She said sometimes you felt guilty about things that were not in any way your fault. She thought perhaps I felt it was my fault that my mother had died, but it could never be a child's fault, as children don't choose to be born, mothers choose to have them, and in any case my mother's death was an accident. I was a miracle baby because she had survived long enough for them to save my life even though they were unable to save hers.'

'What happened to her?'

'She fell down the stairs, about a month before I was due to be born. One day, when you are up to it, I will tell you the whole story, but for now I don't want to upset you. Then my grandmother said perhaps I felt it was my fault that my father didn't care about me, but that was his fault, not mine, because he was too twisted and bitter to love anyone. She said she had always tried to help him, but he would never talk to her. She told me he had been a difficult, withdrawn boy, always unhappy and always arguing with his own father. But when he had fallen for my mother, it had completely changed his life and his outlook on the world. When she died, he had blamed God for it and had become bitter and twisted. He hadn't wanted to love me when I was born because he was afraid that I wouldn't survive, but that is the wrong way to look at it. The joy of loving someone far outweighs the grief of losing them. She told me his father—her husband—had been difficult as well. He had been traumatised by serving in the First World War, and he never got over it. It was called shell shock, and it affected a good many returned servicemen. He would get very depressed and go off by himself for days on end. He had lost both his brothers. My grandmother had been engaged to the eldest one at the start of the First World War, but he had died, and she had married my grandfather after the War ended. He was very hard to live with, but she had loved him absolutely as she loved Daniel absolutely and me as well.

'So then I explained it wasn't me who had tied the knot in the rope; I had simply found it. She said it would have been my father, and we took the rope back to the kitchen, untied the knot, and cut it into small pieces, which we then burnt on the fire in the kitchen stove. We had coal then, so you could do that; it runs on oil now. After that I thought about my father a lot differently to how I had before.

'So now I am wondering what she would have said to you. That perhaps you feel guilty because you are alive and your parents are dead, but that is the wrong way to see things because everyone else is thankful you are still here. Or perhaps you feel guilty for not coping by yourself, but we are all glad you came to live with us, and we love having you here. It may take you a while to get over losing your great-aunt. No one here minds how long it takes you. I lost my grandmother when I was the same age as you are now, and it took me a long time to come to terms with it. For a long time afterwards, I would wish I had told her more often how much I loved her, and I would think of times when I should have said sorry for something I had said or done, knowing that now I would never get the chance to make amends. We all still miss her. She was the only person who could keep my father under proper control. The rest of us just do what he says so he doesn't fly into a rage. He yells at Mary if the coffee is too cold, and he accuses her of watering down the whisky. If he gets really drunk, you can't reason with him. He has been much better since you came. Mary told me that he hasn't once been angry with her, and he drinks a lot less.'

'He has never got angry with me. We get on okay.'

'It is good that you are helping him. He does seem happier. If you're really feeling down, we could get you some anti-depressants.'

'I have something for when I panic, but I don't think it's an anti-depressant.'

'Probably Valium, like I have when I can't sleep. Give it to Mary to look after. She keeps all the pills in the kitchen. My father had barbiturates to help him sleep after my mother died, and my grand-mother once told me she locked them away for fear he would take an overdose and kill himself. He had to ask, and she would give him just one. She did the same with my Valium, but it's nowhere near as danger-ous. It's still kept in the kitchen, but the cupboard isn't locked any more. Mary trusts me.'

'I can give them to Mary. I sometimes took one before I came here, when I stayed with Sarah after my aunt died, but I have never had one since, and I had almost forgotten about them. I don't think I need anything else. Just sometimes it would be nice to have someone to hug. I think that's what I miss most. My mother was never a huggy sort of person; she always seemed wary of anyone being close to her. She didn't trust people, and she would never allow me to go anywhere on my own. But my father always hugged me and so did Aunt Ellen.'

'I can hug you any time you want.'

She remembered Mary saying he didn't like to be hugged, and he didn't like to be close to people. Yet he was offering to hug her because he thought she was unhappy. Had she said the wrong thing? Suppose he misconstrued it and thought she was making a pass at him? He was sitting quite close to her—you had to sit close on the swing seat—but perhaps he was getting used to being near her.

'Your father might come in, and we would get into trouble. But thank you for offering; I know you don't like hugging people.'

'Then give me your hand instead. My father wouldn't see that under the blanket. I don't think I would mind hugging you. You always seem quite safe.'

It felt rather nice to have her hand held in secret. She leaned against him; she couldn't help but lean against him in the narrow seat.

'The first time I ever saw you was when you were sixteen, and you looked so lost and unhappy that I wanted to hug you, but I would never have dared. My father wanted you to come and live with us, but your great-aunt wouldn't hear of it, not even for a visit. You looked as if you needed to be cared for, and I wished I could look after you. We had photos of you, but none of us had ever seen you before, and we hadn't realised how beautiful you were. Then at your great-aunt's funeral I thought the same thing again. I wanted to hug you because you looked so forlorn, and I wanted to make you happy again. Your great-aunt had only ever sent us one photo—or rather Allanstone sent it, but he did ask her first. You hadn't changed much since the first time we saw you.'

'My great-aunt was always very good to me. She brought up my mother, as my grandmother had died when my mother was a baby. Aunt Ellen was my grandfather's sister, my mother's aunt. When my parents died, she came with Mr Allanstone to fetch me from boarding school. It would have been so hard for her to do that. She had lost a niece who was like a daughter to her, but she still kept herself together for long enough to come for me so I was not told what had happened by strangers.'

'She came here with your mother when I was very young. I do remember your mother, she married my uncle Peter, but I don't remember your great-aunt from then, only from when I saw her at your parents' funeral. I saw her again a few weeks before she died. Allanstone's wife had died, and Mary wanted to go to the funeral, so I drove her there. Your great-aunt was very courteous to us. She said you had been unable to get the time off work as some of the other girls were sick, and you felt you had to do the right thing and work that day. I was disappointed, as I had hoped you would be there, and I would see you again. We asked her about you, and she seemed very proud that you had a job in the bank and wore smart suits to work. I asked if Pat and I might call on you some time, or take you and your great-aunt out to lunch, but she said that although she had nothing against me, Pat or Mary, she thought it was better just to leave the past alone. She said she was very glad I had grown up unharmed after what had happened to me.

'When you came here it was supposed to be for two months, but that will be up soon. I asked my father what happens then, but he said you can stay for as long as you want to, and he would like you to live here permanently. So would Mary, and so would I.'

'I hadn't thought about it. I feel like I belong here now, that this is my home, and you have all been so kind. I wish you were here all the time. You are always so good to me. I felt very alone when my great-aunt died because I thought I had no family left in the world. It's a dreadful feeling to have no one left to love, but now I have four people. I've only been here for six weeks, but I feel like I've lived here for a lot longer than that. I would need to go back and get more of my things if I'm staying here for longer.'

'I could drive you over to Richmond tomorrow. Colin is taking his group bowling and Linda will help with that. It's only the walks that she can't manage.'

'If it's no trouble, I would like that. Bowling isn't my thing. We'd better go inside. It's getting dark in here, and there are no lights. Thank you for the hug. It felt like a hug even if it was just holding my hand.'

'I've bought you some chocolates and some for Mary as well. I left them in the kitchen. Chocolate is good if you're feeling a bit sad.'

He put the cat down, rose from the seat, gave her his hand to help her up, and then he really did hug her, in the cold gloomy twilight of a dismal day, and she felt very safe with her face resting against his shoulder, breathing in the soft wool scent of his jacket, her arms meeting behind him. He seemed so warm and solid and strong.

'Thank you,' she whispered, and she felt him relax a little, pull her closer to him.

It felt nice to be hugging him, with his heart beating against hers, his fingers caressing her hair, his thumb stroking her cheek, sending a little flame through her core. If Daniel had done that, she would have pulled away from him, but she didn't mind Ryan touching her face. She knew he would never let his hands stray to places where they weren't wanted. Not that Pat or Jimmy did either, but Daniel was a bit free with his hands, and she had once briefly had a boyfriend who was worse than an octopus.

But he only held her for a moment, and she felt rather shaky when he released her so they could return to the kitchen. She wondered if it had made him feel shaky, too.

She thought again how strange it seemed that they knew all about her, yet she had known nothing about any of them. It was spooky. And then there was that rather odd thing her great-aunt had said about him growing up unharmed after what had happened to him. She hadn't liked to ask what that meant. Then she recalled he had told her he had broken his arm as a child. Perhaps her great-aunt had known that.

When she went into the den to get the cheques for Ryan to sign after dinner that evening, she told Daniel they were going to Richmond the next day to collect some of her things, but she wanted to check first that he was happy for her to stay longer.

'I could have driven you there any time,' he said. 'Why did you bother Ryan? Why didn't you ask me? I would have loved a chance to drive the Jaguar on the motorway. You have cheated me, Jane.'

'Ryan asked if I was staying. He said you told him I could stay here as long as I wanted. I hadn't thought about it before.'

'Of course you can. Stay here forever, if you want. You belong here with me. If you need more money than Allanstone gives you, I can give you an allowance like I give the boys.'

She assured him she had plenty for the few things she bought, he was giving her board and lodging, she didn't expect more than that. She told him she knew she was happier here than she would be if she went back to Richmond to live by herself, and she was glad she had come to live with him; he had been very kind to her.

He took her hand, looked into her eyes, kissed the inside of her wrist, his breath hot on delicate skin, and whispered, 'Ah, Chanel.'

Then he told her he was very glad she wanted to stay, retaining her hand and making a circle with his finger on her palm.

She was not sure she liked him kissing her wrist, or caressing her palm, but she didn't want to be rude to him by snatching her hand away. She didn't like him looking at her directly like that either. It was not the undressing her look. It was the predator look that said they both understood what he wanted. She wasn't sure she wanted to understand what he wanted. He was only flirting with her a little, and he meant no harm. Some men were like that.

She remembered to give her sedative pills to Mary to look after. She compared them with Ryan's sleeping pills. They were the same diazepam, but hers were a lower dose because they were just to calm her down, while his were to help him sleep. She worked out that one of his was equivalent to five of hers.

Saturday 22 November 1975

Ryan offered to take Mary to London with them on the Saturday morning, but she preferred to be left at the station in town as usual. Was it because she didn't want them to know exactly where she went on Saturdays? Or was it to give Jane and Ryan a chance to be by themselves for the day? Mary often encouraged them to do things together, and Jane knew it was because she wanted him to spend more time at the Hall.

When they had dropped Mary off at the station in town, they drove to Oxford on the main road, then took the motorway towards London. She told him what Daniel had said about wanting to take the Jaguar on the motorway, and about driving it on an old airfield to see how fast it would go.

She didn't tell him Daniel had put his hand on her knee, or that he had kissed her wrist. She had coped with that, and she didn't want to complain. Sometimes when she was typing, he would lean over her to see where she had got to and breathe gently on her neck or her ear, smooth her hair as if he was tidying a stray lock of it, slip a finger inside her collar, caress her hand if he took a letter from her, or touch her shoulder while his thumb made little circles on her neck behind her ear. And he was getting bolder at touching her thigh and her derrière when he was standing close to her. At least Ryan never behaved like that.

She felt free driving away from Hayward with just the two of them in the car. It would have been better if it was Pat, but she liked Ryan as well. He might be a lone wolf, but she could still spin dreams of taming him. Last night he had given her a hug, and although it was only meant to be comforting, it had felt good to be close to him, with his fingers caressing her hair and her face. It would be a triumph to get a kiss from him. But she was immediately ashamed of the thought. She remembered Mary saying he didn't like to be hugged, and she knew she needed to respect that he didn't want her to get too close to him. If he really didn't like girls, it would be unfair of her to flirt with him.

They reached the house, and he parked the car in the driveway. It looked a little forlorn with the garden full of sodden autumn leaves, but inside the house was neat and clean. Mrs Brennan came twice a week and she had kept it perfect.

While Jane went through her clothes and selected what she wanted to take back with her, Ryan attempted to tidy the garden. She found him some old wellingtons and a showerproof jacket of her father's, and he swept up the leaves as best he could with them being so wet, putting them in a wooden compost bin in the back corner of the garden, behind the shed.

She left the work suits in the wardrobe as well as the miniskirts, which she did not like to wear at Hayward, partly because of the galleries above the stairs but also because she liked to sit in the evenings with her feet tucked up, and that needed a longer skirt, particularly with a man like Daniel in the house. She did pack a dark-blue satin dance dress, a little above knee length, the circular skirt with a layer of wispy lace in a matching colour. Pat had once told her that Colin sometimes took them out to a dance in town, although so far they had only gone to the cinema. She recalled the dress had matching dark-blue knickers, essential for a dance dress with a short full-circle skirt, so she found those as well. She had only worn the dress twice, once at a dance at school and once when she had gone out to dinner with a young man she had met at Sarah's wedding. But nothing had come of it, and she had never gone out with him again. She needed more winter clothes, so she packed jumpers and warm skirts, and also her tennis clothes as there was a tennis court at the Hall.

They walked to a little café in Richmond for lunch, and it felt good to be in his company in her own part of the world rather than in his. He seemed so different away from Hayward, much more carefree, ready to joke with her about his father speeding in the Jaguar, telling her Daniel drank so much that he was probably never sober enough to be driving at all, laughing when she told him she wasn't bringing back any miniskirts because of the galleries above the hallway. It was good to be sitting here with him. Hayward seemed far away, and she felt there were only the two of them in the world.

He asked if she had thought what she would do with the house if she stayed at Hayward.

'I want to keep it for now; it gives me somewhere to bolt to if I ever need to run away?'

'Why would you need to run away?' He seemed surprised.

She hesitated before she answered.

'Sometimes your father gets a little too close to me. It's nothing I could really object to—he just touches my neck or my hair—but I don't like it. I find it rather creepy. I like to know I have somewhere to go if he goes too far. I do cope with it. He's just like that, and I don't think he means any harm. I don't encourage him, and he usually stops when I ask him to. Sometimes during the week he goes away to London for a day or two—I think he goes to see the publisher or Mr Allanstone—and I find it easier to do the typing then, without him breathing down my neck.'

'If he goes too far, tell Mary and she will talk to him. I can as well if you want, but he would listen to Mary more than he would to me. It would be good to keep this house anyway, even if you do stay with us, as having somewhere so close to London where you can park a car and stay for a few days would benefit all of us. It would feel like being on holiday.'

'I don't think I could fit everyone,' she said, doubtfully. 'We only have three bedrooms, although there are some attic rooms as well.'

'I was thinking just you and me.'

'Your father may not allow that, and it may not be considered respectable.'

'We wouldn't tell my father. He would think I was at Oxford, and no one else would know or care. Mary would trust me, and I hope you would too. You said you have three bedrooms. We would only need two of them. It wouldn't be any good me staying here on my own, as I can't cook anything except toast, so I would have to eat out all the time I was here. And you didn't want to stay in the house by yourself. You could do some shopping and catch up with your friends, and I could look up ancestors at the General Register Office.'

'I would trust you—we already live in the same house, after all—and I know I couldn't stay here by myself. I have never been alone at night in any house. My mother never wanted to be alone in the house at night either, and she never allowed me to go anywhere by myself. On the rare occasions when my father had to be away for the night, Aunt Ellen would stay with us. Aunt Ellen once told me that my mother had been attacked by a man when she was young, and that was why she was so afraid for me to go out alone. But after my parents died, my great-aunt let me go shopping by myself, and I always enjoyed going on trains, although even she liked me to be back before dark. But if I wanted to run away from your father and come back here, I suppose I would have to stay here alone.'

For a moment he looked at her rather strangely, as if he was disturbed by what she had said, and it was a while before he spoke.

'Jane, I don't think my father would harm you, but if you don't like what he does, and he won't leave you alone, then tell Mary, and she will give him a talking to. She's good at that. I'll ask her to, and I'll talk to him as well. Perhaps you shouldn't be in his company all day.'

'I do some gardening with Pat, and I help Mary, and I walk down to the village by myself at times. I have been trying to get your father to drink less. He does try. He says he works better when he's sober.'

'Well, good luck with that, but I think he is beyond redemption. He did manage to give up cigars though. That was a couple of years ago now.'

'He is improving. He drinks his whisky with dry ginger ale now so it lasts longer. We tried lemon soda as well, and he liked that, so I added dry ginger and lemon soda to the order from the off-licence. We started by deciding if he wanted a drink in the daytime, he had to mix it, and now he sometimes dilutes it in the evenings as well. For a while he got me to mix it for him, but one time I just put in the dry ginger without any whisky, hoping he wouldn't notice, but he did. He said if I was one of you boys, he would have given me a clip around the ear. He drank it without the whisky, but then he went back to mixing his own. He said I was a minx and he didn't trust me any more. So I asked Mary to get in a lime, and I mixed him a drink with lemon soda and a slice of lime, and then he let me do the mixing again. We made a rule that if he wants the slice of lime, he has one ounce of whisky and not two. He is only supposed to have two ounces a day altogether, but we rarely achieve that. I do try.'

'It seems I underestimated you,' he said, amused. 'I'm so glad you came here. You have helped all of us.'

When they returned to the house, she put her packed suitcase on the landing, and he carried it downstairs to the car. She left a note for Mrs Brennan to say they had called by to get some of her things and to thank her for keeping the house so tidy.

It was late afternoon when they returned to Hayward Hall. Ryan went back out to collect Mary from the station. Pat had gone out for the afternoon with Colin's group, so he had taken the Rover.

Jane was not sorry she had missed going bowling. It wasn't her thing, and she had enjoyed spending the day with Ryan. She hoped Linda had coped, with the baby due in only a week or two.

Sunday 23 November 1975

On Sunday afternoon Mary made Christmas puddings with Jane helping. She used all the usual ingredients but added two jars of the brandied cherries, which Ryan fetched from the cellar for her, and a surprising amount of additional brandy. There was no silver sixpence, as Pat had once broken a baby tooth on a Christmas pudding sixpence.

Ryan sat at the kitchen table, talking to them as they put the pudding together, then helping Mary with the stirring, as the mixture was quite heavy. He had rolled up his sleeves and Jane saw a long white scar on his forearm that she assumed was from when he had broken his arm and it had been pinned. He had once told her the bone was no longer quite straight, but it looked all right to Jane.

They were making an extra pudding for John Phillips, whose son would be with him over Christmas, as well as his two grandsons. Jane wet the cloths and floured them before they were spread into two bowls and the mixture spooned in. Then the tops of the cloths were tied, and the puddings were cooked in two saucepans on the Aga.

The kitchen smelt like heaven.

Wednesday 26 November 1975

Daniel's behaviour improved a little for the next few days. Jane thought either Ryan or Mary had said something to him, as he now rarely touched her. It helped that she was now typing in the library on the new typewriter, while he worked in the den, although she did try to keep a check on him so he didn't drink in the mornings. For a while now he had stuck to his two drinks in the evening, as he knew he worked better when he restricted it to that.

The weather had been fine, and she had walked with him most afternoons. He said he liked walking as it allowed him to get his ideas in order, and she was happy to stay silent and not distract him.

She went out with Pat again on Wednesday evening. They thought about telling Daniel that they were just going for a drink at the Black Horse Inn in the village, but they would have walked there rather than taking the car, so they said they were going to a film with some other young people.

Daniel didn't seem too concerned, but he waited up and was sitting in the kitchen when they returned. Jane knew he would not have seen them kissing at the back door, but she hoped he didn't wonder why it was so long between the car returning and them coming inside. She made cocoa for all three of them, and told Daniel the plot of the film they had watched so he knew they really had been at the cinema.

Friday 28 November 1975

Pat took Mary to town for shopping on Friday morning, and Jane was left working with Daniel. She made the coffee, and he suggested they drink it in the conservatory in the late autumn sunshine.

'This place cheats on the weather. You can sit in the sun here and pretend it's spring. In the summer it can get rather hot, but the front windows can be opened, and the shade of the building comes over in the afternoon so only the very front section gets the full afternoon sun. On really warm days, you can sit out on the terrace instead, and we always move the plants outside in summer.'

He wanted her to sit on the swing seat with him, but she didn't want to sit close to him, so she said they might spill the coffee. She put the tray on the coffee table and sat in one of the cane armchairs. He pulled the other armchair so it was closer to hers.

'You love this house, don't you,' he said.

'Yes, I do love it. It is a beautiful house.'

'I could leave it to you. Ryan doesn't want it. All he wants is to spend his entire life living like a monk at his college.'

'I am sure you will still be with us for a very long time, Daniel, and I wouldn't want to cause a rift between you and your son.'

'There's already a rift; you can't do much about that. I could leave it to Pat, he at least does the garden, but he's lazy and he expects every-thing to be handed to him.'

'He works hard in the garden. I have helped him sometimes. You should appreciate more what he does for you. You would need to pay a gardener full time if you didn't have Pat. And Ryan does love this house. You know that. He knows all the history, who lived here and when. He wouldn't want it left to someone else.'

'Coffee's finished,' he said abruptly. 'Now come and sit with me on the swing.'

She felt she didn't have any choice, so she sat as far into the corner as she could, conscious that they were alone in the house. She couldn't relax sitting this close to him, but she stayed where she was. It was nice to sit in the sunlight, gently rocking. He didn't say anything, and she was used to remaining silent with him, as she did when they walked, because she knew his mind was miles away in his fantasy world. He put his hand on her knee, but she put it firmly back onto his knee.

'Please keep your hands to yourself, Mr Linden. There are rules here. The boys are not allowed to do that, and neither are you.'

'I make the rules, Jane. They haven't touched you, have they? I won't have them pawing you. And you're not to go anywhere with either of them without asking me first. I could have driven you to Richmond. And my name is Daniel. Why are you calling me Mr Linden?'

'When you misbehave, you are Mr Linden.'

His arm was along the seat behind her and his fingers caressed her neck inside the collar of her blouse, beneath her hair, his thumb stroking her cheek as Ryan had done when he had hugged her. She hadn't minded Ryan doing that, but she didn't like Daniel touching her. She pulled further away from him, but there was not much further she could go.

'I'm not doing you any harm. I like it here with you. I can enjoy your Chanel. I used to sit here with Caroline all those years ago. She wore Chanel. It all seems like yesterday to me. I can still hear her voice in my mind. I left her old room as it was when she died, and sometimes I sit there and feel her close to me. I still see her on the stairs, waiting for me, on nights when the moon shines. She talks to me but I can never quite catch what she says, and when I reach the landing, she is always gone. Now come here and lean against me.'

He had his arm around her shoulders, pulling her against him, and she didn't resist—it was only a hug after all—but she could feel his breath close to her ear, and she didn't like it. She wished Pat and Mary would come back.

'Why don't you and Ryan get on?' she asked him, not really expecting any sensible answer.

'He despises me because I like women, and I despise him because he doesn't. Maybe sons never get on with their fathers. I never got on with mine. I wish he would just stay in Oxford with his other monk friends instead of hanging around here after you, setting you against me.'

'He doesn't set me against you. I like his company, and he looks after me.'

'Don't I look after you?'

He was very close to her, his tongue flicking at her ear. It tickled.

'Yes, you do, and I am grateful for it. Now please stop that, Mr Linden. We need to go back to the typing.'

When Ryan came home that evening, Jane was in the kitchen. She didn't want to sit in the conservatory after sitting there with Daniel, and it was in any case quite dark when Ryan returned. She felt her heart beating fast when he came in, and she remembered the thrill that had touched her last Friday night when he had hugged her. She wished he would hug her again, but she knew she had to be careful not to fall for him.

It seemed a long time since she had seen him, although it was only a few days, but she had thought about him all the time. She wanted him to get on better with his father. She didn't like Daniel saying he wished Ryan would never come home. At least he came home every Friday now, whether there was apple pie or not. Jane knew Mary wanted him to be at home more often, and she did too.

He had bought chocolates again, cherry liqueurs, for her and for Mary.

There was a film on television that she and Mary wanted to watch, but none of the men were interested, so they played snooker in the billiard room, while she and Mary sat in the lounge.

Later that evening when Ryan had swapped her book in the library, and they were drinking their cocoa and sharing the cherry liqueurs, she asked him why he didn't get on with his father. She was interested in his side of it. Her attempts to involve them both in the same conversation at dinner times had so far been fruitless, but she was not giving up entirely yet.

'It's because of something that happened many years ago,' he told her. 'Something that is better forgotten. We get on well enough if we keep out of each other's way. I told him you had complained he was always touching you, and I was concerned you would want to go back to Richmond and we would all lose you. I hope he has improved.'

She didn't tell him his father had wanted to hug her in the conservatory, or what he had said about his son. She didn't want Ryan and his father to fall out over her. Daniel was just like that. He didn't mean her any harm. She would not have thought twice about it if her father had fiddled with her collar, or hugged her or even put his hand on her knee. Although Daniel flicking his tongue in her ear was a step too far. Her father would never have done that. She had gone upstairs afterwards and washed her ear with soap.

Saturday 29 November 1975

Colin had arranged table tennis on Saturday afternoon. With Linda's baby now due any day, he didn't want to be far from home. Mary had gone to London. She had left some jam tarts for Jane to take for the afternoon tea.

This time Jane played with Jimmy, as Ryan was not needed for the numbers and was supervising with Colin and talking to Linda, who was watching the game. Jimmy asked Jane if she would go out with him again, so she suggested they spend Wednesday evening at the Black Horse Inn. Pat might come as well if Jimmy didn't mind.

She thought Daniel couldn't object to her and Pat meeting friends at the local pub. She would have a chance to talk to Jimmy, and she would still get her kiss goodnight from Pat when he walked her home.

While they enjoyed their afternoon tea after the game, Ryan read them the remainder of *The Canterville Ghost*, and promised to find some other ghost stories for them.

'We once had table tennis at home,' Ryan told her that evening as they sat in the library. 'It was set up in the billiard room. Unfortunately,

Pat heard a rumour that the balls were highly flammable, and he set light to one on the floor in the kitchen. They are quite spectacular when they burn. He was given a talking to and a second chance, but when he did it again, my grandmother confiscated the bats and balls, and Daniel put the table away in the stables. It's still there somewhere, so we could set it up again if you like. I'm sure Pat has grown out of playing with matches.'

Sunday 30 November 1975

After lunch on Sunday Ryan took Jane to look over an open house that was built in a similar stone and a similar style to Hayward Hall but was much larger and much older. It was one of the few local houses still open this late in the year.

She always enjoyed going on excursions with him, as he knew such a lot about the history of the places he took her to. She sometimes wished he would hold her hand when they walked together, but she knew he never would. He always treated her like a sister as his father had asked him to.

They were a little early for the tour, so they chose a tea towel for Mary from the souvenir shop. The lady serving them seemed to know Ryan. He paid for the tea towel, but she wouldn't let him pay for the tour or the optional afternoon tea that was served afterwards. She said how lovely it was to see him after all these years, and he introduced Jane as his cousin who now lived with them. He had called the lady Mrs Howard, but she told them both to call her Felicity, as they were not schoolchildren now.

The guide also acknowledged Ryan at the start of the tour, so Jane assumed Ryan knew him as well. They looked a similar age. After the tour was finished, and the visitors who stayed were being served tea, he sat with them while they ate their scones. His name was Martin Howard, and he was an old school friend of Ryan. It was his father's house, but he still lived there. They opened it every Sunday afternoon in the summer, and once a month through the winter, to help with the cost of the upkeep.

Ryan had stayed there at times in the school holidays, and he and Martin talked about mutual friends. Martin's sister Hayley was now married to Luke Tremorne, another of Ryan's classmates. Martin recalled Hayley had been sweet on Ryan when he had stayed there all those years ago. Martin was now an accountant, working in Cheltenham. There was no sign of him having a wife or a girlfriend, so Jane wondered if he was another lone wolf.

Mrs Howard asked them to stay for a while after the other visitors had left so she could hear Ryan's news. She made fresh tea for them all and found more scones. Martin's father joined them.

'Ryan came to stay here in the summer after he and Martin finished school,' Mrs Howard told Jane. 'Luke was here with us that year, and two of my daughter Hayley's friends came as well, so there were six of them. Luke is now married to Hayley. He was a timid boy, and at the time his parents were going through a rather messy divorce. His father was a member of parliament, and a newspaper reporter had snooped around and found he had set up a teenage girl as his mistress in a house in Cheltenham. His career survived, as the girl was eighteen, but his marriage didn't. His mother asked me if Luke could come here for the holidays so he had some young company, and to keep him from being involved with it all. She was, and still is, a good friend of mine, and she has since remarried and put the scandal behind her. Luke was in the same class as Martin and Ryan at school, so they were all friends together.

'All three of the girls fancied poor Ryan and flirted with him relentlessly. Sometimes they really did go too far, so Ryan and Martin would disappear together by themselves all day. They would have taken Luke with them, but he was sweet on Hayley, and he hung around with the girls. They treated him dreadfully, teasing him and asking him to fetch them books and lemonade and carry their things, but he stuck with them like a pet puppy all through the summer.

'Luke and Martin were at university together in London after that, and after they graduated, they shared a flat that belonged to Luke's father. Hayley would go and stay with them on weekends, and she and Luke became engaged. Eventually Luke and Martin set up in partnership together in Cheltenham, and Hayley and Luke were married. He's a lovely boy, we love having him as a son-in-law, and we now have two beautiful grandchildren.'

Martin told Jane how he and Ryan had gone swimming in the nude in the lake at the far end of the park and the girls had found them. There had been a standoff, with the girls refusing to retreat and threatening to run off with their clothes, and the two of them unable to come out of the water. At least the water in the lake was murky, even if it wasn't very deep.

Luke had shown great presence of mind. While the girls were fighting like vultures over what to do with their clothes, Luke had found their towels, and he had sat on them while he took off his shoes and socks and rolled up his trouser legs. He had taken the swimming trunks from inside the rolled towels and waded out as far as he could. Then he had thrown them the rest of the way, and they were able to put them on under the water. The girls had tossed all their clothes and their shoes into the lake, so they had to walk back to the house in their bathers and towels with a pile of wet clothes. Ryan's shoes survived, but Martin's were wrecked. The top came away from the soles.

Martin and Ryan had decided to tell Martin's mother that they had been skylarking and had overturned the boat, but Luke had told her the truth, and the girls had been in trouble. Martin's father had wanted to send the other two girls home, but they had sworn it wouldn't happen again. For a couple of days Luke had sided with Martin and Ryan and had spent the day with them, deserting the girls, but Hayley had cornered him in a corridor and given him a kiss, so he went back to being her slave.

Before Jane and Ryan left, Martin invited them to come over one Saturday afternoon. He would show them the whole house, not just the rooms that were open, and he would ask his sister and Luke over for tea. Spring or summer was better than winter, as the garden would be nicer then. They could have tea outside on the terrace, and row the boats on the lake where they had gone swimming.

As they drove home Jane was thinking about the three girls teasing the two young men swimming in the lake. It would have been fun to come upon them, but not to tease them. She would have sneaked a quick look and then turned her back for them to come out. They would all have been younger than she was now though, even the boys. It was a pity there wasn't a lake at the end of the garden at Hayward Hall. She would rather like to see him without his clothes. Well perhaps not all his clothes, she would allow him some privacy. But then she thought she wouldn't want him to see her without her clothes, so it was unfair of her to even think about it. It was nice to see fit young men with their shirts off and in tight hipster jeans so it left something to the imagination, and she was happy to compromise with that. He did have jeans, black ones that he wore with his cable jumper, but she didn't know if they were hipster or tight because the jumper covered the top of them. What she could see of them looked rather tight, and he seemed very fit.

He asked why she was laughing, so she told him she was thinking about the story of them swimming in the lake. She asked him what the boys would have done if they had come upon the girls swimming.

'We would have behaved like gentlemen and turned our backs for them to come out of the water. Or just gone away and left them alone. I hope you would have turned your back, Jane, if you had found us at the lake.'

'Yes, of course, but I may have sneaked a look first. I've never seen a man naked. I promise I would never have thrown the clothes into the water or treated Luke like a slave.'

He laughed. 'Not all girls were like them. At one of the other houses where I stayed in the holidays, there were two very nice girls, and we were all friends together. We would row them around in boats and play tennis with them. It was like Colin's group where everyone gets on with each other, and the boys look after the girls. But Hayley and her two friends were poisonous. They said nasty things to us and even nastier things to each other. They did nasty things too. They took Luke's glasses and left him lost in the grounds. His eyesight was quite poor without them. Although he could see quite well close up, anything beyond a few yards was a blur.

'When the girls came home without him, Martin and I went out to look for him. If he had been on a path, he might have made it home, but they had left him across the park near the lake, and he would not have been able to get his bearings to find the way back to the house. It would all have been a sea of green to him. We were really concerned because we knew he was upset about the divorce, and we were worried he would drown himself in the lake. Martin's mother had asked us all never to leave him by himself. She even had us three boys sleeping in the same room together.

'We found him on a bench looking over the water. He was really miserable, and we knew he had thought about it. So we sat down with him, and I told him what my grandmother had said to me about hanging yourself yesterday. We said that the divorce was not in any way his fault, he didn't have to take sides, and both his parents still cared about him even if they no longer loved each other. We suggested he would feel better if he talked to someone. If he didn't feel like talking to us, then perhaps he could talk to Martin's mother. She would help him to get it all in perspective.

'When we got back to the house, Mrs Howard was furious with the girls. I will never forgive them for doing that to Luke. They knew he was fragile the same as Martin and I did. A moment's stupidity could have been tragic. I think both Martin and I grew up a little that day, and I hope the girls did as well.

'After that the girls went back to school, and us three boys had another few weeks together before we started at university. I always remember how happy we were for the remainder of our time there. We had Luke boating and swimming with us, but we never swam nude again. I hope Hayley treats him better now they are married than she did then. I'm glad you never behave like they did.'

He told her that tomorrow he was taking the car into Oxford and would return in the evening, as there was a serial of *North and South* that he wanted to watch on television. There was only one more week of term, and then he would spend another week in Oxford tidying up his research before coming home for the holidays. He usually stayed at the college all year even when there were no classes to teach, just to keep away from his father, but now she was here he wanted to spend the holiday at home.

He offered to take her to Richmond for the day again in December or January so she could shop and he could look up ancestors. She said she would enjoy that, and she knew she really would enjoy it. It was nice when it was just the two of them doing things together, and she wanted to get away from Daniel at times.

3 WINTER FIRES

Monday 1 December 1975

Ryan came home for dinner as promised on Monday, and Jane was glad of the chance to spend the evening with him, even if it was only watching television. Mary suggested they sit in her room, as it was warmer.

Daniel was upset because Jane was not playing chess with him as she usually did on Mondays, so Pat offered to play snooker with him, and Mary sat in the lounge, telling them she was watching a different channel.

It was cosy with both of them side by side on the sofa, a blanket over their knees, the cat on his lap, with a glass of port each and a bowl of popcorn that Mary had prepared for them in her electric frying pan. Mary had closed the door to the sitting room, saying it was to keep in the warmth, but the kitchen was always the warmest room in the house, so Jane was not sure that was the real reason. Ryan didn't appear to mind that she was sitting close to him, leaning slightly against him as she did on the swing seat, or that she sometimes reached out to stroke the cat on his lap. But she was careful that her fingers didn't touch his.

When the episode had finished, she asked him if Miss Hale married Mr Thornton by the end of the story. He admitted he had never read the book, but said he hoped so.

'You are just a little bit romantic, aren't you,' she said, and he laughed.

'Yes, of course. If everyone was a lone wolf like me, humans would have died out. If you still like the story after we've watched all four episodes, I'll buy you the book.'

They stayed talking in Mary's room until everyone else had gone to bed and it was time for cocoa.

But the next morning he had returned to Oxford once more.

Wednesday 3 December 1975

On Wednesday Pat and Jane walked to the Black Horse Inn after dinner, where Claire, Jimmy and David were waiting for them.

Linda's new baby boy had arrived on Monday evening, perfectly on time, and Linda and baby Brett would be coming home from the hospital in Oxford on Friday.

They talked about the baby, about the table tennis, the walks to Peddleton and the turkeys at John Phillips' farm, which were definitely not looking forward to Christmas. His son Robert was coming home from Geneva for a few weeks over Christmas so he could be with his father and his sons at the farm. Ryan was spending the holidays at home for a change, Jane offered as her news, but not until the middle of December. He would then be home until the middle of January.

Daniel hadn't waited up for her and Pat to return this time. Jane assumed he trusted that they really had gone to the pub. But even in the winter you could still kiss outside, although you could not have got up to much else in the freezing cold on a frosty night.

Saturday 6 December 1975

On Saturday afternoon Jane, Pat and Ryan walked to the vicarage with a cardigan that Mary had knitted, little sheepskin boots from Iceland that Ryan had found in a shop in Oxford, and a warm blue snowsuit with a little halo of swansdown around the hood that Jane had bought yesterday in town. Ryan had also bought a Beatrix Potter book for Daisy so she didn't feel left out.

There was no Saturday outing that week, and Mary was in London. Some of the other teenagers from Colin's group had come to see the baby, and Colin's mother Betty, who lived at the vicarage with them, made tea for them all. Julie's mum had sent knitted bootees and a little hat, and Candy's mum had sent a teddy bear.

Daisy sat on the sofa between Ryan and Jane while he read her the story about naughty Tom Kitten losing all his clothes.

It reminded Jane of Ryan and Martin swimming in the lake. He flashed her a smile, and she knew he was thinking the same thing.

The girls were allowed to hold the baby. Jane found it a bit frightening, as he was so small, but he felt surprisingly warm, and he fell asleep while she held him, so she knew he felt safe with her.

Sunday 7 December 1975

Ryan was once again visiting his grandfather on the Sunday afternoon, and he asked Jane if she would like to go with him. He was the father of

Ryan's mother, and lived in a nursing home near Bath. He was ninety-five and was not very lucid at times. Ryan tried to get there every month or so, as he was the only family the old man had left.

Jane recalled Ryan had asked her for a poppy to take to his grandfather early in November, but she had not gone with him then because she had been sewing squares together to make blankets.

'He will think you are my girlfriend,' he said. 'Would it be too much to ask you to just go along with it? It would make him happy, and anything else would just confuse him. He is always telling me I should have a girlfriend.'

'That depends how far you want the pretence to go,' she said with a laugh, thinking it might be rather nice if she really was his girlfriend.

'You might hold my hand. I wouldn't expect any more than that. It would make an old man happy. It would make a young man happy, too. Mary has bought him some silk pyjamas for Christmas, and we will take him some chocolates. He has been at Grey Friars for around twelve years. It's called a retirement home, but it's really a nursing home. My grandmother on my mother's side died when I was twelve—it was my first ever funeral—and my grandfather was eighty then. He was a lot older than my grandmother. He didn't manage very well on his own, so he moved to the home, and my father pays for him to live there.'

They left after lunch, driving southwards along the main road to an old house outside of Bath which was now a retirement home. It was a grand house, much larger than Hayward Hall, with beautiful gardens, beautiful rooms and lovely staff. It looked and felt very exclusive. They were shown into the lounge, where an old man in a smart suit, sitting in an armchair with a blanket over his knees, was waiting for them, Jane's poppy in his lapel.

'Got a girlfriend at last, have you? Lovely to meet you, Miss Walters. I'm sorry not to stand up for a lady, but my old bones make it difficult. He's a nice boy, and you could do a lot worse. Has he given you a ring yet? His mother had a beautiful diamond ring from Daniel. The diamond had belonged to Daniel's grandmother, and they had it reset. He could give you that if he can't afford a new one. He will have all my money, but not for years yet. You're Peter's girl? I do remember Peter. He was Daniel's best man when he and Caroline married.'

Tea and cakes were brought in for them all, served by a classically dressed maid, and a lady who was clearly in charge of the establishment came over to meet Jane, staying to talk to them for a while. Her name was Pamela Betteridge. Jane was just to call her Pamela, as everyone was on first name terms here. She asked Jane if she could write out the pattern for the poppy for their craft lady, Judy.

'Most of the gentlemen here served in the First World War,' she told Jane. 'On Remembrance Day they all wear their medals for a service with our chaplain, Paul. Our ladies can make the poppies. It would be very special to have such lovely ones instead of paper.'

They told Ryan's grandfather everything that was happening at Hayward and in the world beyond, but Jane realised he was hardly taking in what they said, although he had moments of lucidity and he had remembered her father. But he talked of the past as though they had shared it all with him, of Sir Winston Churchill, who had by now been dead for ten years, as though he was still in charge, and by the time they left, he was calling them Caroline and Daniel.

In some ways it was heart breaking, but he lived in this beautiful house and was clearly well cared for. And he wasn't alone in the world. He had lost his daughter and his son, who had never married and had died in the War, but he still had a grandson, a last family link. Jane realised his son was Nicholas, Caroline's brother, whose photo hung on the wall on the landing at Hayward Hall.

The old man had been born in eighteen eighty, the youngest of six children, Ryan told her. Their mother was an autocratic Victorian matriarch who had dominated their lives and never allowed any of them to marry. He had fought in the First World War and survived. He was in his forties when his mother died, and he had finally married, the only one of his siblings to do so.

Ryan and I are both here by a tenuous thread of fate, Jane thought, the last heirs of families who would otherwise have died out.

'Thank you for coming with me,' he said as they drove away. 'I hope it was not too sad for you. He is my grandfather, and I've always loved him although I saw him only occasionally when I was young. He wasn't always like this. I try to come every month or so. If you could come with me again, I know it would make him happy.'

She asked Ryan what he would like for Christmas. She had already given it some thought, but nothing had seemed good enough. 'Do you buy each other presents at Hayward? Some families don't.'

'My father always buys jewellery for Mary, usually earrings, so I imagine he will buy some for you. It is not usually appropriate for an unrelated man to buy jewellery for a lady, but Mary is his sister so that is okay, and you are, at least unofficially, his ward. He always buys her Joy perfume as well. Pat and I are not allowed to, as it has to come from him. If you want to buy presents, chocolates are fine.'

'May I get you some silk pyjamas.'

'I would like that, Jane, but it might be misconstrued.'

'You are always laughing at me. But I do see your point. If you bought pyjamas for me, it wouldn't look good. I have thought of lots of things you might like, but you have everything already. You have done so much for me, and I never do anything for you except iron a few shirts. I wouldn't feel confident choosing a book for you since you have read just about everything. What about a new scarf? Your usual scarf has got rather tatty.'

'It's my college scarf,' he said defensively, 'and I don't mind if it's tatty. It shows I've belonged there for a long time. You have done things for me, Jane. You have taken over the paperwork for my father, and you seem to be better at it than I was. I was never sure if I had already paid things. At least you see them come in every day and can sort them. I was just given a pile at the end of the week, and some of them looked like bills I had paid the week before, so I had to do a lot of checking back to what I had done the previous week. You write *Paid* on them. I never thought of doing that, but now it seems so simple.

'And I am grateful for the ironed shirts. If I ironed them, I would burn holes in them. We had an accident with a shirt once. My grandmother had an old-fashioned iron that you heated up on the kitchen range. It ran on coal then, so you couldn't control the temperature as well as you can now. She was ironing a shirt of my father's, when Pat picked up a baited mousetrap that he had pulled out from under the dresser in the kitchen. He was quite small, about five. My grandmother yelled at him to drop it, and she rushed to take it from him before he sprung the trap on his fingers. The iron was left on the shirt, and it made a brown mark in the shape of the iron.

'I was in trouble because I was supposed to be looking after Pat, and we all tried to work out what to do. We considered burning the shirt in the kitchen range, hoping he wouldn't notice it was missing, but it was a special shirt that you wore with a dinner suit, and he only had two of them, so we thought he would miss it. Mary found some vinegar to try to get the mark out.

'But then my father walked in. The mousetrap was still on the floor where Pat had dropped it, and Daniel trod on the edge of it so it went off with a bang, hit him on the shin and landed in the cuff of his trousers. The cheese had fallen off, and he trod on it. Pat and I fled and hid in the boot room because we knew he would be cross and would somehow blame us and clip us around the ear.

'Mary suggested he could still wear the shirt if he didn't take the jacket off, because the mark was at the back, but he got really cross with us all and said there was no point in taking a lady out to dinner if you were going to keep your jacket on the whole night. My grandmother was trying to tell him it was only a shirt, and they could buy him a new one.

'In the end Mary did get the mark out—she was always good at those things—but the next day Daniel bought an electric steam iron for my grandmother. He had seen them advertised on television.

'If you really want to buy something for me, I could use a new watch. Something very plain, with a black leather strap. Mine is rather old and keeps stopping, which is a nuisance, as I rely on it for catching trains. But don't get anything expensive. The shopping is rather limited in town, but if you want to shop in Oxford, you can go into town on Friday when Pat and Mary do the shopping, take the train to Oxford, and you can come home late in the afternoon on the same train as me. Pat can pick us both up at the same time. The Michaelmas term has ended, and I'm staying home tomorrow for our television serial, but I'll be back in Oxford for most of this week to catch up on some research. Then I'm spending the rest of the holiday at home.'

Wednesday 10 December 1975

Daniel had gone to London on Wednesday morning and was not expected back until Friday, so Jane and Pat went out to a film. She told him it would be the last time for a while, as she didn't want to go out with him while Ryan was home. Daniel seemed to accept them going out if he thought they were with some of the other young people, but Ryan would notice and she didn't want Ryan to know. She and Pat had gone out together several times now. They would hold hands through the film, and when they returned home, they would kiss at the back door.

Tonight when they came home, they sat by themselves in the kitchen and talked about escaping from Hayward Hall and living somewhere together. Maybe at Jane's house in Richmond, he suggested. Did she have enough for them to live on for a while? Daniel had once said she had enough money that she didn't need to work. Perhaps they could afford a car as well.

Jane never responded to his questions about her money. It didn't seem right that he wasn't offering to at least try to get a job if she ran away with him. They had never gone further than a kiss goodnight, although Jane was starting to hope that sooner or later they might. She liked the thrill she felt when he held her close to him. But inside the house, and even in the garden, they behaved impeccably, as they didn't want Daniel to find out they were breaking the rules.

Jane was not sure she wanted Ryan to know either. He would be home for about five weeks. She would need to be really careful for that time, but after that she and Pat could return to going out for one night a week.

Friday 12 December 1975

On the Friday when Pat drove Mary to town for the shopping, Jane took the train to Oxford to buy Christmas presents.

She found Ryan an electronic Omega watch with a battery, which lasted a year, instead of the usual wind-up mechanism. She chose one with a black leather strap, which looked as close as she could remember to the watch he already had. It cost more than she had earned in a fortnight at the bank, but she knew she could afford it, and she wanted to give him something special.

For Daniel she bought a black cashmere scarf. He never seemed to wear anything but black. Even his trilby hat was black; only his shirts were white. She wasn't sure about his underwear, as she left Mary to deal with washing and drying the men's socks and underclothes. Just one look at all the black socks tumbling around in the dryer gave her nightmares about how you would get them back into pairs, before you even started to think about whose was whose. But perhaps all the black socks were the same, so you could simply pair them at random and assign them at random.

She found a book on sports cars for Pat with lots of glossy pictures. She lingered at the perfume counter, wanting to buy Mary the Joy perfume that she wore. Jane loved the scent. It filled the room with a memory of roses blooming in the warmth of summer in her parents' garden in Kent. But she recalled that Ryan had told her that his father always bought perfume for Mary. So she chose a silk Liberty scarf with red and yellow flowers on a black background.

She knew Ryan was catching the train home earlier today at three twenty, as he had told Pat which train to meet, and Pat had suggested she catch the same train back so he only had to drive into town to meet it once.

After she had finished the shopping, she walked for a while around the town, past the colleges, wondering if he was somewhere inside one of them, and she returned to the station in time for the train. She saw him standing on the platform, with his overnight bag and an attaché case, so she assumed he was bringing home paperwork for the Christmas break. She touched his arm, being careful not to stand too close to him, called his name, and he turned and flashed her his beautiful smile. He really did seem pleased to see her.

She sat opposite him in the train carriage, but they did not have it to themselves, so they said very little. He did ask her what she had bought, but she told him it was only presents and was all top secret. All the time he looked at her in that half-amused way he had, almost as if he knew what she was thinking. She hoped he didn't because she was thinking how beautiful he looked when he smiled at her and wishing he would take her out to the cinema in town, hold her hand through the film, and kiss her goodnight at the back door.

They reached the station, and she stepped onto the platform where she had once stood feeling completely alone in the world. She felt so much better now than she had then. The porter remembered her, even recalling her name.

Ryan was now back at home for the Christmas break, and there was less than a fortnight to go until Christmas. Jane had decided she would not go out with Pat with Ryan in the house. She guessed that Mary would have told Ryan that she and Pat had been going out to films together, but she rather hoped that she hadn't. Jane was glad to have Ryan there, to talk to him about books and the family history and his research at Oxford, to sit with him in the evenings in the library, to watch their serial by themselves in Mary's room, or play snooker or pool with him and Pat in the billiard room, then have cocoa and biscuits late in the evening, just the two of them, when everyone else was in bed.

She had not told Ryan she was falling in love with Pat, that they had spent nearly every Wednesday evening together in town, or that they were planning how they could escape from Hayward to be together. On Saturdays they were just friends, joining in with Colin's outings, Pat treating Jane no differently than he treated Claire, Jimmy flirting with her, Ryan aloof yet always watching her, seeming unaware of what was happening between his cousin and Jane. She felt that she was heading for a disaster, that when this came out, it would be like them driving over a cliff, yet she was helpless to change course. She had never slept with Pat, she had never done anything more than kiss him, but when she was with Ryan or even with Jimmy she was starting to feel as though she was cheating them both by saying nothing.

Saturday 13 December 1975

Mary went to London as usual on the Saturday.

Jane helped Daniel for a while before going to the kitchen to make the ten-thirty coffee. She went outside to find Pat and Ryan, who had told her they would be chopping wood for the fire at Christmas. She could hear the sound of the axe and found them near the stables.

Ryan, in his jeans and cable jumper with his sleeves rolled up, was axing the rounds of wood, while Pat picked up the cut pieces between Ryan chopping each round and stacked them. The wood was from a tree that had died in the woodland at the back of the garden, and had been cut into rounds when it had been felled. Ryan stopped for a moment and pulled off the jumper, so he was left in his shirt and jeans. It was December, and cold, but axing wood was hot work. His jeans were hipster and they were tight, but Jane knew there was no way he would be taking off his shirt in this weather.

Pity, she thought as she stopped to watch for a while.

Daniel came out to find them, presumably wondering what had become of his coffee. It was nice to watch men axe wood, especially fit young men like Pat and Ryan, but she didn't say that to Daniel.

He seemed to sense it, however, as he decided to have a go, taking off his jacket and rolling up his shirt sleeves. Ryan handed his father the axe and stood back, and she saw him exchange an amused glance with Pat.

Daniel was surprisingly fit, whacking the wood just as hard as Ryan had. Pat asked Jane to go inside and make the coffee. Daniel was showing off, but he would stop if she went back to the kitchen. He might seem strong because he did push-ups every morning—a habit he had kept up from when he was in the army—but he had a dicky heart, and Pat was worried he shouldn't be exerting himself by chopping the wood. He had heart pills that Mary kept in the kitchen. If his heart beat too fast it could become unstable, and he would need to take one of the pills.

Jane hurriedly did as she was told. Daniel did get out of breath much more easily than she did when they were out walking, but she had thought it was just because he was old. She recalled he always took a bottle of pills in his pocket when they went out. He always looked very fit though, not an ounce overweight, and you wouldn't expect him to have a dicky heart. Perhaps it was the whisky that did it.

When the coffee was ready, she went outside and called them all back in. Pat was now chopping the wood, this time into smaller pieces with a hatchet, and Ryan was back in his jumper.

Daniel told her the wood was for the fire at Christmas. The fireplaces were designed to burn coal, so you had to use small pieces of wood to get the fire going initially; you could put on slightly larger pieces later. Jane wondered why they didn't just buy in some coal, but perhaps you weren't allowed to burn coal here.

They spent the afternoon playing rounders on the village green with Colin's group and the younger children as well. Mary had baked a banana cake the previous day for Jane to take for the tea in the village hall after the game. Linda had brought the baby out in a pram, and Daisy joined in the game, running between bases beside the players. This time Ryan came to help, and he and Colin kept score. Jane was umpire. Not that anyone really minded about the score or the rules. It was just fun to run around in the winter sunshine.

Wednesday 17 December 1975

Ryan was now at home during the week. Jane spent the mornings helping Daniel with the typing as she normally did. On the Monday and the Tuesday Ryan had brought his typewriter down to the library so he worked near Jane, but Daniel had continually interrupted him, and on Wednesday he gave up and retreated back to his study upstairs. Jane knew Daniel had done it deliberately to discourage Ryan from working in the library.

On the Wednesday morning when Ryan stayed upstairs, Daniel said it was good, they didn't want him there bothering them.

Jane didn't say anything. She had liked having Ryan there, not only because she liked his company, but also because Daniel never touched her with Ryan in the room.

In the afternoons she normally helped Mary with the housework and the ironing, or walked with Daniel in the garden or to the village, but with Ryan home she walked out with him that afternoon.

He stopped at John Phillips' farm and borrowed the younger dog Casper and a dog lead to take with them on the walk. It was cold but fine, the frost still crunching beneath their boots in odd places along the path to Peddleton. Jane realised she had never actually walked a dog before. Ryan said he often borrowed the dog; he had once had one of his own, called Wolf. John Phillips didn't mind, and the dog was always happy to go adventuring. Where they could, they let Casper off the lead and threw sticks for him to retrieve. He always came straight back if Ryan whistled, as he was a beautifully-trained farm dog.

Jane was glad to be out of the house and away from Daniel. She felt more at ease walking with Ryan. Daniel was always touching her when he helped her over stiles, standing so she was very close to him when she stepped down, not giving her enough distance. Ryan gave her too much distance, she would happily have stood closer to him, and he only helped her if she looked unsteady or held out her hand to him. She became quite good at looking unsteady.

The dog was quite adept at stiles, although most of them had a small dog gate that you could lift, or were beside a real gate you could open. Casper would run up to the stile ahead of them and wait until they opened the gate. But sometimes, while he waited for them to catch up, he would jump over the stile himself, then jump back again before waiting for the gate.

The sun shone, although the day was cold, and Jane felt very free walking with Ryan and playing with the dog. It seemed a long time since she had felt so happy.

They had coffee at the tea shop at Peddleton, glad to be inside in the warm. The waitress found a bowl of water and a dog biscuit for Casper. She seemed to know it was John Phillips' dog. Jane was not sure how, as most of the local farmers had border collies and they all looked the same to her, but perhaps Ryan and the dog were regular visitors.

They walked home slowly, the dog still full of energy, running ahead and returning to them, trying to hurry them along, occasionally bringing Ryan a stick to throw. They reached a stile, and he put the dog back on the lead ready to walk across the field ahead, lifted the dog gate, and helped Jane over the stile, retaining her hand for a moment.

'You, me, a dog, a path and a sunny day,' he said. 'What more could I ever want.'

She laughed, as she knew he intended her to. But when she met his eyes, she felt that she could never want more than that either.

When they returned, he helped her take off her coat, and he pulled off her boots as he always did. She sat beside him in Mary's room, both of them in their socks, warming their feet with a fan heater, laughing together as he touched her toes with his, pretending they were fighting over the best spot in the stream of warm air. The cat was on his lap and their fingers occasionally touched as they both stroked her.

Daniel came down to the kitchen without them realising, and saw them sitting laughing together in Mary's room, with their toes touching. He was clearly rather cross, asking why they had gone out without asking him to go with them, telling them he had been looking for Jane all afternoon.

Jane said nothing, thinking it was up to her where she went and with whom, but she didn't want to antagonise him or increase the animosity between him and Ryan. It crossed her mind that he was jealous of her being with Ryan. That would exactly explain how he was behaving. She put on her sheepskin boots, which had been left to warm by the radiator, and Ryan switched off the heater. Her toes still felt tingly from touching his toes.

Pat was going out to the Black Horse Inn to meet Jimmy that evening, so Jane and Ryan went with him. There were six of them with Claire and David. Jane was rather conscious that she was sitting with two men she had flirted with and kissed and one that she would like to flirt with and kiss. She tried not to flirt with any of them while they were all together. There would be no goodnight kiss for Pat tonight with Ryan with them. She hoped Pat realised that.

She thought, as she had once before, that it would be a triumph to get a kiss from Ryan, but she felt mean even thinking that. She knew he was a lone wolf who didn't like girls, and she should respect that. He always treated her with respect. She couldn't imagine him scheming to get a kiss from her or thinking it a triumph if he did.

Thursday 18 December 1975

On Thursday afternoon Ryan, Daniel and Jane all went walking to town and back. Jane hoped that Ryan and Daniel might get on together on a walk, but it was a disaster. Although they could walk three abreast, with Jane in the middle, where the path crossed fields, there were long stretches where the path was only wide enough for two, with Daniel trying to elbow his son out of the way so he could walk beside her. For most of the walk no one said anything. Jane was used to allowing Daniel to pursue his own thoughts when out walking, and today Ryan was equally silent even when she managed to walk beside him. It seemed he didn't want to talk to her with his father there.

Then there were the stiles, where Daniel was quick to help her and was deliberately staying very close to her when she stepped down so she practically fell into his arms, with Ryan glaring at him.

When they reached town, they had coffee and cake at the café, with Daniel lamenting he would have preferred a real drink. He took one of the pills from the bottle that he carried with him in his pocket, and Ryan was instantly concerned, offering to phone home and ask Pat to bring the car.

'I'll be fine. I just need to sit here for a while until it works. You walk far too fast; I don't know how you expect us to keep up with you. Jane doesn't walk fast when she's just with me.'

It was true that Ryan walked much faster than Daniel did—Jane could sometimes scarcely keep up with him—but he did slow down if he thought she was struggling. He was used to walking by himself, he had once told her, and she was to remind him if he went too fast for her.

They returned home along the path, a little more slowly. Jane stayed beside Daniel, as she wanted him to set the pace. Ryan fell behind where they could not walk three abreast so he did not get ahead of them.

When they reached home, Jane decided they were never doing this again. She took off her own boots. She didn't want Daniel touching her feet, and she didn't want him to get jealous if Ryan did.

She asked Mary about the pills when they were washing up after dinner.

'His heart beats too fast if he gets out of breath, and sometimes it won't come back to normal without the digitoxin. It's not always exertion that causes it. Sometimes it's just stress. I'm not sure that too much whisky doesn't set it off as well, since he sometimes needs one in the night, and he's not out of breath then. He always knows when he needs to take one. His doctor says he won't last much longer unless he gives up whisky altogether. I'm grateful that you are helping him with that.'

Over cocoa that evening Ryan talked about them going to Richmond for the day, and Jane suggested they should wait until Daniel made a trip to London so they could do as they pleased without him knowing where they were. They could stay overnight if he wanted, so they had more time there, as she had three bedrooms. She reminded him that he had once suggested that. Daniel always stayed overnight in London, sometimes two nights, and Mary wouldn't mind what they did.

Friday 19 December 1975

Daniel was taking Mary to town for the shopping on the Friday before Christmas, and he asked Jane to come with them. He wanted her to go to the bank with him to take out cash for the young men for Christmas. Last night he had asked Ryan to sign a cash cheque without the amount on it, on the excuse he hadn't worked out the amount of cash he needed for the week. Once the cheque had been signed, he told Jane the amount to fill in, and said he didn't want her taking that much out at the bank by herself. In the past he had given the boys a cheque each for Christmas, but Allanstone had said it was better now to give them everything in cash. It was to do with the recent changes to death duties. Everything he gave them would now be added back to his estate and taxed when he died regardless of how many more years he lasted. If it was cash, it would be difficult for it to be traced and included.

When they returned home, she carefully tied a red ribbon around each of the two bundles of banknotes before she put them in the safe. They were twenty-pound notes and there were a lot of them. They each had more than she would have earned in three months at the bank. Even the allowances that he normally paid them were far more than she had earned. He did always offer her money when they took out the cash for the young men, but she didn't like to take money from him. It would make her feel as if she was exploiting him when she had plenty of her own, and it didn't seem right for a girl to take money from a man. She would feel that she owed him a favour.

That afternoon she did some typing for Daniel while Ryan was outside helping Pat in the garden. She needed to catch up after being out all morning for the shopping. Daniel came into the library to check where she was up to, and he caressed her cheek, pushed her hair aside, leaned over her and kissed her neck.

'Please don't do that, Mr Linden.'

But he only laughed and told her he was not doing her any harm.

Saturday 20 December 1975

On Saturday afternoon the children who attended Linda's Sunday School put on a nativity play at the village hall, with Colin's group and the parents of the children watching.

Jane was surprised how many children there were in a village with at most a couple of hundred souls, but she did recognise a few of them.

Alice was Mary, and Jenny was a shepherdess. Daisy was one of a group of small children dressed as lambs in little woolly costumes. The baby Jesus was a lifelike vinyl baby doll wrapped in a shawl.

Unfortunately, the shawl got caught in a shepherd's crook, and the baby was pulled out of the manger onto the floor, landing head first and losing his shawl in the process. He wasn't wearing anything underneath. But Alice managed to scoop up the doll and the shawl and quickly rewrap him. Thank goodness they didn't have Brett as baby Jesus, Jane thought, he might have broken his neck.

The three wise men brought their gifts, two small cedar boxes and a net bag of gold coins. Two of the coins spilled out as they were handed to Mary. One of the lambs realised it was a chocolate coin, picked it up and unwrapped it, ate it, then crawled under the manger in search of the other dropped coin.

Jane sat in the audience between Ryan and Pat on a hard and rather uncomfortable chair. Mary was in London, and Daniel had wisely stayed at home. Jane hoped he wouldn't have too many whiskies with no one there to restrain him. When they went out on Saturday afternoons, they often returned to find him more than a little tipsy.

Jane phoned Sarah that evening, just to keep in touch with her friend, telling her she was staying at Hayward Hall indefinitely now, but would be back at times to check the house while she decided what to do with it in the long term. Sarah offered to have Tony tidy the garden occasionally since it was only up the road from them.

Wednesday 24 December 1975

On Christmas Eve Reverend Colin held a carol service in the church, and mince pies and tea and coffee were served in the village hall afterwards. Mary and Jane had made mince pies to bring, and even Daniel came along to sing carols, have supper, and chat to Colin and the farming families.

Jane had spent most of the afternoon ensuring Daniel didn't have more than one whisky before dinnertime. He could drink a fair few glasses before he was noticeably drunk, but she wasn't taking any chances. She promised he would be allowed another when they returned to the Hall. He negotiated for two more.

Jimmy cornered her and gave her a present, which she was to take home and not to open until the morning. It was a small, soft package that fitted easily into her handbag. Pat was with Claire for most of the evening. Jane assumed he was trying, as she was, to keep their relationship a secret.

Robert Phillips was there, home from Geneva to spend three weeks with his father and his sons. He talked to Jane about her father. They were the same age and had been best friends, and Peter and Josie had visited him every year when they were on holiday in Switzerland.

'I was at your parents' funeral,' he told her. 'But you were very upset at the time, so I don't think you would remember me.'

She didn't remember meeting him, she admitted, but he didn't seem to mind, and he told her about Switzerland, and how lovely the lakes were in the summer. He owned a small chalet by a lake, and her parents had stayed there with him. If she ever wanted to come to Switzerland, with Ryan or Pat perhaps, she would be welcome to stay there. He was grateful to Pat and Jimmy for helping his father with the farm. The Hall and the two farms had been like one family during the War, and they had all helped each other get through.

Afterwards she sat in the kitchen with Ryan and cocoa as she always did when he was at home. He had smuggled two of the mince pies home in his jacket pocket, carefully wrapped in a serviette. He joked about leaving her mince pie out for Father Christmas instead of her eating it, and asked if she had been good all year.

Thursday 25 December 1975

Christmas day was cold but fine. There was a rule at Hayward Hall that presents were opened after church, but Jane opened Jimmy's present in her room before she went down to breakfast, so she could thank him if she saw him at the church, and so no one else knew he had given her a gift. It was a small beanbag teddy, the fur a dark russet brown like Jimmy's hair. Someone had stitched *Jimmy* and *Jane* across its front in yellow thread with a little heart between the two names. Since she didn't think Jimmy could sew, she assumed he had asked Claire to do it. She felt rather guilty, for she had only gone out with him a few times, and although she liked him, she was now more than half in love with Pat. She was glad that she had not brought the present downstairs to open.

Mary had made wreaths of yew and holly for the graves, as there were no flowers in the garden this late in the year. Jane asked her about the children, Charles and Eloise, who had been born between Daniel and Mary. Mary told her they were Rhesus babies, although at the time it had a different name that she couldn't recall, and no one then knew the cause. It had something to do with blood groups, and was inherited, but she herself had not been affected because she inherited the same blood group as her mother, and Daniel had been all right because the first baby was always okay. Nowadays it could be treated, but then it was usually fatal for the baby. Mary had been a late and unexpected baby when her mother had been close to forty years old. Mary did not think it likely that Jane would inherit it, as Mary's mother was not a blood relative of Jane, and she didn't think it mattered if the father of the baby inherited it. She thought it had to be the mother.

'My mother had a lot of tragedy in her life. She had two brothers who died in their infancy. Her father was an officer on the Titanic, and he went down with the ship when she was seventeen. She came here from Ireland to stay with a cousin who had married an Englishman and lived in town, and she became engaged to my father's eldest brother, but he died in the First World War. After the War she married my father. She lost two of her own babies, and my father was missing presumed dead near the end of the last War. But she always worked hard to keep the family together, and she doted on her children and her two grandsons. Ryan in particular was the light of her life. She was so proud of him, and he loved her. She did everything she could for Ryan because Daniel never cared much for him.'

Christmas was a happy season with the church decorated with a nativity scene and wreaths of holly. The lifelike baby doll was in a manger near the font, on straw provided by one of the farmers, this time wearing a sleeveless baby bodysuit beneath his shawl to avoid him further embarrassment. He was such a pretty baby that Jane wished she could pick him up and give him a cuddle.

Everyone was in good spirits on a cold but sunny day. Jane managed to get Jimmy alone for long enough to thank him for the teddy and confirm Claire had embroidered the names. He told Jane that Claire had embroidered one for Pat as well. He lamented that he didn't see her much. Why didn't she come over to the farm sometimes? His mother would love to see her, and so would he. He had the idea that her uncle didn't want her to go out with him—he understood that—but they could walk out sometimes. If she came down to the farm, her uncle would think she was there to see his mother or Claire.

Jane liked him, and she liked his company, but she was starting to feel very guilty about flirting with him, especially now he had given her the teddy. She was falling more and more in love with Pat, but now that Ryan was home all the time, she and Pat couldn't go out together without him knowing. She wasn't absolutely sure why she didn't want him to know; she only knew that she didn't. It was odd about the teddy for Pat. Why had Claire done one for Pat? What had she written on it? Was she sweet on him? Jane recalled they had both been missing on bonfire night. Well, he was hers now, and Claire would have to find someone else.

Daniel had bought diamond teardrop earrings for her and for Mary, as well as perfume for them both. He told them he enjoyed buying beautiful things for his two beautiful women. Pat gave her the cherry liqueur chocolates that she liked, and her present from Mary was Liberty cotton pyjamas.

Ryan gave her the book for *North and South*, which they had both been watching on television on Monday nights, and a scarf with a matching hat and gloves, hand made in Iceland from soft fluffy wool, with a pattern of snowflakes, knitted so one side was white with cornflower blue snowflakes and the other was blue with white snowflakes.

Jane wasn't sure how it was done, but Mary said it was called double-knitting because you used two strands of wool. Her mother had once knitted a scarf like it for Ryan in similar colours, and he had worn it until it fell to pieces. He had called it his magic scarf because of the two colours. Jane wondered if he had only owned two scarves in his life, the snowflake one that he wore until it fell to pieces and the college one that was now nearly in pieces.

She also had a little parcel from Mr Allanstone, which had arrived in the post a few days before. He always gave her a present at Christmas and on her birthday. She had left it wrapped to open on Christmas day. It was a small black mesh Oroton evening purse. He always found beautiful things for her. At least he always treated her with respect, and he always kept his hands to himself. She wished that Daniel behaved more like Mr Allanstone.

Mary had bought silk pyjamas for the men, and Daniel had given Pat and Ryan the neat bundles of banknotes.

Ryan loved his watch, but he later told her he hadn't meant for her to buy such an expensive one.

'Whenever I look at the time, I will think of you,' he told her. 'It will take me a while to get used to not needing to wind it up each day.'

There was no Christmas tree at Hayward Hall, or any decorations, but there was a turkey from John Phillips' farm for dinner, served with Mary's redcurrant jelly, and the Christmas pudding that Mary had cooked four weeks ago. There were extra brandied cherries spooned over it in the dishes, and brandy sauce. Ryan had opened a bottle of elderberry wine. For once they ate in the dining room instead of the kitchen, all five of them at one end of a table that could seat eighteen.

Jane remembered the turkeys running free in their enclosure on the farm and knew she could never be a farmer. It was no different from buying a chicken at the supermarket, she told herself, but then you never actually saw your particular chicken running around free before you ate it.

Mary asked if she could borrow *North and South* when Jane and Ryan had both finished reading it. She said she had enjoyed watching the serial.

Jane realised then that Mary had in fact watched it herself in the lounge while she and Ryan were watching it together in Mary's room on

Monday evenings, both of them believing that Mary wanted to watch something else. Had Mary done this to avoid Daniel interrupting them? He had been annoyed that Jane was not playing chess with him. She knew that Mary encouraged her and Ryan to do things together because Mary wanted him to come home more often, but it all seemed a little odd. The three of them could have watched it together. Although Jane had rather enjoyed it being just her and Ryan, sitting close-up and cosy with their popcorn and port. She said nothing to Mary, realising that she was unaware that she had blundered.

After dinner they all sat in the lounge, watching an old black and white film of *A Christmas Carol* on television. As well as the radiators, which merely took the worst of the chill off the rooms, Daniel had lit a fire in one of the two fireplaces, burning the wood that Ryan and Pat had chopped a couple of weeks before.

Jane was on a sofa between Pat and Ryan, with a blanket over all three of them. Pat held one of her hands secretly beneath the blanket. Her other hand stroked the cat, which had settled onto Ryan's lap. He was stroking the cat as well. Sometimes their fingers touched, and he would look sideways at her, sharing a secret. She felt rather naughty, flirting with both of them at once, but she felt happy. She knew she was finally recovering her joy in life. She had sat like this with Ryan in Mary's room when they watched *North and South.* With each episode they had seemed a little closer together, and during the final one she had accidentally touched his hand as she stroked the cat, and his finger had stroked hers, gently and scarcely perceptibly. He had seemed a little tense, so she had been careful not to do it again. But tonight he seemed to accept her fingers touching his, responding with a slight caress and an amused glance. He had once held her hand in the conservatory, and given her a hug, but he had never done that again. Perhaps he hadn't liked it. She knew he didn't like people being too close to him.

'That's one very lucky cat,' said Daniel when the film had finished. 'I hope that's all you've been fondling, sitting there all of you so cosy and with your hands hidden. Next time Jane can sit beside me.'

Wednesday 31 December 1975

The rivalry between Daniel and his son for her company in the afternoons was becoming a little tiring. She would no longer go out walking with either of them except in the garden or to the village. The weather had been so bleak and cold since Christmas that walking long distances was not very appealing in any case.

There appeared to be an unspoken truce. After lunch each day she walked with Daniel in the garden, and later in the afternoon she walked with Ryan, usually to the village and back. When it was raining, they could walk around the conservatory.

On Wednesday afternoon Daniel suggested they get some exercise by climbing the back staircase a couple of times. She easily beat him to the top floor and stopped on the landing, not sure if they were to go through the door and up the last flight to the attic. She remembered he was not to over-exert himself because of his dicky heart.

When he caught up with her, he suggested she come and look at his room so she could see the view from the window. She reminded him that was forbidden; she was not allowed in the bedrooms on the top floor.

'That's only the boys' rooms,' he told her. 'You're always allowed in mine. But we can look at the view from one of the other rooms.'

He opened a door and they stood at the window of a cold empty bedroom, looking out over the garden wall to the sloping fields, stone walls and hedgerows of John Phillips' farm, and beyond that the village of Peddleton, grey against the hillside, solid old stone houses nestled and peaceful beneath a grey troubled sky.

Daniel was standing behind her, far too close to her, and he slipped his arm around her waist, pulling her against him, moving his body against hers. He pushed her hair aside and kissed the back of her neck. 'Come on, Jane. Come to my room for a while. You're old enough to know what I want. No one will miss us for the rest of the afternoon. If we don't come down for coffee, Mary will think we are out walking.'

He took her hand in his and guided it to touch his crotch. For a moment she froze with shock, before spinning around in complete panic and pushing him away. He laughed and let her go.

She wouldn't go up the stairs with him again; she didn't trust him.

They all sat in the kitchen for afternoon coffee, as Pat was at home that day. She tried hard to talk normally, although she was shaking inside. She saw Ryan look at her a little oddly, and she knew he sensed she was upset, but he said nothing.

She asked Ryan if they could set up the table tennis, so on wet days they could play at that instead of walking. Pat promised he would not set light to any balls, assuring them he had grown out of his pyromaniac phase.

Pat and Ryan found the old table tennis table, cleaned away the dust and the cobwebs, and Jane helped them set it up in the billiard room. They would need a new net and some new bats and balls, which they could pick up on Friday when they did the shopping in town. If they played table tennis for exercise, Daniel would be at the other end of the table and couldn't touch her. But of course she didn't say that. She didn't tell Ryan that his father had asked her to go to his room, or what he had done. She didn't want to think about it.

Colin had arranged a New Year's Eve party for the young people in the village hall, the children as well as the teenagers, with the usual arrangements for supper. There would be dancing from eight o' clock, and Jack McCann had kept back some fireworks from bonfire night to set off at midnight. Anne McCann had set up a record player and had borrowed some extra singles from Mary, so they had some variety in the music.

The hall was cold, but there were a couple of convection heaters and a lot of people, so they managed quite well. They started with folk dances, Linda arranging them all in groups of eight, although some of the younger boys had to dance the girl's part. They were good-natured about it, however, and Linda swapped them around, so they all had a chance to partner one of the girls. After a while they went on to more modern music and more modern dancing.

Ryan didn't dance. When Jane asked him, he told her it was not his type of dancing, he only did formal dances. But she jived with Pat and with Jimmy, and did the twist with David, while most of the young people just danced with no one in particular. Since there were more than two boys for every girl, that was perhaps not a bad thing.

At ten they had the supper. Colin had asked them all to bring a blanket or a sleeping bag, and after supper they all sat on the floor while Ryan read a ghost story about a screaming skull. It was the spookiest story Jane had ever heard, and Ryan read it with so much atmosphere that Jane thought she would be too scared to sleep that night. David had brought his guitar, and they sang folk songs to round off the evening.

Just before midnight they all walked over to the village green, their feet crunching in frost, to wait for Jack McCann to let off the fireworks, with a transistor radio on to get the exact time.

Then after some cheering, and shouts of Happy New Year, they returned to the farms and the cottages, Jack ensuring all the younger children and the girls were accompanied home by himself or at least one of the older boys, while Jane, Pat and Ryan helped Colin and Anne McCann tidy the hall.

4 FALLING SNOW

Friday 2 January 1976

When they went into town for shopping on Friday, Jane bought some new bats and balls and a net from the sports shop for the table tennis.

Ryan and Pat had moved some of the timber garden benches into the stables to be mended and painted. Pat had set up a heater so the wood could dry out, and Jane spent Friday afternoon helping them sand off the old paint. Mary had found her some old clothes of Pat's so she didn't get dust on her own. Pat's jeans were rather too large for her, and she had to turn up the cuffs. Ryan joked about it, telling her to be sure to fasten the belt tightly or they might fall down.

They all spent the evening at table tennis, and even Mary had a turn. Jane thought how good it was when everyone did things together.

When Mary went to bed at ten and Daniel returned to the den, Ryan asked to borrow *North and South* from Jane and found *A Christmas Carol* for her to read. Pat joined them for cocoa, and they all stayed up rather late.

Saturday 3 January 1976

There was no outing on Saturday as Colin had arranged the New Year's Eve party for them on Wednesday instead. Linda's parents had been staying at the vicarage since Christmas to meet baby Brett, who was now a month old.

Mary went to see her friend in London, and Jane and Pat spent Saturday morning painting the benches. Ryan had stayed in town after taking Mary to the station, to get his hair cut, and Daniel didn't offer to help with the painting. But Jane didn't mind, as it gave her a chance to be alone with Pat, although there had been no mention of them going out together, or escaping to have a life of their own, since Ryan had come back home for the holidays. Not that Jane minded. She was happy just to work on the benches. She was not even sure now that she did want to leave here.

They would need to wait a few days between coats as the weather was so cold, so would continue on Wednesday.

Jane wanted to check the house in Richmond, but Daniel showed no sign of disappearing to London. If she was going out for the day with Ryan, she preferred Daniel not to know, as there was enough friction between them without her adding to it. She could go to Richmond and back by herself on the train quite easily in a day, but she knew if she suggested it, Daniel would want to drive her there. From the few times she had been in the car with him driving, she knew she wouldn't feel safe with him on the motorway. She wouldn't feel safe alone with him at the house in Richmond either. He was always a bit free with his hands, although never when Ryan was in the room, but lately he had got worse. She hadn't liked him wanting her to go with him to his bedroom, and she didn't want to think about him trying to make her touch him.

She asked Daniel if he was intending to go to London soon, but he said he didn't need anything there for now, so he would wait until Ryan was back in Oxford for the new term. She wondered if this was because he didn't like leaving her and Ryan here together, as he appeared to be jealous of his son. Which was odd really, as it was Pat that Jane wanted, not Ryan, for all that she enjoyed Ryan's company. Daniel didn't seem to mind her doing things with Pat, which was good of course, as it meant they were hiding their attraction to each other quite well.

She talked to Ryan about Richmond, telling him Daniel was not going to London, and she was considering going there by herself on the train. He suggested she get up early one morning and he would drive here there, leaving Mary to tell Daniel they were spending the morning shopping in Oxford. Daniel couldn't have any objection to that.

'He might be cross when we get home much later,' she said doubtfully.

'Then we'll tell him we spent the whole day shopping. We're not children, Jane. He can't dictate what we do.'

Tuesday 6 January 1976

She felt like a truant child as they drove away from Hayward on Tuesday morning. Mary was happy to tell Daniel they had gone shopping when he came down to breakfast. The forecast was for widespread snow late on Wednesday, but today was fine although bitterly cold.

She thought Ryan would want to spend the day doing research in the city, but he said that could wait. They would check the house and garden, have coffee at the café in Richmond, take the train to the city, do some sightseeing, and have lunch somewhere. After that she could shop if she wanted to, before they returned to the house and then drove home. He could go to London at any time by himself if he wanted to research their ancestors.

She was flattered that he wanted to spend time with her, although she did feel a little guilty that she was planning to run away with Pat.

The house at Richmond was cold, but everything was neat and clean. Tony had tidied the garden on the weekend, so that was looking quite respectable as well. She found a few more clothes to bring back to Hayward; she would smuggle them indoors in a shopping bag as if she had bought them that day in Oxford.

They went out for their morning coffee.

She remembered she had sat here in the café with him when he had driven her to Richmond in November, and she felt the same freedom that she had felt then, as though nothing in the world mattered except the two of them sitting by the window in the warm café with the world outside just a faraway illusion. Even Hayward seemed far away and unreal.

At first they talked about things they had done at school, and he said he had often thought about her as he grew up, wishing he could meet her, and wondering what she was like.

He told her he enjoyed his work teaching the undergraduates. Teaching history wasn't just about the students learning events and names and dates, they also learnt to look at the past from the perspective of those who made the decisions. Sometimes things that seem wrong to us now would have seemed right to them. The students learnt values and ethics that would stay with them for all of their lives. He taught Latin as well. Some people just considered it a dead language, but he loved the logic and discipline of it, and it was good to read old texts in the language they were written in.

Some of the young men he taught were challenged by the move from school to university, and he could sometimes help them find their feet. Professor Hanson often put the more vulnerable ones in his tutorials. Others were very privileged young men who thought themselves superior to everyone else and had never looked at the world from someone else's point of view. They were sometimes difficult to deal with, but he had been at school with young men like that, so he was patient with them.

He enjoyed living at the college. He had always thought of his future as staying on living there and teaching full time, but lately he was no longer sure that was what he really wanted. He said it was a long time since he had been at home for more than a few days at a time because he had never got on with his father. He loved Hayward Hall, but he had never seen it as his permanent home. It was his father's home, and he had been happy just coming back on weekends. But now Jane was there, he thought it might be good to live there all the time. He was managing to get on with his father fairly well. Daniel seemed to get on better with all of them since she had come to live with them.

She remembered Daniel telling her he would leave the house to her, not to Ryan, but she didn't say anything, as she doubted that Daniel had really meant it. She also remembered the disastrous walk to town, and thought if that was Ryan's idea of getting on fairly well, it would be interesting to see what life would be like if they didn't get on at all.

She found she could talk to him about her life more easily away from Hayward. She had recovered a lot, and she could think of the past now without collapsing into tears. She told him she had liked school, had loved the weekends and holidays in her parents' house in Kent. She had enjoyed outings with her parents to small heritage railways; her father had loved steam trains.

Ryan recalled her father—his uncle Peter—had once taken him to ride on a miniature railway when he was very small. They had both loved trains.

She talked of the time she had been a bridesmaid to Sarah. She still had the dress somewhere in the attic. She told him how she had met a guy at the wedding and had gone out to dinner with him, but he had wanted her to go back to his flat afterwards, and she hadn't wanted to, so he had never asked her out again. His hands had been all over her, and she still didn't like the thought of it. Perhaps if he had gone a bit more slowly, she might have got used to it, but she hadn't felt safe. She didn't like the idea of sleeping with someone she hardly knew.

She knew Ryan would understand that. She still had not told him that Daniel had asked her to go to his room with him. She didn't like to complain to him about his father because she didn't want them rowing over her.

'He was a very foolish young man to waste his opportunity,' he said. 'But I am very glad he did, or you might have married him and never have come to us. I am so happy that you did come to us. We all are. Mary loves having you at Hayward, and so do I. Pat is good company if you want to play snooker or talk about gardening or cricket, but he doesn't read the same books as I do, and he gets bored with historic houses. Although we often visit open gardens together, and he enjoys that. You and I seem to like the same things, and I just like being with you.'

She looked up at him, meeting his eyes for a brief moment before he dropped his. She wanted to tell him she liked being with him, but she felt too shy to say something so forward to a man. He looked down at his empty cup, his long slender fingers playing with the handle. His hands were beautiful, even if two of the fingers were not quite straight.

They had been sitting in the café for well over an hour. He ordered them another coffee, and still they sat, talking about her father and his job as a statistician in the civil service, which had given them a decent income, about the house in Kent where she had lived, the garden with the roses and the apple trees and pear trees and the monkey puzzle and the high brick wall around it, similar to the garden at Hayward Hall. Except the wall at Hayward was stone not brick, and the garden in Kent had only been an acre. Hayward Hall had ten acres, and the monkey puzzle there was much larger. She only realised now that her father had been trying to recreate the garden at Hayward Hall on their acre in Kent, with the monkey puzzle, the roses, the apple trees, and they had raspberries as well, and a pond with stone edging and koi. There were even a couple of small gargoyles. She wondered if her father had missed the garden at Hayward Hall.

She said it would be nice if Hayward Hall had a lake so they could have a boat, and Ryan offered to take her rowing on the river near Oxford in the summer. There were places that hired out boats, and he would enjoy that. He was in a rowing team at Oxford, but he had never made the top team for the race against Cambridge. And they could go and see Martin again. He had enjoyed the afternoon they had spent there in November, and it would be good to see Luke again. Those last few weeks he had spent with just Martin and Luke boating on the lake that summer, after the girls had gone back to school, had been one of the few times in his life he had really felt happy. School was behind them and they were looking forward to their university days and life in the world beyond. There had been a row with his father because he wanted to read history at Oxford, instead of law, so he had been glad to be away from home. He had always loved history. He felt part of it when he walked in the hills around Hayward.

They talked about *North and South*. Jane had been surprised that John Thornton saving Margaret from the inquest had been left out of the serial, as she thought it an important part of the story. But she had not liked the ending of the book, even though the lovers were reunited. She thought the heroine acted far too shyly, particularly as she had spent the whole book going from being a sheltered parson's daughter to an independent young woman in charge of her own life and her own money. And they had become friends, in spite of misunderstandings, both of them gradually coming to understand each other's world. Surely Margaret could have simply told him she loved him.

'That may be harder than you think, Jane, especially if you are not sure the other person feels the same. It could spoil a friendship. I did feel very sorry for Henry, though, having to help the woman he loved give herself and her money to a rival.'

They were still sitting in the café at lunch time, so they ordered soup with hot bread rolls. After lunch they walked in the heated glasshouses at Kew Gardens, talking about the plants, and in the end they didn't go into the city at all.

On the walk back to the house Jane saw a beautiful hand-knitted Fair Isle jumper in a shop window that she thought would be good to wear with jeans. The pattern was similar to the sleeveless pullover that Ryan sometimes wore. It was an exclusive shop and an expensive jumper, but he told her to go in and try it on, and if she liked it, he would buy it for her. She was not to worry about the cost, as his father always gave him far more than he needed. It fitted her well, and he paid for it, telling her it was a present for giving him such a wonderful day, and he had enjoyed spending some of his Christmas money buying her something she liked. He smiled at her, and she thought how beautiful he was when he smiled. It was good to see him happy.

He hadn't touched her, he hadn't even held her hand, but she felt very close to him, and she had felt so good talking to him in the café. They had plenty of time to talk together at Hayward, but somehow here it felt different. She felt she knew him better now, that he was part of her world here instead of her being part of his world at Hayward. It was good to be with him without Daniel constantly watching them, and away from Hayward Hall it seemed as if they belonged with each other rather than them both belonging with Daniel. She knew she was more than a little in love with him. Perhaps she didn't really want to run away with Pat. She would rather run away with Ryan. But he was a lone wolf, and it would be dangerous to fall in love with him.

They put her shopping bags with her extra clothes and her new jumper in the car, locked the house, and headed home to face the music.

They stuck to their story about Oxford, telling Daniel they had spent the afternoon walking around the town. She knew Daniel was cross about it, but he really had no right to be cross.

Wednesday 7 January 1976

Jane wondered if Daniel thought they had spent the afternoon in Ryan's room at the college, for the next morning he made a comment about how small and dark Ryan's room was there. She said she didn't know, she had never seen his room, they hadn't been to his college.

In the afternoon Pat lit a fire in the stables so it was warm enough for them to continue with the painting. This time Ryan helped them, so she and Pat were not alone together as they had been on Saturday, but Jane didn't mind. She was beginning to wonder if she really did love Pat. He was good company, kissing him made her feel good, and it was fun to plan a life for them together, but she hardly thought about him when she was away from him. She thought about Ryan almost all of the time.

There was snow on Wednesday night and all day on Thursday, not too deep but enough to lay on the ground for a few days. On Friday morning the snow had been cleared from the road between the town and Hayward village, and Ryan, Pat, Jack and Jimmy had cleared the lane from the village to John Phillips' farm, with help from Robert Phillips and his sons, so they were able to do the shopping in town as usual.

Saturday 10 January 1976

Colin had arranged snow games on the village green for Saturday afternoon. This was for everyone, the farmers, the cottage residents and the children, as well as Colin's teenagers.

There were snowmen and snowballs, and the two youngest McCann boys made bricks out of snow and built an igloo with help from Alice and Jenny, the two girls Jane had helped with sewing the squares. Daisy was placed inside it for a photograph. A small sled had been found in the vicarage shed, and Jimmy pulled it along, with Daisy and two other small girls sitting on it, Jane following to ensure they didn't fall off.

Ryan was taking photographs again, of the children beside their snowmen, of Daisy in the igloo, of Jane in her hat and scarf from Iceland. Brett, now nearly six weeks old, was asleep in his pram, wearing the little blue snowsuit that Jane had given him. He had his photo taken as well.

Jane saw Claire talking rather earnestly to Pat, and she seemed upset about something. Jane saw her brush away a tear, and Pat seemed rather angry, but Jane was not too concerned. Claire had been a little cold to her lately. Jane thought it was because Claire liked Pat and could sense he preferred Jane to her. These things happened. If she and Pat were married, Claire would get over it and fall for someone else.

At half past four afternoon tea was served in the hall, with each family bringing a plate of scones or biscuits or cake. Anne McCann had brought along a birthday cake for Jimmy with twenty candles, as today was his birthday, and everyone had a tiny slice of it.

Mary was in London, but she had left a plate of cupcakes for Jane to take for the tea, and a scarf she had knitted for Jimmy. Jane had given him toffees.

Saturday 17 January 1976

For nearly a week they had been holed up indoors, all of them seeming under the weather. Although the snow had thawed by Monday, covering the lane with dirty brown slush, the wind had returned with rain and sleet, so walking was unpleasant. Even umbrellas were no help, as the blustery wind sent them out of control.

The house was cold, even with the radiators, so Ryan had set up a fan heater in the library, and he and Jane had sorted papers for Daniel. At first Ryan had tried to work on his thesis downstairs, but it was impossible for him to concentrate with Daniel interrupting.

Daniel continued typing in the den, but he constantly snapped at his son, and when Jane had suggested taking away the decanter to help him resist having yet another drink, he snapped at her as well.

'It keeps me warm. You two have a heater.'

Mary had refused to allow him to run an electric heater in the den, as she considered it too dangerous with all the clutter and loose papers.

Pat stayed indoors, seeming unable to apply himself to anything and wandering around the house in sulky silence. The weather had made gardening impossible, and when Mary suggested he go over to the McCanns' farm, he yelled at her.

'Why should I help him? He doesn't pay me for it. Besides, there is nothing to do there either in this weather.'

Pat being anything but calm and good-natured was unusual enough for Ryan to ask what was troubling him, but he did not respond.

Eventually Mary set him to cleaning the cellar. Ryan helped him some of the time, as he didn't want Pat to be left brooding on his own, but Jane stayed sorting the papers, as she didn't much like being in the cellar. On her last incursion into its shadowy depths to fetch a jar of jam for Mary, a mouse had startled her, jumping onto her skirt. Jane was not sure whether she or the mouse had fled the fastest.

Thus the week had passed, with Jane glad to have Ryan's company, but unhappy that both Pat and Daniel seemed so stressed and bad-tempered.

Although the weather had improved by Saturday, it was still very cold, so Colin arranged table tennis in the village hall. At least it was active and helped them all to keep warm. Linda stayed at the vicarage with Brett, who had a slight cold, but Ryan came to help.

He played beside Jane, as he had once before, against the Phillips boys. Even with the small amount of practise she had from playing at home, Jane felt she was much better at the game than she had been the first time she had played it at the village hall. Pat was beside Claire, playing against Jimmy and David. Colin always spread the six girls out over the five tables, with the two youngest girls together, but he did allow some preferences and he always put Jane with Ryan.

It was good to be out of the house, good to hear the laughter and chatter of the teenagers, good to look forward to the tea and cakes that Jane and Candy were to serve since Linda was not there.

Pat played a shot with rather too much enthusiasm and his bat hit Claire in the face as he stepped back on the rebound. All may have been well had he simply apologised—she was a little stunned but not badly hurt—but instead he completely lost his temper.

'You were in the way, you stupid girl. You're always in the goddamn way,' he yelled at her, and she instantly dissolved into tears.

Jimmy hugged his sister and faced Pat. Everyone else stopped their game while the two young men glared at each other.

'Don't talk to my sister like that,' said Jimmy menacingly. 'Haven't you upset her enough already?'

What did he mean? Jane wondered again if Claire had once been Pat's girlfriend. He didn't usually show her any particular attention. But although Colin always encouraged the boys to be nice to the girls, he discouraged any show of romantic attachment.

'Sorry,' Pat said, rather sulkily.

'Come, Claire,' said Jane, taking her arm. 'Pat didn't mean to hit you. We need to get the urn heating. You can help me set it up. Pat has been really cross with everyone this week. He can't work in the garden in this weather, so Mary made him clean out the cellar. Mary and I didn't want to do it because it's full of spiders, mice as well. One ran up my skirt once, so now I only go down to the cellar with jeans on.'

'That happened to me once, in the barn,' Claire responded.

Jane exchanged a relieved look with Candy, who had followed them into the kitchen.

'We have mice in our cottage,' said Candy, 'but I never got one up my skirt. I'll put the kettle on and make you a cup of tea while Jane sets up the urn.'

Candy made tea for all three of them, and found a jam tart for Claire.

When they returned to the table tennis, Ryan was talking on the sidelines with Colin, Winston had taken Claire's place with Pat, and Adrian was playing at the table where Candy had been.

Ryan handed the girls their bats and they played on the table with him.

'I get three girls,' he said, trying to cheer Claire up. 'A man can't get luckier than that.'

Jane flashed him a smile, wordlessly thanking him, as he sent gentle easy shots to Claire.

Had Claire been Pat's girlfriend? Or had she just been upset at him yelling at her? Since Claire lived in a house with four brothers, Jane thought it unlikely that she would get upset over a few unkind words. Last week she had thought that Claire would have to accept that Pat now belonged to her, Jane, but she was coming to realise that she didn't really want to run away with Pat. It would be good, at times, to get away from Daniel groping her, but what she most wanted was to always stay at Hayward Hall with Ryan. It was so good having him there all the time, not just at weekends.

He was returning to Oxford on Monday for the start of the new term. Jane felt very bleak at the thought. She would miss his company during the week. She knew it would not be sensible to fall in love with him, but they could stay friends as they were, with both of them always together at Hayward. At least on the weekends.

Sunday 18 January 1976

On Sunday afternoon Pat asked Mary for the key to the lodge. He checked it occasionally to ensure there were no roof leaks or any damage from rats. He asked Jane if she would like to come with him, as she had never been inside it before.

Mary had made a carrot cake—there was usually a cake for tea on Sundays—and it was cooling on a cake rack while she made the icing. Ryan was cracking walnuts for her to put on the top. She asked them not to be too long.

The rain had finally gone, the sky a weak wintry blue, but it was still cold outside. Pat opened the door to the lodge, and the two of them stepped into a quiet world of their own. A fortnight ago she would have been glad for them to be alone together, but now she was not so sure. She wished Ryan had come with them.

'I thought we could ask Daniel if we could get married and live here,' he said as they stood in the cold empty hallway, the door now closed behind them. 'I could still do the garden, and you could still help with the typing, but we would come home to our own life in our own house. Then when you are twenty-one, we can use your money to buy a house in town, and I can buy a car. I asked Daniel how much you had, but he said he didn't know. I know it's a lot because I remember him telling that awful bank manager of yours that you didn't need to work. Do you know how much?'

She didn't respond to the question. She was a little shocked that he was asking it, although she recalled he had asked her the same thing once before.

The house was tiny. Downstairs there was a living room with an open fireplace, and a kitchen with an old porcelain sink, a range that backed onto the living-room fire so they shared the chimney, and a door out to the garden. Another small room behind the stairs had once been used for storing coal. Upstairs there were two bedrooms with fireplaces and sloping ceilings, and an ancient bathroom. There was no furniture, the wallpaper was mildewed and peeling, and a damp smell from the lino floors pervaded the whole house.

They sat on the staircase, and he was kissing her for the first time in weeks, his hands in her hair, her eyes closed as she enjoyed the moment, the thought of the two of them living here together, sleeping upstairs. She did want him, of course she did.

'Jane, we can't go on like this. I want to sleep with you. I can't come to your room because it's next to Mum's, and you can't come to mine with Ryan home. Even when he is away again my room is above Mum's room so it wouldn't work. It's hard to make love quietly, especially in the creaky old beds we all have at the Hall. We could say we were shopping in town and spend an afternoon at a hotel, maybe further afield where nobody knows us.'

Jane wasn't sure she wanted to do that, but she was happy to let him go on kissing her, planning how and when and what they would tell Daniel.

She heard the door open, and she opened her eyes, pushing Pat away from her. For a long silent moment they met Ryan's, and she could see how deeply hurt he was. She remembered them sitting together in the café in Richmond, and how she had thought they belonged together. Had he felt like that too? It dawned on her that this quiet, patient man had fallen in love with her, but she had betrayed him for a shallow young man who offered a bit of flimsy romance and a stolen kiss in a corner in exchange for living off her money.

He looked shocked, his face white and his hand on the doorjamb for support. But when he finally spoke, he seemed to have recovered. 'Holy socks! What are you two playing at?'

'Jane and I are going to get married and live here.'

Jane wished Pat hadn't said anything. She could have told Ryan it was a game, that it meant nothing. She was suddenly ashamed that things had gone so far and very glad that they had gone no further.

'Does my father know?'

'He can't stop us,' said Pat. 'He can accept it and let us live here, or we can leave and he won't have a gardener or a secretary.'

'I take that answer to mean he doesn't know. Oh, dear, what a sorry mess. Pat, I came to find you. You are to go back to the house. Jack McCann has turned up with Jimmy and Claire to talk to Aunt Mary and my father. He didn't bring a shotgun, but I got the idea what this is about. The young lady has a baby on the way and claims you are responsible. You always liked her, and you don't have any choice but to do the right thing by her. Jane, stay here with me, and let Pat go by himself.'

Pat said nothing, gave away nothing. He walked back towards the house without a glance at either of them.

Jane was still sitting on the stairs, too shaken to move. He had left the door open and an icy breath of wind slipped into the house like an evil goblin and gripped her face, making her even colder, but she scarcely noticed it. She was trying to take in what had happened, and she knew that disappointing Ryan was more devastating to her than losing Pat. Why, oh why, had she let Pat kiss her? She didn't love him. It had only ever been a game.

Ryan closed the door and sat down next to her, and she knew he was hurt. Well, he had said he was a lone wolf. How was she expected to know he would be so upset at her kissing his cousin?

'How far has this gone?' he asked her, his voice soft and showing no trace of anger or reproach.

She knew she would have to be careful what she said if she wanted him to forgive her, and she did want him to. In a single moment she had realised how much she wanted to retain his respect, and she knew she was on the brink of losing it, had probably already lost it. Yet for a moment she could say nothing as she tried hard not to cry.

'It hasn't gone anywhere. I have never said I would marry him. He made that up. I went out with him a few times before Christmas when you were in Oxford, and when we came back, he asked for a kiss good-night. He said that was the right thing to do when a guy took you on a date. But that's as far as it went. It was nice to be kissed, and it was fun to be keeping it secret, knowing it was forbidden. He said he knew I was not really his sister so it didn't matter if we broke the rules, so long as we weren't found out. It was just a game. Then when we came in here, he suddenly asked me to marry him and said we could live here. I would never have married him. He never even said he loved me. He just said that when I was twenty-one, we could get a place of our own with my money and he could buy a car.'

Her voice shook and she held back tears. It had been a silly dream, but it had been real to her, much more so than she was pretending. She had liked being loved, and now she was starting to wonder if Pat had loved her at all, or whether it was all a scheme to get his sports car.

Ryan put his arm around her, rather shyly, and she leaned against his shoulder while he held her, his face against her hair. Although at first she felt like it, she didn't cry. She just enjoyed for a moment being held and cared for by this wonderfully kind man. But she knew that he was hurt, and she didn't know what she could do or say to make things go back to the way they were. He was trying to comfort her because he thought she was upset, while she was wondering if it should have been her trying to comfort him.

He touched her cheek with his fingers, brushing back a strand of her hair. 'I don't like to see you unhappy. He should not have treated you like that. But the way he has treated Claire is appalling. He would have known. I saw them arguing about something at the snow games, and she was upset. Then he yelled at her yesterday over nothing. I felt so ashamed of him treating a girl like that after my grandmother brought us both up to always be nice to women. I can't believe he has behaved like this, getting Claire pregnant then chasing after you. Jane, you will stay here, won't you?'

Perhaps that was all it was, she thought. He was worried she would leave and go back to living by herself in Richmond. He knew she didn't want to live alone, and he cared about that. Perhaps he was just shocked at the way Pat had behaved. He had looked shocked yesterday when Pat had yelled at Claire. But when she raised her eyes to meet his, she knew that he was disappointed and hurt.

'Yes, I'll stay here. I don't want to live at Richmond by myself, and I have nowhere else to go. And I don't want to marry anyone. All I want is to always stay living here with you.'

She felt him go tense as she leant against him, and his fingers on her face were suddenly absolutely still, so she hastily added, 'And Mary.'

For a while he was silent, and she wondered what he was thinking.

'It's freezing in here,' he said at last. 'I imagine Mary will be serving them tea, so let's slip in through the back door and sit in Mary's room, and I'll make some coffee for us. Hopefully, there is some of that carrot cake left. We had better keep out of the way for the moment. I'm grateful at least that he's not leaving you in the lurch with a baby as well. We'd be in a fine mess then.'

'Ryan, I'm so sorry you walked in on this. I feel like I've let you down, and you are always so kind to me.' She looked up at him again, knowing he was hurt but that he would never say so. 'I was never in love with him, but it was nice to be taken out and kissed goodnight, and it never went further than that. I went out with Jimmy a couple of times, too. I get a kiss goodnight from him as well, but I'm not marrying him either.'

'Perhaps some time you'll go out with me,' he said. 'Then I might get one.' She knew he said it to make her laugh, but it was a sad attempt at humour. She didn't laugh and neither did he.

She knew he was being defensive; she had disappointed him, and she didn't know what to say. If she asked his forgiveness, he would say there was nothing to forgive, that he was a lone wolf, that she could kiss whomsoever she liked, that it didn't matter to him. But she knew it did matter to him, so she said nothing. She suddenly thought how she would feel if it had been her walking in on him casually kissing a girl. She knew it would have hurt her dreadfully.

'Please don't laugh at me,' she said, trying to regain some dignity, and raising her eyes to meet his. 'It's nice to be kissed, it's romantic, and it didn't mean anything. You can have one if you want, but you have to take me out to a film first.'

He smiled then, asked if taking her out to dinner would qualify or whether it had to be a film, and told her she was a naughty minx.

'Come on, Jane, let's go back indoors. This house is colder than a fridge. It could have been worse. If my father had come here to find Pat, he would have exploded at finding you two like that, and he would have given you both a clipped ear.'

Jane rather wished that it had been Daniel who had found them. She would gladly have put up with the clipped ear to have avoided Ryan walking in on them.

They sat in Mary's room. It was always warm because the radiator had only a small space to heat and was the closest one to the Aga. It was the only room in the house with a radiator that was adequate for the job. He had taken her coat, pulled off her shoes, found a blanket for her knees and the fan heater for her toes while he made the coffee. He came back with the mugs on a tray, and two slices of carrot cake that Mary had left for them on a plate on the table, covered with a clear glass mixing bowl in case the cat thought the cake was left for her. She warmed her toes with the heater, but this time he didn't warm his as well or play with her toes.

After a while he slipped quietly into the hallway to check what was happening, and came back to say they were in the lounge having afternoon tea, all looking amicable enough.

'Jane, Pat was always sweet on Claire, since they were both children. There was always a plan that they would marry this coming summer when she was eighteen and he was twenty-one. She was a bit upset when you first came, as he seemed to prefer your company to hers when we were out walking with Colin on Saturday afternoons. I heard him explain to her a couple of times that he had to look after you as you were a guest. I wondered at the time if he was outgrowing the relationship, but I didn't realise he had slept with her. It was very unkind of him to treat her like that. She would have been worried sick, knowing he had got her pregnant then lost interest in her. Jane, I know you would never say anything about this to Claire, but please don't tell Mary either, or my father. Mary would be disappointed with him, and Daniel would be angry.'

The visitors were leaving. They could hear voices in the hallway, the door closing, Pat carrying the tea tray into the kitchen, Mary following. Daniel had presumably gone back to his den. Jane hoped he had still seemed sober. He usually had a drink or two after lunch on Sundays, telling Jane he deserved an extra whisky after sitting in a cold church all morning being lectured on how to behave by a sanctimonious parson. And he paid twenty-five pounds all up for that dubious privilege. Life would be pretty boring if you never sinned. Just ask Ryan.

Mary saw them in her room and checked that they had found their cake. Ryan picked up their tray, and they returned to the kitchen.

'At least he didn't actually bring the shotgun,' Pat joked, but Mary chided him.

'Pat, you know Ryan doesn't like talk of guns. He had a bad experience as a child,' she explained to Jane, 'but the gun wasn't loaded and no one was shot.'

'I can cope with shotgun jokes,' Ryan said, 'just not with real guns. I still sometimes check that the door to the gun room is locked, and I wish we could just get rid of them all. I don't like to remember that day. It wasn't me holding the gun, Jane, in case you're thinking that, and it wasn't pointed at me either. I didn't know it wasn't loaded, Mary. No one ever told me that. But she wouldn't have known. She would have been terrified.'

'Your grandmother checked it before she put it away. It wasn't loaded then, and if it had been fired in the garden, we would have heard the shot. Perhaps you can tell Jane and me about it. Sometimes that helps.'

'One day I will, but not today.'

'I assume that Jane knows what has happened,' Mary continued. 'Pat and Claire are to be married shortly. April would be about right, perhaps Easter Saturday, so there is some time to organise the details and the weather will be nicer. They were always sweethearts, right from when they were children. Anne will talk to Reverend Colin about the date.

'Most weddings here involve the whole village. Not all of them of course, as some couples like to keep theirs private and no one minds that, but I imagine this will be a village wedding. We have the reception at the village hall, with a buffet dinner, and everyone contributes to the supper which is held later, during the dancing. It helps keep the costs down. Weddings are expensive, and they are really about the families and the community celebrating, not people showing off how much they can afford. We keep the presents small, optional and anonymous, and Linda keeps a list of things the couple want, so those who do want to buy something can consult her. It saves on doubling up. At one wedding we had here a few years ago, the couple were given two electric frying pans, four toasters and three orange fondue sets, but not much else.

'Everyone enjoys weddings except Ryan, who hates crowds and never dances. He normally stays in Oxford for the weekend whenever there is a wedding, but this time that won't be possible. He will be Pat's best man, so he will have to come to the wedding. You will have to dance with the bridesmaid, Ryan, but one dance will do.'

'I wouldn't mind dancing with Jane,' he said. 'But not with anyone else. That's if Jane doesn't mind.'

Jane flashed him a glance, relieved that he was treating her in this almost flirting way, and for a tiny moment her eyes met his, before he looked away. Perhaps he would forgive her, but she rather doubted it. She thought he would never trust her again.

'Then Jane will need to be a bridesmaid. The groom's family usually chooses one of the bridesmaids, so we will have Jane. Are you both happy with that arrangement?'

Earlier today Pat had asked her to marry him, to spend the afternoon making love in a hotel room, and now she was to be a bridesmaid when he married someone else. But she didn't feel upset about it, just relieved that things had been resolved. Kissing him at the back door was one thing, marrying him and living in a tiny cold cottage was another. She had been getting out of her depth. She was glad that Mary didn't know what had happened, and she hoped that Daniel never found out. She wished Ryan had not known either, but it was too late now. She would dance with him at Pat's wedding. She hoped he would have forgiven her by then.

He was rather cold towards her over dinner, however, and he spent the evening upstairs in his study while she watched a film on television with Mary. After the film had finished she waited in the kitchen, brushing the cat, until he came down for cocoa, rather later than usual. She had wondered if perhaps he wouldn't come down at all, or if he was deliberately late, hoping she would have already gone up to bed. He was polite enough to her, but he wouldn't meet her eyes, and she knew she had disappointed him. Their usual friendly conversation and the glances they had shared at amusing stories were gone like the ghost of a long-ago and long-regretted love affair, leaving bitter-cold ice where once there had been the warmth and promise of a small but steadfast flame.

Just look at me once, she silently pleaded, her eyes brimming with tears. Suppose she reached across the table and touched his fingers, which were wrapped around the warmth of his mug. Would he shake off her touch? Or would he finally look at her?

Almost as if he felt her thoughts, he abruptly rose from the table, picked up the empty mugs, rinsed them at the sink and left them upside down on the draining board to join the breakfast washing up. Her chance was gone.

She hurried to keep up with him on the stairs and heard his polite and quiet *Good night* as he continued up to his own floor, leaving her to find the way to her room with her vision blurred by tears.

Monday 19 January 1976

The following day Ryan was back in Oxford for the start of the new term. Jane had tried to get up early so she could talk to him before he left, but she was not early enough. He had already gone to the station with Pat.

Oh, how far away Friday seemed, when she would next see him. Would he have forgotten their discord and be friends with her again? She couldn't banish the fear that he might not come home for the weekend, but would simply stay in Oxford to avoid seeing her.

She found an opportunity to ask Mary why he had such an aversion to shotguns. What had happened?

'We don't actually know,' was all Mary would say. 'Perhaps one day Ryan will tell you. We only know that something did happen. After that Ryan had nightmares and walked in his sleep. He said yesterday that he wasn't holding the gun and it wasn't pointed at him. Even that much was news to me. We have never known what happened.'

Jane knew that Mary could have told her much more, that she was being evasive, but she didn't persist. Something had happened in this house that they didn't want her to know about. There was this vague story that two men had been in love with her mother, but would that be enough to cause a family rift that had never healed? Not once, ever, had her father mentioned this house where he had grown up, the house where he had met and fallen in love with her mother. Aunt Ellen had been here at the time, and she had never mentioned the house either. There was even a photo of Jane's mother in a blue hat standing outside the front of the house. It was on Daniel's desk, and it was in her parents' photo album, now at Richmond.

Her father had been a romantic husband. There was always a valentine card for his wife, birthday cards with beautiful messages, and every year they would spend their wedding anniversary in Switzerland, where they had gone for their honeymoon. As a small child she had gone with them, but later she had been away at school so they had gone by themselves. That was the reason she was still alive. If their wedding anniversary had been in school holiday time, she would have been with them when the train crashed. So why had they never mentioned the house where they had met? Had Daniel threatened to shoot her father? Was that what had upset Ryan? She thought it unlikely there was a real old-fashioned duel, as they used pistols for duels, not shotguns.

'Jane, has something gone wrong between you and Ryan?' Mary was asking her. 'Last night he seemed upset, and he hardly spoke to you. Have you two had an argument?'

She couldn't tell Mary what had happened, so she just said that as far as she knew everything was all right.

She barely slept that night, wracked with worry that he would stay away, that he no longer cared about her, and they would no longer be friends, just when she was beginning to hope they might one day be lovers.

Wednesday 21 January 1976

It was Wednesday morning. Jane had walked down to the vicarage after coffee to give Daisy some red mittens that she had knitted with a bit of help from Mary. Daisy was always losing mittens, and Jane thought red ones might be easier to find.

She returned to the Hall feeling cold but glad of the walk in the fresh air. She left her coat and shoes in the boot room and put on her sheepskin slippers. There was no one in the kitchen, so she checked if Mary was in the cellar.

Pat suddenly cornered her near the back door, as if he had been lying in wait for her, trapping her against the wall with his hands each side of her, pinning her there but not actually touching her.

'Jane, we could run away together, just the two of us. You have a house and some money. We could just pack our stuff and take the Rover until we can buy a car of our own. She trapped me, Jane. She was jealous of you and threw herself at me. I don't want to marry her. I only love you.'

He tried to kiss her, but she pushed him away, every vestige of feeling she had for him fading away into total revulsion. He had made love to a trusting girl, his childhood sweetheart, clearly with a careless disregard for the consequences, and now he wanted to desert Claire so he could get his hands on her money. She felt like slapping his face, but she had to keep her dignity.

She didn't know what to say to him, so she said nothing, ducked beneath his arm, and went out into the garden, hoping he wouldn't follow her.

She was upset, and angry that he had chosen a time when Ryan was away. She had Ryan's phone number, so she could phone him and ask him to come home. But she knew that she needed to stand on her own feet, that she was becoming far too reliant on his support whenever anything bothered her. He had his own life to lead, and she had lost any regard he may have had for her. And she knew, too, that she had brought this on herself. She didn't like to complain about Pat to Mary, and she didn't want to tell Daniel either. She had to face this alone.

She was cold. Although she was still wearing her warm sheepskin boots, she had neglected to put on her coat, so she turned back to the house and almost walked into Pat. He had followed her outside.

'Jane, please, Jane, listen to me. She will be fine. Her father would never throw her out. I don't even know it's mine. It was when you first came here, before I fell in love with you. You loved me, you said you would marry me, that we could run away together, and I can't let you go.'

Still she said nothing, bolting past him back into the house. Where was Mary? She went to the library, looking for Daniel in his den, but there was no one there. Pat had followed her and was standing in the hallway.

'Where is everyone?' she asked him.

'They went into town. The lady from the wool shop phoned to say Mum's wool order was in, and she wanted to choose some baby wool as well. I said I was expected at the farm, so Daniel drove her to town to pick it up. Mum looked for you to ask if you wanted anything from town, but I said you were still out walking. I didn't want you to go with them. I wanted you here alone with me. Daniel took Ryan's Jaguar, so we can take the Rover and go to your house in Richmond. Please, Jane, this is our chance to leave here and have a life together.'

'I'm sorry Pat, I don't want to go with you. And I have never once said I would marry you. Please respect that and stop asking me. When you make love to a girl you know there may be consequences. You made your choice, and I have made mine. I did once like you in that way, but now I just want to stay here and be with Ryan. But now even that has all been wrecked.'

He looked at her hopelessly for a while, as if he was deciding whether she really meant it. Then, defeated, he returned to the kitchen, took his jacket from its peg in the boot room and went out into the garden to sulk.

She knew he would never ask her again. How could they even stay friends after this? Perhaps she should just leave here.

The phone was on the desk near the front door, and there was a tall stool you could sit on when you used it. The hallway, with its cavernous high ceiling, was always cold. It didn't even have a radiator because a radiator would have been useless in that vast space.

Ryan had once written down his number for her on the back of a leaflet that was in her room. But she checked Mary's little notebook next to the telephone to save going upstairs. It was the top entry, Ryan. The next entry was Peter, with the phone number of the house at Richmond and, crossed out, the number for the house in Kent where Jane had lived as a child. Then John. Who was John? It was a London number, with another Kent number beside it. After that was McCann, Phillips and several other names she recognised as being neighbouring farmers. Then Allanstone, vicarage, post office, doctor, taxi, train station.

Who was John? Was it Mr Allanstone? He was John, but he was in there further down with a different number. She knew he had a house in Kent, as he had lived near her parents. Was one his office and one his home? Or was there another John? Phillips was John Phillips, but he wouldn't be in there twice either, and he wouldn't have a London number, or a number in Kent. Was John Mary's mysterious friend? No, that was a woman, a girl she had gone to school with.

She phoned the number for Ryan, surprised at how shaky her fingers were. Perhaps it was the cold. She knew you didn't get him directly; you left a message, and he would ring back when they found him. She wasn't sure exactly what she would say to him, but she desperately wanted to talk to him.

'Please will you ask Ryan Linden to phone Jane,' she asked the man who answered the phone.

'Yes, of course, Miss. I saw him come past a few minutes ago. I'll find him and ask him to call you back. Will he know the number?'

'Yes,' she assured him. He sounded nice, and he didn't seem to mind looking for Ryan. She thanked him and put down the phone, waiting for the call.

It was so cold in the hallway. She found a blanket from the lounge and returned to her perch on the stool. It seemed like an age, and she couldn't get warm, even with the blanket. The phone rang, making her jump even though she was expecting it. She picked it up, wondering what she was going to say to him and wishing now that she hadn't bothered him.

'Jane, is everything all right?' She nodded, but then realised he couldn't see that.

'I just wanted to talk to you. Things are all right, really. Mary and Daniel are out shopping, and I was just a bit upset. Pat asked me to run away with him, but I said no. I thought about leaving here, because I don't know if Pat and I can be friends after this. I hope it was okay for me to ring you. I thought you were cross with me on Sunday, and I was worried you wouldn't come home on the weekend.'

'Jane, please don't leave. Would you like me to come home tonight?'

'No, I'll be all right. I just needed to talk to someone. Pat has accepted I'm not running away with him.'

'Would you like to come here to Oxford for the afternoon? I teach classes until half past three, but you could take the train, do some shopping, and I could meet you for coffee at four. I could come back home on the train with you afterwards if you wanted, so you weren't going home by yourself in the dark.'

'I can't. Pat would have to drive me to the station, and I wouldn't trust him. It's too cold and bleak today to walk that far. But thank you for asking me. I'll be all right. I'll stay here. I just panicked and wanted to talk to you. I can't talk to Mary or Daniel. I'm sorry for phoning you.'

'I'm always happy to talk to you, and I was never cross with you. I did tell Pat I may not go home this weekend, but I didn't mean it. You can phone me every day if you want, but it's easier for me to call you back in the evening. I'm very glad you're not running away with Pat, but he should not have asked you. He brought this on himself. How is everything going apart from that? Anything interesting in the post?'

'The credit card statements—yours is here as well—but not much else. Daniel's was huge because of the jewellery at Christmas, and he went to London in December so there was the hotel as well. Ryan, what does he do in London?'

'Not sure,' he said rather guardedly. 'Perhaps he meets the publisher. Was there much on my card?'

'You know I don't open yours.'

'I wouldn't mind if you did. You could pay mine off from my father's bank account by mistake. He'd never notice, especially as I would be signing the cheque. We could pay off your card like that as well.'

'Your father owes you some petrol. He took your car to town.'

'Did he? I don't mind him driving it since he paid for it. He usually fills it up for me when he does drive it. In any case the petrol just goes onto the account at the garage, and he pays that. I sometimes wonder if he really bought the Jaguar for himself since he drives it in preference to his Rover. I think he wanted it for himself but didn't want the neighbours to think of him as anything but old and staid, so he pretended it was for me. He is the squire here, and he has to keep up appearances. But I was grateful for the car. It's beautiful to drive, and it was the only time he ever gave me a birthday present.

'Jane, why don't you go across to the farm after dinner and see Claire. Make your peace with Pat and take him with you. Tell her you would like to be a bridesmaid otherwise I won't be best man because of the dancing. Anne will understand that even if Claire doesn't. That will tell Pat once and for all that he's not going to get out of it by running away with you. I can phone you tomorrow evening if you want, to see how it went. I'll call about nine thirty, when you're back from yoga.

'If it's fine on Friday you could come here to Oxford and have lunch with me. If you go into town when Mary does the shopping, then catch the train to Oxford like you did before Christmas, you can go to the shops here, meet me for lunch, and I'll show you over my college. We have a lovely thirteenth-century chapel here with very old stained glass, and our college has a really beautiful garden. You can go back to Hayward with me late in the afternoon. Would you like that? I'll talk to you tomorrow night, and we can see what Friday's weather forecast is like. In any case I'll be back on Friday evening. Can you cope? I can still come back tonight if you want me to. I've been worried all week that you would be upset about this and leave, and when I came home on Friday you would be gone. You won't do that, will you?'

'I won't leave, and I'll manage until Friday. I thought you might never come back here, and I feel so much better now I've talked to you. I feel like I've been hugged. Thank you for ringing me back.'

'I'll give you a real hug on Friday.'

She could hear the car on the drive. Mary and Daniel had returned. She knew she would come to no real harm from Pat, but she was relieved all the same.

Pat quietly apologised when he came back in, and Jane suggested they walk over to the farm to see Claire after dinner. Mary rang ahead and spoke to Anne so she knew to expect them. Mary suggested to Pat that he arrange to take Claire into town the following afternoon, when she had her half day off from working at the shop, and buy her an engagement ring.

It all went smoothly. Pat asked Claire if she would come to town with him to choose a ring, and he asked if it was okay for Jane to be a brides-maid. Jane explained about the best man having to dance with the bridesmaid and Ryan not wanting to dance with someone he didn't know—he was rather shy with girls—and Mary had said the groom was allowed to choose one of the bridesmaids. It turned out that Claire was glad to have her anyway. She had wanted to ask her, but she had thought she should ask Mary about it first, with Jane being from London and from a posh school.

Anne had a wedding planning book that Linda lent out for weddings held at the Hayward church, and they went through the details, with Jimmy and Pat working out what they would do about the cars.

Before they left Jane agreed to go out to a film with Jimmy the next Wednesday, and as they walked home Pat asked if they could remain friends, and he promised not to bother her again. He asked her to suggest to Daniel that a sports car would make a good wedding present, so Jane said she would ask him. A Mini would be perfect, she told him, until he was twenty-five. She remembered the rule. A sports car wouldn't do at all, as they would need space in the back for the baby.

He unlocked the back door, making no attempt to claim a kiss good-night. There was no one else up, so Jane made them both cocoa and found the biscuit tin. They had reached a truce; the romance between them was dead and gone, and they agreed to be friends. Pat complained again about how mean Daniel was with the allowances.

'He'd marry you if you encouraged him a bit, and you could have everything you want. He would give me a car then if you asked him to. And you could ask him to give me and Ryan more money. Daniel would do anything for you. He's in love with you.'

'Daniel?'

'Yes, Daniel. You could wind him around your little finger. He's crazy about you.'

Jane wasn't sure she wanted to hear this. 'He has been very kind to me,' she said guardedly, suddenly seeing him in a new light. Was this true? Or was Pat imagining it in an attempt to benefit from her supposed influence over his uncle? Yes, Daniel did look at her in a sleazy sort of way, and he got a bit close at times, touched her sometimes, and he had offered to show her the view from his bedroom, had put his arm around her and kissed her neck, tried to make her touch him. But that was just the way he behaved. She was used to it now. He had done nothing to harm her, and he always respected it—well, at least for an hour or two—when she told him to mind his hands, treating it as if it amused him to flirt with her. It was just his way of flattering her. At Christmas he had said he enjoyed buying beautiful things for his beautiful women. He had included Mary in that, and she was his sister.

'He's got pots of money. He would give you as much as you wanted, and the only difference would be that you would have to sleep with him. During the day things would be just like they are now. It wouldn't be that bad. You could just close your eyes and pretend it was Ryan. Men are all the same in the dark, and I know you like Ryan. Daniel would be good at it, he's had heaps of women in his time, and he's old too, so he probably wouldn't want it all that often, old men don't. Ryan would be upset—he's in love with you too—but you could have an affair with him as well if you kept it discreet. He'd be grateful for a bit more money, so he'd accept it, and he could have the extra money and get you as well some nights. Probably most nights, as Daniel's really old now. He has a dicky heart, so he may only last another couple of years, and then you would get everything, and you could have Ryan as well. Although I'm not sure you would be allowed to marry him, at least not in a church, son of your husband and all that. I'll ask Reverend Colin about it, as he would know. Daft rule if you're not actually closely related. I know you like Ryan, and that was why you were so upset when he walked in on us.'

'Pat, will you please stop this. I am not marrying Daniel. He has never asked me to, I hope he lives until he's a hundred, and I would never, ever, treat him or Ryan like that. And yes, I do like Ryan, and I was upset, but he doesn't like girls, he told me that, so I don't think he would care.'

'You could at least have a think about marrying Daniel. You could do heaps for me and Ryan. Daniel's really mean and gives us scarcely anything. He would save a fortune on those trips he makes to London, too.'

'Why? What does he do in London?'

'Jane, don't be so naïve. He stays at a top hotel with a high-class escort.'

'But there is only the train fare and the hotel account on the credit card, nothing about an escort.'

'You pay cash to the agency, so it's untraceable, and then you can't be blackmailed. Check his bank statement, and I bet you'll find he takes out a heap of cash when he's in London. He might pay cash for a taxi or two, and those sleazy magazines he reads—no one would risk buying those on a credit card—but most of it would go to the agency and the girls. It's expensive because a man like him would only want the best girls from a really high-class agency. I think he likes them young, too, and that would cost more, but the girls would not be underage. Even Daniel is not that bad, or that stupid. The agency would look after that, as some of the men who use the services would be really high profile. You pay the agency for an escort to take out to dinner or wherever you want to go, anything else you do for the rest of the night is entirely between you and the girl, and you pay them directly for that bit in cash. I'm not even sure it's legal. He spends way more on those girls than he gives Ryan and me. They earn more in a night than you would have earned in a fortnight working at the bank, and they have day jobs as well.

'Mum has nightmares about him dying from a heart attack while he's in bed with one of the escorts, and it getting in the papers. We live here very quietly, but he's actually quite famous. She also worries about him getting drunk and doing something indiscreet, but he doesn't drink when he goes to London. If you're paying that much for a girl, you don't want to be drunk and not able to enjoy it.

'He used to bring women here when we were younger, but then one of them tried to seduce Ryan when he was about sixteen, and my grand-mother exploded and said he had to meet them elsewhere. Ryan, Mum and I were cowering together in the kitchen while she was yelling at him. We had never had a row quite like that here before, or since, and it was a bit scary. I was only about ten, so I had no idea then what it was about. It was only years later that Mum told me. She thinks Ryan got put off by the woman groping him, and that's why he never wanted a girl-friend. She says he feels safe in that college of his because there aren't any girls there. She says it's like he's still at school, and he never has to grow up and leave.

'Daniel was always awful to Ryan. Nothing he did was ever good enough, and he would clip both of us around the ear if we got in his way. I don't suppose you ever got a clipped ear, but it really hurts, much more than you'd expect, so we avoided him when we could. Ryan was good to me when I was small, keeping me out of trouble. He sometimes took the blame for things I'd done. We were united against a common enemy. It would serve Daniel right if you married him then slept with Ryan on the sly. Ryan would enjoy getting his revenge. And I know he likes you because he was so upset when he found us together. When I took him to the train on Monday morning, he said he might not come home for the weekend. He said he would let Mary know by tomorrow.'

Thursday 22 January 1976

Thursday was cold and wet, the forecast for Friday no better.

Jane couldn't help thinking about what Pat had said. She was suddenly more wary of Daniel when she helped him in the morning, trying to keep her distance as much as she could, and in the afternoon she played a game of table tennis with him, then helped Mary with the ironing and housework. In any case she could not have gone out walking with him, as the weather was awful.

She checked her account book. It was true that he took a lot of cash out when he was in London. She had never thought about it before, as it was his money and his business how much he spent. She had simply accounted it.

She also thought about what Pat had said about Ryan. It would help explain why he had been so wary of her being close to him when she first came to Hayward Hall, but he seemed to have got used to her now. She recalled him once telling her that he wouldn't mind hugging her as she seemed quite safe. And Pat had said he thought Ryan was in love with her.

Had he really thought about not coming home on Friday? How could she face a whole weekend without him here, knowing that he was staying away to avoid her? But when she had spoken with him yesterday, he had said he would see her on Friday. Yes, he had definitely said that, so he must have changed his mind and forgiven her.

When Ryan phoned late that evening, she said things had gone very well, Pat was happier, he had taken Claire to choose a ring, and everything had been arranged about her being a bridesmaid, so he would only have to dance with her. With the weather being so wet and cold she suggested they postpone her outing to Oxford.

'You will come home this weekend, won't you?' she asked, still worried. 'I could ask Mary if we can make an apple pie.'

'Yes, of course. Ask Pat to meet the three-twenty train.'

Friday 23 January 1976

Jane had intended to be in the conservatory when Ryan came home, so he would sit close beside her, but instead she was still cutting leaf shapes from the leftover pastry to decorate the top of the apple pie.

He gave her a book he had bought for her that explained confusing words and grammar rules. He knew she had been typing up the manuscript for Daniel, and he thought she might find it useful. The editors normally looked after those details, he told her, but she might like to get it right when she did the typing. Not the most romantic of presents, but she liked knowing that he sometimes thought of her in his other life.

She spent the evening in the library with him, selecting another book and playing chess, but he seemed to have forgotten about the promised hug. She felt he was still rather cold towards her, and she understood why. He would feel that she had betrayed him. She was beginning to realise that this self-sufficient and very controlled young man was falling for her, although perhaps he didn't yet know it himself, and perhaps he had taken her loyalty to him for granted. She told herself again that she would feel betrayed if she found him kissing a girl, although she knew she would have no right to. She just didn't know how to make things right between them again.

But she was glad that he had come home, glad that he was trying to keep things normal between them.

The book he had selected for her this time was *The Eustace Diamonds*. She found this an interesting choice because it was about a rather naughty young lady named Lizzie, who flirted with several young men, one of them her cousin.

Saturday 24 January 1976

After the rain on Thursday and Friday, Saturday was sunny, and Colin had arranged another walk to Peddleton. Jane wore the Fair Isle jumper that Ryan had bought for her, with her jeans and her duffle coat. The jumper was not long enough to cover her derrière, but the duffle coat was. She could change when she got home so Daniel wasn't tempted to fondle her derrière in the tight jeans. It really wasn't fair that she had to think like this. Ryan had never touched her, and neither had Pat.

Ryan had the photographs he had taken at the snow games. There were photos of Daisy in the igloo, the baby in the pram, Jimmy pulling the sled, Jane in her blue snowflake hat and scarf, Pat with Claire. He gave some of the photos to Linda before they left for the walk, to pass on to the families of the young people in them.

Pat was walking with Ryan, so Jane left them alone, as they appeared to be discussing something, probably Pat and Claire living in the lodge as that was now the plan. Claire was close to Pat, but she was talking to Julie who was to be the other bridesmaid. Jane stayed beside Jimmy.

They had tea at the same farm, but this time they all piled into the kitchen, as it was so cold outside. She sat next to Ryan, and Jimmy came to sit on her other side. She enjoyed the scones and the warm mug of tea. On the way home she tried to keep closer to Ryan so he helped her on the stiles.

Ryan took off her boots when they returned, and they sat in Mary's room warming their feet with the fan heater, while Pat went to fetch Mary from the station, and Daniel was safely in his den. Ryan was sitting close beside her, his toes touching hers.

He asked if that was the jumper she had bought in Richmond, and told her he had enjoyed that day.

'Have you forgiven me?' she asked him. 'We are still friends, aren't we?'

He glanced at her, and she knew that he understood what she meant, but he looked down again, seeming unwilling to hold her gaze with his. She thought he might just say there was nothing to forgive, he didn't care, but he didn't quite say that.

'You did nothing that needed to be forgiven, and I hope we will always be friends. I haven't forgiven Pat for treating you like that, or for the way he treated Claire. I would have been very unhappy if you had married him. You are way too good for him. I did consider staying away for a while, I needed time to think, but I was terribly worried you would leave here. You don't owe me any loyalty. I'm a lone wolf.'

He had been so kind to her from the first day she had come here, and she was used to thinking of him as strong and dependable, her port in a storm, but just for once he sounded rather vulnerable. She remembered the hurt she had seen in his eyes when he had walked into the lodge. She wished she could say she loved him; she knew now that she did love him. But she was not sure that he loved her, or even if he could love her. He might truly prefer to stay independent and alone.

'I owe you a lot,' she said. 'You have been so good to me and you have helped me so much.'

'I enjoy looking after you, it makes me feel useful.'

After dinner he cleaned and polished her boots as well as his own, Pat's and Daniel's.

She sat with him in the boot room for company and brushed the cat, knowing they were friends again, in spite of his silence.

Wednesday 28 January 1976

Daniel had gone to London on the Tuesday and would be returning on Thursday. Jane was glad to have a couple of days free from him. She didn't mind the typing—she continued with it—but she found his constant attention tiring. He was always watching her, sometimes touching her, and constantly hinting that he was glad his son was back at Oxford and not there to interrupt them. She wished he had gone to London while Ryan was at home, but she sensed he hadn't wanted to leave her in the house with Ryan there but not him.

Sometimes when she typed, he would pull up a chair and sit beside her to check what she was typing, and his hand would tuck itself beneath her skirt and stray to her knee, sometimes a little higher. She would always pull his hand away and tell him off, but the next day he would do it again.

On the Wednesday she went to see a film with Jimmy as she had once before. He could have picked her up from the house in the Land Rover as Daniel was away, but she thought it wise just to do what they usually did. He walked over to collect her at the back door, and they walked back to the farm then went into town in the Land Rover. He was nice to date, never expecting too much, happy just to hold her hand, chat to her over coffee afterwards, tell her she was gorgeous, tell her that he didn't have much to offer a girl like her but he liked to be with her, joke about looking over his shoulder for the gargoyles when he walked her back down to the house, kiss her goodnight on the doorstep, never trying to go any further.

Pat had waited up for her, rather sulkily. He made them cocoa and asked if she was serious about Jimmy. He thought she wanted Ryan. He had even gone to the trouble of apologising to Ryan on the weekend when they were walking to Peddleton. He had told him it was all his own idea to marry her, and she hadn't agreed to it.

'I told him you liked him a whole lot better than you like me, and you were cross with me for taking you unawares and kissing you in the lodge because you thought it had upset him.'

'What did he say to that?' she asked, genuinely curious, and amazed that Pat would help her cause like this.

'He admitted he liked you, and he had some funny name for it, *smitten*. He said he was smitten with you, but he didn't believe you liked him the way he liked you. I promised him you had never let me go any further than kissing you, and it didn't mean anything. Young people nowadays kissed all the time, and it was just harmless fun. He was old now and wouldn't know that. He said he thought you were a bit young for him, and casual kissing behind haystacks wasn't his idea of a relationship. He said you just liked playing games with him. I did my best. He was always good to me, so I wanted to make things right. You never know with him whether what he says is serious or joking, and he rarely says anything about what he thinks or feels, so I was surprised he said as much as he did. But I think he really does like you. Even Mum thinks that. She asked me last week if I knew whether you two had argued about something, but of course I didn't tell her the reason. She was worried that Ryan had told you he loved you, and you hadn't been happy about it and had fallen out with him. She was so relieved when he came home on Friday.'

Jane thanked Pat for trying, wondering if he had just made things worse. But after the walk Ryan had said he had forgiven her, or at least told her there was nothing to forgive, and she knew she had Pat to thank for that. Ryan had said he was smitten with her, that much was gratifying, but he thought her too young and prone to casual flirting. Even worse, he thought she was playing games with him. She wasn't sure what she could do about that. She had to admit to herself that at least some of it was true, but for all that she didn't like him saying it to Pat.

Friday 30 January 1976

On the Friday the weather was fine, so when she went into town with Pat and Mary for shopping, she caught the train to Oxford. Mary and Pat knew where she was going, but none of them had told Daniel.

She bought some more jeans. She liked jeans and now usually wore them instead of a skirt when she went out walking, as well as for gardening and hiking with Colin's group. She bought a blue cable knit jumper to wear with them. Ryan had a black one. She bought a navy-blue corduroy layered maxi skirt from Laura Ashley. If she was wearing a maxi skirt, it would be difficult for Daniel to get his hand beneath it when he sat beside her. She found some black leather lace-up boots, above ankle length, with a high heel and a warm fur lining that just peaked over the top and along the lace-up section.

She met Ryan outside his college at noon as they had arranged. He had drawn a map for her and told her if she was lost, she only needed to ask someone.

The college was much older and larger than she had imagined, built in a style that was reminiscent of Hayward Hall, with three floors with bay windows and smaller windows high in the gables.

He took the bags with the clothes and shoes back to his room, to leave them there while they had lunch. He would then show her the college chapel with its old stained glass, and the very beautiful college garden, and they could walk around the narrow streets surrounding the colleges. Later they would have coffee somewhere, collect her shopping and his weekend bag, and return on the train. He normally phoned home from the station at Oxford to let Pat know the arrival time of the train.

He had a small study and an even smaller bedroom, panelled in oak and rather dark. There was a desk with his Olivetti typewriter and a neat pile of papers, a rather shabby leather armchair, and a bookshelf with the books neatly arranged in height order. On the top shelf was a chess set and a coffee mug. The bedroom had just enough room for a narrow bed, a wardrobe, and a small chest of drawers beside the bed. There was a photo of his mother on the wall—without his father—one of Mary standing with his grandmother, and a small photograph next to his bed of Jane in her snowflake hat, with the crocheted poppy clipped to a corner of the frame. She was flattered, but she didn't say anything. The wolf calendar she had given him was on the wall in the study, with *Jane* written in the square for today's date and a little rose drawn below.

The only heating was a small plug-in oil-filled radiator, but it did warm the small space. It seemed sad that he was exiled here, instead of living with all the space and luxury of Hayward Hall. Although this room was at least easier to keep warm. There were no radiators on his floor at Hayward, and the small electric heater he had in his bedroom there would have been just as useless as the radiators were in most of the downstairs rooms.

He asked to see what she had bought, so she showed him the jeans and the jumper and the skirt and the fur-lined boots.

'Will you be hiking in those?'

'No, I don't think so, the heels are too high. I would only wear them for shopping and church to keep my feet warm.'

'That's good because I'm not sure how I would clean them if you got mud on the fur. It would be challenging.' He smiled at her and she felt forgiven.

They left the bags and went out to find somewhere for lunch, and they spent a wonderful afternoon walking around the town in the winter sunshine. It was nice to be free of Hayward for a few hours, just the two of them, without the watchful eyes of his father. She wished he would take her hand, but he didn't.

But the time passed too quickly. They returned to the college to collect the bags, and he stopped in the quad to talk to Professor Hanson, introducing Jane as his cousin.

'Are you the young ward living with Linden's father?'

'Yes, Sir. I lost my family, and I was left on my own. It was a bit frightening to have no family at all, but my uncle offered me a home. He is my late father's cousin. I am recovering now. My uncle and Ryan have been very kind to me.'

'I am sorry for your loss, Miss Walters, I hope you are recovered soon. But it generally takes about a year to get over losing someone, and life has to go on. Linden gave up some of the tutoring so he could be available to look after you when needed, and we especially miss his company on Friday evenings after dinner. We would like him back. The students all like him, and his students generally do a lot better than the others. We even have students asking to be transferred into his classes. We have given him an extra tutorial to run with some students who are struggling, and he has worked wonders with them. But he wants to teach less and spend more time at home.'

They returned on the train, with just the two of them in the first-class carriage, sitting opposite each other so they did not touch.

'Ryan, I'm sorry I'm taking up so much of your time,' she said, trying to hide that she was upset by the implied criticism from the professor.

He looked at her in his half-amused way, and for a while he said nothing.

'I really don't mind,' he said at last. 'I enjoy looking after you. He wasn't as polite as I would have liked, but don't get upset about it. He is always like that. He expects everyone to lead completely uneventful lives, as he does, so they can just do their job every day without a hitch. He never married, and the college is his whole life. He is used to me being available when he needs extra help. I've lived at the college for nearly nine years now, so he takes me for granted.'

'What did you do on Friday evenings, when he misses you?'

'About a dozen of us go for drinks and conversation in his study. But I would rather be at home with you. I made that choice, so you don't need to feel bad about it.'

For a while he looked at her and she looked at him, saying nothing.

'May I have a photograph of you to put next to my bed?' she asked at last, feeling like she was flirting and hoping he wouldn't mind.

'Oh, dear,' he said, 'I forgot to put that away in the drawer. You'll have to take the photo; I don't have one to give you. I don't generally take photos of myself. I'll lend you the camera. I keep it at Hayward.'

When they reached their station, Pat was waiting with the Rover. The bags were put into the boot, and she was back at Hayward Hall, her day out with Ryan at an end. But now when she thought about him at Oxford, she would know where he lived, what his room looked like, and that he had a photograph of her next to his bed. She thought about him rather a lot.

Saturday 31 January 1976

Colin took his group bowling on Saturday afternoon, but Jane didn't go with them, as Ryan was visiting his grandfather in Bath, and she preferred to spend the afternoon with him. He had his camera with them, and took some photos of his grandfather.

Jane had the pattern for the poppy. Mary had written it out for her and had made a poppy for the craft lady so it was easy to see what they were supposed to look like. Pamela, the lady who ran the establishment, thanked Jane and took a photo of them both with the old man and one of the two of them together.

Jane took some photos of Ryan on the forecourt before they drove away, hoping at least one of them would be steady enough for her to frame so she could have her photo of him.

When they returned Pat told her that Jimmy had missed her and they had arranged to meet at the Black Horse Inn on Wednesday evening. Claire would be there as well. They could discuss the wedding arrangements, and the renovations needed for the lodge, where Pat and Claire hoped to live.

5 ANCIENT STONES

Sunday 1 February 1976

On Sunday afternoon Claire came over, and they all looked around the lodge to decide what needed to be done to make it habitable. Jane was conscious of the last time she had been inside it, but she had to get over that, so she chatted as though nothing had happened there, as though she had forgotten the whole incident. She wished they had done this on a day when Ryan was at Oxford so he wasn't with them.

She wrote notes as they went, for Daniel to give to the builder when they showed him over it for a quote.

The outside needed new paint on the fascia boards and gutters, the doors and the metal window frames, but inside it needed a complete overhaul.

The old wallpaper would be replaced with new. New carpets would be laid, with quarry tiles to the hallway and the kitchen. The kitchen and bathroom would be completely refitted, and the coal store behind the stairs would be converted to a downstairs cloakroom, accessed from the kitchen. There would still be enough space to have a washing machine and dryer in a little nook near the back door. The house needed rewiring. Electric heating would be easier to install than oil-fired radiators and in the small space would work as well. There was no piped gas here.

Jane suggested they could add a small conservatory, covering the whole of the back wall so you looked out into it from the kitchen window and accessed it through the back door. Ryan helped her measure the distance across the back of the house. She thought a half hexagon shape would work well, with the roof rising to a point in the centre of the back wall, and gothic-arched timber windows to match those of the conservatory in the main house. There would be french doors out to the garden.

Claire stayed to have afternoon tea with them. Mary had baked a cake as she usually did on Sundays. Pat and Claire were then left alone together in the lounge until it was time for him to walk her home.

That evening Jane drew up a list of the work needed, with help from the three men. Daniel suggested they make the conservatory octagonal instead of hexagonal, with two half-length parallel walls coming out from the corners of the house, then three full-length walls forming three side of the octagon. The roof would still peak against the wall of the house.

Jane drew up some sketches. It was nice, she thought, that they were all collaborating together almost like a normal family. She didn't like the hostility she often felt between Daniel and his son.

Wednesday 4 February 1976

On Wednesday the builder, Mr Fletcher, came to look at the lodge. He was a friendly man—Jane thought in his sixties—with a lifetime of experience in renovating the old stone houses in the Cotswolds. He brought his architect Alex Miller with him, a surprisingly young man who worked in partnership with his father in town. He would draw up the plans for the internal restructuring and the new conservatory.

Jane and Daniel showed them over the lodge, as Pat was at the farm and Ryan at Oxford. She gave them the sketches she had drawn for the new conservatory.

The architect thought their conservatory addition too small, asking if they had realised that it would be only eight feet from the wall to the french doors, as the house was so narrow. The existing lodge was very small, so it would be good to make the extra room a little larger. He suggested the same half octagonal shape at the back, but four feet further out from house so there was a length of pitched roof before the centre of the half octagon. The room would have french doors out to the garden and gothic-arched timber windows above a low stone wall around the base. The floor would be tiled to match the new tiles in the kitchen. It would be double glazed so it could be heated more easily in winter.

He suggested they use electric wall-mounted radiators in each room to heat the house. If you were using electricity, you didn't need to pipe around hot water. The heating was only like that in the Hall because the radiators were heated with oil, although the boiler would have originally been coal-fired. Oil was now so expensive it was hardly worth the extra cost to install it. He also suggested they had a new half-glazed door between the lounge and the kitchen and added a window or a hatch between the two rooms so you could look from the lounge through the hatch and the kitchen window into the conservatory. It would make the house feel larger and lighter. He would draw it up and send it for approval by the following week.

Jane showed him the conservatory of the main house so he could take some photos and design something in the same style. He was interested in the layout of the house and the staircase as they walked through the hallway. Their conservatory had the same octagonal shape at the end, but closer to the house it was rectangular to fit the space between the wings of the building. The roof peak was just below the window on the stair landing, as the conservatory was a few steps down from the level of the house. Jane told him it was a lovely space on a sunny winter day, but there were no electric lights, so you couldn't sit there at night.

He asked if it became too hot in the summer, but Jane didn't know that, as she had only come to live there in the autumn. She did recall Daniel saying it was sometimes hot in summer, but you could open the windows then or sit outside on the terrace.

The architect told her that he thought the current conservatory had been added after the original house had been built, probably around the turn of the century, possibly as late as the nineteen twenties. It had most likely replaced an earlier, smaller one. You could still see the line on the wall where the original conservatory had ended.

He offered to come back at some time and look at what would be involved in adding lights, and he said he would love to look over the house. Charles Linden had been a highly-regarded architect in his time. He was happy to advise on the lights in exchange for a tour of the house. He asked if the house had ever been rewired but Jane didn't know.

Then he returned to the lodge to take measurements and discuss the renovations with the builder.

In the evening Jane and Pat met Jimmy and Claire at the inn, the four of them seated in a warm quiet corner, discussing the renovations planned for the lodge. She enjoyed her half pint of cider, and she enjoyed Jimmy's company. He could always make her laugh. She knew he liked her but he thought he had nothing to offer her. At least he was not in love with her money. She wasn't even sure he would know she had any, although it was generally known that Daniel was well off.

When they walked home, he kissed her goodnight at the farm gate before she and Pat headed back to the Hall, and asked if she would go out with him the following Wednesday. He seemed to understand it had to be Wednesday, not the weekend.

Friday 6 February 1976

Jane was once again in the conservatory when Ryan came home on Friday evening. The day had been sunny, and it was always good to sit there in the warmth, feeling as if it was nearly spring. She loved to curl up with the cat on the swing seat with her latest book and an apple.

She picked up the cat and moved over so there was room for him to sit. It was good when he sat with her because he could work the swing while she sat with her feet up, hugging her knees, and the cat loved it too, as she could sit on Ryan's lap and be rocked as well as stroked. He didn't seem to mind sitting close to her now. His arm was stretched out along the back of the seat behind her so she had more room, and she leaned her head back slightly so it rested against his shoulder. She recalled that he had hesitated the first time he had sat beside her on the lovers' seat, but then he had hugged her. Perhaps he felt safe with her as she did with him.

It was nearly dark, but they sat for a while in the twilight while she told him about the builder and the architect coming to see the lodge and their suggestion to extend the conservatory and make it into a larger room. She said she had asked the architect whether they could add lights to their conservatory here, and he was happy to come and discuss how it could be done in exchange for looking over the house. She had checked with Daniel, and he was happy for her to arrange it.

She remembered how Ryan had come upon her and Pat kissing in the lodge, but that seemed like weeks ago now, although it was only a little over a fortnight. He had told Pat he thought she was too young and her attitude to relationships was a bit casual for him. He had said he had forgiven her, but she knew it would take a lot for him to really trust her again. She didn't like him thinking badly of her. But then she had kissed Jimmy McCann. She needed to stop doing that if she wanted Ryan. She knew she did want Ryan, but she was not at all sure that he would ever want her.

He had the photos in his jacket pocket that they had taken in Bath, but it was too dark to look at them. He suggested they go into the kitchen, but she preferred to linger there with him until the room had grown cold and the darkness was absolute. There was not a lot of room on the swing, so she was leaning against him, feeling him warm and strong beside her. He seemed content just to sit there with her, both of them stroking the cat, neither of them saying anything. She wished he would remember that he owed her a hug. She wanted to feel him closer to her.

After dinner, when they were alone in the library, she chose one of the photos she had taken of him, and Ryan gave her a silver frame for it that he had found in an antique shop in Oxford. She felt that she was sharing a secret with him. He had her photo by his bed and now she would have his by her bed. They put a photo of the two of them together in another frame to take to his grandfather. She took her photo upstairs in case Daniel decided to join them in the library, and she put it on her bedside table. Mary would see it when they changed the sheets, but Daniel would never know she had it.

Saturday 7 February 1976

On Saturday Colin took the group to the ruined castle that Jane and Ryan had once visited. Some of the younger children came as well, so they needed extra cars, as it was too far to walk. Jimmy drove the Land Rover, Pat the Rover, and Ryan took Jane in the Jaguar with two girls in the back, Alice and Jenny. Jane remembered them from the sewing bee with the blanket squares, and the nativity play.

A few of the parents came with the group as well as Colin, so with eight cars and nearly thirty young people it was a larger group than they normally had.

Colin told them the history of the castle—when it had been built and how it had been besieged in the civil war and left in ruins—and they were then allowed to explore it on their own, scrambling around walls, finding hidden rooms.

Jane lost Ryan in the maze of rooms, and Jimmy jumped out at her from behind a wall, looked around to see if they were out of sight of the others, and gave her a kiss. Jane half expected Ryan to come round the corner and catch them, but thankfully he didn't. She needed to try harder to avoid running this sort of risk.

Afterwards they all had tea in the nearby café, and Ryan told them ghost stories about the castle, although Jane thought he was making them up as he went. He was considered an expert on ghosts after the stories he had read to them all at the farm near town and in the village hall on New Year's Eve. Jane still had nightmares about the skull.

After dinner Ryan cleaned all the boots, as the grass at the castle had been muddy, but he seemed rather distant and cold to her that evening. She sat in the boot room with him for company, but he was silent and seemed preoccupied. The previous night he had been so friendly, and they had shared the secret of the photographs. She hoped he hadn't seen her with Jimmy, but there had been nobody in sight.

Sunday 8 February 1976

On Sunday afternoon Jane and Ryan played tennis. Pat had gone to the farm to be with Claire. The weather was warm for February although not warm enough for usual tennis clothes. Wearing jeans and a warm jumper with tennis shoes was fine in the winter. She wondered what she would do in the summer though, since her tennis skirt was quite short, and she didn't like the thought of wearing short skirts with Daniel around. The shorter the skirt, the easier it would be for him to get his hand up it. He often touched her thigh beneath her skirt. Perhaps shorts or culottes would be safer. Then at worst he would pat her derrière, as no gentleman would put his hand inside a lady's shorts. But then no gentleman would put his hand up a lady's skirt, either.

Mary called them in for afternoon tea, and afterwards they tidied up the net and the racquets and sat in the conservatory on the swing seat talking about books. He seemed to have recovered from whatever had troubled him yesterday. She wished he was home all the time; she missed him on the days he was at Oxford.

Wednesday 11 February 1976

On Wednesday Jimmy took her out to a film. She told Daniel she was going to the pub with Pat and Claire. Pat was happy to back her up, and they walked together to the farm, where he collected Claire while Jimmy took Jane into town.

She offered to pay for them this time, but Jimmy wouldn't hear of it. She respected that, but she knew his father couldn't pay him much, and he didn't have a job in the town like David did. She liked his company. He was always cheerful and amusing, not expecting too much, happy just to hold her hand in the cinema, share Maltesers with her, and he never wanted more than a kiss goodnight.

When they had coffee afterwards, they talked about his sister's wedding, the lodge renovations, what was happening on the farm, how it made him feel old to think he would soon be an uncle. He said he was running some extra sheep on land that John Phillips wasn't using, and he had discussed taking over the management of his farm, leaving the old man with his beehives and his hens and turkeys and a half share of the profits on the sheep. Robert worked in Switzerland, and neither Adrian nor Winston wanted to take over running the farm when they left school. Jimmy thought he could make the farm pay better if it was properly stocked, and it would give him an income of his own.

He walked her to the back door again, gave her a kiss, told her she was beautiful, he was in love with her, he thought about her all the time, he wanted to earn enough for them to get more serious, he wished he could see her more often, and he wished he could make love to her.

When she went inside, Pat was still up, but thankfully not Daniel, as he would have wondered why Pat had come home before she did. She drank her cocoa, thinking she was getting out of her depth with Jimmy as she once had with Pat. She just couldn't see herself married to Jimmy. She liked to flirt with him and laugh with him, but that was all. Perhaps it was best if she and Jimmy didn't go out by themselves again. She knew it was Ryan that she wanted, but she also knew that was danger-ous, as he didn't like girls. He had told her only a couple of weeks ago that she did not owe him any loyalty, that he wanted to remain a lone wolf.

Thursday 12 February 1976

Daniel had been getting bolder at touching her when she was typing in the library. She would ask Mary to say something to him again. She picked up a letter that had slipped from his hand and fallen onto the floor under the desk, and he fondled her derrière as she bent down, then slid his hand beneath her skirt and up between her thighs, trying to get his fingers inside her knickers, but at least that wasn't possible with tights. It was unexpected and it made her jump so she hit her head on the edge of the desk.

'Mr Linden, that is not allowed,' she told him, cross because her head hurt.

'There's nobody watching. You are beautiful Jane, and you should be glad to be beautiful. Men like to touch beautiful women.'

'I prefer you keep your hands to yourself. If you do that again I shall go to the kitchen and help Mary, and you can do your own typing.'

'Sorry, Miss Walters. Suppose I write it out a hundred times. *I must not touch Jane's pussy.* Perhaps you could type it out for me to sign. But, no, that wouldn't do, as Ryan would have to sign it for me, and he would know I got into trouble. Suppose we get him to write out the lines instead. Does he touch you?'

'No, he doesn't, not ever, and neither should you.'

After lunch she told Daniel she didn't want to walk with him, so he went out by himself. He looked very contrite and said sorry, but he was smiling. He didn't stay out for long, as he had only walked in the garden and through the wood.

Some suits were delivered from the dry cleaners in town, and Jane helped Mary remove the soft plastic wrap and the little tags with their safety pins, and put the suits on wooden hangers. The trousers went over the rod, then the waistcoat with all the buttons undone except the top one, and the jacket went over the top of both. They arrived back with all the waistcoat buttons fastened, but Daniel got cross if he had to unbutton a waistcoat before he could put it on, so Mary or Jane always unbuttoned them. The pins went into a tin in the kitchen drawer. The suits were all black or dark grey, but there was a tweed jacket that she knew belonged to Ryan. Jane didn't know how Mary could tell whose suit was whose, so she hung them on the clothes airer for Mary to take upstairs later.

When Daniel came back in, he asked her again to walk in the garden with him, promising not to touch her, and she relented. He behaved perfectly, as usual lost in his own world.

Friday 13 February 1976

Friday was shopping day, so Daniel drove Jane and Mary into town. Pat and Jimmy were helping John Phillips set up the incubator for the turkey eggs, which would arrive from the breeder next week. Daniel went to the bank with Jane, then left her with Mary at the supermarket while he did some shopping of his own.

In the afternoon she did the typing for him then helped Mary with the ironing. There were always so many white shirts that the pile seemed endless. Every so often there was a blue shirt of Pat's—that did relieve the monotony—and there were her own liberty blouses and her pyjamas. The men had silk pyjamas, and they needed to be ironed carefully. There were jeans as well, and she knew the black jeans were Ryan's, since Pat wore blue jeans and Daniel didn't wear jeans at all. She ironed the black jeans absolutely perfectly for him, imagining what he would look like wearing only the jeans.

When Ryan came home, he had a box of heart-shaped chocolates for her. They sat on the swing seat and she leaned against him, occasionally taking a chocolate from the box for herself and dropping another into his hand. The chocolates were rather soft, and a little of the chocolate melted onto her finger. She looked down at it, her other hand reaching in her pocket for her handkerchief. He took her hand in his, raised it to his face and licked the spot of chocolate from her finger. It was sudden and surprising and somehow intimate and provocative. She looked up at him, meeting his gaze, a brief moment of embarrassment between them.

'We can't waste good chocolate,' he said, and they both laughed.

He had retained her hand, and was gently stroking her finger where the chocolate had been. Whatever had made him cold last week seemed to be forgotten.

Saturday 14 February 1976

On Saturday morning Jane picked up the post from the doormat on her way to the kitchen. There was rather a lot. Perhaps it was somebody's birthday. But then she realised it was Saint Valentine's Day. As well as the usual letters and bills for Daniel, there were two cards addressed to Jane and one for Mary.

Mary was staying at home this Saturday, rather than making her usual visit to her friend. There was no sign of Ryan although he was usually up long before she was.

Jane handed Mary her card, and put her own cards on the table in front of her. One was typed, and it was postmarked from Oxford. That would be Ryan. She was flattered he had thought of her, but then she remembered their conversation on the day she had first come here, when she had told him that her father always sent a valentine to her mother. Perhaps he remembered everything she said to him as she remembered everything he said to her. The other was handwritten, and postmarked from the village, so she knew it would be from Jimmy.

She opened Jimmy's first.

He had written: *To Jane, Love and Kisses, Jimmy.*

'Doesn't he know you're not meant to sign you name?' she said, showing it to Mary.

She opened the one she guessed was from Ryan, slitting the envelope carefully with a sharp kitchen knife. She wanted to keep the envelope, as he had written *SWALK* on the back of it. The card was soft yellow, covered in pink roses. She instantly recognised his very fine spidery writing.

For my beautiful Wild Rose, Thank you for the sunshine you have brought into my life, Love always from the Lone Wolf.

He had added a little picture of a wolf, a picture of a rose, and below that a heart with *te amo* in tiny letters inside it. She knew that *te amo* was Latin for *I love you.* She was strangely touched that he would write that to her, that he would have even thought of sending her a card at all, but she also knew he had done it at least partly to amuse her. She slid the card back into the envelope, reluctant to share it even with Mary.

'Ryan went out earlier to post the letters from last night. He probably didn't want to be here when you opened it. What did he write?'

Jane read out the middle line but did not show Mary the card.

'That sounds just like him. Nothing you couldn't say to a sister, but enough to tell you he cares about you. He is in love with you, Jane, although I'm not sure he even realises it himself. When he comes home on Fridays, the first thing he asks is where you are, and when he is in a room with you, he can't take his eyes off you. I have to say I would welcome it if you two made a match of it. Best thing that could happen to him, and he would always look after you well. He'll never rule the world, but he is good at what he does, and he is always kind and caring. You could do a lot worse. But it is up to you, of course. A couple of weeks ago he was upset about something, and I was worried he had told you he cared for you, and you had rebuffed him. Sometimes I think you like him, but sometimes I'm not sure.'

'Not in that way. He's far too old,' Jane said guardedly, reluctant to admit even to Mary that she did like him, and wondering how she could explain Ryan being upset without involving Pat. She owed it to Mary to come up with something, however vague.

'We did have a slight misunderstanding, but it was entirely my fault, and we sorted it out. He is very kind to me, and he has never said anything out of place. I thought we had to be brother and sister. Wasn't that Daniel's rule?'

'Jane, we suggested that as a precaution. Attraction between unattached young people can quickly turn into an obsession which can cloud their judgement. Neither of them is actually your brother, and if they were we would have told you. But we were worried if you got romantically involved with one of them and it didn't work out, then you would be left with nowhere to go. If you genuinely cared for each other, neither Daniel nor I could have any valid objection. He isn't too old for you, Jane. He is only twenty-six. Although sadly Daniel will never let us celebrate his birthday because it was the day that Caroline died. I always try to have a special afternoon tea for him on the nearest Sunday, but he has never once had a proper birthday cake or blown out a candle.

'Your father always sent both Ryan and Pat a birthday card and a present right up to when he died. When they were younger it was Meccano or books. Pat loved the Meccano and Ryan loved the books. The last present he sent Ryan was his camera, which he treasures. Peter always loved taking photos, and he bought his first camera by saving up what was left of his wages after he gave most of it to my mother. She would never take it all. But the only time Daniel even acknowledged Ryan's birthday was when he was twenty-five. He went into Oxford the next Saturday morning, when Ryan was at home, and he came back driving the Jaguar. He parked it out on the forecourt; then he came in, handed Ryan the keys, and told him it was his birthday present.'

Jane knew when Ryan's birthday was because she had laid flowers on his mother's grave. She had died on the fifth of March in nineteen forty-nine. His birthday was less than a month away. She would remember the date and give him a birthday card.

'You would think that once Daniel had got over the worst of losing his wife, he would be glad that their son had survived.'

'Yes, Jane, you would, but in some ways my brother is a rather strange man. I know that my mother and I were very thankful they were able to save Ryan. Caroline would have been thankful as well if she had known, but sadly she didn't.

'She was eight months pregnant; the baby was five weeks from due. I was fourteen then. We were about to go shopping in town. She could drive the car, as she had learnt to drive when she worked for the army during the War. She was very glamorous, always insisting on wearing high-heeled shoes. She came down the stairs to just below the landing, dressed to go to the shops, and she recalled something she had forgotten. We never knew what it was. When she turned, her heel caught on the top step, and it broke right off, so when she put her foot down, she lost her balance and fell backwards. She was heavy with the baby, and that made it worse. She hit her head on the edge of a tread and broke something at the base of her skull.

'We called the ambulance, and they rushed her to the hospital in Oxford. My mother and I went with her, leaving Peter to look after the house and the guests. It was Saturday, so he was at home, but Daniel was away in London for the day. They said there was nothing they could do to save her life, she would last a few hours, then she would die. But they did think they could save the baby.

'After they had delivered Ryan and checked he was okay, they wrapped him up and laid him to sleep close to her so he could hear her heartbeat for the first few hours of his life, and they managed to keep her alive for long enough for Daniel to get there. She died in his arms, but she was not conscious. They said she would not have known he was there, or her baby, but my mother and I like to think she knew her child had been saved.

'Daniel was inconsolable, completely devastated. My mother locked the gun room, hid all the kitchen knives and took his razor blades. That night he drank himself unconscious, and we nearly lost him as well. He wanted nothing to do with his son. I think he saw Ryan as the reason she had died.

'The baby was really small, less than five pounds, but they were hopeful he would pull through. Every day I went to the hospital to look after him. Peter was studying at Oxford, but they allowed him to take the last week of term off, and after that he was on holiday for a while. He would drive me to the hospital each day then go back to help my mother with the house and Daniel. They taught me how to sterilise the bottles, mix the evaporated milk and get the temperature right, bath him and wrap him up, and I would stay there with him all day. Peter would come to collect me in the evening, and he would stay for a little while and play with him, holding his little hands and talking to him, telling him he was getting big and strong and soon they would be playing with toy trains together and climbing trees. I think your father willed him to survive. Some of the visitors would look at us a bit strangely, as I was fourteen and looked much younger because I was always very thin, and Peter was only nineteen. But the nurses were very supportive, and the other mothers were as well when they knew what had happened. It was over a month before they would let him come home; he had to be eight pounds. Daniel never once came to the hospital to see him, and when we got him home, he wanted nothing to do with him. But the baby had me and my mother and Peter and he did very well. We were all so glad he was saved. He was my mother's pride and joy; she adored him.'

Jane asked who had sent Mary's card, but Mary just said it was an old friend from years ago who always remembered to send her a valentine.

Mary washed up the breakfast dishes, then took the rest of the mail to Daniel's den while Jane dried them.

Ryan came in before she had finished putting the plates away, and he helped her. They were alone in the kitchen. She thanked him rather shyly for the beautiful card, but he only smiled and told her not to tell his father. She said she thought it was from him because she didn't know any other wolves. She didn't tell him she also had a valentine from Jimmy, but she did ask him if he knew who had sent Mary's card.

'She gets a card every year, every birthday as well. Pat and I think it's from Pat's father, but we don't actually know that. Apparently, he was married already, so he couldn't marry her. That is all we know. Flowers usually arrive as well, red roses.'

The flowers arrived mid-morning, the lady who delivered them ringing the doorbell, handing them to Pat when he opened the door, telling him that there were two lots of roses; Mary's were ordered from London while Jane's had been ordered yesterday morning in their shop in town. Then she rushed off with an apology for not stopping to chat to Mary because it was their busiest day of the year.

There were red roses for Mary and pink roses for Jane. Her card just said *To Beautiful Jane*. She asked Ryan, but he said they weren't from him, he wished he could afford to send her roses, he would send them every day.

She guessed they were from Daniel. She knew Jimmy could never afford to send flowers, and there was no one else. She wasn't sure she liked Daniel sending her flowers on Valentine's Day, but perhaps it was by way of an apology. She told Ryan and Mary that Daniel had been a bit too free with his hands on Thursday, so she thought the flowers were an apology for that.

Mary promised to talk to him again. She found two vases, and they put the roses on the dresser in the kitchen.

Later Jane put the card from the flowers and both her valentine cards on the mantelpiece in her bedroom next to the teddy from Jimmy, and thought about what Mary had said about Ryan liking her. He had even written *SWALK* on the back of the envelope. She touched it to her lips, hoping he really had kissed it, then put it up to lean on the wall behind the cards. For a moment she closed her eyes and imagined him kissing her in the garden, her fingers in his beautiful black curly hair, the two of them lost somewhere in the maze on a warm summer day, away from the eyes of his father. She rather liked the idea. Except that you could see the maze and anyone in it from the top floor of the house, and Daniel had eyes everywhere. And Ryan had caught her kissing Pat.

She knew that would take a lot of forgiving for a man like him. Yet he had sent her a valentine, he clearly thought about her sometimes in his other life in Oxford, and he had a photo of her in his room. She had tried not to fall for him, as he had said he liked his own company and didn't want a girlfriend, but whenever he came home from Oxford, she felt her heart beat faster and recalled the thrill of him hugging her in the conservatory. She knew she was hopelessly in love with him. She would never be able to talk herself out of it.

Colin had organised a film night for the Saturday evening. This time it was *Murder on The Orient Express*. He had asked for Ryan's help, as Linda was very tired with the baby still keeping her up at night. They were to take Winston and Adrian. Winston could drive now, but his grandfather didn't like him driving at night, even if it was only into town.

Jane spoke with Jimmy in the foyer while Colin and Ryan were arranging the tickets, thanking him for the valentine card and asking why he had signed it. Didn't he know you were not supposed to? He said there was not much point sending a valentine if the girl didn't know it was from you, and Jane had to agree there was a certain logic to that.

He offered to buy her chocolates, but Ryan had already bought her Maltesers. Jane sat next to Ryan, Jimmy on her other side, but she would not hold Jimmy's hand with Ryan with them. She told Jimmy that Ryan might tell Daniel and get her into trouble. She put the box of Maltesers on her lap, and handed one to each of them every so often during the film. It was easy to give one to Jimmy, his hand was always waiting for the touch of hers, but slipping one to Ryan was more exciting. She would touch his sleeve, then slide her hand down to his in the darkness until she felt his palm below hers, his fingers curling up to close around the chocolate, and she would open her fingers and drop it into his hand, then caress his closed hand and his wrist as she pulled her hand away. You had to do it all fairly quickly, of course, to avoid the chocolate melting in your hand during the transfer.

By the interval the Maltesers were all finished, so he bought her another box, telling her he enjoyed her sharing them with him. She protested they would both make themselves sick, and she put the new box in her bag for later, telling him she would just pretend to give him one occasionally.

When they were back watching the film, she pretended to give him another one, and left her hand in his. His fingers twined with hers, and then he caressed her palm and the inside of her wrist, slipping his finger beneath the cuff of her blouse, and she caressed his hand and his wrist with her fingers, making circles on his palm as his father had once done to her, all the time wondering how such a simple thing as holding hands could feel so sensual, like they were making love with their hands. She leaned against him, ever so slightly.

After the film they dropped the two Phillips boys at the gate to the farm. John Phillips had waited up for them, and Jane waved as he let them in the door. She had hoped to get a kiss goodnight from Ryan, but Pat had returned and was putting the Rover away as they reached the garage. He had taken Claire and the two youngest McCann boys, while Jimmy and David had picked up Candy and Julie in the Land Rover.

The three of them went in the back door together, so there was no opportunity for her to negotiate a kiss goodnight. Ryan made them all cocoa. At least Daniel had trusted them and hadn't waited up. This time she would not have been able to tell him the plot of the film; she had been so preoccupied with Ryan that she had scarcely watched it.

Wednesday 18 February 1976

The plans had come back from the architect, and the builder came on Wednesday afternoon to discuss them with Daniel. The next step was to get the council approval before he gave them a final quote for doing the work.

Jane and Pat met Claire and Jimmy at the Black Horse Inn on Wednesday evening. Pat realised Jimmy was to be his brother-in-law. They had not thought about this before, and it gave them all a moment's amusement. Jane was glad to get away from Daniel for an evening, as he hadn't gone to London for a while, and she found his constant attention to her a little tiring at times. Although she chatted happily enough, she was all the time thinking that Ryan had sent her a valentine card and Mary had said he liked her. He had held her hand in the darkness of the cinema. She was used to thinking of him as a lone wolf, as someone she would rather like to fall in love with, but there was no point, since he would never think of her in that way. Now she was wondering if perhaps he did really like her, if he might one day ask her out to a film by herself, buy Maltesers for her again, give her a kiss goodnight.

Friday 20 February 1976

Daniel had behaved well all week, hardly touching her at all. He took her and Mary shopping on the Friday morning and went into the bank with Jane when she collected the cash. It was a lot because it included the money for the young men's allowances. Jane sat in the back of the car going home, trying to ignore the continual glances he gave her in the rear-view mirror, hoping they wouldn't encounter a sheep in the lane.

She did some typing for him in the early afternoon, as there were some cheques and envelopes to prepare for Ryan to sign that night. He came and sat with her with a glass in his hand.

'That's one less you're allowed tonight,' she reminded him, without looking up from her work.

'Jane I've been good for weeks, you know I have. And this is mostly dry ginger with only a tiny bit of whisky. You've bewitched me. I could give it up altogether for you.'

'That's probably not necessary, and I doubt you really could. Just keep it to a sensible amount.'

She suddenly recalled Pat once saying that his uncle wanted to marry her and she could have anything she wanted from him. She didn't like him talking like this. He sat and watched her with his predator look while he drank his whisky.

'You're beautiful, Jane. I could sit and look at you all day.'

'That would be a terrible waste of time, Mr Linden.'

'I could make love to you all day, too, if you'd let me. That wouldn't be wasting time. You could come upstairs with me now. I promise you'll enjoy it. You'd look even more beautiful without your clothes. Young women always have beautiful maidenhair and beautiful pussies.'

She was so shocked she nearly fell off her chair. She hardly knew what to say to him.

'Please don't talk to me like that, Mr Linden. This time I will forget you said something so completely out of place, but if you talk like that again I will go back to my home in Richmond, and you will have to do your own typing. Now please go away so I can finish these. Then it will be time for afternoon tea, and after that we can walk in the garden.'

It didn't take her long. She left the cheques and their envelopes on the desk in the library and went into the kitchen. She was shaking when she sat at the table, but when Mary asked her what was wrong, she just said nothing was wrong, she was okay.

She knew it was all only empty threats. She could never leave here and return to Richmond. She would be far too frightened to stay there at night alone, and there was nowhere else for her to go. She didn't know what to do.

Late in the afternoon she waited in the conservatory for Ryan to come home, sitting on the swing seat with a book and the cat, hoping he would join her there and hoping Daniel wouldn't. She was not even sure where Daniel had gone, as he was not in the den. Perhaps he had gone to collect Ryan from the station.

Ryan came in and sat beside her. He had bought chocolates for her again, and a jigsaw puzzle with a picture of a steam train. He didn't seem to mind now being close to her. She gave him a chocolate, slipping it into his hand as she had at the cinema, but these chocolates, like the Maltesers, were not so inclined to melt as the heart ones he had brought home for her the previous weekend, so he didn't lick her fingers. She told him what they had all done in the week, but she didn't tell him what his father had said. She didn't even want to think about it.

'Jane is something the matter?' he asked.

She knew she hadn't disguised well enough that Daniel had upset her.

'Your father said something inappropriate. I'll get over it.' She couldn't hide her voice shaking.

'What did he say? I can talk to him if you like.'

'I would rather not repeat it. And I don't want you rowing with him. I wish he behaved more like you do. You never say anything out of place or touch me where you shouldn't. I wish he would go off to London so I was free of him for a few days.'

'You can stop helping him if he bothers you, and stay with Mary all day. We'll get Mary to talk to him again. She is better at it than I am. Last time he told me you like it really, and I was just jealous. I felt like knocking him out, but I didn't.'

'Did he pick you up from the station? He seemed to have disappeared.'

'Yes, he did. He was waiting with the car. He had a box with him when he came in. It's now on the kitchen table. I think it's flowers for you.'

They returned to the kitchen, as it was nearly dinner time. The box was on the table, but Daniel was back in his den.

He had bought her a dozen roses again, red ones this time, with a card that simply said *Sorry*. Mary found a vase for them and asked Jane what had happened.

'He asked me to go up to his room,' was all she would say, and she saw Ryan and Mary exchange a look.

When he came in for dinner, she didn't thank him for the roses. She didn't speak to him at all. But she knew that things could not go on like this.

He spent the evening watching television with Mary, whisky glass in hand. Pat was at the farm with Claire. Jane and Ryan sat in the library, with the door closed, working on the jigsaw and talking about books. She had been reading *Gormenghast*, which was rather a fun book to read and talk about.

Saturday 21 February 1976

On the Saturday Mary was in London again. Jane wanted to avoid being with Daniel so she went outside to help the young men in the garden. They were planting seeds in trays in the glasshouse so there would be flowers to plant in the spring. Jane was given the job of sowing sweet peas into their own cute little clay pots, neatly nestled together in a wooden tray.

Daniel came to find them, as no one had brought him his coffee. He joined them in the glasshouse, helping with the seeds, while Jane made the coffee and brought it out to them, and he remained with them until lunch time, not bothering her at all. She thought how good it was for them all to be working here together like this with no antagonism, only cooperation.

Pat, Jane and Ryan went to the village hall at one o' clock. This time they were walking towards the town and would have tea at a farm just this side of it, as they had once before. She had also walked this way with Daniel several times, so she now knew who lived in all the farms and cottages between Hayward and the town. Some of them were the families of the teenagers in Colin's group.

She stayed close to Ryan when she could, but Jimmy wanted to walk with her and swing her down from stiles, and she couldn't be rude to him. She tried walking with Candy, who was only a year or so younger than Jane and was interested in hearing about Jane's life at boarding school. Jimmy had to swing both of them down from the stiles, so it didn't look so much like Jane flirting with him.

Candy was in sixth form at the local girls' grammar school, her mother managed the lingerie shop in town, and her father was the headmaster at the primary school. She told Jane that her uncle, her father's brother, was coming to stay with them at Easter and would be with them all summer. He had been teaching in South Africa, but was now returning to live in England. Candy also told Jane that Julie was her cousin; Jane hadn't known that. Julie's father had been Candy's mother's younger brother. He had died very young, only three years after he was married. He had ridden a motorbike, and one night he had skidded on black ice and been killed. Her aunt Alison always said he was the only love of her life, and she had never wanted anyone else. Candy's mum had told Candy that no one in the family would have been upset if Alison had remarried, since it was hard to bring up a child alone. Julie and Alison had lived with Alison's mother as they couldn't afford to rent a house of their own. When Candy's family came to live at Hayward, Candy's mum had offered Alison and Julie the cottage to live in. It came as part of the house they had bought, and had previously been let out for holidays, but Candy's mum hadn't wanted to run a holiday let, as it was quite a lot of work. It was nice having Julie next door.

'Your uncle is the same,' Candy told Jane. 'Mum said he never got over losing his wife, and he never wanted anyone else. He's a nice man, and he is always so polite. If I see him in the village, he always raises his hat and calls me *the beautiful Miss Morgan*. He looks at me in a nice way too, like he really does think I'm beautiful. Mum says he looks at everyone like that—he's a ladies' man and quite harmless. Dad calls him *The Squire*. You are so lucky to have him for an uncle. He is the patron of our youth group. He gives Reverend Colin the money so he can pay for us all to go to the cinema and pay for the farmers to give us tea on the walks. Without that some of our group wouldn't be able to afford to come because the farms don't make much money. Everyone buys synthetic jumpers now, so there is less wool needed.'

Jane hadn't known that Daniel helped fund the youth group, although she did recall having typed out a cheque to the parish, which she had been asked to take to the vicarage and give to Linda. She hoped Daniel wouldn't start groping Candy behind a tombstone after church. Her father might call him something less polite if he did, *a randy old goat* perhaps, and her mother wouldn't think him so harmless then.

'Ryan's nice too,' Candy was saying. 'He found out about the history of our cottage for my dad. He knew when it was built and the names of the people who lived there for quite a long way back. When he came to give us the notes, he helped me with some Latin translation. He reads it like it's English. I didn't like Latin much before that, but he explained it so simply, and made it all seem so interesting, that now it's my favourite subject. He said learning Latin helps you understand how languages go together and that when you read the old texts, you can hear the voices and share the thoughts of people who lived hundreds of years ago, so you realise that they were not any different from us. He told me he sometimes thinks in Latin because it can seem less complicated than thinking in English. I didn't really understand what he meant, but he made me laugh. Dad says he's a natural teacher. I'm glad he helps with our group now. Mum says it's because you're here, and he wants to look after you. She thinks he fancies you, but I told her not to be so silly, as he's much too old for that. You're only a year older than me, and he must be nearly thirty. The ghost stories are good, though. Everyone here loves ghosts.'

Ryan had been talking to Colin, but Jane managed to get back beside him, leaving Candy with Jimmy, and Ryan helped her at the next stile. It was nice to touch his hand. He gave her a quick look and a smile. Was he remembering that he had held her hand last Saturday? She thought they were almost lovers now, so perhaps they would be soon.

It was not such a long walk as the Peddleton one, but it was a cold day, and when they reached the farm, they were glad of the warmth of the kitchen and the hot tea and toasted raisin bread. They had a while to rest, so Ryan read them all another ghost story, *The Signalman*. Even the farmer and his wife enjoyed listening to it.

When they reached home, Daniel had already left to pick up Mary, so Jane and Ryan sat in Mary's room warming their feet with the heater as they had before, his toes caressing hers in their socks while they pretended to be vying for the best spot in the stream of warm air. Jane still had some chocolates, and she occasionally gave one to him as she had in the cinema. When they were all gone, they linked their fingers and he caressed her wrist again. They were alone in the house, as Pat had stopped at the farm with Claire and was having dinner with them, except at the farm they called it supper. She leant against his shoulder, and she felt very close to him. It was only a small step from here for him to kiss her, for her to melt into his arms, bury her fingers in his hair. He touched her cheek with his fingers, tilted her head so she was looking into his eyes, and she realised that he felt like she did, but she sensed that the feeling had taken him by surprise. She knew that things would have to go slowly with him, he wasn't going to kiss her, at least not yet.

But all too soon they heard the car returning, so they put on their sheepskin boots, and Jane moved to the separate armchair.

He asked if she could manage another walk tomorrow afternoon in an ancient forest a few miles south from Hayward. He used to walk there from Hayward when he was younger, but it was a long way, so they would drive to Charlford and walk from there. There was a circular path, about three miles around.

Sunday 22 February 1976

Daniel seemed rather annoyed that they were walking again on Sunday afternoon when they had gone out yesterday, saying he had wanted to walk in the garden with Jane, but Ryan ignored his attempts to argue with them over lunch, and they left as soon as they had changed from their church clothes into jeans.

Jane always felt an exhilarating sense of freedom driving away from Hayward Hall with him, even though she loved the house. She enjoyed the feeling of it just being the two of them together. Yesterday he had nearly kissed her, perhaps today he would, and there would be no one to interrupt them while they were alone in the woods. Perhaps that was why he had asked her to come here with him.

They found the path, escaped into the depths of a forest, leaving the rest of the world behind, surrounded by oak trees still bare from winter, pine trees dark and old, thickets of yew guarding ancient secrets, hazel with soft yellow catkins, ivy twining near their ankles and moss on the path beneath their feet. She put her hand in his. He didn't seem to mind, and it seemed a natural thing for her to do. She felt that they were lovers even though no word of love had ever been spoken between them.

He was silent, and she did not like to disturb the sounds of the forest, the rustle of small creatures and the constant song of birds that only deepened the stillness.

After a while they left the main path and stepped deeper into the woods, their feet on a faint narrow way through the tangle of ivy, the bare oak twigs above them dark lace against a light grey sky. Jane felt that they could walk on into another world, a primeval forest where only the two of them existed, entwined in the shadowed memories of past lives, leaving care and toil behind.

A red squirrel darted above them in the trees, scolding them for intruding, its beautiful chattering telling them the woods belonged to squirrels, not to humans.

The path ended in a small clearing with two standing stones, green and soft with moss, one taller and seeming to lean over the other like a man shielding a woman or a mother protecting a child. A little way ahead of them was a mound of earth beneath the trees.

'It's a barrow,' he told her. 'I don't think it has ever been disturbed. The trees around it are very old. The Victorians liked to dig them up, and sadly a lot of the contents became lost as a result. One part of me would like to see what it holds, so we can date it, but the spirits of the those who are buried here tell me it should be left alone.'

Jane put her hand on the taller stone, the moss soft, cool and damp beneath her palm. His placed his hand over hers, standing quite close to her.

'I used to come here when I was still at school. I would walk here all the way from Hayward. I felt like I was part of the history of this place. Our ancestor Charles Linden lived near Charlford before he built Hayward Hall, so he may have come here when he was young, and his ancestors before him. If they hadn't lived, you and I would not be here. We are all a small part of one long continuous process of life. The people who once lived in this place thought and felt just like we do, tried to find patterns to explain their world and plan their lives, as we do, except we have more science and less superstition to guide us. We could be standing here like this any time in the last four thousand years, with the same sounds and the same forest and the same feeling of there being no one but us two in the whole world.'

She looked up at him, wishing he would kiss her. He was showing her this place because it was precious to him, and she was content with that. He didn't have to tell her he loved her. In the deep quiet of the forest, she knew he did, and she felt that he knew she loved him. For a moment she looked into his eyes and she felt very close to his soul. They were meant to be lovers.

He faced her, held both of her hands, their palms touching, fingers intertwined. She closed her eyes, willing him to pull her closer to him and kiss her, waiting for the touch of his lips on hers.

But there were voices on the narrow path behind them, beyond a thicket of hazel.

'Damn,' he whispered, and she opened her eyes. He smiled at her, amused that they had been interrupted.

She looked around to see two elderly gentlemen approaching them, and their moment of magic together was gone. One of them recognised Ryan—he had taught him at Oxford—and he introduced his friend, also an Oxford professor. They were both now retired, and lived together in Charlford. Jane was thankful that they had not come upon her and Ryan smooching on the path, but she did wish they had not turned up at all. It had been getting rather interesting.

The second professor took a hazelnut from his pocket and placed it on the smaller standing stone. He motioned them to stand back and quietly wait. The squirrel, swift and delicate, came down from the trees, crossed the open space, snatched the nut from the stone and returned to the safety of the canopy, watching them as it devoured its prize.

They spoke for a while about the barrow and the stones, before they all returned to the main path, pausing on a bridge where it crossed a stream, looking down into the cool clear splash of the water. Jane hoped the two old men would wander on, but they lingered by the water with her and Ryan. They all continued together along the circular path back to Charlford, Ryan's former tutor talking to him about friends and acquaintances from his college, and his friend offering Jane his arm, telling her about a red squirrel that lived in their garden and fed from their bird table, asking her if they had squirrels in the garden at Hayward Hall. Jane didn't recall seeing any, but told him there had been grey squirrels in their garden in Kent. He asked her about her old school and what books she liked to read, and it turned out he was also a fan of *Gormenghast*.

Back at the village the two professors treated them to tea and scones at the tea shop, Jane resigning herself to the lost opportunity to have Ryan to herself and enjoying their company and their talk of books and squirrels. She knew they were being kind, and were themselves glad of the opportunity to catch up with Ryan's news of the college where they had spent so many years.

When they reached home, Ryan asked her if she would go out to dinner with him the following Saturday night, somewhere quiet where it was just the two of them. He said he hoped this time they didn't run into anyone he knew; perhaps they should go in disguise. He took off her boots, sitting on the floor beside her, and caressed her toes, but Daniel had seen the car return and had come to find them.

Thursday 26 February 1976

It was a Thursday morning, now nearly the end of February. Jane was typing up the hand-corrected manuscript for Daniel in the library, checking the grammar from the little book Ryan had given her. After this it would be taken to the library to be photocopied before it was sent to the publisher. A few more minor hand corrections at the end didn't matter, as the editor would look after the final step.

Mary brought them coffee at ten thirty as she always did, and they sat in the library to drink it.

Normally Jane would go back to typing, but Daniel decided he wanted to walk in the garden. The day was fine and not too cold, so she didn't need her coat. He took her into the centre of the maze as he had once before. She remembered thinking that the maze was overlooked from the house, but with him beside her there was no one to do the overlooking. Mary was in the kitchen, Pat had gone into town, and Ryan was in Oxford. Something in Daniel's manner made her a little apprehensive, and she could smell the whisky on his breath. He was not supposed to drink in the mornings.

She sat on the stone bench. It was sheltered in the maze but colder than she had expected. The hedges shielded her eyes from the low winter sun but closed in on her so she felt trapped. He sat down beside her, very close to her, and took her hand. She felt panic rising in her, thinking that she knew what he was going to say and wishing he wouldn't say it.

'Jane, I'm in love with you, I just can't help it, and I can't go on like this any longer. Marry me, Jane.'

She had to keep control of this. She looked up at him. 'Mr Linden, please stop this. I am years younger than you are, and I am not in love with you.' She wished he would just say sorry and let her go back indoors, but she knew it was not going to be that easy. One part of her felt sorry for him, another said this was her fault, but she knew she had never deliberately done anything to lead him on.

'Please marry me, Jane. I can't go on just wanting you like this. I can't concentrate on anything. All I think about is having you naked in bed with me and making love to you. Nothing would change here except you would sleep upstairs with me. You can still have your own room if you prefer, and you would just come to mine at night. Or you can have the room next to mine, my wife's old room. You don't have anyone else. Pat is marrying the little girl from the farm who trapped him, and Ryan's no use to you. He's gay, and he can't make love to a girl even if he wanted to. He damaged his spine when he was a child. I can give you money, diamonds, travel, anything you desire. We live very quietly here, but I have the money to give you any lifestyle you want. You don't have to be in love with me. All you have to do is sleep with me. I'm an experienced lover, and I promise you'll enjoy it. I'll have you wanting me as much as I want you. It feels better for the man if the woman enjoys it. You can just lie on the bed, and I will do the rest. We can try it out first if you want.'

Ryan was gay, he had said. Jane had never once thought of that, and it hit her like a bolt of lightning. He had said when she first came here that he didn't have a girlfriend or a boyfriend either, he was a lone wolf. Yet he had her photo, he had kept the poppy, had sent her a valentine, he treated her like he cared for her, and he had held her hand that evening in the cinema. On Sunday they had stood by the standing stone, and she had felt that he loved her. Mary thought he loved her, and he had even told Pat he was smitten with her. But he had never treated her as if he wanted to make love to her. Not once had he ever touched her, beyond holding her hand, or attempted to kiss her. Was it true that he couldn't make love to a girl, or was Daniel just trying to upset her? Did he know she wanted his son? Did he realise how affected she would be by his casual spiteful words?

But she had to concentrate on Daniel. He wanted her to sleep with him, that was all he wanted. Perhaps if she did, he would get over wanting her. But she knew that wouldn't happen, and sleeping with a man because you felt sorry for him didn't seem like a sensible thing to do. And she knew she couldn't do it. The thought of it revolted her. He was an old man. And he made her feel as if he was a predator and she was the prey.

'Jane, please listen to me. I want you so much. I'm offering you marriage, everything I own. You can control all the money, have anything you like, and all I would want in return is to make love to you. I know you'll enjoy it. I promise it'll feel good for you as well. I don't care if you don't think you love me. I wouldn't expect you to. Lots of people marry someone they don't think they love, and it can still work out. I may only be around for another few years, then you would have everything I own and the rest of your life to do as you please.'

She remembered Pat telling her that Daniel was in love with her, that she could marry him and then he would give his son and his nephew all the money they wanted, suggesting she could have an affair with Ryan on the side, and she had been appalled at his attitude to marriage.

'Please stop this,' she pleaded, getting to her feet, trying to stay in control, but she was shaking. She had to remember the way out of the maze, or he would trap her in a dead end.

But he didn't stop. He stood up and was holding her shoulders, and she thought he would try to kiss her. 'Jane, please just sleep with me once, and I promise you'll want to do it again, please Jane.'

Then he did kiss her, first her face, then her mouth, then her neck, and she was too shocked to even try to move away from him. 'I love you, Jane. I can't live without you.'

He was holding her against him, his hand on her behind, then sliding further down, trying to get beneath her skirt.

'Mr Linden, please control yourself. I would like to go back to the house.'

'Jane, will you at least think about it?'

'I don't have to think, Mr Linden. The answer is no. Now please let me go.' She tried to push him away, suddenly panicking. 'Let me go!'

He released her. She remembered the way out of the maze, and he followed her back to the house, not touching her and saying nothing. She went in the back door, into the kitchen, sat at the table, trying to stop herself from shaking.

Mary looked at her, clearly guessing something had happened, before Daniel walked wordlessly through the kitchen and across the hallway to his den.

'I can't stay here,' Jane said. 'I liked living here, but I can't stay. I've had enough of it. I'll pack my case and leave. Pat can take me to the station.'

'What happened? Did he make a pass at you?'

Jane nodded, for a moment unable to say anything.

'He said he was in love with me and wanted to marry me. I don't want to marry him, and I have never led him on, or said anything to him that could make him think I cared for him in that way. I said no, but I don't think we can live in the same house after this. He is always trying to get his hand up my skirt, asking me to sleep with him, and I've had enough of it.'

'Will you take a bit of time to think about it before you go. We all like having you here. I can talk to him again if you want, and ask him to leave you alone. Would you like me to ask Ryan to come home? Would you stay if he was here every night? I know he wouldn't mind.'

Jane knew that Mary didn't really understand, that she would always take Daniel's side, would never see him for the predator that he was. And she knew that if she stayed here, nothing would change no matter how much Mary spoke to him. Mary was always afraid he would lose his temper, and she never said a cross word to him. And Pat would never help her, as he wanted her to marry his uncle. It was best that she left. She didn't like the thought of being by herself in Richmond, but she had no other choice. She was not staying here any longer.

'I want to go now. I can't be relying on Ryan all the time, and I don't want them rowing over me. I have my own house; I will go back there. Mary, Daniel said Ryan was gay. I don't mind if he is, I would understand, I know some men are like that, and I want him to be happy. But I'd rather know that before I fall completely in love with him.'

'I don't think so Jane. I suppose it's possible—I have never thought about it—but I know he does like you. Daniel is jealous of him, and he's just trying to get between you. He was jealous of him from the first day you came here. Pat is shopping in town, so I can't contact him. Would you like me to ask Daniel to take you to the train?'

'I don't want to be alone in a car with him, and he would want to stop me leaving. I'll walk.'

'Call by the farm and see if Jimmy can drive you. I can phone them.'

'Mary, please don't get anyone else involved in our problems. It's not far to walk, and it isn't raining. Please don't tell Daniel that I've left or where I'm going, or he will come after me, and I don't want him turning up at Richmond. I wouldn't feel safe just with him.'

'I'll pack your case for you later, if you like, and ask Ryan to bring it to you on the weekend. He won't mind. You can't walk to the station with a heavy suitcase. For now just take what you need for a night or two.'

Mary took the car keys from their home in the kitchen drawer and put them in her pocket. 'He won't be able to follow you unless he walks to the station. But if you change your mind, come back here, and we will sort it out. Ryan will know what to do. Phone when you get to Richmond so we know you're safe.'

Jane had not quite reached the village when John Phillips drove past on his way to the library, and he gave her a lift into town. She chatted to him as they went, asking him if they had any baby turkeys yet, if his grandsons were well, all the time hiding that she was shaking inside, not just from Daniel wanting to marry her, but from what he had said about Ryan.

'You're not running away, are you?' he said, half-jokingly but with more perception than she had expected from him, as he took her bag from the back of the car.

'No, I'm just spending a night or two with a friend in London. The shopping is much better there. After I get back, I'll come and see the baby turkeys. Thank you for the lift.'

It seemed so strange to be suddenly adrift and on her own, no longer part of the family at Hayward Hall. She was by herself in the first-class carriage, the train rushing her back towards Richmond, her overnight bag in the rack, but the pain of leaving Hayward would not leave her. She had loved it there, it had become her home, but now she felt she couldn't live there unless she agreed to marry Daniel. It seemed so unfair. She recalled that he had made the young men promise to treat her like a sister. Why had he not treated her like a daughter or a niece? He had spoiled everything.

She remembered the garden, the flowers, the pond with the fountain, the maze in the back garden, helping Pat to keep it trimmed. She remembered them all sowing seeds for the flowers that would colour the garden in spring and summer. She remembered the house hugging her, helping her to regain her joy in living, helping her to face the sad memories of the people she had lost. She had felt close to her father when she walked in the garden, feeling that she might turn a corner in the path through the trees and find him sitting on a stone seat, waiting for her. He had lived there and loved it too. He had tried to create a garden in Kent that reminded him of his old home.

She felt the loss of her father's protection very keenly as the train passed through countryside that was blurred for her by tears. If he was still alive, she would not have been living at Hayward Hall at the mercy of a man who should have loved and cared for her as her father had, but instead had treated her with only barely disguised lust, as if she would fall into bed with him if he seduced her skilfully enough, or negotiated a high enough price. Her great-aunt had been so right in not allowing her to live with him when she was orphaned at sixteen.

But if her father had been alive, she would not now be friends with Ryan. She remembered Mary saying Ryan liked her, and she remembered that cursed day when he had found her kissing Pat in the lodge. But then she remembered standing with him in the stillness of the wood, knowing they were destined to be lovers, knowing he was the only man she would ever want to spend her life with. If only Daniel had not got in the way.

She had cared about Daniel. She had sensed his loneliness. She had given him her company in his rather secluded life, made him laugh at things, tried to help him get on better with his son, although that had not worked out well. She had encouraged him to reduce his dependence on whisky, had come to understand when he wanted her to talk to him and when he wanted her to stay silent when they walked.

Perhaps she should have stayed. Perhaps they could have sorted it out. She could have just said no. But she had said no, and Daniel had persisted. She could have gone to talk to him in the den, told him that she liked being there with him, that she didn't want to marry him or sleep with him, but she did care about him and she didn't want to leave. She could have asked him if they could go back to how they were before. But she had panicked as she always did whenever anything went wrong. It was time she stopped panicking and got a hold on running her own life instead of needing other people to cling to.

The train stopped at Oxford. For a mad moment she thought about getting off there and going to find Ryan at the college. She would tell him what had happened, and he would know what to do. At least he would hug her; she badly needed him to hug her. But what could he do?

She couldn't stay there in his room with him. Even if it had been allowed, the bed was so narrow that one of them would have had to sleep on the armchair or the floor.

The train pulled away from the station, and the opportunity was gone. She would telephone him tonight. It would be good to hear his voice even if he was far away from her. She fought back tears, glad there was no one to see her, feeling totally lost and alone in the world. Things had been so much better at Hayward. She had recovered from being an emotional wreck, and she had felt part of a family. She had enjoyed looking after the accounts, helping Daniel with the typing. She had enjoyed the yoga class on Thursdays, going to the pub with Pat and Jimmy, helping Mary make the apple pies that Ryan loved, spending weekends with Ryan. She belonged there. She had four people to love and who cared about her. Except one of them had loved her too much. The wrong one.

She changed trains at Reading, went on to Richmond, her troubled thoughts soothed by the steady clatter of the wheels on the rails, the soft green of the fields and trees beyond the window. She walked the mile from the station with her bag getting heavier with each step.

Richmond no longer seemed her home; Hayward was now her home. Mary had promised that Ryan would bring the suitcase to her in a day or two. It would be so good to see him, and perhaps he could stay the night here in her father's old room. She knew that she could telephone Sarah, move back to Sarah's house, but she also knew that was not fair on her friend. She would have to face staying here by herself, alone with the ghosts of her parents and her great-aunt. They had loved her in life; their ghosts would do her no harm. She would take up her life where it had left off, perhaps try to get her job back, go to the shops in Richmond and Knightsbridge, see her old friends. The first night would be the worst; after that she would be used to being here alone. Perhaps Ryan would come and see her on the weekends instead of going home to Hayward. He loved her, she knew he loved her, and he would want to come and see her. He could still be part of her life.

How would Daniel manage the accounts on his own? Ryan would have to go back to helping him. At least now he knew to write *Paid* on the bills and he could fill in the account book as she had. But then he would need to spend some weekends at Hayward.

She unlocked the front door, her hand scarcely steady enough to hold the key, stepped into the familiar hallway. But it seemed so bleak and empty, so silent and cold. There was no Aunt Ellen to take her coat, make her dinner, ask her what she had done that day. She closed the door, leaned for a moment against it, then got as far as the stairs before she sat down on the second step, shaking uncontrollably, and cried. She could not even make a cup of tea, as there would be no milk. She would need to go out to the shop, buy some milk and bread, make herself a meal for tonight. But for now all she could do was to sit and weep for the life she had lived for such a brief time in the most beautiful place in the world. She realised she had left her sedatives in the cupboard in the kitchen. If she had remembered them, she could have taken one and felt at least a little better.

She just needed to get through tonight, and perhaps tomorrow Ryan would bring her suitcase. But she knew it was unfair on him. He had his own life to lead, and she couldn't expect him to be at her beck and call. She would phone him tonight; she needed to talk to him. She hoped he wouldn't chide her for running away, but she knew he would understand because he always understood. She had his number on the leaflet he had given her. It was in her bag along with the valentine card with *te amo* written in the heart, inside its envelope with *SWALK* on the back.

It was nearly three o' clock. Mrs Brennan had been keeping the clock in the hallway wound up. Jane could hear the cars on the street, voices of people walking by, time passing, the clock chiming three, then half past, and still she sat, no longer crying but unable to rouse herself from the misery that overwhelmed her. Her whole world and her whole future life seemed total emptiness. She was back here with no one to care for her and no one she could love. She knew she should not have left. Perhaps tomorrow she would go back—it was too late to return today—but for now she needed to get up and walk to the shop.

Then she heard a car slow down in the street, turn into the driveway, a car door quietly close, feet on the front steps, a dark shadow behind the frosted stained glass of the front door, the bell ringing, and her own heart racing. It couldn't be Ryan. He was coming on the weekend, not today, and he couldn't possibly have got here this soon, as he had been in Oxford. Perhaps it was Daniel, following her here to persuade her to come back. Please don't let it be Daniel. She couldn't cope if it was. She couldn't be alone here with him. She might feel sorry for him and say yes. Mary had taken the car keys, and she would not have given them to Daniel. Unless he had forced her to. Please, oh please, don't let it be Daniel.

There was a chain latch on the door. If it was Daniel, she wouldn't need to let him in. But if she didn't, he might wait outside, trapping her so she could not even go to the shop. Perhaps Mary had sent Pat. That would be all right. She trusted Pat.

She forced herself to get up. She carefully put the chain in place, suddenly realising that until she had done that, he could have simply turned the knob and come inside. She opened the door a sliver.

It was Ryan. The relief that flooded over her left her shaking.

'Hang on a second,' she said, closing the door so she could remove the chain. The moment that it took steadied her a little. She opened the door and let him into the hallway. But then she fell into his arms, clinging to him.

'Steady on,' he said as he closed the door. 'Mary said you had left Hayward. She phoned me and asked me to come after you and make sure you were all right. I got a taxi home from Oxford to get the car, and I drove here. I have your suitcase with me that Mary packed for you, and your sedatives as well. Mary remembered them at the last minute, and they're in my pocket. I can stay here tonight if you want. Mary said you have a spare room where my uncle Peter used to sleep, and I'll need to stay because it's getting a bit late to drive back, the traffic would be awful, and you look like you need company. I'm not leaving you here by yourself. You should have been here an hour ago on the train, but it looks as if you only just arrived. You still have your coat on.'

'I have been sitting on the stairs for ages,' she admitted. 'I feel like I have made a total mess of everything and I should have stayed and sorted it out. I have run away from the only people I care about. I always panic when things go wrong. Thank you for coming and for bringing my case. When you knocked on the door, I thought it was your father coming after me, and it shook me a bit. I would be so grateful if you would stay, I would feel safer, and I don't like being by myself. I've never been alone in a house at night. I'm so sorry to mess up your life like this, but I am glad to see you. You are always so kind to me, and I know I don't deserve it.'

'We'll get this sorted out. Mary said my father had shut himself in the den, so he didn't know then that you had gone or that I had come home. She intended to go in to him and try to stop him getting drunk, but she wanted to wait until I had gone after you before she let him know you had left. Let's take off your coat, and I'll give you a hug. Can we make a coffee or a cup of tea?'

'There won't be any milk, or bread or anything. We will need to shop.'

'Let's see what we do have, and we can make a list. Is there any heating?'

He helped her take off her coat, and hung it on a peg in the hallway. Then he hugged her, and she cried again although it felt good being close to him.

'Now please calm down and stop crying. I'm here with you, you are safe, and you don't have to face the ghosts alone. We'll get this all back in perspective. My father proposed to you, and you refused him. He is no doubt disappointed, and you are upset, but nobody is dead or injured, the sun will set tonight and rise again tomorrow, you have a roof over your head, and no money has been lost.'

He had come all this way to help her, and he always knew how to make her laugh. She needed to make an effort to be cheerful. She felt much safer with him there. Daniel coming after her no longer mattered.

She took him into the kitchen. The water for the radiators was heated with gas, and he wasn't sure what to do, as they didn't have gas at Hayward. She showed him how to light it, and they turned on the taps for the radiators in the downstairs rooms. They could heat the upstairs rooms later. For now they needed to shop.

There was sugar and tea and a small can of evaporated milk because Mrs Brennan made herself a cup of tea when she cleaned the house, but there was not much else.

He wrote down milk, bread, butter, cheese, jam and coffee.

'Do you have a percolator?' he asked her. 'Or do we make do with instant?'

'We have a cafetière and a grinder, so we buy coffee beans. It tastes just as good as percolated.'

'We'll buy strawberry jam,' he decided. 'We always have raspberry jam at Hayward, but when you are used to Mary's raspberry jam, the shop stuff seems tasteless, so we'll have strawberry jam while we are here. Mary made strawberry jam once, but most years we eat the strawberries as fast as they come ripe, so there are none left for jam. The hedgehogs get most of them before we do. They aren't so fussy about them being ripe.'

She knew he was just trying to cheer her up with trivial things. It was so good to have him here with her.

Then he added porridge, cocoa, chocolate biscuits, fruit cake and apples to the list.

'I'm not much good at this,' he apologised. 'Mary always does the shopping. We can have dinner at a café somewhere—maybe that one we went to before. I don't think you are in fit state to go anywhere upmarket, and if I tried to cook dinner, we might both be poisoned. If you're feeling better tomorrow, I'll take you out to dinner somewhere really nice. Last weekend when we came home from the walk I asked if you would have dinner with me this Saturday, just the two of us, but that can be tomorrow instead. Now come with me to the shop so I know where to go. Is there somewhere close enough to walk, or do we drive?'

'Close enough to walk. I'll find a shopping bag.'

She walked beside him down the familiar street to the shop. The assistant remembered her and said she hadn't seen her for a while.

When they returned with the groceries, Jane showed Ryan how to light the gas stove, and she put the kettle on.

He asked if she had an electric kettle, but she didn't.

'You do get used to gas,' she assured him. She ground the coffee, poured the hot water over it in the cafetière and timed the four minutes.

'This is beautiful coffee,' he said as they sat in the kitchen with their mugs and a slice of fruit cake.

Jane felt a lot better. She had not had any lunch, and she realised just how hungry she was. He took the bottle of sedative pills from his jacket pocket and handed it to her, hastily retrieving something else that fell from his pocket onto the floor. But she knew she would cope without one now.

'First tell me exactly what happened to make you leave. Then you can show me the rest of the house. I've only been upstairs once to get your case when we were here in November. Mary just said my father had proposed to you, and it had upset you. He didn't threaten you, did he?'

'Threaten me? No, I don't think so. He asked me to marry him, and he wanted me to sleep with him. We had walked in the garden. He said he wanted some fresh air, and I had been typing all morning, so I went outside with him, and he took me into the centre of the maze. I didn't know if I could remember the way back out, and I felt trapped. We sat on the stone seat in the centre, and he told me he was in love with me and he couldn't help it, and he wanted me to marry him. I said no, as politely as I could, and then he said other things that I didn't like very much. That he would give me money and diamonds, and all I had to do was sleep with him. Apart from that, things would be just the same. He said he knew I would change my mind if I let him make love to me, and if I wanted, we could just try it out. He said he didn't care that I didn't love him, he didn't expect me to. I panicked, and I asked to go back to the house. I told Mary what had happened and that I wanted to leave. Pat was in town so I walked to the station, and Mr Phillips came past and gave me a lift. He said he has some newly hatched baby turkeys that we can go and see. Not that I will see them now.

'Mary said she would ask you to bring my suitcase in a few days. I didn't expect you to drop everything and come after me today, but I am grateful that you did. I don't want to marry Daniel. He is a nice man, but he is years older than I am, and I don't love him except as a kind of uncle. He's always trying to get his hand up my skirt, and I don't like him doing it. All the way here on the train I was worried he would follow me. I don't know what I would have done if he had turned up here; I would have been very frightened of what he would do if I was alone here with him.

'I liked living at Hayward. We all got on. I liked helping Mary, and she was always good to me. I felt that she cared about me. And you were so kind to me, and I looked forward to when you were there on the weekends. But I can't stay there with your father treating me the way he does. He gets really close to me, touches my knee, breathes on my neck as I do the typing, puts his hand up my skirt, and sometimes he really frightens me. He's much stronger than I am.

'I'm sorry that I don't want to marry him, but I just don't. I like him and I get on with him. He's nice looking and polite, but the thought of him making love to me gives me the creeps. He makes me feel like he's stalking me, like a hunter, waiting for me to tire out and give in and agree to sleep with him.

'Pat once said if I married Daniel, it would be good because he would give you and Pat more money and everything would still be the same for us all, except I would have to sleep with him. But that would be all right if I closed my eyes and pretended that he was someone I liked, since all men are the same in the dark. But that isn't my idea of being married.'

'Pat said that? When did he say that? Not today, as you said he had gone out to town.'

'It was the night we went to see Claire at the farm to arrange for me to be a bridesmaid. He said Daniel was in love with me, and it would be good for everyone if I married him because then I could ask him to give you both more money. He thought you would like that as well. Pat already gets far more than I used to earn working at the bank, so I don't know what he expects. Although I suppose he is older than I am, and men earn more than women. He wants some sort of expensive sports car; I can't recall the name of it. I have never encouraged your father. I do feel sorry for him if he really does like me, but I can't sleep with him just because of that.'

She didn't tell him the bit about Pat suggesting she slept with Ryan as well. She still couldn't believe Pat would say that.

For a long time he said nothing, but his fingers were restless, caressing the warm mug.

'Jane, for once I really am lost for words. My father treating you like that is bad enough, but for Pat to talk to you like that is appalling. He was always selfish, but that is about as low as you can get. He wants you to marry my father so he can have more money, and he actually imagines I would like that as well. We were all supposed to be looking after you, and this is what happens. I can't help but be angry with both of them. Hayward Hall is your home now, and you have the right to feel safe living there. My father asked Pat and me to treat you like a sister, and then he goes and treats you like this. He was in a position of trust; you were in all respects his ward and under his protection. We all like having you at Hayward, so I am still hoping we can sort all this out, find some strategy for you to deal with him, call some sort of truce.'

'You have always been very kind to me, and so has Mary. I know I should have coped with it rather than running away, and I wish now that I had stayed and tried to sort it out, but I panicked. I always panic when things go wrong. Now I feel as if I have messed up your life as well as mine, and I'm sorry you had to come after me, but I am very glad you did. If you hadn't turned up, I think I would still be sitting on the stairs, petrified that he would follow me here and persuade me to sleep with him. I only realised when you rang the bell that I hadn't even locked the door.'

'You haven't messed up my life, I promise. Looking after you feels like the best thing I have ever done. We'll sort this out, and the door is locked now. You need to show me the rest of the house and where I am to sleep.'

He had already seen the downstairs rooms when he had been there previously, so they went straight upstairs. She showed him her aunt's room at the front of the house, with the bay window. Jane had never been in there since her great-aunt had died, except to show the room to Mary, but it still looked exactly as Aunt Ellen had left it that morning. For a moment, in the stillness, she imagined her great-aunt calling her name, felt her close by. Aunt Ellen's ghost would never harm her.

Then she showed him her own room, where her mother had slept until she married, the bathroom and her father's old room. He had stayed here for a month or two before he married her mother, and then both of them had slept there until they had a house of their own. So that room at least had a double bed.

'That's better than your room at Oxford.' Jane remembered the small room with the narrow single bed. She had never been in his bedroom at Hayward Hall.

'We only have one bathroom,' she apologised, 'and the cloakroom behind the kitchen, but your room does have its own hand basin and a mirror, so you can use that for shaving. We can have a roster or some-thing.'

'Not a problem. We share bathrooms at Oxford, although not with ladies. I promise I am perfectly house trained. And I promise you are absolutely safe here with me.

'It seems so strange to think of Uncle Peter living here. I only ever saw him once after he left Hayward, and that was not long afterwards. His father's medals are still here on the wall. They used to hang in the hallway at home, and he knew what each one was for, but I don't recall that now. Your grandfather fought in both World Wars, the same as my grandfather. I loved your father. I always wished he was my father instead of Daniel, and I always thought how lucky you were to have him for yours. When he lived with us, he always read me stories, and he taught me to read long before I went to school. We both liked the stories about the railway engines the best. Trains were nearly all steam engines then. He played with me, and he was really good fun. On wet days he would put sheets over tables, and we would play at indoor camping. Mary used to get cross if there were guests in the house—she said it looked untidy—but my grandmother didn't mind.'

'He played that with me too,' Jane told him. 'And he read me the steam engine stories. They were his favourite. Our books are still up in the attic.'

So long ago now, she thought, yet she could recall every picture in the books, and every story.

'I still have happy memories of when he lived with us,' Ryan continued. 'He invented an imaginary animal, called a wobby, that lived in our garden and was very shy. We would creep along the paths, hoping to catch a glimpse of it, and we would follow tracks that Peter said were its tracks, but were probably a cat's.'

She laughed. 'We had a wobby in our garden as well. There was a hole at the base of the brick wall—I think it was for drainage. The grate had rusted away, but my father never repaired it because it was where the wobby went from our garden to the next one.'

'Ryan, do you know why he left? I know they both wanted my mother, but something happened, didn't it? He never once mentioned his life at Hayward Hall to me. He never even saw Mary again except at his wedding, and she would have been like a sister to him. He always wrote to her.'

He was silent for a long time, leaning against the door jamb while she stood inside the room. The daylight was dimming, the last rays of the sun fading tired into the dusk of another passing day.

'It was a long time ago, Jane, and I was only six. My father and your father were both in love with your mother. My father was jealous because she preferred Peter, and, yes, something happened that I hope he later regretted. I don't like to remember it, but sometimes it still comes back to me deep in the night, and I try to shut out the memories and think of other things, but I can't. I had nightmares for a long time, and I used to walk in my sleep. I've grown out of the nightmares, and I know I should just get over it, and perhaps I have to some extent. There was a row and Uncle Peter left with your mother. Can we just leave it at that?'

'Yes, of course. But sometimes it does help to talk about things. Was that when you broke your arm?' He had once told her he had broken his arm as a child and he didn't like to think about the day it happened. Was it all the same memory? She was trying to be helpful, and wondering what on earth could have happened. Was it to do with the shotgun? She wondered again whether Daniel had threatened to shoot her father.

'Yes, it was when I broke my arm. I was collateral damage. Your father was in no way to blame. Perhaps, one day we can talk about it, but for now please just leave it alone. I don't want to think about it.'

He had broken his arm and his ribs, and Daniel had said he had damaged his spine. Had he tried to come between two men fighting? Is that what he meant by collateral damage? And where did the shotgun fit in? If someone would tell her what had happened, then perhaps she could help him.

'I have thoughts like that too,' she told him. There was the nightmare of her parents in the train crash. Were they conscious for a while, lying there in the darkness of the tunnel, knowing they would die, worried about each other and how she would cope with losing them? Or had they died instantly? No one had ever told her. Perhaps no one had ever known or could ever know.

He looked at her in that kind way he had, as though he understood without her having to say anything.

'I think about them lying in the dark in the tunnel, and I wonder how long it was before they died, and I think I could have been with them.' There, she had told him, the words dark as a nightmare, yet it was a relief to say them.

He hugged her then, and she tried not to cry. He had dropped what he was doing to come and look after her, and she was grateful for that. She owed it to him not to be a complete wet blanket.

'I am very glad you weren't. Try not to dwell on the past, and don't get depressed. Just keep the happy memories alive. We will sort something out between you and my father. For the moment we are here, we are together, and you are safe. You don't have to face things by yourself. We need to turn on the heating up here, and then you can show me the attic.'

She turned on the radiators in her room and his, found some clean sheets, and they made up the bed for him.

'What about Oxford?' she asked. 'Don't you need to be back there in the morning?'

'Not tomorrow at least. I don't actually do a lot there. There is research for my PhD, which is now nearly finished, and some tutoring, and marking assignments and exam papers. But there are always other graduates needing a bit of extra cash to do the tutoring, so I don't do as much now. I really only keep the room there so I can get away from living with my father, but with you at Hayward I wanted to come home more often, so I dropped the teaching as much as I could. It goes with the room. If you want a room and you are not an undergraduate then you're a tutor, and you need to teach. I don't need the money; I don't spend much, what I earn pays for the room, and my father gives me an allowance. I don't even need that, as I have some money of my own that my grandmother left to me.

'I need to be at Oxford on Mondays, Tuesdays and Wednesdays. I usually teach one class on Thursday, but Professor Hanson said he would look after that one if it made it easier. I can catch the train from here until we sort something out. Or I can drive instead. It may be faster with the motorway going the whole way now, and I would be going in the opposite direction to the worst of the traffic. I will need to leave here really early, but we can cope with that.

'When Mary phoned the college to ask if they could give me a message to call home urgently, I was with Professor Hanson, whom you met. We were discussing extra classes for some of the students. He told me to call from the phone in his study. Since he heard my part of the conversation, I told him that the ward had run away from home, and I needed to go after you. When he asked couldn't my father do that, I thought about it and decided to tell him that my father had asked you to marry him, and you had fled the house. I told him I felt it was my responsibility to ensure that you were safe. He was a bit shocked, and I know Mary would be cross with me for telling him, but at least that way I had him on my side. He couldn't refuse to let me go, and I think he realised that if he didn't give me some leeway, I would have quit Oxford altogether. He gets a bit annoyed about people having private lives, he thinks they should just be either students or dons with no life outside of the college, but he does have some concern for us all. I am to call him tomorrow to let him know you are safe and to tell him if I need someone else to take all my classes next week, but I should manage the three days.

'Apart from going to Oxford three days a week, I can stay here as long as you want me to. In any case there are only two weeks left of this term. After that I don't need to be back there until late April. We will have sorted things out by then.'

'Do you still walk in your sleep,' she asked, remembering what he had said, for she had also been a sleepwalker. She wondered if it ran in families.

'I don't think so, not for years. I would wander around at night, and then wake up somewhere strange. My grandmother always closed the gate at night so if I went outside, I could go no further than the garden. It was actually quite frightening, waking up somewhere and having no idea where you were or how you got there. Once I woke up outside the house, on the path in the wood. There was no moon, and I didn't recognise where I was in the dark, so I found a bench and stayed there all night, and it was very, very cold because I was just in pyjamas and bare feet. I would have been nine. In the morning, when they realised I was missing, they all came out looking for me and my father found me. I was right at the end of the wood, near the standing stone. It was nearly winter, and still quite dark. He wrapped me in his jacket and carried me back to the house because I had no shoes on, and that was the only time ever that I thought he did actually care about me.'

Jane thought that was a terribly sad thing for him to say. Her own father had always treated her as though she was the most precious thing in the world to him.

'I used to walk in my sleep too, but only after my parents died. I would get up and walk around the house. Sometimes I would do something strange and then go back to bed, but in the morning I would have forgotten what I had done. Usually I took things out of cupboards and put them somewhere else, so things often became lost. But then a few days later, sometimes weeks later, I would suddenly remember where the missing things were. Something would jog my memory, and I would recall in perfect detail getting up in the night and moving the things, and I would even remember the twisted logic of why I had moved them. My great-aunt thought it was the diazepam that made me sleepwalk, but I don't know if that was true because most times I didn't know when I had sleepwalked, I only remembered that I had.'

The bed was made, and she showed him the rooms in the attic, now full of old furniture and pictures and clothes, tennis racquets and ice skates, musty books, old lamps and shabby suitcases. A furtive flash of movement in a corner of the room made her jump, but it was only her own reflection in a dusty mirror.

They went back downstairs and Ryan phoned Mary to tell her they had both reached Richmond safely. Then he fetched his bag and Jane's suitcase from his car, and he left her to unpack her things while he unpacked his. She knew this could not last forever, but she was very glad he was here. If Daniel turned up on her doorstep, she would have Ryan to protect her.

It was now past nightfall; the last of the daylight had gone. They went out intending to eat at the café, but came back with fish and chips instead and a bottle of wine.

She found plates and glasses, laid the table perfectly in the dining room with the best linen and the best silver, and she even found some candles, stored in the kitchen for use in power cuts. She had set the places at either end of the table, but he asked if she would mind if he moved them so they were opposite each other across the table and much closer. They ate their fish and chips by candlelight.

'We were to go out to dinner on Saturday,' he reminded her again, rather sadly. 'I was looking forward to having you to myself for the evening. You once offered me a reward for taking you out to dinner. But now it has all become a lot more complicated.'

'Perhaps you could think in Latin,' she said, remembering what Candy had once told her. He looked at her blankly, and she realised he didn't know what she meant.

'Candy said you once told her you sometimes think in Latin and it makes life seem less complicated. After you helped her, Latin became her favourite subject.'

'Did it? I'm flattered. Yes, I do recall saying that. It was only to amuse her. I don't often think in Latin, except perhaps when I write out a valentine card.'

Jane remembered the *te amo*. 'Do you send a lot of valentines?'

'No. I have only ever sent one. I am a hopeless failure at valentine cards because the lady I sent it to knew straight away that it was from me. They are supposed to be a mystery. There you see, Jane, you are laughing. I have cheered you up.'

She understood what he meant about life becoming more complicated. She had not forgotten that she had promised him a kiss for taking her out to dinner—knowing that he remembered that sent a little quiver of excitement through her heart—but now anything between her and Ryan would mean disappointment and jealousy for Daniel. And she knew that Ryan would never try to take advantage of her while they were here together.

For the remainder of the evening, they sat close together on the sofa in the lounge, going through the photo albums from her childhood while she told him about the life her father had led after he had left Hayward.

'I felt very rejected when your father left us,' he told her. 'I was only a small child, and he had always been there for me in a way that my father never was. When I was older, I understood why he had left. There are some things that no man could ever forgive. I wanted to get back in touch with him, talk to him instead of just hearing news from his letters to Mary, but I could never face the memory of the day he left, and I thought he might want to talk about it. When he died, I was very sorry that I had never phoned him. I will regret it for the rest of my life. I like to think he would be glad if he knew that you and I are friends now. When your mother first came to stay with us at Hayward, when I was six, I thought she was a princess because she had long yellow hair. He told me he wanted to marry her, and I said I wanted to as well. So he told me I wasn't old enough, but if he married her, they might have a little princess, and she could be my princess when I grew up.'

She laughed. It sounded just like her father to say that. 'He always called my mother his princess,' she told Ryan. But she still wondered what had happened to make him leave.

'Daniel has that picture on his desk.' He indicated a photograph of her mother at about the same age as Jane, wearing a dusty-blue suit and a matching blue felt hat with a feather in the band. She was standing in front of Hayward Hall. 'You are the image of her. I saw that hat hanging on a peg up in the attic, so we could do a photo of you looking the same. You would just need to change your hairstyle a bit. We'll get it copied, and we can take the copy back with us and work out exactly where it was taken.'

There were photographs of Pat and Ryan in her father's album. Jane had seen the pictures before, but had not known who they were of. She had scarcely even thought about it. Mary had sent them, and her father had put them in the album, but he had never talked about them, and she had never asked. There was the same graduation photo of Ryan that was on the wall in Mary's sitting room, and a photo of Ryan at twelve, with the border collie puppy Wolf, the same photo that was on her wall in his grandmother's old room at Hayward. Jane had known that she had seen both photographs before. She found a photo of herself with the white rabbit Muffin to show him her childhood pet.

There was a photo of her parents on holiday in Switzerland with a man Ryan immediately recognised as Robert Phillips. She recalled Robert telling her at Christmas that her parents had visited him each year when they were in Switzerland.

Ryan was putting her family on his family tree, and he took down some notes on names and dates for her mother, her great-aunt, the brothers who had died In the First World War and her grandfather. He would look them up at the General Register Office in the next few days.

Eventually they had their cocoa and went to bed, Jane finding it strange to be back in her old bed in her old home, yet feeling as though she no longer belonged here. Hayward Hall was her real home, and now she was exiled from it. It was terribly unfair of Daniel. He was making her choose between marrying him and living at Hayward, or being banished from the house and the life she had made for herself there. Everything had been fine as it was. Why couldn't it have just stayed that way?

It was also strange having Ryan sleeping only a few yards from her instead of up on the forbidden top floor of the house. She felt safe with him. She would never have trusted his father sleeping so close to her. His door was shut, but she liked to sleep with hers ajar. She wondered where the cat would sleep tonight at Hayward Hall.

Friday 27 February 1976

In the morning she cooked the porridge for Ryan, but made toast for herself as she was not a fan of porridge. He ground the coffee in the wooden grinder, and she was reminded that he did things that needed strength with his left hand.

There was so much she didn't know about him. He had come and gone at Hayward, and she was always glad to see him when he was home, had looked forward to him returning each weekend, and the days without him always seemed longer and bleaker than those when he was there. He had always been very kind to her, and she liked his company even though he was often silent. It was good just to have him there with her. She liked to walk with him, sit with him, tell him things that made him laugh, and she knew she was in love with him. Yet he always seemed completely self-sufficient. Mary had once told her that she didn't think he had ever had a girlfriend, he was just not interested in girls. She had wished that he would be interested in her, and sometimes she had thought he was, but he had never said anything. But then Mary had said she thought he was in love with her. He had sent her a valentine that was now on the mantelpiece in her bedroom. That evening he had held her hand at the cinema, and last Sunday they had walked together in a wood, and she had felt very close to him, had felt that they were lovers.

As she sat across the table from him, she again imagined him kissing her in the garden at Hayward Hall on a warm summer day, lost in the maze, the sun on their faces, her hands in his hair. She knew that if it had been him wanting her instead of Daniel, she might have said yes. But Daniel had said he was gay, that he was unable to sleep with a girl, and it nagged at her. Was it just spite on Daniel's part? She didn't like to ask Ryan if it was true. You could perhaps ask a man if he was gay, now that being gay was no longer a crime, but you couldn't ask the other thing. Was that why he was always so controlled and aloof? Was she just spinning dreams of an impossible future?

She recalled Martin's mother telling her that Ryan and Martin had spent the summer going off by themselves to get away from the girls, and Martin had said they had swum together nude in the lake. Perhaps they both were gay. Could he still love her if he was? Could a man be both?

After breakfast a box was delivered for Miss Jane Walters, red roses and a card with *Please come back to me.* Jane put the flowers in water and put the card on the mantelpiece. It was troubling, she was not sure what she should do, but at least Ryan was here with her.

She said she hated to think what the credit card balance would be this month with all the roses, but Ryan said the cost would be nothing compared to what Daniel spent when he was in London. He had plenty of money, and she should enjoy the roses. The fragrance was beautiful. Red roses always had the best scent.

He picked up the card she had put on the mantelpiece and asked her if she minded him altering it. On the back he wrote *For my beautiful Wild Rose, with love from the Lone Wolf.*

He drew a little heart with *te amo* inside it. Then he added, in his neat spidery hand, *Forever thou art mine only true love.*

'There, you see, I sent the roses to you. Now you can enjoy them totally free from guilt. They didn't cost me anything.'

She laughed; she knew he meant her to laugh. She took the card from him, and for a moment she looked at him, meeting his eyes, wondering if he really was just trying to amuse her, or if this was his way of letting her know he loved her.

He phoned Professor Hanson to say Jane was fine, he was with her in Richmond, and he would be in to teach his classes next week.

He helped her to do the shopping so there was something for dinner. He would take her out on Saturday evening, but tonight they would dine at home.

Then he went into the city to have lunch with Mr Allanstone. Mary had arranged it. He would have taken Jane with him, but she needed some time to recover, and she knew that Ryan wanted to talk to him about Daniel and what they could do to sort things out.

She went up to the attic and found the hat. It was a schoolgirl style, with a faded pheasant's feather in the band.

She phoned Sarah and explained she was back in Richmond for shopping, and Ryan was staying with her. Sarah immediately asked them both to dinner the following evening. She knew Tony would be glad to see Ryan, and she was dying to hear what Jane had been up to.

How long was she back here for? Jane thought a week, maybe longer. Had she liked it at Hayward? Jane said yes. Was she going to marry Ryan? Jane said no. Were they dating, then? Jane said no. Was she in love with him? But Jane didn't say no to this. She said she thought perhaps she was. Was he in love with her? Jane said no, he doesn't like girls much. Sarah told her that makes him a challenge. Had the older man behaved well? Jane recalled Sarah had predicted he might make a pass at her, and she had been proven right, but Jane just said yes, he had behaved well enough. She didn't want to talk about it, even to Sarah.

Jane took the photo of her mother with her to the hairdresser, who trimmed her hair a little at the sides and curled it under, creating a style that was a remarkably good copy of it. The hairdresser told Jane the style was called a pageboy, and it had been very popular in the fifties. To maintain it she would need to curl the ends under when she set her hair after she washed it. Between washes she could keep it perfect with an electric curling wand and a touch of hair spray. If she wanted to flick the ends of the side sections back the other way, she would have a modern shag hairstyle.

She then took the picture to a photographer to be copied, arranging to pick it up on Monday. They were happy to copy the print, as she was not sure where to even start looking for the negative. Perhaps there was no negative. It may have been printed from a colour slide as she knew some of her father's early ones were. There were boxes of slides, but it would take her a long time to go through them.

Ryan was back when she returned to the house—she had given him a key—and he told her that Mr Allanstone sent his regards and would have loved to have seen her.

He had bought an electric kettle that turned off automatically when it boiled. He wasn't keen on gas, and he was used to having a kettle that looked after itself; he was worried with the gas that he would go away and forget he had put the kettle on.

He made coffee for them both in the cafetière, cut some more of the fruit cake, and they sat at the table in the kitchen to eat their afternoon tea. He noticed her hair was different and said it looked very like the photograph, and she told him she had found the hat.

'Sarah and Tony asked us to dinner tomorrow night,' she told him. 'I accepted, as I thought you would like to talk to Tony again. I hope that was all right. You had wanted us to go out together.'

'Yes, of course it's all right. We can go out together any time.'

She felt rather relieved. She didn't want him to think she was trying to avoid going on a date with him.

He said he had phoned home while she was still out and had spoken to Pat about him encouraging her to marry Daniel. Pat had sent his apologies.

'Pat said he had felt bad about it afterwards. It was his own idea. He could see my father was crazy about you, and he thought you might persuade Daniel to buy him the car he wants. He also recalled that he had said something else to you that he particularly regretted because you had taken it rather badly. He wouldn't tell me what it was, but he knew you would remember, and he was very sorry he had said it.'

Jane was not sure she should tell Ryan what Pat had said. But she did, as there was no point in hiding why Pat had upset her. 'He said that if I married your father, I could have an affair with you on the sly, and you would enjoy getting your revenge. I don't think I will ever forgive him for thinking I would treat you or Daniel like that.'

'I don't think I will either. Pat is rather selfish and sometimes thoughtless, but he means no harm. He and I grew up together, and we understand each other. You haven't been treated very well at Hayward, by Pat or my father.'

'At least you have always treated me with kindness and respect. I can understand your father falling for me when I remind him of a lost love and I am so much in his company, but I expected better than that from Pat, especially as only that morning he had been swearing he loved me and he wanted us to run away together. I didn't believe him when he said you would like having the extra money as well. I know you would never have said that. But he was right about your father being in love with me, and I hadn't realised that then. He had seen it, although I hadn't. But it was several weeks ago, and I have got over it. I don't want you and Pat to fall out over me, or you and your father.'

'Jane, if I thought you loved my father and wanted to marry him, I would cope with it, although I could never be happy about it. I know he would treat you well, and I know he really does love you, or at least he believes he does. I would even have coped with you marrying Pat if that was what you wanted, although I would have done my best to talk you out of it. You would be wasted on him, since he thinks of no one but himself. I could not have been best man for either of them though. I would have stayed in Oxford and never returned to Hayward.'

Pat had wanted her for her money, and Daniel wanted her for her body. Perhaps one day Ryan would want her because he loved her. He had told Pat he was smitten with her, he talked as if he was smitten with her, and he had written on the card that she was his true love.

'I promise I am not marrying either of them,' she said, meeting his gaze, 'so you don't need to be exiled.'

He told her then that he had asked Mr Allanstone about the train crash. Peter and Josie would have died instantly, as they were in the first carriage behind the engine when the train hit the collapsed earth in the tunnel. Robert Phillips had identified them, and had arranged for them to be returned home so Allanstone didn't need to leave England and could be there for Jane and her great-aunt. Her parents had visited Robert each year when they went to Switzerland. He had been her father's best friend as they grew up. Allanstone had given Ryan the phone number for Robert so Jane could phone him if she ever wanted to talk about it.

Ryan gave her a hug; he always knew when she needed to be hugged. It felt good to have him looking after her. She wished she could do something for him.

'Thank you for asking for me. I do feel much better knowing that. I will talk to Robert at Christmas. I should feel more able to talk about it by then.'

They went for a walk around the block, a chilly wind whipping at their hair, and he sat in the kitchen while she cooked the dinner, helping where he could by finding the plates and cutlery.

After dinner there was a phone call from Daniel, but she let Ryan answer it and relay the messages to her. He sent his humble apologies and would be grateful if she would return to Hayward Hall. He hadn't wanted her to leave, he wanted her back, and he was sorry that he had upset her. He would never mention marriage to her again and would accept any other conditions she cared to make. He wanted to be allowed to talk to her himself. He could even drive over and talk to her tomorrow if she wanted him to.

She asked Ryan what Daniel meant by conditions.

'Mary has suggested that he agree never to talk to you like that again, to keep his hands to himself, never to be alone in a room with you with the door closed, that sort of thing. Will you talk to him? Don't agree to him driving over here, as he may have a whisky or two before he leaves home and be over the limit.'

Jane didn't want to talk to him, but she gave Ryan a wicked look and asked him to thank Daniel for the roses. Next he asked if she would talk to him if he phoned again tomorrow, and she eventually agreed to talk to him in a few days' time.

She returned to the kitchen and the washing up, but it was several minutes before Ryan hung up the phone and joined her.

'We would all like you back,' he told her. 'We can stay here for a week or two while you think about it.'

'After that will you go home?' she asked, rather disappointed.

'Not unless you want me to. I am quite happy to live here with you for as long as you'll have me. Forever if you want. I can easily find something to do. London is full of libraries and museums, and I can do some research at the university here and the General Register Office. I could get a job somewhere close to here, and you could go back to your job at the bank or do a course—accounting perhaps as you are good with numbers.

'If you decide you don't want to return to Hayward and you prefer to stay living here by yourself, then that's okay as well. I can go back to live in Oxford at any time. Although it would be good if I could still come and see you on weekends, or at least keep in touch. I would like us always to stay friends. Even if you do agree to go back, we can make my father wait for a while. If he has few days without you, he will come to appreciate you more, and it will encourage him to behave.

'You said we are dining with Sarah and Tony tomorrow evening. Would you like to have coffee tomorrow morning in that little café where we sat in January? I really enjoyed that day. It changed the way I thought about what I wanted to do with my life. We could spend the afternoon looking around Kew Gardens. We were only in the greenhouses last time. Or we can take some flowers to the cemetery. Next week you can do some shopping while I'm in Oxford, and next weekend we can do some sightseeing. We can enjoy ourselves for a while before you make up your mind.'

He spent the remainder of the evening sketching out the family trees for both their families to show her how they were connected through Peter. Coincidentally both Peter and Josie had two uncles killed in the First World War and a father killed in the Second World War. Ryan and Jane both had a great-aunt who was a nurse, although Ryan's great-aunt, Jane's grandmother, had been killed in the Blitz.

He had put Jane's mother Josie near the centre of the page, next to Peter from his side of the family, and he drew a dashed line between them to show they were married, then a line down for Jane. It did make it easy for Jane to see how they were connected. Grace Linden, her father's mother, had been the sister of James Linden, Daniel's father. Grace had married Edwin Walters, Jane's paternal grandfather, and Peter was their only child. Ryan didn't know much about the Walters' side of the family and neither did Jane. Aunt Ellen had been her mother's aunt.

Ryan drew a small picture of a wolf below his entry on the family tree and a rose below Jane's.

Saturday 28 February 1976

The following morning they sat in the café at the same table by the window, remembering the time they had sat there in January. It was much busier today because it was a Saturday. Yet in spite of the people coming and going, she still felt there were only the two of them in the world. She had enjoyed that day with Ryan, playing truant from Daniel, sitting for the whole morning in the café, thinking she belonged with him. That was the day she had first realised she was a little in love with him, and she had wondered if he thought the same way about her. Last night he had said that day had changed the way he thought about his life, so perhaps he had fallen in love with her as she had with him.

They talked about things they would do in the summer. They would spend an afternoon with Martin and Luke, and there were other open houses they could visit. He would hire a boat and row her on the river. They could walk around the colleges at Oxford again, and they could go further afield if she wanted, stay for a few days in Wales or Scotland, follow some hiking trails, ride on a steam train, even spend a weekend in Paris. He was weaving dreams for her of a life where the two of them were together, but he didn't say he was in love with her. She knew he wouldn't say that because he was here to look after her, and he wouldn't want her to feel he was taking advantage of her when she was vulnerable. She wished she could tell him that she was in love with him, but perhaps he knew that without her saying it, as he often seemed to know what she was thinking.

In the afternoon they took flowers to the cemetery where her parents and her great-aunt were buried. It was sunny, and the graves with their white marble and bright flowers were so peaceful that she found she could cope. How could she be sad in such a tranquil place? Her life in Richmond seemed long ago, and her life in Kent seemed in the distant past. She was the only one left who remembered the years she had lived there.

It helped to have Ryan standing beside her with his hand holding hers, and she hoped that if her father could see them from the life beyond, he would be glad they were there together.

The dinner with Sarah and Tony went well. It was easy walking distance, and they arrived with flowers for Sarah and a bottle of port for Tony. They had steak and salad for dinner, and raspberry souffles in small ramekins. All way beyond Jane's cooking skills, but she enjoyed everything except the worry that she could not match this if she invited them back.

Jane and Sarah left the men to sit in the lounge with their port, talking about school, while they took the dishes from the dining room to the kitchen. Sarah's house, although similar in age and original layout to Jane's, had been altered to be much more open plan, with french doors between the lounge and the dining room and a hatch to the kitchen, so you could sit in the lounge and see right through the house to the kitchen window and out to the back garden. The house had the same three bedrooms on the first floor, but there were two bathrooms on that level and another one on the top level for the two attic bedrooms. It was Tony's stepmother's house. When she had married Tony's father, she had moved in with him, leaving her own house available for Tony and Sarah.

Sarah lent Jane a pinny, and Jane rinsed the plates before Sarah stacked them in the dishwasher. It was like old times when Jane had stayed there, sleeping in one of the attic rooms.

'Ryan is a real dream. He is just so good looking. I hope you're going to marry him.'

'I don't know,' said Jane. 'I like him but I don't think he likes girls very much, and I'm not sure he's the marrying sort. He is always very independent and self-sufficient.'

'But you would have him if he asked?'

'Yes, I think I would. I would like him for a boyfriend first. I hadn't really thought about marrying him. Sarah, they may be listening to us.'

'I turned the extract fan on,' Sarah assured her. 'They won't hear what we are saying over that. It's obvious he likes you, just by the way he looks at you.'

'Not like he is mentally undressing me, I hope.'

'No, Jane, not like that, more like an adoring puppy. If you glance back, you will see that he changed where he was sitting so he can look through the dining room and see you in here.'

'Jane, I wish you had come to the Swiss school with us when we finished school here. I know it was because you wanted to do sixth form and you liked to spend the weekends with your aunt, but I really missed you. Some of the other girls were so snooty. They joke about those schools only teaching you to fold dinner napkins, and make canapés, and walk with a book on your head, but we learnt so much more there about men, not just at the school but from each other.

'We learnt how to recognise a man making a pass at you, how to avoid getting into situations where things get out of control, how to drink slowly and keep count of drinks so you don't get drunk. And we learnt how to be sexy in a subtle way, how to seduce a guy without being too forward. You may have to encourage him a bit. Touch him sometimes, as if by accident.'

'Touch him? Touch him where?'

'No, Jane, not that. That's only when you are very intimate with a man, and there's no going back if you do that. It says *I want sex, now right now*. No, much more subtle than that. Brush the back of his hand with the back of yours when you're walking next to him, lean against him if you're sitting beside him in a train, flick an imaginary ladybird off his jacket lapel, look into his eyes when you talk to him, flatter him, ask his opinion about things. Dancing is the best thing; it really breaks the ice. Next weekend we can all go out for dinner somewhere where they have dancing. When you dance with a man, it's just the two of you in your own space, and you can get right up close against him, and no one can think you forward. Men enjoy being really close to a girl they fancy. And you need to wear something sexy, not those boring midi skirts. Have you got a little black dress?'

'No,' said Jane, 'not any black dress except the suit I wore at the funeral, and that's still at Hayward.'

'Jane, come to the boutique on Monday. I work there on Mondays. I'll fix you up with something that's top class but still very sexy. Not too skimpy because that isn't you, but we'll find something that suits. We have some new wrap dresses in black silk jersey that would be perfect. And you'll need silk pyjamas, there's nothing quite like silk when you're in bed with a man, except no pyjamas at all, of course. We don't sell pyjamas, but Selfridges or Harrods will have them. Pyjamas are much sexier than a nightdress. It's more of a challenge for a man to get them off you.

'That's the dishes loaded, so now we'll make coffee. He's still watching you. I expect he is wondering what I am saying to you, whether we are talking about him and why you are laughing so much. Jane, don't lead him on unless you really do want him. A deep quiet man like him will get badly hurt if you love him then change your mind. He won't want a casual affair. Some men only care about the physical pleasure side of it, and don't care if it's casual, and some men just want the thrill of conquest and seduce a girl then lose interest, but most men get far more enjoyment from making love when they know the girl chose them over the other guys, and cares about them enough to want to sleep with them.'

Jane and Ryan walked home just before midnight, the air cold and the sky clear and bright with stars. He didn't ask her for a kiss goodnight and she didn't offer, but she couldn't help a feeling of disappointment.

Sunday 29 February 1976

On Sunday morning they went to the church in Richmond so Jane could talk to the vicar who had buried her great-aunt, and to her great-aunt's friends. She told them she loved living at Hayward, and everything was going well there. Ryan had come back with her for a few days while she did some shopping in London. They remembered him from the funeral, and were all delighted to meet him again. No one asked whether they were staying alone together in the house, but she knew some of them would have been thinking about it.

After the service Ryan helped her light three candles, two for Peter and Josie who had died in darkness, and one for her great-aunt.

'I've forgiven her for trying to keep you away from me. I know she meant well, and she was right about my father, so she deserves a candle.'

She met his eyes above the tiny points of flame, amazed as she always was at how kind he was to her, how well he knew how to make her feel better.

'Ryan, thank you for being so good to me,' she whispered, not wanting to disturb the quiet timelessness of the church. For hundreds of years people had lit candles here for their precious dead, tiny lights to connect them with the souls of those in the shadows of the unknowable world beyond ours.

'Thank you, Jane, for always making me feel glad that you and I are both alive and both here together.'

In the afternoon Tony and Sarah came over and helped Ryan tidy up the garden. Tony had been working on it occasionally, but it needed a spruce up. They had arranged this the previous evening when Jane and Sarah were in the kitchen. The girls helped where they could, and they had coffee and angel cake for afternoon tea.

Tony recalled how much they had enjoyed cricket at school on lazy summer days, sitting on the benches with the other boys, waiting for their turn to bat, or standing by themselves on the field in the warmth of the sun, hoping for the ball to come their way so they could make a miraculous catch and be the hero of the day.

'We all loved cricket, but in the winter we played rugby, and we hated it. You end the game wet, freezing cold, battered and bruised, and covered in mud. And the showers at school were always running out of hot water. Not my idea of a good time, being covered in mud and only a lukewarm shower in a freezing changeroom to wash it off.'

Ryan invited Tony to spend a Saturday at Hayward in the summer. He could join in the cricket, Sarah could talk to Jane about knitting, and they could stay overnight. He knew Mary wouldn't mind.

Jane was secretly a little worried about whether they could keep Daniel sober enough to safely entertain friends. She would need to insist he came along to play cricket, or at least watch the game with her, so he was not alone all afternoon with no one between him and the decanter. She realised that she was assuming she would return to Hayward, but she knew that in the end she would return. It was her home now.

Daniel phoned again on Sunday evening, spoke to Ryan for a while, and this time she agreed to speak to him. He apologised for having upset her, promised he would never do so again, told her he accepted that she didn't want to marry him, he would learn to live with that. He and Mary were both missing her. Ryan had told him off for not treating her with the respect she deserved and so had Mary, and he had been given a list that Mary had drawn up with help from Ryan. He promised that he would never be alone with her in a room unless the door was open, he would never touch her again, he would never say anything that he wouldn't say if Mary was in the room, he would never get closer to her than she allowed, and he would only have his two permitted whiskies a day and never in the morning.

He said he missed her, he could no longer live without her, the sunshine was gone from his life, he would do anything to have her back, anything she wanted. The bills needed to be paid, the banking done, she was part of their life now, and they couldn't manage without her. Even the cat was wandering around dejected, looking for her. Ryan had agreed to stay every night at Hayward Hall if that made her feel safer. It was close enough for him to go into Oxford by train each day.

She told him she needed a few days to think about it, made him promise he would not come here after her, and she passed the phone back to Ryan. She didn't listen to what they were saying. She went into the kitchen and washed the dishes, worried that he was still obsessed with her, that nothing would change.

When Ryan came back to the kitchen, he had a message for her. His father had said he would write out the hundred lines.

Jane laughed. She couldn't help it. If Daniel wasn't such a predator, he would be fun to have around.

'What was he to write?' Ryan asked her.

She wasn't sure whether to tell him, but in the end she did.

'*I must not touch Jane's pussy*. It was his idea, not mine. I was puzzled at first because I thought he meant the cat. I had never heard the word used like that before, but then I guessed what he meant. He said he would write out the lines, or perhaps I could type it for him, and he would sign it. But then he said you would have to sign it for him like you do the cheques, and then you would know he had got into trouble. Your father can be very funny at times, but he shouldn't have touched me where he did. He jokes about it, but he knows I don't like it. He deliberately dropped a letter so I had to bend down and pick it up from under the desk.'

She had expected him to be amused, but she could see he was shocked.

'He shouldn't be talking to you like that, or groping you. If you had told me at the time, I would have flattened him.'

'Please don't fight over me. He doesn't mean any harm, and I don't mind him joking, but I don't like him touching me. He knows I don't like it, but he does it anyway. That was why he sent me the flowers on Valentine's Day, to apologise. The week after that he asked me to go upstairs with him to his room, and he said something else that was a bit sleazy about young women being beautiful without their clothes. He said it feels much better for the man if the woman enjoys it. I do ask him not to talk to me the way he does. I suppose I should be firmer with him, but I'm not very good at that.'

'Jane, he is the one in the wrong, not you. It is disgraceful for him to be talking to you like that. You are a bit of a church mouse, a beautiful church mouse, but that is all the more reason for him to leave you alone.'

'I'm sorry if I'm just a mouse. I do try to keep him in control. Sarah would tell me I should slap his face, but I know I could never do that.' She was rather hurt that he thought her a mouse.

'Jane, I love you being a mouse. It makes me feel safe.'

She looked at him, thinking at first that he was joking, then realising he really did mean it.

'I'm glad you don't behave like he does so I can feel safe with you. Do you really think I should go back? If you are in love with someone, I don't think that it would be easy to suddenly stop thinking of them in that way. Sometimes older men do go crazy over younger girls. Would I be torturing him just by being there when he knows I don't want to marry him?'

'Pat and I manage to live in the house with you without harassing you, and I am sure he can. I have talked this over with Mary and neither of us knows what to do for the best. Allanstone thought you should stay here, and we shouldn't trust Daniel, but I don't think that is what Mary was hoping for. She has loved having you with us. We all have. You are part of our family.'

'Have you told Mr Allanstone? Oh dear!'

'Mary suggested I talk to him, as she has great faith in his judgement. I haven't had a lot to do with him before this, as he was my father's friend rather than mine. They were best friends at school. He seems to know a lot about us. Mary must talk to him at times, as he knew things that I know my father would never have told him.'

Jane recalled the telephone list with John and two phone numbers, one London and one Kent. That would have to be Mr Allanstone, so not the friend Mary visited. She must know her friend's number by heart, as there had been no one else on the list who was unaccounted for.

'He told me he thinks of me as a nephew and you as a niece. He had a daughter who died a few hours after she was born, and he always imagines his daughter might have grown up like you. He said your father understood that. He would have taken you to live with him when your parents died if your great-aunt had not been able to look after you, and if the age was still twenty-one, he would now be your legal guardian, as that had been in your great-aunt's will. He does care about you. When he suggested you stay with us for a couple of months after your aunt died, he never imagined you wouldn't be safe with us. He never understood why your great-aunt disliked my father so much, and I didn't enlighten him. He thought it would be good for you to have Pat and me for company, and he knew Mary would look after you. He wanted you to have some family around you, and he hoped it would help you to become a little more independent, so you had the confidence to return here to live if that was what you wanted. He was concerned if you stayed here after your great-aunt died, you would marry the first man who asked you so you didn't need to live by yourself.'

'He was right, you did all help me. It was what I needed, and I was getting over losing Aunt Ellen. I loved being part of your family at Hayward, and if your father had treated me properly, I would have stayed. And I didn't marry the first man who asked me, or the second.'

'I hope the third man will be luckier.'

He looked at her in his amused way, and she wondered if he meant he wanted to be the third man, but she said nothing and he continued.

'Allanstone said if we need his help with anything, he can come over and talk to us one evening, or we can phone him. He gave me his home number. He said if you are not happy at Hayward, and don't want to be here at Richmond by yourself, you are welcome to live in his house in Kent. But he is only there on Sundays, so you would still be by yourself most of the time. During the week he lives in a flat near to where he works, and the flat is too small for more than one. For the moment I am here with you, and he is happy with that. But if it doesn't work out, and you don't want to live here alone, he will help you arrange something better. He said he could move to a larger flat so you can live with him if you wanted that, or he could buy you a flat in the same building as his so you were independent but he was close by. He thought you might be all right by yourself in a flat where there were no past memories to cope with.

'What would you like to do with the remainder of the evening? Do you have a chess set?'

She played chess with him, but her mind wasn't on the game and he easily beat her. She was thinking about his comment on the third man being luckier.

6 DARK SECRETS

Monday 1 March 1976

On Monday morning Ryan drove to Oxford, promising to be back by six that evening. He had offered to take her with him, telling her she could sit in his room at the college, or in the library, or wander around the town and the shops, and then come back with him. But she thought she would manage by herself during the day. Daniel had promised not to come to Richmond, and he didn't know that Ryan would be spending the day in Oxford. Mrs Brennan would be here for most of the morning, and Jane intended to shop in the afternoon.

She had set her alarm to get up very early to cook the porridge for him. It was the least she could do when he had been so good to her. She had dressed first, as by now she was used to never going downstairs in pyjamas.

Mrs Brennan came at nine to do the cleaning, and she seemed pleased to see Jane. They enjoyed a cup of tea together, chatting about Aunt Ellen, before she got to work on the vacuuming.

Straight after lunch Jane took the train into the city for shopping, picking up the photos on her way to the station.

She went to the boutique where Sarah worked, and bought a beautiful black silk jersey wrap dress, sleeveless and figure hugging, not too low cut and not too short. The overlap in the front allowed room to move when she danced, while the skirt kept its beautiful flared A-line. She also bought a sleeveless summer dress, the mid-length skirt with gathered layers of fabric in different floral patterns, and lace and ribbons, all in shades of blue, the dress fastening down the front with small pearl buttons. She found a blue lacy silk cardigan to wear over it on chilly days. It felt good to be thinking about summer clothes.

Sarah offered to drop the bags back at her house on her way home from work that evening, as Jane had other shopping to do.

Next she needed shoes to go with the black dress. She bought some strappy black leather platform shoes, high enough to look glamorous, but not so high that she would risk breaking her ankle if she danced in them.

She found a dusty-blue suit that matched the colour of the felt hat, a white silk blouse to wear with it, a blue Liberty scarf with a William Morris pattern, and two sets of silk pyjamas, all from Harrods.

On her walk home from the train station, quite late in the afternoon, she passed a straw hat in a shop window in Richmond that she thought would go well with the summer dress. It had blue ribbons and lots of small lifelike flowers around the brim. It was the shop where she had bought the Fair Isle jumper when she had been here with Ryan in January. He had paid for it, and had thanked her for giving him a wonderful day. It had been a wonderful day for her as well. She had realised that day that she was in love with him.

Even without her purchases from the boutique where Sarah worked, she was carrying a lot of bags, so she returned to the house and left her new clothes in the hallway before returning to buy the hat.

She had often shopped at the Richmond boutique, and she stayed for a while to talk to the assistant, who recalled that she had come there a month or two back with a very attractive man.

But she needed to return home as Sarah would soon drop off her bags on her way home from work. As Jane made her way back to her house in the familiar street, she thought that in some ways it was nice to be back in Richmond.

Ryan came back as promised just before six. She was cooking, and it felt good to have a man coming home from work to her making dinner, especially when the man was him.

Her shopping bags were still in the hallway. Sarah had dropped off the dresses, and they had chatted for a few minutes, so she had not yet taken anything upstairs.

After dinner Ryan asked to see what she had bought, so she showed him the suit, the summer dress and the hat, but not the pyjamas. He said the dress and hat looked very pretty and romantic, making him think of a garden party or playing croquet on a lawn, and he would photograph her in the garden in that as well when the weather was warmer. He looked amused, and she asked him why he thought it was funny.

'Sorry,' he said. 'I was thinking something rather wicked.'

She wasn't sure what to make of that. It sounded a bit like he was making a pass at her. Not that she minded. She was perfectly happy for him to think wicked things about her, since she had once thought rather wicked things about him swimming naked in the lake. She knew she was safe with him.

She took the black dress from its bag and held it up against herself, her heart giving a nervous flutter as she wondered what he would think, what he would say.

'That looks a bit sinful, and not like you at all. Would you try it on and show me?'

She went upstairs, taking the shopping bags with her, and put on the wrap dress. One of the ties went through a slit in the waistband, so they could cross at the back then tie at the front. She found some tight navy-blue gym knickers, left over from school, to go over her tights in case her underwear showed if she bent over. She would have to buy something a bit sexier to wear under the dress. She mentally put tight black knickers on her shopping list. A black bra would be good too, in case a strap ever showed, perhaps even a push-up bra.

She brushed her hair, swept it up into a loose chignon and pinned it, the newly trimmed sides still loose around her face, giving a slightly shaggy look that she thought rather attractive. She redid her lipstick, checked that her eye makeup still looked good, put on the diamond pendant earrings that Daniel had given her, and the strappy black shoes, and gave a last look in the mirror. Her upswept hair showed off the earrings, and she thought the dress made her look surprisingly tall and slender. She rarely wore anything this close-fitting, and since she had first gone to Hayward Hall, she had never worn anything this short.

She walked slowly down the stairs, conscious that he was standing below her, hoping that the wrap skirt was not too revealing, although she knew it overlapped quite a lot, so at worst she would be showing a small amount of thigh. She wouldn't mind him seeing that, as she did have tights on, and she wanted him to think she looked sexy. She had never thought about looking sexy before—attractive and neat and elegant, perhaps, but not sexy. He cared for her, she knew that, and he had written romantic notes to her, he had even held her hand, but there was never any lust in the way he looked at her or treated her. Perhaps he kept it under impeccable control. Or perhaps he just didn't feel it. She knew she wanted him to feel it. She wanted him to make love to her.

He was standing in the doorway to the lounge, leaning against the jamb as he liked to do, waiting for her.

'You look amazing,' he said, still seeming amused, when she reached the bottom step. 'Not like the usual Jane at all. I've never seen you in anything before that showed your knees, and you look somewhat taller, nearly as tall as me. Those heels must be five inches at least. Is this the city-girl Jane? May I take you out to dinner tomorrow? Somewhere I can dance with you.'

'I was thinking we might ask Sarah and Tony out to dinner on Friday or Saturday, since we had dinner with them. I wouldn't be confident enough of my cooking to ask them here. But I am happy to go out just with you any time you want. I would like that. I wasn't sure if you would want to dance. I know you don't like girls.'

He laughed. 'Don't I? Who told you that? I like you, and you are very much a girl. I haven't had a string of girlfriends—in fact I can't actually recall any at all—but that doesn't mean I don't like girls. It just means I'm a lone wolf. I like my own company, and I enjoy being independent. I never really wanted a girlfriend, it seemed too complicated for me, and I wasn't sure I would know what to talk about. When I was younger, there were a couple of girls at Oxford that I liked the look of, but every time I thought about asking a girl out, I would remember that sooner or later you have to bring a girlfriend home to meet your father, and the thought of that was just too awful to contemplate.'

He was always laughing at her, so she never knew when to take him seriously. For a long moment she imagined bringing him home as a stranger to meet her parents, and she knew she would have been proud of her father and proud to be introducing a boyfriend like him. It was so unfair that they had died. Fathers were supposed to live long enough to meet their daughters' boyfriends, and walk their daughters down the aisle when they married.

'Your father is not that bad,' she told him. 'He is sober most of the time, and he looks respectable. You could warn the girlfriend not to get too close to him, and not to wear a short skirt.'

'I might find a girl who knows my father already, and then it wouldn't be a problem. I would enjoy dancing with you. We learnt at school, same as you did, so I might be a bit rusty. I have been out of school a good many years longer than you have.'

He held out his hands, and she came up close to him as if to dance with him, but not too close because she knew he didn't like it. Although he didn't seem to mind hugging her now, or sitting close beside her on the sofa. His hand on her back felt warm and deliciously thrilling through the thin silk, she could feel each of his fingers, and his other hand met hers, their palms and fingers touching in a soft caress. His face was very close to hers because the shoes had platform soles and were quite high.

Time paused its flow as she looked into his eyes, remembering them standing close together by the standing stone, hovering on the brink of eternity. Did he feel the same way about her as she felt about him? She had thought that day that he did, and she found herself wishing he would pull her right up close against him and kiss her. But of course he didn't. And he had warned her only moments ago that he didn't want a girlfriend.

There was a soft scent of sandalwood and citrus about him, and she recognised the same Taylor Sandalwood aftershave that her father had always worn. She touched his sleeve, slipping her hand up to his shoulder. It was thrilling to touch him, and she wished she had the courage to bury her fingers in his hair, wondered what he would do if she unfastened a button on his shirt. She knew he didn't like her too close to him, and she could feel that he was tense, nervous even, so perhaps she needed to be careful. She had once gone out with a young man whose hands were all over her, and she hadn't liked it. She didn't like Daniel touching her either, but she knew she wouldn't mind if Ryan did, provided he didn't get too personal too quickly.

'We could still go out by ourselves between now and Friday,' he suggested. 'I would need to bring my dinner suit here from Oxford. That dress deserves nothing less.'

He was still holding her, but not close up, his hand on her back, his fingers moving over the silk of the dress. Her hand was on his shoulder, and she moved her fingers as well. Would he feel it through the jacket? She slid her hand between his jacket and the waistcoat, her fingers reaching the warm white cotton of his shirt sleeve, caressing his shoulder. She wished he would hold her closer, she wanted to feel his body against hers, but she knew it had to come from him. It would be a mistake for her to get too close if he didn't want her to.

'You look very beautiful in that dress, Jane—I could stand here and look at you all night—but then you always look beautiful in everything you wear. Now go back up and change out of it. We still need to wash up the dishes.'

'Thank you,' she said very graciously. He had released her hand, but she lingered where she was, playing with one of his shirt buttons beneath his tie, wanting to stay here with him, wanting this all to go further. Much further.

His fingers touched her throat, gentle as a breath of air on a misty morning.

'You had a necklace in the photo.' It was a statement, yet it felt like a question.

'What photo?' She did not understand.

'I have it in my room. Allanstone sent it to Mary. You were at a school dance, in a dark-blue dress, looking totally beautiful. I had an enlargement made and hung it on my wall. Pat laughed about it, but my father liked it so much that he stole it. I came home one Saturday and it was gone. At first I thought Pat had taken it, and that was the closest we ever got to a row, but Mary guessed it had to be Daniel, and she found it hanging in his room. So I rowed with my father instead, and for once Mary backed me up. She gave him the smaller photo that Allanstone had sent—she put it in a frame for him—and he was happy with that. You were wearing a necklace on a ribbon. It looked very Victorian.'

'It was a pendant of my mother's. I don't have it here. Mary didn't pack the jewellery box with my case, so it is still at Hayward.'

'May I buy you something to wear with the dress?'

'That might not be proper.'

'Jane, who would know or care? This is the nineteen seventies, not the eighteen seventies. My father bought you the earrings.'

'They are beautiful, and it would be sad if I never wore them. I was happy at Christmas, when he gave them to me. He bought some for Mary, as well. Do you mind if I wear them when we go out to dinner?'

'No, of course not.'

'I will find a necklace to wear with the dress. There might be one with my great-aunt's things. I recall your father once told me about the photo. I thought it odd that you were arguing over a photo of me, when I hardly knew any of you.'

'We always felt that we knew you.'

She was about to turn and go upstairs, but she needed to know if what Daniel had said was true. She continued playing with his button, but not unfastening it as he still seemed tense, just caressing it with her finger. She was looking at his tie and not at his face, still so close to him that she felt surrounded by the scent of sandalwood. Her heart was beating nervously. She would never know unless she asked.

'Ryan, your father said you were gay. I don't mind if you are, we would still be friends, but I would prefer to know. It's only fair to me to know where I stand. He said that you didn't like girls and couldn't make love to a girl even if you wanted to.'

She was immensely relieved when he laughed. 'Holy socks! What a spiteful old devil he is! How low can you get? I never thought I'd see the day he was jealous of me over a lady, but I suppose it's always good to know who your enemies are. He has always thought I was gay, I know that. He once hired an escort for me, back when I was still at school, but I didn't want to sleep with her and I asked him not to do it again. He asked me then if I was gay, and said some pretty nasty things to make me feel I was inadequate to be his son, so perhaps he really does believe it. But I haven't answered your question. I am definitely not gay, and I would be happy to make love to you any time you want, with one condition.'

'What's the condition?' she asked him, rather intrigued at the way the conversation was heading and rather surprised at what he had said. He was usually rather shy. She stopped fiddling with the button and looked up at him, still trying to take in what he had said about Daniel being so awful to him. He was looking at her but no longer touching her, his gaze soft and his face still close to hers.

'It would have to be for real.'

'For real?' She was trying to interpret what he meant.

His fingers strayed to her face, lightly touching her cheek, and his eyes still held hers.

'Forever. You wanting me as much as I want you, and you caring for me as much as I care for you. I don't play games, and I don't want a casual affair, even with you. Especially with you. I would rather stay your friend than be your erstwhile lover. I'm not a teenager happy with a kiss and cuddle on a staircase, or behind a castle wall. Now please go up and change before this gets out of control. I can't think sensibly when you're this close, and I'm supposed to be looking after you. And be careful on the stairs with those shoes.'

She fled up the stairs, almost tripping over in her high heels, wishing he wasn't always laughing at her, but thinking perhaps he really was in love with her. He had said he cared for her, and he just needed her to commit to wanting him. She knew she did want him. But the reference to her kissing Pat on the staircase smarted. She knew he had never really forgiven her for that, and a part of her didn't blame him. How had he known about Jimmy kissing her at the castle? No one had been in sight. And how could Daniel have treated Ryan like that, trying to humiliate his own son, instead of supporting him, and telling her such spiteful lies?

She changed back to her usual skirt and jumper, hung the dress in the wardrobe, wishing she could hide under the bed and not go down and face him after what he had said about the castle. But she had no choice. She knew she had no choice.

She came back down to where he was waiting for her in the kitchen, ready to wash the dishes from dinner. She tried to stay dignified and keep things normal although she felt rather shaky. She asked him whether the traffic had been slow, had he got to Oxford on time, was the professor well, had they sorted out the students who needed extra help, had the tutorials gone okay, anything to keep away from the subject of her kissing Pat on the stairs, all the time knowing from his amused look that he was still laughing at her. But in the end she couldn't resist asking him about the castle. Who had told him that?

'The two young ladies who came with us in the car. I have spies in the camp, Jane. They asked me if you were my girlfriend, so I said no, you were my cousin. Then they said that was a relief because you were kissing Jimmy McCann behind the wall.' He was laughing at her. He was always laughing at her.

Well, Jane thought, if I pull off a miracle and get married to him, those two girls won't be on my bridesmaid short list.

She thought about telling him it was all Jimmy's fault, he had taken her by surprise, but she decided to keep her dignity and say nothing at all. She had only herself to blame for asking him how he had known. In fact she had only herself to blame for kissing Jimmy at the castle. If Ryan really did like her, he would have been very hurt, even if he did laugh about it. Instead of blaming him for not forgiving her, she should be blaming herself for treating him like that and expecting forgiveness.

So she changed the subject, reminding him where to put the dishes he had dried, all the while thinking that if he hadn't brought Jimmy into it, she might have told him she did care for him, and right now they might have been upstairs in bed together. Well, perhaps not that far that fast, but at least he might have kissed her.

Tuesday 2 March 1976

Ryan went to Oxford again on the Tuesday, leaving her to shop for the black push-up bra and the plain black knickers to go over her tights beneath the dress. The shop had some rather scanty black lace knickers, and she bought some to wear under the tights. They didn't leave much to the imagination, and it made her feel rather wanton. She wanted to look sexy if they ever got as far as him taking off her dress and tights when they got back from the dinner. Perhaps she should wear black underwear all the time; white was for schoolgirls. The lingerie shop had new range of bikini knickers in bright colours, so she bought one of each colour. That was more interesting than white, but safer than black.

She passed a jeans boutique and bought some denim shorts to wear for tennis in the summer, and a couple of tee-shirts. If she was playing with Ryan or Pat, Daniel was unlikely to touch her, and she could change back to jeans or a skirt when the tennis game was over. If she was playing with Daniel, he would be at the other end of the tennis court.

She bought a denim oversize newsboy cap, which she could wear with her jeans on Colin's walks in the summer. She could tuck her hair up beneath it, so it was cool around her neck. Perhaps she and Ryan could borrow the dog again and walk to Peddleton by themselves. She would make one of the conditions for Daniel that she and Ryan were allowed to walk out together whenever they wanted to.

She also bought a box of toffees and a birthday card for Ryan because she remembered his birthday was this Friday. But it didn't seem enough. What else could she buy for him? For Christmas she had bought him a watch. She stopped by a jeweller's window, looking at the watches, but no one needed more than one watch. Then she saw the silver wolf cufflinks. He always wore cufflinks with his suit when he worked at the university and at church. What could be more fitting?

When she reached home, she washed the underclothes, in case someone else had tried them on in the shop, but she took the clothes airer up to her bedroom to dry them, as there was no dryer here. If she left the airer in the kitchen, she risked forgetting and leaving them in sight when he returned home. She didn't want to embarrass them both, and she would die if he joked about the black lace knickers. He might ask her to try them on and show him. She wouldn't, of course, but the thought of it flooded her with a warm feeling of wanting to be close to him. She wanted him to think she was sexy and want to make love to her.

While she ate her lunch, alone at the kitchen table, she thought what she would write on the birthday card.

What was Latin for lone wolf? *Lupus solus* would do, and wild rose was *rosa fera*. What about happy birthday? *Felix natalis*?

Even if it was not quite right, it would amuse him. She wrote out the card, drew a little heart, as he had on the valentine, and wrote *te amo* in tiny letters. There, it was done, and he could make of it what he liked.

She managed to look after herself for the remainder of the day, although she did wish he was with her. At least it gave her a chance to have a bath without worrying about him being there and opening the bathroom door by mistake, as there was no lock on it. He had been very good so far, though, staying downstairs when she bathed, and she had always used lots of bubble bath, just in case.

She remembered it was Shrove Tuesday and after dinner she made pancakes, which he seemed to enjoy. Tomorrow she would make an apple pie. She felt good to be cooking for him, having him help with the dishes, then sitting very close to him while they watched the detective programme she liked on television. The young detective didn't seem half so attractive now she had Ryan to compare him with.

Wednesday 3 March 1976

On Wednesday he was once again in Oxford, and he brought back his dinner suit from his room at the college. They would go out to dinner on Friday, with Sarah and Tony. Tomorrow they would go into the city for sightseeing, so after dinner she found a map and they planned their route.

Thursday 4 March 1976

On Thursday they walked around London in the morning sunshine, and she slipped her hand into his as if it was the most natural thing in the world. He gave her a quick smile, but said nothing, and he kept hold of her hand for most of the day. In the afternoon they visited the British Museum, as rain had set in, and she felt happy and carefree.

They were to take Sarah and Tony out to dinner on Friday night, and then return to Hayward Hall on Saturday afternoon. Daniel had accepted all of the conditions that Mary had suggested, and some others that Ryan had insisted on, even her own condition about allowing them to walk out together, and Jane wanted to go home.

Ryan had a bath while she made the dinner that evening, and she thought about him being upstairs in the bath without his clothes on. She tried not to think about it, but she couldn't help it. She wondered if he thought like that about her. She wouldn't mind if he did, so long as he didn't accidentally open the bathroom door. The bubble bath was on the shelf next to the tub, so he could have used it if he had been concerned about her coming in by mistake.

She hadn't seen too many men without their clothes, none at all in fact, but she had seen pictures that some of the girls had sneaked into their rooms at school. And there had been a magazine with a male centrefold that one of the girls had at the bank, but the man in the picture had his hand carefully placed, so he was not showing everything. The manager had found the magazine in the tearoom, and there had been trouble over it, but it was completely out of sight of the customers, so Jane didn't know what he had against it. There had been an article in the magazine about making love, and Jane had borrowed it to read one lunchtime. At least she now knew what was supposed to happen. She could have bought her own magazine, of course, but she would not have wanted her aunt to find it in her room.

She thought she would be happy with just a kiss from Ryan after they went out to dinner. Anything else was just a bit frightening.

Friday 5 March 1976

On Friday morning Mary phoned to wish Ryan a happy birthday. Jane gave him the card and toffees at breakfast, and he was surprised she knew it was his birthday, as it was never celebrated. He laughed at the Latin, as she had hoped he would, and thanked her. He didn't say anything about the *te amo*, but she knew he would have noticed it.

Then she gave him the box with the wolf cufflinks, wondering what he would think, watching his face light up with joy, his eyes meeting hers.

'Thank you, Jane. This is the best present I have ever been given. Do you know why I always wear cufflinks?'

'I thought it was because you always have to wear a suit at Oxford. Are there not rules?'

'No strict rules, just conventions, and I prefer to wear a suit. I damaged the nerves in my hand when I broke my arm, and although I can write and draw perfectly well, I have trouble with cuff buttons, but not with cufflinks. That is also why I wear my watch on my right wrist. I can't fasten a watch buckle with my right hand.'

She remembering he had once told her that he couldn't quite straighten two of his fingers and his arm had healed with the bone slightly crooked. She reached out and touched his wrist above the watch, and he rolled up his sleeve and let her feel the slight bump in the bone. It was electrifying to feel the soft dark hair of his arm beneath her fingers, to meet his eyes in surprise at the warmth that swept over her when she touched him, and to know that she wanted him, desperately and forever. She put her palm against his and they laughed at how much longer his fingers were than hers, and how his ring finger was longer than his index finger while hers was shorter. He told her it was a natural difference between men and women. Then he caressed her hand as he had at the cinema, circling a finger around her palm, and she knew they were lovers. He didn't need to tell her that. She felt it with her soul.

He was spending the day looking up ancestors, but she decided to stay at home and wash her hair. She wanted to look perfect when they went out to dinner. She was not sure what she expected from the evening, but she hoped it would end with at least a kiss and an admission that he loved her. He had liked the dress when she had tried it on, and she would be dancing with him. He seemed to accept her being close enough to dance.

She set her hair in rollers, dried it with her hair dryer, and laid out the clothes she would be wearing on her bed.

He had promised to be back by four. She went out to the shop after lunch and bought a small cake for them to share for his birthday, and a box of birthday candles. She remembered Mary saying he had never had a birthday cake or blown out a candle.

When he returned, he had a necklace for her, a beautifully sculptured wild rose with a clutch of small diamonds in the centre, on a delicate rope chain, all in white gold to match her diamond earrings.

For a moment she looked at the necklace in its black velvet box, and she knew he would not have been confident buying jewellery for her, but he had done so anyway, wanting to please her.

'Do you like it?' he asked, sounding a little doubtful.

'Of course I do. It's beautiful. But it's your birthday, not mine.'

'I'm a wolf. I don't always follow the rules.'

'Wolves can be dangerous, especially when they don't follow rules.'

'So can roses. They ensnare us poor wolves with their thorns. Once entangled, there is no escape.'

'Are you ensnared?' she asked, and he laughed.

'Utterly, hopelessly and irredeemably. But I don't want to escape. It's rather exciting to live dangerously. I enjoy it.'

She looked at him, her heart light with joy, knowing he really did mean it, even if he never sounded serious.

She thanked him for the gift, but he said nothing more, so she made the afternoon coffee, and he dutifully blew out his candles, although there were not twenty-seven of them, as the cake was too small for more than the dozen that had come in the packet, and even that was a squash.

He said he was rather sorry they were going home, it had been fun just the two of them living here for a few days, but perhaps they could stay here together again, even if things worked out better between her and his father at the Hall when they returned.

She was relieved at this, as she had been worried that she was messing up his life by needing him to look after her.

Carefully choosing her words, she told him that she had enjoyed being here with him, and she would be happy to do this again, but for now they were expected back at Hayward, and she knew he really wanted to go home. She said she understood that commuting to Oxford from here was impractical, and someone would need to sort out the bills at the Hall. If Daniel signed the cheques himself the bank might not accept the signature as his.

In the evening the four of them had dinner at a hotel in Mayfair. Ryan had consulted with Tony on the best place to go, and checked with Jane that it was not the hotel on his father's credit card statements. Ryan knew he looked enough like his father that the staff would see the connection if he booked in the same surname at the hotel where his father stayed.

Jane was in her little black dress, now with black knickers beneath it over her tights in case the skirt flared out when she danced, and the scanty lace knickers beneath the tights in case the evening ended with them making love. She had styled her hair so the top was pulled back from her face to show off the diamond earrings that Daniel had given her at Christmas, with the trimmed sides flicked backwards in the shaggy look, and the back falling in cascading waves. However much she disliked the idea of marrying Daniel, it would be a shame to waste the earrings. And of course she wore the rose pendant. She wanted to ask Ryan to fasten it, as the thought of his fingers on her skin sent a thrill coursing through her. But it might be beyond his skill, so it was safer to do it herself. She had her small black Oroton mesh purse for her lipstick, her compact, two five-pound notes and her credit card. She had been taught never to go out without sufficient cash to catch a taxi home.

She felt slightly nervous sitting beside him in the taxi, her hand in his, his fingers caressing her palm and her wrist. Less than a week ago he had told her he was still a lone wolf, and she had considered herself the girlfriend of Jimmy McCann. But now here she was on a real date with Ryan, feeling strangely like she was in love with him and hoping he was in love with her.

The doorman took her coat. She assumed he had some sort of tagging system, as there were a lot of ladies and a lot of coats. Most of them seemed to be fur, but Jane didn't really like the idea of fur coats, as you thought about the animal roaming wild and free in the forest. Although these days they were probably all on farms, so perhaps it was no different from leather for shoes.

Sarah and Tony were already there. Ryan guided her across to them, his hand on her waist. She was glad that he was at last treating her as if he was her lover. Perhaps he would want to sleep with her when they got back home, and the thought was slightly frightening but rather thrilling. There would need to be precautions, but men looked after those things. She hoped he had thought of it. She did know there was something she could do, and she would ask Sarah how you organised it.

They enjoyed the meal, the beautiful fruity red wine, Ryan and Tony reminiscing about school, telling the girls about pranks they had played, hilarious incidents with other students, teachers they didn't like and teachers they did like. There was a story about a science master who sported a very fancy moustache and regularly met his girlfriend in the evenings for a cuddle behind the sports shed, until two of the boys hid on the roof of the shed with a long-handled feather duster and gave the young lady the fright of her life while she waited in the darkness for her lover to appear. Ryan promised it wasn't him or Tony wielding the duster.

There was strawberry pavlova, and Champagne to celebrate Ryan being twenty-seven, and Tony, who was normally rather reserved, assuring the girls that he and Ryan were the luckiest men in the world because they were with the two most beautiful women. And then there was dancing.

She left the mesh purse on the table. Ryan asked if she had money in it, so she gave him the banknotes and the credit card, and he put them in the inside pocket of his jacket.

'I hope I don't get your card mixed up with mine when I pay for the dinner,' he teased.

It was thrilling to be dancing so close to him, first a foxtrot and then a tango. He danced very well, and she easily remembered the steps, following him as though they had done this on every day of their lives. The touch of his hand through the soft silk of the dress was seductive and sensual. All the time he looked at her, and she knew he wanted her.

By the end of the evening the steps no longer mattered. They just held each other close, bodies pressed together, her hand on his shoulder, his around her waist, their other hands folded together and gently resting on his jacket, his cheek touching her hair, his thigh against hers as they moved, dancing to slow old-fashioned love songs. She had never been this close to him before, except for the odd brief hug, but he didn't seem to mind. She had never wanted a man like she now wanted him. It was a delicious, thrilling feeling that she wanted him even closer to her. All the time she was dancing with him she was wondering what would happen later, whether they would spend the night together when they returned home, what it would feel like to be naked in bed with him, what it would feel like if he made love to her.

It was time to go home. Ryan paid the bill, and Sarah and Tony thanked them and left, Sarah wishing her luck. The doorman called them a taxi and returned her coat, and Ryan held it for her to put on. She leant against him in the back seat of the taxi, holding his hand, laughing when he told her he really had got the credit cards mixed up. He had thought she wanted to take him out for his birthday. She suggested she could pay off his credit card from Daniel's bank account. Since Ryan would sign the cheque, Daniel would never realise he had been cheated. She remembered he had suggested that to her once before when she had phoned him that day from the Hall. Better still they could write out a cheque to Ryan and Jane for a million pounds and run away together. Daniel was so hopeless at accounting, he would never miss it.

They were back in Richmond, the taxi paid for, the lights disappearing down the street. He unlocked the door, guided her through, took her coat and hung it on a peg.

The porch light was still on, but he hadn't yet turned on the light in the hallway, so it was lit only by the soft light through the frosted stained glass of the front door. She could still hear the cars on the street, but they seemed far away. Nothing in the outside world mattered. With the door shut it was just her and Ryan alone together in the house, alone together in the world. She was standing close to him, and she found his hand, wishing he would kiss her. Just touching his hand was magic, but she was nervous about what might happen later.

She thanked him for taking her out.

'Thank you for coming with me. May I have my kiss for taking you out to dinner?'

'Yes, of course.'

She knew that both of them were a little intoxicated from the dancing as well as the wine. His hands were holding her face, steadying her, his fingers in her hair, his thumbs caressing her cheeks, and he was covering her face with gentle kisses, soft like the touch of the wings of a butterfly, his mouth on her forehead, her eyelids, her cheeks, his lips brushing against her mouth, catching her lower lip then pulling away, teasing her. He finally kissed her, the tip of his tongue finding the tip of hers, playing with hers for a long while, his fingers soft on her face, her neck and her hair, and then he pulled her against him and was kissing her passionately, and a warm thrill washed over her like nothing she had ever felt before. His hand was on her derrière, pulling her closer to him, but she didn't mind. She knew he wanted her as much as she wanted him. There was no disguising that when he held her so close. Yet she felt he was still totally in control. She was a ball of jelly in his clasp, his strength a little frightening but deliciously thrilling. He could have done anything to her, and she would not have stopped him. She wanted him to touch her, and she wanted him closer to her. Her fingers were in his thick dark curls. She had for so long wanted to touch his hair.

He ran his fingers down her back, pretending he was unzipping her dress, and she jumped back, checking the dress was still fastened, before she remembered that there was no zipper.

'There is no zipper. It's a wrap dress, so you need to undo a tie here at the front.'

He released her, and they both collapsed into laughter. He switched on the light.

'Thank you, Jane. I have never enjoyed an evening so much in my whole life, and I have never had such a wonderful birthday.'

'Where did you learn to kiss like that?' she asked him. 'You said you have never had a girlfriend. That wasn't just a kiss, it was a total experience.'

'From a young lady, but she wasn't really a girlfriend. A man has to have some secrets. One day I'll tell you about it. Now can we have our cocoa and go back to behaving properly before this gets out of control?'

'I thought you never got out of control.'

'There's always a first time, and I was dangerously close. Good thing there is no zipper. I have been thinking all evening that there is only a bit of flimsy silk between me and heaven. You will need to show me how the tie works. I wouldn't want to accidentally knot it so you couldn't get the dress off.'

He locked the front door, switched off the porch light, followed her into the kitchen and made the cocoa. He sat opposite her at the table, not even touching her, looking at her in his usual amused way, as if they shared a secret.

But when they finally went upstairs, he kissed her again on the landing outside her door, told her she was beautiful, she had bewitched him, he was hopelessly in love with her. He held her against him and she could feel his body responding to hers. She wished that this time he really would untie the dress. She wanted to be closer to him. She wanted to tell him she loved him and wanted him to make love to her, but she didn't dare.

'I came here to look after you,' he said when he at last released her. 'I'm not doing a very good job of it. I don't know how we allowed this to happen. I promised you would be safe here with me, and I would be a cad if I took advantage of you when you are a little bit tipsy. I wouldn't want you to regret it in the morning. You came here to get away from my father, and if you wanted to run away from me as well, there would be nowhere left for you to go. Now go to bed, Jane, and no sleepwalking. I think we should both lock our doors.'

She didn't mind. She was happy with what she had achieved so far. He was hers and the rest would follow. But as she lay in the darkness wondering what it would feel like to have him make love to her, wondering if he was lying awake only a few yards away from her thinking the same thing, she did also wonder about the expert young lady who wasn't really a girlfriend.

Saturday 6 March 1976

It was past eight o' clock when she awoke, and she didn't feel well enough to make him porridge. She had a headache from too much Champagne, so he found her an aspirin and made them both toast and strong coffee. He didn't say one single word about the previous evening, and she wondered if he was now regretting it. She knew she never would.

They walked around the block to help her recover, and he held her hand, but he said very little. When they returned, she did feel a lot better. She packed her case, and he took it downstairs and out to the car while she made lunch.

He suggested they take the photo albums back to Hayward so Mary could look at them, and Jane found a bag for them. The diagram he had drawn for the family tree was still beside them on the coffee table. At some time between when he had drawn it and now, he had pencilled a dotted line between his name and hers with a heart and a question mark above it. She folded it and tucked it inside one of the albums.

He asked if she wanted to take her grandfather's medals back to Hayward for Mary to restore to their place in the hallway. She went back up the stairs to her father's old room, sat for a moment on the bed, then kicked off her shoes and lay back against the pillow, wishing now that she had slept in here last night with Ryan. He had followed her and was standing in the doorway, looking at her rather wistfully. She wondered if he wished it too. He seemed to guess what she was thinking.

'I had to be responsible. Getting a lady drunk and then making love to her is not my idea of how a gentleman behaves, and I was here to protect you. Would you have regretted it?'

'No, not at all. But it's too late now, we're going home.'

She took down the frame with the medals and handed it to him to take downstairs, all the time wishing he would kiss her again and say they didn't have to leave, they could stay here forever, they could sleep together tonight when both of them were sober.

She wondered if he had been worried that he might regret it as well, since he had been a little tipsy too. He was always telling her he didn't want a girlfriend.

'Would you have regretted it? You were a bit tipsy as well.'

'No, not unless you did. I never do anything I regret, and I don't think I was tipsy. I'm always careful about that. We could come back and stay here again in a couple of weeks. I will be on holiday then, and hopefully we will have sorted things out between you and my father. And between you and me. Would you like that?'

She looked at him, knowing he meant they could be lovers then. 'Yes,' she said. 'I would like that.'

He had taken her hand. Why did it feel so good just to touch him? Why didn't he just kiss her again, say they could stay here tonight?

'Come on,' he said. 'We need to leave.'

The car was warm, walnut and leather luxury, quietly purring as it covered the miles. She fell asleep as they drove and woke when he stopped for a break in a small town.

They had coffee at a café. She remembered he hadn't given her back her credit card, and he pretended he had left it in the bedroom at Richmond. Then he gave it to her but without her banknotes. 'What about my ten pounds?'

'I used some of that to pay for the coffee,' he teased, but he gave it to her.

The town had a leafy park beside a river, where they sat for a while watching two young children feeding ducks. He had taken her hand and was stroking her fingers, and she leant against him, enjoying the sunshine and the quiet companionship, knowing that he was hers and she was his, that they would soon be lovers as well as friends, knowing that being with him was all she would ever want.

'Jane there are things about my father that you should know,' he said at last. 'You would have realised already that he is not exactly a saint, and I don't know how much Mary has told you. To the outside world we are a perfect family, with my father the local squire, now wealthy from writing the books, so we no longer have to let out rooms. He has money in the bank like most people could only dream of, a beautiful house, his sister to look after it, his son at Oxford, his nephew doing a wonderful job on the garden, a beautiful niece staying at his house, all of us in church on Sundays, involved with the local village life. But underneath all the veneer he is a serial womaniser and a hopeless alcoholic.

'Pat said he told you about the trips to London. They are called escorts, but however high class they seem, those girls are prostitutes and my father is a kerb crawler. He told you it was better if the woman enjoyed it, but they are paid to make a man feel good and would fake it. When we were boys, he would bring his women back to Hayward, and my grandmother tolerated it as long as he didn't do anything indiscreet in front of the guests.

'There were times when he did indiscreet things in front of me and Pat, and we both kept away from him. He would fondle his women in the garden and the wood, sometimes in the den, even in the library where I liked to sit, immersed in all the books. It was how we grew up. He was always angry with us, sometimes with Mary too, and he yelled at us over little things. But he never yelled at my grandmother. She was always wary of his temper, as he occasionally smashed plates, and she needed to keep him under control when we had paying guests in the house, but she always stood up to him on things that mattered. I spent the holidays with other boys when I could. I knew it disappointed my grandmother, but I think she understood I didn't like to be with my father. But I did feel very guilty about leaving Pat with him without me there.'

'Why are you telling me this,' Jane asked. 'His love life is his own affair. I'm not intending to marry him.'

'Perhaps I'm still afraid you will marry him because you feel sorry for him. But you are a lady, and he is not fit to lick your boots. He says he loves you, and I think he believes it, but if he really loved you, he wouldn't harass you like he does. If you did marry him, he would probably be faithful, he would treat you well, and he might even drink a bit less, but it would be a travesty for a disgusting man like him to have a girl like you. He was told he will only last a couple more years unless he gives up the whisky altogether. He used to smoke cigars, but he gave that up completely, so I'm sure he could give up whisky as well. I know you've done a lot to help him, and Mary and I are both grateful for that.'

'I do care about him, really I do. I want to help him, but I don't want to marry him. I just want him to accept that and treat me like his niece or his daughter.'

'He has promised to, and at least now he knows that you really will leave if he doesn't behave. There is more I want to tell you. When I was a teenager, he was always trying to get me to drink whisky and smoke cigars, Pat as well, and when I was sixteen, he asked one of his women to seduce me. She was an awful woman who came here quite often and treated my grandmother like dirt. Nothing was ever good enough for her. I was very polite to her as I had been taught to be with all the guests, walking with her in the garden if she asked, but sometimes she would touch me and try to get me to touch her. I'll spare you the details, but she revolted me, and I never responded to her, so she did her best to humiliate me and to get me into trouble with my father. I avoided her whenever I could, but I didn't know what to do, and I have never liked to be in situations where I don't feel in control. I was worried she would try to come to my room, and I felt completely out of my depth.

'So I went to my grandmother and asked if I could have the key to my bedroom door so I could lock it, and of course she got the story out of me. There was a huge row, the like of which Hayward Hall had never seen before and has never seen since. Pat, Mary and I were petrified. My grandmother was by then quite frail, and she was nowhere near as tall as you or Mary. He was nearly twice her weight. We were afraid he would kill her. Pat was then about nine or ten, and he hid under the kitchen table, while I was working out how I could defend her if we needed to.

'She said she couldn't throw him out of the house because it was his house, but he was never to bring that woman here again, or any other woman. If he wanted a mistress, he could keep her in London. He had plenty of money. He could set up a flat and meet her there. She told him he was setting a terrible example to me and Pat, and she wasn't standing for it any longer.

'After that, with the exception of one incident, he behaved better at home and things improved. I'm not trying to be vindictive towards him. I just want you to know what he is really like.

'Mary will tell you that's why I never liked girls, but I got over it. I was always a lone wolf. I like my own company, and I like to be independent, so I never really wanted a girlfriend. Girlfriends were for other people, like parachuting out of planes or climbing Everest. Good if you like that sort of thing, but you don't feel like you're missing out on anything if you don't. Before you came to live with us, I found the whole idea of making love to a girl rather distasteful. But now I know I was just waiting for the right girl.

'When you came to live at Hayward with us, I wanted to do things with you, instead of being on my own. One evening when I came home from Oxford, I sat beside you in the conservatory and gave you a hug, and I realised how good it felt to hold a girl you liked up close. I spent that whole of that night thinking about you. I scarcely slept, and I hoped you would want a hug again. Then I got to thinking perhaps one day we might be more than friends, that you might like to be with me as much as I like to be with you, but it was difficult when we lived in the same house. I was afraid that you would leave if I said I cared for you, and I didn't want that, for your sake as well as mine, because I knew you were happier living at Hayward than you would have been on your own in Richmond.

'Then I walked in on you and Pat, and that night I was totally miserable. I had been so patient, and I had started to hope you might care for me. I decided I would stay in Oxford and never come home, so I could forget you and never see you again, but then I remembered you saying you wanted to stay at Hayward to be with me, and I wondered if you had really meant that. I found myself wishing it was you and me kissing on the stairs. I thought how good that would feel, and I knew that if I was allowed to make love to you, it would be the greatest privilege of my life. By lunchtime on Monday, I was worrying that you would leave Hayward because of Pat. I could think of nothing else. I wanted to phone you and ask you to stay, but I couldn't think what I would say if my father answered the call. Then on the Wednesday you phoned me, and I was so happy that you wanted to talk to me. I knew then that I could never stay away however hard I resolved to, and I would have forgiven you anything,'

He was silent for a while, and she was not sure how he wanted her to respond. Was he telling her that he was in love with her? She thought she remembered him telling her last night that he loved her, but she really had been a little bit tipsy, and she was not quite sure.

'You said there was another incident. Was that the escort? Do you want to talk about that too?'

'I'm not sure it would be wise. And I don't feel bad about that one, I never have, because that time I felt I was in control.'

'If you slept with a girl, I don't want to know about it. If I had slept with someone, I would never tell you. It's just between two people, and no one else's concern.'

'I didn't sleep with her. She was hired by my father to sleep with me, but I didn't want to. Even back then I despised him for the way he treated women, and I would never have let him drag me down to his level. My father sees sex as something you pay for, like a haircut. I see it as a privilege a man earns by caring for a woman. I don't doubt that he loved my mother—no one could doubt that—but since then his women are just there for his pleasure. Pat thinks he likes the girls to be young. He found magazines in Daniel's room with explicit pictures of teenage girls. At least he didn't leave those lying around the house when we were younger. My grandmother would have exploded. Would you like the story of the escort? It's not at all sordid, although I never told my grandmother or Mary, and it might amuse you.'

'Yes, please tell me if you want to.'

'I was still at school so no more than eighteen. A lady friend of my father was coming to stay as a guest and would be bringing a younger sister. He had organised a booking for them and selected which rooms they would have. By then my grandmother had the rooms you are in, so he had put them on the top floor. I think my grandmother was a little suspicious, but we still had some guests, and sometimes my father took the bookings. They arrived in the afternoon, and we picked them up from the station as we often did for guests as part of the service. Daniel was taking the older lady out to dinner in town, and he asked if I would come as well as company for the younger one. She was eighteen, the same age as I was then. She was really good to talk to, asking me about school and what I wanted to do when I left, and afterwards I realised it was all part of what she did. We had wine with the dinner, but I was always very careful about how much I drank because I had seen what too much alcohol did to my father.

'When we returned to the house, he asked me to entertain her for the remainder of the evening in the library with him and the older woman, and we all played cards. The ladies were given gin and tonics, and I was given a Scotch. Eventually it got late, and my father asked me if I would take the younger lady up to her room so she didn't get lost in the darkness. She had been given the room adjacent to mine. By then I had my corner bedroom, but my study was still a bedroom for guests. She took my hand as we went up, and I thought it was because she felt scared at being in an old house. When we reached the room, she kept hold of me and tried to pull me inside. I told her as politely as possible that I would rather not, and she said she was confused, as she was being paid to sleep with me, and hadn't I realised that. Then she said that she would never try to persuade a man to do anything he didn't want to do, that was one of the rules for the job she did, so perhaps we could just talk for a while. She was worried she would have to give the money back to my father if I just left her at the door to the room. So I went into the room with her. I did trust her, and I knew she could never persuade me to change my mind.

'For a while she just talked to me, and her life was so different from mine I was totally fascinated by what she said. She was from a poor background. Her mother was single and struggled to make a living. She had left school at fourteen to work in a shop, but she had tried to get a better life. She had taught herself to speak well and she learnt how to dress and make herself up to look beautiful but not cheap. She had moved jobs to eventually work in the makeup section in an upmarket department store, and she joined an escort agency which specialised in high-class placements. One of the girls who worked in the shop with her was an escort, so she had the connections. She hoped to eventually find a client who would set her up on a more permanent basis as a kept mistress. It was called having a sugar daddy. Some of the escorts even got married, usually to older men. She said that most of the men she escorted were very nice to her and were grateful for the service she gave, but sometimes they were awful and those were reported back to the agency, and she didn't have to go out with them again.

'She told me that my father had asked her to sleep with me, but she would not tell him what did or didn't happen as there was client confidentiality involved. She said if I didn't want to, then she respected my decision, and it was good to have someone who talked to her like she was a real person.

'I never saw her again, but I do sometimes wonder what became of her. In the morning I went out for a walk before the women came down to breakfast, and I didn't come back until I knew they had gone. Then I told my father not to waste his money doing that again, and if he did, I would tell my grandmother. He said a lot of unpleasant things to me at the time, telling me how disappointing I was, not even having the gumption to make love to a girl. At the time I tried not to care, but I was very hurt, and it was something that I could never share with my grandmother. I knew she would have helped me to keep it in perspective, but I didn't want to snitch on him, as I knew she would be angry with him. He was always awful to me, so I was used to it. You get over things, and I got over it. But sometimes I wished he would tell me just once that he was glad that I had survived although my mother was dead. I still wish that, but he has never said it.'

'I'm glad you survived, and I know Mary is too. I can't imagine my life without you in it.'

'I haven't upset you, have I, by telling you about the girl?'

'No, I found it quite fascinating. I hope she found someone. Was she the girl who taught you to kiss like that?'

'No, that was a girl called Lynne, who was with us at a house where I stayed in the school holidays. Not Martin's place. She taught all of us. We had a lot of fun that summer.'

'Did she teach you anything else?'

He laughed. 'Only how to hold a girl's hand in a cinema. After I hold your hand and kiss you goodnight, we're on our own. Although nothing could beat the seductive way you handed me those chocolates that night. I was wishing we were by ourselves on the swing and I could lick melted chocolate off your fingers.'

The children had gone, the ducks were now lazily floating on the water, the afternoon shadows lengthening along the soft lawn, the air still, another day slipping into memory. A day Jane knew she would never forget.

'I could sit here with you forever,' he said, 'but we need to go home.'

She was more alert when they resumed the drive, but he was silent, seeming wrapped in thought. She didn't mind. She was happy to watch his long slender fingers on the steering wheel, thinking about the things he had told her, knowing they would be lovers now. Perhaps tonight they would sleep together, upstairs in his room. They were always the last two up, so no one would know.

They reached Oxford, left the motorway, followed the main road to town, and finally reached Hayward village then Hayward Hall. He stopped the car on the driveway inside the gate so they could look at the house, glowing warm in the glancing rays of the late afternoon sun, welcoming them home.

'I'm glad I have come back, I feel like this is my home and I have always lived here,' she told him. 'I always think of this place as loving us all, wanting to comfort us, and sad that it is unable to help us sort out the mess we have all got into.'

'I love this house, Jane. I love watching the sun and shadow on the stones, the old staircase, the way the moonlight lights up the hallway through the landing window. I love sleeping in my room below the attic and the stone tiles. I love the history, all the people who have lived here and loved the house. I loved my grandmother, and I still really miss her. I used to save up things I wanted to tell her when I next saw her, things we could laugh about together, and I still did that for years after she had died. I would feel her near me in the house, see her in the movement of shadows in the hallway, hear her voice calling me. And I love Mary. But I have never liked being with my father, and that was enough to keep me away. Then when you came here to stay, I wanted to come home to be with you, and now I save up things to tell you.

'Like you, I see the house as powerless to stop us from making a mess of our lives. It can only watch us do it, then comfort us when we try to pick up the pieces. I believe that everything that happened here, every word that was ever spoken, every thought and memory of the people who lived here, is locked up somewhere within the stones, and would be there for us if we could only find a way to decipher it. Sometimes I think about the four children playing in the garden here, in the years before the First World War, our two great-uncles, my grandfather James and your grandmother Grace. All four of them were killed in one or other of the World Wars. I feel them close to me in the garden, echoes of their voices all around me, I feel that I could reach out and touch them, talk to them, share their laughter, but they are never quite there where I am. You, Pat and I are their legacy, and I always think it sad that you were not brought up here with us, even if you had only visited us in the holidays. That was my father's fault, and I always feel that he cheated us.

'There are other ghosts here too, not just Linden ghosts. We were a bed and breakfast right through the War. Servicemen would stay here with their wives or girlfriends, and for some of them it would have been the last hours they ever spent together. After the War and right into the nineteen sixties, we had honeymooners and holidaymakers and visitors from abroad. Some of them came back every year. There are people out there with memories of this house that would be very precious to them. Perhaps their memories are here too. We still have all the registers, and when I was younger, I would sometimes look at the names and wonder where the people were now.

'Jane, we can still change our minds. It's a bit late to drive back to Richmond today, but we could stay at a hotel in town for the night. Then tomorrow we could return to Richmond and live there together. I could quit at Oxford and get a full-time job in London. Even without your money, I could earn enough for us to live on quite well, and I do have some money of my own that my grandmother left to me. When I talked to Allanstone last week, he said if we wanted to stay together in Richmond, he would let you have as much as we wanted from your trust until I was earning enough to keep us, but I don't think we would need that. It would be your choice whether you wanted it to be permanent, but I know I would want it to be. We always get on well together, and we would make a good team. I can do the heavy lifting, and you can iron the shirts and cook the apple pies.'

She laughed at that, but she was suddenly serious again.

'You can't quit at Oxford, not until you finish the year. I would never want you to do that. But we could work something out. The hotel, Ryan, would that be separate rooms?'

'Your choice, Jane. You know the condition.'

'Would you let me have a glass of wine with my dinner, so I wasn't so nervous?'

'Yes, of course. If you are too frightened, you can just sleep next to me, and I won't touch you. I have spent so many nights just wishing you were there beside me.'

She imagined them booking into a hotel as Mr and Mrs Linden when she didn't even have a wedding ring. She would need to keep her hands in her pockets. But she knew it would make her feel cheap, and the idea of other people knowing they were sharing a room was somehow sordid. Wanting him to make love to her when they had been out dancing, were alone in the house and she was a little tipsy was one thing. Lying in bed with a man in a cold impersonal hotel room, too frightened to go through with it even with the promised glass of wine, was another. It would not be fair on him.

'I think I would be too frightened, and that might be torture for you, in bed with a girl but not making love to her, like the old chivalry where they slept with a sword between them. It wouldn't be fair on you. It was different last night when we had been out dancing and were kissing on the landing. I wanted you to make love to me then, but a hotel room seems so cold and impersonal.'

'Being with you could never be torture, and sleeping with you would be heaven even if we really were only sleeping. But if you want to go back, we can book separate rooms. Or we could return to Richmond tonight if you prefer that. It would be late when we got there, but we could stop for a coffee in town and have dinner somewhere on the way back.

'Jane, this is one time in my life when I really don't know what is the right thing to do. I wish now we hadn't come back here. He is not going to stop wanting you, and I think we are chasing rainbows. Do we turn around? Or do we go on and give this a go?'

'We go on and give it a go. I don't want you giving up your life here for me, and I don't want you quitting at Oxford. We need some time to work this out. I will handle him as best I can. I think you and I had better go back to being friends as we were before, at least for now, and in front of Daniel. There is a room full of shotguns, and I don't want him deciding you are a rival and shooting you.

'I do like you, and I am very grateful for what you have done for me. I also like the idea of us having a life together, but we need to seriously think about all this. Only a week or so ago you were a lone wolf, and I thought you didn't ever want a girlfriend, and me loving you would be hopeless. I have tried for months now not to be in love with you. I thought it was safer to be the girlfriend of Jimmy McCann.

'I wasn't even sure about the valentine. I thought you just sent it to amuse me because you imagined I was upset about Pat. Then you took me out to dinner and kissed me, and fireworks happened. I would happily have slept with you last night. I hoped you would come to my room. I wanted to go to yours, but I didn't dare. I wish now that I had, as then we would have stayed together in Richmond and not come back here. But we are back here, and for now I think we just need to go on as we were. I don't want to upset Daniel. And I also have a better plan.

'If we are serious about wanting to be together, I could buy a house close to Oxford, and you could live there with me. I think I would have enough money for that, but I don't actually know how much a house costs. We could ask Mr Allanstone if we could afford it. We could sell the house in Richmond if we needed to. My father was never able to save much because as well as keeping my mother and me at our own house in Kent, he had to help Aunt Ellen and pay my hideously expensive school fees, although they were reduced a bit because I had a scholarship. But when my parents died, the train company paid out compensation, the house in Kent was sold, and there was a huge life insurance payout. My father had taken it out so that if he died, my mother would be left with enough to keep me at school, look after her aunt, keep the house in Kent and not have to work. To me it was a frightening amount of money, but after looking after your father's accounts it doesn't seem quite so much. If we lived close to Oxford, you could finish your degree and get a full-time teaching job at the university, I could go back to working in a bank, and we could come here every Sunday to see Mary and Pat and Claire and the new baby.'

He took her hand in his, ran his fingers around her palm and the inside of her wrist.

'That sounds perfect. Are you still the girlfriend of Jimmy McCann?'

'I would rather be the girlfriend of Ryan Linden, but you always tell me you don't want a girlfriend.'

He looked at her, and she knew he was thinking what to say, and when he did speak it took her by surprise. 'I'm not quite sure whether you do really like me, or whether this is just a game to you, and you just see me as a conquest because you think I don't care for girls. If so, then you were successful. I am totally smitten. You are the most beautiful thing that ever happened to me. I have been trying to tell you I love you since that day in January when we sat in the café, and I knew I didn't want to be a lone wolf any more. All I wanted was to spend my whole life with you. We walked in Kew Gardens, and I wanted to tell you I loved you, but I was afraid I would frighten you off, and I didn't even have the courage to hold your hand.

'You said you would like to be the girlfriend of Ryan Linden. Would you like to be the wife of Ryan Linden?'

She could feel her heart beating rapidly, as she struggled to keep her words in order and her voice calm. 'Is that a proposal or just a hypothetical question?'

'Yes, Jane, it is a proposal. I can't go down on my knees in a car. But if the answer is no, then I will accept it, and I won't ask you again. I don't want you feeling that you need to run away from me, and I would want us to stay friends. This is your home and you don't have to marry my father or me to stay living here. If you're not sure, then you can have as long as you like to make up your mind. I will never change mine. But I want total commitment, not a casual affair. Jane, please say yes.'

He was caressing the inside of her wrist while he waited for her to answer, looking at her in that kind way of his that made her feel he was hugging her.

'I promise I really do like you, Ryan. It's not just a conquest. I think I love you, but until this last week I didn't think I was allowed to. One day you write me love notes, and the next you tell me you want to stay being a lone wolf and would rather jump out of an aeroplane than make love to a girl. It's you who plays games with me. And I don't know how we would tell your father. He would be upset about it.'

'I don't run my life to oblige my father, and neither should you. We don't need his permission, or his forgiveness, or his money. It would be his choice to accept it and be happy for us, or not accept it and be miserable. We don't have to live here. He needs us more than we need him, and he can't stop us from seeing Aunt Mary and Pat, even if he disinherits me.'

'I think the answer is yes, but I want some time to get used to the idea. I hadn't thought about us being married, only about us being lovers, at least to start with. Could we just wait a bit, perhaps until Pat is married. That's only six weeks, and they need our help for the wedding to go smoothly. Then we can think about what we want to do and where we would live. And meanwhile Daniel might accept us being lovers. I don't want to be the cause of you falling out with him, or of you losing this house. I know you love it.'

'Not as much as I love you. But we had better go in. If my father sees us here, he will wonder why we stopped.'

'Tell him we were admiring the way the afternoon sunlight falls on the house.'

The first evening was easy. At dinner Daniel appeared to be making more effort at conversation, asking Ryan what they had done in the week they were away, asking Pat how the plans for the wedding were progressing, and after dinner there were letters to be opened, bills to be paid, envelopes for Jane to type and cheques for Ryan to sign.

Daniel offered his son a whisky while Jane sat typing at the desk in the library, and for once Ryan accepted. The two men sat on leather armchairs near her, discussing the ever-increasing cost of the home heating oil, and she was immensely glad that there was no open animosity between them.

When Ryan had taken the letters to the kitchen to be posted the next day, Daniel asked Jane why they had stopped on the driveway before they came in. He had seen the car stop as he was walking through the lounge.

She told him they were talking about how the sun touched the windows and the stone walls in the afternoon, and why the house faced northwest when it meant that there was scarcely any sun on the front of the house in the depths of winter. They assumed it was so it was parallel to the lane. In the end one side had to face towards the north.

Daniel seemed to accept this, and said he thought they had used the same footprint as the previous house, incorporating the original cellar, which was below the kitchen and the dining room.

He noticed she had changed her hair style, telling her it looked different, but he didn't seem to realise that she had done it to look like the photograph of her mother.

Ryan returned to his seat in the library, Mary and Pat both joined them, and Daniel talked about Caroline, telling them how he had met her when she first worked with him, when she was sixteen and he was nineteen, how he had loved her from the day he first saw her, had dated her for eight years until they could marry in nineteen forty-seven, two years after the War ended. They were all trying to put the War behind them and get their lives back together. They had lost his father, both of Peter's parents, his friend Jim McCann and Caroline's younger brother Nicholas. In the end they had only another two years together before she died.

'I still see her sometimes on the landing when I go upstairs to bed. She stands there with the moonlight shining through the window behind her. Sometimes she talks to me, whispering things I can't quite catch, but when I reach the landing, she is always gone. One day I will reach her, and she will still be there, and I will know then that I am dead and back with her. I can still hear her voice in my mind. I remember the scent of her and the feel of her beside me in the night as though it was yesterday.'

Jane felt sorry for him, and she wished she could somehow change what had happened so his wife had lived. She still felt tearful when she thought of the beautiful young woman dying so young, and how grateful she would have been if she had known her baby son had survived. Jane felt she could have loved Daniel as his daughter-in-law and brought some sunshine back into his life, but he had wanted to possess her. She still hoped he would come around to accepting her and Ryan being lovers, and she was glad that he seemed to be making an effort to repair his relationship with all of them.

Later that night she sat with Ryan over cocoa, sharing the toffees she had bought for his birthday, their fingertips touching across the kitchen table, planning how they would cope until they could escape. She wished she could go up to his room, but they did not want to antagonise Daniel. They would make it a game. It was only a few weeks, and it would give them both time to think about what they wanted to do, and how it would work.

He suggested they could go back to Richmond together for a few days in a couple of weeks' time. She could say she was staying with Sarah to do some shopping, and he would tell his father he was taking the opportunity to spend a few nights in Oxford. He would be on holiday then, and they could spend every day together. And every night as well if that was what she wanted.

Sunday 7 March 1976

On Sunday they walked to church, taking the basket with the usual bunches of flowers from the garden for the graves, all of them beautifully dressed and seemingly united, with not a hint of the turmoil that had sent her fleeing to Richmond a little over a week before. Everyone would have noticed that last Sunday she and Ryan had been missing from the family pew.

Jimmy found her after church, said he was glad she was back and he hoped she would go out to a film with him on Wednesday. She told him that Ryan was staying at home in the week at the moment, and he liked her help with things, but she would see him on Saturday for whatever Colin was arranging for them. Claire wanted her to come over one evening to plan the bridesmaid dresses and work out a time for her and Ryan to teach them all to dance the waltz. The wedding was six weeks away in mid-April, on Easter Saturday.

After lunch she walked with Ryan to John Phillips' farm to see the baby turkeys hatching in the incubator. She had expected them to be yellow, like baby chickens, but they were mostly a soft colour between honey and grey, although some were nearly white.

Winston picked one up and carefully handed it to her. They were soft and warm to touch, and they wriggled when you held them. They had to be kept warm for a couple of weeks before they went out into their barn and their enclosure. John Phillips said it was good to see her back and asked if she had enjoyed the shopping with her friend.

Did he know that she really had been running away? She hoped he didn't know why. He would have known that Ryan had gone after her because neither of them had been at church last Sunday.

When they returned from the farm, Jane and Ryan stood in front of the house, trying to work out where the photo of her mother had been taken, and eventually they found the right place with one of the bay windows in the background. She went upstairs and changed into the blue suit and hat, then returned to the forecourt and stood for her photo.

She thought about her mother standing here more than twenty years ago, with her father taking the photo, Ryan only six and herself not yet born. It still seemed strange to think that this house had been her father's home, where he had grown up under the care of Ryan's grandmother. Jane often imagined him here, walking in the garden or running up the stairs. Sometimes she felt him close to her, heard his voice calling her name. She would ask Mary which room he had slept in, as she didn't even know that. Perhaps there were still things here that were his, books he had loved, clothes he had worn, photos from school. She thought she could face them now.

Daniel had seen them from the window in the hallway. He came out onto the front steps, and asked what they were playing at. He was ashen and appeared rather shaken, and Jane wondered if for a moment he had thought she was a ghost.

'We're trying to recreate the photo of Jane's mother,' Ryan told him, seeming rather surprised at his tone.

But Jane understood that they had upset him, and she tried to appease him. 'We meant no harm. We were trying to work out where my mother was standing. I found the hat in the attic in Richmond, and my mother's suit was very like one I had.'

She didn't want to tell him she had purposely bought a suit that more or less matched it, at least in colour, although the design was much more modern. Her mother's suit had been a closely-fitting design with a peplum.

'Did you think I was a ghost?' she asked him.

He seemed to have recovered a little. 'Yes, I did think that. It was taken from about here, before church one Sunday. It was summer then, in August, so the light would have been different. Peter took the photo. He had saved enough to buy a camera from what was left of his salary after he gave most of the money to my mother. She would never take all of it. It was originally a colour slide, as that was the easiest and cheapest way to do coloured photos then. He had to be sparing with photos, as it cost so much to get them developed. But Josie was so beautiful, he wanted to photograph her. He did some nice shots of Ryan as well, and Mary will still have them somewhere. He sent the photo of Josie to Mary in a letter. I recognised his writing on the envelope and took the letter from the hallway. Mary was angry with me for taking her letter—she caught me reading it—but in the end she let me keep the photo of Josie and she just had the ones of Ryan. Peter often sent photos, but after that he typed the envelopes, so I didn't recognise his writing and couldn't steal them.

'Now come inside both of you. Mary sent me to ask you to come in for afternoon tea. Claire is here.'

Mary had made a Black Forest cake with the last jars of the brandied cherries. Jane realised it was for Ryan's birthday, but nothing was said. Claire had come to spend the afternoon with Pat.

Daniel asked if he was allowed the cake with the brandied cherries as well as his two whiskies for the day. Jane told him if he was in any doubt about it, she would be happy to eat his slice of the cake. Claire looked at Jane, seeming a little surprised at her talking to him like that. Claire called him *Sir* and only spoke to him when he directly asked her a question.

Jane thought afterwards that trying to replicate the photograph was ill-judged. It was not good to be disturbing the ghosts of the past in this house, and perhaps the memories were better left sleeping. Unleashing them could be healing, but might instead be destructive. How could she judge that, when she still did not know what had happened to make her father leave here and never return? She recalled Ryan saying that there were some things that no man could ever forgive. Daniel had been thwarted once before when he had loved her mother, and he was to be thwarted again now that he loved her. She felt very sorry for him, for in the end he would have to accept that he would lose her to his son.

That evening Jane brought down the photo albums for Mary to look at, and gave her the framed medals to hang back in the hallway. Their hook was still empty, patiently awaiting their return for over twenty years.

She wanted to think that the rift was now healed, that it had died when her father had died, but she knew it still lived on, smouldering in the memory of a young man who had been collateral damage in a fight between two men over a woman more than twenty years before. Once Ryan had told her he didn't get on with his father because of something that had happened in the past but was best forgotten. There had been a shotgun involved, and he had broken his arm, badly enough that he still had the scar from where the bone was pinned, badly enough that it had not mended quite straight, he had trouble fastening cuff buttons, and he had never regained enough strength to make the top rowing team. Afterwards he had walked in his sleep, and the thought of what happened that day still haunted him in the night. Perhaps one day she could help him to heal from the memory of it as he had helped her to heal from the grief of losing her parents and then her great-aunt. But before she could help him, she needed to know what had happened. Why was there this conspiracy of silence?

Daniel sat with them in the lounge while Jane showed Mary the photos. Mary and Daniel knew some of the people in the older ones. Jane had not realised before that some of them were of Caroline and some were of Mary's mother Kathleen. Daniel recognised Jane's grandmother, who had been his aunt Grace, and her grandfather Edwin Walters who had been Peter's father. The medals were his, but they knew very little about his family. Ryan said he would see what he could find out.

The family tree that Ryan had drawn for her fell to the floor—she had forgotten she had tucked it into the album—but luckily it remained folded. She hastily retrieved it so Daniel didn't see the line that Ryan had drawn between his name and hers, took it upstairs to her room, found an eraser to rub out the pencilled question mark next to the heart, and put it on the mantelpiece beside the valentine card and its envelope, and the card that Ryan had altered, which had come with the flowers. *Forever thou art mine only true love* he had written, and she now knew that he really had meant it.

When she came back down, they were looking at the photos from Sarah's wedding, with Jane in a blue bridesmaid dress with Sarah and Tony, the two other bridesmaids, and Tony's best man Scott. There was a photo of the three bridesmaids with Jane's great-aunt and one with just Jane and Scott. She told them he had once taken her out to dinner.

Daniel demanded to know who he was; she had never told him about a boyfriend in Richmond.

'I only went out with him once,' she said. 'I wouldn't go out with him again because he wouldn't keep his hands to himself.'

That wasn't strictly true, as he had never asked her out again, but she enjoyed saying it to Daniel.

Over cocoa that night Ryan outlined his plan for them.

He needed to be in Oxford every day this week to do the tutoring, but he would come home each night. He would drive the car into Oxford and park there, so if she fled the house again, he could more easily come after her.

This was the last week of the Hilary term, so he could then stay at home until late April. They would spend a few days together in Richmond in a couple of weeks' time if she wanted, but longer term they needed something more permanent. Living in Richmond and working in Oxford was simply not practical as the trip took nearly two hours. Pat would be married by the time the Trinity term started, and if Daniel wouldn't accept that they were lovers and was still harassing her, they would leave here if she still wanted to be with him. If necessary, they could rent a house for a while, and not tell Daniel where they were. They would tell him they were going to Oxford to shop for the day as they had once before, and he would telephone his father late in the afternoon to let him know they were not coming home. That way Daniel would have time to get over his anger without them being there. After a few days he would phone Daniel again, and suggest they could both come back during the day on Sundays to help with the paperwork. For at least the first Sunday they would come directly to the church, as Daniel would have to behave there. He didn't think Daniel would do them any real harm if he had some time to get over being angry with them.

At least now they had a way forward, but Jane still hoped Daniel would accept that she didn't want to marry him, and they could all stay here together. She liked living here; she enjoyed helping Daniel with the accounts and the typing, helping Mary with the housework, and Pat with the garden. She felt she was part of a family who loved the house, tended to its needs, and kept it running smoothly.

Monday 8 March 1976

On Monday morning Ryan drove to Oxford, leaving before Jane was up.

Daniel wanted to walk with her in the garden again after morning coffee, but Mary insisted he was not to be alone with her. The Olivetti typewriter was still in the library, so she was not in his den while she worked.

She tried to talk to him as she normally would, all the while knowing that this was not going to work, and he was not going to stop being in love with her.

He sat near her in the library, watching her as she typed.

'When Mary told me you were gone, I wanted to go after you and bring you home, but she wouldn't give me the car keys. I didn't like to think of you there by yourself. Then Mary said she had sent Ryan after you. She should have let me go instead. You're mine, not his. You should not have left without asking me; I was not going to harm you.'

'I know now that I should have stayed, and we could have sorted it out.' She really did want there to be a solution that made everyone happy, but at the moment she couldn't see one.

'I could have looked after you in Richmond just as well. I would have taken you out to dinner somewhere nice. If you'd had a bit of Champagne and danced with me, you'd have relaxed a bit, and we could have enjoyed ourselves in peace back at your house for the rest of the night. Or we could have just booked a room at the hotel.'

'Mr Linden, please don't talk like that. We have an agreement.'

'It's not *Mr Linden*, it's *Daniel*.'

'Yes, Sir. Sorry, Sir.'

He laughed as she hoped he would.

'Did you sleep with him?' he suddenly asked her. 'You were alone together in that house. He's gay, and he'll never sleep with you. He can't do it with a girl, he's simply not capable. If he'd slept with you, neither of you would have come back, so I know he didn't. If you'd slept with him there, you'd be sleeping with him here, and I know you're not. I checked your doors, and both of you slept with them ajar. If you had been together, you would have closed the door.'

She didn't like the idea of him prowling around at night, checking her door; perhaps she should lock it.

'Mr Linden, please stop this or I will go back to Richmond.' She knew he was setting a trap for her, trying to goad her into telling him whether she had slept with Ryan, while at the same time trying to make her doubt that Ryan wanted her if she hadn't.

'He would want to marry you first, knowing him. Where would you be then if you married him and he couldn't make love to you? It's always best to have sex before you make up your mind to marry someone. Sex and marriage parted company when rubbers were invented. Once you're married to me, he can't get his hands on you. I'd kill him if he touched you.'

'Mr Linden, we have another condition on me staying here. You don't say anything to me that you wouldn't say if Mary was in the room.'

He laughed. 'She knows all about rubbers. She used to put them in the drawers when we ran the bed and breakfast and she helped my mother set up the rooms. My mother wouldn't put them in the same drawer as the bible. She was a very religious woman. She was a Catholic before she married my father, and they don't believe in them, but she cared about the girls that came here with their young men in the War. Mary wouldn't have known what they were for. She was only a kid. Pity someone didn't tell her though. She may have avoided getting pregnant when she got older.'

'And your garden would now be a complete mess without Pat looking after it. I think this conversation has gone far enough. Now please allow me to concentrate. If I make a mistake, I need to type the whole page again.'

He went back to the den, but she could see he was still watching her through the open doorway.

After lunch she walked down to the farm to see Claire, just to get out of the house, forgetting that Claire worked in town. But that didn't matter, as Anne wanted to talk to her about the dresses. Jane sat patiently listening, a cup of tea and a biscuit in front of her, while Anne explained the problem.

Alison, the mother of the other bridesmaid Julie, didn't have much money, but she would be too proud to take charity and would insist on paying for Julie's dress. The wedding planner book that Linda had lent them said that the bridesmaids normally bought their own dresses, and although Anne had tried to pretend that the bride's father always paid for the dresses, Julie's mother believed the book and wouldn't hear of Anne paying.

There were cheap bridesmaid dresses you could buy off the peg in the chain fashion stores, but Anne was worried they would not be good enough for Jane, and it would look dreadful if Jane had a really nice dress but Julie had a cheap one. They needed to match. Anne had looked at the dresses in the shop, and they were all ribbons and bows and frills and would make the girls look and feel about ten years old. That may have passed for Julie who was scarcely sixteen, but she knew that Jane would not want to be dressed like that. The shop also had some tight low-cut satin dresses in rather loud colours, but Anne thought they would be difficult to dance in and they would make both girls look cheap.

She knew that Jane could choose something beautiful in London for them from somewhere more upmarket, but that would leave Julie's mother in an awkward position, wanting to pay for something that she couldn't possibly afford.

Anne asked if Jane could think of anything they could do to get around this. Was there any way they could buy something more expensive and cheat about the cost? Anne was of course happy to pay for Julie's dress even if Jane preferred to pay for her own. She wanted Julie to have the chance to be a bridesmaid, as she had always been Claire's best friend, and she had dressed for most of her life in hand-me-downs from Candy. It would be dreadful if she couldn't be a bridesmaid because her mother couldn't afford the dress.

Jane thought for a while, nibbled at the biscuit, and came up with a plan. She and Rebecca had been bridesmaids to Sarah less than a year ago, along with another girl she hadn't known very well, Tony's cousin Sonia. Only last night she had been looking at the wedding photographs of the girls in their dresses. She still had her own dress, and she would phone Rebecca that evening and ask if she still had hers. Rebecca was a friendly and obliging girl, and Jane was sure she would lend it if she still had it. Then Jane could take the train to Richmond one morning, pick up both dresses, and return in the afternoon.

Jane's dress was a cornflower blue, Rebecca's a deep rose pink, and Sonia's apple green. The sleeves were fitted to the elbow, then had a flounce which fell to a point so they looked medieval. The bodice was covered with matching coloured lace and was fitted to hip level, with ribbon lacing which added to the medieval look. The skirt was a full circle, beautifully draping in a soft cascade of satin.

Julie was a girl of waif-like thinness, so at worst the dress would need taking in, and possibly taking up as well, as Rebecca was slim but tall.

Jane could sense Anne's relief at this suggestion, and she hoped it would go as planned. Weddings were not as straightforward as you would expect.

Claire was to have worn her mother's wedding dress, but post-war brides were naturally thin from living on rations and doing outdoor work that the men had previously done. It was already obvious it would never fit Claire in her condition. There was a lot of fabric in it, however, and Anne seemed confident she could alter it to fit.

There was also to be a very small bridesmaid, Reverend Colin's daughter Daisy. She was already a seasoned bridesmaid, as this was to be her third wedding, and she was still only four. Colin's mother was making her dress.

The McCann boys were all to have new suits. The two youngest were to be the ushers, along with Winston and Adrian Phillips, while David and Jimmy would drive the wedding cars. Daniel's Rover would be borrowed for the bride, but the bridesmaids would have to make do with Jack McCann's Land Rover. The Jaguar was needed for the groom and the best man. Daniel and Mary would walk to the church.

With the dresses, suits and cars now sorted out, they went through the arrangements for the service. Pat and Claire were to be married in the church at three, followed by photographs in the churchyard if the weather permitted or in the porch if it didn't, and the reception would be held in the village hall. Most of the village was invited, but the hall was large enough to fit everyone who was likely to come. The caterers from town would provide a buffet meal, and everyone brought a contribution to the supper which was served later, partway through the dancing. The landlord of the Black Horse Inn, Craig Austin, would arrange the drinks, with only a skeleton staff left at the pub for the evening. His brother would come to help out. After the speeches and toasts and meal, there would be dancing until ten o' clock. That left only the rings, the flowers, the photographers, the programmes for the service, the wedding cake and the band to arrange.

The bride and groom would spend the night at the farm or the Hall, and would leave the next morning for their honeymoon in Devon. Daniel was lending them the Rover for the week. When they returned, they were to live in the lodge. The renovations would be started soon. The plans had been drawn up, and they were waiting for the approvals to come through from the council and the final quote from the builder.

Jane was still at the farm when Jack and Jimmy returned to the farmhouse. Anne had been telling her stories about her father. She had grown up on one of the neighbouring farms before she married Jack, and they had both been friends with Peter. He had been the best man at their wedding. She had shown Jane the wedding photos.

Jimmy walked Jane home, but she wouldn't let him hold her hand in case Ryan passed them in the lane on his way back from Oxford. She tried to keep her distance because she knew that eventually she would have to tell him that she only wanted to be friends. She knew that she should tell him now that she and Ryan were planning to get engaged, but she didn't altogether trust him not to chat to his family about it, and it could get back to Daniel.

When they reached the back door, Mary asked him in, but he couldn't stay, as his mother was making supper, and he didn't want to hold everyone up. Ryan was not yet back. Jane couldn't resist Jimmy's offer of a quick kiss before he went home, but only after she had checked that Mary was not watching them, and she wouldn't agree to go out with him on the Wednesday, reminding him she didn't like to go out while Ryan was at home.

Jane phoned Rebecca and arranged for the pink dress to be left with Sarah later in the week. Rebecca said she would get it cleaned first, and that Julie could keep it if she wanted, as she was unlikely to wear it again. The matching shoes might fit Julie, so she would send those as well. She didn't need the shoes to be returned either, as no one would wear pink shoes anywhere but a wedding. She would contact Sonia and ask if she still had the green dress. Then Julie could choose which colour she preferred, and it would give two chances for a dress to fit her.

Jane then phoned Anne with the news that the arrangement had gone to plan. She would collect the dresses from Richmond next week, and bring Rebecca's to the farm on the following Sunday. If they could arrange for Julie to be there, she could try it on in case alterations were needed. It might also be a good time for some dancing lessons, so Claire, Julie and Jimmy would know the steps for the waltz. She would bring Pat of course, and hopefully Ryan as well, as he had to dance with her. She suggested Claire might like to ask Candy to the dancing lesson so David had a partner. Jack and Anne McCann would know how to dance because when they were young, everyone could dance. Jane assumed Daniel would dance with Mary to complete the bridal party, but they could look after that themselves. She couldn't imagine Daniel practising dancing at the farm, and she didn't want him to. He would want to dance with her, while she wanted to dance with Ryan.

Tuesday 9 March 1976

'I hope you don't think I'll let you marry that McCann boy,' Daniel said when she was typing in the library the following morning. 'I saw him kissing you at the back door. Does Ryan know about that?'

'Only if you're mean enough to tell him,' Jane replied. 'I hope you will behave like a gentleman and keep it to yourself.'

'Give me a kiss, and I'll promise not to tell on you. You kiss him, why not me?'

She had been back here for only three days and already this was becoming insufferable, she thought.

'No, Mr Linden. I only kiss men who keep their hands to themselves.'

'You're not to do it again. I won't have it. And that young architect had his eye on you. I hope you haven't been kissing him behind my back.'

'Alex Miller? No of course not. I showed him the conservatory so he could design the one at the lodge to match it. That was weeks ago. Really, Mr Linden, please try to keep your imagination under better control.'

'It's not *Mr Linden*, its *Daniel*. I've told you that before.'

'Yes, Sir. Sorry Sir. I do call you Daniel when you're good.'

'Don't call me *Sir*, either. Escorts do that. It's usually because they've forgotten your name. You're not one of them. Although I wish you were. You'd sleep with me then. I'd pay you anything you want.'

'Mr Linden, please don't talk to me like that.'

She told him about the wedding plans, going through all the details, trying to steer the conversation away from his constant harassment and innuendo. She said he would need to dance the opening waltz with Mary, and she hoped he knew how to waltz.

'You could show me,' he suggested, but she said nothing. 'Can't I dance with you instead?'

'Only if you're best man instead of Ryan. There are rules. The best man dances with the chief bridesmaid. Jimmy is second groomsman because he drives the wedding car, so he dances with Julie.'

'Too complicated for me. What about the second dance. Will you dance with me then?'

'Second dance the best man gets the bride, the groom gets the chief bridesmaid, the other bridesmaid gets David, as he drives the bridesmaids' car. You get Anne McCann, and Mary gets Jack McCann.'

'Maybe I'll sit that one out. She might tread on my toes, and she looks rather heavy. She was only a wisp of a thing when she was first married, like Claire is now, and quite pretty, but the years catch up with us all. If I am very patient and can stay on my feet for long enough, will I get the third dance with you? What about the third dance and every dance after that.'

'Let me see. The third dance you get the bride, Pat gets Mary, I get Jack McCann,' she smiled so he knew she was teasing him. 'Yes, you can have the third, Daniel, but you must promise to behave. No wandering hands.'

As long as he kept to this light-hearted flirting, she could cope with it, tiring though it was. She knew the best response was to make him laugh. She hoped he wouldn't tell Ryan about her lapse with Jimmy McCann, but she really did need to be more careful. Ryan had joked about having spies in the camp, but Jane knew she had a dangerous enemy who would be overjoyed to snitch on her.

As the days passed, she coped with Daniel, moving away when she found him too close to her, reminding him of his promise not to mention marriage to her although he frequently did. For the first few days after she had returned from Richmond, he had behaved well enough, but he was now gradually slipping back to his old ways. She wished he would go to London and leave her alone for a day, but he seemed to have lost interest in that. He hadn't gone to London since late January.

Sometimes he touched her neck as she typed, sliding his finger beneath her collar, and once he leaned over her and breathed in her ear. She knew she had to stop this before it went any further. He was getting bolder, telling her that she would enjoy being married to him, asking her to sleep with him, but doing it in an amused way as if he was just flirting with her and not expecting her to take him seriously. At least he was keeping his hands under better control.

'Mr Linden, I have a suggestion for you. Why don't you go up to London, hire a young lady from the agency, and when you sleep with her, pretend it's me.'

He laughed at this. 'Who told you what I do in London?'

'Pat told me. He thought if I married you, I could persuade you to give him more money so he could buy the car he wanted.'

'He wanted you to marry me, and he goes and tells you that?'

'He thought it would save the cost of the London hotel, and I might care about that. Perhaps he hoped you would pass the saved money on to him.'

Daniel had a better solution, much less bother for everyone. Jane could sleep with him and pretend he was Ryan, or Jimmy if she preferred him. Men were all the same in the dark. She could just lie back on the bed and close her eyes and he would look after everything else, and he promised it would feel good. He would even undress her if she would let him. He would enjoy doing that. He would have her wanting him as much as he wanted her.

She didn't like this, and wished she had said nothing.

'You think my son is in love with you, don't you?' he said.

'Your idea of loving a girl is sleeping with her. Ryan's is caring about her.'

She remembered him looking after her blistered feet, polishing her boots, buying socks for her and a warm scarf, sitting with her on the swing in the conservatory concerned that she was unhappy, holding her when they sat on the stairs in the lodge, caring that she was upset about Pat marrying someone else, although he was himself hurt by finding her there, not taking advantage of her at Richmond when she was a bit tipsy and would happily have slept with him. That was love, not this *I have to sleep with you, you're driving me insane* kind of love that seemed to be all Daniel understood.

'You know I care about you. You can have anything money can buy. He acts like a besotted lovesick puppy wanting to lick your boots, but he doesn't like girls, and he won't make love to you. Sleep with me and pretend it's him. He won't care. He could still idolise you. That's all he wants. Then all of us will be happy.'

She knew making him laugh usually defused the situation when he got into this way of talking to her. 'I promise he has never once licked my boots. He cleans my boots, but he does it in the usual way with a brush. You have never once offered to clean my boots.'

'Boots are Ryan's job, and always have been. He gets all this money from me, and he hardly does anything around the house. He can't even make his own porridge. He expects Mary to get up early to make it for him. No one else has porridge. Horrible stuff. It's what they serve up for breakfast in that college of his, like something out of Dickens. It stops them from wanting women. At least Pat does the garden.'

Friday 12 March 1976

She told Mary she needed a new prescription for the sedatives, and Mary found her the phone number for the doctor in town. She booked an appointment for the Friday when Pat would take Mary to town for shopping. It was easy. She asked for the sedatives and explained that she was shortly getting engaged and would like to go on the pill. There were a few checks and some instructions but nothing complicated. Jane asked about the Rhesus babies as her boyfriend was related to her and his grandmother had lost two babies. She was assured it was no longer a problem if they did blood tests beforehand. If Jane was planning a baby, she was to come in, and they would arrange it.

Jane came home that day with what she needed to make it safe for her to sleep with her lover. It made her feel in control of her life, being able to organise that by herself. But she didn't tell Ryan, as she didn't want him to think her too forward, and she was starting to wonder if he still wanted to sleep with her at all. He really had gone back to treating her the way he did before they were at Richmond together. He had once told her he found the thought of sleeping with a girl rather distasteful. Did he still think that way about her?

She and Ryan spent the evening in the library. Daniel was watching television with Mary, and Pat had gone down to the farm to be with Claire.

They finished the jigsaw of the steam train and talked about books, the renovation of the lodge, the upcoming wedding, but not about their time in Richmond or them living together in Oxford, and he didn't touch her or even try to hold her hand, even though they were well out of sight of his father.

She didn't tell him Daniel was still harassing her. She was coping with it by herself for the moment.

It was now the end of the term, and Ryan would not need to return to Oxford for several weeks, although he would work in his study in the mornings while she helped Daniel.

Saturday 13 March 1976

On Saturday morning Ryan took Mary to the station and stayed in town to do some shopping of his own. Pat was at John Phillips' farm, helping to fix a tractor that had broken down. Jane was left alone in the house with Daniel, so she kept out of his way, putting her clothes into the washing machine and doing some ironing for Mary.

She took Daniel his coffee at ten thirty, but managed to slip back to the kitchen without him realising everyone else was out. When she had finished ironing the men's shirts, she took her clothes from the washing machine, put her liberty shirts and her pyjamas on the clothes airer and put her underwear and the mesh washing bag containing her tights into the tumble dryer.

Then she found her wellingtons and walked up the lane to John Phillips' farm to see how the tractor was going and to see the baby turkeys. She liked the old man, and he was always pleased to see her. He remembered her father and liked to talk about him, and about his son Robert who worked in Geneva. They didn't see him much although he usually came home at Christmas. Jane reminded him that she had met Robert at Christmas, and he had talked about her father.

There were some new very small turkeys, but the others seemed much larger than they had been last week, and some were now quite recognisable as turkeys. Their greyish-honey colour had turned to medium grey, but they were still cute and fluffy.

After an hour or so she returned to the Hall, leaving Pat and Winston still working on the tractor. They had put it back together and were testing that the repair had been successful.

She knew that Ryan was back from shopping because the garage door was now closed. She passed the dryer in the scullery. Her load had finished, so she pulled out the underclothes, folding them into her cane washing basket.

She realised with a cold flood of horror that the black lace knickers were missing. Everything else was there, the white underwear and the new coloured knickers, the black bra and the plain black knickers. She checked the depths of the dryer and the washing machine, but there was no sign of the lace ones. She knew she had washed them, because she had wondered whether it would be safer to put them in the mesh bag with the tights. She continued into the kitchen where Ryan was making himself a coffee. Had he seen them through the glass door of the dryer and stolen them?

'Did you take something from the dryer,' she asked him as casually as she could. Not that she would really have minded if he had, as it was about time he got interested in what she wore beneath her clothes. She had bought them to look sexy for him.

He denied it, and she believed him, as he seemed completely surprised at the question. He asked her what was missing, but she didn't immediately reply. She saw that Daniel's coffee cup had been returned to the kitchen and knew straight away he was the culprit. She didn't like the thought that he had something so intimate of hers, or that he knew she wore anything so scanty. He wouldn't realise she wore them beneath her tights with more respectable knickers over the top, and she could hardly explain that to him. Now when he looked at her, he would be thinking about her wearing them.

'I think your father has taken something of mine. I'll take more care not to go out of sight of the dryer next time.'

'Would you like me to ask him to return it?'

'I prefer you don't mention it. I don't want him to know it has upset me. I can easily replace it; it's not worth an argument. But before I do, I'll ask Mary to check his room.'

She took her remaining washing up to her bedroom then made lunch for them all. Pat was now back from the farm, so she sent him to get Daniel from his den. She didn't mention the missing knickers, as she didn't want him to make some joke about them in front of Pat and Ryan, or even worse, take them out of his pocket and hold them up.

They were walking to Peddleton again that afternoon, and she was glad to get out of the house and be with Ryan for the afternoon. She stayed close to him when she could, wishing he would hold her hand.

Tea was once again served outside at the farm, as the day was warm for March. It was good to be away from Daniel. She couldn't talk about him to Ryan with everyone else there, so she tried to forget about him and enjoy the afternoon. But she couldn't enjoy it; she could only think about the missing knickers. She knew that coming back to the Hall was a mistake, that nothing was going to change and nothing had changed, except that he was getting bolder in what he said to her. He was never going to just hand her over to Ryan without a fight.

Colin was asking her about her trip back to Richmond. Had she sorted out what she went back there for? But she could only give him a non-committal answer, trying to hide that she was upset. It was only a pair of knickers. Daniel had probably seen hundreds in his time. But these were hers, and she had bought them so she could feel sexy with Ryan, not for Daniel to crow over. She didn't like to think what he would do with them. Maybe he just collected them. Ryan was beside her, and he reached for her hand under the table; she knew he could see she was unhappy.

She made an effort at conversation, asking Colin if he had seen the baby turkeys, and telling him how surprised she was at how much bigger they had grown in only a week. Winston and Adrian were sitting opposite them at the table, and they were consulted about how long it took for the turkeys to lose all their cute fluff and become fully grown.

Sunday 14 March 1976

On Sunday afternoon Jane and Ryan went to Bath to see Ryan's grandfather. It was so good to be driving away from Hayward. She wished they were never coming back. At least here in the car she could talk to Ryan with no one else there to listen to what she said. She tried to talk about safe things, the wedding, the renovations, the turkeys, the grandsons of John Phillips.

Ryan told her that they came to stay with their grandfather every weekend because their mother had left their father years ago and now lived with a new husband in Scotland. They boarded at a school near Oxford. With their father working in Geneva, only their grandfather's farm was close enough for them to go to on weekends. They went to Scotland to stay with their mother for the summer holidays, and only saw their father for a couple of weeks at Christmas.

Other people had problems and conflicts, Jane thought. At least she had been brought up with parents who loved each other and were there for her when she needed them. Until they weren't.

But inevitably she returned to talking about Daniel. Things were not going well, she was not sure how much longer she could cope, and she didn't know what to do. Ryan reminded her he would be at home for the next few weeks, and any time she wanted they could leave. Pat's wedding was now less than five weeks away. They would spend a few days together in Richmond in a week or so. He could bring his typewriter down to the library so he was there when she did the typing for Daniel in the mornings. It hadn't worked in the Christmas holiday, but they could try again. Or they could both work on sorting some of the papers in Daniel's den. Jane seemed to have given up on doing the sorting, as typing the manuscript was taking so much of her time. Daniel could hardly harass her with him in the room. Why had she got so upset about the stolen underwear? It was only clothes.

She knew he didn't understand, perhaps a man wouldn't.

'Please don't be cross with me. I'm sorry I was upset. They were black lace knickers and rather sinful,' she said, remembering the word he had once used to describe her dress. She could scarcely believe she was telling him this. 'They didn't leave much to the imagination. I bought them to wear under the tights when we went out to dinner, but I wore something more respectable over the top of the tights to keep them up. I don't like the idea of Daniel thinking about me wearing them. He said something very sleazy to me once about young women looking beautiful without their clothes, and I don't like him thinking like that about me. He wouldn't understand that I would have tights on as well, and I don't like him knowing what I wear under my clothes. I only bought them to look sexy for you, and I only wore them once when we had dinner at the hotel. They were meant for you, not for him.'

He laughed. 'Maybe I should have untied the dress. Perhaps one day you'll give me another chance. Suppose we steal something of his and offer him a swap. What about his credit card?'

'He would keep that in his pocket, and I'm not putting my hands in his pockets for anything, especially his trouser pockets.'

'It will be in the inside pocket of his jacket. We could turn up the heating in the den and wait until he gets hot and takes the jacket off. I'll distract him, and you steal the card. Then we'll negotiate with him. Mary can arbitrate.'

She laughed, and she felt better. It was only a silly pair of knickers.

'I wouldn't have minded if it was you who had taken them,' she told him. 'I'll cope with him. You don't need to work downstairs. It really didn't work before in the Christmas holidays. I still hope he will accept that I don't want to marry him so we can both stay here.'

They arrived at the retirement home to find themselves in the middle of a party. One of the ladies was a hundred years old today. There were balloons and a cake with a hundred candles; the lady's two great-granddaughters helped to blow them out.

Ryan gave his grandfather the framed photograph of them both to put in his room. The old man asked if they were engaged yet, so Ryan told them he hoped they would be by their next visit, and he seemed happy with that. Pamela overheard and congratulated them, saying she would be happy to see Ryan settled with such a lovely girl as Jane. He had been coming to see his grandfather for a good many years now, and it was always a pleasure to have him there. He had helped her put together the history of the house a few years back, and she would always be grateful for that.

Here they both were, Jane thought, talking like lovers, accepted as lovers, everyone happy for them, no one imagining that back at Hayward Hall they had to contend with Daniel's jealousy of his son and his constant harassment of Jane. She wondered what Pamela would think if she knew Jane's future father-in-law had stolen her underwear from the tumble dryer.

Wednesday 17 March 1976

On Wednesday the final quote arrived from the builder for the renovations to the lodge for outside painting, new wallpaper, rewiring, new paint, carpets upstairs, tiles downstairs to replace the musty lino, new bathroom fittings, new kitchen cupboards, converting the coal cellar to a cloakroom and a little space that would fit a washing machine and dryer, and adding the new conservatory. Then there was heating to both floors and hot water.

'He gets a young lady into trouble and expects me to supply them a house and an income.' Daniel grumbled, as they both looked at the quote. 'He's lazy and spoilt, always pestering me to buy him an expensive car, telling me he's no good at anything so he can't get a proper job. He can fix up cars. He's good at that. He can buy himself an old Mini and fix that up.

'His father sends money to Mary for him as well, and some for herself. He paid Pat's school fees. Although I would, of course, have been happy to do that.'

'Daniel, do you know who Pat's father is?'

'No, Jane, I don't. It is all arranged through Allanstone. When I was his age, I was in the army and working in the War Office as an aide to one of the generals. We looked after mapping and strategy and arranging supplies, and sometimes I drove the general about. It was difficult during the War, as we didn't know then that our side would win. For a while it all looked rather bleak. Not that anyone really wins in a war. I recall a day we were all in a bunker on the south coast, watching a practice run for a beach landing. Churchill was there with my general, and Eisenhower and the King. My father was there as well, commanding the men on the beach. I remember thinking that a lot of them would never make it home. But there was nothing any of us could do to stop the madness. We could only do our best to minimise the damage. If good men don't fight evil, it takes control of the whole world. In the end it all worked out, and our side won, but my father was one of those who never made it home from Normandy.

'My mother had to keep this place going on her own. Mary was only four when the War started, I was nineteen, and your father was ten. My mother had the worry of looking after guests, keeping chickens so there were eggs, finding enough tea and sugar to give them breakfast, paying the bills, keeping up the maintenance, doing the garden herself, and never knowing if her husband and son would still be alive at the end of each day. She was grateful for the rabbits that your father, Jack McCann and Robert Phillips shot for her. They were still all teenagers then and too young to fight, but they could shoot rabbits, and they all helped keep the farms going. Jack's older brother Jim was killed at Dunkirk. He was the same age as me, and we had always been friends.

'In the end my father was missing presumed dead near the end of the War. He still lies at the bottom of the sea near Normandy. It nearly destroyed my mother. Every time the phone rang, she would be hoping there was a mistake and it was him returning, but it was always just a guest making a booking. We couldn't even bury him—just a brass plaque on a cold stone wall in the church. Eventually she gave up hope of course, but she still worked like a slave to keep this house going for me and Mary and Caroline. Before she died, she told my sister that she wanted her ashes scattered on the sea where he had died, but in the end we decided to bury her in the churchyard with the rest of the family.

'Caroline was sixteen when the War started. She worked with me for a while, then went to work at Bletchley Park, decoding the messages. She was clever with numbers, same as you are. We dated when we could, and wrote to each other, and after the war she married me, but not before I made sure we had enough to live on. I finished my degree and got a job at a solicitor's office in Oxford. I adored her, Jane, like nothing you've ever experienced or ever could. There's nothing in the world that feels better than making love to a woman you are in love with. Sex with escorts never comes near it. I'd have died for her. She was always glamorous—everyone wanted to look like film stars in those days. She always wore high heels, and one day she fell on the stairs, and they couldn't save her. She and I had gone through a war together, celebrated that we had both survived to the end of it, and then she died because a heel had broken on her shoe.

'I wanted to die with her, but my mother had locked away all the guns, there wasn't even a knife to be found in the kitchen, so I got a bottle of whisky from the cellar thinking if I drank the whole lot, I'd be dead in the morning. But I wasn't. I threw up all night, and the next day I had a hangover that was complete misery. I swore I'd never have another drink, but the whisky didn't kill me.

'Your father helped me get through it. He helped me write a memoir of my time in the War Office, and that led me to take up writing books. He was at school during the War and for a year or two afterwards, then he went on to Oxford to get his degree. He was still at Oxford when Caroline died; he would have been nineteen then. For a while he worked as a maths teacher at a boys' school. He gave most of what he earned to my mother to help with running the house, same as I did.

'One summer your mother came here with your aunt, and she was just like Caroline, beautiful and clever—she even looked like Caroline— and I thought fate had sent her to me. But she fell in love with your father, and they went away to live in Richmond. My mother missed him terribly, and she blamed me for antagonising him. He was nephew to her husband, but she loved him just as much as she loved her own children, Mary and me.

'Then you came, and you looked like Caroline and Josie, and I thought fate was giving me another chance at love, but all you did was chase after my son. Don't pretend he slept with you at Richmond. I know him well enough to know he didn't. You would have come back engaged, or more likely the two of you would never have come back here at all. He'll never marry you; he doesn't care for girls. I think he's gay, but he did once deny it. I brought a young lady here to sleep with him. It was supposed to be a present for him when he was eighteen. She came from an agency in London. I asked them for their best and youngest girl for my son, and the woman who ran the place sent a stunner. I was a good customer. She was high class and really lovely to look at, beautiful big blue eyes like yours. In the morning he told me not to waste my money doing that again, so I asked him if he preferred men to women, but he just said he didn't want either, he just liked to be by himself.'

'Do you know what became of her?' Jane asked, rather intrigued to be hearing his side of the same story.

'Actually, Jane, I do,' he said, seeming rather surprised at her interest. 'Do you really want to hear it? I don't want to upset you. I'm not a saint, but if you married me, I would only want you.'

'I promise I won't be upset. And I'm not marrying you, Mr Linden. I am quite happy for you to sleep with anyone you like as long as it's not me.'

'As I said, she was really beautiful, so the next time I went up to London I asked them for the same girl. She was called Lily, but that was not her real name. They never use their real names. I took her out a few times, and I actually thought about bringing her here to live, maybe even to marry her if my mother got upset about her living in sin here with me. But I had brought her here before for Ryan. I knew he would recognise her, and I couldn't face what he would tell my mother. She would have been horrified at what I had done.

'So I set the girl up in a rented flat near Regent's Park, and met her there as often as I could. Sometimes I would stay there all week with her. She was attractive and skilled at pleasing men, but I was never in love with her, and she knew that. She was allowed other dates, but she wasn't allowed to bring them to the flat; that seemed fair to me.

'It lasted about six months. Then she told me she was marrying a client, and I let her stay in the flat until the wedding. He had been married twice before, but his second wife had left him for his best friend. They had gone to Canada, leaving him with his two teenage children from his first marriage. He had wanted a girl to take out for the night, and the lady who ran the agency gave Lily the date, as she was still the best girl there. After he had dated her a few times, he decided to marry her. He would get a beautiful young bride who was good in bed and who would be completely loyal to him, as she had too much to lose by being unfaithful. He was a wealthy man, and a real catch for a girl like her. There was probably spite towards his ex-wife involved as well, since he was replacing her with a beautiful younger woman. She became stepmother to his children, and as far as I know she is still with him.'

She could actually like him if he wasn't such a predator, Jane thought. He was a complex and unhappy man who had been treated badly by fate. But she could never love him the way she would want to love a husband. However much she felt sorry for him, she knew that was no basis to marry him. If there had been no Ryan in her life, would she have accepted him? She didn't think so. She would have forgiven his past, but she could never love him enough to overcome her aversion to sleeping with him. The constant smell of whisky on his breath revolted her, and she hated him to even come close to her.

She typed up the cheque for the deposit for the builder and phoned their office to say it was on its way and to arrange a date for them to start.

Ryan was working on his thesis in his study. Mary took the cheque up to him to sign.

Daniel asked her to walk with him down to the village to post it. He needed fresh air, and they would be in full view of everyone.

The day was cold. He helped her put on her coat, and he wrapped her scarf around her neck and pulled her beanie down over her ears, then adjusted it, as it was now covering her eyes as well. Ryan was at home, so Daniel couldn't take the duffle coat. He put on his black Burberry coat and his black trilby hat, and she remembered Sarah saying the Lindens all looked like black vampires. For all that, he looked every inch the squire, and he was still a good-looking man. She knew a lot of girls would be happy to marry him, even without his wealth. She wouldn't take his arm, as she didn't want to touch him, and this walk was all in the lane, so there were no stiles for him to help her over. He was silent as he usually was when they were out walking, but she didn't mind. She understood he liked to think out in the fresh air.

When they had posted the letter, they walked past the war memorial and across the green to the church and went inside.

They were by themselves in the stillness, and Jane sat wordlessly beside him in their pew. The plaque remembering his father was on the wall at the end of the row, above the plaques for his two uncles who were killed in the First World War.

COL JAMES EDWARD LINDEN

MISSING IN ACTION

NORMANDY 6 JUNE 1944

There was no sun today to make the dust dance in the sunbeams, but it was always peaceful here, with the scent of flowers and the gentle stillness of ancient places. She couldn't even begin to comprehend the heartache of that plaque, but she had finally got over crying at every sad thought, and if there was an afterlife then James and Kathleen

Linden were back together. You couldn't take on everyone else's sorrows as well as your own. There were a lot of things she would like to be able to go back and change, but it was futile. Bad things happened, and you just had to pick up the pieces and get on with your life. Kathleen Linden had done that. She had still had two children and an orphaned nephew to love and care for, and later two grandsons. Jane was sad that she had never met her, and grateful that Kathleen had cared enough to knit a cardigan for her and have photographs of her on the walls. If she was still living, she might be glad if Jane and Ryan were married. She would want them both to be happy.

'I once did something that I have regretted all my life since,' Daniel told her. 'I try to drown the memory of it, but it haunts me and always will.'

He didn't continue. He just sat there beside her in the stillness for what seemed a long while. She looked at his profile as he raised his eyes to the stained glass behind the alter. He was beautiful like Ryan, but the years and the whisky had etched lines of sadness on his face. She could never love him as she would expect to love a husband, but she did care about him. Lately he seemed to be talking to her about the past, as if he was finally coming to terms with it, as if his soul had gone through torture and come through into the peaceful light of acceptance. Life had not been kind to him, but was life kind to anyone?

'Are you going to tell me about it?' she asked at last, knowing that she was finally close to discovering the secret that this family was burying away from the world and from her.

'I had been shooting with John Phillips, and I came back through the gate in the wall from his farm to the garden. Your mother was walking by herself along the path through the wood, and I threatened her with the shotgun and raped her. My son came from nowhere to defend her, and I completely lost my temper and nearly killed him. He was a little child, only six years old, trying to protect a woman from a grown man.

'I still don't know what possessed me to do either of those things. I did sometimes lose my temper, but I was never a violent man. I thought she was sent by fate for me, but she loved my cousin. I was just very angry at what life had dealt me.

'Josie tried to help him up, but he couldn't stand. He was stunned. His eyes were wandering all over the place, and he didn't even whimper. I could see I had broken his arm. Even after what I had done to her, she only cared about Ryan. I knew I had hurt her; she was bruised and bleeding from trying to fight me off. She asked me for my jacket and I just handed it to her. She wrapped Ryan in it to keep his arm supported, then she picked him up, trying to comfort him, and stood there facing me, with her dress ripped. She asked me to hand her the gun that was lying there between us. She couldn't pick it up herself because she was holding Ryan. She said she didn't want me shooting her or Ryan or myself. It wasn't loaded, but she would not have known that. She was so calm, and I was so shocked at what I had done that I just did as she asked.

'That was the last I ever saw her, and that is how I remember her, bravely facing me, knowing I could have shot both of them. She took him back to the house, and I sat all day in the garden thinking he would die, and I couldn't move from where I was. Eventually darkness fell, and I went back inside. Everyone was asleep, and I didn't know what had happened to him. I went to his room, but the bed was empty. I sat in the den and tried to kill myself with whisky again, but it didn't work. It never works. I was sick the next day, but I wasn't dead. In the morning Mary found me, told me that Peter had taken Josie away, and that Ryan was in hospital in Oxford. I was so relieved he wasn't dead.

'I should have gone to prison for what I did to both of them, but Josie never said anything. I suppose she told your father, but I was never charged. Men often get away with rape. It's hard enough now for a girl to stand up in court and say a man raped her, but it was even worse then, and I dare say she didn't want to face it. She would have been made to feel that she was the one on trial and that she had asked for it. There were no witnesses except Ryan, and Peter didn't want him traumatised any more than he had been. And my mother kept quiet about what I did to my son, she covered it up, because she was afraid he would be put into foster care.

'If I had killed him, it would have been the ultimate betrayal of my love for my wife, and I could never have lived with the guilt. He was all that was left of her life. I don't believe in God, Jane, but I still thank him that Ryan recovered. A lot of his bones were broken, and at first they thought his spine was damaged, as he couldn't stand up. I was frantic with worrying about him, imagining all sorts of terrible consequences, and knowing it would be my fault if he died, or was brain-damaged or paralysed. My mother still had the guns locked away, but there was rope in the old stables. I found a length of it, worked out which beam I would hang it from, then hid it away.

'Mary had to run the house and look after the guests with Pat only six weeks old and Peter gone, while my mother went each day to the hospital. I wanted to ask her if he would recover, but I couldn't face the anger in her eyes when she looked at me. So I just hid in the den, and Mary would bring me coffee and food and whisky. Each day I expected my mother to come back saying he had died, and I would have gone to the stables when everyone was asleep and hanged myself from the beam.

'But in the end he was all right, and he came back here just as bright and active as he had ever been. His right arm was weak, but he tried really hard to overcome it. He took up rowing when he was a teenager, and he still does that. He learnt to use his left arm where strength mattered—he plays cricket left-handed. But from that day forward he hated me, and I never blamed him for that. He even tried to keep Pat away from me to protect him. And every time he looked at me with his mother's eyes reproaching me, every time I saw him patiently struggling with a button, or a nut and bolt on the Meccano, I was wracked with guilt over what I had done to her son. I still feel like that, but there is nothing I can ever do to change what happened.'

Jane didn't know what to say to him. She wasn't sure what she had expected, but she was shocked at what she heard. She felt very young and completely out of her depth. This was why her father had left here with her mother, and this was why Ryan avoided his father. He had broken his arm as a child, he had once told her, and he didn't like to think about the day it happened. She could only begin to imagine the effect of that day on a child of six, the absolute loss of faith in someone who was supposed to love and protect you. And her own father had left here that day as well, Ryan's uncle Peter who was more of a father to him than Daniel was. Ryan had once told her he felt rejected when Peter left, but later he had understood. Now she understood too. Daniel had raped Jane's mother knowing that she was in love with his cousin Peter, who had been brought up as a brother to him. There are some things that no man could ever forgive.

She was coming to realise that now the same story was happening again. Daniel wanted her, but she wanted his son. She was afraid of him, and she could see no way forward. Was this all to end in an ugly confrontation, or could it be controlled, talked about, some resolution reached?

'There was another incident, Jane, where I got the blame unfairly. I had a mistress who came here sometimes on the weekends, and she tried to seduce my son when he was sixteen. My mother thought I had put her up to it, but I swear I didn't. I was as shocked as she was. I don't know what happened between them, but I think that was what put him off women. He would never talk about it, and after that he became really depressed and cold and withdrawn. He wouldn't even hug Mary or my mother. That was why I hired the girl for him when he was eighteen. I wanted him to have a better experience—those girls know how to make a man feel good—but he didn't appreciate it. Has anyone here ever told you any of this?'

'I was only told there was a row because you and my father were both in love with my mother. My mother is dead, but Ryan still lives with the memory of what happened that day. You can never change the past, but perhaps you could atone for it a little if you let me marry Ryan. Please, Daniel, give us your blessing and let us live here together with you. You have been given another chance, and this time you could do the right thing. You and I were happy here for a while, and we could go back to that. I type things for you, I play chess with you, I walk with you, we laugh at things together, we play table tennis, and you talk to me about Caroline. None of that would change. I really do care about you, but I don't want to sleep with you. You can go to your escorts in London for that. I could have been your daughter. Could you not think of me in that way?'

'If you were my daughter then you couldn't marry my son,' he said with undeniable logic, but she knew he was just putting off answering her.

'Sometimes I imagine what life would be like if Caroline hadn't died. I have money now. I could give her anything she wanted, and our son might have grown up confident and successful. He was always clever; he could have done anything. He might have respected me, and I could have been proud of him. And Mary could have gone to live with her lover. He wanted her to live with him, but with Caroline gone, and then Peter as well, my mother needed Mary's help to run the house and look after the guests. We could all have been so happy here. You would have come here with your father for holidays, perhaps he and Josie would even have stayed living here, and Ryan may have fallen for you and married you with the blessing of all of us. But instead he's a wimp who hides away from the world, clinging to the safety of staying at school for the whole of his life, living like a hermit in that awful little room at Oxford working on the Doomsday Book. It's clever enough stuff, I dare say, because you have to interpret the writing and the language and the place names and relate it all to what we have today, but it seems dull and dead end to me. He lives there to get away from me. I know that he despises me. And he doesn't even have the gumption to make love to a beautiful girl who throws herself at him. You two were alone together in a house for a week, and even I can see he is hopelessly in love with you. I was frantic with jealousy, imagining you in bed together, thinking he had won. I was desperate to go after you, but Mary wouldn't allow me to. She said I had brought it on myself, and she wouldn't give me the car keys. She said you and Ryan had every right to be together if that was what you wanted. She even told me I was a ridiculous middle-aged man besotted with a teenage girl. Then you both came back and I knew nothing had happened.

'When Mary and I first talked about asking you here after your aunt died, I did think perhaps he would fall for you, that he might finally get over his aversion to women, and I wanted that for him and so did Mary. He even has a photo of you on his wall. But you are so beautiful that as soon as I saw you again, I wanted you for myself. I didn't want him driving over to fetch you from Richmond or even picking you up from the station. I wished he would just stay in Oxford and leave you for me.'

'If you loved us both, you would let us be together. I will never marry you, Daniel. You know that.'

'I never really loved him. He was a tiny little baby unlikely to live, so there was no point in loving him. He survived by the sheer willpower of Mary and your father. Then when he was older, he would look at me with his mother's eyes, and I resented that he was alive and she was dead. Even though he hated me for what I had done to him, he still tried his best to please me. He always worked hard at school, and he did as he was told. There was an argument when he wanted to read history at Oxford while I wanted him to read law, but my mother stepped in and said he had the right to choose what he wanted to do. She died not long afterwards. He always loved finding out about the past. He once told me that he talks with the ghosts of the ancient people who once lived in the hills here.

'He'll never marry you. He worships you like a goddess, but he would never make love to you. It would defile you for him, and he would hate himself every time he touched you. He could never get any pleasure out of it and neither would you. You need a man who can give you real love, passion and pleasure like you've never even dreamt of. You said if I let you marry him then perhaps I could atone for the past, but I just can't do it, Jane. You were meant for me. If you slept with him, I would kill you both, and myself as well.'

He was completely mad, she thought. She had no idea what she should say, or even how to extricate herself from sitting here with him in the quiet of the church. She was becoming really frightened of him and what he could do. Even if she and Ryan left, he might come after them. How could they stop him?

When she had first come here it had all seemed so safe, so healing for her to have a family she was a part of, so much better than feeling alone, uncared for, and afraid of being unable to cope. Daniel had seemed such a gentleman, the village squire, the perfect uncle who would care for her as her father had, his home the haven that she needed to recover from the darkness that shadowed her soul. Yes, he had flirted with her, often going too far in his attentions, but until now she had never feared for her safety.

'Please can we go home,' she said, and he followed her out of the church and along the lane to the Hall.

She said nothing to Ryan about what Daniel had told her although it troubled her deeply. She needed some time to consider it, to get over the shock she had felt at finally learning the truth of that sad long-ago day. She knew Ryan didn't like to think about the day her father had left, and now she understood why.

Thursday 18 March 1976

The following morning Ryan, Pat and Jane drove to Richmond. The two young men took the train into the city from there to have their suits fitted for the wedding. Jane had arranged to collect Rebecca's dress from Sarah and would look for her own dress in the attic. She would meet Pat and Ryan in the city at one o'clock for lunch with Mr Allanstone. Then they would return to Richmond, put the dresses in the car, and drive back to Hayward, before the worst of the commuter traffic left London.

It was so good to have a day away from Daniel's pursuit of her, even though his confession still gripped her thoughts in spite of every attempt she made to keep it at bay and think of something less confronting.

Jane found her dress in the attic, carefully folded in tissue paper in a box with the matching high-heeled shoes.

She thought back to when she had worn the dress at Sarah's wedding last summer. She had been eighteen then, only slightly younger than Sarah but much less worldly. Sarah and Tony had been married in a church in London, and the reception had been held at Sarah's father's beautiful house that bordered the Thames near Hampton Court. Jane had danced with the best man, and they had walked down to the river in the darkness, leaning their elbows on the low wall that separated the back garden from the tow-path by the river.

His name was Scott. She had asked him about his family, his job, where he had gone to school, and everything else she could think of. She wanted to be polite and friendly towards him because she liked him, she liked the way he looked, and she liked the idea that she might finally get a boyfriend. She met so few young men, as her great-aunt's friends were all old and she was too timid to go out to dances with the girls she had worked with.

He had kissed her in the warm night air, with the music far away in the background, the gentle splash of a night bird on the river, and soft reflections of the house lights on the dark water. She had never been kissed like that before, and it felt good. But then he had become an octopus. No sooner had she pulled his hand away from her derrière, his other hand was down the front of the dress, and he had asked her if she wanted to go upstairs and find a bedroom. She had pulled away from him rather warily and politely said no, she didn't know him well enough for that.

She had thought him a rather self-centred young man. He hadn't asked her a single thing about herself, not even where she worked, and she wasn't sure she liked the idea that you slept with a man first, then decided whether to fall in love with him. But he had seemed to accept her refusal with good grace, and he had gone back inside with her and stayed beside her for the whole evening. He was quite nice to talk to on the rare occasions he wasn't talking about himself and his achievements. He traded in futures, made vast sums of money for the firm he worked for and quite a lot of commission for himself. Jane had only a vague idea what a future was, but if he made money from them, then perhaps it didn't matter.

At the end of the evening, he had asked if she wanted to go back to his flat, but she had told him her aunt would be worried, and she had taken a taxi home as originally arranged. Aunt Ellen had come to the wedding but had left when the dancing started. Sarah's mother had understood that. Jane had always been Sarah's best friend at school, so Sarah's mother knew Jane's great-aunt was old and tired very easily.

The following Monday flowers had arrived for her. Aunt Ellen had put them in water and put the card aside for when she came home from work. He had phoned later that week and asked her out to dinner, and she had worn the dark-blue dress that she had once worn for a school dance. He had picked her up in an expensive sports car, and had been very polite to her great-aunt, promising to have her back by midnight. They had gone to a hotel, the car left at the door in the care of a valet to be parked until he wanted it. She had tried not to drink too much wine because she knew she needed to keep her head when she danced with him. She didn't want to be persuaded to go back to the flat, although she had been tempted by the thrill of being so close to him as they danced. She had politely refused his offer of booking a room at the hotel for an hour or two.

It had been late when they left, the car delivered to the door for him, and for a while he had parked near the river, his hands once again wandering all over her. She had been happy to kiss him, but she didn't want anything else at this stage, and she didn't want to go back to his flat. Perhaps they could do something together on the weekend, walk in a park or play tennis, visit an art gallery, so they could get to know each other better before they had an affair. Eventually he had taken her home and had said something vague about them spending the weekend at his father's country place, but there were no more flowers, and he had never contacted her again.

She phoned Sarah to say they had reached Richmond, and she was on her way over to collect Rebecca's dress.

Sarah seemed glad to see Jane, and she had the green dress and shoes as well. The other bridesmaid Sonia had been happy to lend her dress. Sarah said her mother was pleased that the dresses were being used again, as they were so beautiful.

Jane told her the evening had gone well after the dinner, without going into too much detail, and that she and Ryan were planning to get engaged but were waiting until after Pat's wedding to announce it.

She mentioned to Sarah that she had gone out to dinner with Scott last year, after meeting him at Sarah's wedding. Sarah had been on her honeymoon at the time, so she might not have known about it. Jane said she had only gone out with him once, and he had seemed a bit offended that she wouldn't go back to his flat. She asked after him. Did Sarah still know him?

Sarah seemed horrified. 'Thank goodness you didn't sleep with him. He chalks up his conquests, so you would be a name and number on a board. He probably puts up an extra star if he gets a virgin. He's Tony's cousin, brother to Sonia, otherwise I wouldn't be friends with him. I did see you together, but I didn't know then what he was like, or I would have warned you. Rebecca fell for him, but she got the last laugh. She's had a few lovers, so it didn't bother her. She said he was so hopeless in bed that no girl would want to make love with him twice, so every time he wanted to sleep with a girl, he had to find a new one. He lasted about ten seconds, and didn't seem to understand that the girl was supposed to enjoy it too. I'm not sure if anyone ever told him what she said about him, but I hope someone did.'

Jane wondered how long it was supposed to last, but she didn't like to ask.

'If things don't work out between you and Ryan, and you come back here to live, we can find you a much nicer boyfriend than Scott. Tony has lots of friends. We could set you up a blind date in a safe way—say dinner at our place—so you could get to know each other before you went out together. There are lots of nice men around, and you could be choosy since you look good and have money of your own. They don't all demand sex on the first night out.'

Jane left the dresses at the house and caught the train to the city to meet up for lunch with Pat, Ryan and Mr Allanstone.

Pat explained that he and Claire would be living in the lodge, but Mr Allanstone thought it would need a lot of renovation, as it hadn't been lived in for years. They would need some sort of heating if a baby was to live there. Perhaps they could find a better house in the village or the town.

'I would need to ask Daniel for the money,' said Pat. 'I have none of my own. Perhaps he would help, but he likes to keep us all poor so he can control us and tell us what to do. I work in the garden, but he only pays me pocket money, and Jack McCann can't pay me much. Farms don't make a lot, and he has four sons. Sometimes Jimmy and I help Mr

Phillips on his farm, but he can't afford to pay anything at all. He gives Mary a turkey at Christmas, and the odd pot of honey, and the redcurrants that she makes into jelly.'

'If you had a formal job, I could arrange a mortgage for you. What are you good at?'

'Nothing, Sir,' said poor Pat.

'Pat is good at gardening, and he knows a lot about cars,' said Jane helpfully. 'He helps Jack McCann mend the Land Rover, he fixes Daniel's car, and he has helped Mr Phillips with his car as well. He and Jimmy mend all the tractors. And he is an expert on sports cars. He can tell you how fast they go, and how many seconds it takes from starting to going sixty miles an hour. He could be a car salesman, or run a garage, or service farm machinery.'

Mr Allanstone liked that idea, and said he would talk it over with Mary and check if he had any contacts for car dealers.

Jane then asked him about buying a house near Oxford, and he said he would let her have whatever she needed within reason. He wanted to look over any house she chose to buy, as he did have a duty of care. He thought she could easily afford anything that wasn't absolute river frontage on the Thames.

This was the first Pat had heard about the Oxford house plan, and Ryan told him to say nothing to Daniel. They were waiting until after the wedding and would plan their escape then if things hadn't improved between Daniel and Jane. Ryan would live in the house with her, as she didn't like being in a house by herself. He would finish his PhD and then teach full time.

'That would leave Mum and Daniel by themselves,' said Pat.

'Unless your mother wanted to leave as well,' said Mr Allanstone. 'Would Daniel cope on his own?'

'No way, Sir,' said Pat. 'He'd drink himself to death within a week. I think poor Mum is stuck there forever. She could only leave if Ryan and Jane stayed, but they can't stay because Daniel is so jealous. All her life she has had people to look after. She was only fourteen when she took charge of bringing up Ryan, but I suppose you would know that. Then she looked after our grandmother until she died, and now that Ryan and I can manage by ourselves, she has Daniel to look after.'

'I don't think she really minds,' said Jane. 'She is a very caring person. But if she did want to leave, I'm sure Daniel could afford a housekeeper.'

'That could backfire,' said Pat, clearly alarmed. 'Unless she was an absolute dragon, he might marry her and leave her everything. That's the last thing we all want.'

'Maybe we could find an absolute dragon,' Jane persisted. 'But I don't think Mary would want to leave. She has always lived at Hayward and she really cares about Daniel. She loves him unconditionally, knowing all his faults.'

Mr Allanstone had to get back to his office, but he said he would see them all at the wedding. Mary had asked him to stay for the night afterwards. Meanwhile if he could help with anything, they all knew how to contact him. He paid for their lunch on the way out, and they walked to the station to get the train back to Richmond.

Jane asked Ryan if Mr Allanstone was somehow related to them. He treated them all like family, and he looked rather like Pat. Ryan didn't think so, but he hadn't traced the family beyond direct ancestors. It was quite likely he was related somehow. He had been to the same school as Daniel, so the families would have moved in the same circles, and they did tend to intermarry. Perhaps he was related to Pat's father. They didn't actually know who Pat's father was. He may be Allanstone's brother or cousin.

They returned to Hayward Hall in time for dinner, with the dresses and matching shoes, and Jane checked her dress still fitted.

She phoned Anne and said they had three dresses. They had been made to measure at the time, but the green dress looked about a size ten, the same as Jane's blue dress, while the pink dress was closer to an eight—Rebecca was quite thin—so that one was more likely to fit Julie. She suggested Claire might like to ask Candy to be a third bridesmaid if she fitted the third dress.

Friday 19 March 1976

Ryan drove Mary into town for the shopping on Friday morning, and Jane went with them. She wanted to avoid being alone in the house with Daniel. She would look for some new black lace knickers to replace the stolen ones. And this time she would only do her washing while Mary was around to help keep an eye on the dryer. Mary sat in the back seat of the car, as she always liked to have Jane and Ryan together.

Jane found the lingerie shop where Candy's mother worked. She had spoken with her after church and when they had sewn up the blankets, and she sometimes came to the yoga class. Her name was Sylvia, but Jane just thought of her as Candy's mum and called her Mrs Morgan. She was not used to calling older people by their Christian names.

It was a lovely shop selling beautiful underwear and pyjamas. Candy's mum seemed to understand that a girl wanted nice underwear beneath her clothes. She didn't seem at all surprised at Jane asking for black lace and choosing something quite scanty.

Jane bought the new black lace knickers and some blue ones to go with the bridesmaid dress. The dress was ankle length, but it was better to be safe and have matching underwear. She also chose some more silk pyjamas. They were sky blue with pink and yellow flowers, and were much prettier than the plain ones she had bought in London.

Jane hoped her choice of underwear wouldn't be the talk of the village by Sunday afternoon. She imagined the whispers. *Jane Walters wears skimpy black lace knickers under those dowdy midi skirts.* Even worse would be whispers that the wealthy and smartly dressed squire had stolen her skimpy knickers. She hadn't told Candy's mum that of course, but she imagined them falling out of his pocket when he took out his five-pound note for the church collection, and someone in the pew behind picking them up, then tapping her on the shoulder and asking if they were hers.

Candy's mum asked how the wedding plans were going. Candy was going to the McCanns' farm to practise the formal dancing on Sunday afternoon so Jimmy and David both had partners; Claire had phoned last night to ask her. Jane didn't tell her that she was hoping Candy could be a bridesmaid as well, as she wanted it to be a surprise for Candy, and it would only work if she fitted the green dress. They didn't want to have to start again on finding bridesmaid dresses.

She told Jane that her brother-in-law was coming to stay with them and would be here in time for the wedding. He had taught in a school in South Africa for many years. The life there suited him—living out in the wilds—and it was over ten years since they had seen him. But now he was returning to England, as her father-in-law had been ill. Nothing too serious, but Maurice had decided to come home. He intended to stay in England and find a teaching job locally. He was a bit of a loner and had never married.

Another lone wolf, Jane thought.

She met Ryan and Mary back at the car as arranged. When Mary was safely in the back seat, and Ryan was holding the door ready for Jane to sit in the front, he asked if she had found what she was looking for.

'Yes, thank you. Next time I'll sit next to the dryer.'

'Next time I'll untie the dress.'

She laughed. She liked him talking to her like this, as he hadn't exactly behaved like a lover these last two weeks. Next week they were going to stay at Richmond for a few days. Jane would say she was staying with Sarah to do some shopping, and Ryan would say he was taking the opportunity to stay in his room at Oxford while she was away.

Nothing more had been said between them, but Jane knew they would sleep together when they were alone in the house. They would go out to dinner again, dance together so she felt the thrill of him holding her close to him. When they returned home, he would kiss her in the hallway as he had before. They wouldn't bother with cocoa this time, but would go straight upstairs. She would lie on the bed in his room while he untied her dress and pulled off her tights, and she would unbutton his shirt. She didn't like to think beyond that. She assumed his trousers would just unzip the same as her jeans did, although he might not like her doing that. She would need to ask him first. But if he wanted her as much as she wanted him, their clothes weren't going to get in the way.

7 COLD MOONLIGHT

Sunday 21 March 1976

With four weeks to go before the wedding, they were to spend the Sunday afternoon at the farm, for Julie to try on the dresses and choose which colour she preferred, and for everyone to practise the waltz.

The pink dress was slightly too loose and slightly too long for Julie even with the high-heeled shoes. Jane carefully pinned it where she needed to make alterations, but there would not be much to do. She was reluctant to shorten the length, as she would need to trim the fabric, but it was not so long that Julie would trip over it. With Julie's dress out of the way, Jane asked Candy if she would like to try on the green one. It fitted her well enough, as the bias-cut satin fabric was quite forgiving on size. Claire asked Candy if she wanted to be a bridesmaid as well; Candy was thrilled.

Julie and Candy were dressed again, and the young men were rounded up for the dancing. The farmhouse kitchen was a large room, and the table and chairs had been taken out into the hallway.

Anne found some old seventy-eight records for the waltz music. Ryan and Jane were to demonstrate the steps, and then everyone else would follow. To practise the dancing Jane had worn the flared dark-blue dance dress, with the matching knickers over her tights for safety. If the dress swept too high in a turn, or she fell over, they would look like part of the outfit, which in fact they were. The dress was sleeveless, and the fabric was lightweight and silky, but farmhouse kitchens were always warm.

Ryan's hand was on her back, his other hand holding hers, and she was very conscious of the last time they had danced together, and what had happened afterwards. She knew by the amused way he looked at her that he was conscious of it as well. It was a secret they shared.

The steps were easy, the timing easy, the others keen to learn.

Pat danced with Claire. He had learnt to dance at school, and she picked it up quite quickly. Jimmy danced with Candy, and David with

Julie. Even Anne and Jack joined in, for they had danced together when they were courting after the War.

When they had all learnt the waltz, Anne found some jazz music for the foxtrot, Jane and Ryan dancing it perfectly along with Anne and Jack, but the others finding it confusing at first. Jane reduced it to a few basic steps for them. She didn't want this one to be declared too hard because she knew Ryan enjoyed it, and they had danced it together at the hotel in Mayfair on the most beautiful night of her life. So far.

All they needed to do, she said, was *forward, forward, side, side,* then they could add a few backwards moves and even a dip or a spin for the girl if they wanted. It didn't really matter if they were not strictly fox-trotting, as long as they were following the music and enjoying it. If there were too many people on the floor, they could just go forward then back so they stayed more or less in one spot. As long as they held their hands correctly, the man could lead the girl in which direction to go, and they would be fine.

Jimmy wanted to practise the jive, which most of them could do already. This was not Ryan's idea of dancing, so Jimmy danced with Jane. She was conscious that the skirt of the dress flared right out when she spun around in the jive—it was meant to do that—and she was glad of the dark-blue knickers that perfectly matched it. She knew her worst fears were realised when David wolf-whistled, and she wondered what Ryan was thinking. When she looked at him, he was laughing, but at least he hadn't whistled.

She asked if he wanted to jive, but he said it was more fun watching. After the jive Jane and David did the twist as they had at New Year. David was smaller than Jimmy and much more agile, and Jane thought him a natural dancer.

Anne made them tea and scones to finish the afternoon. The table had been returned to the kitchen, and the pinned pink dress was back in its bag for Jane to alter on the treadle sewing machine in Mary's room. Over tea they all went through the arrangements for the wedding day.

When Pat, Jane and Ryan finally walked home they were all rather tired. It was nearly dinner time, so Jane didn't have time to change out of the dress, although she did have a cardigan over it.

Over dinner Pat told Mary they had all enjoyed their afternoon, and how good Ryan and Jane were at dancing. Mary asked them to show her after the meal. They could dance in the hallway, there was plenty of space without moving furniture, and she could find them a suitable record. Ryan wasn't keen, but Jane didn't want to miss the chance to dance with him again. Perhaps later tonight they could slip away to his room and resume where they had left off on the night they had danced in London.

In all these two weeks he had never kissed her, never said he loved her, never talked of them living together except for the day they had lunch with Mr Allanstone, and even then it was her asking about buying a house near Oxford, not Ryan. But he had joked about untying her dress, and he had said they would go to Richmond for a few days, perhaps this week. She hoped he still meant it.

Mary went through the singles and found them a record to dance to. Pat, Mary and Daniel watched from the doorway to the lounge. Jane found the high-heeled shoes that she had worn that afternoon, took off the cardigan, and stood in the dimly-lit hallway, cold in her sleeveless dance dress.

Mary was the perfect ally, for the music she had chosen was *This Guy's in Love With You*. For three long minutes, she felt that there was no one in the world but the two of them, dancing to the beautiful song, although he didn't hold her close, and his hand was high on her back because he knew his father was watching them. But all the time he looked at her and she looked at him, and they were close enough for it to be seductive, his thigh brushing against hers as they moved in the dance, all perfectly controlled, yet hinting of a passion just out of reach. She knew they danced it well. It was their show-off dance that had impressed everyone at the farm, even Anne and Jack.

'This may have been a mistake,' Ryan whispered when the song ended.

It was a mistake. Daniel told Mary it was his turn and asked her to play it again, same song. Jane heard Mary ask why he couldn't just leave the two of them alone, but he insisted. She looked at Jane, but Jane could find no real excuse to avoid dancing with him.

He danced just as well as Ryan had, but holding her much closer, and his hand was on her waist, sometimes much lower. Twice she asked him to move his hand from her derrière. She knew he was doing this to spite Ryan, who was standing in the shadows, leaning against the doorjamb of the lounge, and she knew Ryan was deeply hurt, watching his father holding her right up close, touching her in an over-familiar way, yet helpless to object.

She realised there was a downside to dancing with a man. It wasn't quite so exhilarating when your partner was someone you preferred not to be so close to. Why, oh why, couldn't Daniel just accept that she loved his son? Why couldn't he just treat her like a daughter? He could still have danced with her, with a polite distance between them. He could even still have flirted with her a little, provided it didn't extend to groping her or asking her to come up to his room.

She was still troubled by his confession to her only three days before, but she was trying to treat him as she always had. He couldn't change what he had done. She needed to help all of them go forward.

After the record had finished Daniel asked her if she would like to tango.

'It's much more fun than the foxtrot,' he assured her. 'Find the *Caro Mio* record, Mary. Can we still play the old seventy-eights?'

'No, Mr Linden,' Jane said as firmly as she could, facing him. 'I told you I would only dance with you if you kept your hands under control.'

'Please indulge me, Jane. I promise I'll be good. The foxtrot is such a formal, safe dance, but the tango is much more fun. Caroline and I used to tango. *Caro Mio* means *My Darling*, but to me it meant *My Caroline*. I always called her Caro. We used to dance to it here in the hallway. I'll tell you what I want you to do; just keep looking at me the whole time.'

She relented, and Mary found the record. They started by facing each other a foot or so apart, not touching at all, and he told her which direction to step. Then he took one of her hands, holding it high in the air, a few steps later putting his other hand on her waist, telling her to still keep her left hand behind her for a few more bars of the music, then to touch his shoulder. They slowly got closer, and he added a spin and a dip, strides and a lunge, and then he turned her so he was pulling her back against him as they moved together, his arm around her waist, his breath very close to her ear, so he was almost kissing her neck, his fingers encircling her wrist as he held her hand very high above her head. It was like a courtship dance, she thought, rather wishing Ryan would dance with her like this. Turning her to face him again, he pushed her away then pulled her hard against him, finishing with her leaning back, supported on his bent knee, with his face almost on hers and her whole body stretched against his. It was perfectly timed at the end of the music. Had he remembered the routine from all those years ago? Or did he tango like this with his escorts at the London hotel?

He whispered to her to put her arms around his neck, then he picked her up, spun around with her in his arms, and set her back on her feet. She was amazed how strong he was, and how surprisingly fit for an old man. She hoped he hadn't overdone it, as he seemed rather out of breath, and she recalled his heart was dicky.

'Are you okay,' she asked him quietly. 'Do you need a heart tablet? I can fetch the bottle for you.'

'Thank you, Jane, I'm fine. It is years since I danced like that, and I enjoyed it immensely. Dancing is supposed to be passionate and seductive. Even when you are married to a woman, every time you dance with her you are courting her all over again. Now admit you enjoyed it as well. We can do it again at Pat's wedding. We'll practise it a couple of times before then. It will give those boring farmers' wives a shock. Ryan would never dance with you like that.'

'It's my turn, Sir,' said Pat, taking Jane's hand, and she was grateful to him for intervening. Daniel was still breathing heavily, and it had become a bit difficult there for a moment. She wished he had left Ryan out of it.

'Mum is worried he is overdoing it,' Pat whispered to her as they waited for Mary to change the record.

The first song was played again, and she danced with Pat, this time a slow jive, defusing the animosity between Ryan and his father that for a moment had been tangible in the room, just as Daniel dancing with her had spoilt the magic between her and Ryan. But then she remembered that the dress didn't behave when she jived, and she felt very self-conscious with Daniel watching her. She would have died if he had wolf-whistled like David had. She wouldn't have minded what the dress did while she was dancing the tango, as Daniel would not have been in a position to see. At least the lights were dim here in the hallway. She tried not to spin too fast, and mercifully this song was slower than the one she had danced to with Jimmy. It was fun to dance with Pat. She remembered that she had once thought herself in love with him, but now she thought of him as she might have thought about her brother if she had been lucky enough to have one. He had his faults, like being selfish and spoilt, but she still cared about him and enjoyed his company; he was part of her family.

'If you dance with Jane at the wedding, Daniel, please keep your hands away from her derrière or you'll embarrass us all,' said Mary when the record had finished. 'Gentlemen do not behave like that, particularly old men with young girls. And I don't think you two should tango like that in public either. It looked a bit risqué. Ryan and Jane might get away with it, but not you and Jane.'

The dancing over, Daniel retreated to the den and his whisky. Jane found Ryan in the shadows, stayed beside him while Mary and Pat returned to the lounge and the television.

'Mary meant well,' she said, 'and your father enjoyed the tango. I didn't mind doing that for him.'

He took her hand. 'Maybe one day you could dance like that with me. Jane, as soon as the wedding's over, we'll leave here if you still want to. Can you manage that long? I can't take too much more of this. We can go back to Richmond for a few days later in the week. What about Tuesday? We can leave here early.'

'I would like that. Ryan, what if he comes after us? I'm afraid of him.'

'It will be okay. He knew we were together in Richmond before, and he left us alone. Eventually he will accept it.'

She saw him look furtively towards the closed door of the library, which led through to the den, before he pulled her body close to his. She caught her breath, desire flaming through her, her knees weak and her heart fluttering, and she hoped he felt it as strongly as she did.

'Two more days,' he whispered, but he didn't kiss her, and she knew it was because he was worried things would get out of control if he did.

Later that evening Pat and Ryan played snooker. Jane sat in the billiard room, back in her normal skirt and jumper, reading the latest book Ryan had selected for her, *Dr Thorne*, while the men enjoyed their game. Mary had left a long-playing Frank Sinatra record on in the lounge so they had some music; she was watching television in her own room.

It was still a ritual, having her book selected every Friday night. Jane was tired, and was happy to sit quietly reading, absorbed in the plot, safe in the knowledge that the heroine Mary Thorne would marry her lover Frank Gresham in the end. Some twist of fate would intervene to allow their union.

Daniel came in and asked for her help, something about the renovations and how much had been paid so far, so she left the young men and went with him through the deserted lounge and the library to his den where she had left her account book. He turned up the volume on the record player as he went past.

She scarcely noticed that he had closed all the doors until she realised that he had trapped her. He was between her and the door. He was slightly unsteady on his feet, and she knew he had been drinking far more than the two whiskies that he was allowed. She tried to get past him but he grabbed her, held her close to him and started kissing her face, telling her he loved her, he had to have her, he would give her anything she wanted, please would she come upstairs with him. He promised she would enjoy it, she just needed to lie back, and he would do everything. If she didn't like it, he would make love to her that once then leave her alone. She was nineteen. He couldn't believe she hadn't slept with anyone by now; people did it every day and thought nothing of it. Even if she had never done it before, he promised he wouldn't hurt her.

He was still kissing her face, kissing her mouth. She did not respond, but she did not push him away. She was unable to resist him because he was holding her so tightly.

She didn't know what to do. She felt panic sweep over her, as she desperately tried to think. Knee in the groin, she had been taught at school, but he was holding her so tightly she couldn't move her knees. Her hands were free, so she tried to pull his hair, but it was cut very short. She tried thumping her fists against his chest, but he caught her hands, held them behind her in one of his. Men were so much stronger than women, and she knew he was a strong man, as he had effortlessly lifted her and swung her around only an hour ago.

'Jane, don't resist. Just relax and you'll like it. I promise you'll enjoy it.' His hand was up her skirt, tearing her tights, his fingers in places they had no right to be, and his other hand was gripping her hands behind her so tightly that it hurt. And suddenly the panic overwhelmed her, and she screamed hysterically.

His response was instant. He released her and slapped her face. 'Stop that Jane, someone will hear.'

She managed to pull away from him and get behind a chair. Her cheek hurt, and her head was spinning. She wanted to scream again, to get the attention of Pat and Ryan, but the sound would not come. She felt stunned. She tried to lift the chair, with a vague idea that she could smash it over his head, but it was far too heavy for her to raise from the floor. Please, please, could someone come. He was between her and the door, so she stayed where she was with the chair between them.

He took off his tie, stood for a moment holding it in both his hands, watching her with his predator eyes. But this time it wasn't a look that said they both understood what he wanted, it was a look that said he was going to get what he wanted. She felt hunted and trapped.

There was another door, she remembered, out to the back staircase, somewhere behind her. She pushed the chair over, hoping the clatter would be loud enough for the young men to hear from the billiard room, and then she took a step backwards, another and another, until she reached the door, but he came around the fallen chair and grabbed her again, winding the tie around her neck, pressing her back against the door, thrusting himself against her, pulling on the ends of the tie so she could only clutch at it with her hands, trying to loosen it, his other hand holding her so tightly against him that she could do nothing to free herself.

'I won't harm you,' he said. 'Come upstairs with me.'

He loosened the tie a little so she could get her breath back, but he was still pressing her against the door. She tried to reach the handle, thinking if she could open it, they might both fall into the passage. But when she turned the handle, nothing happened. The door opened inwards into the room.

'Even if you force me to sleep with you, you can't force me to marry you,' she told him, trying to stay calm, still hoping she could talk him out of his madness. 'Please leave me alone.'

'No, but I can spoil it for him. He won't want you if I've had you first.'

His hand was once more inside her tights. She found her voice and she screamed, ducking as he slapped her again, but at least he had let go of the tie. She tried to pull it away from her neck, but he caught hold of it once more, looking at her with that relentless gaze, leaving her feeling helpless and trapped, her spirit unable to resist his. She needed someone to hear her. Pat and Ryan were only in the room next door, but the sound would not travel through the stone walls and the shelves of books. She would have to go upstairs with him, lie on the bed while he raped her. If no one helped her, she would have no choice. She would ask him to take the tie away first. She may have to pretend she enjoyed it, or he might kill her anyway. He seemed completely mad. She recalled Ryan telling her the escorts faked it, but she had no idea how you did that.

'If you take the tie away, I'll come upstairs with you.' She tried to fight the panic and think what she could do. It would give her some time to get the attention of Ryan and Pat, and if she stayed calm, she still might talk him out of it. She could climb the stairs much faster than he could; she might get away from him.

'Of course you will. I promise it'll feel good. I'll take it off when we're upstairs, but I won't hurt you. You were meant for me Jane, and I could never hurt you.'

Then at last she heard the door open, and Pat grabbed him from behind, dragging him away from her. She sank onto the floor.

Ryan was beside her, pulling the tie from her neck, asking if she was okay.

'I'll be all right now you're here. He wasn't trying to strangle me. He was just trying to get me to go upstairs.' But she couldn't stop shaking, and for a moment she clung to him.

Pat had released his hold on Daniel and was on her other side, helping her to her feet. For a moment she stood supported between them, before Ryan handed her to Pat, who gave her a hug.

She watched mesmerised as Ryan took his father by his shirtfront and stared at him in total disbelief. God, please don't let them kill each other, she thought.

He had recovered enough to speak, and she had never heard him so angry, yet he was still so totally controlled.

'My God, you're a hypocrite. You lectured Pat and me about treating her respectfully and we did. She was the best thing that ever happened to this house. She was like a breath of fresh air, like someone had turned on the sunshine. Even Mary has loved having her here—I have never known her so happy—and for the first time in my life I actually looked forward to coming home on weekends. She has helped you enormously. The bills are paid, the cheques get to the bank, and she even types your sordid stories for you. Pat and I were both in love with her, but we never once touched her. But you had to spoil it for all of us because you can't control your urge to get up her skirt.

'I am taking her away from here, and neither of us is ever coming back. You can keep the money you pay me. I can easily get a job. If you come after us, or if you ever touch her again, I will kill you. I've always dreamt about killing you as once when I was a child you nearly killed me. In all the years since, you have never once said you were sorry for what you did to me and to Josie. How can you live with yourself after what you did to us? And now you want to spite me by hurting Jane just like you hurt Josie to spite Peter.'

He released his hold, pushing Daniel away from him. 'If you had killed her, you wouldn't be leaving this room alive. But you're not worth hanging for. You're a pathetic lecherous drunkard. The whisky will kill you, and not soon enough.'

Daniel staggered backwards, but managed to stay on his feet. He seemed a little shaken, but he poured himself another glass of whisky.

'Have you quite finished?' he said curtly. 'I would never have harmed her. She knows that. She just plays hard to get. She wants a real man, not a limp wimp like you. Now get out! All of you get out!'

Pat helped Jane stay on her feet while he took Ryan by the arm and pulled him from the room before he could attack his father any further. She was shaking and in tears, feeling hopeless and inadequate. She should have been better able to control a man trying to make a pass at her. Now everything was spoiled for all of them, and it was her fault.

When they reached the kitchen Ryan pulled her towards him, hugged her like he would never let her go. 'I am so sorry. I should have looked after you better than that. I should never have trusted him anywhere near you. I wish now we had never come back.'

'I wish you had knocked him out,' said Pat. 'I felt like flattening him. He deserved it. I still can if you want.'

'No, leave him be. Fighting won't achieve anything, and if we killed him, we would be in a right mess. Jane's here with us, and we won't let him near her again.'

Pat tried to explain to Mary what had happened. Jane was still shaking, but Ryan released her so she could sit at the table. Mary wrapped some ice cubes in a towel for her to hold against her cheek and made her some tea.

'Jane, you gave me some tablets you had to calm you down, would you like one?'

Jane took the sedative with the tea. She knew she shouldn't rely on them, but she also knew it would make her feel better.

'I didn't lead him on,' she said. 'I have never led him on. His hands were all over me, and I couldn't get him to stop. He had his tie around my neck. He said he wouldn't harm me, but it was very frightening to think he could easily kill me. I think he was drunk, much more so than usual, and I didn't know what to do. I could scarcely breathe, and I panicked. I didn't know how he could be so strong. I don't want anyone fighting over me. I thought Ryan was going to kill him, and he would get hanged. This is all my fault, and I am so sorry.'

'They don't hang people these days,' said Pat. 'And there were witnesses. I would have said it was self-defence. He was trying to strangle you, and no one could blame Ryan if he had killed him. Ryan, what did you mean about him nearly killing you when you were little? I've never been told about that.'

Ryan said nothing. He just sat at the table, and Jane realised he was too shaken to say anything.

'We never knew what happened,' Mary answered. 'It was back when Jane's mother was here. You were only a few weeks old, and Ryan was six. Jane's great-aunt was staying with us while she visited a terminally-ill friend who lived in town. The friend was the sister of a man Jane's great-aunt had once been engaged to, but he had died in the First World War. We were a bed and breakfast, but we sometimes did full board as well. My mother knew Jane's great-aunt, from when they were younger, so she didn't mind. Jane's mother Josie came with her aunt—they lived together in Richmond—but she stayed here with us each day, as she scarcely knew her aunt's friend. They stayed for about a month. It was school holidays, in August, so Peter was home, as he was a teacher then. Josie was nineteen, the same age as Jane is now, and both Peter and Daniel fell in love with her. She and Peter just seemed to get on from the start, and within about three weeks he was talking of marrying her. Neither my mother nor her aunt had any objections except that it happened so quickly, and they both thought they should wait a while and get to know each other better. But Daniel had fallen for her as well, and he was beside himself with jealousy. He had been a bit unstable since his wife died, but we had never seen him like that. Jane's mother looked a lot like Caroline, and I think he imagined that she had been sent by fate to replace his dead wife.

'Josie loved Ryan, and she was always ready to play with him as Peter always did. One morning, when Peter had gone to help at the farm, she took Ryan to walk in the woods. Daniel was out shooting with John Phillips. She came back an hour later with the shotgun in her hand, carrying Ryan who was hurt. He was a sturdy boy, and I have never known how she could have carried him so far. Her dress was torn, she was bruised and bleeding, and she was shaking, and we thought she had been raped. But she said she was okay, and we had to look after Ryan. His arm was clearly broken, and he was covered in bruises. When she put him down, he couldn't stand. She told us that Daniel had attacked them both, but he hadn't shot anyone.

'I phoned for an ambulance for Ryan and phoned the farm to ask Peter to come home. We also phoned Josie's aunt who was with her friend in town. My mother took the gun from Josie and put it back in the gun room, but she did check it, and it wasn't loaded. I went with Ryan in the ambulance to the hospital while my mother looked after Josie. She told me to say he had fallen from the tree house. We didn't actually know what had happened, but we were worried that the welfare people would get involved. If they thought Ryan had been hurt by his father, they would have put him in foster care, and I was worried they would take Pat away as well. My mother and I would have done anything to prevent us losing the boys, and I know that we did the right thing.

'His arm was broken, his collarbone and two of his ribs. At first they thought he might have damaged his spine because he would just collapse when he tried to stand up. They asked him at the hospital what had happened and if someone had hit him. He told them he had fallen from the tree house. He seemed to accept that was what he had to say. They believed us because his injuries were consistent with that. They told me he would survive, but they didn't know whether he would ever recover completely. They needed to keep him in hospital, and lying flat, so I stayed for as long as I could then went back home on the train. I had Pat to look after as well. I dreaded what would happen if Ryan said it was Daniel who had hurt him, but he stuck with the story about the tree house.

'When I returned here, Josie and her aunt had left, and Peter with them. He had taken them back to their house in Richmond. My mother phoned him there to let him know that Ryan would be all right, as she knew he would be worried. Peter said Josie didn't want Daniel charged over what he had done to her, so we never really knew the extent of it. It was hard then for a girl to bring a charge of rape, she would have been treated like she was on trial, not him, and they didn't want Ryan to have to testify in court. He also wanted to protect my mother from the shame of having Daniel in prison. She had brought Peter up, and he loved her.

'Daniel finally returned late that night and went into his den. He drank himself unconscious, and in the morning he was really sick. He recovered, but he didn't say a word to either of us for days. He just sat there in the den brooding and drinking, and I would take in his meals.

'Ryan was in hospital for three weeks, but at the end of that he could stand up and walk, although his arm was still in plaster. My mother went in every day to be with him, leaving me here to run the house and look after Pat.

'Peter never returned here, but he did offer for Ryan to go and live with him. For a while he stayed with Josie and her aunt as their lodger. He had been a teacher, but he got a job in the civil service, and he married Josie. He invited my mother and me to the wedding but said he didn't want Daniel there. We left the children with Jack's mother Ethel at the farm, and went to London for the wedding. Jack and Anne came with us, and Robert Phillips. He was Peter's best man; they were always close friends.

'That was the last time I ever saw Peter, but he wrote to me frequently and sent me a postcard from Switzerland where they went for their honeymoon. Daniel had stolen one of the letters that had some photos of Josie and of Ryan, but I caught him and he gave it back. Then he found the postcard when he collected the mail, and he tore it into pieces. After that I asked Peter to type the envelopes and not put a return address so the letters were anonymous. Peter and Josie were married for ten months before Jane was born, and my mother and I were both greatly relieved at that. We never knew if Daniel had actually raped her. We never really knew what had happened to Ryan that day either.'

Ryan had regained his usual control. 'Peter was helping at the farm, so it was just Josie and me in the wood. I had run ahead, and I was hiding behind the standing stone ready to jump out at her. My father came by carrying the gun, and he stopped to talk to her. He hadn't realised I was there. Then he pointed the gun at her. I thought at first it was a game, but I wasn't sure. When there are guns in a house even very small children are taught that you never point a real gun at a person, so it didn't seem right. He said he would kill her, and Peter as well, if she didn't give him up. She stood there in front of him looking like a scared rabbit. Even from where I was, I could see she was shaking with fright. Then he ripped her dress and pushed her backwards onto the ground. She was trying to fight him off. She was screaming, and I knew he was hurting her. He was lying on top of her, so I jumped on him and hit him as hard as I could. He turned on me and hit me with the butt of the gun. My arm took the blow when I lifted it to protect my face. If I hadn't done that, I think it would have cracked my skull. He kept hitting me, and then he picked me up and threw me back against the stone. I can still remember the force of the impact when I hit it. I remember Josie helping me, but I couldn't stand up. I felt really strange, and she had to carry me. She asked him to hand her the gun, and she took me back to the house. I was worried he would follow us, but I don't remember much else.

'Peter came to see me at the hospital, and he told me he was going to marry her, but they couldn't live with us any more. He thanked me for trying to rescue her. I never saw him again, but I never forgot him. When I came home from hospital he had gone away to live in Richmond. I always wished he had been my father instead of Daniel. For a long time after that I hated my father. I avoided him whenever I could, and I always tried to keep Pat away from him. Even when I was older, I could never like him. It was only years later that I realised he had been trying to rape her, and I still don't know if he actually did. It has stayed with me all my life, the image of a man forcing himself on a terrified woman, and the sound of her screaming. For a while, when I was old enough to realise what he had done, I thought Jane might be my sister. So I asked my grandmother, and she told me it wasn't possible because Jane was born nearly a full year afterwards. She said she knew why I thought that and asked me if I wanted to talk about it, but I didn't, and she respected that. I used to look at the photos of Jane and think she was lucky that Peter was her father and not Daniel, and I was glad she didn't live with us in case Daniel attacked her as he had attacked me. He had nearly killed me, and he has never once said he was sorry.'

'I know he was deeply ashamed of what he had done,' Mary told him. 'But he has never talked about what happened, to your grandmother or to me. I sometimes think he just wants to obliterate the memory of it, and that's why he could never apologise. Peter was very unhappy at leaving you here, but he didn't have much choice. He and Josie offered to take you to live with them, but my mother would never have let you go. He always asked after you when he wrote to me. I sent him photos of you as you grew up, and he sent me photos of Jane. He would never phone here in case Daniel answered it, but I sometimes rang him.'

'Daniel was sorry.' Jane had recovered sufficiently to remember their conversation in the church. 'He told me he had once done something that he deeply regretted, and he hadn't known what possessed him to behave like that. He said if he had killed you, he couldn't have gone on living because it was the ultimate betrayal of his wife, and he thanked God that you recovered. He said he often imagines what life would have been like if Caroline had lived and how much better things would have been for you. He thinks he has failed you.'

'But this isn't about me,' Ryan remembered, taking Jane's hand. 'This is about Jane. I am taking her away from here tonight. We'll go somewhere he'll never find us. She will never be safe here with him. I wish now we had stayed in Richmond and never returned here.'

'Tomorrow,' Mary insisted. 'It is far too late tonight to be driving so far, and neither of you is in a fit state to leave here. Jane can lock her door tonight, and tomorrow you can both leave. Pat, go and lock the cellar door and bring me back the key so Daniel can't get another bottle of whisky, then just check he's all right. Ask him if he wants to come in here with us and talk about this. We all need a way forward. You are the most neutral person in this.'

Pat came back to say Daniel was still sitting in the den drinking, and he didn't want to talk to any of them. Mary went in to him. She was gone for what seemed a long time.

When she came back, she had negotiated to some extent. He had said he was happy for Jane and Ryan to leave, he would not go after them, he was sorry for what he had done to both of them, he would not have harmed Jane, and he would keep paying Ryan's allowance until he had a decent job so Jane could be looked after properly. Mary had asked if he would talk to his son, but he said he didn't want to see either of them again.

Mary made them all cocoa and suggested Ryan take one of his sleeping pills, but he said they made him feel groggy the next day, and he had to drive Jane to Richmond.

When she went up to bed, Jane locked her bedroom door and the door to her sitting room, and put a chair in front of each so it would fall over and wake her if the door was forced. Ryan had offered to sleep in her sitting room, but his room was above hers, and she was content with that. She knew he needed to sleep properly if he was to drive her to Richmond tomorrow. And Daniel was by now so drunk he would be unlikely to harm anyone.

She slept only fitfully, nervously straining to hear the least noise in the corridor, dreading a hand rattling the door handle, reliving the helpless feeling of the tie around her neck, of being held in his grip while he thrust his hands beneath her clothes. But then she pushed the thoughts from her mind and turned to thinking about Ryan's story. Finally she knew the whole history of what had made her father leave and what Ryan had tried all his life to forget and how the two were entwined. Perhaps now he could face the past and commit to loving her. She knew he loved her. He had even said so. The two of them could make a life together, far from Daniel and the fractured dreams she had held of them living here with him.

This house had seemed so welcoming when she had first come here. She had felt it embracing her, welcoming her back to the place where her parents had met, placing her at the heart of a new chapter in its life, where she and Ryan fell in love and lived out their lives here, helping the house overcome the sorrow of all the lives lost in the two World Wars and the years that followed. The old yellow sandstone and the beautiful garden had been so healing, and so had Mary, with her quiet wisdom and her acceptance of what life had dealt her. Jane would miss her. And Mary would be left here to care for Daniel on her own, with Pat married and Ryan and herself gone.

Jane knew that none of this was her fault, but she still felt she had torn this family apart. Could she have done anything differently that would have prevented this? The photo Ryan had taken of her in her mother's hat had been a mistake, and perhaps they should not have danced together in the hallway, but they were small lapses of judgement. From the first day she had come here, they were all being precipitated to this seemingly inevitable end. Daniel had said then that he had loved her mother. It was only to be expected that a middle-aged man in the constant company of a young woman who reminded him of a lost love would fall for her.

There was no way she could have loved him in return. He was nearly three times her age, and she had found his constant passes at her wearying. Even the way he looked at her made her feel uncomfortable. He looks at you as though he is thinking what you look like without your clothes, Sarah had said, and Jane knew exactly what she meant. She had always behaved perfectly towards him, and she had never once worn a miniskirt or a low neckline in his house. She had never by word or look encouraged him. She had tried to stave off his advances with light-hearted rebuttal. She had helped him with the typing and the accounting. She had walked with him, made him coffee, tried to help him reduce the amount of whisky he drank, treated him as she would have treated her father, or her uncle if she had one. But that hadn't been enough for him.

Surely even he could see it was Ryan that she wanted. Why couldn't he just have been content to see her love his son instead, to play out his dream by his son marrying the daughter of the woman he had loved. Or at least professed to love. How could any man love a woman then rape her at gunpoint? Had he just wanted his revenge on Peter because Josie preferred him? Had he wanted revenge on Ryan by attacking her? Or had he just been so angry with the blow that fate had dealt him that he hated anyone else to be happy? If Pat and Ryan hadn't helped her, she would have had to go upstairs with him. He would have raped her and then probably strangled her as well. She remembered him saying he would kill her and Ryan and himself. He was completely mad.

Through the long night her thoughts went back over everything Ryan had ever said to her, every smile, every touch of his hand, every hug, the books he had selected for her to read so she had some romance but not too much tragedy, the beautiful moment in the stillness of an ancient wood when they had been alone together and had felt outside of time, the night in Richmond when he had kissed her and told her he was hopelessly in love with her.

She tried to obliterate the memory of Daniel touching her. She wished she could go downstairs and make another cocoa to help her sleep, perhaps take another diazepam or one of Ryan's sleeping pills, but she didn't dare unlock the door. Tomorrow they would go away from here, start a new life together, and she would make sure he never wanted to leave her. Tomorrow night he would make love to her in the house in Richmond, and life would be beautiful again. What had happened tonight would no longer matter. There would just be the two of them back together in their own world. They would need to return here for Pat's wedding, but perhaps they could stay in the town.

She heard the mantel clock in her sitting room striking midnight, then one, then two, before she finally slept.

Monday 22 March 1976

She awoke to someone banging on the locked door of her room. It was Pat.

'Jane, Jane, get up quickly. Something terrible has happened, and we need your help.'

She was instantly alert, grabbing her dressing gown and slippers and unlocking the door. It was not quite seven o' clock.

'Jane, get dressed, as quick as you can. Just do it, and I'll explain what's happened.'

For a moment she imagined that Ryan was dead, that Daniel had killed him.

'Is Ryan okay? Please tell me Ryan's okay.'

'Ryan? Yes, Ryan's okay. It's Daniel. He's fallen down the stairs in the night and we think he's dead. Mum is in hysterics and Ryan is trying to revive him. Just get dressed, and keep calm. I just need to check the den, and then I'll come back for you. Just wait if I'm not back when you're dressed.'

She trembled as she pulled off her pyjamas, put on her skirt and blouse and tights, found a cardigan and her shoes. She looked in the mirror and realised her face was bruised, and her neck was as well. She found a silk scarf. At least she could hide the bruise on her neck. Pat was not yet back, so she made up her eyes with her blue eyeshadow, black eyeliner and mascara. The familiar routine steadied her.

She returned to her door to wait for Pat, vaguely recalling that she had put a chair in front of it before she went to bed last night, yet now the chair was back in its place by the dressing table. Had she moved it when she opened the door to Pat? She didn't remember doing that. But she didn't have any more time to think about it, as Pat was returning.

'It's a bit confronting, but we all need to stay calm and think what to do. Just hold my hand.'

He led her along the corridor to the stairs, then down the first flight to the landing beneath the gothic window.

At first she thought herself within a nightmare, yet she was swamped by an overwhelming feeling of déjà vu. She felt she had known what she would find. There on the floor of the hallway below, Daniel lay still, spread out on his back in his black suit on the black and white tiles like a dead bat pinned out in a display case. Mary was sitting huddled on the second step, completely distraught, with Ryan holding her. Even from where she stood, Jane knew Daniel was dead.

She went slowly down the stairs and knelt on the floor close to him. She touched his hand. The fingers were still soft, but his hand was cold. She held it in hers, stroking his palm and his wrist, wanting to warm him, wishing she could do something to make him wake up.

'Has someone called the ambulance,' she asked, knowing it was hopeless, but it was still the correct thing to do.

'No, no,' said Pat. 'You can phone them in a minute. He's dead so a minute won't matter. They will bring in the police, and we have to come up with a consistent story before they get here.'

He sat on the step on the other side of Mary and took her hand.

'Mum, please just try to listen for a minute. We all need to think this through. We don't want them to think that Ryan killed Daniel. In a minute I'll make you a cup of tea, but for now just keep calm and listen. Can you manage that?'

She nodded.

'First, was it one of us who pushed him downstairs? If it was, then we could brick up the body in a corner of the cellar, and everything could go on as normal. Ryan signs everything for him anyway, and he was a recluse and might never be missed. Or we can make up an alibi, or one of us could be witness to it being self-defence. I know it wasn't me. Ryan?'

'No, of course I didn't. Last night I felt like killing him, but I didn't push him down the stairs.'

'I didn't either,' said Jane. 'I was in my room all night with the door locked.'

'So we can assume it was an accident. He was drunk and he fell down the stairs. But we still need a plausible story. Last night he made a pass at Jane and tried to strangle her, and Ryan threatened to kill him. This morning he is dead at the foot of the stairs. If we tell them that, they will think Ryan murdered him. We all have separate rooms, so none of us have any sort of alibi, although Jane and Ryan could say they were together even though they weren't. We also have Jane with a bruise across her face which looks like someone hit her. We will have to explain that, so we can't just say last night was a normal night. So what do we say? We need it to be as close to the truth as practical so we don't contradict each other. That he made a pass at Jane and she was upset, yes. That he hit her when she got hysterical, yes. That he tried to strangle her with the tie, probably not. Ryan grabbed him by the shirt, no. Well, maybe we have to. Ryan, check if his shirt is torn. Although Jane could have torn it when he attacked her. Ryan threatened to kill him, no, absolutely not. Ryan being injured as a child, no, none of their business. Jane and Ryan saying they were leaving, not that either. Just tell the truth but not the whole of it. We all have to keep calm. I very nearly punched him in the face when we found him attacking Jane, and I wouldn't have blamed Ryan if he had, but thank goodness neither of us did. Things would have looked very bad for us if we had hit him.

'So is everyone okay with that? We tell them he made a pass at Jane, that she screamed, and he slapped her. There was an argument, and

Ryan grabbed his shirt when we pulled him off Jane, but play that down a bit. We don't tell them about Jane and Ryan dancing and Daniel getting so jealous over it, or about Ryan saying he'd kill him. We can say Daniel stayed up drinking after we went to bed. That much is true. We don't actually know when he fell. Did anyone else come down here to check him so we know a time? I got up and checked he was okay a little after midnight, because I knew Mum was worried about him, and he was still in his den. He looked like he was asleep, so I left him alone. He can't have been dead then, or he would still be there.

'It all gets worse. While you two were trying to revive him, while I was waiting for Jane to dress, I checked the den. He had finished the decanter, and a bottle of Ryan's sleeping pills was sitting next to the glass. I don't think he overdosed on them. I picked up the bottle to see what they were, and it seemed quite full. If he did take some of them, then I hope his fingerprints are on the bottle so they can't accuse one of us of spiking the whisky. I thought about putting the pills back in the kitchen, but if he took one of them, they would find traces of it in his blood. I found his tie and put it on the desk so it would look as if he took it off and put it down there. Last night I picked up the fallen chair, so that is back in its right place. It fell on the carpet, so it isn't damaged. We heard it fall, though, and that was when we realised that something was wrong. We were already on our way to check when we heard Jane scream. I don't think either of us has ever moved so fast as we did then.

'It won't end with the police, of course, because he was famous. We will have the press here as well. God, what a mess. I wouldn't have blamed Ryan if he had pushed him down the stairs after he treated Jane like that. I'm sure he attacked her just to spite Ryan. He knew Ryan's in love with her. When they danced together last night, Daniel looked at them like he wanted to kill Ryan. Then he was groping her bum in front of us all and dancing that tango like he was about to make love to her on the floor in the hallway. Even I felt like knocking him over for treating Jane like that in front of Ryan. I understood then why they wanted to keep quiet about being in love with each other and getting their own place in Oxford. Ryan, you were checking his shirt.'

'It isn't torn,' said Ryan, 'but a button is missing, and some of them are undone. His waistcoat is open. Did someone unbutton it, or did he?'

'I think it was already unbuttoned,' said Mary, who had recovered enough to be following what Pat was saying. 'I don't remember doing it, but I may have, trying to find a heartbeat. Perhaps he unfastened it himself when he was sitting in the den.'

'You can all say I manhandled him but please not that I threatened him. I could never have killed him. Although I never liked him, he was my father, and even I understood he was a deeply unhappy man and that was why he behaved like he did. Jane, we won't be leaving here today after all. Will you call the ambulance? Can you manage that?'

'No, wait just a few more minutes,' said Pat. 'He has magazines upstairs in his room that are nobody's business but his. I saw them there once when Mary and I were making the beds. He had left a drawer partly open. We don't want the police finding them and the press getting their hands on the story. I remember hoping that if he got married to Jane, he would get rid of them so she didn't find them in the drawer. I'll take them up to the attic, and we can dispose of them later. If they search the whole house, I'll say they were mine. I'll check the room looks okay otherwise. Can anyone think of anything else we need to do? Ryan, find his wallet and take out any banknotes. He usually carried a lot of cash around with him, and we don't want it disappearing with the body. Check he doesn't have a card in it with the phone number for the escort agency. What about the time he was found?'

'I got up at half past six,' said Mary. 'I was trying to revive him when Ryan came down, and he went to find you.'

'That gives an hour before we called the ambulance. I suppose that is believable. Probably better to tell them you got up a bit later, ten to seven say. If you don't want to lie, just say you can't remember. We don't want them knowing we had that long to plan what we would say. They will say we should have rung for the ambulance straight away. Now hang on until I get back from his room.'

Jane was amazed at how calm and in control Pat was. He was thinking of everything. They waited, Jane still holding Daniel's hand, until Pat came back down. He had a bundle of banknotes he had found in a drawer. Ryan had found the wallet and taken out the cash and a card.

'What do we do with the card from the agency?' Ryan asked.

'Jane can tear it up and flush it down the loo in the cloakroom behind the kitchen.'

Pat went to put the money in the safe in the den, while Jane disposed of the card. Then she walked across the hallway to the desk, past where Daniel lay, and with shaking fingers she dialled for an ambulance.

'I am calling from Hayward Hall,' she told the operator, feeling strangely calm when all she wanted to do was to give way to panic. She was trying to stop herself from shaking, all the while hearing her own calm voice as if it was someone else talking. She gave them the address and the phone number. 'My uncle has fallen down the stairs in the night and we think he is dead. Please send an ambulance.'

The operator wanted to keep her on the phone, telling her how to check for a pulse, turn him on his side, check for breathing, but Jane knew it was hopeless. 'Please just send someone,' she said. 'We are doing what we can, but we know he is dead, and we need to look after my aunt.' She hung up the phone.

She took a few steps back towards the stairs, but she suddenly felt that she was somewhere else, that her body was no longer hers, and she knew she was going to faint. She clutched at the edge of the desk, trying to stay upright. She saw Ryan jump up from where he was sitting on the stairs, still comforting Mary. Pat had returned from the den and he caught her as she fell. She felt Ryan pick her up as if she was weightless, and he laid her on a sofa in the lounge, swinging her feet over the arm so they were above the level of her head, while Pat found a blanket for her, and Mary went to fetch her a glass of water.

After a while she could hear the sirens on the drive, but everything still seemed far away and unreal.

The men from the ambulance could only confirm he was dead, probably for at least a couple of hours. They would need to call in the police, as any death that was not obviously natural causes would need to be investigated. It was just routine, they assured them. They didn't need the phone, as they had radio contact.

But they did look after Jane, checking her pulse, untying the scarf she had put around her neck and keeping her warm. They asked Mary to get her a cup of tea with lots of sugar, and one for herself as well. One of them went to the kitchen with Mary to help her make it. Jane recovered enough to sit up and drink it, but she still felt very light-headed and sick.

A police car arrived with two uniformed officers, one of them a very young policewoman. They were unable to contact Daniel's usual doctor, so they would call in their own; he would arrive shortly. They also called in CID. They apologised for it, but it was routine if someone had died from a fall or other apparent accident and there were other people in the house at the time.

Everyone was allowed to go into the kitchen, and Ryan made coffee, as none of them had eaten breakfast. The cat had caught and killed a rat, and had brought it indoors, so Pat had to deal with it and give the cat her food for the morning. Jane wondered where the cat had slept, as her bedroom door had been locked. Perhaps that was why Jasmine had gone out for a prowl and found the rat.

They were all to stay in the kitchen until the detectives arrived, and would then be asked to make statements individually. They would need somewhere quiet for that, and Ryan suggested they could use the guest dining room, as it could be accessed from the kitchen through the family dining room so Jane didn't have to go back through the hallway.

Pat showed the policeman the room, then took him across to the library and Daniel's den, while the policewoman stayed in the kitchen. Jane thought it was so they were not able to collaborate before they were interviewed. Another police car arrived with two more men in uniform. One was stationed outside, the other with Daniel in the hallway.

Ryan made toast, found the butter and jam, encouraging Jane and Mary to eat something. Jane knew he was just trying to keep things normal, and she wondered how he could seem so calm, but he was always controlled. Her cup rattled in the saucer as she drank her coffee. He pulled his chair closer to her and put his arm around her, but she couldn't stop shaking. Mary found her another sedative, after checking how often she was allowed to take them.

They waited.

The doctor arrived. He was a sympathetic man and quietly spoken. He confirmed Daniel had been dead for at least a few hours, but the cause was not clear, as there were no obvious traumatic injuries. He waited with them until the forensic team arrived, the pathologist and the photographer and finally the detectives, one old, one young. For a while they could hear them talking to their team in the hallway, then looking over Daniel's den. Eventually they came into the kitchen.

They were very courteous to everyone. This was just routine. They always attended when someone died if it wasn't clearly natural causes. Jane's face was bruised, so she knew there was no hiding what had happened. Her neck was bruised as well. Her scarf had been taken off and left in the lounge, so she had no way to disguise that. She tried to recall what they had agreed to say and what not to say.

At first they wanted background information, Daniel's name, their names, how long they had lived there, where they worked, who owned the house, who would inherit, the name of Daniel's doctor so they could access the medical records. Pat did most of the talking, but none of them knew who would inherit. They assumed Ryan. They gave him the name of the solicitor, Mr Allanstone, who would have the will.

'In any case,' Pat added with rather candid honesty, 'we were all better off with him alive. He wrote books, they made a heap of money, and we all had a share of it. It would have been like killing the goose that laid the golden egg.'

They asked if any doors had been left unlocked or forced open, if there was any sign of an intruder, anything missing, who had found him, and if he had been moved. Mary said she had found him when she came downstairs around seven to make breakfast. She may have moved him a little so she could try to revive him. She hadn't known when she first found him whether he was dead or just unconscious. Ryan had come down a few minutes later, and he had gone back up to fetch Pat. Then Pat had woken Jane.

Pat and one of the policemen went around the ground floor checking the windows and the french doors and that the safe was still locked.

The detectives went back into the hallway, spoke together for a short while, then returned to the kitchen and asked them again if he had been pulled away from the stairs. Mary didn't recall moving him, but she had been frantic and had hardly known what she was doing. Ryan said he had tried to get him lying flat, so they could check his heart, but he didn't think he had moved him far, maybe a few inches. Had they unbuttoned his waistcoat? Mary said she didn't recall whether she had, yes, maybe she had, she didn't know, he had spent the night asleep in the den, so he may have unbuttoned it himself.

They took Mary into the hallway, with the young policewoman supporting her, and asked if she could recall exactly where he was when she had found him, but she thought he was more or less where he was now.

They were to make statements individually, Jane first.

'Jane will need someone with her,' Ryan insisted. 'She is emotionally fragile, even before this happened. Can Mary or I sit in with her? Do you have a social worker?'

After some negotiation with Ryan, the detective allowed the policewoman to sit with Jane. She was young, scarcely any older than Jane. She sat beside her and held her hand, and Jane was grateful that she did not have to face the detectives on her own.

The inspector was a middle-aged man, unsympathetic, ugly and smelling of sweat and stale tobacco. Jane took an instant dislike to him, but she knew he was only doing his job. She had to talk to him because if she didn't, he might think that Ryan had killed his father. The sergeant sat silently beside him, taking notes, but Jane avoided looking at him, as she sensed he was looking at her. He was a much younger man, tall and slender, but with a wiry strength.

Who found him? She didn't know. She had been woken by Pat, and the others were already there. What time? She thought about seven o' clock, perhaps a quarter past.

The inspector told her she had phoned for the ambulance at half past seven. What had happened in between? She had to dress, that took some time, and they had discussed what to do. She had thought you rang for an ambulance even if you thought the person was dead, in case they weren't actually dead. But they had known he was dead.

When had she last seen him alive?

'Last night. He was still in his study at about eleven o'clock when I went to bed.'

He asked her to tell him everything that happened last night.

'He was rather tipsy. He often drank too much. He made a pass at me, and I was upset about it. Ryan and Pat told him off, and he told us all to get out. We went back to the kitchen and left him to his whisky. Mary told Pat to lock the cellar and give her the key so he couldn't get another bottle.'

'Who hit you, Miss Walters. It is obvious that someone did, so we don't want to hear that you walked into a door.'

'Daniel did. I was panicking. I panic very easily. My parents died and then my great-aunt who looked after me died too, and I was an emotional wreck. I was left by myself in the house, so I had to stay with a friend. The Lindens are my only family, and they brought me here to recover. I was hysterical, so Daniel slapped me. It's what you do, you know, when people get hysterical.'

'Not that hard, it isn't. And there is never any excuse for a man to hit a woman. So how did you bruise your neck? Did he try to strangle you?'

She didn't answer. She didn't want to think about the panic of his tie around her neck while she struggled to breathe. The inspector didn't pursue the question. She thought that was because he already knew the answer.

'Were you in a relationship with him? You don't have to answer that, but it would help if we knew.'

'My father's cousin,' she told him helpfully, not understanding what he meant. 'My father lived here during the War and afterwards until he married my mother. That was before I was born of course. His parents had both died in the War. There are a lot of dead people in our family. Nearly everybody is dead. I'm the only one left.'

'Were you having an affair with him, Miss Walters? Sleeping with him. Sex. In love with him.'

'No of course not. He had asked me to marry him, but I didn't want to. I have never, ever led him to think I wanted to. He loved my mother years ago before she married, and I think he had some idea I was sent to him by fate to marry him. I look like she did.'

'You said he made a pass at you. What did he do?'

She fell silent, suddenly shaking. Last night he had touched her in a very intimate place, and now he was dead. She didn't want to think about it. The policewoman told her it was okay, she didn't have to answer if she didn't want to, or if she preferred, she could just talk to her.

'He had his hand up my skirt, and he ripped my tights,' she said at last. 'He was telling me I would enjoy having sex with him. I was very frightened of him, as he sometimes seems like he's completely mad. I get upset very easily. I think I screamed, and he hit me to try to stop me screaming. I don't think he meant to hit me so hard.'

The detective said nothing at all for a while, and Jane thought he seemed rather shocked. He had been writing things down, but now he was drawing or circling something with the pencil. The sergeant had also been making notes of what she was saying, but she scarcely paid him any attention.

'Miss Walters, a man many years your senior, and in a position of trust, tries to rape you, and you make excuses for him. He wanted you because you remind him of a lost love, you scream only because you are easily upset, and you think he didn't mean to hit you so hard. If he had still been alive and you had told me all this, we could have charged him with assault. What happened next?'

'Pat and Ryan came in because I had screamed. By then I had managed to get a chair between us, but he got past it and was holding me against the door. Pat grabbed him from behind, and Ryan yelled at him. No, he didn't actually yell. Ryan never yells. He is always very controlled. I think he may have grabbed his shirt. He told Daniel he was a hypocrite because he had told him and Pat they were to treat me like a sister then he had tried to get up my skirt. He said that he would take me away from here. Then Daniel told us all to get out, so we went back to the kitchen, and Mary gave me some ice for my face and one of my tablets to calm me down. I don't take them all the time. They were given to me when my great-aunt died. No, before that, it was when I lost my parents. Then I went to bed and locked my door. That was about eleven o' clock. I think Daniel was still in his den. That's what we call his study. Mary had spoken to him, and he had said he was sorry.'

She remembered that she wasn't supposed to have said that she and Ryan were leaving, but she was upset and confused. She wished he was with her; he was always so calm and controlled, and she would have coped much better.

'You stayed in your room all night?'

'Yes, absolutely. We all have our own adjoining bathrooms, and I would have been too scared to come out. Usually I leave my door ajar, and the cat comes up and sleeps on my bed near my feet, but last night I locked it. Pat banged on my door this morning and asked me to dress and come down to help. I called the ambulance, but then I fainted.'

'Did you hear anything in the night? Voices or arguments? A crash?'

'No. I heard nothing.'

'Has he done anything like this before?'

'He asked me to marry him about a month ago, but he has never hit me before. I said no, and I went back to my old home in Richmond, as I didn't think I could live here with him after that. He phoned me and apologised, and said he wanted me back, and it would never happen again. So I came back, but I wish now that I hadn't trusted him.'

'And the two young men. What is your relationship with them?'

'Second cousins. Our parents were cousins. And I haven't had an affair with either of them if you mean that.'

'Have either of them made a pass at you?'

'When I first came here, Pat and I did have a bit of a romance, but not an affair. We went to the cinema a couple of times. But now he is marrying someone else, and I am to be a bridesmaid. Ryan is very kind to me and always treats me with the utmost respect.' That much was true. She didn't want to tell him about Richmond, or that she was in love with him. That was her and Ryan's concern, not the detective's.

'Miss Walters, you have been very helpful. I understand how difficult it would be for you to talk to me like this, a man and a perfect stranger. You are a very brave young lady and I sincerely appreciate your honesty. I know you are upset, and I am sorry we needed to speak to you.

'On the face of it, it would seem your cousin had too much to drink and fell down the stairs, but I would not be doing my job if I didn't consider other scenarios. Someone may have pushed him. I expected this to be purely routine, an unfortunate and very tragic accident. Then I find that the previous evening the deceased man has both sexually and physically assaulted a very conservative young lady, only nineteen years old, who is living in his house under his protection, and who is now trying her best to make excuses for him. There are two young men in the house. Both of them would have been angry at what had happened. I also find it very strange that a man who was drunk would fall backwards down a staircase. He was much more likely to collapse at the knees and fall forwards, or simply trip on a step and again fall forwards. The staircase is not at all steep, quite the reverse in fact. And he landed a long way from the bottom step. If he had fallen from one of the lower steps, he may have landed there, but the fall would then have been unlikely to kill him. Did you see anyone move him?'

'No, they were just sitting there. Mary was upset, so Ryan was hugging her. If he had been moved, it was before I came down.'

'Later this morning we will write this down as a formal statement for you to sign. At some stage you may need to testify at an inquest, but we will make everything as easy as possible for you by using the statement you give us today. Constable Wilson will take you back to the kitchen, and she will stay there with you and look after you.'

Jane sat at the kitchen table, no longer able to fight back tears, but the policewoman assured Ryan she had done very well and hadn't been at all upset when they questioned her.

They wanted to talk to Pat next.

Here they all were, Jane thought, in this beautiful house, educated in some of the country's top schools, all Daniel's money at their disposal, with the dirty laundry now showing beneath the expensive clothes. Daniel had assaulted a young girl who was living in his house under his protection. He was a drunkard, a rapist, a philander and a child beater, and Mary had managed for all those years to keep her family together and functional for the world to see. A lovely extended family living in beautiful harmony in a beautiful house, scones with homemade raspberry jam in the village hall after cricket matches, Mary visiting her friend in London each week in a bespoke silk dress, church every Sunday with the three men all lined up in Savile Row suits, Daniel now famous and rich, quiet studious Ryan doing so well at school then at Oxford, Pat keeping the house and garden immaculate. But all the while Mary and her mother had Daniel to cope with, locking the gun room, locking the cellar, dealing with him raping a young woman who was a paying guest in their house, pretending to the hospital that Ryan had fallen from the tree house when he had been beaten by his own father, sending Daniel's mistress packing when she had tried to seduce his teenage son, covering up the real purpose of his frequent visits to London.

She wished now that she had not said so much in her interview. Telling them that Daniel had made a pass at her and she had taken fright would have sufficed. Although it would scarcely have resulted in her screaming so much that he was justified in slapping her. None of them had killed Daniel, so it was really their own business what had happened the previous night.

This was just a nightmare, she told herself, and soon she would wake up and find none of it had happened. Why, oh why, had she agreed to come back here after the first time Daniel had proposed to her? How could she have thought things would just go back to how they were before? How could she have trusted him? And now here they all were with Daniel dead and Ryan likely to be suspected of his murder. Daniel was a successful and popular writer, and every aspect of the inquest would be in the papers, horrible details of what he had said to her, where his hands had strayed to, speculation that someone had pushed him down the stairs or put Valium in his whisky so he was too unsteady to make it safely upstairs to bed.

She sat close to Ryan, his arm around her shoulders, unable to stop herself from crying. No one else there was crying, not even Mary, but Jane couldn't stop. The young policewoman was holding her hand with a depth of sympathy that was surprisingly comforting.

Pat returned and the detectives went into the den, returning with the bottle of sleeping pills carefully sealed up in a transparent plastic bag. The inspector put it on the table.

'Tell me about these.'

'Valium,' said Ryan. 'They are mine. I have been a poor sleeper all my life, but I rarely resort to them. They are kept in a high cupboard here in the kitchen. Daniel would have known they were there, but I have never known him to take one.'

'Who would have touched the bottle?'

'Mary would have picked it up from the chemist, I would have touched it of course, Daniel if he took one last night, and Pat said he picked up the bottle this morning to check what it was. So everyone but Jane.'

'I did touch them,' said Jane. 'I once checked them against my diazepam. Ryan's are diazepam as well but a much higher dose. And Mary took the bottle down last night, to ask Ryan if he needed one.'

'We have counted them, and there are four missing from the original thirty in the bottle. Can you recall how many you took yourself since last July when the label is dated.'

'Not precisely, but certainly two or three of them.'

'In a few days we will get back some results on whether he took any of them. Suicide is unlikely, as he would have taken the lot, but it is possible he just put the bottle on the table and thought about it, and didn't take any of them at all. How much did he normally drink? He was obviously a whisky drinker, and he appears to have drunk it straight. How long would a bottle last?'

'Perhaps three or four days,' Mary told them. 'I don't count them. Jane may be able to work it out from the accounts from the off licence. He was trying to reduce how much he drank, but sometimes he would just sit there and drink glass after glass, once or twice most of a bottle in a night. But that was years ago, and he always regretted it the next day. He had been mixing it with dry ginger lately. Jane has been trying to help him to drink less, and she worked out the bottle was supposed to last him for nearly two weeks, but it never did. He was allowed two one-ounce drinks a day, but he always cheated and had two ounces in each drink, and usually more than two drinks.'

'Do you know how much was in the decanter at the start of yesterday evening?'

'No, I'm sorry, I don't. I asked Pat to lock the cellar so he couldn't get another bottle, but I'm not sure he didn't already have the next one in the room somewhere. There is another decanter in the library, and one in the billiard room. We didn't go into his den much, except Jane if she was doing paperwork for him.

'He may have got the pills mixed up. His digitoxin is kept in the same place in the cupboard. It's high up, so you have to take the bottle down before you can read the label. He takes them if his heartbeat gets unstable. He has another bottle of them beside his bed.'

Mary took down the bottle of digitoxin. It was similar to the bottle with the Valium and the pills were a similar size and shape. The sergeant took that as well.

They wanted to interview Mary next, asking her if she wanted the policewoman with her, but she declined. The other three sat silently around the kitchen table, but Mary was not away for long.

When she returned, the detectives asked Pat to show them Daniel's bedroom, but they then sent him back downstairs. He gave his mother a hug, asked her if he could do anything, but she told him she was okay.

Jane was gradually calming down, but she felt weary and numb. One of the policemen came in to tell them that Daniel had been moved from the hallway, but they were to leave everything as it was for the moment. They had drawn chalk marks on the tiles where he had been lying, and they wanted those left in place. He would be taken to the mortuary. When they had determined a cause of death, they would release him for burial, but they could contact an undertaker in the meantime. The policeman asked if there was anyone else they needed to contact? Relatives? Their solicitor? Would they like the local vicar to call by, a neighbour, or a doctor to check on Miss Walters?

She was very conscious of how she looked with her face bruised. She didn't want anyone to see her because she would need to explain how it happened. She still desperately wanted to wake up and find this was all a terrible dream.

The detectives returned to the kitchen and took Ryan to the guest dining room. He was gone for an eternity. They think he murdered his father, Jane thought, that is why they are talking to him last so if he contradicts what someone else said, they can confuse him over it. They would think he had killed Daniel while he was trying to protect her. They would force him to confess to it whether he did it or not. It was her fault, and she had ruined his life. They would take him away with them, and their dreams of a life together would be shattered to dust.

Tomorrow would be Tuesday, when they had planned to leave early and spend a few days at Richmond, pretending to Daniel that she was staying with Sarah and Ryan was staying in Oxford. They would have slept together, lovers for the first time and for all time, and perhaps they would never have returned. She tried to stay calm. She had to stay calm. Mary was calm, and Mary had known and loved Daniel for all of her life.

Pat tried to comfort her, sitting beside her as Ryan had, with his arm around her. 'Jane, it's okay, really it is. It was an accident. You saw how drunk he was last night. I am amazed he could stand up at all. Nobody pushed him. He fell when he was climbing the stairs. There was a moon last night, so it would have been quite light, and he had probably forgotten to turn on the lights. Jane, I'm sorry you had to see it. I wish now I had brought you down the back staircase and straight to the kitchen. Ryan didn't hurt him, we all know he never would, and they don't convict people for things they didn't do. Not very often, anyway. The police are just doing their job.'

She asked if she could go up to her room to get a warmer jumper, saying she could go up the back staircase. The policewoman told her it was okay provided she didn't go down the main stairs, and kept away from the hallway. She offered to come up with her, and so did Pat, but Jane said she could cope alone. She found the jumper and tidied the room, picking up her pyjamas, which she had left on the floor when she had dressed that morning, and making the bed. Last night she had started to pack her suitcase, ready for when she left with Ryan this morning, but now she put the clothes away. They would not be leaving today, and she didn't want the police to find her half-packed case if they searched her room.

When she came back out into the corridor, she could hear the detectives talking in the hallway below, so she guessed they had finished talking to Ryan. She slipped quietly along the passage almost to the gallery above the stairs, but she only made out some comments that they were all hiding something, they were not giving them the whole story, and it would have been easy for someone to shove a drunk man down the stairs. The sergeant made a few disparaging remarks that toffs like him thought they were above the law and that blonde chick was a stunner, she wouldn't want a nerd like him. She would want the old man, as he was the one with the money.

I certainly wouldn't want a creep like you, she thought, as she returned to the kitchen down the back staircase, suddenly regaining her energy in the face of his criticism of her lover. Ryan was now sitting at the table, looking shaken and exhausted. It was unfair on all of them, being questioned as if they were criminals. Daniel had a dicky heart, and none of them had done anything wrong, except perhaps Daniel himself. The policewoman asked her if she was okay, as she had been a long time finding the jumper.

When the detectives came back into the kitchen, she was still seething at the sergeant's comments about Ryan. She felt angry with them, and she stood up and faced the older man across the kitchen table. She wanted nothing to do with the younger one.

'Why are you treating us all like criminals? My uncle is dead. He had a weak heart, he was drunk, and he fell down the stairs. None of us killed him and all of us are upset that he died.' She knew she was getting hysterical.

Ryan jumped to his feet, pulled her towards him and hugged her close. 'It's all right, Jane,' he whispered, his hand stroking her hair and her face. 'There's no point getting angry and upset.'

She knew they had given away that they were more than friends. But it was none of the inspector's business anyway. It was Daniel who was dead, and she wasn't hiding a relationship with him.

'I'm sorry, Miss Walters, but we are only doing our job. If he died from natural causes then the post-mortem will show that, and you have nothing to worry about. If he has been murdered, perhaps by an intruder, you would want justice for him.'

They were polite enough, saying they would be in contact tomorrow as soon as they had checked how much alcohol he had in his blood and whether he had taken any of the pills. Once they had the results of the post-mortem, they would decide if they would charge anyone, and prepare a report for the coroner, who would then determine if an inquest was needed. They said that nobody was to leave the area, but that Ryan could go as far as Oxford when he was ready to go back to working there. They wrote down the name of the policewoman for Jane, and the phone number for the police station in town. They said if she wanted to talk to her about what had happened, or to one of their social workers, she could ring that number.

At last they were gone. They had left the chalk marks on the tiles, taken the whisky glass and decanter, the sleeping pills and the digitoxin, the tie and some of Daniel's shirts. They had apparently found a button somewhere. They had asked them to leave the den and the bedroom as they were for twenty-four hours. By then they would have their photographs developed and would know if they needed more.

'They said they may want to talk to me again,' said Ryan. 'The inspector seems to think we had a fight, and I pushed him down the stairs. Can we each tell exactly what we said to him so I know where I stand. Particularly Jane.'

'I told him nothing at all about us. I said he had groped me, and he hit me because I was hysterical, but I didn't say he tried to strangle me. He asked that, but I didn't answer. I said Pat had pulled him off me, and you had grabbed his shirt and told him he was a hypocrite, and then he had told us all to get out. He asked if I was having an affair with you, or if you had made a pass at me, and I told him that you behaved with the utmost respect towards me. I didn't tell him we had been at Richmond together or anything else about us. I told him Pat and I had gone out together to a film a couple of times, but I hadn't had an affair with him either. I think I said you told Daniel you would take me away today. I forgot we weren't supposed to be saying that.'

Reverend Colin came by. The police cars passing through Hayward village had not gone unnoticed. They explained that Daniel had fallen down the stairs, but said nothing about him being drunk at the time, nothing about Jane's bruised face, and she hoped he would be too polite to ask. She had retrieved the silk scarf from the lounge, so at least the bruise on her neck was now covered.

He accepted a cup of coffee and a biscuit, sat with them at the table, told them the police often got involved when people died and agreed it was very stressful, said all the right things about Daniel, and Jane realised that the right things were actually quite comforting when they came from him. He said Daniel was with Ryan's mother.

'No, he's not,' Mary chimed in with some asperity. 'She's in heaven, and there's no way whatsoever he would be allowed anywhere near the place.'

Jane wanted to fall into hysterical laughter at this, but she managed to confine it to a hiccup. She knew that Mary was deeply upset, and that, however badly her brother had behaved, she had always loved Daniel above anyone else.

'This has been a great shock to you all. I do understand how you are all feeling and if Linda and I can do anything, contact anyone, deal with the undertakers, anything at all, just ask. I assume you want him to be buried with his late wife.'

'Yes, of course,' Mary told him.

'I think we will need to put off the wedding, Pat, at least for a couple of weeks. Would you like me to talk to the McCanns?'

Pat nodded. 'I'm not sure whether it's necessary. It's still four weeks away. We'll be over it by then. We can't leave it too long, baby bump and all that.'

'I will call there on my way home and tell them what's happened. They would have seen the cars as well, since they came past the farm in the lane. Shall I ask Anne to call on you?'

'No,' Mary replied. 'Not today. She'll understand that. Perhaps tomorrow.'

'Tomorrow afternoon? I'll talk to John Phillips as well. I'll ask them to leave you alone for the rest of today, and in the morning there will be things for you to arrange. But if you need anyone, or any help at all, just give me a call. Are you all right, Jane? You look as though you have taken a knock.'

'I walked into a door,' she said, knowing that he would never believe her. At least the bruise on her neck was now covered. It would have been a strangely shaped door to bruise her neck as well as her face.

That night she couldn't sleep. Every time she closed her eyes, she saw Daniel lying in the hallway, splayed out on the tiles. Nothing she could do would shake the image from her mind, or the nagging voice that kept telling her all this was her fault. She heard the mantel clock striking midnight, then one o' clock. She would make herself another cocoa and take another sedative. She put on her dressing-gown. She would not normally go downstairs in her night clothes, but she didn't think anyone else would be up.

The house was silent and seemingly asleep. It was dark, for the moon had not yet risen to light the mullioned window and spill its rays across the hallway. Another life lived here had slipped away, soon to fade into the past with all the others. There would be nothing left but the photos of him on the walls, and he would be gone from here like the souls behind the dead faces in the other photographs. But she could never think of the house as evil. It was just a sad and helpless witness to the destruction he had wrought on his own life. She knew it was not her fault that Daniel had died. She may have been a catalyst for what had happened, but she was never the cause of it.

For a moment she stood on the landing, a strange feeling creeping over her, the flicker of a memory stirring in her mind. The moon had been shining then. She had stood here once before, recently, in the soft silver glow of moonlight, and something had happened, but she could not recall what it was.

When she reached the bottom of the stairs, she saw there was a light on in the kitchen. Was someone else up? Or had it simply been forgotten?

Ryan was seated at the table, a mug set up for cocoa, waiting for the kettle to boil. She told him she couldn't sleep, and he set up a second mug.

'I came down here to get one of the sleeping pills, but then I remembered the police have taken them so I am trying another cocoa. I can't sleep either.' He found the biscuit tin and put two chocolate biscuits on a plate. 'We can drink the cocoa in Mary's room.'

'You can have some of my diazepam. It's the same as Valium. I checked the dosage once, and one of yours is five of mine.'

'I'll try that if the cocoa doesn't work.'

She sat beside him on the sofa, a blanket pulled over their knees. When the cups were empty and the last biscuit crumbs consumed, he put his arm around her, and she leaned against him. It was so comforting to have him warm and strong and close to her.

'Jane, last night after you had gone to bed, did you come up to my room to find me?'

'No. I stayed in my room with the door locked.'

'I thought I heard someone in the corridor. When I opened the door, there was no one there, but I could smell your perfume, it lingers in the air after you leave a room. Was it definitely not you?'

'No, definitely not me. It may have been the cat. She usually sleeps in my room, but the door was closed, so she may have been prowling in the corridor looking for someone else to sleep with. I don't think she smells of Chanel, though.'

'I walked along to the stairwell, and I saw a woman on the landing. She had the moon behind her. I remembered that my father always said he saw my mother's ghost on moonlit nights. Last night I saw her too. You were in your room, and the woman was not tall enough to have been Mary. And her hair was fair and loose, while Mary's hair is black and she always plaits it at night. But I was still half-asleep, and I went back to bed, thinking I was dreaming. I was not sure in the morning whether I had simply dreamt it all. I didn't say anything to the police. But now I wish I had checked the time, and I also wish I had gone downstairs. If he had only just fallen, I may have been able to save his life. I feel guilty that I didn't.'

She told him she had also felt guilty, but then she had thought about it, and she knew Daniel had brought it on himself with his constant drinking and his refusal to believe she didn't want to sleep with him.

'But I feel that if I hadn't come back here, he would still be alive. If we had slept together that night, we may never have come back. None of this would have happened. I would still be in Richmond, you might still have been with me there, and I would have been out of his way. If I had been able to stay there by myself, you could have gone back to live in Oxford during the week, and come to see me on weekends, so we would not have needed to return here. It was only you commuting so far that made it difficult. We would have worked something out so we could be together while you finished the year at Oxford.

'He was really unhappy. He often told me that. I was awful to him at times, but he had this obsession that he wanted to sleep with me. If it wasn't for that, I would have been nicer to him. I did like him, but I just didn't want to marry him. I wish you two could have made up. He told me he had always regretted what he had done to you, and I asked him to try to make amends for it by not standing in the way of us being lovers. But he said if I slept with you, he would kill us both and himself as well.'

'Jane, bad things happen in life. You can't have foreseen that us coming back would lead to this. I can live in the same house as you without harassing you, and I don't see why he couldn't. If you had wanted to marry him, there is no way I would have attacked you like he did. I would have taken it on the chin and coped with it. But in the end, no matter how badly he behaved, he was my father. I said some awful things to him too, and he deserved them, but I will live the rest of my life wishing I had been kinder to him. He was never a happy man, and he buried himself in the stories he wrote to help him cope with losing my mother. All my life I just wanted him to say he was glad he had a son. It was never enough for me that my grandmother and Mary both loved me; I wanted my father to as well. Even if he had accepted that you were mine and given us his blessing, I would have felt that he cared enough to make that sacrifice for me, and it would have made up for all the years that nothing I could do was good enough, however hard I tried. He knew you would never marry him. But in the end he would have raped and strangled you rather than accepting that and leaving you for me.'

He pulled her closer to him, and she nestled her head on his shoulder while he rested his face against her hair. They stayed there together, comforting each other, until she slept.

He shook her awake. 'Jane it's past two, and we need to go back upstairs. Try to get back to sleep. We may have a long day tomorrow. I don't think we've heard the last from the police.'

Moonlight was now spilling into the hallway through the diamond panes of the arched window, casting strange shadows, stirring strange memories. Tonight there was no ghost on the landing. But when Jane reached it, she looked down into the hallway, expecting to see Daniel still lying on the tiled floor, and she looked up at the bridge, remembering she had once seen a ghost there, but unable to recall when it was. But there was only moonlight, silver and cold, and the reassuring touch of Ryan's hand holding hers. Had Ryan seen a ghost last night? Was it the same ghost that she remembered seeing? When had she seen it? Had it been part of a dream?

He left her at her door with a final hug, and she heard his steps on the next flight of stairs to his room.

Tuesday 23 March 1976

The inspector called on them in the morning, arriving with the sergeant in their sleek new black car. They had their photographs and needed no further access to the den or the bedroom for the moment. They were sending a team who were experts in falls to do some calculations on where Daniel had fallen. They would arrive at about eleven.

'I'm just being cautious,' the inspector told them. 'Where he was lying just didn't look right. We have the blood alcohol reading but not the drugs yet. The post-mortem was inconclusive, so we need an autopsy, and that will take a bit longer. At the moment all we know is that his blood alcohol level was high, but not enough to kill him by itself. At that level some people would be lucky to still be standing up, but if he normally drank a good deal, it would not have the same effect. Our expert said that for someone who drank a lot, he may have still seemed quite sober. We believe he died between three and four o' clock.'

Ryan spent a lot of the morning on the phone, first to Mr Allanstone, then the publishers, then the undertakers. The publishers were to make a press release. Daniel Linden had died after a fall down the stairs in his home in Oxfordshire, and the family were asking for their privacy to be respected. They wrote it up in more detail and phoned Ryan back so they could check it with him before they distributed it.

Anne McCann had phoned and had spoken to Mary. Reverend Colin had phoned. One of the newspapers had phoned, but Ryan told them they had the wrong number.

Mary, Pat and Jane changed the sheets just as they normally did on a Tuesday, but they left Daniel's bedroom as it was. They all tidied the den and closed the door with its *Private* sign, left over from when there were paying guests in the house. Perhaps in a few days they would sort all the papers, tidy the pens and pencils in the drawers, clean the leather seats, close the curtains, vacuum the carpets, and it would go back to being an unused room. Perhaps one day Ryan would take it over, sit in his father's chair and work at his father's desk. But not yet.

The experts arrived, two young men who chatted incessantly to each other. They asked to be left alone in the hallway while they worked, for safety reasons, as they would be dropping things. But they said it was okay for Jane to watch them from the doorway to the dining room, as they could then ask her questions if they needed to. They measured the hallway, the height of the landings and the bridge across the top floor, the height of the balustrades, the distance from the floor to the landing. They had graph paper and plumb lines, slide rules and calculators, and small beanbags with numbers on them. These were dropped from various spots on the gallery, and from the bridge on the top floor. They took photographs each time of where they fell.

The cat came in to see what was happening and pounced on a bean bag that had just been dropped from the bridge, landing within the chalk marks where Daniel had been lying. Jane came to rescue the cat, and they asked her to do an experiment with them.

They rolled up one of the rugs from the hallway and put it on the stairs, with the lower end just reaching the tiles, and they asked Jane if she could pull it down onto the tiled floor. She was easily able to. They lifted it between them to judge the weight and asked her if she knew how much Daniel had weighed. She didn't, but she was able to tell them he was a similar build to Ryan and Pat, as they could all wear each other's clothes. He was perhaps an inch or two shorter than Ryan.

They found another rug and rolled both rugs together for her to try. It was heavier, but she was able to move the rugs down the last few stairs and out onto the tiled floor. They thanked her, and she helped them put the rugs back in their usual places.

They had left the front door open to give them more light. The sunshine through the window on the landing fell in dusty shafts, warming the stone tiles on the floor, merging with the light from the open doorway to give a last glow of colour to the worn old rugs, a memory of a past life to the old wood grain of the oak balusters and rails and newels and finials and treads of the staircase, as though the wood was remembering the long ago years when it had been absorbing the sun, proud and free and alive in a forest.

For fifty-five years, almost half of the life of this house, Daniel had walked in the hallway, climbed the stairs, touched the banister and the newel posts. His wife had died after falling on that staircase, and now he had too.

Mary made coffee and sandwiches for the two young men at lunch time, and they thanked her and apologised for the intrusion. But when they left, they would not say what their conclusions were. They needed to do more calculations, and they needed the results from the post-mortem. They would only know how far he had fallen from the extent of his injuries.

The van arrived for the linen, the driver cheerful as always, for he knew nothing of their loss, Mary responding to his greeting as she normally would, Jane handing him the calico bag with the sheets and towels, then helping Mary stack the clean linen. How calming and healing it was to do ordinary routine things. She recalled thinking the same thing when she had first come here to live.

Anne and Jack McCann called by at three that afternoon, with Jimmy and Claire, Reverend Colin and Linda, and John Phillips. Claire had been allowed the afternoon off work due to the tragedy in her fiancé's family. Her employer had sent a note with her condolences to Mary, who often bought wool from the shop.

Anne gave Mary a hug, Claire hugged Pat, and Jimmy hugged Jane. Nobody hugged poor Ryan, but Jack McCann did put a hand on his shoulder, asking if he was coping.

The McCanns had brought scones and cream, and Linda had made egg and cress sandwiches. Mary found a jar of her raspberry jam for the scones, and made tea in a huge teapot. They all sat in the dining room, as the kitchen table was too small for so many. Jane sat with her back to the window, hoping they would not notice her bruised face. Her neck was once again covered with a scarf.

Jack McCann was eight years younger than Daniel, but he reminisced on the days when he and his older brother Jim, long dead in the War, had shot rabbits with Daniel, had gone swimming in a pool on the stream between his farm and the next one, had shared drinks and stories, seasons with snow, lazy days in long-ago summers. He talked of the years when they were children before the Second World War, of hardship and good times, runaway bulls and bogged tractors, mutual friends now lost, some in the War, some along the path of their lives since.

He shared his memories of Mary's mother and the brave face she had put on running the place after her husband was missing near the end of the War, memories of Jane's father, much closer to Jack in age than Daniel was, best friends with Jack and Robert Phillips. The three of them had shot rabbits together when they were teenagers during the War, and his mother and Mary's mother and Margaret Phillips had always been grateful for the extra meat. They had tried to pretend they were seventeen so they could sign up to be in the Home Guard, but it hadn't worked. John Phillips had been in the Home Guard, as he had been too old to enlist in the army and in any case would not have not been fit enough. He told them he still had his tin hat. He had helped Jack's mother with her farm during the war, as well as running his own, as Jack's father and older brother were both away fighting.

Then there were the kinder memories of the years after the War, village hall teas, cricket matches when Daniel had played well and the opposing team had gone home soundly beaten. Daniel had always been good at cricket. They would miss him in the older men's team this summer, as he had still been their best bowler. Ryan clearly took after him, as he was the best bowler in the young men's team, even though he played left-handed. Jack recalled Ryan had broken his right arm falling out of a tree when he was a child.

'It was around the time that Peter left. I remember that because his arm was still in plaster when we went to London for the wedding. Ryan and Pat were left at our farm with my mother for the day. Peter and Josie were married in a church in Richmond, and afterwards we all had a wonderful afternoon tea at a posh hotel. It had to be early enough so we could return to Hayward by train that day, as Mary couldn't leave Pat overnight, and Anne was expecting Jimmy then and tired easily. For some reason Daniel didn't come with us. I think he was sick at the time. Robert was best man, and he first met Susan that day. She was Josie's bridesmaid. A few months later they were married. He worked in London then, before he took the job in Switzerland. Susan didn't like living abroad, so after a few years she brought the boys back to live on the farm here, so they could go to an English school, and a few months later she ran off with someone and left her boys with Margaret.'

This was all new and interesting to Jane. Clearly Jack didn't know the story of the rivalry between her father and his cousin over her mother, and Jane had not heard the whole story before about why Adrian and Winston lived with their grandfather and not with either of their parents.

'Maggie never quite forgave her for leaving Robert, or for going off without the boys, but I did.' John Phillips took over telling the story from Jack. 'Susan's brother and his friend came to stay with us for a few weeks in the summer, so he could see his nephews. The two of them camped out in the barn. They both worked together in a hospital in Edinburgh. It turned out Susan and the friend had been sweethearts before she married Robert. She left a note for us. It wasn't just about the school for the boys. Robert was never one for the girls, although he fathered his two sons. He had a friend in Switzerland, and Susan said she was sick of playing second fiddle to a man. She did want the boys; she said she would come and collect them in a couple of weeks. Her brother and his friend shared a tiny flat, so they were finding a house with room for them all. But Robert wouldn't let her have them, and he wouldn't give her any money, even though by law he was obliged to. He was a lawyer and he had a lot more money than she did, so she didn't fight it through the courts. She knew it was hopeless. He threatened to take the boys to live in Switzerland with him if she contested it, so she would rarely have seen them. They spent a lot of their time at school—he paid for that—and he grudgingly let her have them for the summer holidays. Robert didn't really want them either, at least not with him, so Maggie and I brought them up.

'It's a sad thing to be ashamed of the behaviour of your own son towards his former wife, but in the end everyone came to accept the arrangement. He eventually let her have a divorce, naming her lover as co-respondent, and by then she was expecting another child. Robert still lives with his friend in their flat in Geneva and they have a summer place by a lake. Maggie and I never went to Switzerland, and we never met the friend.'

When the scones and sandwiches were all eaten, Jane fetched the biscuit tin, and that was emptied as well. When the guests finally left, life seemed a much friendlier place to Jane than it had last night.

It was on the news that evening from the press release by the publisher. Daniel Linden was dead after falling down stairs at his home in Oxfordshire. There was some footage of Daniel and Mary with a teenage Ryan in a dinner suit and bow-tie, with shorter hair, looking amazingly like his father and surprisingly neat, arriving at the premiere of one of the films.

Wednesday 24 March 1976

The following morning *The Times* had an obituary that Mary carefully cut out. There were no reporters, for Daniel had always kept the telephone number silent, and the publisher dealt with any correspondence. No one knew where they lived, and never had they felt more grateful for it.

Two days passed quietly enough. Ryan and Jane started work on the den in earnest, sorting the piles of papers, finding unopened letters—much of it fan mail sent on from the publisher. But there were old bills that they weren't sure had been paid, cheques that had never been banked, bank statements that would give them the means to reconcile all of it, share certificates still in their envelopes instead of the safe.

Since Jane had arrived, the new paperwork coming in had been kept under control. Before that it was only things that Daniel himself had set aside for Ryan to deal with that had been done, and Ryan had only been there for one night each week. Jane had tried to gradually sort some of the old letters and papers, and Ryan had helped her over the Christmas holiday, but she had only touched the surface. There were shares in Ryan's name, shares in Mary's name, even Pat's. Ryan told her he was sometimes given a dividend cheque to bank, but he hadn't taken much notice of it. It was all money and Daniel had looked after where it was invested.

It gave them something to do, and they were grateful for anything that would take their minds off the police investigation. The detectives didn't appear to be happy that Daniel's death was an accident, but they had not yet revealed what evidence they had.

Friday 26 March 1976

The inspector returned on Friday morning with his sergeant. The preliminary toxicology report was in, but they did not yet have the autopsy results. There was still some question over why Daniel had died, and another specialist was being consulted. He had taken one of the Valium pills at some time before he died, but the only clear fingerprints they had found on the bottle were Jane's and Pat's, with a fuzzy print that could be Mary's.

He had also taken his digitoxin, possibly two of them, but they were not able to say precisely when he had taken them. They had an expert doing further analysis.

Mary explained he took them as needed, not on a regular basis. His heart would sometimes beat too fast, and if it hadn't slowed down after he sat still for five minutes, he took one to slow it down. He would only take one, as taking too many could actually precipitate heart failure, your heart could slow down too much, so you had to be very careful with them. He always knew when he needed one, and it was not all that often.

Jane told them he always took the bottle with him when they went on walks. She had only seen him take one once, when Ryan was with them, although he often seemed out of breath on hills. She always tried to walk at his pace when she was just with him, but when Ryan had been with them, they had all walked faster.

Mary showed them the cupboard where the pills had been stored, explaining that it had once been kept locked, as many years ago Daniel had barbiturates to help him sleep, and their mother hadn't trusted him not to overdose on them. There were no barbiturates there now, and Mary trusted Ryan with his sleeping pills. The shelf was very high, above eye level even for the men. Daniel's pills would usually be at the front, as he took them with him when he went out walking in the hills. Ryan's and Jane's were usually at the back, as they were rarely used, but Mary had taken them down the night before he died so she could give

Jane a sedative. She had taken down Ryan's Valium as well to ask if he needed one. When she put them away, Daniel's heart pills would have then been at the back, so it was possible he made a mistake and took a Valium, thinking the bottle was his digitoxin. He may have realised it was a mistake and taken the digitoxin afterwards.

The inspector wrote all that down, then continued with his next question.

'We have looked at the bank and credit card statements. He took out a lot of cash. What did he spend it on?'

Jane decided she should answer this, as she kept the accounts.

'This house costs a lot to run, and he gives some money to Pat to pay him for the gardening, and a little to Ryan as he is doing research and doesn't work full time.'

'Did he give you money, Miss Walters?'

'No. He always offered, but I wouldn't accept it. I have means of my own from my father's life insurance.'

'He took out large amounts of cash when he was in London. We also have hotel payments on the credit card that correspond to the dates he took out the cash. Did you go to London and stay in a hotel with him, Miss Walters? Did he give the money to you?'

Jane was not sure she liked what the inspector was implying.

'No, I didn't go with him, and I never took money from him, ever, except that he always gave each of us a five-pound note for the church collection.'

'Do you know what he spent it on, Miss Walters?'

'No, I don't. I helped him by doing the accounting, and I keep track of all the withdrawals, but I didn't ask him what he did with his money. That was his affair, not mine, and I don't see it has any bearing on why he died. Perhaps he went to concerts or paid for taxis.'

'The relevance is for us to decide, Miss Walters. The withdrawals were for a significant amount of money, hundreds of pounds. Is it possible someone was blackmailing him?'

'He was a wealthy man, Inspector. If someone was blackmailing him, they would want more than a few hundred pounds.'

'Do you know what he did when he visited London?'

'No, I don't. I imagine he talked with the publisher.'

'Only occasionally. We have checked that with them. Did he have a mistress there?'

'If he did, he was unlikely to tell me. I really can't see how this can be relevant. He died here, not in London.'

The inspector gave up on that line of enquiry, but he wasn't finished.

The fall experts had said that there were five likely scenarios. The inspector held up his pudgy stained fingers as he counted them out.

He died elsewhere in the house and the body was moved to the foot of the stairs so it looked like an accident.

He was moved away from the stairs after he fell from the landing.

He fell backwards from the second or third step.

He fell from the bridge on the top floor.

Or he was pushed backwards with considerable force while standing on the landing.

Since he had died in the early hours of the morning, rather than the night before when there had been an argument, they thought the first scenario unlikely, although they were not eliminating it. If he had been injured in a fight it might have been several hours before he died, or there might have been another altercation during the night.

Everyone had denied moving him, and if he had fallen from the lower steps, the fall would have been unlikely to kill him, so they were discounting both of those scenarios.

If he had fallen from the bridge then it might have been an accident, he might have deliberately jumped or he might have been pushed. The results from the post-mortem and the autopsy would help as they would then know the cause of death and the full extent of his injuries from the fall. The experts thought that if he had fallen from the bridge, he could possibly have landed where he did with his feet on the stairs, particularly if someone trying to revive him had straightened him out.

They seemed to think he had reached the landing, although they did not say why they thought that, and everyone had denied moving the body by more than a small amount, so the most likely scenario was that he was pushed with some force from the landing following a confrontation at around the time he died.

They thought it unlikely that he was pushed downstairs earlier in the night and left lying there for three or four hours before he died, as Pat had checked him after midnight and he was then still in the den. All four of them being involved in a cover up and leaving an injured man to die hours later on the floor of the hallway was unlikely.

At least they don't think us capable of that, Jane thought, but the inspector's next words sent a chill through her.

Ryan was to go with them to the police station in Oxford to answer more questions. At this stage they were not arresting him or charging him with anything, they just wanted more information and would appreciate his cooperation, but they said he might prefer to have a solicitor with him.

Mary rang Mr Allanstone. It was not in his line of work, but he contacted a colleague in Oxford and arranged for him to meet Ryan at the police station there in an hour. He rang Mary back, confirming the arrangement, saying that the solicitor Mr Jameson was an old friend of his and Daniel's, promising if Ryan was charged, they would find him the best defence lawyers that money could buy. He would come to Hayward tomorrow and bring the will with him. He asked to talk to Ryan. Later Jane learnt that he had told Ryan to say as little as possible without refusing to answer reasonable questions. From the information Mary had given him he considered it would be difficult for any jury to convict him beyond reasonable doubt, and he thought the police would try to get a confession from him. Just keep calm, stay polite, try not to sound insolent and don't let them make you angry.

Ryan fetched his jacket from his room, hugged Mary then Jane, asked Pat to look after them both and followed the inspector outside.

Jane watched from a front window as the car disappeared through the gate, the sergeant driving, the inspector sitting in the back with Ryan. She was unable to conquer the fear that she might never see him back here again. How would he cope with them questioning him? He always seemed confident and in control, but beneath the calm surface was a child who had been bashed by his father and had never fully recovered from the trauma of it. Her heart ached for him, and she felt how keenly he would be hurt by their suspicions. She wished she could have gone with him, sat beside him, but she knew she would have gone to pieces long before he did. It was her fault, she had dragged him into this mess, he had been defending her, and she had ruined his life, perhaps forever.

Pat was beside her, his arm around her, but she could not stop shaking. Her legs felt like jelly, but she tried to stay calm. If she felt like this, what would he be feeling like?

'Bear up, Jane. Tears aren't going to solve anything. We all know he had nothing to do with it. We have a justice system in this country, and no jury would convict him on the flimsy evidence they have. Provided he doesn't say anything stupid like confessing to something he didn't do, he'll be fine. Ryan is always absolutely in control of everything he says and does.'

'Jane, Mr Jameson will look after him,' Mary assured her. 'He knew Daniel well. They were at school and Oxford together, and they worked together after the War. Ryan will cope. He always does. He didn't kill Daniel, so he has nothing to fear.

'I should have known that it wouldn't work, having you back here, in spite of all Daniel's promises. I was hoping that you and Ryan would come back from Richmond engaged. The two of you were alone in the house there and quite obviously in love with each other. I told him when I sent him after you not to miss his opportunity. He knew what I meant. Daniel would never have touched you if you had been engaged to Ryan, although he would have been bitterly disappointed. He did have some principles.'

'I hoped so too, but Ryan told me he had never wanted a girlfriend, and he preferred just to be a lone wolf. Then the last night we were there, he took me out to dinner, and afterwards we nearly slept together, but he said I was tipsy and he wouldn't take advantage in case I regretted it the next day. He was a bit tipsy as well and I thought he was also concerned he might regret it. I wish now we had slept together because then we would have stayed in Richmond and not come back here. Even when we got back to the Hall, we stopped at the gate and talked about just driving away again. I had some idea that Daniel would see we were lovers and forgive us, and we could all live here happily together. I like living here. I didn't want them fighting over me, and I didn't want Ryan giving up his home here for me. He thought Daniel would disinherit him, but he said he didn't mind. He did ask me if I wanted to marry him, but it took me by surprise. Only half an hour before he had been telling me he liked to be by himself. So I said perhaps we should both think about it for a while, but I wish now I had said yes. I feel that this is all my fault.'

'Daniel may still have attacked Jane, just to get back at Ryan, even if they had come back engaged,' said Pat. 'He was always awful to Ryan. When he danced with Jane and was groping her bum in front of us all, it was just to spite Ryan. And he persuaded her to tango with him, then danced like he was trying to seduce her. I thought Ryan was going to flatten him. He would have deserved it. Even I felt like flattening him. Then he wanted to force Jane to sleep with him. That was just to spite Ryan as well so he could crow that he had her first. He knew she would never agree to marry him, however good he was in bed. I thought Ryan would kill him that night, but he kept his temper, thank goodness. He always does stay calm. But Daniel will have really got his revenge for Jane preferring Ryan to him if Ryan hangs for murdering him.'

Jane dissolved into tears, and Mary was angry with Pat. 'That was a very unkind thing to say in front of Jane. They don't hang people in England any more. Not for the last ten years at least. And this is not your fault Jane. Not at all. The only one at fault was my brother.

'Mr Allanstone is coming here tomorrow morning. He will spend Saturday night here and go home on Sunday afternoon. Jane can help me set up a room up for him. He is bringing the will with him. Normally we wouldn't see it until after the funeral, but the police have been asking about it, so he thought we should at least know what is in it before they do. Tomorrow afternoon Mr Jameson is coming for afternoon tea with us so he and Mr Allanstone can talk about what is to be done for Ryan. They are old friends.'

Pat took Mary and Jane into town for the weekly shopping and Jane picked up a new bottle of Valium for Ryan; Mary had found the prescription. It was difficult to concentrate on the shopping, but at least they were occupied, and she felt glad to be doing something for him, however small.

After lunch, Mary and Jane dusted and vacuumed the corner room at the front of the house on the other side of the stairwell from Jane's, made up the bed, found towels for the bathroom and turned on the radiators. It was years since there had been a guest at the Hall. Mary had picked some daffodils from the garden, a bright splash of yellow in a white vase on the dressing table; another bunch had been put on the table in the conservatory ready for tomorrow's lunch.

'My mother always put flowers in the rooms if she had any in the garden. She wanted to make people happy when they stayed here. She thought of everything. She would put a French letter in the drawer by the bed so if a man brought a girl here, they had what was needed to keep the girl safe. But she never put them in the same drawer as the bible. Of course I had no idea then what they were for. I was only ten when the War ended, but I still helped my mother run the house.

'We had a lot of servicemen here during the War. Sometimes they needed somewhere to meet their wives if they were stationed away from where they lived, but more usually it was their girlfriends. She didn't judge them. She understood how hard it was for young people in those days. She simply signed them in, showed them the room, suggested they could walk in the garden if they wanted to. Some of it was casual, but sometimes it was an otherwise respectable girl who just had to take what opportunity she could to be with the man she loved. If a girl had a boyfriend, she would be in constant dread of losing him, and getting married in the usual way with family and friends present was next to impossible. Some of them would have planned to marry after the War, but none of us knew then whether the War would ever end, and if it did, whether we would still be here to celebrate.

'We kept chickens so we had enough eggs for the breakfasts, and there was always milk and butter from the farm. Jack's mother had a few cows then. And John Phillips would always give us honey if he had any to spare. With rationing on, it was hard to get bacon, tea and sugar, even marmalade, but we made raspberry jam with what sugar we could save by having honey in our tea, and my mother always managed to feed the guests somehow. We were allowed some extras as we were a hotel. Even after the war ended, we still had rationing. We had a ration book for Ryan, but it was over by the time Pat was born. Bread was the worst thing. The only loaves the bakers were allowed to sell were made from dirty brown flour. They could only sell bread that was a day old, so it was stale, and they were not allowed to slice or wrap it. It was so good when rationing ended and we had enough white flour and sugar to bake cakes again.'

Jane knew Mary was trying to keep both of them thinking about trivial things to keep their minds from the non-trivial ones. She had talked about the War, but today there was no mention of the lives lost, Mary's father and both of Peter's parents. They were both depressed enough without that. Jane thought about Mary's mother, who had spent day after day, month after month, year after year, with her husband and son away fighting in a war and two children to look after at home. She had coped, as we all cope, because in the end there is no alternative.

The cat came in, exploring a room that was normally shut for any trace of mice, jumping onto the bed to test how soft it was, then purring around Jane's ankles.

They finished the room and Jane ironed some shirts. Mary took them up to Ryan's room, returning with his black cable jumper and asking Jane if she would like to hand wash it, to keep busy. But instead, Jane sat at the kitchen table hugging it, while Mary made the afternoon tea.

The jumper smelt of Ryan, a mixture of warm wool scent and the Taylor Sandalwood aftershave that he used. Her father had used it too. She and her mother had bought a bottle for him every Christmas, and it had always been given to Jane to wrap for him. She felt her father near to her. He had loved Ryan as well. The scent of the jumper was surprisingly comforting, and Jane hoped that by hugging his jumper, she was making Ryan feel hugged wherever he was. He would be stressed. She knew he would be stressed.

Mary was making an apple pie for that evening's dessert, so Jane helped her cut up the apples. Ryan always enjoyed Mary's apple pies. Was Mary really so confident that he would be coming back today? Why were they questioning him for so long? Could they keep him locked up? Jane knew that Mary was trying to keep them all from worrying—even Pat was on edge—so she tried to stay calm and be useful.

Mary sent Pat to the village shop to buy some cream for the pie, and Jane went with him, glad to be doing something to ease the agony of waiting. Then she washed the jumper in soap flakes, spun it in the washing machine, and laid it flat to dry on a towel on the coffee table in the conservatory. Would he ever wear it again? Why wasn't he back yet? Would he ever return?

It was late afternoon when the sergeant dropped Ryan back at the house. He was exhausted and dispirited, saying nothing while they made him a warm mug of coffee. Jane found the cat on Mary's sofa and brought her to sit on Ryan's lap. She found the cat brush as well so when he finished his coffee, he could brush the cat. It was a very relaxing activity and Jasmine enjoyed it too.

'I was grateful for the solicitor,' he said at last, absently brushing the cat. 'I'm not sure they wouldn't have belted a confession out of me otherwise. They clearly think I pushed him, but Jameson doesn't think any jury would convict me on the evidence they have. Allanstone was right in saying they would try to get me to confess to it. Jameson said that as well. He is coming here tomorrow afternoon to talk with Allanstone about representing me if the police charge me, or whether we go for a really top lawyer from London. He was at school and Oxford with both Allanstone and my father, and they worked together for a few years after the War. It was good to have someone who knew him, and it was good to have someone on my side.'

'Jane and I will make scones for tea tomorrow. Did they give you some lunch?'

'Yes, sandwiches and coffee, for Jameson as well. They treated us very courteously in that regard at least. I did my best to tell them as little as possible, but Jameson said if I refused to answer everything, they might keep me in custody. I do always think carefully before I say anything, but I had the idea the inspector found it irritating.'

Pat wanted to know what they had asked, but Ryan said he would rather not think about it. Perhaps he would talk about it tomorrow. But after a few minutes while he sat silent and absorbed, still brushing the cat, he did tell them.

'It was completely nerve-wracking. I really understand now what that term means. At first they wanted background information, where I had been to school, what I had studied at Oxford, was Jane my girl-friend, did I have a girlfriend, past girlfriends, why had I never had a girlfriend, was I gay, was that why didn't I get on with my father. I was as non-committal as I could be, telling them I had never wanted a girl-friend or a boyfriend either, and my father and I got on as well as any other family. Jameson said I didn't have to answer when they asked if I fancied Jane, so I didn't.

'They seem to think he was pushed quite hard backwards from the landing, or from partway down the staircase. Their best theory is that he reached the landing, was pushed progressively backwards down the stairs, then given a really hard shove. The stairs are not at all steep, so if he had simply fallen backwards onto the stairs from the landing, he might have slid to the bottom, but he would have stopped as soon as his head reached the tiles. He was much further away from the bottom of the stairs than that. All of us denied moving him, but they agreed it was possible Mary had moved him without realising how far she had dragged him.

'They said he may have fallen, jumped, or been pushed from the bridge, but from what they know so far, they think that unlikely. They didn't say why they thought that. They don't think either of the ladies would have been strong enough to push him that hard from the landing or to have got him over the railing of the bridge, so that leaves Pat and me. I know it wasn't me, and Pat knows it wasn't him. I suggested a stray bat may have flown into his face or he may have fallen over the cat, but they said he would have collapsed where he was or fallen forwards, and told me this was not a joking matter.

'They had another nutcase theory that we had a fight the night before, but he hadn't died until around three o' clock, and then we had moved him to the stairs to look as if it was an accident. I told them that was getting a bit far-fetched. He couldn't seriously believe that Mary wouldn't have called an ambulance if I had injured my father in a fight. They even suggested he died making love to Jane, and we made it look like an accident to spare Jane embarrassment. They said Jane's finger-prints were all over his buttons, as though she had undressed him, and how could I explain that? I couldn't of course, but I assume it was true or they would not have said it. He asked if I had found her in bed with him and killed him. He even suggested it was me who had hit Jane when I found her sleeping with my father.

'The inspector was trying to make me admit I was angry about what my father did to Jane. He had tried to strangle her, didn't that make me feel like killing him? He asked me if he had been strangling her with his hands or with his tie. I didn't answer that. It was difficult at times to keep my cool, but I did. I said that of course I was angry with him, but if everyone killed anyone they got angry with, there wouldn't be many of us left.

'They were continually asking me to tell them what really happened that night. They were convinced that there was something that none of us were telling them. They suggested Jane had pushed him down the stairs, and they threatened to bring Jane in for questioning. Were we all hiding what really happened to protect Jane? They really knew how to get at me. They were hoping I might confess to it if I thought they were going to hassle Jane. I reminded them that they had already said they did not consider Jane to be strong enough to push him that far, and to the best of my knowledge Jane had stayed locked in her room all night.

'Then they said if I had killed him in a fight, and confessed to it, so it was easy for them, they would only charge me with manslaughter. By the end of it I was starting to wonder if I really had killed him, but had forgotten I did it. Maybe I had been sleepwalking. I hope they don't turn up again wanting to take Pat or Jane in for questioning because it was not a pleasant experience.

'In the end Jameson told them they had to release me because they couldn't charge me with anything until they knew more precisely why he had died. They could only detain me for twenty-four hours, and that was pointless unless they knew they would have the autopsy results by then. He may have died from natural causes while he was climbing the stairs, since he did have a weak heart. Jameson seemed to know that, so Allanstone may have told him. I don't think I did.'

'How do they know he reached the landing before he fell?' Pat asked. 'If he had been a few steps up and fallen backwards, he would have landed where he did.'

'The missing button from his shirt was on the landing, so they assume he had got that far before he fell, and there was then some sort of altercation which resulted in the button being torn off. I told them I had grabbed him by his shirt front, but in the den, not on the landing. If I am to be convicted of murdering him, it will hinge on the position of one shirt button. Jameson said no jury would convict me on the evidence they have so far, as the button could have been dropped at any time. He could have reached the landing, then gone back down the stairs to get something he had forgotten from the den. Jameson thinks they will only be able to charge me if I confess to it, which he doesn't recommend, even if I did do it.

'And Jane, thank you for answering the questions about the money this morning. You were brilliant. It was so good to see my little church mouse standing up to him. I was trying hard not to smirk when you said my father was unlikely to have told you he had a mistress. They asked me about the money as well, but I just said that you look after the accounting, and I don't usually live here except at weekends, so I have no idea where my father goes or what he spends. I imagine they have some idea where the money went. Unless he had a serious drug or gambling problem, there is really only one explanation. At least we got rid of the card from the escort agency. They would know what some of those agencies are a cover for, and they know from the hotel account that he always paid for dinner for two.

'Mary, can you find me the cellar key after dinner so I can find some brandy. I don't think I could face Scotch at the moment after it killing my father, but some brandy would be good. We'll give Jane some as well, she can have it with lemonade, as she looks very stressed. God, I'm tired, and I need some fresh air. It was stuffy in that interview room, and they were all smoking. I am totally exhausted, and I never want to go through that again. Jane, will you walk in the garden with me while Mary cooks dinner? Can you spare her, Mary?'

'Yes, of course, but don't stay out too long. If you get the brandy before dinner, you can bring up a bottle of wine as well. We made an apple pie for dessert. Pat can whip the cream for me.'

Jane took her duffle coat from its peg in the boot room and followed him obediently into the garden. He took her hand. It was rather cold outdoors, and neither of them had gloves, so she tucked her hand and his into the pocket of her coat.

They walked in silence, down through the garden and into the wood, past the door in the wall where Jane had first met Jimmy McCann, through the trees, the gargoyles menacing in the shadowy light, Jane recalling that Jimmy thought they came alive at night. They passed the standing stone, the door that led through to John Phillips' farm—now disused and overgrown with raspberry canes—then back past the tennis court, the maze and the coach house, and around to the front of the house with the banks of flowers and the pond and the fountain, rather gloomy in the last chill remains of daylight on a cloudy day. The shadowed shape of the monkey puzzle tree loomed above them, gaunt and threatening, as if it would extend one of its twisted branches and clutch them both, then devour them with its sharp teeth.

 They continued along the drive to the open gate, now dark and sinister beneath the trees that bordered the lane. And all the time he said not a word, so she stayed silent, her hand still in his, warm in her pocket. They returned towards the house, solid against the evening sky, and Jane felt it wanting to hug them both, to comfort them even though it could not help them.

Through the front door, into the hallway, the chalk marks still on the tiles, the oak staircase leading up, the last faint glow of daylight lingering behind the gothic window, the photos of long dead Lindens on the walls, all now gone into the forgotten depths of the past, the photo of Daniel with his bride, the bright promise of her life cut down so soon. But she had left a legacy, her beautiful tall son with his father's gaunt features and black hair, but her eyes and her curls, who now stood weary and troubled in the hallway in the last light of another fading day. Jane wanted to comfort him, but she didn't know what to say. She could only stand in silence with him, still holding his hand.

'They're all dead,' she said at last. 'The people in the photos are all dead. And now your father is too.'

'Actually, Jane, not all of them. Somewhere there is one of Pat and me as children, one of those beautiful fifties black-and-white studio photos that everyone has of their children, except that we were cousins not brothers. There is a similar one of you as well, but sadly not one of us three together.

'Most of them are dead, some so long ago that no one alive now remembers them. But they are still part of the lifetime of this house. When people we love die, we keep their photos on the walls so we remember the good times. When we stop thinking that we can't go on living without them, we remember that we loved them and they loved us and how good life was when they were still here. My father never got that far. After my mother died, he spent the remainder of his life cursing fate and drowning his sorrow in whisky and women and the fantasy world he created. My grandmother once said he had let grief and loss define his life, and that was never a good thing to do.

'In all the history of the world no one has ever found a way to go back and change one single moment of the past. We can study it, perhaps learn from it, but we can never change it. We can only accept it, and only then can we go forward.

'At the moment I'm not sure how we do that, but in the end we will both cope with what has been thrown at us. Right now life looks pretty bleak to me. I have never felt so depressed in my whole life. If I am convicted of murdering my father, I will lose any chance I had of marrying you, I will lose my freedom, and I will lose my inheritance as well. Under British law you can't benefit financially from a crime you committed. I don't know whether it would go to the state or they would let it pass through to Mary. I will ask Allanstone tomorrow. I can only hope so. If my father has left everything to me, then this beautiful old house, all of the money, and the income from the royalties might be forfeited and Mary would be destitute. She has very little money of her own, and she has never had a job. Pat would look after her as best he could, of course, but he has no money either, and he has only ever done the gardening here and casual farm work for Jack McCann and John Phillips. But you have a house and some money of your own, and you did at least have a job that you could perhaps go back to. Jane, you would look after her, wouldn't you, like you looked after your aunt?'

'Yes, of course. But she does have someone else to protect her. Pat's father sends her money, and he paid for Pat to go to school. Your father once told me that. If she had some income of her own, we could manage very well together in the house in Richmond, and she could still afford her beautiful clothes and her Joy perfume.'

'Then there's my grandfather. He's always saying I'll get his money, but the truth is he has none. My father pays for him to live at the nursing home in Bath, and that costs a good deal. God, what a mess this all is!'

'I promise I would do everything I can. I do have money of my own, nothing like as much as Daniel had, but still quite a lot. You didn't kill him and you won't be convicted, but even if you had, and you were, I would wait for you forever. You know that. I could never love anyone else. I feel this is all my fault. I would love a hug.'

He took her coat, hung it on the newel post, and pulled her close, his cheek touching her hair, her arms around his neck.

'I need a hug as well. Jane, please don't get depressed, and try not to cry.'

She was close to tears, and she thought perhaps he was as well, but she tried not to give in to the weary despair that threatened to suffocate her. She felt incapable of helping him, she couldn't be strong, and she just wanted to cry with the unfairness of it all. She knew he wanted comfort. He needed to know she was there with him, that she understood his desolation. Yet she felt the thrill of his body against hers, the magic touch of his fingers on her face and in her hair.

'After dinner you can have some brandy. It will make you feel better. None of this is your fault in any way. We were so close to leaving here and being together, but for now that has to wait. This will all blow over, and everything will be good again. I loved him. We all loved him. I understood that he just wasn't capable of loving me, but I always tried to help him, even if all I did was sign the cheques and play billiards with him. Losing him the way we did was bad enough for all of us, but to be suspected of murdering him is more than I can take. They tried to confuse me, and they made me feel powerless and no longer in control. They knew I felt bad because I hadn't protected you, and they played on that. I was glad I had Jameson. He kept reminding me that I didn't have to answer every question, and I didn't have to prove I was innocent, they would have to prove I was guilty.'

There was just enough time for them to get the brandy from the cellar before dinner. The key was now back in the door. Mary had only taken it to stop Daniel drinking too much, but that no longer mattered. Jane went down the stairs with Ryan, the electric light barely adequate, the small rooms, shadowed and spooky, filled with velvety blackness. Anything could be hiding in the murky corners of those unlit rooms, formed here hundreds of years ago, much earlier than the current house.

Jane remembered Pat saying they could brick up Daniel in one of the dark corners, hide away from the world that one of his family had murdered him, except that none of them had. How could it possibly have worked? Colin would wonder why he was not at church. Jack McCann would wonder why he never saw him out walking. Mr Allanstone would wonder why he was never there if he phoned. The publishers would wait forever for the next book to be sent to them.

Pat was all right, for he had been leaving here, at least as far as the lodge, but she, Ryan and Mary had all been set free by his death. She had seen no way forward from his mad desire to possess her, yet suddenly everything had changed. It was a relief to her that she no longer had to cope with his advances, but she felt guilty even thinking that, and she also felt guilty that she had not wanted to sleep with him when he had desired her so much. But he hadn't loved her. He had tried to strangle her, had deliberately terrified her, and you don't do that to someone you love.

The cat had followed them down the stairs, happy to pursue the smell of mice, but staying close to them, wary of being left behind when they returned to the warmth of the kitchen. They came back up from the cold depths of the cellar with the bottle of brandy, and a bottle of elderberry wine to have with dinner, waiting for Jasmine to come through the door before they closed it again, trapping the mice and the ghosts of that dark underground space where evil things could lurk unhindered for all time.

Were there other bodies walled up beneath the house? Long ago secrets, ancient whispers, deceit and lies that would rest there until the house and the garden and the cellar were one day all gone.

Saturday 27 March 1976

Mr Allanstone arrived around mid-morning on Saturday. He hugged Mary for what seemed a long time, shook hands with the young men and briefly hugged Jane. Mary took him upstairs to his room, although he clearly already knew his way around the house. It was a while before they came down.

He was given coffee, and he walked in the garden with Ryan and Pat while Jane and Mary made a quiche and salad for lunch, which they ate in the conservatory. Ryan brought up a bottle of white wine from the cellar, and if it wasn't for what had happened to Daniel, and what was now threatening Ryan, it could have been old friends enjoying a leisurely lunch in a beautiful setting on a beautiful day.

The conservatory was warmed by the spring sunshine, for once the soft rays had ventured in, they were trapped by the glass, warming the room, so although it was not yet April, it felt like a long lazy summer day.

After lunch he fetched his briefcase from his room and took out the will. It would normally have waited until the day of the funeral, but it was important that they all knew where they stood, as the police had been asking him for the details.

'So far I have told them nothing. I said I needed a couple of days to retrieve it from a safe deposit box at the bank. I have now done that, and I will give them a copy on Monday.

'There is a recent change to the will. Daniel came to see me in London when Jane first came here late last year. We added her name to it, and we updated it, since Ryan is now over twenty-five and no longer needs a trustee. Apart from that it has been the same for many years.

'I will also tell you something that I normally would have kept to myself, but I think it best to tell all of you. I have already spoken about this to Ryan when he and Jane were in Richmond, and Mary also knows.

'Back in January Daniel phoned me to say he wanted to change his will. He wanted to leave everything he had to Jane. With no ill intent to Jane, naturally I tried to talk him out of it. Men in their fifties falling for young girls and wanting to leave them everything is something we do sometimes see, but I was rather surprised to see it from Daniel.

Normally I would have drafted up the new will, as that is my job, but taken a good week to do it so the man had time to cool off. And I would have warned of potential challenges.

'But as well as the professional relationship, Daniel and I have always been friends. We were at school and Oxford together. I suggested that he think about it for a few weeks at least, and if he still wanted to do this, only then would I write it up for him to sign. I reminded him that both Mary and Ryan would have reasonable grounds to challenge it. I asked him if he really wanted to see his sister and his son in the courts, in the unseemly process of challenging the will of a besotted middle-aged man who wanted to leave everything to a teenage girl. I was not sure he would ever speak to me again after that, and he didn't contact me about it again, so I hoped he had thought better of it. I spoke to Mary at the time, to check that everything was working out with Jane living here, that Daniel was treating her properly, and Mary assured me it was under control.

'I haven't told the police this, and I don't intend to. If I tell them that Daniel wanted to leave everything to Jane, then it gives Ryan one heck of a good motive to push him down the stairs before he signs the new will. In the unlikely event that Ryan is charged and they make it stick, then if they believe he killed his father in a fight over what he did to Jane, he might get away with a charge of manslaughter. Then at most he would get ten years, probably six before he gets parole. But if the motive is the inheritance, it looks a lot more like murder.

'There is, of course, a possibility that he did have a new will written up by someone else because I wouldn't do it, but as far as I know the will that is on the table in front of us is the current one.

'I have been named as executor and trustee. The house goes to Ryan, with Mary having the right to live here for her lifetime. The royalty income from the books is Ryan's. The remainder, after the tax is paid, is divided so Pat and Jane are each to have one tenth, Mary gets three tenths and Ryan the remaining half. Pat's is held in trust until he reaches twenty-five, while Jane gets hers at twenty-one. So whatever happens to Ryan, Mary at least is well provided for. Pat will eventually also inherit something from his father, as well as his mother's share, which is why Daniel gave Ryan more than half of the estate. And Jane already has her father's money, which she can control herself in a year or two. There will be death duties of course, so we could lose up to three quarters of it, but I hope it will still be a considerable sum. At this stage I don't know exactly how much, as I don't run Daniel's financial affairs beyond looking after a trust set up some years ago for Pat, Ryan and Jane, which I will talk about shortly. I am hoping that Jane will have some idea of the total as she has been doing the accounting.

'Now, before Pat complains that he has to wait until he is twenty-five when Jane gets hers at twenty-one, there was some reasoning behind it. Ryan had to wait until he was twenty-five as well, but he is now twenty-seven. Daniel thought it pointless for Jane to wait so long, as she already has some money coming to her when she reaches twenty-one from her father's estate. She also has the proceeds from the life insurance. I am still managing that money for her, but it was hers to control when she reached eighteen, as it was never part of the estate. If Pat needs some of his money before then, we can come to some arrangement, but not for expensive sports cars.

'There is also a trust that was set up with all of the money that Daniel was paid for the rights to make the films, and the trust receives the ongoing film royalties. This amount is outside of Daniel's estate, as it was set up over seven years ago, so there is no tax to pay on it. Daniel arranged for the money to be split between Ryan, Pat and Jane when Jane reaches twenty-one. Most of Jane's money is from life insurance and a compensation payment. Apart from the two houses, in Kent and Richmond, her parents didn't have all that much to leave to her. Peter's father's estate had been used to pay for his school fees and there was just enough over for him to buy the house in Kent. Peter was brought up here more or less as a brother to Daniel and Mary, and he helped Mary's mother keep the house going after the War. He also helped Daniel when he first started writing the books. So I suggested to Daniel that he include Jane in the trust. It was set up before Jane's parents died, and Peter knew about it. At first he didn't like it, but I persuaded him to accept it rather than depriving Jane of a considerable sum of money. At that stage I didn't fully understand the rift between Daniel and Peter; I have only very recently heard the full story from Mary.

'I have made a copy of the will to leave here with you, and I have been asked to give a copy to the police. I need the original to arrange the probate.

'If Ryan is convicted of murdering Daniel, he would not be allowed to inherit, and his share of Daniel's estate would go to Mary, as she is Daniel's next closest living relative. However, I think it unlikely that they will charge Ryan. I don't imagine for one moment that he killed his father, and they don't appear to have any credible evidence at all so far. Although miscarriages of justice do occur, they are extremely rare, and usually involve men being persuaded to confess to things they didn't actually do. When Jameson comes here later this afternoon, we will talk about what we can do for Ryan if he is charged. We can certainly afford to get him the very best defence lawyers.'

'I am very glad to hear that Mary would get the inheritance,' Ryan told him. 'I thought it would go to the state. I was worried if Daniel had left everything to me, then Mary would be homeless. Jane and I were planning for Mary to live with her in Richmond if that happened.'

'We could have fixed that,' said Pat. 'We would have written up a new will leaving everything to Jane. Ryan signs all his cheques, so if he signed the will and Mum and I witnessed it, no one would ever know it wasn't genuine. Then we could all still live here with Jane.'

Mr Allanstone looked a little surprised at Pat's idea but said nothing.

'What about bail?' Pat continued. 'If they arrest Ryan, we might be able to get him back here on bail so he can still be with Jane. But they would want millions. None of us has any money at all. Daniel paid for everything. All he gave any of us was pocket money. Jane has some money of her own, and I know she would offer it, but it is all in trust, so she wouldn't be able to access it. We can't use the estate money until the probate is through, and that could be months.'

'If it comes to that, we will manage it between us all. It is never excessive. I would have enough to cover it, and Jane does have access to some of her money, so we could use that. Unless Ryan flees the country, the bail money is safe; it is only a temporary arrangement.'

Jane thought how kind he was, this man who had been both her father's and Daniel's friend, and who was now helping them as though they were his family.

'Everything will be all right,' he continued. 'They don't even know what caused Daniel's death at this stage. They are only making assumptions. And they certainly can't charge Ryan with murder before they have the results of the autopsy.'

Mr Jameson arrived, and the tea and scones were brought out to the conservatory.

He was a quiet but confident man, and Jane felt that he could help Ryan not only with the technical aspects of dealing with the police, but also by keeping them all calm and rational.

He said how sorry he was that Daniel had died, assured Ryan he had handled the questioning well, and talked with Mr Allanstone about possible defence lawyers if Ryan was charged. Mr Jameson was happy to take it on, but he rarely defended murder charges, and suggested it might be better for them to engage someone more experienced in that field.

They filled him in on what had happened the evening before Daniel had died. He looked at Daniel's den, and the staircase, and the chalk marks on the floor and said, as Pat had, that the most likely explanation was that he had fallen backwards from a few steps up. That only left a button which could have been dropped at any time. He could have gone upstairs, dropped the button and then returned to the den, before finally going up to bed. It might even have fallen earlier in the day.

'I doubt that they have enough evidence to charge Ryan,' he concluded, 'but if they do, I can help him if the inspector questions him again. Although Ryan was every bit his match, it is always better to have someone there who is on your side. It helps to keep them from going too far.'

He walked in the garden with Mr Allanstone for an hour, but declined Mary's invitation to stay and have dinner with them, as his wife was expecting him home. Mary wrapped the daffodils in paper and gave them to him with a jar of homemade raspberry jam to take to his wife, along with their thanks for allowing him to give up his Saturday afternoon.

After dinner Mr Allanstone went with Jane and Ryan into the den and helped them check the safe for share certificates, gilts and securities, showing them what to look for when they sorted the filing cabinet and the piles of letters, in case there were more certificates that had not been stored in the safe.

Jane had the latest bank statements for two accounts, and so far there was no indication he had others.

'We need to find all the assets,' Mr Allanstone told them, 'and then we can value Daniel's estate for death duties. Unfortunately, it will diminish the total considerably, but you know the old saying about death and taxes. Once we have sorted the papers, we can list all the shares and work out their value. If you have a newspaper with the share prices from last Friday it would be a great help. Daniel used the same stockbroker as I do, Alan Ennis. He went to the same school as we did, although he is older than us. His son is the husband of the young lady Jane stayed with in Richmond. He works with his father. They will be able to suggest which shares to sell to pay the tax, or whether it is better to sell the gilts. And sorting this lot will at least keep you all occupied until the police investigation is complete.'

Sunday 28 March 1976

In the morning they went to church as usual, all of them dressed in black, taking the flowers for the graves of Mary's mother, the lost children and Caroline.

Mr Allanstone was with them instead of Daniel. He was rather surprised that Jane included him when she handed out the five-pound notes from the stack that Daniel had always kept in the safe ready for church on Sundays.

After the service everyone had a kind word or a memory to share. As far as the village was concerned, he had died from a fall on the stairs, and the police had been there because that was what the police did when someone died and it was not immediately clear it was from natural causes. There had been no word leaked about murder, or Ryan being a suspect, even to Reverend Colin. Jane's bruised face had recovered enough to be disguised with a little makeup, and she hid the bruise on her neck with the black Liberty scarf that she had given Mary for Christmas. Mary had lent it to her, carefully arranging it around her neck in a gesture that made Jane think tearfully of her own mother.

Mr Allanstone was introduced to Claire, who sat with them in the Linden pew now that she and Pat were engaged. He congratulated her and said he hoped to get to know her better when she was part of the Linden family.

Jane spoke to Linda about the money for the youth group. She appeared to have been delegated running the household finances now that Daniel was no longer there.

'Mr Linden gave me a few hundred pounds each year, so Colin could take the teenagers out without their parents needing to find the money. It was an informal arrangement, but I account it carefully, and I would let him know when we needed more. In the summer we play cricket, and we don't need any extra funds for that. There is rarely any new equipment needed, and the parish pays for the tea and coffee. We have sufficient for the moment, but if Ryan can afford to continue with sponsoring the teenagers, Colin and I would be very grateful for it. But only if he really can afford it.

'Ryan was not originally a part of the youth group, as he was already over twenty when we first came here. Colin asked him to help with running it, and he did for a short while, but there were a couple of late-teenage girls who had a crush on him and he didn't cope with it. I offered to talk to them, but Ryan said he wasn't enjoying it, and it was not really his thing, so we accepted that. But Pat, Jimmy, David and Winston were among our original members, so Mr Linden was happy to help with the cost when Colin suggested it. He was a lovely man, Jane, and we will all miss him terribly. We all called him *The Squire*, and he stood for everything that was traditional in a village. He was an absolute gentleman.'

If you only knew, Jane thought.

But then she realised with horror that if Ryan was charged with murdering Daniel, there would be a trial, and every detail of their lives at Hayward Hall would be all over the newspapers and the television news. Mary's years of effort to hide her brother's sins from the world would be in vain. It would destroy her. God, what a mess this all was.

After lunch they worked in the den once more, Mr Allanstone copying a list that Jane had made of the shares and the gilts and noting down the bank account balances. This would at least give him some idea of what the estate would be worth, except for the house which would need to be valued.

He reminded Ryan not to sign any more cheques on his father's behalf. Ryan said he was happy to pay the household expenses from his own account for the moment, as well as the cost of the funeral and the renovations, which were starting in a week or two. He had some money that his grandmother had left him, and it was plenty for that. He would keep all the receipts, and the estate could pay back the funeral cost before the tax was calculated. There was also a good deal of cash in the safe, which Jane thought would cover the usual household costs until the probate was granted.

There was a banana cake for afternoon tea, partaken slightly early, and Mr Allanstone left to return to Kent, shaking hands with the young men and kissing both Mary and Jane on the cheek.

Monday 29 March 1976

On the Monday Jane and Ryan returned to the sorting. Pat helped them, and even Mary stayed in the den with them after she brought in their morning coffee. In the afternoon all four of them worked in the garden. They were staying together in the face of a threat from the outside, supporting Ryan and trying to keep themselves from the dark clutches of worry.

Tuesday 30 March 1976

On Tuesday morning the detectives returned. They were shown into the kitchen, accepted the offered coffee, and they sat at the table, facing a rather hostile family group.

Jane recalled the comments she had overheard from the young sergeant, so she carefully avoided looking at him, although she sensed he was looking at her. She would never go out with the likes of him, so he could keep his admiring glances to himself. No one got away with calling her a chick and her lover a toff and a nerd.

The inspector assured Ryan they were not there to arrest him—they were still not yet sure how his father had died—but their investigations were continuing. They had brought back the two shirts they had taken from Daniel's room. They were shirts that were missing a button, but their buttons did not match the one found on the stairs, so they had no bearing on the case. The button they had found had been from the shirt he was wearing. They also returned the glass and the decanter, as they had only Daniel's and Mary's prints on them, and the contents had been analysed and found to be nothing but whisky, no Valium at all. The pill he had taken would have been swallowed, not dissolved in the whisky.

They were not yet releasing the body for burial, as they were waiting on an expert second opinion for the autopsy and some further analysis on the amount of digitoxin he had taken. They could not yet arrange a date for the funeral, but the inspector hoped they would have the information shortly.

At this stage they knew he hadn't been pushed or fallen from the bridge, as he had no broken bones at all. He could not have fallen that far without breaking something. They were discounting suicide altogether, as there was no evidence that he had taken a deliberate overdose of the Valium or the digitoxin. If you want to overdose, you take more than one or two pills.

Jane was relieved at that, as she did not like to think he had been so unhappy at her refusing him that he had taken his own life. She knew that she would have felt very guilty if he had. She wished that she had gone back to him in the den that night, Ryan with her for protection, and talked to him so they had parted friends before he died.

The detectives also wanted to talk to Jane about the button. It was too small for any definite prints, but they had found a fragment of a print that matched Jane's. Did she recall handling a button from Daniel's shirt?

She told them she ironed the shirts, so she could have touched it then, and she had occasionally sewn on a loose button. Or she may have touched it when she tried to push him away. Then a memory stirred of a button coming off in her hand. In her mind she felt it slip through her fingers.

'Yes, I do recall a button coming off in my hand. I think I grabbed his shirt to try to push him away. I remember it because I was thinking I would need to look for it so I could sew it back on.'

Could she account for it being on the landing, they asked her next, but she had no explanation for that, except that it may have caught in her clothes when it fell, then dropped out as she went up the stairs. She couldn't recall picking it up. She asked if they had considered the button might be from a shirt belonging to Pat or Ryan. Even her own Liberty shirts had similar small mother-of-pearl buttons. The inspector acknowledged that, and asked them all to check for missing buttons.

They asked Jane next if she had undone the buttons on his waistcoat. It had been undone when the police arrived, and her fingerprints were on all of them.

No, she told them, she didn't recall unbuttoning it. She hadn't ironed it either. The suits were always dry cleaned. But of course, she would have undone the buttons when the suit came back from dry cleaning. She took off the plastic and the pins, and put the suits on wooden hangers for Mary to take upstairs. The wire hangers were returned to the dry cleaners the next time the suits went for cleaning. The waistcoat buttons were all fastened when the suits came back from the cleaners, but she always undid them so Daniel didn't have to do that himself when he put on the suit. She always left just the top button fastened so the waistcoat stayed on the hanger under the jacket. The suits were mostly black or very dark grey, and she never knew which were Daniel's and which were Ryan's or Pat's. They all looked the same to her, and they all came from the same tailor in Savile Row, but Mary always knew. Perhaps it was because Daniel's trousers had cuffs, while Pat's and Ryan's were flares.

The sergeant had written down what she had said, and she signed it, borrowing Ryan's spidery pen because she didn't want to touch the sergeant's grubby ballpoint. He always looked at her with that same predator look as Daniel had.

The detectives went away, promising to be back within a day or two when they had the results of the autopsy, and their report for the coroner could then be completed.

Ryan was silent and abstracted. Always at the back of Jane's mind was the nagging worry that they would charge him, and she knew if it was this bad for her, it would be dreadful for him. She wished she could give him some comfort, but she felt that nothing she could say or do would help him. She wished she could sleep with him, hold him through the night, but he was rather cold and aloof and did not encourage her. She knew he didn't sleep well, and she thought of him lying awake at night, faced with losing his freedom and everything he owned and cared about for something he hadn't done. She knew he would never say he loved her or ask her to share his life with this hanging over him because it would cause her more hurt if he was convicted.

She asked him what she could do to help him. She even found the courage to ask if he wanted her to sleep upstairs with him so he wasn't by himself, but he just looked at her in his amused way and told her he was not going to risk her having a child with its father in prison.

'Stay here and stay in good spirits,' he told her. 'This will blow over, and then we can think about the future. I didn't kill my father; none of us did. They will eventually realise that—I think perhaps they have already—and things will work out. You're not to worry. None of this is your fault. I have the new bottle of Valium, but I don't need it. It's months since I've needed it. After you came to Hayward, all I had to do was think about you, and then it didn't matter to me if I was asleep or not. Now I think about the day we walked in the woods near Charlford, and we watched the squirrel take the nut, and I always sleep.'

In the evening they sat together in the lounge, and he let her lean against him while they were watching the programme she liked on television. Afterwards she found a book of Alfred Tennyson's poems in the library and read *The Lady of Shalott* to him. It was her favourite poem, even if it was a little mournful. But she knew he was still tense and worried, and she was too.

She went to sleep that night thinking about the walk in the wood, the squirrel, and the soft cool moss on the standing stones, and she knew things would work out. They were meant to be together.

Two more interminable days passed while they sorted the papers and made the funeral arrangements. The funeral was to be a private affair with invited guests only and no announcement in the newspaper. After the burial service the guests would return to the Hall for sandwiches and tea and coffee in the guest dining room, with the undertakers arranging the catering. All they needed was for the body to be released so they could set the date.

Jane and Ryan continued to work in the den in the mornings, with both Pat and Mary helping them for at least some of the time, and all four of them spent the afternoons cleaning the windows in the conservatory. Jane knew this companionship was to help them all get through the days while they waited for the autopsy results and for the police to decide if they would charge Ryan.

Jane found a handwritten manuscript and some journals, and Mary said Daniel had once written a memoir of his time at the War Office, and Peter had helped. It was in the first few years after his wife died, and Mary thought it had helped to keep him sane. They had sent it to a publisher, but although they liked it, they were not be able to publish it, as it was still too soon after the War, and the information might still have been sensitive. They suggested he write fiction, and that set Daniel off on his career as a writer, with the money he made very welcome in a house where making ends meet was difficult, with visitor numbers unreliable, and the farms that the family had once owned and rented out now all sold.

Mary told them they had only just managed to stay on in the house after the War. There were a lot of final notices on bills, and when Peter had gone away with Jane's mother, it had left a hole in the finances, as he had previously given most of what he earned to his aunt, Mary's mother, to help with running the house. He had sent her some money after he left, but she had sent the cheque back, telling him he had other priorities now he was to marry Josie.

But by then cheques were arriving from the publisher for Daniel's first book, and Pat's father was giving her money to help with raising him, and things had become much easier after that.

8 WARMER DAYS

Friday 2 April 1976

On the Friday morning the inspector and the sergeant returned. They seemed friendly enough and didn't appear to be immediately arresting Ryan, so they were offered biscuits and coffee again. Jane once more carefully avoided the glances of the younger man. Who did he think he was, looking at her like that? And he had eaten at least four of the biscuits. She hoped Mary had another packet, or there would be none for cocoa that night. But of course, it was shopping day, so when the detectives left, they would go into town and could buy some more.

They had the results of the autopsy. Daniel had died from heart failure, and had been dead before his head hit the tiles of the hallway floor. They now believed he had fallen from the second or third step. The fall may have injured him, but would not have been enough to kill him by itself. He would have been unstable on his feet with the alcohol and the Valium, and his heart had succumbed as he went up the stairs.

He had taken the Valium around half an hour before he died. Perhaps he had mistaken it for the digitoxin, or perhaps he had wanted something to help him sleep. He had taken the digitoxin at around the same time, so he could have confused the bottles, and then realised his mistake. He would have gone into the kitchen to take the tablets. He had then taken the Valium into the den, so it was possible he had considered taking an overdose. His heart was so weak and damaged that the digitoxin had slowed his heartbeat down too much, with the Valium contributing to that. Valium and digitoxin can be a lethal combination. The experts had said he was lucky to have lived for as long as he did with the state his heart was in.

They no longer thought he had been pushed, as the injuries from the fall were not consistent with that. If he had been pushed with enough force from the landing to land on the tiles where he was found, he would have broken bones. If he had fallen from the landing and been moved from the stairs onto the floor of the hallway, it would need to have been very soon after he died. The blood tends to puddle after death, and they knew that he had been lying flat from very soon after he fell. If one of them had moved him from further up the stairs during the night they would have phoned for help at that stage, and there would have been no point in denying moving him.

The button on the landing didn't indicate conclusively that he had stood there when he fell. They believed Miss Walters had pulled it off in the den. They didn't know how it reached the landing, but they said there were usually loose ends like that in any investigation. They would send their report to the coroner. There may be an inquest—that was up to the coroner—but they were satisfied he had died from natural causes.

They were returning the bottle of Valium, the bottle of digitoxin, the tie and the button. The inspector put the Valium on the table, and suggested Ryan try something safer. Although Valium was less dangerous than the old barbiturates because an overdose was less likely to be fatal, it was addictive, and there was a new product that was safer. He suggested Ryan ask the chemist about it. They also returned Daniel's watch, his wallet and credit card, and some loose change that had been in his pockets. His suit would be given to the undertakers. If they wanted him buried in something else, they could talk to them and ask for the suit to be returned.

The inspector thanked Mary for the excellent coffee, thanked them all for their cooperation, told them they had only been doing their job, said he hoped the young lady had recovered from her ordeal, and wished her and Ryan well.

They left, shaking hands with Pat and Ryan on the forecourt, and when the car had disappeared through the gate, Ryan lifted Jane clean off her feet, swung her around, and hugged her.

'I can't believe it is only a week since they took me into Oxford with them. It seems like the longest week of my life. Mary, do we have any Champagne in the cellar?'

Saturday 3 April 1976

Mary still did not go to see her friend in London, the second Saturday she had missed. After lunch all of them went into Daniel's bedroom to tidy it up, change the sheets and find something for him to be buried in. Pat and Ryan checked the pockets of the jackets and the trousers in the wardrobes and found some banknotes and some stray loose change.

Jane had never been in his room, nor in the other front room adjoining it. In fact she had only been upstairs on the top floor twice before, once when she had first come to Hayward Hall and Mary had shown her over the house, and once when she had come upstairs with Daniel for exercise and he had wanted her to come to his room. She still felt cold at the thought of him kissing her neck and trying to make her fondle him.

The bed was neatly made, as he had not slept in it that night. The pyjamas were still folded beneath the pillow. But the clock had stopped, as he had no longer been there to wind it. It was strange to be in the room of someone who was gone. All their clothes and the things they had owned and cherished were now no longer loved or needed. Yet there was the feeling that they were only a little distance from you in the stillness, in the timeless shafts of sunlight with the dust moving slowly in its warmth. She had felt the same at her great-aunt's house, and at her parents' house in Kent, which had been sold.

If he had behaved better towards her, he might have died peacefully overnight in his sleep, up here at the top of the house with the ghost of his wife in every photo on the wall.

Jane made an effort not to cry. He had wanted her to come up here to sleep with him on the four-poster bed, telling her all she had to do was lie there and close her eyes and he would do the rest. If she had said yes, he might still be alive. He would not have drunk so much that night, and he might have survived the heart attack without the Valium in his blood. But then if she had come up here with him, he might have had a heart attack and died while making love to her. The thought of that was totally horrifying. Imagine having to tell that to the police. And to Ryan.

There were only Daniel's things in his room, nothing of his wife's, although the walls were covered with dozens of photographs of her.

'Did Caroline share this room with him when she was alive?' she asked Mary.

'No, she didn't. None of us had the front rooms then. We all had the smaller rooms overlooking the conservatory, so the best rooms could be let out for guests. As the number of guests dropped off, we spread out a bit. Daniel wanted this room on the corner, as it has the view from both windows. Ryan has the corner room the other side, and he was older than Pat, so he got first choice. Pat could have had the other front room, which is now Ryan's study, but he chose the one behind because that way he had his own bathroom. My mother had the rooms you are in, and I chose the one I have now, so I could be close to her if she needed help in the night. We left the other corner room on the first floor free so it was available if anyone came to stay. Daniel still had all of Caroline's things in their old room, so he set up the room next door to this as if it was her room, with her perfume and her hairbrush and her clothes in the wardrobes, and he never let me clear anything out. It is still set up as if she still lives there in the room connecting to his, even though it was never really hers.'

They came across Daniel's army uniform in the wardrobe, and Jane thought it would be good to bury him in it. It would be easier for

Caroline to recognise him, dressed as he would have been when they had first met. There were moth holes in it, and Jane said she would darn them.

In spite of Mary thinking they would be poles apart in the afterlife, Jane wanted to think of them back together. It was strange that they had both died falling backwards down the same staircase. She remembered what he had told her about seeing the ghost of his wife at the top of the stairs. One day he would reach her and she would still be there, and then he would know he was dead and back with her. He had spent his whole life since she died tortured by grief at losing her, yet twice he had tried to go forward with a new love, and twice fate had mocked him for it. Had Caroline's ghost been on the stairs the night he died? Was she the figure that Ryan had seen? Could ghosts control who could see them and who couldn't? Had she intended her son to see her that night, as well as her husband?

They took the uniform for Jane to darn, found a shirt to go under it, and closed his room. One day they would have the heart to sort his things.

Then Mary opened the door to the room they called Caroline's, although she had never once slept there.

Her Chanel perfume was on the dressing table, her silver-backed hairbrush with still a few strands of her hair, her matching hand mirror, face powder in a cut-glass bowl with a lid that fitted over the top—the two matching halves held together with little triangular teeth in the glass—and even the powder puff was still there, waiting forever for the touch of her hand. Her rings were together in another glass bowl and another held earrings. Her wedding ring had been buried with her, but the engagement ring with the beautiful diamond that Ryan's grandfather had remembered was there along with some garnet and sapphire rings. There was a photo of her brother Nicholas in a silver frame, looking younger here than he had in the air force uniform. Such a beautiful young man, with a lovely boyish smile and thick wavy hair, shot down over France and dead at nineteen.

Caroline's clothes were hung in the wardrobe, high-heeled shoes on the wardrobe floor, petticoats in the drawers, white handkerchiefs embroidered with flowers and her initial, old-fashioned underwear from the forties, camiknickers and silk stockings and suspenders, once-white lace nightdresses now yellow with age.

Dust and shadows, the cold quiet things Caroline had once owned and cherished waiting, waiting forever, for the beautiful young woman who would never use them again. She had now been dead for over twenty-seven years. Longer than both Jane and Pat had been alive.

Mary told her that Daniel had set this room up around ten years ago, when he had moved out of his room at the back of the house. He had set it up as a shrine to his dead wife, and it was not even the room she had shared with him. Jane remembered him saying he had left his wife's room as it was when she died and he sometimes sat there and felt her close to him. Yet it had never actually been her room. How could his mother and Mary have allowed him to do this, seventeen years after she was gone? It was totally morbid.

'Should we put the rings in the safe?' she asked Mary.

'Yes, perhaps we should, at least the diamond one. The stone was from a pendant that had belonged to my grandmother. She was the boys' great-grandmother and yours as well. It was reset for Caroline. Daniel could not then have afforded a ring with a diamond like that. He wanted it left here so it seemed as if she had just taken it off to sleep. Mr Allanstone said it was left to Ryan when she died, so we don't need to include it with the estate valuation. He joked that it is worth more than the house, but I don't think that is really true.'

Jane sat at the dressing table, looking into the mirror, half expecting to see the face of Caroline staring back at her, but of course she saw only her own face, with Mary behind her and the two young men standing silently in the doorway.

She opened one of the top drawers of the dressing table. There were old lipsticks and compacts, jars of nail polish, all neatly arranged. The top drawer on the other side held a bundle of letters, tied with a yellow ribbon, and Jane recognised Daniel's handwriting, although it was steady and bold then, not the sad shaky hand that she knew. He had written to Caroline throughout the War and until they were married.

In the drawer below, laid out carefully by themselves, were Jane's missing black lace knickers.

'Those belong to me,' she told Mary. 'They went missing from the dryer.'

She folded them and put them in her pocket to take back to her room. She would wash them again, since he had touched them. At least he hadn't put them in his own room. The police had looked inside it when he died, and they might have found them. She imagined the horror of the young sergeant holding them up in front of everyone and asking if they were hers, saying they had been found in his bedroom, asking if she had been telling the truth when she denied sleeping with him. She would have died with embarrassment.

She remembered Daniel saying if she married him, she could have his wife's old room next to his. Would he have cleared out all of Caroline's things, finally accepting she was gone? Would he have set them up in another room for her somewhere else in the house, another shrine? Or would he have left them there to merge with Jane's things? Perhaps he would have wanted Jane to dress in the old-fashioned underclothes.

Mary found some darning wool that matched the uniform, and Jane spent the evening in the library carefully darning the holes while Ryan sat close beside her and read her a ghost story by Montague James. The cat sat purring on his lap, occasionally waving a paw at the loose end of the darning thread.

Friday 9 April 1976

They buried Daniel on the following Friday, a bleak, cold, wet day. Even the weather was mourning, Jane thought.

Ryan and Pat were pallbearers, along with Mr Allanstone, Jack and Jimmy McCann, and Winston Phillips. John Phillips had offered, but he was over eighty and walked with a limp, so he followed the coffin into the church, his hat in his hand, with Mary holding his arm and Jane on his other side. Adrian Phillips and David McCann walked behind them with Claire between them, then Anne McCann with her two youngest boys.

Most of the local Hayward families were there. Two men from Daniel's publisher had driven across from London, and they had arranged for a reporter and cameraman from the BBC to cover the publicity for the service. The two detectives showed up, although Jane was not sure who had invited them. Mr Jameson and his wife had been invited. Professor Hanson came from Oxford with three of the younger dons who lived at the college, friends of Ryan.

For Jane it was yet another funeral. Everyone who had ever looked after her had died, and she wondered if she really did want to marry Ryan in case he was next.

The church was dismal under the grey sky, the rosewood coffin dark beneath the wreath of burgundy roses. Ryan held her hand through the service except when he stood at the pulpit to talk about his father, but she could not help crying, in spite of the sedative that Mary had given her before they had left the Hall.

Ryan didn't actually say Daniel was the world's best father, but no one listening could have imagined how much they disliked each other. He spoke as though they were a normal family with Daniel the perfect father and the perfect village squire. Mr Allanstone talked of Daniel being his friend through school and during the War, and how much he would be missed by his friends and relations. They were still the perfect family, farewelling their beloved brother, father, uncle, cousin and friend.

They followed the coffin out into the churchyard, the undertakers holding big black umbrellas to give them some shelter from the cold incessant rain, and it was lowered to sit deep in the dark damp earth above that of Caroline Ann Linden. Reverend Colin read the order of committal, and the handfuls of earth fell on the rosewood. They were finally together after twenty-seven years.

The headstone was leaning against the next one. Before it was replaced, it would be taken away to be engraved with his name below that of his long-dead wife.

They returned to the Hall, where sandwiches and tea and coffee were served by the caterers in the guest dining room, with sherry and whisky for those who preferred it. At least in here it was warm, as fires had been lit in both of the old stone fireplaces to augment the inadequate radiators. Ryan kept Jane beside him, his hand holding hers, while he talked to the publishers, the reporter, the men from Oxford and the local families. No one watching them could doubt they were lovers, she thought, but they weren't lovers. Not yet.

Mr Allanstone was with Mary, talking to Pat and Claire. Mr Jameson and his wife were with them.

In the warmth of the room Jane recovered enough to talk to the guests with more ease. It was strange that when someone had been buried, you could start to look forward and carry on with your life. Professor Hanson was very kind, remembering that she had lost her aunt not long before, hoping Linden was looking after her, with no mention of what he knew of Daniel proposing to her, of her running away and Ryan coming after her. He hoped Linden would be able to return to them shortly. It was a critical time for his students as the end of the academic year was fast approaching. Ryan promised to be back for the new term in the last week in April for the tutoring.

The three younger men were delighted to meet Jane. Linden had spoken very highly of her, and they had been covering for him at times by taking his classes, but they were more than happy to help. At the end of the year, they would all go out for dinner together, and they looked forward to seeing her again in happier circumstances. Jane felt glad that he had friends at Oxford, and even more glad that all of them were men. She wondered if they were all lone wolves like he was.

Then she was telling the publishers that she had typed up most of the manuscript for Daniel's latest book. She thought she remembered him saying it was finished, they were on the correction stage, so if it seemed complete once she had typed up the remaining pages, Ryan would send it to them. There was also the memoir from his days in the War Office. That was hand-written, but Jane offered to type that up as well. Perhaps now they could publish it, as it was over thirty years since the end of the War. Her own late father had helped with it, she told them, and she thought it might be a tribute to both of them.

It had been written while her father still lived here on good terms with his cousin, Jane realised, and perhaps if it could be resurrected it would help to heal the rift between them, too late for both of them in this life, but it might help Mary, Ryan and herself, who had all lived with the sad aftermath of what Daniel had done on that long ago August day. One single day had changed forever the course of both their lives, but it didn't obliterate the years they had spent together before that, brought up here as cousins who cared about each other, by a woman they both loved.

The publishers asked Ryan to speak to the reporter and the cameraman, with Jane beside him, to say they were hoping to get his father's last book to the publisher soon, and they were hoping to publish his memoir of the time he had worked at the War Office during the Second World War, the first thing he had ever written with the help of his cousin, Jane's father. Ryan obliged. It was in his interest to have the income from selling the books, so a little publicity was a small price to pay. Jane was grateful for tear-proof mascara and hoped it hadn't smudged, as she had no time to find a mirror to check.

A little while later she saw Ryan talking to the detectives while she spoke with John Phillips, who was always very kind to her. Winston was with his grandfather, and she thanked him for helping carry the coffin. She didn't want to talk to the detectives again after the worry they had caused them all, and the comments she had overheard from the sergeant. But the inspector seemed friendly enough to Ryan.

The sergeant approached her, and she didn't want to be rude to him. However much satisfaction it would have given her, he was a guest in their house. She stepped aside a little, as she didn't want to speak with him in front of John Phillips.

He was very polite, asking if she was recovered and telling her he regretted the inconvenience she had been put to. He offered her his card, which she politely accepted, holding it by a tiny corner.

'If we can ever be of service, don't hesitate to contact us,' he said, rather formally, before continuing in a lower and more hurried tone. 'My home number is on the back. If you have a free evening, give me a call, and I can take you out to dinner or a film. What about tomorrow night?'

She kept her calm, and her manners. 'Thank you, but I don't go out except with my cousin.'

'He's in Oxford during the week. I could pick you up one evening after work, and we could go for a drink.'

'Thank you, I will keep it in mind.'

'Are you and he an item, Miss Walters? The inspector and I never worked it out.'

Mind your own damned business, she thought. But she didn't want him persisting in asking her out, so she decided to admit to it.

'Not yet, but I'm hopeful,' she said. That should be enough to let him know that neither of them had lied about their relationship, but put him off from asking her out again.

'He's a lucky man to have a lovely chick like you, Miss Walters. But if it doesn't work out, you have my number.'

He wished her well and rejoined the inspector, who was still talking with Ryan, and she saw them both shake Ryan's hand as they left. The inspector caught her eye, so she waved her hand, but she still considered both of them beneath her contempt.

She stood by the window, remembering the day they had taken Ryan to Oxford and she had felt so powerless to help him, had wondered how he would cope, had wished she could be with him, and had blamed herself for what had happened that night. How could that man think she would go out with him after they had treated Ryan like that? And he had the hide to call her a chick to her face. She had to admit he was a good-looking young man, although not her type, but she would never have gone out with him under any circumstances. He looked at her in the same predator way that Daniel had. He had waited until Ryan was talking to the inspector and was separated from her before approaching her. Ryan had been beside her for the rest of the afternoon, so the sergeant would have been waiting for his chance.

After she saw their car drive away from the forecourt, she threw the card onto the fire, delighted to watch the flames consume it, and returned to her conversation with John Phillips and Winston.

'Why did you throw that man's card on the fire?' Winston asked.

'He asked me out, and he's a creep.'

'If he bothers you again, I'll flatten him,' Winston promised, and they both laughed. Winston was mild-mannered and usually rather timid, and the sergeant was a lot taller and heavier than he was. The dismal day suddenly brightened for Jane.

'Thank you, but that's probably not a good idea. He's a policeman.'

The sandwiches were all finished and the guests were leaving. Candy and her father came over to take their leave. Candy gave her a hug and passed on her mother's condolences. Jane thanked them for coming, and she was grateful for the hug. At first she thought they had taken time off, but she recalled it was now school holidays, which was why Winston and Adrian were also at home. She was glad the young people were there to support her. She had felt so much better when she had joked with Winston. It was good to have friends.

Once today was over, they could go forward, she thought, as the last guests drove away. The men from Oxford had gone, the Jamesons had gone home in their yellow Range Rover, and the farmers had returned to the farms.

The caterers cleaned up from the sandwiches and cake and coffee, washed up the glasses and the china, and returned it all to the dressers in the guest dining room before they left. Mr Allanstone was to spend the night here once again so that tomorrow they could go through the paperwork that Jane and Ryan had sorted so far.

Next would be the wedding of Pat and Claire, and then only Jane, Ryan and Mary would be left in the house. Tonight they were all more relaxed. Mr Allanstone was becoming part of the family, asking them all to call him John as Mary did. Over dinner he once more broached the subject of Pat getting a job, asking him what he was good at besides fixing cars.

'Nothing, Sir. I was hopeless at school, and Oxford wouldn't take me. Daniel let me work in the garden and paid me an allowance for that, and Jack McCann is always happy to have an extra pair of hands available at busy times. He sometimes pays me a bit, but Daniel always said he was happy for me to help at the farm as part of the money he paid me. Jimmy and I help John Phillips on his farm as well, but he can't afford to pay us. He helped Jack's mother with her farm during the War, and my grandmother with the garden here, so it's repayment for that. He's so old he only keeps a few sheep now, and his bees and some hens and turkeys, and he doesn't make much. He lives off his pension. Claire and I are going to live in the lodge. Before all this happened to Daniel, we were tidying it up. He was going to continue paying me to do the garden. He liked to keep us on short rations, as that way we did what he wanted. He saw the gardening as just idleness, but it is actually quite a lot of work, and he would have to pay someone to do it if I wasn't here. I won't have to worry now anyway, with all the money Mum will have, she can afford to help us out, and I get a bit as well, even if I do have to wait years for it.'

They watched the news with a snippet on the funeral of Daniel Linden, footage of the coffin being taken into the church and of Ryan, with Jane beside him, talking about his father's latest book. Jane hoped that no one would recognise the church and know where they lived. She found it very strange to see herself on television, and she was glad she had taken the trouble to do her eye makeup perfectly for the funeral. She would have looked a sorry mess without it. At least the mascara had coped.

They all spent the evening together in the lounge, talking about Daniel, and Jane realised how much more relaxed everyone was with him no longer there. Yet she had loved him in her way. He had taken her in when he knew she was alone in the world, and had offered her a family life with him. He had meant well, at least at first, and she had got on well with him, she had liked to talk to him, and they had laughed at things together. Perhaps it was inevitable that he had fallen in love with her. Middle-aged men did sometimes fall for young girls. They had done so throughout history—it was just nature—and Jane knew that when older men fall for young girls sometimes their common sense goes out of the window. She did feel that she was to blame—she would always feel that—but she couldn't change what had happened. She remembered the day he had talked to her about the War and how he had felt so helpless on the day in the bunker knowing men would be killed, how he had tried to kill himself with whisky the day that Caroline had died, how he sometimes imagined his life with Caroline still there, and his guilt at what he had done to his son. If Ryan had not been there, and if Daniel had not been constantly harassing her, she might have loved him, might even have felt sorry enough for him to marry him. Could she have got over her aversion to sleeping with him? She didn't think so. Yet, she would be happy enough to sleep with Ryan. The physical attraction thing—the intoxicating thrill of being right up close to someone, of wanting to be as close together as two people can get—was completely different from just caring for someone. She knew she could never feel that for Daniel, and for a marriage to work you would need both.

Ryan had brought up a bottle of port from the cellar for the men, and Jane and Mary had a glass as well. She sat beside him on a sofa, leaning against him, hugging her knees, with a blanket carefully wrapped around them, his arm along the back of the sofa behind her, his fingers playing with a lock of her hair. The cat jumped onto his lap and Jane stroked her, being very careful her hand didn't slip from the cat into his lap. He stroked the cat as well, and her fingertips played with his, hidden deep in the black fur of the cat. She recalled they had sat together stroking the cat at Christmas, with her other hand in Pat's. But she didn't really understand why they still needed to keep things between them a secret. There was no Daniel to mind that they were lovers, no one to care if they slept together in the darkness on the top floor of the house.

She knew he needed more time to get over losing his father and being suspected of murdering him. She needed time to get over losing Daniel as well. Did Ryan blame her for what had happened? She had come to live in this house with this family who fronted the world as a perfect household, not quite the usual husband, wife and children, but an extended family who got on well with each other and lived a life of perfect happiness together. Except they didn't. There were already rifts even before she had come here. She was just a final straw that had torn them apart, with Daniel jealous of his son and Ryan confronting his father, stirring up the secrets and the grudges of the past. Would Daniel still be alive if she hadn't come here? Could she have done things differently to avert the final showdown? Should she have accepted her fate and married him, or at least slept with him? But she knew that if she had, she would have lost Ryan forever. She was just as much in love with him as his father had been with her. She had the right to choose her lover.

Saturday 10 April 1976

Colin had arranged a cricket game on the green for Saturday afternoon, the first game for the season. Ryan and Pat played while Jane helped Colin with the scoring. Mary had made scones for the tea that was always served in the village hall afterwards. She and Mr Allanstone were spectators. Mary usually went to London on Saturdays, but Jane knew Mary's friend would understand why she didn't come on the day after her brother's funeral, and with a guest to look after.

It was good to be back doing ordinary things, to be going forward with their lives, and Jane knew both Ryan and Pat loved playing village cricket.

Sunday 11 April 1976

On Sunday morning they had the usual English breakfast and went to church, still in their black, Mr Allanstone with them once again.

They spent part of the afternoon sorting papers in the den. It seemed less daunting with all five of them working on it. They were still sorting them into piles, as it was pointless trying to rearrange each pile into date order until all of the paperwork had been found and sorted.

Mr Allanstone left before four in the afternoon. He was to come and spend most of the Easter weekend at the Hall, to help Jane and Ryan finalise the paperwork so he could work out the value of the estate. Jane assumed Mary would not be going to London that weekend either. But she didn't like to ask her, as Mary was very private about her friend in London. Jane didn't even know the friend's name. She asked Ryan, but he didn't know either.

Pat and Claire were to have been married on Easter Saturday, but the wedding had been postponed for four weeks.

Monday 12 April 1976

Jane continued typing up the manuscript, using the golf ball typewriter in the den, while Ryan sorted the pages and put the chapters together. They both wanted it to be complete so it could be published as Daniel's last book, along with the memoir, and there were no loose ends left.

Ryan still seemed rather quiet and depressed, so she didn't ask him again if he wanted her to sleep with him. She felt he would come around to being more like her lover in his own time. He needed to get over losing his father and nearly losing his freedom. He told her that the few days he had been worried about losing the Hall had changed the way he thought about it. Once he had seen his life as living in the college in Oxford with no interest in making a life for himself here, then he had thought about living somewhere else with her, but he now knew he wanted to keep the house and live here if he could. He hadn't cared about the money either, as he spent very little, but now he realised he would need it to keep the house maintained and to keep his grandfather in the nursing home.

Jane helped Mary run the household as normally as they could without Daniel. He had done very little work around the house, so that much was easy. They were waiting for the wedding to be over before they sorted his clothes and set up the den for Ryan to use. With Pat gone the household would be different and they might feel the loss of Daniel less keenly.

She felt herself between one phase of her life and another. It was hard to adjust to thinking that there was now no hindrance to her loving Ryan except his own reticence. She had been so used to Daniel opposing her and Ryan being lovers, that she could scarcely come to terms with the opposition being gone.

Jane and Ryan went through Daniel's bedroom in case there were any stray letters or papers. His room felt like Caroline's room, with clothes that were no longer worn, books that were no longer read, the photographs of his wife—which had meant so much to him—now just ghosts fading on the wall, things once owned and loved now forlorn and dead.

She took off her shoes, lay on the bed and closed her eyes, remembering that Daniel had asked her to come up to his room so he could make love to her. He had told her she could just lie there and close her eyes, and he would look after everything else. It would have been such a simple thing for her to do, she knew that, but she had been unable to do it, and she felt guilty that she had disappointed him. Yet she knew she shouldn't feel guilty. She felt that she would agree to it now if it would somehow bring him back.

'Jane, what on earth are you doing?'

'Having a rest for a minute,' she said, opening her eyes.

He was laughing, and he suddenly pulled off his shoes and jumped onto the bed so he was lying beside her, supported on his elbow, leaning over her, but not touching her.

'He told me if I was married to him, I could just lie here and close my eyes and pretend it was you making love to me. He said he didn't care if I didn't love him.'

'Wouldn't it be fun to make love in his bed,' he said, his fingers caressing her face. 'You could lie there and close your eyes, and I could make love to you. You wouldn't need to pretend then. It would be the ultimate revenge.'

She laughed at this, knowing he didn't really mean it, but wishing he did.

'Come here,' she whispered, putting her arms around his neck and pulling him on top of her. He seemed to understand what she wanted. She had never had a man on top of her before. He wasn't as heavy as she had expected, but he was still leaning on his elbows, so she wasn't taking his full weight. Her fingers were in his hair. She twined her ankle around his, and it felt exhilarating, having him so close to her. If they had been wearing less, he could have been making love to her, on top of her like this.

'I don't think I want revenge. I wish he was still here. Well, not here right now with me on the bed, although if that was what it took to bring him back, I would do it. I feel it is my fault he is dead because I wouldn't sleep with him, but I do know that isn't really true. I wanted us all to be able to live here together. I wanted to make him happy but still have you. I liked his company. He was usually wrapped in his own world, but I got on with him, and I understood when he didn't want to be chatted to. He could still have flirted with me a little if he wanted. I just didn't want to sleep with him. We could have bought him a sex doll for Christmas, or a season ticket to his escort agency.'

'I wish he was still here too, but I couldn't see any way we were going to resolve the situation except by us leaving. It's not your fault because you couldn't love him enough to want to sleep with him, but my fault for bringing you back here when I knew it could never work. He was never going to stop wanting you. I understand that now because I know I would never stop wanting you even if you had married him. I couldn't have stayed living in the house if I knew you were sleeping with him. That last night when you and I were dancing in the hallway, I felt we were taunting him; I wish now that we hadn't done that. I felt like killing him when he tried to strangle you, and Pat said he did as well. If he hadn't attacked you that night, and he had lived for a few more days, we would have gone back to Richmond. And if you had decided then that you wanted us to be together for always, we may never have come back here. He would have died anyway, as his heart was so damaged. It was only a matter of time.'

'I still think about what could have happened that night if you and Pat hadn't come in when you did. I would have had no choice but to come up here with him and let him make love to me, but I would have tried to get him to take the tie from around my neck first. It was not a nice feeling that he only had to pull it tight and he could kill me. I tried to reason with him, but he had gone completely mad. I don't think he would have strangled me—he said he wouldn't hurt me—but he was no longer rational, and he was so strong. If I had come up here, he may have had the heart attack anyway, when he was up here with me. That would really have been a nightmare, having to explain to the police why I was in bed with him. If I hadn't left the billiard room with him that night, he might still be alive. I just didn't realise he was trapping me.'

'If he hadn't attacked you, and we had left, perhaps he would have come round. I did hope he might. We could have come back during the day on Sundays to help with the accounts so he didn't have to think of us sleeping together here in the house. When the whisky wasn't paid for, and they wouldn't send him any more, he might have wanted us back.'

He was still lying on top of her. She was hoping he would at least kiss her; he was looking at her as if he wanted to. The whole length of his body was pressed close to hers, and the feeling of wanting to be even closer to him was overwhelming. She understood how a girl who loved a man could easily be persuaded into sleeping with him. It was difficult to think properly when a man was this close. She wanted him to kiss her, then for both of them to tear off their clothes and make love.

They had left the door open, and Pat came in.

'Sorry,' he said. 'But you did leave the door open. What's this? Paying him back by making love in his bed? I like that, and I hope he's looking down from somewhere. It would be hot where he is now. They have radiators in all the bedrooms there. Mary sent me up when she remembered the magazines. She thought I should be helping up here instead of Jane in case there were more of them. But I can go away and shut the door if you want.'

Ryan stood up, held out his hand to help Jane up, and they put their shoes back on. She went downstairs, leaving him and Pat to finish looking for paperwork in the bedroom, and she helped Mary for a while, all the time imagining Ryan making love to her in Daniel's bed. But she knew they would never do that. It would seem sacrilegious, like making love in a churchyard.

Later they also checked the library and found some papers in the drawers there and some files with old bank statements shelved with the books. Jane continued sorting the papers into piles, each pile with a label on the desk beside it with its category.

Ryan would keep Daniel's Burberry coat, but he couldn't see himself wearing the trilby hat. For now they left it on its shelf in the boot room, and eventually they would take it upstairs to his bedroom for sorting at some distant time when they could face clearing out his things. Ryan might wear some of the suits and the shirts. Cuffed trousers were coming back into fashion now, and shirts were timeless.

Jane knew from her own experience that if you waited even a few months, it was easier to dispose of things that dead people had owned.

You just kept a few things that they had loved, and you cherished them as they had.

Thursday 15 April 1976

On Thursday Ryan spent the day in Oxford. He told Jane and Mary he was talking to a friend of Professor Hanson regarding a new position he might want to take up at the end of the academic year. He could stay on as a don at the college even if he didn't live there. However, although he enjoyed teaching the students, he wanted to try something different. Professor Hanson had said he would be sorry to lose him, but he had asked around and found a couple of possible things that Ryan could do.

After he left, Mary told Jane she was glad that he was finally wanting to leave his cloistered life. She had never liked the idea of him staying there forever, however good he was at the teaching. She still hoped he and Jane might get engaged.

Jane said she was hoping so as well, but it hadn't happened yet.

'He just needs a bit more time,' Mary told her. 'In the last six months he has had to adjust to falling for you and losing his father. Both things turned his safe world upside down. Being suspected of murder didn't help, either. It upset him far more than he let on. The police should have waited for the autopsy before they treated him like that. They would have looked very silly if they had persuaded him to confess to something he didn't do, then the coroner had found Daniel died from natural causes.'

Friday 16 April 1976

On Good Friday they went to church in the morning. Mr Allanstone was coming over on the Saturday, as he was spending the Friday catching up at his house in Kent. Mary seemed to know that he only lived in Kent on the weekends and had a flat in London where he stayed during the week. Jane recalled Ryan saying something similar when they were in Richmond.

They all spent the afternoon planting out the flowers that had grown from the seeds they had sown in February. Jane remembered Daniel helping them, and how happy she had felt that they were all working there together with no antagonism between Ryan and his father. She asked Ryan if he remembered that day, and he told her he did remember it being a happy day. They had walked to town in the afternoon and later they had warmed their feet while she had given him chocolates. His father had gone to meet Mary, and Pat had stayed at the farm. It was the first time he had ever been alone in the house with her. He had wanted to kiss her, but he wasn't sure how she would respond. He was afraid he would frighten her off. The following day they had walked in the woods at Charlford, and he had enjoyed that.

She had meant she had been happy with them all working together, but she said nothing. She was glad that he recalled being happy because he had been alone with her.

She wished she could sleep upstairs with him, but he didn't encourage her to. In the evenings they had their cocoa then went upstairs and said goodnight at the foot of the stairs to the second floor. Although he said nothing to her, she understood he needed more time to come to terms with his father being gone. And she sensed that the day he had spent being questioned by the police had really shaken his belief in himself. She knew he didn't like situations where he didn't feel in control.

Saturday 17 April 1976

With the wedding no longer occupying Easter Saturday, Colin arranged an Easter Egg hunt on the village green and along the lanes. Each family hid some eggs in the morning, and everyone with any claim to being less than a full-grown adult was allowed to search for them in the afternoon from two o' clock, when they would meet on the green for the start of the hunt. Mary and Jane took a basket of chocolate eggs in bright coloured wrappers, and hid them along the lane and on the verge outside the wall, but none of them were joining in the hunt, as Mr Allanstone was expected later in the morning.

John Phillips was near the gate of his farm with his two border collies and his two grandsons, so they stopped to chat and gave them an egg each. Winston joked that they could put them in the incubator and hatch three chocolate turkeys.

Mr Allanstone arrived before lunch and the afternoon was spent on the paperwork, the piles by now completely categorised, each one waiting to be sorted by date. The filing cabinet was empty and ready to be refilled in some logical order.

The old newspapers had already been thrown out except for the one from the Friday before Daniel had died, which would be used for the share prices when valuing the estate. The old company reports were thrown out, and only the current ones were kept. The bills were sorted, and those from the last three years were put aside for Jane to work on. Jane would go through them all, checking them against the bank statements and the cheque book to make sure they had been paid. The share certificates were separated into those belonging to Daniel, to Ryan and to Mary. There were even a few for Pat. Jane would need to match them with the pile of contract notes. There were some dividend cheques which had never been banked. Jane put them aside to take to the bank when they did the shopping on Friday. She would use the statements from the publisher to work out what Daniel had earned this year.

Jane had counted all the cash in the safe including the cash that Pat had found in Daniel's room. Mr Allanstone suggested they use that for household expenses for the moment since there was no point banking it, as they would then be unable to withdraw it again until the probate had been finalised. He would leave it up to them how much of it they wanted to include as part of the value of the estate.

They would need a surveyor to value the house. Mr Allanstone would organise it and let them know the appointment time. The surveyor would need to look over the house and garden, and some adjustments would be needed for the work on the lodge which was not yet fully paid for. He would try to arrange a Friday, when Ryan would be there.

But sorting out the income and totalling the assets was only the beginning of the paperwork for the tax. The money that Daniel had given to Pat and Ryan since Pat left school and Ryan finished his first degree needed to be included for calculating the inheritance tax. Mr Allanstone stressed it didn't have to be paid back to the estate, just included for the tax. Although any money Daniel had given to Mary for running the household was exempt. If the allowances he had paid Pat and Ryan were paid in cash and they hadn't banked the money, then it would be nearly impossible to account and couldn't be traced. There was in any case a minimum amount for each year that was not taxed, and an exemption for gifts below a certain value. The shares that Daniel had bought for all of them during the last seven years would also need to be included, but only at the price Daniel had paid, not their current value, and only the amount above the exempt allowance for each year. Jane needed to find the contract notes for those so they knew the original date and cost. She would also need to find the receipt for the Jaguar, which they would need to include as a gift to Ryan, unless Daniel had paid cash for it, in which case there was nothing to say that Ryan hadn't bought it for himself. The Rover was old, and had belonged to Daniel, so they would include a small nominal value for it, and Ryan was happy for ownership to be transferred to Pat. When Jane learnt to drive, he would buy her a new car.

They also needed to work out the income for Daniel for the current year and calculate the tax on that, as the tax owing was not included as part of the estate. The cost of the funeral could also be deducted. The trust for Ryan, Pat and Jane had been set up more than seven years before, so mercifully was exempt. Mr Allanstone would let Jane know the current balance of it. None of them could access it until Jane reached twenty-one, but that was now only sixteen months away. The trust would then be wound up, and they would each have one third of the money.

Mr Allanstone gave Jane a detailed list of all the calculations that needed to be done. When she had finished sorting all the papers, she would then be able to work out all the required amounts. She would type the list up, then go through item by item, with Ryan's help, and tick off what had been done. Mr Allanstone would come down again in a week or two so they could go through the amounts together.

Jane had the ledger that she had started six months before when she had first come to Hayward Hall. She would buy another account book and work backwards to fill in the last three years or so. The bank statements were not a lot of help, as they only gave vague descriptions like *cheque* for the entries, with nothing to say who the cheques were to or from. But if she started with the statements, she could pencil in amounts she had bills for, and amounts she knew were dividends or payments from the publisher. She had the remains of the old cheque books for the last twenty years tucked away in one of the drawers. Most of the stubs had a description and an amount although a lot of them were just for cash. Ryan had generally filled them in when he wrote out and signed the cheques for Daniel.

Ryan offered to take the bank statements to the library in town on Tuesday to photocopy for her so she could write notes on the copy without affecting the originals. If she came with him, she could pick up the new account book and bank the stray dividend cheques.

By the end of the afternoon, they were exhausted, so they all spent the evening in the lounge, playing scrabble. Ryan was the best player as he knew more words than anyone else. But when he put down *te amo*, and gave Jane a wicked look, she disallowed it because it was Latin. Pat asked what a *teamo* was, but Jane wouldn't tell him. Mary looked at them blankly, but John Allanstone laughed.

Sunday 18 April 1976

On Easter Sunday they went to church, still all in their black. The day was warm and felt like spring. Mr Allanstone was once again with them.

They had not yet picked up the suits for the wedding from London, and Claire still had no wedding dress, for Anne was at a loss to know how to alter her old one to fit. After church she asked Jane if she could come over and advise her on how they could make something more modern out of it. She admitted that the silk had become very yellow, and there were marks on it that she was not sure the dry cleaners would get out. She was worried that Claire would look shabby against the beautiful bridesmaid dresses. Perhaps Jane could help them choose something new.

Jane suggested they could buy something for Claire in London with Pat paying for it from his expected inheritance money. Meanwhile, if necessary, Jane herself would cover the cost. She asked Anne to arrange for Claire to have a day off work in the week to come to London with them. Thursday would be good, as that was half day where Claire worked in the wool and haberdashery shop. Jane hoped Claire's employer would allow her the whole of that day off to buy her wedding dress. Claire would still wear her mother's veil, but the old dress would go back to its mothballed box in the loft at the farm.

As they walked home Jane asked Mr Allanstone if Pat could be given some of his inheritance money to pay for Claire's wedding dress, and he offered to pay for it himself as a wedding gift.

After lunch Jane played tennis with Ryan, Pat and Claire, the men versus the girls, while Mary and Mr Allanstone remained indoors. After an hour or so, Jane went inside to fetch them all a drink. There was no one in the kitchen, so she took a bottle of lemonade from the fridge, found four glasses and some biscuits and put them all on a tray.

From the kitchen window she could see into the conservatory, where Mary and Mr Allanstone were sitting together on the lovers' seat, gently rocking. His arm was resting along the back of the seat behind her, and they were deep in conversation, facing each other, laughing together, looking for all the world like lovers, and Jane found it rather jarring.

Those two seemed to know each other rather well, she thought. Was he courting her now she was to inherit a good deal of money from her brother? Or had they always been better friends than it appeared on the surface? He had been friends with Daniel, she remembered, and he had once stayed here; Mary had a photo of him with Daniel in the garden beside the koi pond when Ryan was three.

In the evening they all watched a film on television, Jane once again next to Ryan, leaning against him, both of them stroking the cat. Mr Allanstone was staying with them until the following afternoon. He suggested they spend at least some of the next day talking about what they planned to do when the probate was through and Ryan had control of the house and the money, and how Pat planned to keep his wife and child fed and clothed.

Monday 19 April 1976

On Monday morning Pat and Jane showed Mr Allanstone around the lodge and explained how the renovations would work. The plans had now been approved, and the builders were to start the following morning. They were hoping for it to be finished in about six weeks, not quite in time for the wedding, but certainly before the baby arrived in early August.

Over lunch in the conservatory, they talked about what they would do in the future to manage the money and make enough to keep this expensive house running. Jane had done some calculations of the value of the estate, with Mr Allanstone's estimate for the value of the house, and had calculated how much would go in death duties, sadly rather a lot.

But it did give them some idea of what Ryan would have remaining after Mary's share was accounted for. After six months of managing Daniel's expenditure, Jane knew roughly what it cost to run the household. You added up what had been spent over the six months, then subtracted Daniel's visits to the London hotel, the cash he withdrew when he was there, the cash for the young men at Christmas and the cost of the earrings he had given Jane and Mary. You then multiplied the six months' costs by two for the whole year. She didn't take off the cost of the whisky, as she would have needed to separate it out from the other items on the account from the off license.

Mr Allanstone thought they could easily cover the household expenses if the money was invested sensibly and not squandered. However, he did think it wise for Ryan to have some sort of career when he finished his PhD, since money had a way of shrinking with inflation, and costs were going up at a faster rate than the return you could get on investments, especially after you paid tax on the investment income. There were the royalties from the books, but that would not last forever, as writers eventually went out of fashion, and there would be no new books now Daniel was gone unless Ryan wanted to write them himself.

'Ryan is good at ghost stories, and he knows a lot about history,' Jane suggested.

But it seemed Ryan already had something planned.

'Since Professor Hanson knew I may not be staying on at the college after the end of this year, he asked around, and I have spoken to a friend of his about a job with the National Trust, working on the history of some of their houses and writing up the brochures, starting in August. It is Oxford based, and would not be full time, so would suit me well. I am also considering a job at the boys' grammar school in Oxford, teaching history and Latin to sixth form. Their current history master, another friend of the Professor, is retiring. I could stay working at the college as a tutor even if I no longer lived there, but I would like to try something new.'

Mr Allanstone said he knew he could rely on Ryan, and he told Pat he was in contact with a car dealer in Oxford, and was arranging for Pat to get an interview with him after they returned from the honeymoon. He hoped that Pat would make an effort to impress a potential employer. He only needed to be polite and smartly dressed to sell cars, and to know why the cars he was selling were better than the ones the other dealers sold. Mr Allanstone was confident Pat could manage all that. He was not to expect his mother or Ryan to keep him indefinitely, although he did acknowledge that Pat did a good job on the garden. Another option was for Pat to run a gardening business and work on the gardens of some of the other houses in the district as well as the one at Hayward Hall. His work on the garden at Hayward Hall could be paid for by having the lodge rent free.

Ryan said he didn't want rent for the lodge. Hayward Hall was just as much Pat's home now as it had been when Daniel was alive, and Mary's and Jane's home as well. He would use the royalty income to cover the household expenses for them all, as well as the cost for his grandfather to live at Grey Friars, and he was happy to share anything remaining with Pat, Mary and Jane for as long as it lasted. However, he was not sure that he could afford to pay Pat the current allowance indefinitely with Daniel no longer there to earn the money, as Daniel had paid each of them more than Ryan could earn himself. But for the moment Pat and Claire would need something to live on, so Ryan would continue paying Pat for the gardening until he could get a permanent job and could access his inheritance, and he would give Mary whatever she needed for her own use before the probate was through and she had her share of the estate. After that he and Pat could look after the garden together on the weekends. Pat would have the money that their grandmother had left them when he reached twenty-one in June, so he and Claire would have something of their own. Ryan said he was confident that if he and Pat both worked, they would all have enough to live on. And they could afford to keep the house maintained if they all helped with the work.

Jane wasn't sure that Pat was convinced he needed to get a real job, and she knew he was happy doing the gardening, but she saw the sense of it. Their inherited money was unlikely to last them all of their lives, so they would all need some way of earning an honest living. She wanted to go back to working herself when the wedding was over. She would talk to the bank manager in town, and ask if they needed a temporary when the other girls were sick or on holiday. It would give her a head start there until they had a permanent job for her. She had enjoyed working at the bank in spite of the behaviour of her old boss. She had often spoken to the manager here and had no concerns that he would behave the same way. If Ryan was working in Oxford, she could even get a job at a bank there, as they could go in together each day, perhaps even meet at a park at lunchtime.

Tuesday 20 April 1976

On Tuesday the builders started on the lodge, stripping wallpaper and lifting the old carpet and lino, taking out the old kitchen cupboards and bathroom fittings. Jane and Pat went to the lodge to talk to Mr Fletcher. Everything was under control, so they left him with his two workmen to carry on.

The architect, Alex Miller, came to lay out the pegs for the conservatory. Jane saw his car drive in and walked to the lodge to talk to him. She had not seen or spoken to him since Daniel had died. He said he was very sorry that she had lost her uncle. He believed the late Mr Linden was her uncle and not her father since their names were different, and he apologised if he had got it wrong. She thanked him and explained about Daniel being her father's cousin.

The pegged-out area still looked rather small, but he told her it always looked small until you built the walls. It would be a decent-sized room when it was finished, and the extra space would make the lodge a much better place to live. They would pour the concrete floor by the end of this week, and next week the stonemason would build the low wall up to the level of the windows. He would call by as the work progressed to check it was all going to plan, and on one of the days she could show him the house as she had promised. He was a friendly and polite young man with a smile that lit up her day, and his love for old stone houses was infectious. He had been working for his father since he qualified last year, and his father had spent all of his working life on designs for renovating old stone houses in the Cotswolds.

In the afternoon Ryan drove her to town to pick up her new account book, bank the cheques and photocopy the statements at the library.

He told her he was grateful to have her to sort out the accounting, but he was happy to go through it with her and give her any help he could.

Thursday 22 April 1976

On Thursday they had arranged to pick up the men's suits for the wedding and organise a dress for Claire. They drove to Richmond as they had a few weeks previously, left the car at the house, and headed into the city on the train. Sarah had recommended a shop that sold wedding dresses off the peg and could, if necessary, alter them on the spot, and she had arranged to meet them there to help with the selection. She had phoned ahead to say they needed something for a six months' pregnant bride, size eight, five foot three tall.

They found something beautiful with an empire line, medieval sleeves similar to those on the bridesmaid dresses, and a little extra fullness to allow for the four-week delay before wearing it. The hem would be adjusted by two that afternoon when they would have a final fitting and could then take it home with them.

Jane told Sarah that she and Tony were welcome to come to the wedding and could stay the night at Hayward Hall. But that weekend was Tony's father's sixtieth birthday, and they had a party planned. Sarah said if it had been Jane marrying Ryan, she wouldn't miss it for the world. Surely, they were engaged by now.

Jane said it was still too soon after his father had died. It was taking them all a while to get over it. The police being involved had been very stressful even though it was only routine. She hoped they would be announcing they were engaged fairly soon now.

Mr Allanstone took them all out for lunch, Sarah as well. He remembered her from when Jane had stayed with her before her great-aunt's funeral.

Claire seemed a little overwhelmed, but Mr Allanstone helped her select what she wanted to eat, and asked her how the house renovations were going and if they had a name chosen for the baby. She told him Mary had suggested they call the baby Rosemary if it was a girl and she liked that. Mary had said that Pat had once had a half-sister called Rosemary who had died as a baby, but they knew nothing else about her or about Pat's father. Mary would not tell them any more than that.

Mr Allanstone said he thought Rosemary was a beautiful name, he was glad they had chosen it, and he rather hoped they had a girl.

Claire said if she had a boy, she would like to call him Daniel, but she wasn't sure yet, as Mary had said to ask Ryan first. Mary thought that he and Jane might want that name kept for their baby if they had one. Pat's grandfather had been James, and Claire's uncle who had died in the War was James as well, but they didn't want James as that was her brother Jimmy's real name and it might cause confusion.

Jane flashed a questioning glance at Ryan, who hadn't answered Claire about the name, but he just looked at her helplessly. It was clearly something he had never thought about. So she said for her part they were welcome to Daniel, as she had already decided if she had children, they would be Charles and Eloise, the Linden babies who had never had a chance at life. They had never felt the sun on their faces or the wind in their hair, and she liked the thought that she could give them another opportunity. Claire liked that idea and recalled her mother had lost a baby in between her and Paul. His name was to have been Michael, so perhaps they would use that.

Mr Allanstone gave Jane a signed blank cheque so she could pay for the dress when it was collected, as they were not yet certain of the final price. There was the inevitable joke about them all having a holiday at his expense on the French Riviera, but he said he trusted Jane completely. She could phone him tonight when they returned to Hayward and let him know the amount so he could account it.

They collected the dress—the length was now perfect—Claire chose some shoes to wear with it, and Jane wrote the amount on the cheque. The young men had picked up the suits from the tailor, and they all returned to Richmond on the train, before driving back to Hayward Hall, leaving Claire and the dress at the farm. Jane remembered to phone Mr Allanstone with the amount of the cheque.

Friday 23 April 1976

The surveyor came on Friday morning to value the house and garden. Jane and Ryan showed him around, and he made notes about the size of the rooms and the age of the furniture.

Jane pointed out that the house might need rewiring, it was very cold in winter even with the radiators running, the heating was expensive to run and there were often mice and occasionally rats in the kitchen and the cellar.

He laughed and said he would do his best to give a fair valuation for them. It was actually quite difficult to sell these large houses. They were expensive for people to take on, and very few families were large enough to need twenty bedrooms. These days they were often divided up into separate apartments, which were each given a section of the garden.

This house could be divided very readily into two, reasonably easily into three with a large apartment on each floor, into four with a bit of imagination, or into six smaller apartments. In each case the hallway, the conservatory and perhaps also the attics would be communal space.

He asked if they were intending to sell. If they sold within a few months at a price higher than the valuation, they might be required to pay more tax.

Ryan said he wanted to keep the house, and he hoped to have enough to cover the tax without needing to sell their home.

Jane discussed with the surveyor how they would handle the issue of the lodge renovation that had not yet been paid for.

He told Jane the correct approach would be for him to do the valuation on the assumption the lodge was as it was when Daniel had died. This would also give them the best outcome. A derelict cottage would add very little to the value of the house, whereas a cottage that was modernised and habitable would add more to the value than the outstanding renovation cost.

She left it to Ryan to show him the bedrooms on the top floor while she waited downstairs in the hallway. She had shown him her own and Mary's rooms, which had been tidied for the occasion. Even with Daniel gone they still stuck to his rule about bedrooms. Jane thought it unfortunate that they did, as it was about time she was allowed to sleep with Ryan in his room.

Saturday 24 April 1976

On Saturday afternoon there was cricket again. There would be one more game next week with just the Hayward men, then a match against Peddleton, held on the Hayward village green as Peddleton had only a very small one. The Saturday following that was the wedding, so there would be no cricket that day.

Mary hadn't gone to London to see her friend. Jane was surprised she was missing so many weekends. She helped Mary make the scones for the afternoon tea.

The game was similar to the one the previous fortnight, with the younger men playing the older men. The children ran around the edge of the green with ice creams from the village shop. Linda's baby Brett was in a pushchair, laughing in excitement at the children playing with him.

The older-men's team won the game, with a lot of help from Candy's uncle Maurice, who had been put on their team to help with the numbers although he wasn't particularly old; Jane thought him only mid-thirties. The younger men would have another chance to win next weekend, and they would decide then which team members would play against Peddleton the following Saturday.

Colin had left a quarter of an hour of playing time to give the girls a turn at batting, but he wouldn't let Ryan bowl to them. David bowled at a much gentler pace. Ryan caught Jane out then deliberately dropped the ball.

Sunday 25 April 1976

On Sunday afternoon Jane walked to the cottage where Julie lived with her mother Alison, so Julie could try on the altered pink bridesmaid dress. They had arranged this after church. Candy was to come over as well to help with the fitting.

The dress now fitted much more snugly and looked much better, as the design was meant to be figure hugging, but it still looked a little long. Julie said she could keep hold of the skirt when she wore it, so she was less likely to trip over the hem, but Jane decided it really did need to be a few inches shorter. Jane discussed with Alison what could be done. They could turn up a wide hem and hand sew it carefully in place, but it would not look as good as the original small rolled hem. Jane decided to contact Rebecca to ask if she minded if they trimmed the hemline to reduce the length, since Rebecca had said Julie could keep the dress.

Alison offered to do the hemming, but Jane had more leisure and was happy to do it herself. If Rebecca was happy for them to reduce the length, she would stitch a new rolled hem by hand.

Alison had been a teenage bride and was now in her early thirties. Her husband had been killed in a motorbike accident years before when Julie was a toddler, and Alison found it difficult to make ends meet. She cleaned the church and the village hall and did some housework for Candy's mother so she was free to work in the lingerie shop. She also cleaned the post office and sometimes worked in the local shops and the tearoom when extra help was needed in the summer months. Occasionally she stood in for the usual barmaid at the Black Horse Inn. She lived in the other half of the cottage where Candy's family lived, so Julie and Candy were next-door neighbours as well as cousins. She was delicately beautiful, slender and pale, with the same wispy fair hair as her daughter, usually in a neat bun. She looked too young to be Julie's mother; they could almost be sisters.

The cottage was rather small but was light and neatly furnished. It was in fact only one third of the building. There had originally been three cottages, but the other two had been combined to give Candy's family one decent sized house. Alison's cottage had once been a holiday let owned by Candy's family, but now Alison and Julie lived there for a very small rent in exchange for Alison doing the housework one afternoon a week for Candy's mother.

Candy told Jane her Uncle Maurice was now staying with them. He had come back from South Africa just before Easter and would be with them for most of the summer. Jane had seen him at cricket and at church but had only spoken to him briefly when they were introduced.

Monday 26 April 1976

Ryan was returning to Oxford on the Monday and staying there until Thursday afternoon to catch up with his students and his research, and run the extra tutorials for the students who were struggling. There was now no reason for him to come home each day, as Jane was no longer at the mercy of his father. Pat was there at night, so Jane and Mary were not alone in the house.

He did offer to telephone her every evening, and she agreed to Tuesday evenings. He would do this for three weeks until Pat's wedding, then return to commuting each day so Mary and Jane weren't by themselves at night. It would not have worried Mary, but it did worry Jane. When he commuted, he didn't mind leaving the car parked at the station in town during the day. He just didn't like it being left there overnight.

After the wedding there were only five more weeks of classes and another week or two of tidying up, then he would be home for the whole summer, his degree would be completed, the estate would be finalised, and they could plan their future.

Jane was disappointed at his decision to stay in Oxford, but she said nothing. She was even more disappointed that they were now to wait for six weeks following the wedding before their future was sorted out. She was beginning to think he wanted to go back to being a lone wolf.

She phoned Rebecca that evening to ask if she minded them reducing the length of the pink dress by trimming the hemline, as Julie was not as tall as Rebecca. Jane didn't think it would hang right if they hemmed a full three inches.

Rebecca said she was happy for them to do anything they wanted, as she knew she would never wear it again, and she was glad it was getting a second use. Julie was welcome to keep it. Sarah's father had paid a small fortune for the bridesmaid dresses, and they would have been a lot of work for whoever made them. It would be a shame if they were only ever worn once. Even Rebecca's mother was glad the dresses would be used again.

She told Jane about her latest boyfriend Clive. This one was the right one. They were getting engaged shortly, and the notice would be in *The Times* next week. She would invite Jane to the wedding, and she was welcome to bring a boyfriend if she had one, or one of her two good-looking cousins if she didn't. Sarah had mentioned that Jane had gone out with Scott. Rebecca said Jane hadn't missed anything by not sleeping with him. He was hopeless. If you had never slept with anyone before, he would have put you off sex for life. It was good that nowadays you could try a guy out before you married him. Imagine getting married to a man you thought you liked then finding he was hopeless in bed.

Tuesday 27 April 1976

Ryan phoned her late on Tuesday evening after her television programme had finished, but he didn't have much to say. She told him how the renovations were going and what bills had come in, that the cat had caught another rat and brought it indoors, so Pat was setting traps in the stables. She said she missed him at cocoa time, and he told her he thought about her all of the time.

She had to be content with that. She knew she needed to be patient with him. He had once seen his future as living a celibate life as a fellow of his all-male college, teaching history and Latin to young men like himself. Then he had been her knight, protecting her from her own fears of living alone in Richmond, hoping to get a permanent job so he could marry her and look after her, planning a life for them together away from his home at Hayward Hall. Now he had to adjust not only to losing his father, but also to returning to live at his home as the unofficial local squire, and starting on a new career. He had accepted the research job with the National Trust.

He really had wanted to make love to her at least on that one night— she knew that—and the next day he had asked her if she would like to marry him, but now she was beginning to wonder if he still wanted her at all. He was not behaving like a lover. He had lost his father, and Jane remembered how disorientated she had been when she had lost her parents. She knew it took a long time to adjust when your life changed so much in such a short time. She was trying not to throw herself at him. He would make up his mind in his own time, and perhaps he just needed some space to adjust. She couldn't even begin to think of what she would do if he really didn't want her. She still could not face the idea of living by herself in the house in Richmond, and she didn't think she could stay living here with him unless they were lovers. She would be miserable wanting him and knowing he didn't want her.

Wednesday 28 April 1976

Pat was meeting Claire and Jimmy at the Black Horse Inn on Wednesday evening, so Jane went with him, and Jimmy was pleased to see her. He was always good company, telling her what they were doing on the farm. John Phillips had been troubled by a fox trying to get at the hens and turkeys. It had dug a hole under the fence, but the dogs had set up such an uproar that John had woken up and found it.

Jane didn't like to ask the fate of the fox. It was just being a fox, trying to find food for itself, trying to survive in a world where foxes were unloved, unwelcome and underfed, while hens were plentiful and mouthwatering, but difficult to access.

Jimmy said he had missed her company. He understood about her not wanting to go out with him while Ryan was at home, and he understood that she was still upset about her uncle, but he was always glad to see her.

She didn't tell him she was in love with Ryan, even though Daniel was no longer there to care. She was beginning to wonder if anything was going to come of it. If she announced it but then it went nowhere, she and Ryan would both look pretty silly. She didn't want to keep stringing Jimmy along, but he was always good company, and it was hard not to respond when he flirted with her.

They left the inn and returned along the lane. Pat was kissing Claire at the farm gate before they continued to the house, so she let Jimmy give her a kiss goodnight. If Ryan found out and didn't like it, he had only himself to blame, leaving her alone for days on end like this. But she did ask Pat not to tell him. She remembered Ryan's comment about teenagers kissing behind castle walls, and she did feel just a little bit guilty.

Thursday 29 April 1976

The stonemason had started on the wall. It went up remarkably quickly, and by the end of the day you could stand within a bounded room, even if it was just a low wall open to the sky. The rewiring was well underway, the coal store was now a cloakroom, the pipes were in and the painters were working in the rooms upstairs.

Ryan came back late on Thursday afternoon. There was still plenty of daylight, so she showed him how the lodge was progressing, and was grateful he didn't mention a previous time they had been there together. She told him it was good to have him back at home, but he didn't respond as she had hoped. He just talked about the renovations. She told him that next week the timber framework would go up for the roof and windows of the new conservatory, and by the end of the following week the glass panels and the doors would be in.

After dinner he walked with her to the yoga class, and he picked her up again at nine o' clock. They played table tennis for a while before they had cocoa.

Friday 30 April 1976

The valuation came back from the surveyor on Friday morning. Ryan opened the letter, and Jane was glad to see it was lower than Mr Allanstone had estimated. She now had the last of the amounts they needed to finalise the estate. Ryan would photocopy the letter at the library in town the following morning, and they would send the original to Mr Allanstone, along with the list that Jane had made of all the shares and bank accounts, and the transfers to Pat, Ryan and Mary that were to be included, although that was mainly only the shares they had been given and the cost of the Jaguar. She had found all the contract notes and the receipt for the car.

In the afternoon they all worked in the garden, planting out flowers, trimming hedges and sweeping paths.

That evening she sat beside Ryan in the library while she worked on hemming the dress, and he read her another ghost story as she stitched in the light of a table lamp. The Montague James stories weren't quite as nightmarish as the screaming skull story he had read to the group on New Year's Eve, but they were atmospheric, and she felt they were meant to be read aloud. He always translated the Latin quotes for her. He knew it was easier to understand Latin if you saw it written down rather than listening to it spoken. The cat was perfectly content on his lap. Perhaps she loved the sound of his voice as much as Jane did. Jane had to be careful the cat didn't get her claws anywhere near the dress, so she couldn't sit as close to Ryan as she would have liked.

She wanted to ask him if he still wanted her, but she knew she needed to be patient. It was now only two weeks until the wedding, so perhaps he would make his mind up then. He had talked about deciding what he wanted to do at the end of the term, but that was still weeks away. She couldn't imagine how she would cope with waiting for that long.

9 SPRING FLOWERS

Saturday 1 May 1976

On Saturday Mary went to London. She set up the Crock-Pot as she usually did, even though Jane would have been happy to cook the dinner.

Jane spent the morning making scones for the cricket tea, the cat watching her from a corner of the kitchen, ensuring there were no mice to bother her while she worked. Ryan had gone out to the library to photocopy the letter from the surveyor and her typed list of the assets.

This time at cricket they changed the teams from the previous week so some of the other young men had a chance to play. Ryan was umpire, and Jane and Colin kept score again. At the end of the game the team was selected to play against Peddleton the following week. Some of the younger men were to play, along with Candy's father and Candy's uncle, while everyone else would help set up seats and garden umbrellas and the tea tent, and watch the game from the sidelines.

The cricket finished a little earlier than usual so the children from Linda's Sunday school could dance around a maypole while everyone else enjoyed their tea. They had been practising after school all week, and it went as well as could be expected with the varying sizes and skills of the children, as they danced in and out until the ribbons covered the length of the pole.

Jane enjoyed watching the bright colours of the fluttering ribbons, the pretty summer dresses of the girls, and the light-hearted dancing of children too young to know the cares of life. It seemed so traditional and safe.

Sunday 2 May 1976

On Sunday afternoon Ryan and Jane went to visit his grandfather in Bath, taking him chocolates, and flowers from the garden. Jane was conscious that last time they had been there Ryan had hinted that they would soon be engaged.

The old man remembered her name, but if he recalled their imminent engagement, he didn't ask about it. When Pamela spoke to them, Jane told her that Ryan's father had died so they hadn't visited for a while. It had been rather sudden, and it was taking them all a long time to come to terms with it. They were not telling Ryan's grandfather, as they didn't want him to upset him. Ryan didn't talk of their planned engagement, and neither did she. But deep down she was unhappy. Ryan must recall that he had said it, all those weeks ago, and she felt a little awkward talking to the people there without it being mentioned.

They told the old man about Pat's wedding, now only a fortnight away—although Jane wasn't sure he remembered who Pat was—about the baby turkeys now looking more like real turkeys, how good the spring weather had been, and that the lodge at Hayward Hall was being renovated. Did he remember Hayward Hall? They assumed he had been there at some stage, but Ryan couldn't remember his grandfather ever coming there when he was a child, although his grandmother had occasionally taken him to visit his maternal grandparents in Bath.

Yes, Ryan's grandfather did remember Hayward Hall. Kathleen lived there with Caroline and Daniel. There were always flowers in the garden. Caroline was expecting a baby; it would arrive soon and he would have a grandchild. He told them his son had recently died in the War—he had been a fighter pilot—but he still had a daughter.

All the way home Jane was silent, trying to fight back tears at the old man's recollections. Ryan scarcely even spoke to her. He had gone back to treating her as though she was his sister, and Jane was starting to think he was no longer in love with her. She might just have to face the fact that things were not going to work out the way she had hoped.

'Jane, why are you unhappy?' he asked when they had returned to the Hall. 'You've hardly spoken to me the whole way home. Empathy is good, but you can't take on everyone else's sorrow as well as your own. He is happy there and well looked after.'

'I was remembering the last time we were there. Your father was still alive then, and we told your grandfather we wanted to get engaged. I was upset because Daniel had stolen my underwear, and we didn't know how to tell him about us. It all seems such a long time ago.'

He reached over and took her hand.

'We still want to get engaged, or at least I do. As soon as Pat's wedding is over, we can go to London and buy you a ring and put the notice in *The Times*. Would that make you happy?'

She didn't know what to say to him. She didn't care about the ring, and she didn't care about *The Times*. She just wanted him to kiss her and make love to her. She wanted to tell him that she wanted sex, and she didn't care whether they were married or not, but she didn't think that was quite the right thing to say. She might not be happy if a man said that to her. Perhaps he only wanted to make love to her when he wasn't completely sober. Well, she wasn't going to try to get a man drunk so she could persuade him to sleep with her. At least if she was married to him, he would make love to her, or at least she hoped he would. It would be unfair of him to marry her if he didn't want to. She liked Rebecca's idea that you tried it out before you got married.

But you couldn't tell a man that you wanted to try it out first. If it didn't go right the first time, he would feel like a failure.

Had he changed his mind, but didn't know how to tell her? Had he simply been carried away by the moment when he had kissed her in the hallway at Richmond, and asked her to marry him in the car coming home the next day? Was this all a huge mistake? How could she marry a man who didn't even want to kiss her? Perhaps they should just stay as friends.

But that evening he was a little kinder to her. When she sat with him, working on the dress, she leaned against him while he read her the ghost stories, and he caressed her hair with his free hand and called her his sweetheart. The cat was prowling for mice elsewhere in the house, so the dress was safe from her claws.

Wednesday 5 May 1976

Wednesday was Black Horse Inn night. This time David was with them and he and Jimmy had collected Candy and Julie, so there was quite a group of them sitting outside in the last of the evening sunlight. There were tourists around now that spring was here, and there were a lot of people sitting in the garden, so it was rather noisy.

They discussed the wedding and the renovations, the cricket team, the turkeys and the sheep.

Jane wished Ryan was with them. Why did he choose to stay overnight in Oxford? Was it to get away from her? Was she being too clinging? Or was he regretting their relationship, wanting to distance himself from it? He had phoned her last night, as planned, but he had seemed rather cold and uncommunicative and she had rapidly run out of things to talk about.

Mary had suggested Pat and Claire spend their wedding night at the inn, as it would be too late for them to drive down to Devon for their honeymoon after they left the reception. They could have stayed in Pat's room at Hayward Hall, but Mary thought they would feel more relaxed and romantic if they were by themselves at the inn. No one would want to spend their wedding night on a creaky bed with their mum sleeping in the room below.

Pat talked to the landlord and booked the room.

They all walked Julie and Candy home, then continued to the farm gate. Jane was not keen to kiss Jimmy at the gate with David there. She was wary of snitches, and she knew her flirting with Jimmy had to stop. So she just gave him a quick kiss, and she gave David a hug as well so he didn't feel left out. Then she and Pat went on to Hayward Hall.

Saturday 8 May 1976

On Saturday the Peddleton cricket team came over to Hayward, parking their cars at the village hall. They were given a back room in the hall to change, and the Peddleton ladies were shown to chairs on the green where they could watch the game under shady garden umbrellas.

Ryan and Pat were both in the Hayward team, along with Jimmy, David, Winston and Adrian, as well as Candy's father and uncle. Two of Colin's other teenagers and one of the younger farmers made up the eleven. As they had only three hours to play before they all had the tea, a limit was set on the time each team played, regardless of whether the whole team was out.

Jack McCann was umpire and Colin looked after the scoring, along with two older men from Peddleton. Mary and Linda were in charge of pouring lemonade for the players at half time. Jane wondered why Mary hadn't gone to visit her friend. She had missed so many Saturdays and would miss the next one because of the wedding. But she had at least gone there last week.

It was a lovely way to spend the afternoon. Jane enjoyed watching the game, talking to the Peddleton spectators and to Julie's mum Alison, looking for Ryan among the fielders when he wasn't bowling.

By the end of the game Hayward had won but only by a few runs, so any resulting ill will quickly evaporated over scones, jam and cream, brought out from the hall to a couple of canvas gazebos, since the weather was so lovely. Jane served tea and coffee from an urn, with its power cord snaking back across the road and into the village hall. She spoke with the guests as they came for their cups of tea or coffee, chatting for a while with the farmer they had afternoon tea with on their walks to Peddleton. Alison was also helping with the urn, and Candy's uncle Maurice lingered to talk to her when he came for his coffee. Ryan brought over a plate with some scones for them all, as Jane was unable to leave her post, and he talked with Maurice about the finer points of bowling, as Maurice was also an expert bowler. They seemed to get on well. Maurice spoke about the South African school where he had worked and how good he had felt when two of the first students he had taught had graduated from the university in Johannesburg, hundreds of miles from his little bush school.

When the afternoon was over, the opposing team cheered as they drove away, the gazebos were dismantled and returned to the storeroom in the village hall, the cups and plates were washed up, and the village green was left deserted, the game now just a memory but for the scuffed grass and the trampled field flowers.

Sunday 9 May 1976

On Sunday afternoon they had a rehearsal for the wedding. Colin and Linda directed everyone to the correct side of the church, the Lindens in their own pew on the right at the front, the McCanns on the opposite side. The youngest McCann boys were to be the ushers, along with Winston and Adrian. They were given instructions to keep the first three rows on each side free for the wedding party.

Since the church was expected to be packed, they couldn't be too free with space. Normally the front row was only the parents of the bride on one side and the best man on the other, but Colin suggested the McCann boys could sit with their parents, and the row behind was reserved for some McCann cousins who were expected. All of the bridesmaids would sit in the Linden pew for the service after they had escorted the bride down the aisle, as well as Pat, Claire, Ryan and Jane when they had returned from the registry after the signing and witnessing. Mary and Mr Allanstone would sit in the row behind along with the Jamesons who were also invited. Next to them would be Linda, and Colin's mother with Brett. Candy's parents and Julie's mother would occupy the third row on that side so they had a good view of the bridesmaids. Candy's older brother and his wife, who were coming to Hayward for the weekend to see Candy in her bridesmaid role, would also sit with them. John Phillips and his two grandsons would sit in the third row behind the McCann cousins.

Jane thought there was sure to be some confusion in the seating, but as long as the first three rows were kept free it should all work out okay. Linda had some *Reserved* signs to put up, and the ushers knew who was to go where, even if Jane was a little confused.

When the seating had been agreed on, the bride came down the aisle, escorted by her father, with the bridesmaids, including little Daisy, following. The vows were rehearsed, the walk to the registry, the return to the pews and the walk back along the aisle, Ryan and Jane following Pat and Claire, then Jimmy with Candy, and David and Julie with Daisy between them.

After the rehearsal they all had tea at the farm. Jane had finished hemming the dress—the skirt still draped beautifully—and she gave it to Julie so she could try it on when she returned home, just in case anything else needed to be done.

After dinner she asked Ryan if he would like to practise the foxtrot, and Mary found them an Engelbert Humperdinck record. Neither of them wanted the song they had danced to once before, however beautiful it had been when they danced to it. Daniel had spoilt it, and now he was dead.

When the record finished Mary suggested that Ryan might like to dance a tango with Jane as his father once had. She thought it might help them to get over what happened. She found the *Guitar Tango* single for them. It was more modern than *Caro Mio*.

The tango was more interesting than the foxtrot. Jane threw her whole soul into it, and Ryan seemed to as well. It felt like a courtship ritual. The first few steps they danced without touching, both of them with hands behind their backs, his eyes looking into hers, then touching only slightly, then more, then close together, dancing as if they were one, with spins and dips and her thigh against his and his face close to hers. His father had turned her so she was pulled back against him, and Ryan did the same, and he ended, as Daniel had, with her leaning back, her leg stretched out close to his, his hand on her waist holding her against him, his face so close to hers he was almost kissing her. Then he lifted her and spun around, as Daniel had done.

Pat stood at the door to the lounge, saying it could be awkward if the floor was slippery, as they could both end up doing the splits. He told them it was sexy just watching them dance. It felt sexy too, at least to Jane. Pat asked if they would dance a tango like that at the wedding, but Ryan said he would need a few drinks before he would be brave enough to do that. But they worked out a routine that they could follow for the tango if they wanted to, and did more practice at the foxtrot. It did seem very chaste after the tango.

Jane gave Pat a turn at the foxtrot as well. She knew Ryan wouldn't mind. There was never any open animosity between them. Pat had once told her they had always been united against a common enemy.

Dancing in the hallway still brought back troubled memories of the last time they had danced there, so it didn't work the magic that Jane wanted, but they were all a lot more relaxed than they had been then, and even Mary had a dance or two with Pat and with Ryan.

Mary shared her memories of Daniel and Caroline dancing in the hallway when they were first married. She had been twelve then and fourteen when Caroline died.

'She was a beautiful dancer, like Jane is. She had learnt ballet dancing as a child and she was very graceful. I loved to watch them dance. He adored her. We all did. She was so beautiful and glamorous, like a film star. Ten years they had together, but only two of them here after they were married. There was never anyone else for either of them.

They went through the War only seeing each other occasionally, and when they married after the War ended, it was as if we had all come out into the sunshine and life could be good again. Then she died just when they were looking forward to their first child. All of us were completely devastated, but we were so grateful that Ryan was saved. Daniel never got over it.

'The evening before he died, when he danced the tango with Jane, it was the happiest I had ever seen him in all those years. But then he spoilt it. My brother wasn't a saint, Jane, and what he did to you was unforgivable, but sometimes he just got so angry with life. My mother and I always did what we could for him, but we were both rather afraid of him.'

'I did enjoy dancing with him, and I liked making him happy,' said Jane. 'That evening when we were dancing was the closest I got to loving him, but I could never have married him, and he knew that.'

They talked about the music they would have at the wedding. The band from town was versatile, as they covered a range of events. Pat would ask if they could do *Guitar Tango*.

When they were tired out, Ryan gave Jane a hug, and said it was time for cocoa, reminding her he needed to be up early in the morning to return to Oxford. Her hopes of spending the night in his room were dashed yet again.

Wednesday 12 May 1976

Mr Allanstone phoned on Wednesday morning. As Ryan was not there, he talked to Jane. He had now lodged the application for the probate using the amounts she had given him and the valuation of the house from the surveyor. They could expect it to go through by the end of June. Once the probate was granted, they would pay the tax from Daniel's estate account, and ownership of the house would be transferred to Ryan. Mr Allanstone would set up the trusts for Jane and Pat and transfer Mary's share of the balance to her bank account. He was sending Ryan an estimate of what would be left, and how much they could each expect to get, so they all knew where they stood.

He checked that they were managing with the cash they had from the safe and Ryan's bank account. Jane knew they had enough because she was keeping track of it for Ryan. He was happy for her to do that. The funeral had been paid for, as well as the Champagne that had been ordered for the wedding, and the next payment had been made on the renovations.

Mr Allanstone told her he would be on holiday for a couple of weeks in late May, but he would give them contact details, and they could talk about it at Pat's wedding on Saturday. He would be back well before the probate came through, and at that stage he would come to Hayward Hall for a few days so they could work out the details of the distribution. They would talk about how they were intending to invest it. He would like Jane to help with that so she could eventually take charge of her own inheritance money as well as Ryan's.

He seemed to be assuming that she and Ryan would be together permanently. Jane wished she could be as confident.

On Wednesday evening Jane went with Pat to the Black Horse Inn once more, telling herself that this would be the last time. The wedding was on Saturday. If Ryan was still cold and unresponsive to her after that, she was going back to Richmond. He was supposed to have phoned her on Tuesday night, and she had waited close to the phone for an hour after her programme had finished, but he had forgotten to call. Was he regretting that he had once wanted to sleep with her, that he had asked her to marry him that afternoon in the car? It all seemed so long ago now.

She sat with Pat and Claire at a table outside in the last of the daylight. Jimmy, David, Julie and Candy joined them again. The pub garden was much quieter than last week, with just the usual people who came out from town, and a few local farmers. The weather was not as warm as it had been the previous week, so perhaps the tourists were inside.

Jane wondered if Ryan would phone her this evening instead, since he had forgotten yesterday. Mary would tell him she was out at the inn with Pat and Claire. Jane hoped Mary wouldn't mention Jimmy.

They went through the last of the wedding arrangements. Everything had been booked and ordered. Claire had brought home the wide white ribbon for the cars, a gift from the lady who owned the shop where she worked, and some ribbons that matched the bridesmaid dresses for their hair. She would not be going back to work after the wedding and the honeymoon. The baby was due in early August, so Claire was to have a couple of months to set up her new home in the lodge. Jane did some sums in her head and realised the significance of Pat and Claire going missing on bonfire night.

The builders had nearly completed the work. The wallpaper had been replaced, the bathroom was finished, the coal cellar was now a modern cloakroom, the kitchen cupboards were being installed and the downstairs rooms now had quarry tiles on the floors. The glass for the conservatory had been installed last week.

When Pat and Claire returned from the honeymoon, they would spend a few weeks living either at the farm or at the Hall until the lodge renovations were complete, the new carpets were laid upstairs, and they had chosen the furniture. They hoped to be living there by the time the baby was born.

At closing time they all walked Candy and Julie home, and Pat and Jane left Claire, David and Jimmy at the farm gate. As they walked along the lane towards the Hall, Jane asked Pat where he and Claire had been on bonfire night, and he admitted they had been upstairs in his room, taking advantage of a rare time that they could be together in a house by themselves. They had sneaked down the back staircase by the kitchen after they heard Ryan come upstairs.

'Don't you two know you're supposed to take precautions?'

'We did,' Pat said. 'Those things are in drawers in nearly every room in the house. Trouble is after twenty years they weren't up to the job.'

Mary had been watching a film in her sitting room, and she had waited up for them.

'Ryan phoned,' she told Jane. 'The phones weren't working last night, so he was unable to call. I passed on the message from Mr Allanstone about the probate, and I told him you were with Pat and Claire at the pub, working out the last of the wedding arrangements. He'll be back on the four-twenty train tomorrow. He wants to wash and polish the cars on Friday.'

Jane felt very mean for thinking he had forgotten her. Now he would know she had gone out, and he would know Jimmy would have been there. Well perhaps a bit of jealousy wouldn't do any harm. If he hadn't been in Oxford, he could have come with them.

Thursday 13 May 1976

The architect came the following afternoon to check on progress at the lodge. Everything appeared to be going well. They were waiting for the kitchen worktops and the carpets.

Jane took him into the conservatory of the main house, and he showed her ways they could get electricity to it so they could install a light. There was a light in the cupboard below the landing of the main flight of stairs, so he thought they could take the power through the wall to the outside and have a light on the back wall. From there they could take the wires along the rafters to the point of the octagon and hang another light there. There were also wall lights in the billiard room and the kitchen, so wires could be taken through the wall to lights on the sides of the conservatory. All quite simple, Jane thought, surprised that it had not been done before. He recommended they didn't try to disguise the wires, but instead put them in a brass conduit from the lights to the switch. Brass light fittings would look good, perhaps something shaped like an old gaslight.

She showed him over the house, starting from the cellar and continuing through the ground floor to the narrow metal staircase behind the den and the billiard room. Upstairs she showed him the empty front guest rooms on the first floor, and Daniel's room on the top floor.

It still seemed strange to be in Daniel's room. She had only been in here twice before, both times after he had died, and she had felt he was close to her as she stood in the room with all of his things. The clock was still by the bed, collecting dust and forever silent.

The afternoon sun shafted through the window at the side of the house, filtering through the diamond panes, touching the photos of the beautiful young woman he had married all those years ago. Now they were both gone, leaving only a room filled with lingering sadness and silent emptiness.

She explained to the architect that this was her uncle's room and the photos were of his wife who had died many years before. She had brought him in here to show him how the ceiling sloped as soon as it cleared the top of the side windows, how the fireplace had been placed above one of the fireplaces in the lounge downstairs so the chimneys were together, for him to see the way the light came into the room in the afternoons and the view down to the stone-rimmed pond below with the occasional muted glimpse of an orange or yellow koi. The imperfections in the diamond panes of glass gave the view a soft touch of slightly blurred reality, like a Monet painting.

She had thought she could manage coming in here, but she remembered the day when they had found his uniform for him to be buried in, and her voice shook. She knew by the way he looked at her that the architect was a caring young man, like Ryan was, and could see she was upset.

'He used to tell me he would sometimes see his wife's ghost on the stairs, but when he got to the landing, she was always gone. He thought that one day she would still be there when he reached her, and then he would know he was dead and back with her. When he died, we found him in the hallway at the foot of the stairs, so I hope he saw her that night and is now back with her. I don't expect you believe in ghosts, Mr Miller, but he did, and I think that now I do as well.'

'I do believe in ghosts, Miss Walters, and I know they would now be back together. If you work with old houses like I do, you feel ghosts everywhere. Thank you for showing me the room. I am sorry that it has upset you to come in here. You have clearly thought about how the house goes together. Old houses like this need to be cared for by people who love them.'

They went right up to the attic with the lofty ceiling and the glorious round mullioned windows at each end, which illuminated the space, the gentle light filtering through the dust that lingered here with a patient disregard for time, unable to completely dispel the gloom of the shadowy twilit area between the sets of chimneys that came up through the attic. It was months, perhaps years, between the tread of anyone on the floorboards, the breath of anyone in the air.

Ryan had once told her that he felt that everything anyone said and thought was locked up in the stones of this house. Jane imagined the thoughts and the words stored up here beneath the stone tiles of the roof, in this dusty quiet space where time had no meaning. The words and the thoughts would whisper between the rafters, go back and forth in soft echoes in the shafts of light from the windows, touching the soft threads of spiders' silk, never encountering a soul who could hear the long dead voices or fathom the thoughts that were locked up here, adrift for all time.

They stood for a moment in the stillness, and she knew the architect also felt the whispers and the patient ghosts that dwelt here below the tiles. She could almost hear the voices of the four children who had played here more than seventy years before, the gentle echoes of their laughter.

'I feel that I could stand here forever,' he said to her. 'I'm sorry if that sounds a bit strange. This is a really magic place. It feels like time stands still here.'

'I feel like that too,' she told him. 'It doesn't sound strange to me. I do love this house. My father grew up here, and he met my mother here. It was his mother's home when she was a child. I have only been here for six months, but I feel as if I have lived here all my life. I feel like I belong in this house. I have never been up here before, only to the attic on the other side which is similar to this. Mary showed it to me when I first came here. She told me that my grandmother and her three brothers played up in the attics when they were children at the turn of the century, and she could feel their ghosts here.'

'I feel them too. We don't really understand time, and perhaps in some way they really are still here. Perhaps they can even sense us, as we do them. I'm not sure why the attic was designed like this. They could easily have divided it up into rooms for servants, with skylight windows. But it does give you a good way to check the roof beams are still sound, and that there are no leaks through the tiles.'

'Some of the beams are cracked,' Jane noticed.

'They're oak. It does crack, but it doesn't affect their strength, and they always used larger beams than they really needed to. This house is over a hundred years old, but some of the houses around here have beams that are three or four hundred years old. The most important thing with beams is to keep them dry.'

It was only after they returned downstairs that she remembered Pat had taken some magazines from Daniel's room up to the attic. It seemed he had remembered to dispose of them. She thought how embarrassed she would have been if they had still been lying there in full view.

She told the architect that the heating was very expensive to run, and asked what he thought about having individual radiators in each room, as he had suggested for the lodge. Would that cost less? Ryan had told her the cost of the oil had more than doubled over the last three years. In any case only the ground and the first floors were heated. The men slept on the second floor and had to do without.

He thought it would be cheaper, as the Aga would be expensive to run continuously, and the oil heating for the other side of the house would be less efficient than heating each room as required. There was no piped gas here, so they couldn't use that option. They would need to look at the cost of any extra sockets that were needed. They could add electric radiators to the top floor even if they left the other heating as it was at present. He recommended they ask an electrician to check the loading on the circuits so they didn't blow fuses if everyone heated their rooms at once. They might need to rewire, and they could talk to the electrician about that. He could recommend someone with experience in rewiring these old houses if she wanted him to.

Jane made coffee for them both, and Mary found them some fruit cake. He had a sketchbook with him, and he sat with her at the table in the conservatory and drew out a rough plan of the ground floor. Jane was amazed at how accurate it looked, as he had only seen the rooms once.

Then he showed her how the northwest aspect of the front of the house worked with the sun at various times of the day and of the year. In summer the late afternoon sun would touch the front windows, although deep into winter they were always in shade. He said that the aspect would have been dictated by the direction of the lane and the driveway and by the cellar that they had incorporated into the new house. You had to work with what you had.

The conservatory was placed to make the most of the sun in the morning, but was partly shaded in the afternoon by the west wing of the house so it didn't get too hot in summer. The present conservatory had been added later, but it would have replaced an earlier one, most likely smaller. The Victorians liked conservatories, so the house would have been built with one, and the fireplaces had served something. Although even they looked a little more modern, so the original conservatory may have had a stove or two instead to keep the plants warm, probably burning coal, possibly wood.

The guest dining room would have been used in the mornings to make the most of the light, the lounge and the library in the afternoons and evenings to harvest as much as possible of the warmth of the sun. The guest dining room would have been called the morning room when the house was built, while the lounge would have been called the drawing room. The dining room had less window area than the front rooms, but would have been light enough when it was used for breakfast on sunny mornings, and at dinner time light from windows was less important as it would be dark outside anyway for most of the year.

Jane told him how the gothic window on the landing flooded the hallway with sunlight in the daytime and with moonlight at night and how the small diamond panes with their imperfect glass filtered the light so you couldn't always quite make out the clouds in the sky or the stars at night.

He sketched how the staircase worked with the gallery around the first floor and the bridge across the top floor, and explained how the beams supporting the bridge would tie the two wings of the house together.

He gave her the sketch of the house, with the beautiful little suns with smiling faces, and a drawing of what he thought the light fittings for the conservatory might look like, and he wrote his phone number and his name on the corner of the page.

He said he didn't know how she was placed, and he didn't wish to offend her, but if she wanted to go out to lunch or dinner with him after the lodge was finished, he would like to get to know her better. If she was interested in architecture and old houses, he could take her to look at some of the National Trust ones.

She thanked him, said she would have liked to take him up on his offer, but she hoped to be engaged soon to her second cousin who now owned the house. She assured him that she was very flattered and not in the least offended.

He seemed to accept that, and he said that when she became the lady of the house, he hoped she would renovate it where required with the least possible change to the original design. He hadn't yet met the younger Mr Linden, as he had dealt only with her late uncle, but he was looking forward to doing so. He hoped her cousin loved the house as much as she did.

He told her the builder would contact him when the kitchen was finished and the carpet laid, and he would come back and sign off on the renovations so the final payment could be made. He thanked her for allowing him to look over the house, said if she wanted advice on any aspect of renovating it, she had his contact details. He left his card next to the sketch on the table.

When she had shown him out and waved as his car drove away, she returned to the conservatory and sat for a while by herself on the swing seat with the cat on her lap. Pat was working in the garden, Mary was in the kitchen, Ryan was in Oxford and Daniel had been gone for over seven weeks. She was finally getting used to him not being there. Although she did still miss his company during the day, she now had far less to do. She had long ago forgiven him for the night he had attacked her, and his past attack on her mother and Ryan was now deep in history. Nothing could change that, and the world had moved on. She only remembered how unhappy he was, and how he had never come to terms with losing the love of his life so tragically.

It was warm and light in here and very quiet, and she thought about the afternoon she had spent with the young architect, Alex Miller. She recalled Daniel once telling her the architect had his eye on her, although she had thought nothing of it at the time.

He seemed a perfectly nice young man. He had said he would like to take her out to dinner and get to know her better. He had cared that she was upset in Daniel's room, and they had stood for a moment up in the attic and shared their thoughts in the stillness. He hadn't tried to kiss her behind a haystack or patted her behind, or put his hand down her dress, or asked her to come back to his flat. He had simply asked for some time in her company. He wasn't tall dark and handsome like Ryan was, but that would not have mattered to her if she had wanted to go out with him. He was pleasant enough to look at. She was not going out with him, she was already spoken for, but somehow the whole world had changed for her.

She had been at Hayward Hall for over six months. She was still only nineteen years old. In early August she would be twenty, no longer a teenager but a young woman who could shape her own destiny in life. Perhaps Claire's baby would be born on her birthday, as it was due around the same day. She had lost a lot of people that she loved, and when she had first come here, she had been an emotional wreck, desperate for a port in a storm, craving for someone to care for her. She had found Ryan. But now she knew that if she had to, she could stand on her own feet. She was not sure if Ryan really wanted her the way she wanted him. He was a lone wolf, and she thought he liked being a lone wolf. Perhaps lone wolves could never really change the way they felt about themselves and their place in the world. He was smitten, he had told her, as if it was her fault for smiting him. He was concerned he was nothing to her but a conquest. Suppose he had got over being smitten and wanted to return to being a lone wolf? He had already gone back to spending as much time as he could in his college in Oxford, and he never tried to kiss her or make love to her, yet now there was nothing to stop him.

Yesterday she would have felt herself on the edge of an abyss even thinking about it, but today she found she could face it. It would take her a long time to get over loving him, but she knew she could. In the space of a few hours on a warm afternoon her whole perception of things had changed, thanks to a shy offer from an unassuming young man whom she scarcely knew. She now felt she would be able to go back to Richmond and live there by herself. Sooner or later there would be another young man who would ask her out hoping to get to know her better, not just wanting to kiss her and take her back to his flat for the night to make her another of his conquests, not just unashamedly wanting her for her money as Pat had, or for her favours as Daniel had, or in spite of himself as Ryan seemed to.

Today was Thursday. Pat's wedding was on Saturday. Then she and Ryan would decide whether they would stay together or go their separate ways. That was what they had agreed on that long-ago day sitting in the car at the gate. He appeared to be sticking to that timeline even though the wedding had been postponed. He didn't seem to be in any hurry.

There was no in between; she knew she couldn't live here with him unless they were lovers. She wanted him, she desperately wanted him, but if he didn't want her, she knew she would be able to walk away from here and live by herself in her house in Richmond, making herself a new life either on her own or with someone she was yet to meet. It would be hard at first, but she could do it. She recalled Sarah telling her they could find her a boyfriend, assuring her there were lots of perfectly nice young men in the world. She didn't even need a boyfriend. She could live by herself, enjoy life on her own, go back to working at the bank and eventually become a manageress. She could study accounting, she could even go to university, as she had enough money to support herself for a few years without needing to work. She had been offered a place at Cambridge when she had finished sixth form and her headmistress had encouraged her to accept it, reminding her that her father would have wanted her to continue studying after she left school. But with her parents dead and her aunt being rather frail by then and needing Jane to live with her at the house in Richmond, it hadn't been practical, and she had taken a job at the bank instead.

If she went back to live at Richmond, she could still come here and see Mary sometimes, or even buy herself a house closer to here. Perhaps she and Ryan could still remain friends. She could take up the young architect on his offer of dinner, look over some country houses with him as he had suggested. She knew she didn't want to stay at Hayward and marry Jimmy. She could never be a farmer's wife. And it would be unfair on Jimmy because if she stayed living close to Ryan, she would never stop loving him. The only thing she dreaded would be if she left here and then Ryan married someone else. She knew that was one thing she could never, ever, come to terms with.

But she did still hope that things would work out. She wanted to stay here with Ryan, and she would do everything she could to persuade him that he wanted her. He always talked as if he wanted her. He just didn't behave as if he did.

She took the tray with the mugs and the plates with the crumbs from the fruit cake back to Mary in the kitchen. It was nearly time for Ryan to return—Pat had already left to collect him—so she returned to the swing seat, and the cat jumped back onto her lap. It was still light this far into the spring. The sun had not yet set, but it was shaded by the west wing of the house from where she was sitting. She hoped Ryan would not be cross with her for going out last night, but if he had been at home, she would have wanted him to come with them. Not that he was ever cross with her.

He found her, sat beside her, apologised for not phoning her on Tuesday, but he didn't mention Wednesday night and neither did she. It was warm enough in the conservatory without a blanket, but she didn't need a blanket now to hide them holding hands, as there was no one to care. She put her hand into his. It was no good waiting for him to make the first move; he never did. With her other hand she stroked the cat.

She told him that Mr Allanstone had called about the probate and would send them an estimate of how much they each would have when the estate was divided up. It should arrive in the post tomorrow.

She said the architect had called by to check on progress at the lodge. He had talked with her about how they could put lights here in the conservatory and how they could heat the top floor rooms with electric radiators and perhaps eventually replace the expensive radiator system so the Aga was only running when it was needed for cooking. She had shown him some of the rooms in the house, and he had drawn diagrams for her of how it was designed to work with the sun across the year.

The sketch he had drawn was still on the table, with his name and phone number in the corner. His card was sitting next to it. Jane realised that the number he had given her on the sketch did not match the office number on his card. He had given her his home number. She hoped Ryan wouldn't notice that, or if he did, that he would not realise the significance of it.

She asked him if he knew what had become of the magazines that Pat had found.

'We made a bonfire behind the stables and burned them when we knew you and Mary were busy. Pat joked about sending them to the parish jumble sale. They were the real thing; don't even try to imagine what was in them. One was called *Teenage Babes*. They weren't wearing much and neither were the grey-haired men who were enjoying their favours. They may have been legal. The girls may have been eighteen, although they looked much younger. But I'm glad the police didn't come across them, and that you and Mary didn't see them. We don't know where he got them from, but I promise they are now gone.'

But she had something else to tell him, something that she had almost forgotten.

'Your father told me something once that I meant to tell you, but it went out of my head when he died. I know what happened to the young lady he paid to sleep with you. He said he did it to make amends for the other woman who had tried to seduce you when you were younger, and he swore he hadn't put her up to it. He said he was as shocked as your grandmother was, and he never had anything to do with the woman again. He said he brought the young lady here for your birthday because he wanted you to have a better experience after the first one.'

'What did he say happened to her?'

'He liked the way she looked, so he asked for her next time he went to London, and he set her up with a rented flat and visited her there. He would have brought her back here to live with him, but he knew you would recognise her and tell your grandmother what had happened. She still worked for the escort agency, as he only got to see her every couple of weeks. The agency made a date for her with a man whose second wife had run off to Canada with his best friend. He took a liking to her and he eventually married her, so he got a beautiful young wife who was good in bed and who would stay faithful because she had too much to lose if she didn't.'

'When did he tell you this?'

'It was only a few days before he died. I think it was the day before we went to London to collect the bridesmaid dresses. We had walked to the village to post the cheque to the builder, and I sat with him in the church. He told me what had happened to make my father leave here, and he said he was sorry for what he did to you, he had always regretted it, and he never knew what had possessed him. He told me he thanked God that you had recovered even though he didn't believe in God, and that he could not have lived with himself if he had killed you because you were all that was left of his love for his wife. He told me he had found a rope in the stables and worked out which beam to use to hang himself if you died. That would have been the rope you found years later.

'I know you always wanted him to love you, and perhaps he did in his way. But I think he was just incapable of feeling love like you and I would, except perhaps for your mother. Some people are like that, and it isn't their fault, or yours. It's just one of those sad things in life.

'He said he sometimes imagined what life would have been like if Caroline hadn't died. He thought you would have been able to respect him, and you would have grown up more confident and successful instead of living like a hermit to get away from him. And Mary could have gone to live with her lover. He wanted her to live with him as his wife, but she had to look after you and help run the house here with Caroline gone.

'He was a lonely man who had a tragedy in his life that he never recovered from, and I did feel very sorry for him. I couldn't love him the way he wanted, but I did care about him. I enjoyed helping him, and I always understood when he wanted me to talk to him and when he didn't. He said he had loved Caroline beyond anything. They had been through a war together, and then she had died because a heel had broken on her shoe. Then twice he had tried to love again, and both times he had been cursed by fate. There was no excuse for what he did to you and to my mother, but he spoke to me as though he felt he was a victim too. Perhaps that was how he managed to live with himself after what he had done.

'I felt completely out of my depth when he told me all this. I didn't know what to say to him. I did try to tell him that he could make amends by letting us be lovers. I could still be here for him, and do all the things we did together, but I just wouldn't be married to him. I suggested he could go to London if he needed someone to sleep with. But then he said he couldn't do it, he wanted me too much, and if I slept with you, he would kill us both and himself as well. He really frightened me when he said that.

'I have never read any of his books apart from the one I was typing for him, but Tony said the heroes are young men who sleep with women but never actually care about them. I think your father made himself a fantasy world where women were just there for sex. If you don't love someone you can't get hurt.

'I can understand if you never forgive him for what he did to you, but I have forgiven him for attacking me. Although I still feel it was my fault he died that night, and I should have handled him better than I did.

'He was always telling me he wanted me to go upstairs with him. He said he didn't care if I didn't love him, I could just lie on the bed and close my eyes and pretend it was you making love to me, and he would look after everything and it would feel good for me. He said he would even take my clothes off, and he would enjoy doing that. I never agreed of course, but he was so unhappy that I felt very guilty that I didn't want him making love to me. I wished I could love him the way he wanted me to. Please don't laugh. I never laughed at him.'

'Sorry,' he said. 'I would enjoy doing that too. I often think about it.'

'Do you, Ryan? Now please behave yourself and stop laughing.' Well at least he did still want her.

'Jane, you should never, ever feel guilty because you don't want to sleep with a man. It is entirely your right to choose, and he should never have been asking you in the first place. It was completely selfish of him to treat you like that when he knew you didn't want him to. And so totally repugnant. How could any man want to make love to a woman who only agreed to it because she was pretending that he was someone else?

'I know you see him as a victim as well. I think that you were at least slightly in love with him, and I don't begrudge him that. You think it romantic that he loved his wife so much, but can you just try to see things from the point of view of those around him.

'He thought how things would have been different if my mother had lived. But apart from his own loss, which I can understand would have been dreadful for him, all those other good things would still have happened if he had tried to accept that she was gone and controlled his anger at the way life had treated him. He thought your mother was sent to him by fate. He only thought that because he was so obsessed with my mother and couldn't cope with her being gone. He didn't care whether Josie loved him or not. She was just there to replace his wife and make him feel whole again. When it didn't happen in the way he thought it should, he tried to ruin her happiness and that of his cousin, who had been like a brother to him, who had always loved and supported him and had helped him cope when his wife died. I was just collateral damage.

'If he had accepted that my mother was gone and tried to get on with his life as everyone around him was trying to help him to do, then Peter and Josie could have stayed here when they married, leaving Mary free to leave and live with Pat's father, and he would never have attacked me the way he did, so I could have grown up loving and respecting him—perhaps even understanding and accepting that he couldn't love me—and with your father still part of my life. You would have been part of our life as well. Pat and I always thought you belonged here with us when we saw the photos of you that your father sent to Mary. And, yes, perhaps I would have been more confident and more successful.

'Then when you came, he did the same thing all over again. He wanted you because he thought you could replace his wife, and he didn't care that you didn't want to marry him or that I loved you. He tried to keep us apart. You were really good to him and really good for him. He had company when he went for walks, you did the typing for him and paid the bills, you helped him to cut down on the whisky, and you treated him as if you cared about him. You even danced that tango with him because he said he had once loved to tango with my mother. He repaid you by trying to force you to sleep with him instead of accepting that you loved him but not in the way he wanted. It was totally and utterly selfish of him.

'Mary once told me that before you came to live with us—after Allanstone had asked Mary if you could stay here for a while after your great-aunt died—my father had talked to her about you and I possibly getting involved with each other, and how good that would be for me and they hoped for you as well. Then when he saw you, he decided he wanted you for himself so he could go back to having the woman he had loved and lost all those years ago.

'There are some things in life which we can't control, and people dying tragically is one of them. What we can control is our decision to accept that bad things happen and move forward with our lives. However angry we feel, we can control the way we react to things and how we treat others. Our consciousness, and our ability to understand that all of our actions have consequences, gives us the free will to choose between right and wrong. And we have a responsibility to avoid hurting other people.

'I am glad that he told you he regretted what he did to me and to Josie—that does make me feel a little better about what happened—but I can't think of him as a victim the way you do. His obsession with my mother, his bitterness and anger over losing her, didn't just wreck his own life. He allowed it to damage the lives of everyone around him. If he had accepted that she was gone and tried to go forward, all of us would have lived much happier lives here.'

The sun was now low behind the garden wall, so the lawn below the terrace was in shade, but it still touched the treetops in the wood with a soft glow of rose. This late in the spring it was still a while before dusk would merge into darkness.

He sat beside her, saying nothing more, still holding her hand. But it was time for dinner. Pat had been sent to fetch them and the cat had already wandered off to the kitchen in search of hers.

Friday 14 May 1976

Friday arrived with gentle sunshine and warm spring weather. Only one more day to go before Pat's wedding.

Last night Sarah had telephoned while Jane was at yoga, and Ryan had spoken to her, promising that Jane would call her this morning. While Ryan drove Mary into town to do the shopping, Jane stayed at the Hall and phoned her friend.

Sarah wanted to know how the wedding plans were going, and whether the dresses had all fitted well.

'I had a really interesting conversation with Ryan last night,' she continued when Jane had assured her everything was under control. 'I asked him when you two were getting married. I know it was a bit cheeky of me. He said he wanted to marry you, but he had a rival, a handsome young farmer. I told him he was not to allow the farmer to win, you were a city girl, and I couldn't imagine you herding sheep in tweeds and wellingtons. But he just laughed, and said you would look lovely whatever you wore, and you looked especially nice in the dress I had helped you choose for the dinner. He said he was planning to take you to the seaside in the summer so he could see you in a swimsuit. He is so funny at times, Jane. You would be mad if you let him get away. I still laugh every time I pick up my feather duster, although Tony told me that Ryan had made up that story. Promise you'll marry Ryan if he asks you and not the farmer.'

Jane promised, but she felt a tiny bit cross with Ryan. Here he was, telling everyone else he wanted to marry her, but not telling her. She asked Sarah to send her best birthday wishes to Tony's father for his sixtieth birthday party tomorrow. She remembered meeting him at Sarah's wedding.

After morning coffee, she washed her hair, set it in rollers, and sat in her room while she dried it with the hairdryer.

That afternoon Jane helped Pat and Ryan wash and polish the cars. She couldn't wear a swimsuit, but she could wear her new denim shorts. Perhaps if Ryan saw a bit more of her, he might want to sleep with her.

He did tell her, in that amused way of his, that she looked nice in the shorts, but that was all. Even that awful young detective had looked at her as if he found her attractive and would like to make love to her, but Ryan never did.

When the cars were so shiny you could almost see your reflection in them, they had afternoon tea, and Jane gave the men's shirts a final press.

The rings were already in the pocket of Ryan's jacket. All Pat and Ryan had to do tomorrow was to put on their white shirts, the dark-blue brocaded silk waistcoats and the immaculate black suits, tie the bow-ties, and arrange the little floral buttonholes that would be delivered to the house by one of the McCann boys around lunchtime.

But they had to be trusted to do all that by themselves, as neither Jane nor Mary would be there to help.

Ryan was sitting on the bench in the boot room after dinner, polishing his own and Pat's shoes, while Mary was setting up a pastry board and rolling pin to make jam tarts for the supper that would be served at the village hall partway through the dancing. Jane and Pat were still drying the dishes from dinner.

A knock at the back door heralded the arrival of the four McCann boys, with Winston and Adrian, to take Pat to the pub for a stag night.

'We only just remembered,' Jimmy explained. 'The best man should organise it. You're not doing your job, Ryan. You have to come as well.'

'I'm polishing shoes,' Ryan protested. 'We can't arrive tomorrow with scuffed shoes.'

'I'll finish them,' Jane offered. 'Please go with them, Ryan, so they stay out of trouble.'

'You can come with us too if you want, Jane,' Jimmy offered, but David would have none of it.

'Of course she can't. She's a girl. This is men only.'

'Some of you are not old enough to drink,' Mary said doubtfully. 'Does your father know about this?'

'Yes, he does. He will be there himself with Mr Phillips. They usually meet there on Friday night to talk about sheep. Don't worry, Miss Linden. Paul and Brian will have ginger beer, Adrian will as well, and Winston is eighteen now. It's only fair they get included in the stag night, since they are all helping tomorrow.'

'You are all to come straight home after closing,' Jane told them. 'Pat is taking Mary to the station very early tomorrow so she can see her friend and be back in time for the wedding.'

'Yes, Miss,' said Jimmy, saluting her, and the young men disappeared into the night, leaving Jane and Mary to the drying up, the shoes and the cooking.

The shoes were finished, the polish and brushes stowed back in their box in the boot room. Jane washed her hands to help with the tarts.

'Are you and Ryan getting engaged?' Mary asked her. 'You seem to be taking your time about it.'

'I don't think he really wants to marry anyone. He asked me once if I wanted to, but I wasn't absolutely sure then, so he said we would wait until Pat was married and he would ask me again. So I am still hoping. He did actually kiss me once. We had been out to dinner in London, and we were both a bit tipsy, but he never did it again. After Daniel died, he became quite cold.'

'Jane, I think you may have to give him some encouragement. He was always a quiet controlled boy who never did anything he thought was wrong. When two people care about each other, making love is the most beautiful thing in the world. It is only when it's just lust and you don't care about the other person that it becomes sordid. That was the only side of it that Ryan saw. His experiences of relationships between men and women were the mistresses his father brought home when he was younger, and watching his father try to rape your mother when he was a child. He even told us he could never forget the image of a man forcing himself on a terrified woman. You were brought up in a home with a mother and father who loved and respected each other. He wasn't.'

'Mary, how do I give him encouragement? I can't just throw myself at him.'

'Just let him know you're serious about wanting him. It can't be too hard. Tomorrow you will dance with him again; that's a good start. The last evening before Daniel died, it was so good to see you dancing together, although Daniel had to spoil it with his raging jealousy. And Ryan was happy enough dancing a tango with you last Sunday. There is nothing quite like dancing for getting men and women together. You can get right up close when you dance, and it's perfectly acceptable. And it is just the two of you by yourselves even though you are in a room full of people. By their very nature weddings are romantic for the other people there. The married people remember their own weddings, the young people plan for their turn, and everyone wonders who will be married next. And there is Champagne of course. That always helps overcome a bit of shyness.

'And if you want Ryan, don't flirt with Jimmy. I don't say that you have led him on, but don't be surprised if you get a proposal from him before tomorrow's out. Weddings do that to people. He would be more fun than Ryan, he's a steady enough young man and much closer to you in age, and I wouldn't blame you if you made that choice. But I've seen Ryan grow up, and I know he would be desperately unhappy if you married someone else. I don't think he would ever get over it. He's not as confident as he pretends. If he thinks you prefer Jimmy to him, he'll give up at the first hurdle. Men have a deep-down fear of being rejected by women. If you want him, go up to his room in the night—not tonight because you both need to concentrate tomorrow—but one night soon. Perhaps tomorrow after he dances with you at the wedding and while he is still under the influence of the Champagne. He will need to know you want him before he will admit he wants you. I put a couple of extra pillows in his room here when you two were staying in Richmond, in case you wanted to sleep upstairs with him. I don't know what he thought about it, but he didn't say anything.'

The tarts were now in the oven, the timer ticking, the cake cooler waiting on the table.

'Mary, does Pat's father know he is getting married? Do you still see him?'

'Yes, I do see him, and yes, he does know about Pat. He was married, and it was impossible for him to divorce his wife and marry me, or he would have done. He did care about her, but it was all a bit complicated.

'I was very young, not even seventeen, when he came here to stay with Daniel for a few days. They had been at school together and had kept in touch. He was a lot older than me, but I instantly liked him. I was walking in the garden with Ryan, who was three then. He came out and found us. My mother had told him I would show him the garden if he asked. We walked with Ryan between us, both of us holding his hands. He told me he had once had a daughter, but she had died at birth, and it had been soul destroying. Her name was Rosemary, and she would have been four by then if she had lived. He told me he was married, but after she lost the baby, his wife had lost her reason, thinking everyone was trying to kill her and then lapsing into dementia. Apparently, that does sometimes happen when women have children. Usually the women recover, but his wife never did. He loved her very deeply, and he wished he could do something to help her. His mother looked after her in Kent while he worked in London. He had a small flat in Kensington near where he worked, and he just went home on weekends.

'I told him how baby Ryan had been very small when he was born, and how I had gone to the hospital every day to look after him. I showed him over the garden, and he knew the names of all the flowers. He said his mother had a beautiful garden and grew many of the same flowers as we did. We went into the maze because Ryan always liked to do that, and I teased him about leaving him there. He laughed and asked Ryan if he knew the way out, and he followed him. Ryan already knew it by heart. We disagreed on the name of a flower, so we looked it up in a book in the library here, and it turned out both names were right. He said it was good to talk to someone who knew about flowers and asked if I had ever seen Kew Gardens. Then he offered to meet me in London, take me somewhere for lunch with him, and we would go to Kew Gardens and see flowers from all over the world. He seemed very kind and very lonely, and quite harmless, so I said I would come.

'I told my mother I was going across to London on the train to meet with an old school friend for shopping, and she accepted that. I often shopped by myself in Oxford, and I did sometimes meet friends in London. We were never intending to deceive her, but I couldn't tell her I was meeting a married man. She would never have allowed me to go.

'For a long time, well over a year, we had lunch together almost every Saturday, and we walked in parks if it was fine and in museums and galleries if it was wet. He had never intended to seduce me. He just wanted company, and he really did have a love of plants. He was a rather lonely man, living by himself in the week then going home to spend Sunday with his mother, who he dearly loved, and a wife he could no longer hold a sensible conversation with.

'By then I was hopelessly in love with him. I lived for the weekends when I would see him, and scarcely concentrated on anything during the week when I helped with the house and the guests. I don't know how my mother didn't realise it was a man I was meeting, but she didn't. I just liked to be in his company. I would hold his arm as we walked, but he never otherwise touched me or I him. Then one day we were caught in a sudden rainstorm, his umbrella blew inside out, and we were soaked to the skin before we could reach shelter. We were in Kensington Gardens, not far from his flat, so we went back there, and he hung my dress and petticoat and his jacket over a radiator while I stood shivering in a shirt of his, and he found a hairdryer for my hair. I had let it out of its bun, and he was running his fingers through it while he dried it.

Things just happened from there, one thing led to another, and it all got out of control. We were a man and a woman who wanted nothing more in the world than to be with each other. I was scarcely eighteen and he was fifteen years older than me, but neither of us ever thought about that. He asked me to move to London and live with him in the flat as his wife. He would buy me a wedding ring and give me anything I wanted. He would never be able to divorce his wife because she was of unsound mind and would never be legally able to agree. Divorces were much harder to get then. She also lived with his mother, which complicated things because he could never take me to his home. He asked me to think about it. Then he said he was sorry for what had happened, and he helped me put on my petticoat and my dress and said he would understand if I didn't want to come again. He took me back to the station, waited until I was on the train as he usually did, and caught his own train to Kent where he spent Saturday nights and Sundays with his mother and his wife.

'I phoned him in the week to tell him I had thought it over. I couldn't leave my mother to run the bed and breakfast alone with Ryan to look after—he was four by then—and I thought that living a lie would be too complicated for both of us. But I told him I loved him, and I was happy to continue to meet him if that suited him. Of course it did suit him; he was relieved that I was not breaking it off altogether. He said we could go back to walking in parks, he just wanted to be with me, that the year we had been meeting had been the happiest of his life. The next Saturday we had lunch, and walked for about half an hour in Kensington Gardens, and he didn't say anything about what had happened. Then I asked if we could go to his flat. Once you get a taste of it, you get hooked on it. It's just nature.

'In spite of us taking precautions, a little over a year later I knew I was expecting Pat. Again he offered for me to live with him, but again I said no. He wanted me to keep the baby, as he had no other children, and he would support me financially. He hoped that one day we could marry or just be together, and he could be part of our baby's life.

'My mother was shocked when it became obvious that I had a baby on the way, but she took it in her stride. At first she asked if the father was Peter, as I didn't have a boyfriend that she knew about, so I had to tell her the man was married, he had offered for me to live with him, and he was prepared to support us, pay for schooling and so forth, and give me some money for myself. The welfare people sometimes took babies from single mothers for adoption in those days, but there was no problem about our baby being allowed to stay with us at Hayward. If you wanted to keep the child and you had somewhere to live and some means of support, they left you alone.

'Eventually his mother died. She had been ill for some time, and before she died, he told her about me and that she had a grandson, but I never met her. His wife was put into a nursing home, so we could have lived quite openly in Kent with Pat, but by then my mother had arthritis, and it was difficult for her to do a lot of the work she had used to do. So I had the house to run, and I could never have left Ryan with only his father to look after him. He was around sixteen then. Daniel was always trying to get him to drink whisky, and he could never have been left in charge of him with my mother unable to do much. We could have taken Ryan with us as well, but I knew Daniel would never have allowed us to, and neither would my mother.

'So we just stayed as we were, and most Saturdays I met him in London. After my mother died Ryan was old enough to look after himself and he lived at the college most of the time, but we had got used to the way we both lived, and I didn't like to leave Daniel here by himself.'

'Will he come to the wedding tomorrow to see his son married?' Jane asked.

'Yes, he is planning to come back with me. But please don't tell the boys yet.'

The tarts were by now cooling. Mary found a second-best glass plate—in case it was lost or broken—a paper doily and a cake tin.

'We need to remember to bring the plate and tin home,' she said, and the subject of her secret lover appeared closed.

They went back over the arrangements for the following morning. Jane was to go to the farm at eleven, taking the tarts with her for Anne to deliver to the village hall for the supper. Ryan would drive her to the farm in the Rover, leave it there, and walk back. Jane would dress at the farm and help dress Claire and the other two bridesmaids. Pat and Ryan would have to look after their own suits and bow-ties and were to drive to the church in Ryan's Jaguar just after two thirty. Mary would come back from London on the train a little after two and would take a taxi to reach the church by half past. She was taking her dress with her and would change at her friend's house before she returned. At a quarter to three Jimmy would drive Claire and Jack to the church in Daniel's Rover. The bridesmaids would follow in the farm Land Rover with David driving. The distance was short, but the bride still needed to arrive in a car. The smallest bridesmaid Daisy would be at the church dressed and waiting for them. The two youngest McCann boys and the two Phillips boys were the ushers. They were to ensure only the family and close associates sat in the first three pews, and give out the printed leaflets with the programme for the service.

After the wedding there would be photos in the churchyard, and then everyone would walk to the village hall for the reception. The speeches and toasts would be made, and everyone would have dinner. After the meal the wedding cake would be cut up, and there was to be dancing until ten to music by the band from town, with supper served partway through. Most of the people who lived in Hayward village and the surrounding farms had been invited, as well as some McCann cousins.

The caterers from town would supply the buffet dinner, and the guests were bringing cupcakes, scones and tarts for the supper. Tea and coffee would be available as well as lemonade for the children.

Mr Austin, the landlord of the Black Horse Inn, was in charge of the drinks at the wedding. He would provide beer, cider and whisky, and serve the Champagne which had been ordered from London. The inn would stay open with his brother in charge.

Mary went to bed at ten, as she was leaving very early in the morning.

Jane waited up until the men came home, Pat a little intoxicated and Ryan apologising for it. Pat went upstairs to bed, refusing Jane's offer of cocoa and complaining he felt rather sick, with Ryan following to ensure he didn't slip on the stairs.

'If you wait up for a while longer, I'll come back down and make the cocoa,' Ryan offered.

Jane made the cocoa herself while she waited. She opened the cake tin, took out one of the tarts, and carefully cut it in half. Mary would never think to count them in the morning.

'Did it all go okay?' she asked when he returned and was sitting opposite her at the table with his mug and half tart. 'We finished making the tarts, and Mary told me some really interesting things, but it will wait until tomorrow.'

'I have spent the whole evening listening to an upstart and rather tipsy young farmer telling me and everyone else how wonderful you are, and that he is going to marry you. Now Daniel is gone he decided I was the one he had to ask for permission. He actually admitted he would never have dared to ask my father.'

'Did you give your permission?' she asked, trying to keep a straight face. Maybe a bit of jealousy wouldn't be a bad thing.

'I was inclined to say no, and tell him he is nowhere near good enough for you, but I was gracious and said the decision had to be entirely yours. I felt like knocking him over, but he is heavier than me, and I don't think it would have looked good if one or both of us had arrived tomorrow with a black eye. Jane, you are not seriously going to marry him, are you? You must have encouraged him, or he wouldn't be talking like that.'

She wanted to ask him if he would really care if she did, but she knew it was not the time for games. He was clearly upset, and she knew she had no right to blame him for not trusting her.

'No, of course I'm not marrying him. And I have never led him to think so. He is the one who does the flirting. We are good friends and always will be, but we are not lovers, and he should not have talked as if we were. You're not cross with me, are you?'

He seemed relieved. 'No, not at all. But I am cross with him. That's what comes from kissing young men behind castle walls. Sometimes they think you mean it. You are going to have to stop doing that, or sooner or later you will get into trouble.'

You kissed me once, she thought, and I did mean it, but nothing came of it. But she didn't say it.

'These tarts taste good,' he said, and her opportunity was gone. 'The suppers are always good at these functions. No one will go home hungry. Usually Mary makes scones, but that wasn't practical this time, as they are nicer when fresh. Jane, there is something I have been meaning to ask you, and something else I want to tell you.'

He paused for a moment and her heart leapt. Proposal and *I love you*, she hoped. This time she would say yes straight away. She was not going to give him another chance to change his mind.

'When the Trinity term is finished and I am back living here all the time, I would like us to get a dog. I asked Mary and she doesn't mind. Would you mind?'

For a moment she was speechless with disappointment. It was so different from what she had been hoping he would say.

'No, of course I don't mind. But the cat might not like it.'

'That cat will cope with anything, and the dog would not be allowed upstairs, but Jasmine would, so she could feel very superior. Cats enjoy that. There are often puppies available from one or other of the farms, so I will ask around.

'Something else I want to tell you. This morning when I took Mary to the shops in town, I took my father's digitoxin tablets for disposal at the chemist, and I asked about the new sort of sleeping pills. They are doxylamine which is an antihistamine, rather than diazepam which is the ingredient in Valium. You don't even need a prescription for them, so I bought some to try. Then I asked him some things I wanted to know about Valium. It doesn't dissolve in water, so you can't spike someone's glass of water with it, but apparently it does dissolve better in other things. It dissolves to some extent in milk because of the fat content, so okay in coffee if you make it with all milk. But, more importantly, it does dissolve very well in alcohol. He thought you may have a little residue, but if it was whisky, rather than pure alcohol, the base would dissolve almost completely in the water component and the diazepam in the alcohol. He did think you might notice the taste, but he said he wasn't a whisky drinker, so he didn't know. He asked me, jokingly, if I was trying to murder someone or do away with myself, and said it wouldn't work because Valium is not all that toxic, although it is addictive. He said if I switched to the doxylamine, I should bring the Valium back to him to be disposed of safely. I left it at that of course. He knew my father had recently died, and I had Valium in the house, so I didn't want him making the connection.

'So I thought about the bottle being next to the whisky decanter, and I tried to piece together how it could possibly have got there. The police thought he may have taken the bottle back to the den with thoughts of overdosing on them, but if he really had wanted to kill himself, he knew he only had to take two or three of his digoxin tablets. Mary thought he may have got the bottles mixed up, but I honestly don't think he would have. He was too careful for that. He always took the digitoxin bottle with him in his pocket when he went out walking and he didn't get the bottles mixed up then. If he really had wanted to take a Valium tablet to help him sleep, he would have taken it in the kitchen and left the bottle there. Even he would swallow a tablet with water rather than whisky.

'So how did the bottle get into the den? The police didn't even find his fingerprints on it. You were locked in your room, and Pat didn't know we had Valium in the house. I asked him afterwards. He only knew they were mine when he picked up the bottle in the den and my name was on the label. He remembered then that I had sleeping pills, and he was worried my father had deliberately overdosed on them. I knew it wasn't me, so that only left Mary.

'After you had gone to bed that night, Pat and I went up, leaving Mary tidying up the mugs. Pat had checked on Daniel and said he was asleep in the chair in his den. He checked him again between midnight and one o' clock, as he knew Mary was worried about him, and he was still asleep. He told me the bottle wasn't there then because he checked how much whisky was left, and he knew he would have seen it, as it was next to the decanter when he found it in the morning. But he just told the police he couldn't remember.

'I think Mary wanted my father to stay asleep in the den so he didn't try to get into your room in the night. He did sometimes fall asleep in the den and stay there all night. Perhaps she dissolved the tablet in the glass of whisky knowing that if he woke up, he would have another drink before he went upstairs. But then she would have put the tablets back in the kitchen. She would never have left them in the den where he could have seen them. That bothered me for a while.

'But the next morning she had been the first of us to get up. She always gets up earlier than I do to cook the porridge. She knew that Daniel was dead, and she knew that they would find traces of the Valium in his blood, so perhaps she put the bottle in the den to look as though he had taken them himself from the kitchen. I imagine she did something with the glass as well, probably she rinsed it out in the kitchen so there were no traces of dissolved Valium and refilled it.

'I talked to the inspector at the funeral, and he said the Valium by itself was not what killed him. Although if he really had taken it by mistake for his digitoxin, then that may have contributed to his death, as the combination of the two drugs can be lethal. If he had taken only the digitoxin, he may not have died that night. The inspector said we will eventually get a report from the coroner on why he died, and he thought it unlikely that they would want an inquest, as they were satisfied that he had died from natural causes. He said it was to do with bruising. If your heart has stopped pumping blood before you fall, the bruising is a lot less. And he had no injuries from the fall that would have been fatal by themselves.

'He also said that me and Pat manhandling him to protect you had not caused any injuries that would have contributed to his death, so we would not be charged over that. There was nothing that could not be considered reasonable force in the circumstances.

'The inspector was very courteous to me that day. He was sorry that they had suspected me before they knew why my father had died. He explained that they needed to question people as soon as they could so they didn't forget anything. He said it had looked dodgy that there had been an argument the night before, your face was bruised and Daniel was at the foot of the stairs, so they had been obliged to investigate it, as that was their job. If he had collapsed and died anywhere else in the house, or if you had not had a bruise on your face, they would not have pursued it unless there had been a break-in, or the post-mortem had turned up something suspicious. He said he thought you coped very well after what had happened to you, you were a very lovely young lady, he was sad my father had treated you the way he did, and he hoped things worked out well for us all. I told Mary that the Valium was not what had killed him, as I didn't want her to think it was her fault that he had died if she really had given it to him.

'In the end the person who benefits most from my father's death is Mary. You and I would have walked out of the house in the morning to a new life, and Pat was leaving to be married. She would have been left here to look after Daniel, as he could never have managed this house on his own. He was always her adored older brother, and she loved him above anyone else. She would never have deserted him no matter what he had done; she was always making excuses for him.

'But she must have resented all those years of trying to keep him under control, the drinking, the mistresses and then his pursuit of you. It was a terrible strain for us all, trying to keep up the appearance of a civilised household, trying to avoid him flying into a rage, trying to stop him drinking before we went to church, keeping the guns locked up for fear he would kill himself when he got depressed.

'All those years ago when he attacked Josie and me, he would have gone to prison for what he did if we hadn't all kept quiet about it, your mother in particular. I never knew whether he raped her or just tried to, but either way he could have been charged.'

Jane did know, as Daniel had told her, but she said nothing. Perhaps Ryan would feel better believing that he may have saved Josie from the worst of his father's attack on her.

'Mary is scarcely forty. I know you think forty is one foot in the grave, but it is really still quite young. She is beautiful and elegant, and now she is also well off. She could easily find someone to marry if she wanted to, or she could just go and live with Pat's father. All her life she has looked after us. She was fourteen when I was born, and she had to look after me because my own mother was dead. She had to leave school. The headmistress was against her leaving because she always did very well at school, but my grandmother didn't have much choice as she had to run the bed and breakfast and look after a baby and Daniel. After that Mary had Pat to look after, and she couldn't leave here with him because my grandmother needed her help running the place. Peter had left, and I was still only six. Then she looked after my grandmother when she was frail, she still had us boys to look after, and Daniel needed her to run the household. She is the only one of us who has never been free to leave here.

'But now she can leave if she wants to because you and I can look after ourselves. I hope she stays here with us, but I have often wondered if the friend she visits in London each week is actually her lover.'

Jane decided not say anything about Mary's lover because Mary had asked her not to.

'Your father used to take sleeping pills. I think it was you who told me that. Your grandmother locked them up, and he had to ask if he wanted them, and she would only give him one. They were barbiturates, which are much more dangerous than Valium, and he told me that he was sometimes suicidal. I think he was a bit fuzzy that night because he was drunk, and he fetched the pills from the kitchen thinking they were his barbiturates. He may have thought about taking the lot, but then he just took one. He would have been very unhappy that night.'

Then a memory stirred deep in her mind, something from a half-forgotten dream, something hovering on the brink of recollection. She knew that Ryan's mother had fallen down the stairs from the landing, and for a moment she imagined her standing there while Daniel slowly climbed the stairs towards her. A chill crept over her. Ryan had seen her ghost that night.

'Ryan, I have another theory. You can laugh at this if you want to, but it just came to me with a shiver like someone walked over my grave. I think the ghost of your mother pushed him down the stairs. He would have deserved it. He wasn't exactly faithful to her memory, was he, however much he loved her when she was alive, and he didn't treat you well. If she could look down from heaven, I think she would have been appalled, yet probably very unhappy for him.

'Your father once told us that he often saw her on the landing when he went upstairs to bed. She would talk to him, but he could never quite catch what she was saying, and when he reached the landing, she was always gone. He said that one day she would still be there, and then he would know he was dead and back with her again.

'You saw her ghost that night. Maybe she pushed him down the stairs to help us. Daniel once said if I slept with you, he would kill us both and himself as well. She would have wanted to protect you, and it was her way of setting us free from him. Ryan, it was all so sad, and I don't want to get teary again. I am so glad they were able to save you as a baby. I can't imagine my life without you in it.'

His fingertips touched hers across the table, surprisingly tense.

'Jane, do you remember that I once asked you if you had come up to my room that night because I heard a step in the corridor, and the scent of your perfume was there when I opened the door? I told you I thought I had seen my mother's ghost on the stairs, but that was not the whole story. I went along the corridor to the top gallery where the bridge goes across the hallway, and I clearly saw her on the stairs, silhouetted against the window in the moonlight. I know it was her because I heard my father call her name. I saw him come up the stairs and talk to her. Then he kissed her, and I went back to my room. I was still half asleep, and I thought I must be sleepwalking or dreaming. So perhaps he was by then a ghost as well, and he was back with her. I still wish I had gone downstairs at the time, but we can't change what happened. I told Mary I saw my mother's ghost. I know she would find comfort believing they were back together.'

'Your mother wore Chanel, so perhaps the scent was hers. It is really strange that they both died falling down the same staircase.'

'I didn't tell the police that I heard someone in the corridor, or about seeing a ghost on the landing, and I only told Mary after the police had cleared us all of murdering him. I was not sure I hadn't just dreamt it, and they may have thought it was you I saw, and that you pushed him. They knew there was something I wasn't telling them, but I do think they could have waited for the autopsy results before they assumed that I had killed him. As it was, they didn't believe the first report and called in another expert. That week was very stressful, but it made me realise I really do love this house, and I want us to stay living here if we can.

'And, Jane, thank you for not going out with the sergeant. I would have died from jealousy if you had.'

'Who told you that he asked me out?'

'Winston. He asked me this evening if the policeman you didn't like was coming to the wedding. If he was, he would look out for him and make sure he was seated well away from you. He overheard your conversation at the funeral without meaning to, and said that after the man left, you threw his card on the fire because he had asked you out.'

'The sergeant is a complete creep. Of course I would never go out with him. He even suggested he could pick me up after work one day when you were staying in Oxford, so you didn't know about it. I wanted to tell him he had a hide, asking me out after the way you had been treated, but I had to be polite, as he was a guest in our house. Did Winston tell you what I said to the sergeant?'

'No, he didn't. We are both gentlemen, and he said he didn't mean to listen. He only told me what you had said to him afterwards.'

'I told the sergeant I only go out with you. He asked if we were an item, so I said I was hoping we would be. I didn't want them to think we had been trying to cover it up, but I wanted him to know it was you I wanted, so it was no use him asking me out. Winston is sweet. He offered to flatten the sergeant if he bothered me again.'

'I think Winston is a bit in love with you as well. He told me tonight that he wishes you were younger so you would still be available when he graduates. I have so many rivals that I sometimes wish you were not quite so beautiful.'

Jane laughed and picked up the empty cups, taking them to rinse at the sink, but he stayed sitting at the table, so she returned to her chair.

'Ryan, who asked them to the funeral? I know I didn't.'

'The inspector phoned me and asked if it was okay to come, as he knew it was supposed to be private. I couldn't really say no. I imagine the sergeant just came along for the chance of seeing you. I believe they came in their own time. They sometimes work odd hours so they have some flexibility. The inspector just wanted to talk to me, to let me know they were sorry for what they did, although he didn't directly apologise. He spoke to Mary as well, to tell her we would hear from the coroner soon. He can be quite pleasant when he wants to be. Hopefully neither of them turns up at the wedding tomorrow.'

'Ryan, you have written your speech, haven't you? I was going to offer to help you, but you seem to be away at Oxford all the time lately.'

'I don't need to write it. I always know what I want to say. I'm sorry if I've neglected you, but I need the wedding to be over, and then I can start to think where we go from here. I would never have wished him dead, and I am sorry he died, but it turns out very convenient for me. I get the house and the money and hopefully you as well, and I wanted to leave some sort of decent interval before we danced on his grave. He did get some revenge. When I thought they would charge me with murdering him, I felt as if it was his way of getting back at me. I have never been so worried in my life as I was then, or felt so helpless, thinking that it would mean the end for you and me when we had been so close to being lovers.

'The night before he died, we made plans to go back to Richmond. I was intending to phone him from there and tell him if he wanted us back, he had to accept we were engaged. I would have suggested we just came back here on Sundays to look after the paperwork for him until he got used to the idea that you were mine and not his. Then we could have moved closer to Oxford as you suggested, so we were still near Mary. That would have given him a chance to get over his initial disappointment with us safely away from here. He got angry once before, and I have lived all my life with the consequences of it. I was afraid he would get angry again, and I was trying to work out a way forward for you and me.

'But then he attacked you, and I knew neither of us could ever come back here after that. I would never have trusted him near you. He could have killed you that night, and I know I would have killed him if he had. As it was, I felt like taking him by the throat and smashing his head against the wall, but I managed to keep in control. I was so glad afterwards that I had. If Pat or I had injured him that night, we could have really been in trouble. Violence never solves anything.

'Yet I still feel guilty that he died, and I feel guilty about the way he died, alone in the night, desperately unhappy and with all of us hostile to him. I feel we should have somehow prevented it, but I don't know how we could have done that.

'Perhaps it was Mary who gave him the Valium, or perhaps it was just a mistake he made. He might have taken the Valium, then realised his mistake and taken the digitoxin. That is what the police thought. He was intoxicated, and I doubt that he would have known the combination could be lethal. If he had deliberately overdosed, he would have taken more than one of each. But then how did the bottle get into the den? We will never know now. I do know we can't change what happened. We can only go forward.

'We need to get Mary to the station fairly early tomorrow, so I need to set the alarm in case Pat doesn't get up in time. He got a bit tipsy tonight, but not as badly as Jimmy did. We could spend a night or two in Richmond next weekend so we are by ourselves. The wedding will be over by then, so life will be more relaxed. We can go out to dinner again, this time just the two of us. Would you like that?'

'Yes, I would like that. But Mary might not want to be left here alone.'

'I don't think she would mind. If she does, we would need to wait for Pat and Claire to get back from Devon. Or we might persuade Mary to spend next Saturday night with her friend in London so we are by ourselves here.'

She wondered if he needed them to be alone in the house before he could make love to her. Was he was worried it wouldn't work out, and he would disappoint her? Or was he worried about the creaky beds as Pat had been? Perhaps Mary was right, and she would need to encourage him a little more.

10 WEDDING BELLS

When Jane came down for breakfast, Ryan had already returned from taking Mary to the station. He made toast for them both, as there had been no time for Mary to make porridge before she left. They had breakfast by themselves, as Pat was still in his room.

'I forgot to tell you last night. We have arranged another car, so you won't have to arrive at the church in the Land Rover. It was never a good solution. Jimmy wanted to borrow the Jaguar for the bride, leaving the Rover for the bridesmaids. He promised he would take absolute care of it. He didn't think Pat and I would want to arrive in the Land Rover, but he suggested we could walk to the church. I did see the logic, but I don't like lending my car, so I talked to John Phillips. He was there with Jack McCann, and they came to sit with us. I asked if he would lend us his blue Rover. It's the same type as ours, so would match. He is happy to walk to the church as he does on Sundays. Paul and Brian are washing and polishing it this morning in exchange. I can't imagine how we didn't think of it before.'

Jane was rather relieved at this, as it was difficult to believe the farm Land Rover could ever be cleaned up enough to transport three bridesmaids in bespoke satin dresses. She remembered the blue Rover, as John Phillips had once given her a lift to the station in town.

'Jack offered to help me sort out the shotguns when the probate is through and we can get the licences transferred. Pat can keep his at the farm. Jack would like the one my father always used, and he will help me to sell or give away the others. I would like to get them all out of the house. We can use the room for something else then.'

Jane reached for his hand across the table, knowing how relieved he would be to do that simple thing. It would be healing. His fingers twined with hers.

When Pat finally appeared, looking rather sorry for himself, Ryan made him some toast and strong coffee and found him an aspirin.

'Have you taken Mum to the station already?' he asked Ryan.

'Yes, and she caught the early train okay. I didn't tell her you and Jimmy got drunk last night. Hopefully no one else tells her. I just said we had all gone to bed rather late and you were still asleep. Something rather odd happened, though. I carried her bag into the station, and I overheard her when she bought the ticket. She didn't go to London. She bought a one-way ticket to Oxford.'

'Perhaps her friend came to meet her there, as they didn't have the whole day,' Jane suggested, wondering if she should tell the young men that the friend was Pat's father and he would be at the wedding. Better to let it be a surprise as Mary had obviously intended. She was rather relieved that Mary had only gone as far as Oxford; it would be much easier for her to return from there in time for the wedding.

Jane's dress and shoes had been packed ready the previous day. She put on her makeup and braided the top section of her hair, threading blue ribbon into the braids and leaving the lower section in loose waves. She would do Julie's hair in a similar style. She found some small sapphire stud earrings, which Mr Allanstone had given her for her nineteenth birthday. None of the other girls had pierced ears, so she wanted to keep her earrings discreet.

Ryan drove her to the farm at eleven, dropping Pat's suitcase at the inn first so Pat and Claire could carry on to their honeymoon tomorrow morning without needing to return to the Hall.

He left Jane and the Rover at the farm, and walked back to the house. Paul and Brian were tying white ribbons on the blue Rover, having spruced it up with a polish the like of which it had not seen for years. David was sent with the cake tin to the village hall, which was already set up for the reception, and afterwards he took Claire's suitcase across to the inn.

Julie and Candy were at the farm, along with Julie's mother Alison. Jane was to help them with makeup and hair styling before they dressed. She was considered an expert in these things because she had lived near London, and she had gone to a school where they taught you how to look good. The smallest bridesmaid, Daisy, would be dressed by her mother at the vicarage and would join the procession at the church.

Julie had long fair hair, uncompromisingly straight, so Jane braided the top section, leaving the remainder loose, and threaded pink ribbon through the braids so Julie's hairstyle was similar to her own. Alison liked the braids, so Jane offered to braid Alison's hair to match her daughter's. She normally wore her hair in a neat tight bun.

Jane made up Julie's eyes with blue eyeshadow, soft eyeliner and mascara, and she made up Alison's eyes as well. Jane thought it was about time Alison allowed herself to look a little more glamorous. She had thought at the cricket match that Candy's Uncle Maurice was interested in Alison. He had stayed to talk to her when he came for his cup of coffee.

Candy had short brown hair, worn in a Mary Quant style with a thick fringe. Being older than Julie, she did her own makeup.

Claire wanted her hair left loose beneath the veil, but Jane threaded some white ribbon through a few tiny braids to make it look more interesting. The bride and the bridesmaids were each to have a delicate wreath of small white roses.

Jimmy wanted some last-minute dancing practice, but Jane laughed and said there was no time. She helped him with his bow-tie. He was always amusing and cheerful, and she knew if she married him, life would be fun. There would be none of this cold self-control that she had from Ryan. Jimmy would never need persuading to kiss her or make love to her; she knew he would oblige in an instant with either. She always tried to avoid leading him on, although it seemed so natural to flirt with him when he flirted with her. But she knew that she would never marry him, that she was not cut out to be a farmer's wife. And she would never be able to live so close to Ryan. She would never stop wanting him if she did.

Reverend Colin dropped by to see that everything was going to plan. The flowers had arrived, so he took the wreath for Daisy back to the vicarage and the buttonholes for the groom and best man across to the Hall.

It all seemed mayhem to only child Jane, with the five McCann children, the two other bridesmaids, the farmer and his wife, and Alison, all working towards having everyone looking spruce and ready on time. The two Phillips boys arrived in their suits, and Alison checked their bow-ties and arranged their buttonholes, telling them how smart and handsome they both looked.

At two o' clock the four ushers were sent on to the church, their suits impeccable, bow-ties perfect, buttonholes neat, with the box of pro-grammes in hand. Jane wondered whether they would still look neat at ten o' clock when the reception wound up.

She placed the wreaths on the other bridesmaids' hair and over Claire's veil, carefully pinning them so they didn't slip off during the walk down the aisle. Alison fixed Jane's wreath. Jane found a loose white rose in the box that had held the flowers, and she pinned it in Alison's hair where the braids joined together at the back, adding a left-over length of white ribbon.

By half past two they were all finished. Claire looked obviously pregnant but breathtakingly beautiful with her veil and the wreath of flowers in her hair. Julie, in the deep pink satin dress, with her hair braided beneath the white roses, looked like a fairy-tale princess instead of a waif. Candy with her green dress and green eyes looked young and pretty beneath her halo of roses. Jane was in the cornflower blue dress, flowers in her hair. All of them wore the matching high-heeled platform shoes, elegant and glamorous but stable enough to dance in later in the evening.

The farmer looked surprisingly smart in his grey suit with his hair recently cut and his beard trimmed. The mother of the bride was in a dress of pretty pale apricot. Julie's mother wore a blue summer dress in a Liberty print. She told Jane it was a castoff from Candy's mother, but they had taken it in, and Jane thought it looked lovely on her. She looked very young and pretty with her hair braided and loose from her usual bun and her eyes looking soft and large with the makeup.

Jane thought it sad that she had never remarried. She was really beautiful, she worked hard to keep herself and her daughter, and she always seemed good natured although rather timid. She had been so helpful to them all that day, so happy to be useful, so caring of her daughter and so content with her life.

David had been stationed to watch for Ryan's car to drive past down the lane, the signal for them to wait for ten minutes then pile into the cars. Anne and Alison went on ahead to the church on foot.

There were so many details to arrange, Jane thought, but it had all gone well so far. She hoped the young men had put their suits on the right way round, remembered the buttonholes, remembered the rings.

Had Mary and her lover caught the right train back? Would they find a taxi? Had they arrived at the church yet? Things could still go horribly wrong. It would be dreadful if Pat was married without Mary there. Jane couldn't understand why Mary had gone to Oxford today. Why couldn't the lover have just come here? Having Mary's help with the organising would have been so much better, as she could have ensured the young men got everything right. At least Mary would be at the church when Pat and Ryan arrived there, and she could check the buttonholes then.

They were in the cars, driving the scant half mile to the church, with Jimmy driving his father and sister, David driving the bridesmaids, the cars polished and the white ribbons singing in the breeze, the sunny weather a gift from the gods.

Ryan's Jaguar was parked at the church, next to Mr Allanstone's black Mercedes and a yellow Range Rover that Jane recognised as Mr Jameson's.

Everything was good so far. Was Mary there yet?

David handed the girls out, and they were in the porch of the church with Anne waiting for them, and Linda handing over beautiful little Daisy in a white frilly dress with a yellow ribbon sash, and with a wreath of tiny white flowers on her curls. She was placed behind Claire to hold the end of the veil.

Jane and Julie straightened out Claire's dress, the photographers took some shots of them in the porch, and they were ready to go. Jimmy and David escorted their mother to her place at the front of the church.

The music started. The church was packed, with every pew full and people standing at the back. Jane saw the two snitches, Alice and Jenny, in white organza dresses, at the end of one of the rows, jumping around in excitement. She wanted to see who was with Mary, but there were too many people.

She could see Pat and Ryan, who had both turned to watch Claire as she walked down the aisle. Both young men looked very slim and smart in their new black suits with flared trousers, and their dark-blue brocaded silk waistcoats. Their satin bow-ties and buttonholes were perfect, and neither of them had a hair out of place. As they approached, she exchanged a look and a smile with Ryan, but she still could not see Mary's lover.

When they had reached the two waiting young men, and she was level with the front pews, she glanced across. Mary was looking beautiful in a fuchsia silk dress with a corsage of flowers on the front, her hair swept back in a French twist held in place by a silver comb, her diamond and garnet earrings highlighting her perfect cheekbones.

Next to her was Mr Allanstone. Beyond them were Mr and Mrs Jameson, Linda, and Colin's mother Betty holding baby Brett. There was no one else there at all. Mary's lover, it appeared, had not come back with her after all. Jane felt a pang of disappointment.

Jack McCann had given away his daughter and had joined his wife and four sons in the opposite pew. The McCann aunt, uncle and four young cousins, none of whom Jane had yet met, were in the pew behind. Candy's parents, her brother and his wife, and Candy's uncle Maurice with Alison, were behind Mary and Mr Allanstone. John Phillips, behind the McCann cousins, caught her eye and smiled at her.

The bouquet had been handed to Jane. The vows, the rings, the kiss, everything was going perfectly apart from that one thing, Mary's missing lover. Jane and Ryan followed the bride and groom to the registry to sign as witnesses to the marriage. He had taken her hand as though that was part of the ceremony. Perhaps it was. She couldn't remember.

'You look amazing,' he whispered, and she recalled the time he had said the same thing to her at Richmond.

'So do you,' she whispered back.

After the signatures had all been done, the photographs had been taken, and the flowers had been returned to the bride, he told her that something very strange had happened, but he did not have time to finish. She thought he was going to tell her about Mary and her lover, but the lover was simply not there, so what was there to tell?

But as they returned to sit in the front row, and Mary gave her a rather wicked smile, the truth hit her. How could she have not seen it all along? Mary's lover was sitting there beside her, holding her hand in his. John Allanstone was her lover, and the father of Pat. She had once thought there was a family resemblance. Now it all suddenly came together, Mary phoning him whenever anything went wrong, his interest in finding Pat a career, his offer to bail Ryan, the cheque he had written for Claire's wedding dress, all the help he had given them. She recalled the afternoon she had come upon them on the swing seat, laughing together and looking very loverlike. Mary even had his photograph on the wall in her bedroom. But he had stayed in the house, helped them with the paperwork, played scrabble with them. Why had they said nothing? And why had Mary gone to Oxford? Why hadn't Mr Allanstone simply driven here?

Reverend Colin gave a short sermon about marriage, telling them how happy he was to be uniting two lovely young people he had known for so long, and the last hymn was sung. The service over, they followed Pat and Claire out of the church, Jane with Ryan, Jimmy with Candy, David and Julie holding Daisy by the hand between them, past all the guests crowded in the pews, until they emerged into the sunshine to the joyous ringing of the bells in the tower. They waited outside the church while the congregation came out, all with their congratulations and kisses and handshakes.

Then there were photos, the bride and groom, the best man and Jane, the other bridesmaids, the mother and father of the bride, all Claire's brothers with the Phillips boys, Mary and Mr Allanstone, then all of them together and every possible combination, standing in lines before the tripod, or being shot by an assistant who placed them in front of church windows or gravestones or trees. Little Daisy was in whoops of joy, enjoying the attention, as everyone wanted her in every picture, running to Ryan to be swung around. The photographer's assistant caught that on his camera.

Finally Ryan managed to pull Jane away from the group, his fingers twining in hers, to where his parents were buried.

'Jane, something rather strange has happened. Mary and Allanstone were married this morning in Oxford. They met at the Jamesons' house, so Mary could change, and went from there to the registry office. The Jamesons were witnesses at the wedding. Then they all had lunch together and came on here. That was why she left so early to catch the train.

'When we reached the church, they were waiting for us as we drove in. They told us they were married, and Pat said that meant he now had a stepfather. Then Allanstone said he was Pat's real father. It turns out he is the friend Mary visited each week for all those years. I don't think I have ever been so surprised in my whole life.'

But the roaming photographer had caught up with them, wanting them in a photo together, telling them to look at the camera, then telling them to look at each other, to stand together behind his parents' grave with their hands on the headstone, then facing each other, holding hands, then with his arm around her, their faces close together, and she thrilled at the touch of his hand, the glance of his eyes close to hers, his fingers straightening one of the roses in her hair so it looked right in the photo.

At last the photographer went to find the other bridesmaids, Julie and Candy, setting them up with the two eldest McCann boys standing on either side of them.

'Mary said we can announce they are married and have a toast for them, but she asked us to keep quiet for the moment about Allanstone being Pat's father. You spotted the resemblance from the beginning, but I have only seen it now that I know. They will stay in Oxford for the night, then spend a few days in his house in Kent before they go to Europe for their honeymoon. We will be left here on our own, just you and me and the ghosts.'

With the photographs over, Claire tossed her bouquet to Jane, but Jane wasn't sure if Claire had Jimmy or Ryan in mind. They walked across to the already crowded village hall. The room was full with tables set up ready for the meal, and a side table with the contributions for the supper—scones, tarts, cupcakes and biscuits.

The dinner was served from a buffet, and when everyone had filled their plates and found a place at the tables, the speeches began.

Jack McCann thanked everyone for coming, and welcomed Pat as his son-in-law. He didn't see their marriage as losing a daughter, but as gaining yet another son.

Pat gave a speech thanking Claire for marrying him, thanking Reverend Colin and everyone who had helped set up the hall, thanking his mother and Claire's mother, thanking his cousin and best man Ryan for his lifelong love and support and Jane for her help with the dresses and for being like a sister to him, thanking Jimmy and David for driving the cars and the four ushers for the faultless way they had looked after the seating.

Ryan gave a speech with hilarious incidents from Pat's past, including the stories about the mouse trap and the blazing ping-pong balls, and Jane wondered why she had ever thought he might want her help writing it. He had been head boy at his school, she recalled. A speech at a wedding was not going to faze him, and he had spoken very well at his father's funeral.

He went on to say that he was sad, as he was sure all of them were, that his father was not here to celebrate with them, and then he said he had great pleasure in announcing that his aunt Mary and his father's lifelong friend John Allanstone had been married that morning in Oxford. Everyone cheered at that, for everyone liked Mary.

After the speeches there were toasts to the bride and groom, to Mr and Mrs Allanstone, the best man Ryan, the groomsmen Jimmy and David, the four beautiful bridesmaids, and Mr and Mrs McCann for obligingly providing a bride.

There was a break after the meal while the tables were cleared away for the dancing. The wedding cake was cut up, the pieces piled onto a plate and put with the treats for the supper.

Jane and Ryan circulated together, talking to everyone they could, trying to pretend that Mary marrying Mr Allanstone was the most natural thing in the world. Ryan was considered the squire now his father was gone, and he behaved like the squire even though they no longer owned any of the surrounding land. He always knew exactly what to say to everyone, and of course he knew everyone, although Jane still didn't.

David was keeping possessively close to Julie, and Winston came up to talk to her. She looked radiant. A shy dowdy girl of sixteen, usually in hand-me-downs, was suddenly looking like a princess and being treated like a princess. Jane was glad that she had taken the trouble over the dresses, instead of them all being dressed up as larger versions of Daisy in flounces and ribbons.

She found some time to speak to Mary and John Allanstone, but she felt betrayed and hardly knew what to say to them. He had stayed in their house. She remembered them sitting together on the swing in the conservatory, and they would have slept together in the room she had helped Mary prepare, perhaps the first time they had ever spent a whole night together. Yet they had said nothing, preferring to keep things a secret even from their own family. He did apologise for springing this on them all, but they had wanted to keep it all low key so their marriage didn't overshadow Pat's wedding. Jane told them that she and Ryan would have loved to have been there, and Mary said she understood that and hoped they would both forgive her.

The band was in place, tuning the instruments, consulting with Jimmy McCann, who was master of ceremonies. The first waltz was to be the bridal party at least at first, the second waltz everyone was to join in, then there was to be a foxtrot for Ryan, a tango, and a jive for Jimmy.

Jane helped Claire take off the wreath and the veil, so she couldn't trip on it while she danced. Jane took off her own wreath as well so if Ryan danced close to her, he didn't have flowers in his face.

The music started. Pat was waltzing with Claire, Ryan with Jane, Candy with Jimmy and Julie with David, Mary with John Allanstone, the McCanns, Reverend Colin and Linda, the Jamesons. The farmers and their wives joined in, Candy's parents, Alison with Maurice, Candy's brother with his wife, and some of the young people.

Alice and Jenny, looking lovely in their white organza dresses with blue ribbon sashes, were dancing with a couple of smartly dressed boys of about their own age. They would make rather pretty bridesmaids, Jane thought, but she wasn't relenting.

For the second waltz they swapped partners, so Ryan was with Mary and Jane with Mr Allanstone.

'If you marry Ryan, I really will be your uncle,' Mr Allanstone said to her. 'Were you surprised? I rather thought you had guessed and so did Mary. She said she almost told you last night.'

'Yes, I was surprised,' Jane admitted. 'But I'm not sure why I didn't guess. It all seems so obvious now, and I always thought Pat looked like you. For a while there, you were nearly my father-in-law. Pat and I were going to escape together, before I knew about Claire of course. But please don't tell Mary, she doesn't know, and I hope Claire doesn't know either.'

'Does Ryan know?'

'Yes, he does. He once walked in on us kissing, but it never went further than that. He believes I was never serious about Pat, but for a little while I think I was. Ryan kept telling me he didn't want a girlfriend, and I believed him, but I liked him from the start, from the day of Aunt Ellen's funeral. He was always so kind to me.'

'I did once think it would be good if you and Pat got married so you were my daughter-in-law, but I think Ryan needs you a lot more, so I'm happy with you being my niece instead. I know that if his grandmother was still alive, she would have been thrilled. She wanted to see him happy in life, and she always worried about him. It seems a perfect match to me, and I know your father would have been pleased as well. He loved Ryan when he was small. Can I look forward to giving you away to him?'

'I hope so, but it's not settled yet.'

'When you two were in Richmond, before Daniel died, Ryan had lunch with me. He told me he had changed the way he thought about his future life when you had come to Hayward, and he was hoping you liked him enough to marry him. He asked my permission, although he knew he didn't actually need it. He said that his father being in love with you rather complicated things for him. He was in Richmond to keep you safe, so he couldn't ask you to marry him, as it would put you in an impossible position if you didn't want to. He didn't want you to think that your only choice in life was to marry him or to marry Daniel. We talked about ways you could live by yourself without feeling too alone.'

'I do like him enough to marry him, but I'm not sure he realises that.'

The music was over and Mr Allanstone gave her back to Ryan for the next dance. It was the foxtrot, beyond the skills of most of the young people, but some of the farmers and their wives were surprisingly good at dancing. They had all danced in their youth during the War. And of course the Allanstones and the Jamesons knew it and Candy's parents and Alison with Maurice. Pat and Claire had a go. David with Julie and Jimmy with Candy were following her and Ryan, managing to remember the easier steps she had shown them. Alice and Jenny, with their young men in tow, were also pretending they knew how to dance the foxtrot.

Jane loved being held close to him, his hand on her back, his eyes holding hers, moving with him as though they were the only two people in the room. They had practised this, found themselves a routine that worked perfectly for them. She remembered what Mary had said about dancing bringing men and women together. The touch of his hand was intoxicating. His face was so close to hers he could almost reach to kiss her—but not here in the village hall of course. His thigh touching hers was seductive, firing a passion that was perfectly controlled, perfectly respectable, an embrace that could go so far but no further, a taste of forbidden pleasure. Forbidden at least until later, deep into the night, when they were at last at home together. Tonight, she thought, you are sleeping with me, Ryan Linden, and there will be no excuses this time. They would be alone in the house. That was what he had wanted.

When the music stopped Jane saw that Pat and Mr Allanstone had changed partners, so Pat was with his mother and Mr Allanstone with Claire. As he handed her back to Pat, he said something to her that made her smile. Jane assumed Claire had by now been told that he was Pat's father.

The lead singer announced that the best man Ryan and bridesmaid Jane would dance a tango together. This was to be a tribute to Ryan's late father who had loved to tango with his wife many years ago, and more recently with Jane. He had been looking forward to dancing a tango with Jane at the wedding, and they had been rehearsing the steps before he died. They would then play the tune a second time for everyone else to join in. Jane thought this was Pat's idea, but Ryan didn't seem to mind, so she assumed Pat had arranged it with him beforehand.

They danced as they had practised to *Guitar Tango*, facing each other at first but not touching although perfectly in step, circling each other, then gradually increasing contact and getting closer, then very close, with the dips and the spins and Ryan turning her and pulling her back against him, breathing close to her neck, until the end when he was leaning over her, almost kissing her, and her leg was stretched out against his.

Jane knew that they had danced well, and she also realised with some surprise that he had enjoyed it as much as she had, but she still scarcely believed he had agreed to do this. Wasn't he supposed to be shy? Everyone in the room would be wondering what sort of incestuous orgies went on at Hayward Hall, with her having danced like this with Daniel. Many of them would assume he really was her uncle, and would not know he was actually her father's cousin.

Ryan picked her up, spun around with her, set her back on her feet, and gave her a joyful hug. She heard the applause and the odd wolf whistle. The tune was played again for everyone to join in, and this time she and Ryan danced a little more conventionally. Alice and Jenny, with their young men, were trying out some of the tango moves; Jane hoped their partners didn't drop them.

After the tango Jimmy came to claim her for the jive, and she saw Ryan standing at the side of the hall with Mary and Mr Allanstone, immersed in conversation. But she knew Ryan was watching her, so she needed to take care.

'I've finally got you to myself, Jane,' said the irrepressible Jimmy, but it was hard to keep up a conversation when you were jiving at a Jimmy McCann pace. In the times when she was close to him, he was holding her a little closer than was strictly necessary, but she didn't pull away. At least with a dress this long it didn't matter how fast she spun around, she was in no danger of showing her underwear, although as a precaution she had worn knickers that matched the dress. At the end of the song, he picked her up as Ryan had and spun around with her.

'Next wedding could be ours,' he offered, when he put her down.

She was standing with him at the side of the hall, rather out of breath. She suddenly knew she had to be serious with him.

'Jimmy, I like you and I hope we'll always be friends, but I don't want to marry you.'

'Don't you? That's a shame. I didn't really expect you'd want to, but it would be fun if you did. I was rather hoping you'd go outside with me a bit later, and we could talk about it. I hope you're not marrying Ryan. He's so old. Mum thinks you like him better than you let on, and she knows he likes you. I was asking Ryan's permission to marry you last night. I didn't realise he wanted you, or I wouldn't have said it. I feel bad about it now. Mum was furious when she heard what I'd done. There was an explosion at breakfast this morning, and Claire said she thought you and him were engaged. Mum said I should never have said anything like that unless I had asked you first. She said if I married you, she'd be the happiest mum in the world, but it wasn't right for you to be a farmer's wife trudging around in wellington boots.

'I'd fight him, but those top schools teach guys to defend them-selves—judo and such—and although I'm heavier than him, I might come off worse for wear. They don't allow duels any more. Pity. He's never shot anything in his life, so I would have the advantage there. Would you marry me if he wasn't around?'

'Yes, Jimmy, I think I would, but please don't shoot him to get me.'

'I know I could never offer you what he can, but I don't think that would worry you if you liked me enough. Should I apologise to him, do you think?'

'No, I don't think so. It's probably best to just leave it alone.' She liked Jimmy, she knew it was at least partly her own fault for leading him on, and she didn't think a bit of jealousy would do Ryan any harm.

'Will you dance with me again later? We could still slip outside for a bit. He wouldn't see us behind the hall.'

'I'll dance with you, but that is all. What about Candy?' Jane suggested. 'She seems to like you, and she is rather a pretty girl.'

'She's not a blonde,' said Jimmy, 'and no one is as pretty as you.'

Another jive followed, and Jane danced with Winston, who was a year or so younger than she was. He had seemed a little bashful asking her to dance, and he told her she looked lovely in the dress. She was flattered to have a young admirer, but she knew he understood that nothing would come of it. He told her he was going on to university in London when he left school later this year, and he wanted to study medicine. He would still come home to his grandfather's farm on week-ends so he was with Adrian. In August they were both going to Scotland for a month to visit their mother, their stepsister Hilary, who was now ten, and their stepfather. He was a doctor and they both liked him, but not as much as their own father of course. They lived in the Highlands, in a really interesting house with a secret passage, but it was quite remote. His uncle—his mother's brother—lived in Aberdeen, in a stone house with a tower. He was a doctor as well, and he had two children, a boy and a girl, cousins to Adrian and himself. He didn't see his mother much, but he phoned her every week from school to tell her what he and his brother had been doing.

'Jane, you're not really marrying Jimmy, are you?' he asked when the music had stopped. 'He was telling everyone last night that he was going to marry you and he needed Ryan's permission. I tried to shut him up, as I could see it was making Ryan hot under the collar. Adrian and I both realised a long time ago that Ryan likes you, but it seems Jimmy hadn't seen that. My grandfather said afterwards he didn't believe you would marry Jimmy.'

'No, of course not. Jimmy apologised for saying it.'

'My grandfather hopes you will marry Ryan. That way you will always be next door to us. When we all walked home last night, after we left the McCanns at their farm, he told Ryan to get a ring on your finger before someone else steals you.'

After the jive there were the folk dances that everyone knew, the Barn Dance and the Durham Reel and the Pride of Erin, and Jane danced with the younger McCann boys and with Adrian.

There was then a break for the supper, and tea and coffee were served. It gave everyone a chance to circulate and mingle once more.

Mary told Jane that she and John were returning to the Hall for a short while to collect Mary's suitcase and feed the cat. Jane knew she would have forgotten about the poor cat, at least until they returned later that night.

After the last plates were emptied and the cups and saucers tidied away, the young people danced in their own way, most of them scarcely touching each other, which Jane found rather sad. You didn't even need a partner. It was the touching that made dancing so magical.

Jimmy found her, danced with her again, rather close, and she hoped Ryan wasn't watching, but she knew he would be. She tried to keep Jimmy in check, and was far too sensible to agree to his plan of slipping outside separately then meeting behind the hall. Those two wretched girls were there, Ryan's self-appointed spies.

'I don't think it would be wise. Jimmy, please believe me when I say I do like you, but I don't want it to go any further. I want to marry Ryan, I just can't help it, although I am still waiting for him to ask me. I would have told you before now if we really had been engaged. I think I'm a bit in love with you as well, if that makes you feel better, but I can't marry you both.'

'I would be happy to share you. He can have you on weekdays, and I'll have the weekends. Or he gets the daytime, and I get the nights. Better still I'll offer to give you up to him if he lets me drive you to the wedding in the Jaguar, then I can kidnap you and get his car as well.'

'Jimmy, please be serious. We had some good times, I enjoyed going out with you, and I'm sorry it didn't work out. I'm not cut out to be a farmer's wife. You might want me to skin a rabbit.'

'I'm sorry, too. I shouldn't have said what I did last night, least of all to him. I was a bit drunk, and I really do like you. We don't see him much, and he always seems so much older than any of us. I didn't realise before today that he liked you, but I knew when you two danced the tango together that I didn't stand a chance. He and I need to stay on good terms since we will probably be neighbours for the rest of our lives, and we are related now Pat is married to my sister.'

Later she saw Jimmy talking to Ryan, and she hoped he wasn't bringing up the sharing idea. She saw Ryan laugh, and they shook hands. She wondered what Jimmy had said.

She stopped to talk to Mr Phillips. He told her she looked beautiful, and he wished he was young and fit enough to dance with her. He was such a lovely man, she thought, and she wished he was her grandfather. She had never known any of her grandparents. Although Aunt Ellen had been as good as any grandmother could have been.

By nine she was feeling tired. Jimmy was dancing with Candy, who looked slightly tipsy. Jane hoped he was reconsidering his aversion to the colour of her hair. They looked happy enough together.

She found Ryan talking with Mr Allanstone and Mr Jameson, and danced with him again, but this time slowly, very close to him, her face against his shoulder, his cheek against her hair. They had danced like this in the hotel in Mayfair. Surely, he would remember that evening, and what had happened afterwards. Did he want her the way she wanted him? Was he thinking, as she was, that soon they would be back at home, and it would be just the two of them alone together in the house. Perhaps she could say she was scared by herself without Mary in her room along the passage. Perhaps he would let her sleep upstairs with him.

But Jenny came to find her, as Anne needed her help with something that had been torn on Claire's dress. It was easily fixed with a safety pin that Candy's mum found in her handbag.

Anne said she would miss Mary terribly. They had been friends for their whole lives, and neighbours for over twenty years. She was concerned about Jane being alone in the house with Ryan without Mary there, and asked if she wanted to stay at the farm in Claire's room until something better could be arranged.

'Would Ryan ever do anything to harm me?' Jane responded, thinking she wanted to wake up tomorrow in bed with Ryan, not at the farm with Jimmy.

'No, of course not, but it doesn't look good. Not that young people seem to care about those things nowadays. I hope Jimmy has not been bothering you. Jack told me that last night at the Black Horse Inn he was talking to Ryan about marrying you. You know of course that I would be very glad to have you as a daughter, but I don't think it's right for you to be trudging around in wellies on a farm. I told Jimmy so. Claire said she thought you and Ryan were engaged, the way you were talking when she went to London with you, but Jimmy said he knew you would have told him if you were. You have done so much for Ryan, and I hope you will stay here and marry him. He was always a lovely polite boy, and he deserves a lovely wife. I wouldn't like to think of him living in that house on his own. He dances with you like he is in love with you. When you two did the tango together, Jack said he thought you were going to make love on the dance floor. Did you really dance like that with your uncle?'

'He was my father's cousin, so not really my uncle,' she corrected. 'He used to dance the tango with his wife. I didn't mind dancing with him, it was only for fun, and he enjoyed it. I did too.'

'It doesn't seem right though, an old man dancing like that with a young girl, and not what I would have expected from him. You danced very well with Ryan. Are you and he engaged?'

'Not yet. I would have told Jimmy if we were. But I am hoping we will be.'

He had once asked her to marry him, but she had not been ready to give him an answer. So much had happened since then, but he had kept to his word and waited until after Pat was married as she had suggested. Well now Pat was married, and she hoped he would ask her again. She wished she had just said yes the first time, but it had taken her by surprise. They would have come home engaged, and Daniel would have had to accept it. Perhaps he would still be alive.

'Have you thought you might ask him? Girls can do the asking with all this equality that we have now.'

But Jane knew she could never do that.

'I think he is yours if you want him, Jane, but don't lead him on if you don't,' was Candy's mum's advice. 'He is so much more confident now than he was before you came. He helped my husband find out about the history of our cottage, and he seemed very shy and a little otherworldly. I thought perhaps he didn't like girls, some men don't, but I always thought he liked you. The very first day we met you, after church, he stood beside you and looked at you as if you had bewitched him. And tonight, when you danced together in that rather suggestive way, I knew you really had.

'Jane, thank you for making Alison look so beautiful. I couldn't persuade her to let her hair loose, but she said you asked if you could do it to match Julie's, and she didn't want to offend you by refusing. I can only say well done. We think Maurice likes her, and we are all hoping they get together.'

Jane had somehow lost where Ryan was. She eventually caught sight of him sitting on a bench in the foyer, below the noticeboard and across from the cloakrooms, talking to Alice and Jenny who were perched on milk crates at his feet and squealing in excitement at what he was saying. At least she hadn't gone outside with Jimmy, so this time there was nothing for them to snitch about. What on earth was he saying to them?

As she headed towards the doorway to the foyer, Reverend Colin was walking back into the hall. He stopped beside her for a moment, seemingly reading her thoughts.

'He is telling them about the ghosts of Hayward Hall. I eaves-dropped. Although I rather think he is making it up as he goes. Has he told you about any ghosts? I don't recall him ever telling me. There would be plenty to choose from, though, as the house replaced one that was much older. Ryan once told me the original manor house dated back to the fourteenth century. I believe his mother died when he was a very small baby, but I don't know the whole story. If she came back as a ghost, I think she would be very grateful to you, Jane. You have done wonders for that young man. Linda and I are both so glad you came here. A year ago, at an affair like this, he would have been in a corner with the farmers, talking about sheep and cows without having the slightest interest in either, and he would never have danced. Now he is relaxed and happy and talking with everyone. When he was dancing that tango with you, it was the closest I have ever seen him to showing off. You both dance so well, and it was a pleasure to watch you. And this only a couple of months since he lost his father, although I'm not sure they liked each other all that much. There seemed to be a rather complex relationship between them. He never said anything to me, but I got the idea Ryan rather despised his father on one level, but on another level, he wanted to please him as most children want to please their parents. It's built into us. In my line of work, I see a lot of outwardly happy families who are not really so happy beneath the surface.'

'They had their differences, but I know that they cared about each other. Ryan's mother fell down the stairs when she was eight months' pregnant, and they managed to save him but not his mother. When she died Daniel was devastated. Mary said they had to lock the door to the gun room for fear he would shoot himself.'

'Jane, I hope you are going to stay on here with Ryan now Mary is leaving. I heard a rumour that Jimmy McCann was telling everyone at the pub last night that he is marrying you. He is a good enough lad, but I was relieved when Jack told me it wasn't true. I rather hoped you might marry Ryan.'

'I'm not marrying Jimmy. I like him but that is all. I have never led him on. Well, I only respond a little when he flirts. I don't chase after him, and I have never said I would marry him. He said he was sorry, and that if he hadn't been drunk, he wouldn't have said it. I will marry Ryan if he wants me.'

'He will if you give him enough time. You may need a bit of patience, and it may be wise not to flirt with Jimmy. Ryan will need to know that you want him. I don't think he would have the courage to ask you otherwise. I would have been happier if you were a little older and more independent, but you seem to suit each other well enough. Ryan always seems a bit of a loner, rather melancholy at times, but sufficient unto himself.'

That describes him exactly, Jane thought. She knew it was a saying from a Greek philosopher. Ryan would know which one. It seemed there had always been men like him, right back to Ancient Greek times.

'He calls it being a lone wolf,' she told Colin.

'About time you tamed him, Jane. He plays chess with me occasionally—or at least he used to, before you came here—and he was helping Linda work out the genealogy for the farming families from the church register. But we haven't seen much of him at the vicarage since you came to Hayward. I think he wanted to be with you. He may just need a little more time to get over losing his father. Jane, why did you run away?'

'Did I run away? Who told you that?'

'John Phillips. This is a village. Everyone knows everyone, and nothing goes unnoticed. He gave you a lift to town on his way to the library. He phoned me from there, and said he thought something was not quite right. He said you seemed chatty enough, but you looked to him to be shaky and ready to cry. He would have phoned Mary to check she knew you had left, but he couldn't recall the number and you are not in the phone book, so he asked me to phone her. Mary said you were fine and that Ryan was looking after you, but she didn't say why you left.'

'I had an argument with Daniel, and I was a little upset over it, but I mainly went back to Richmond for shopping. I did love my uncle—we always got on really well—but he wasn't happy about me and Ryan. We had been going out to places together and Daniel got cross about it. He thought me too young to settle down, and he had told Ryan and Pat that I was out of bounds. We sorted it out, and I came back. He was a deeply unhappy man. He once told me how he had tried to kill himself when his wife died. He never got over losing her, and he only coped by burying himself in a fantasy world.'

'Was there a fight the night he died? Was it Daniel who hit you? I know it can't have been Ryan.'

'Daniel only hit me because I got hysterical. I sometimes do get hysterical. He didn't hit me hard, but I bruise very easily. Ryan was cross with him over it, and there was an argument, but not a fight. But that had nothing to do with why he died. His heart was weak. The coroner said his heart failed. The fall on the stairs wasn't what killed him. He only fell because he had already died. The police had to investigate, in case there had been an intruder, or one of us had pushed him down the stairs, but they soon realised he had died of natural causes.'

'If you ever want to talk about it, you know my door is always open, but for now go and rescue Ryan from those two before he runs out of stories.'

She went to sit beside Ryan on the bench, and he absently took her hand in his, twining his fingers with hers.

'Have you seen the ghost, Miss Walters,' Jenny asked.

She pretended to think about it. 'Well, I haven't actually seen it, but I sometimes hear it on the stairs at night. I pull the covers over my head, and hope I remembered to lock my door. Not that it would help. Ghosts just walk right through doors, don't they?'

A strange thought suddenly struck her, a dim memory that she had once seen a ghost at Hayward Hall. She had been standing on the landing in the moonlight, and there had been a dark figure on the bridge, looking down at her.

She shivered and Ryan asked if she was okay.

She nodded. 'I just remembered a dream I once had about a ghost on the bridge.'

'Miss Walters, is Jimmy McCann still your boyfriend?' Jenny was asking her, and the ghost on the bridge was forgotten.

'No, I don't think so,' said Jane. 'I'm not sure he ever was.'

'Yes, he was. You were kissing him at the castle. But I hope he's not your boyfriend now because he was kissing Candy Morgan outside the hall.'

'That's nice for Candy,' Jane managed to say, trying not to dissolve into hysterical laughter. Luckily the other girl changed the subject.

'Miss Walters, please would you teach us how to dance properly like you and Mr Linden. You could give us lessons in the hall here. Please.'

'Talk to Reverend Colin,' Jane suggested. 'He may be able to arrange a dancing teacher to come here. I wouldn't mind coming along and helping with lessons, but I don't think I could teach anyone.'

The girls ran off to find Colin, leaving Ryan and Jane to themselves. She was still trying to control her laughter, but she was rather relieved that Jimmy had got over her so quickly. She didn't feel nearly so bad about it all. She stole a look at Ryan and realised he was laughing as well.

He put his arm around her, and she leaned against his shoulder, wishing they could just go home and be alone together with no one in the world but the two of them, hoping that tonight he would let her sleep with him.

Mary passed them on her way to the cloakroom, and she gave Jane a secret smile and an almost imperceptible thumbs-up, so Jane did the same back when Mary returned to the hall.

'I'm exhausted,' Ryan told her, resting his cheek against her hair. 'We all put so much effort into making today work out well for Pat and Claire, in spite of everything that has happened, and it did go well. Even the weather was perfect. It will finish soon. We have to wrap up by ten. We could go outside for a while where it's quieter—the music is rather loud—but you may be cold. I could lend you my jacket.'

'Then you would be cold,' she reminded him. 'And those two girls would probably follow us so they could snitch to someone about us snogging behind a tombstone.'

He laughed. 'I would be happy to oblige, but I was thinking more of a walk across the green.'

'I would love to, but I'm too tired to walk anywhere, and the high heels would sink in the grass. We'll be home by ourselves soon. Can you wait that long?' She looked at his watch, pushing back his cuff and running her fingers across his palm and the inside of his wrist as he had once done to her. 'There is only another quarter of an hour. At ten Claire and Pat will go to the inn for the night, and we all have to wish them well before they leave. Then we can go home. There are plenty of people here to clean up. We need to remember to get the plate from the kitchen.'

Alison came up to talk to them, with Maurice holding her hand, so they stood up, but Ryan left his arm around her waist.

Jane recalled she had thought Maurice might be another lone wolf. It was good to see Alison with a pretty hairstyle and a new lover. Jane hoped the romance of attending a wedding would work for them as well as for her and Ryan. Perhaps Alison could finally get over losing her first husband and marry again.

'I'll get the dress cleaned and sent back to you,' she assured Jane, but Jane had a way around that too. Rebecca had said they could keep the dress, but Jane knew that Julie's mother would see that as charity.

'I think these dresses are silk, so they will need to be cleaned in London. Leave Julie's dress with the McCanns tomorrow, and I can take all three of them across to London later in the week.'

Then I'll hang on to them, she thought. There might be other weddings in Hayward shortly, and if one of them was Alison and Maurice, then Julie and Candy would soon be bridesmaids again.

'You will let me know the cost so I can pay you back, won't you, Jane?'

'Yes of course,' she promised, with no intention whatsoever of doing so. Eventually the debt would be forgotten.

'You two danced so beautifully. It was like the dancing they have on television. You are just as good as they are. Jane, it was so good of you to arrange the dresses. Please thank your friend from me for lending it. Perhaps I could write and thank her myself if you give me the address. I could never have afforded to get Julie anything as nice as that. She looks so lovely, and she is so happy. I was so proud of her when she was dancing with David and looking like a princess. He asked me if he can take her out to a film after cricket next Saturday. She suddenly seems to be grown up.'

'She is beautiful; you have every right to be proud of her,' Jane assured her, thinking Alison would get a shock if she knew how much the dresses actually had cost when they were made. Sarah's father had paid for them.

'The dresses were from my best friend Sarah's wedding in June last year,' she told Alison. 'Everyone is really pleased that they are being worn again. My great-aunt was at the wedding, and she said we all looked like fairy-tale princesses. She looked after me after my parents died, and I adored her. Sarah's wedding was only a few months before my great-aunt died, so I am glad to be wearing the dress again and remembering her. It was such a happy day for everyone. Today has been a happy day as well.'

Jane recalled what Mary had once said about grief fading with time, so you remembered that you had loved the person who had died and they had loved you. She could think of Aunt Ellen now without crying. She was so grateful to have had a great-aunt who had loved her and looked after her when she most needed it, and she would always cherish the memory, and the photograph, of Aunt Ellen with the three brides-maids.

Alison said she had enjoyed the day, and she knew that Julie had too. Everything had gone so well. Maurice agreed it had been a wonderful day, and he put his arm around Alison's waist and smiled at her.

Another lone wolf tamed, Jane thought.

The last dance was announced, and everyone was to be on the floor. They played *Forever and Ever*, Jane's favourite song. It was crowded, so she and Ryan stayed close together, moving slowly, lost in the music and the words of the song. She knew that they would spend the whole night together. Alison and Maurice were also dancing very close to each other. Jane wondered if they would be together all night as well. Dancing did that to people.

The music was over. Pat and Claire were leaving, with everyone lining up to kiss the bride and shake the groom's hand. They were to spend the night in a room at the inn, and tomorrow they were taking the Rover and heading for their honeymoon in Devon. It was only now that Jane realised Mary had suggested they spend the night at the inn instead of at the Hall at least partly so she and Ryan were alone together in the house that night.

Mary and John left as soon as Pat and Claire had gone. They were driving back to Oxford to stay with the Jamesons for the night, and would then stay in Kent for a week, before spending two weeks in Europe. Mary said she would phone them around lunchtime tomorrow to check everything was okay. Pat would phone both his mother and Ryan from Devon. She and John would come and stay at the Hall for a few days after their honeymoon, as there were a lot of things they would need to talk about. Then she pulled Jane aside and told her not to waste her opportunity.

Ryan hugged his aunt, shook hands with his new uncle, and everyone wished them well as they saw them off. Jane wondered if this was the first time in Mary's life that she had slept away from Hayward Hall, except perhaps when Pat was born.

The Jamesons left at the same time, saying they hoped to see more of Jane and Ryan, inviting them to have dinner with them in a week or two, promising they would be in touch.

'He never sent me the account for the afternoon he spent with me at the police station in Oxford,' Ryan told Jane. 'I reminded him, but he told me Allanstone had fixed it up. I don't think that was actually true. I was very grateful to have him there.'

The band was packing up, the chairs were stacked, the glasses were boxed to return to the inn. There were plenty of willing helpers to do the cleaning up. Jane collected the plate and the cake tin, found her wreath of white roses, and they escaped to the Jaguar, which was parked next door at the church.

The car slipped away from the lights and the village, through the gates and into their own private world. Pale moonlight touched the windows of the house, the moon a little past full. Ryan put away the car while Jane waited by the back door in the moonlight.

He unlocked the door and pushed it open, but for a while they stood on the threshold in the stillness, saying nothing, her hand in his. The house was now theirs to look after with Mary gone, theirs and theirs alone, just Ryan and herself, living here forever. She sensed that he felt the same.

'This house is ours, now, yours and mine. This is how life is meant to be,' he said at last, echoing her thoughts. 'I wish it had been our wedding.'

'We could pretend it was,' she said softly.

She felt his fingers intertwine with hers, even as she wondered if it was quite the right thing for her to say. She knew that tonight they would finally become lovers and she sensed that he knew it too.

Without a word, he picked her up and carried her inside, then he set her down, with his arms around her, so she was standing very close to him, leaning against him, her hands on his chest, then slipping up behind his neck.

'You will stay with me, won't you, now it's only the two of us? It seems so strange to be here on our own that I still can't quite believe it. Mary leaving was such a shock. She has always been here. So much has happened today, and so many things have changed that I can hardly even begin to think it all through. We will have to make our own meals, and wash up the dishes. I will need you here to cook the porridge. And I'm not sure I would want to live here alone in this house. It would be too spooky even for me. I always feel the ghosts here, my grandfather, his brothers and your grandmother, all dead before I was born, my grandmother and my mother, your father and now mine. But they are not malevolent ghosts. They know that you and I and Pat are all they have left. Having you here with me just seems right. We have so much we need to talk about, but I am exhausted, so most of it will have to wait until tomorrow. And we will need to pick up your things from the farm after church.'

I'll stay here forever if you want, she thought, as she felt his body warm against hers, his hands in her hair, but she didn't say it. Mary had told her she would need to give him some encouragement, but she was still afraid he might think her too forward. How could she judge the line between? He had kissed her once at Richmond, talked about them living there together forever, but then he had gone cold again.

He released her and switched on the light in the scullery, then the brighter kitchen lights, and filled the kettle for cocoa.

The cat was waiting for them, confused at the house being empty and dark.

The night air had been chilly, but it was warmer indoors. He took off his jacket and the bow-tie, unfastened the top button of his shirt, took out the cufflinks and rolled up his shirtsleeves.

He made the cocoa, found the biscuits, carried the tray into Mary's sitting room, put it down on the coffee table.

She sat on the sofa while he knelt on the rug and pulled off her blue high-heeled shoes, caressing her feet as she stretched out her toes in the tights. It felt good to have the shoes off. He took off his own shoes as well, then sat beside her, his toes touching hers.

The cat jumped onto his lap. Jane needed to protect the dress from Jasmine's claws, so she covered it with a blanket. They drank their cocoa in silence, then she leaned against him and his arm was around her shoulders.

'You will stay here with me?' he asked again, and she could feel his face against her hair, his lips brushing her ear. She remembered Daniel licking her ear, and she wished Ryan would do that. It had felt nice. She had gone upstairs afterwards and washed her ear, but that was only because it was Daniel. Perhaps she should lick Ryan's ear. It might feel good for him. She touched his throat where he had unbuttoned the shirt, and her fingers fiddled with the second button, unfastening it so she could caress his neck beneath the collar of the shirt.

'Without Mary living here, you will have to marry me. No choice in the matter, Jane. We have to think about your reputation.' He was laughing when he said it, as though he had trapped her.

She knew he wasn't being serious, but she thought it was about time he did get serious. He was talking as if marriage was some sacrifice they had to make to propriety so he could keep her here to wash the dishes and make the porridge and so she didn't have to live alone in Richmond. She felt like telling him it was about time he tried instant porridge, but she didn't. That could wait. If he thought he could make his own porridge he might decide he didn't need her after all.

Why can't you just kiss me instead of just laughing at me, she thought, and then you will know how much I want you. Yet she felt good just sitting here close to him, relaxed and warm, while they talked. She knew that tonight she would sleep in his room and they would finally be lovers. But there was no hurry; they had all night.

'Jane, we don't have to live here if you don't want to. We can move to Richmond or Oxford or anywhere else you like. I do love this house. I only realised how much I loved it when I thought I might lose it, and I still can't really believe it's now ours. But I don't know if we can keep it going just by ourselves. It is expensive to run and will take a lot of work. John said he will retire and buy a house in Hayward village so Mary can stay living near Pat and us. He wants to make up to her for all the years they had to live apart. I was going to suggest to him that they could both live here with us, since there is plenty of room, but I wanted to ask you first. Having them here would help with the costs and with the work, and it would give us more freedom.

'They are coming to stay with us for a few days when they get back from Europe. He suggested that we all get together then, and talk about what we want to do. He is giving Pat and Claire some money to help them set up home in the lodge and get by until Pat gets a job and the probate is through. He didn't want me to have that expense. He thought you and he could share the responsibility of looking after the money and the investments for all of us. It would stay in our individual accounts, but you two would look after accounting and managing it. Then if anything happened to him, there would be someone left who knew what to do. He said that my father dying at fifty-five suddenly made him feel old, since he is the same age.

'I like him, Jane, and I already feel that he is part of our family. Pat couldn't have asked for a better man to be his father. He said it is going to take him a while to get used to it, though.

'But I still haven't got over the shock of Mary being married to him. It changes so many things. I thought it a bit unfair of her to spring it on us like that. They should have told us when he came here after my father died. He was telling us who would inherit, and he should have said then that he was Pat's father, and that he stood to benefit from my father's bequest to Mary. He told me tonight that the only person who knew was your father. Mary had told him right from the beginning. He thought that Daniel had guessed as well, but he was never sure, as Daniel had never said anything.'

'I think they were just so used to it being a secret that in the end they just didn't know how to tell us. He was the friend she always went to see on Saturdays. She had this strange secret life with her lover for years, and no one else knew. Last night when you and Pat were out for the stag night, she told me about him, but she didn't say even then that it was Mr Allanstone. I was as surprised as you were. She told me she had met him when she was nearly seventeen. He had stayed here for a few days with your father. She knew he was married right from the beginning because he had told her he was. He walked with her in the garden, and they talked about the flowers. Then he offered to take her to look at Kew Gardens. She told your grandmother that she was visiting a school friend, as she would never have been allowed out to meet a married man. They walked each week in parks and gardens, and on wet days in museums and art galleries, and eventually they had an affair. He wanted her to live with him, but she didn't want to leave here, as your grandmother needed her help. Pat was an accident, but he wanted her to keep the baby. He had once had a daughter, but she had died. His wife was sick, his mother looked after her, and he couldn't divorce her, and they went on like that for years. Eventually his mother died and his wife was put in a nursing home, but Mary couldn't leave your grandmother to run the house alone.

'Then last September his wife died. I remember my great-aunt going to the funeral for Mrs Allanstone not long before she died herself. I couldn't get the day off work to go with her, as we were short-staffed because two of the girls had flu. One of the ladies from the church went with her. I had never met his wife; I hadn't even known he was married. I remember you once said you were there and spoke with my great-aunt. It is strange that we nearly met then. I will tell you the rest tomorrow. I am so tired tonight.'

'Jane, you still haven't said if you will stay here with me. I've been patient for a long time, waiting until after Pat's wedding so it was just you and me left, and you had some space to think about it. You may find living here with me a bit reclusive, and I wanted you to consider that. You can have more time to think about it if you like. And I wanted to leave a decent amount of time after my father died. It's hard to really think straight for a while when things change so much. If you want to leave and go back to your old life, I would understand, and we could still be friends, but I would love you to stay here with me. We could get married in London, with just Pat and Claire, Aunt Mary and John, and Sarah and Tony. We could all go for dinner and dancing at the hotel where we went before, and stay the night there. I couldn't face another village hall wedding. We could honeymoon anywhere you like. You may want to go to Switzerland like your parents did, but only if you think you could cope with that.'

'Yes, I think that now I could cope. We could stay where they always stayed, and we could visit Robert Phillips. But if we were married in London, Reverend Colin would be disappointed.'

She was rather flattered that he had been planning a wedding, thinking out a guest list.

'I think he knows me well enough that he would entirely understand. But if you prefer, we can marry here in the church, same guests, with dinner and dancing in town, and Sarah and Tony could stay here overnight here. Mary and John as well, of course. But absolutely no village hall. Will you say yes to that?'

He sounded a little exasperated, so she didn't think it wise to bring up inviting the McCanns and John Phillips, Winston and Adrian, Julie and her mother, and Candy's family. Julie and Candy could be bridesmaids—they could use the same dresses—and she might even relent and have Alice and Jenny as well. And Ryan's three friends from Oxford could come; they had seemed nice enough young men. They could hold the reception here at Hayward Hall with caterers as they had for the funeral. They were not under any obligation to invite the whole village.

Still she did not answer him. He was always so controlled, but she suddenly felt shy and tongue-tied and rather nervous. When she was this close to him her heart didn't behave in the way it was supposed to, and rational thought fled, along with her ability to put words together in a sensible order. She wanted to say yes, to tell him she would like to sleep with him, but she was worried she would mess things up. She wished he would pull her closer, and at least let her know he wanted to make love to her even if he didn't do it. She went back to fiddling with the next shirt button.

'If you unbutton my shirt, Jane, I might unzip your dress. This one does have a zipper. I checked it out while we were dancing.'

She laughed and unfastened the button. But he didn't unzip the dress. Was it his way of telling her she was being too forward? Please just kiss me like you did once before, she thought. She lifted her head so her face was closer to his, and he would only need to lean over a little to kiss her, but still he didn't. She slid her arms around his neck, and he picked up the cat from his lap and put her down on the floor, so he could hold her closer.

The cat didn't appreciate the gravity of the situation, assumed Ryan had put her down by mistake, and jumped back onto his lap.

Jane suddenly knew what she wanted to say. She was tired of playing games. 'I would like to stay here with you, and I would like to marry you—I don't mind you being a recluse—but so far you've said you don't want to be here alone, you need someone to help wash up the dishes and cook the porridge, and it wouldn't look good if we were here together and not married. You never say you love me, and you never even try to kiss me. Apart from that one night in Richmond and the afternoon when we sat in the car at the gate, you are always so cold. That was a whole ten weeks ago and since then you've never once treated me like you wanted to make love to me. I was afraid you really wanted to go back to being a lone wolf. I would like us to be lovers, and I would like it to be forever. You said you would be happy to make love to me if I agreed to the conditions. I even went on the pill so it would be easier for you if you wanted to sleep with me.'

For a moment he sat in absolute silence, and her heart beat so strongly she could hear it. Had she gone too far? For a dreadful moment she thought perhaps his father had been telling the truth when he said Ryan couldn't make love to a girl, and she would be hurting him with her insistence that she wanted him to. Yet she knew she would marry him anyway, they could still sleep together, do things together, care about each other. Perhaps he just didn't like the idea of being so intimate with someone. She felt a bit like that too.

'Even if you don't want to, I would still stay with you. We can live here together and care about each other.' She knew she was floundering, but she was worried she had hurt him, and she was desperate to redeem the situation.

She said nothing more and still he was silent. It all seemed to be going horribly wrong.

'Jane, I'm rather lost for words,' he said at last. 'Thank you for doing that for me. You can't even begin to imagine how good that makes me feel. You know I want to make love to you. How could you doubt it? I'm sorry I made such a mess of it. Perhaps you will let me start again.

'I have loved you since the very first day you came here. We sat in the kitchen late that night, drinking cocoa, and I knew then that you and I were meant to be together, that I had found the other half of my soul. Even before that, on the day I first saw you when you were sixteen, you seemed so sad and vulnerable that I wanted to protect you and make you happy. For months now I have thought of nothing but you. I would sit in my room at the college trying to work, and I would be wondering where you were, who was with you, what you were thinking, wanting to ask you things and tell you things I had seen and done, wishing I was at Hayward with you. I would lie awake at night, unable to sleep, wondering if you were also awake and whether you ever thought of me in the night like I thought of you. I would lie there wishing you were beside me, and I could reach out and touch you and make love to you. When I came home on Fridays, I always hoped I would find you in the conservatory so I could sit very close to you, and if I was really lucky you might need another hug. Are you happy with this so far?'

'Yes, perfectly.' Well, she hadn't really expected him to be serious. He never was with her.

'I can't have you just live in sin with me. I would worry you were going to run away with the young farmer next door. I want you to be legally mine.'

He put down the cat again and knelt at her feet. 'The lone wolf would be greatly honoured if the wild rose would agree to become Mrs Linden, lady of the manor and wife of the squire, at Hayward Hall in the county of Oxfordshire. Will you marry me, Jane?'

The cat jumped onto Jane's lap, cross at all these unnecessary interruptions. Jane laughed, but she still did not give him an answer. He hardly gave her a chance to. He picked up the cat, put her firmly back in the kitchen and closed the door to Mary's room. Then he sat beside Jane again, pulling her close against him, caressing her hair.

The cat, outraged at the way she was being treated, mewed outside the door, but they ignored her pleading.

'Now where were we, Jane? You were about to say yes.'

'You were telling me why you want to marry me even though you never want to kiss me or make love to me.'

'I do want to, of course I do, but the last time I kissed you we both nearly got out of control. Passion tends to prevent people from thinking clearly, and I wanted to give you the chance to think it over as you once asked me to. There is much more to love than just sleeping together, and I wanted you to feel like that too. I have never wanted a girl before the way I want you. My father's mistress when I was a teenager rather put me off the whole thing.'

She felt more confident, and again she knew what to say. 'Mary said that when two people care for each other, making love is the most beautiful thing in the world. It is only sordid when it's just lust and you don't care about the other person. I don't mind if it takes us a little while to get used to being so close. I may need more time as well.'

She timidly put her hand on his knee as he sat next to her, spreading her fingers on the soft fabric of his suit, sliding her hand along his thigh as high as she dared but not anywhere near the whole way up, as though it was the most natural thing in the world for her to be doing. A little flutter of fire stirred inside her and she wondered how it could make her feel so good just to touch him. For a moment he seemed a little surprised. Then he put his hand over hers. She thought she had gone too far, and he would pull her hand away, but he didn't.

'That feels rather nice,' he said, amused. 'A little further up would be very nice, if you aren't too shy.' He was laughing at her again.

She was hit with a moment of panic, suddenly recalling the day Daniel had tried to make her touch him. 'I'm sorry but I am too shy. Please don't laugh at me.'

She moved her hand back to his shirt, playing with the next button, then unbuttoning the dark-blue silk waistcoat, slipping her hand into the warm space between the waistcoat and his shirt. That seemed safer. She suddenly recalled having done that before, but she couldn't remember when. Perhaps it was the night in Richmond. Had she unbuttoned his waistcoat then?

She had now undone several of his shirt buttons as well as the waistcoat. She swung her legs over his so she was almost sitting on his lap, pulled him down so they were lying on the sofa, and finally he was kissing her, his body warm beneath her touch, close against hers, but never close enough, her fingers finding his bare skin beneath his shirt, his hand stroking her thigh through the soft fabric of the dress. She was lost in the male scent of sandalwood and sweat, the passion overwhelming her like a flame, both of them short of breath, and she knew he wanted her as desperately as she wanted him.

'Will you sleep upstairs with me tonight?' he asked her. 'Just you and me alone together in the house. We won't go the whole way unless you want us to, but if you do want to, we'll work it out. I won't let it get out of control. You can have all the time you want to get used to it. If you just want to sleep that's fine, and I won't feel at all tortured. We have both had a very long and complicated day. Mary gave me some extra pillows recently. I think it was in case you came up to sleep with me. She's good about things like that. You don't need to bring your own pillow.'

'Did she leave a French letter in your drawer?' Jane couldn't resist asking him. 'Mary told me her mother used to do that for the guests. We were setting up the room for Mr Allanstone. You were with the police in Oxford, and she was trying to keep us all busy. Pat once told me that when he and Claire went missing on bonfire night, they had been upstairs in his room, and he had found one in a drawer in one of the other rooms, but it was old and hadn't been up to the job. It was probably about twenty years old.'

He laughed at that as she hoped he would.

'I suppose I should be thankful for that, or he may have been free to marry you. When Mary sent me to Richmond after you, she gave me a packet that she had pinched from my father's room. She handed it to me when she gave me your bottle of sedatives and told me not to waste my opportunity, but we were to talk about it first and not just let things get out of control. She said she didn't want to see you pregnant at nineteen like she was, and she wanted me to have you to myself for a couple of years before I had to share you. And she told me, like she told you, that if you love someone it would never seem sordid, and it would feel like the right thing to do. Mary is the best aunt in the world. The packet fell out my pocket when I gave you the bottle of sedatives, but I managed to pick it up before you saw it. I was horrified at what you would think of my intentions if you had seen it. So we would have been okay at Richmond, but you were a bit tipsy and I didn't want you to be left with nowhere to go if you regretted it the next day. I was very tempted, but I had promised that you were safe with me. I didn't want to take advantage of you when you were vulnerable, and I didn't want you to think you had no other choice than to marry me. Will you sleep upstairs with me?'

'Can you give me a quarter of an hour to change before I come up to your room? Would that be all right?' She could hardly believe she was saying it and even less that he had asked.

'Would you like help with the zipper?' he asked, and she laughed. 'You will come up, won't you? I could wait for you outside your door if you find the stairs a bit spooky at night. My bedroom is directly above yours. I lie there at night thinking how close you are to me. If I fell through the floor of my room, I would land in bed with you. Although you might be cross at being squashed. Do you need a brandy so you're not so nervous?'

'Why can't you ever be serious? No, I don't need a brandy. You would tell me I was tipsy, and you couldn't take advantage of me. I don't need to be drunk to want to sleep with you.'

She went up to her room, carrying the blue high-heeled shoes, while he tidied up the cups from the cocoa. She took off the dress and her tights, wiped off most of the makeup but not the eyeshadow, tidied her hair but left in the braids, freeing the ends of them so they would slowly unravel. She found her silk pyjamas and her dressing gown. High heels would look silly with pyjamas, so she put on her slippers, but they didn't feel very glamorous. Bare feet would be sexier. Upstairs there were no cold stone floors, only oak boards and carpet. She left the dressing gown in her room so she wore only the pyjamas. Indoors it was only slightly cold.

Her heart was thumping as she walked up the stairs to his room. Tonight was her chance to make him thaw. He had been drinking Champagne, dancing very close to her. That had worked magic for both of them once before, but she did still feel slightly nervous. Perhaps he was nervous as well; he had said he had never had a girlfriend before. She hoped he knew how it all worked, since she wasn't absolutely sure she did. But even if things didn't go quite right the first time, she wouldn't mind. They would sort it out. She would never want him to feel bad about it.

She looked down into the hallway from the gallery at the very top of the stairs, and she stood still for a moment with a strange impression that this had happened before. She had gone upstairs to his room, had stood here looking down into the hallway, the moonlight giving a silver glow to the window behind the landing, spilling over the stairs, filling the hallway with cold pale light so she didn't need the lights on, only the night light that was always left on near the desk below. She had walked up these stairs before in the moonlight, and something had happened, but she couldn't quite recall when it was or what had happened. She suddenly knew that it was when she had stood on the landing and seen the ghost standing on the bridge. Had she walked in her sleep? She felt as if she was remembering a dream. Daniel had told her that he sometimes saw his wife on the landing in the moonlight, and Ryan had seen her there on the night that Daniel had died, but tonight there was no one there, and no one on the bridge either. Daniel was with Caroline now. She would have no need to ever return to the landing. Had Caroline come back and pushed Daniel down the stairs to set her son free to marry Jane? Or had she just come back to be there for him when he died?

Ryan had left the lights on in the passage and in his room. She had never been in his bedroom before. It was the reverse of Daniel's room, since it was on the opposite corner of the front of the house, and was very like her own bedroom below, but tidier. The bed was an old four-poster, similar to Daniel's, and much larger than the double bed in her own room. There was the photo on the wall of herself at a school dance, wearing the dress that had misbehaved at the McCanns' farm when they had practised dancing for the wedding that Sunday afternoon. It now seemed so long ago.

For a moment they stood facing each other in silence. Then he held out his hands to her, she came close to him, and he kissed her as he had kissed her at Richmond, holding her against him with only the thin layers of their silk pyjamas between them. She wanted him to continue where they had left off when he had decided he would do the right thing and not take advantage of her. This time she hoped he wouldn't stop at just a kiss.

She pulled away from him and sat on the bed on the other side from the bedside table with his stained-glass lamp, his alarm clock, his watch and a photograph of the two of them together that had been taken when they were in Bath. She pulled back the covers, swung her feet under them, leant back on the pillows and sat hugging her knees.

'Can we please turn the lights off?' She felt awkward in the light, and she knew she would feel better lying beside him in dark.

He left the light on in the passage, with the door ajar, so if she needed to get up in the night, she wouldn't be completely lost in the darkness. There was only one lamp and it was on his side of the bed. He told her he would fix that before tomorrow night, so she had a lamp as well.

'Now come to bed,' she said.

He slipped in beside her, sat leaning back against the pillows as she was, his arm around her, and reached to turn off the lamp. Life was meant to be like this, she thought, a man and a woman safe and warm together in the darkness.

Through the open curtains she could see the stars in the midnight sky, blurred by the diamond panes of glass. There was moonlight on the trees in the garden, but the windows were in the moon's shadow.

For a while he just held her as he lay beside her, asking her if she just wanted to sleep, his fingers caressing her face and her hair, unravelling the braids. She told him she didn't just want to sleep, and she unbuttoned his pyjamas and her own, wanting to get closer to him, so his bare skin was against hers. He was kissing her, those magic gentle kisses, whispering to her, while she got used to the feel of his body against hers, male hair against her smooth skin, the thrill of his fingers touching her and hers touching him, no longer shy, and she was surprised that it all felt so natural and so good.

He was asking her to stay forever, telling her he couldn't believe she was really here with him, asking if she wanted to go the whole way. She did. He pulled off her pyjamas and his own and threw them onto the floor, so there was no longer anything between them, and she was lying beneath him, giving herself to him, his body melting into hers.

She was tense for the first moment, and she sensed he was too. Both of them lay still for another moment while he asked if she was okay, and she felt they couldn't get any closer than this. There were only the two of them, together and outside of time, two halves of one soul, and she wondered how something so physical could feel so spiritual. Did he feel that too? Then she was moving beneath him, her body one with his, lost in a warm glow of pure joy that built up slowly then broke over her in waves, catching at her breath.

She lay back, warm and strangely content, while her heart rate slowed, but he was still moving, and she felt his release, his tension gone, his muscles still strong beneath her hands but his body relaxing against hers and his breath ragged, and she knew they had worked it out. The bed had creaked, but at least they were alone in the house.

She had never imagined how good it would feel, and she hoped it felt this good for him too. She was still too shy to ask him that. He had once told her he had never wanted to make love to a girl. Yet now he had made love to her, and she knew he had wanted to. He had asked her. She had not coerced him.

Afterwards they lay still, his heart beating against hers, and she felt very close to him, as though she could almost feel what he was feeling, think what he was thinking.

'I feel like I belong here with you,' she whispered.

'I felt you belonged here with me the first day you came here and every day since. Jane, you will stay with me, please say you'll stay. You're mine now.'

She told him she would stay forever, would marry him if he wanted, and his fingers caressed her face while they decided whether they would share a room, or have two adjacent rooms, or both stay where they were and she would come up to his room each night. She said she would keep her own room so if they had a row, she could go back to sleeping there.

'We never row,' he murmured, kissing her neck. 'What could we ever row about? We have lived in the same house for six months and we have never once rowed. From the first we were friends, and now we are lovers as well.'

'You won't go back to stay in your room at Oxford and leave me alone here at night, will you?' she whispered. 'And you won't ever go back to being a lone wolf?'

'No, and no. Giving up both of those has its compensations. You have given me your body in exchange for my soul, and I'm happy with the bargain. But you are to honour your side of it. I expect loyalty. From now on you're only kissing me.'

She asked him what Jimmy had said to him, but he just laughed and wouldn't tell her.

'You did really want to do this, didn't you?' she whispered, the thought still nagging her.

'Yes, of course. From the very first time you sat close to me on the swing, I thought sleeping with you might feel rather nice. I knew it would all seem right if it was with you.'

'Why did you make me wait so long?' she asked him next. 'You were rather a reluctant lover. Although I do understand now about the creaky bed, and I'm glad there's no one else in the house. They probably heard it from the McCanns' farm.'

He laughed at that and said he would try tightening the screws.

'I thought we both needed some time to get over what happened. I felt very guilty that my father had died and left me with the house and the money and you. I still feel I have cheated him, but I'll get over it. We can't change what happened. I also feel bad that I didn't protect you well enough that night. He could have killed you while Pat and I were playing snooker in the next room. We all failed you, all of us, right from when you first complained to me about him touching you. I should never have brought you back here from Richmond. You had finally found the courage to leave, and I persuaded you to return. Mary and I were always afraid to stand up to his temper tantrums, and Pat thought only of what you could do for him if you married my father.

'I would never have wished him dead, but it is a great relief to me that we weren't forced into being fugitives. Even without your money we could have managed quite well on what I could earn. We could have bought a house in Oxford with the money I inherited from my grandmother. But we would have been hiding where we lived, and I would have been worried for your safety every time I left you in the house by yourself. We could never have lived like that. Even if he had come around to accepting it, I would never have left you alone with him again, ever.

'And I needed us to be somewhere by ourselves, not sneaking around in the night with other people in the house, even if it was only Mary. I asked you if you would like us to go to Richmond for a few days next weekend. I thought it would be easier for both of us if we were by ourselves, and I wasn't expecting us to be alone here tonight. And you once told me you wanted us to wait until Pat was married. I thought perhaps you were hoping something would go wrong and the wedding wouldn't happen so Pat was still free to marry you.'

She was not sure if he was being serious. 'I would never have married Pat,' she told him. 'You know that. It was his idea, not mine. It was always you I wanted, but you kept telling me you were a lone wolf and didn't want a girlfriend. I never gave up hope though, even when you told me you'd rather jump out of an aeroplane than make love to me. I thought I belonged with you when we sat in the café in January, and when we walked in the wood, I felt that we had been lovers through all time. The first day I came here to this house, I felt I had come home. I'm not sleeping here by myself though. I would never be brave enough to do that. There are too many ghosts.'

The cat, confused at finding Jane's bed cold and empty, had wandered up and found them. Jane heard the slight movement of the door and felt the soft bump as Jasmine jumped onto the bed and settled near their feet. She told Ryan it was just the cat, but he was by then asleep. She felt warm and safe beside him. She couldn't help feeling a little glow of triumph that he was finally hers. She had tamed the lone wolf.

Sunday 16 May 1976

She awoke in the night, well before dawn. The sky was dark and scattered with stars, and there was still moonlight on the garden. She realised she had forgotten to take her pill for the night; the packet was in her bathroom. She didn't want to wake him, and she was glad that he had left the door to the passage ajar so she had some light. She found her pyjamas on the floor beside the bed, slipped out into the lighted corridor as quietly as she could, put on the pyjamas and went to the top of the stairs.

The moon was a little past full, the pale light shining through the gothic window, lighting the hallway with a glow of silver, sending strange twisted shadows of the balustrade across the tiled floor a long way below her. For more than a century, longer than anyone's lifetime, the moon had shone thus through this window. She wanted to see Caroline on the landing with Daniel, but there was no one there, only cold moonlight and deep shadows, and photographs of Caroline and Daniel and the beautiful young man Nicholas who had died in the War at nineteen. All of them gone while the world carried on without them.

She went rapidly down the stairs to her own floor, conscious that she was the only one awake in the house, but she made a mistake and descended one flight too many, finding herself standing beside the photographs on the landing below the window, looking down into the hallway below.

A strange chill came up from the base of her spine and left her shaking, a déjà vu feeling that this had all happened long before in a dream. She tried to keep the memory in her mind, cling to the thread of it, lest it slip away from her as dreams often do when they see the first light of day. She sat down on the carpet and closed her eyes, trying to recall what had happened.

She remembered leaving her room in the dead of night, moving a chair and unlocking the door, wanting to find Ryan, wanting to slip into bed beside him so he could hold her safe all night. She remembered climbing the stairs to his floor with the stairwell bathed in the same weird silver glow of moonlight, then reaching the darkness of the top floor passage. Which was his room? She had thought she could find it in the darkness, but she wasn't sure. She knew it was above hers, but it was pitch dark in the corridor. The moonbeams, cold and uncaring, could only go their own way in their own direction, oblivious to her need for light, for they had no power to turn and illuminate the way along the passage. She had not known where to find the light switch. Suppose she got the wrong room and found herself in bed with Pat or Daniel.

She had taken a few steps along the passage, but the darkness beyond the moonlit hallway was absolute. Defeated she had turned and gone back down the stairs, but she had gone one flight too far, had found herself standing on the landing, just as she had tonight, with the moonlight behind her. Above her the bridge had been touched with moonglow, and she had seen a dark shape standing there, watching her. Was it a ghost? She had not had time to think about it further, as someone had been coming up the stairs. She had known it was Daniel, but she had been unable to move. She had felt like a doomed and frightened rabbit, caught in the glare of a spotlight, mesmerised while it waited for the sound of the shot.

He had been coming upstairs to bed, defeated and weary but still sober enough to climb the stairs. He had seen her in the moonlight, silhouetted against the window. He kept repeating his wife's name,

'Caroline, Caroline, my beautiful Caroline. I love you. I never loved anyone but you. And I'm sorry I hurt him. I am so, so sorry.'

He had reached the landing. Then he had pulled her close to him, still whispering his wife's name, covering her face with gentle kisses, his lips brushing hers, his tongue finding hers, his arms holding her against him as if he could never let her go.

All the while she had let him do it, paralysed by sleep.

He had been kissing her neck, his hand on her breast through the silk of her pyjamas. 'Caroline, you're back with me now, and life will be good again. Come up to bed.'

She had unbuttoned his waistcoat, sliding her hands beneath it, feeling his body warm and lean beneath her fingers. She had started to unbutton his shirt, her body responding to the pressure of his. A button came off, slipping through her fingers. She would need to find it later so she could sew it back on. His hands had been inside her pyjamas, hers inside his shirt. She had wanted to get closer to him. She had felt her mouth responding to his kisses, her body moving against his, her arms pulling him closer to her, the touch of his fingers setting her on fire. She remembered saying she loved him, that she would go upstairs with him.

But then he had suddenly pulled away from her, one hand clutching at his chest, swaying unsteadily and reaching out his other hand for the banister. For a long moment he had stood there, gasping for air, supported against the stair rail, before he crumpled and fell backwards.

She had tried to grab his shirt, but it was too late, and she had watched him fall down the stairs in the soft, cold glow of the moonlight, heard the thud as his head hit one of the treads.

Had she pushed him, finally avenging her mother and Ryan, or had he just fallen? She was sure he had just fallen. She remembered looking up at the bridge, but the ghost was gone. There was only the moonlight caressing the balustrade.

There was a dim light by the desk which was always left on all night. He had been lying on the stairs. She had known she could never pull him back up to the landing, so she had pulled him backwards down the staircase, until he was lying flat on the cold tiles of the hallway floor. She had felt for a pulse, but she had known he was dead. For a while she had held him, lying across him on the cold hard floor, listening for a heartbeat, still whispering she loved him, kissing his face; then she had straightened his clothes, tucked in his shirt.

She had remembered she had come downstairs for a sleeping tablet, so she had gone into the kitchen and taken the bottle from the cupboard, checking it was the right one as she walked back past the nightlight in the hallway. She had thought Daniel might need one so she had gone into the den, lit only by the moonlight through the window, and put the bottle next to the whisky glass. He would take one with his next drink, then he would sleep, and he wouldn't bother her again that night.

Then, still asleep, she had gone back up the stairs to her room and locked the door. She didn't need the chair next to it, he could no longer harm her, so she had returned it to the dressing table, and had gone back to bed.

Had she walked in her sleep on that fateful night? Or was it all something that her mind had put together afterwards in a dream, weaving together the past and the present into a frightening memory of something that had never really happened? It couldn't be real. She would put it forever from her mind, tuck it into a dark corner where it could once more fade into the underworld of lost dreams and never trouble her again.

She remembered the times she had walked in her sleep when she was younger, crushed by the loss of her parents and the total collapse of her safe sheltered life. She would remember in perfectly clear detail, often weeks later, what she had done while asleep. Usually she had taken something from a cupboard and put it somewhere else, with some strange logic for why it needed to be moved. Her aunt had blamed the diazepam, and the night that Daniel had died she had taken one to calm her down. She would never take a sedative again, ever.

She went back up to her bathroom, found the packet, and swallowed the pill for Saturday. For a moment she thought of staying in her own bedroom, she felt too shaken to go back upstairs, but she thought Ryan would wake up and find her gone and think she hadn't wanted to be with him.

She returned to his room, barefoot on the stairs, glancing behind her at the silent moonlit landing, but there were no ghosts there, only photographs, lingering echoes of those who were gone, still alive in our memories, but separated from us by a chasm of time that could never come again.

The passage light was still on, so she had no trouble finding his door. She took off her pyjamas and dropped them back onto the floor, then gently slipped back into the bed, not wanting to wake him. But he was awake.

'Jane, what happened? I woke up and you were gone. I thought perhaps I had dreamt it all, but your scent was still on the pillow. I was about to come and look for you. I was worried you were packing your case to leave in the morning. Jane, you're shaking. Are you okay?'

'I was remembering a nightmare.'

'Was the nightmare finding yourself in bed with me?'

She knew he was trying to make her laugh.

'No, of course not, that was a dream come true. I went down to my bathroom. I didn't want to wake you up. It was spooky with the moonlight on the stairs, and it reminded me of the night your father died. I remembered I had a dream that it was me who pushed him down the stairs. I'm okay now. Ryan, you don't blame me for what happened, do you? Sometimes I blame myself.'

'Blame you? Why should I blame you? You were locked in your room the whole night. He had a heart attack; no one pushed him. He's with my mother now. I know that because I saw them together on the landing. I still don't know whether I really saw them, or if it was part of a dream, and sometimes I think perhaps I did push him down the stairs, but forgot I did it. When the police questioned me, I started to feel confused about the whole thing. I knew I couldn't tell them that I saw my mother's ghost. They would never have believed me, and they would have thought it was you or Mary I saw. But they seemed to realise I was not telling them the whole truth, and I don't even know what the truth is. I only know that something strange happened that night, something that I will never be able to explain. I think he really did reach the landing, but if he had died there, he would not have been lying where he was. I wish I had gone downstairs, as I still wonder if I could have saved his life. At least then he would have had someone with him when he died, and I could have told him that I cared about him, even if he could never love me.

'For a long time I felt so bad about that night, I could think of nothing else. I had failed to protect you from him, and then he had died, and I felt so guilty that I had not gone downstairs when I saw him on the landing. I know I should have checked he was okay, but I was still so angry with him, and seeing my mother's ghost left me confused and unsure if I was simply dreaming.

'But time does help you to get things back in perspective. We can't change the past, and now it all seems a lifetime ago. I did ask the inspector if my father could have survived if there had been someone else there when he fell, and he said he thought it unlikely. The police were satisfied he died of natural causes, but I will always wonder what really happened. You're safe from him now, and nothing matters tonight except you and me. Come here, Jane.'

He held her close until she stopped shaking.

'Did you really think I was leaving?' she asked him.

'I will always worry that you will leave. I was afraid you wanted it all to be perfect, and I would make a mess of it. But it was perfect for me, and when you responded like you did, it all seemed so right. I will happily be your slave forever if that is what it takes for you to want to stay here with me.'

Had he been afraid of disappointing her? He had tried all his life to please his father, but had always failed. Was he worried he would fail to please her?

'It was perfect for me as well. And even if it wasn't, even if it had all gone wrong, or you hadn't wanted us to do this, even if you never wanted us to, I would still stay here with you for as long as you want me to. Wherever you are is home to me, and I will always think you are the most wonderful man in the world. I don't expect things to be perfect. I am happy with life being good.'

He made love to her again, moving slowly. She whispered she loved him, she felt very close to him, she would never leave him, and she asked if it felt good for him. He told her it was the most exquisite thing he had ever done, the closest he had ever felt to heaven, and she always made him feel glad to be alive.

The cat was still asleep near their feet, occasionally a little restless, stalking a mouse in her dreams, but otherwise oblivious to the disturbance of the bedclothes and the soft words of the lovers, and unaware that she would soon have to contend with a dog in the house.

Jane awoke to the morning sun shining through the windows, filling the room with joyous soft light. He was sitting beside her on the bed, touching her face, already dressed except for his jacket.

'Jane, wake up. I let you sleep as long as I could, but it's half past eight, and we have to be at church at ten. I found where Mary keeps the porridge, but I don't know how to cook it, so we will have to make do with toast again. I've fed the cat and picked the flowers. I tried to do the paper for them, but I've made a bit of a mess of it. You may need to do it again. Are you okay? Do you have a headache from the Champagne?'

'I'm fine. I didn't drink very much of it. Can't we just stay in bed today? I hardly had any sleep.' She was conscious that she wasn't wearing anything, so she pulled the sheet up around her neck and held onto it warily in case he pulled it off and left her exposed.

'Jane, I still can't believe last night really happened. But here you are in my room, and you're not wearing much, so I know I didn't dream it. I asked you to stay here and marry me—I remember that—downstairs on the sofa, but I don't think you actually answered then. The cat kept getting in the way. I asked you again when you were up here in bed with me, and I think you said yes, but you were saying yes to quite a lot of things by then. Is it still yes? You haven't changed your mind? You will stay, won't you? You're not regretting last night?'

'I will stay, and I haven't changed my mind.'

'Jane, can you keep it a secret just for now. Will you do that for me? After coping with all those people at Pat's wedding yesterday, I don't think I could face them all congratulating us today. Yesterday they were all hinting I ought to marry you, since you were staying alone in the house with me. If we turn up today engaged, they may think we have spent the night misbehaving. If we don't turn up at all, it will look even worse. Can we just leave them guessing today?'

'Can't I even hold your hand?'

'Yes, but do it discreetly. Then when we do announce it, there is the problem of what to say when they ask you where you were when I proposed, or worse still they ask me where I was when you accepted. People always ask that. It is part of the ritual. We need to have a very serious discussion about this. If we say on a sofa having cocoa before bed, it would be okay, as it sounds only slightly suspicious. What happened next, and where we slept, would be left to their imagination. But you didn't actually accept until you were in bed with me *sans* pyjamas. That won't do at all. Since we can't tell the truth, we need to agree on what we do say so we have a consistent story.

'Later this week, perhaps Friday, we can go to Richmond. I need to be in Oxford each day until then. You'll be here by yourself, but I'll be back before dark. If you can't cope with that, you can come with me and sit in the library or my room at the college. On Friday we can drive across to Richmond, get the dresses cleaned, and I'll buy you an engagement ring. I could propose to you again in Kew Gardens—we enjoyed walking there—or in that little café. That morning in January when we sat there, I realised that I wanted to live my whole life with you. We sat in the café again when I stayed with you in March, and I wanted to tell you I loved you then, but I was there to protect you, and I wanted you to feel safe.

'We can ask Sarah and Tony to have dinner with us on Friday night to celebrate being engaged. Same hotel so we can dance, and you can wear the sexy black dress. And this time I really will untie the dress, but I promise not until we get back home. Then next Sunday you can show off your ring at church here, and say I proposed in Kew Gardens. That sounds romantic and quite respectable, as you would obviously have been fully clothed at the time. In the afternoon we can go to see my grandfather. Are you happy with all that?'

By this time Jane was shaking with laughter.

'We'll have to ask Anne to feed the cat if we go to Richmond. And your mother's engagement ring was sitting in a glass dish in her room, so Mary found it a box after your father died, and we put it in the safe. We could reuse it as your grandfather once suggested, although Mary said it was probably worth more than the house, so perhaps I would be too frightened to wear it, in case it was lost. I'll be okay here by myself in the day. We're supposed to have a cooked breakfast on Sunday, but it's too late for that now. We're already missing Mary; I'll never be able to run this house as well as she did. Now be a gentleman and turn your back while I retrieve the pyjamas that have mysteriously folded themselves and jumped onto a chair. I don't recall folding them.'

'I like my room to be neat,' he explained, turning his back, but Jane saw there was a mirror beyond him, and he was laughing at her.

'Yes, I see that won't work unless you promise to close your eyes as well. I'm not sure I trust you quite that much. Go down and make the toast so I can get up, and make the coffee quite strong, or I will fall asleep in church.'

He picked up a length of blue ribbon, which had fallen from her hair when he had unravelled the braids, and he tied it around the bed post.

'Trophy,' he said with a wicked smile.

He put her pyjamas on the bed beside her and pretended to pull the sheet away. Then he picked up his jacket, and she heard him whistling as he went down to make the breakfast, his feet light and swift on the stairs. She knew that he was happy, and free from the last of the ghosts of his past. The rift between her father and his could never be healed, but it was finally buried with them.

She returned to her own room, put on the layered summer dress she had bought when they were together in Richmond, wiped off the last of the eye makeup and did it anew—the blue eye shadow, the smudgy eyeliner and the dark tear-proof mascara—brushed her hair, sprayed on her Chanel perfume. She picked up her shoes and her silk cardigan, the straw hat with the lace and the flowers, put a lipstick in her handbag, and went downstairs.

'I remember that dress,' he said. 'You bought it when we were in Richmond, and I thought about us lying on a picnic blanket deep in a forest on a summer day.'

'Just lying?' she asked him, remembering he had laughed when she had shown him the dress, and said he had thought something wicked.

'No, Jane, not just lying. Those buttons looked very tempting.'

'I always wanted to see you in just your jeans, without your shirt. We have our own forest here; perhaps we could do both things this afternoon. We could shut the gates.'

'How will I get through church, thinking of that?'

Her coffee and toast were waiting, and she still had twenty minutes for breakfast before they needed to leave. She ate the toast, drank the coffee, adjusted the paper around the flowers, placed them in the basket for Ryan to carry, put on her lipstick, the silk cardigan, the shoes and the hat. The wreath she had worn at the wedding was still on the kitchen table, so she added it to the flowers in the basket. At the last moment she remembered the five-pound notes, and Ryan fetched them from the safe.

He put on his jacket and picked up his father's black trilby hat from the boot room, and she laughed as he checked how the hat looked in the mirror by the back door.

'I'm the squire now,' he said by way of explanation, 'so I need the squire's hat. And you are now the squire's lady. What more could I ever want?'

'A dog?' she suggested. He flashed her his beautiful smile, and she knew he was finally feeling relaxed and happy. And he was now hers, eternally and irrevocably hers.

She followed him out into the already warm sunshine. Summer was here a little early. There was blossom on the apple trees in the orchard, blossom on the cherry trees. She would ask Mary how to bottle the brandied cherries so she could make Ryan a Black Forest cake for his birthday next year.

Only the future mattered, their future. She knew Ryan had now broken free from the past, from the conflict with his father, the worry of being accused of something he didn't do, and the safety of being a lone wolf. She would still need to encourage him to trust her, and both of them still needed time to fully heal from the guilt. He had helped her so much, and she knew she had helped him. And she had come to terms with her own past. She could think back on her childhood in Kent, and her schooldays, and her life with her great-aunt in Richmond, without collapsing into tears, grateful for the love that had always surrounded her. Although the pain never fully went away, if you allowed the sorrow to heal, the memories of the love would overcome it. You couldn't let grief and loss define your life. You had to go forward and care for the people who were left, glad that you still had someone to love. Her parents were dead, her great-aunt was dead, Daniel was dead, but she still had Ryan and Mary and John and Pat and Claire and soon the new baby.

In all the history of the world no one has ever found a way to change one single moment of what happened in the past. We need to accept it, and only then can we go forward.

She looked back at the house, warm and mellow, its darkest secrets still safely hidden, the beautiful garden enjoying the gentle touch of the sunshine. She could always feel her father near her when she walked in the garden, and she could feel the laughter of the long-ago children who still haunted this place, their voices surrounding her, their childhood living on forever in the sunbeams and the soft warm scent of spring flowers.

Perhaps there would be children here again, her and Ryan's children, Pat and Claire's children, cousins together, Rosemary and Michael and Charles and Eloise, excited young voices in the corridors, childish laughter echoing in the stairwell, light steps running across the hallway and bursting out into the bright sunshine in a beautiful garden. The house would embrace them as it had embraced her, patient, loving and forgiving, sharing their joys and feeling their sorrows. There would be another generation of Lindens whose hopes, dreams and memories would become locked until eternity in its warm stones.

Locked away forever with them would be the last fractured shards of the memory of what had really happened on the night that Daniel had died. It was just a dream. Of course it was just a dream.

But then she remembered Ryan asking her if she had come up to his room that night. He had heard a step in the corridor, her scent had lingered there after she had gone back downstairs, and he had seen her on the landing and thought her the ghost of his mother, returning to finally free her son from the madness of his father so he could marry the girl he loved. She had seen him standing on the bridge, a dark shadow in the moonlight, and she had thought he was a ghost. But Daniel hadn't been pushed. He had died from heart failure. He had reached the landing, and this time the ghost of his wife had still been there, waiting for him, returning his kisses, her body responding to his embrace, and he had died believing he was back with her. Jane knew it wasn't just a dream. She really had given him that one last precious gift.

One day she would tell Ryan what really happened that night, but not today. Or perhaps never at all. Would he be happier believing he really had seen his mother's ghost on the night his father died?

She put her hand in his as they walked down the lane to the church in the sunshine, with just enough time to lay the flowers on the graves before the service began.

Kathleen, who had lost the love of her life but had still cared steadfastly for her family. Jane placed the wreath of white roses on her grave, thinking how she had lived for so much of her life under the shadow of what her son had done to hurt her grandson, her nephew and Josie. She knew Kathleen would have been glad that she and Ryan were together.

The children Charles and Eloise, who had died as babies, never feeling the warmth of the sun on their faces or the soft touch of the wind in their hair, never hearing a bird sing or knowing that the sky is blue.

Caroline who had died so tragically, leaving a husband adrift in a lifetime of heartache and bitterness, and a miracle baby to grow up without his mother's love and protection.

And there was Daniel, whose obsession with his dead wife had damaged the lives of everyone around him, now back with Caroline somewhere beyond time.

A new inscription now filled the space beneath the one for Caroline, above the line of Latin.

IN LOVING MEMORY OF

CAROLINE ANN LINDEN

DIED 5 MARCH 1949 AGED 26

LOVED WIFE OF DANIEL MOTHER OF RYAN

AND OF HER HUSBAND

DANIEL JAMES LINDEN

DIED 22 MARCH 1976 AGED 55

LOVED BROTHER OF MARY FATHER OF RYAN

UNCLE OF PAT AND COUSIN OF JANE

FINIS VITAE SED NON AMORIS

In her mind she added another line. There was just enough space below the Latin.

REUNITED WITH HELP FROM JANE ELLEN WALTERS

HOUSE LAYOUT AND FAMILY TREE

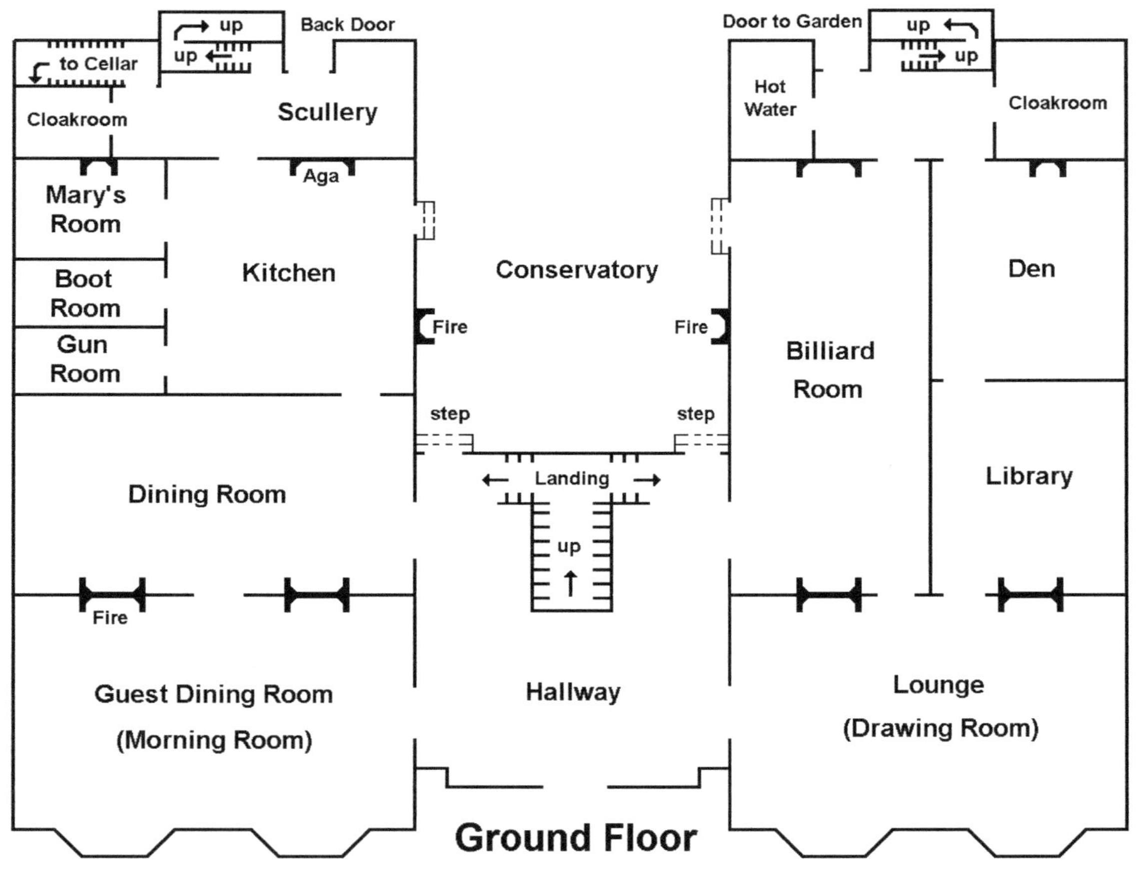

up
to Cellar
up
Back Door
Door to Garden
up
up
Cloakroom
Scullery
Hot Water
Cloakroom
Mary's Room
Aga
Kitchen
Conservatory
Den
Boot Room
Fire
Fire
Billiard Room
Gun Room
step
step
Dining Room
Landing
Library
up
Fire
Guest Dining Room
(Morning Room)
Hallway
Lounge
(Drawing Room)
Ground Floor

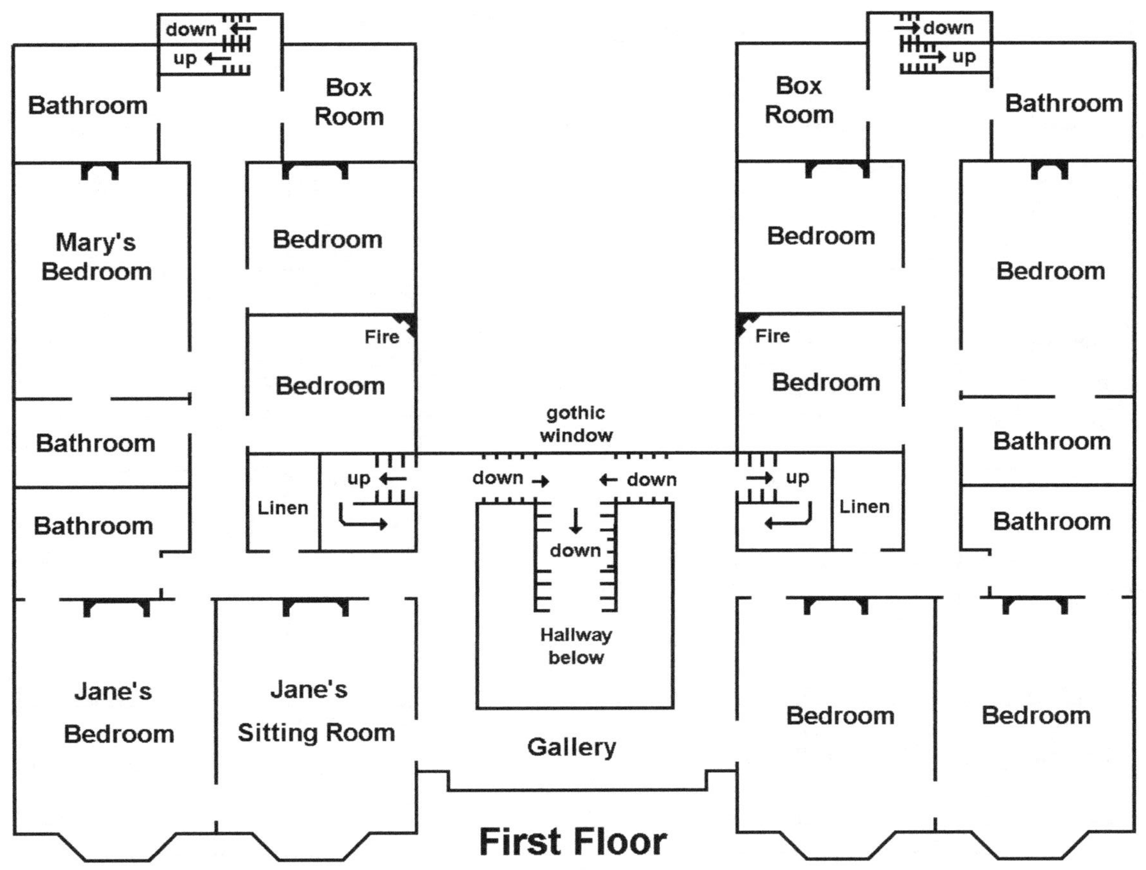

Bathroom
Box Room
down
up
Box Room
Bathroom
Mary's Bedroom
Bedroom
Bedroom
Bedroom
Fire
Bedroom
gothic window
Fire
Bedroom
Bathroom
Bathroom
up
Linen
down
down
up
Linen
Bathroom
Bathroom
down
Hallway below
Jane's Bedroom
Jane's Sitting Room
Gallery
Bedroom
Bedroom
First Floor

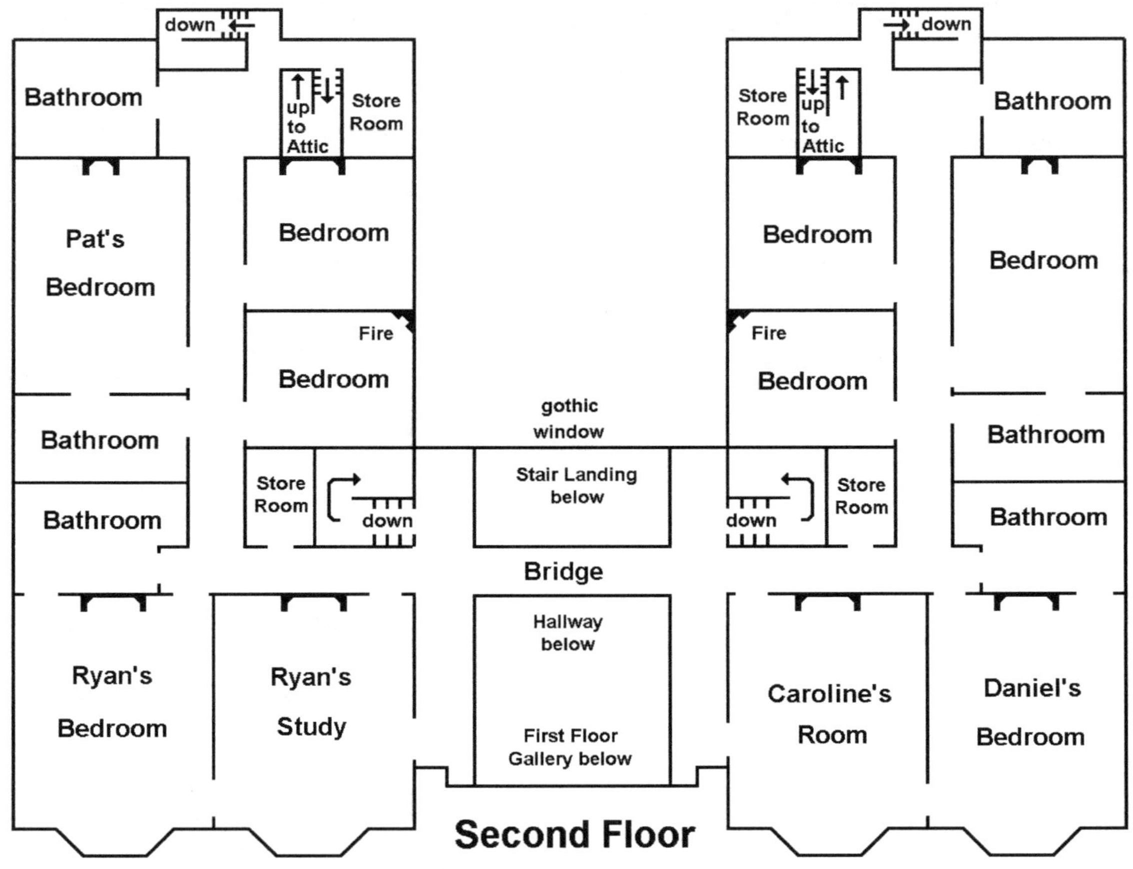
down
up to Attic
Store Room
Store Room
up to Attic
down
Bathroom
Bathroom
Pat's Bedroom
Bedroom
Bedroom
Bedroom
Bathroom
Bathroom
Bedroom
Fire
Fire
Bedroom
gothic window
Bathroom
Bathroom
Store Room
down
Stair Landing below
down
Store Room
Bridge
Ryan's Bedroom
Ryan's Study
Hallway below
First Floor Gallery below
Caroline's Room
Daniel's Bedroom
Second Floor

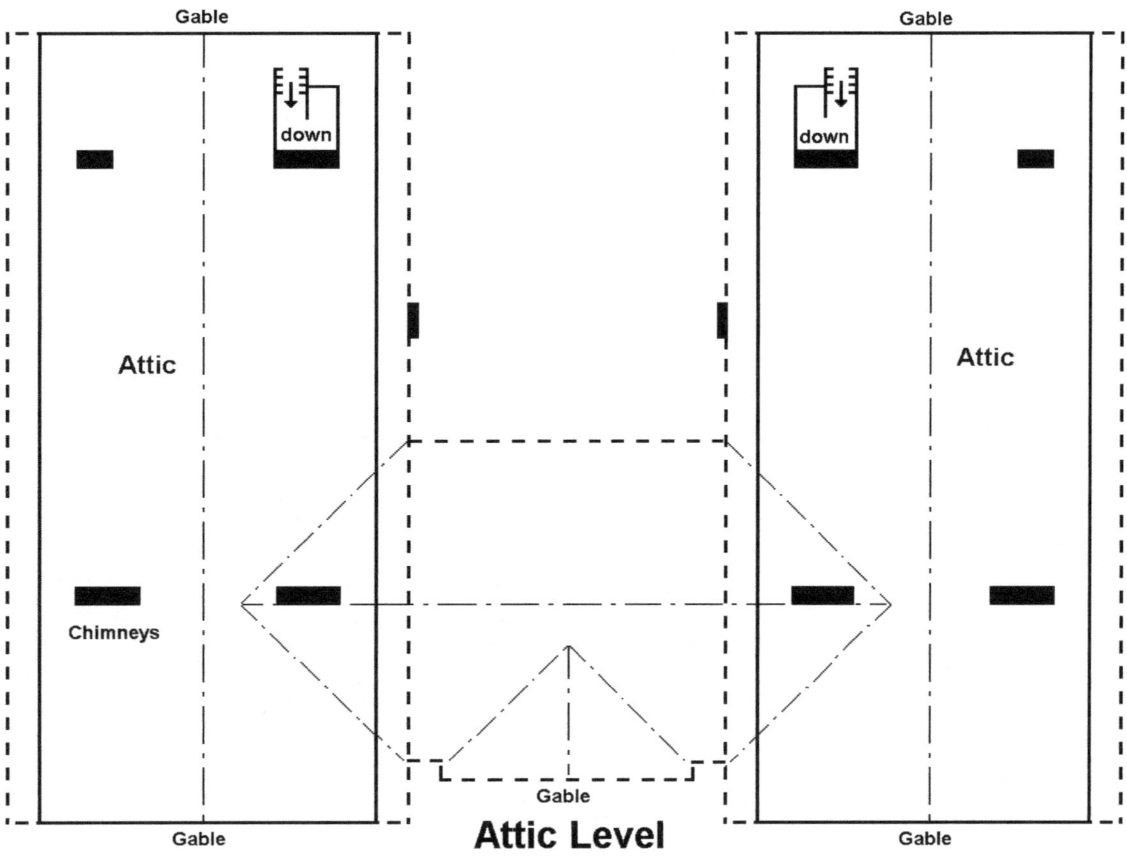

Gable
down
Attic
Chimneys
Gable
Gable
down
Attic
Gable
Gable
Attic Level

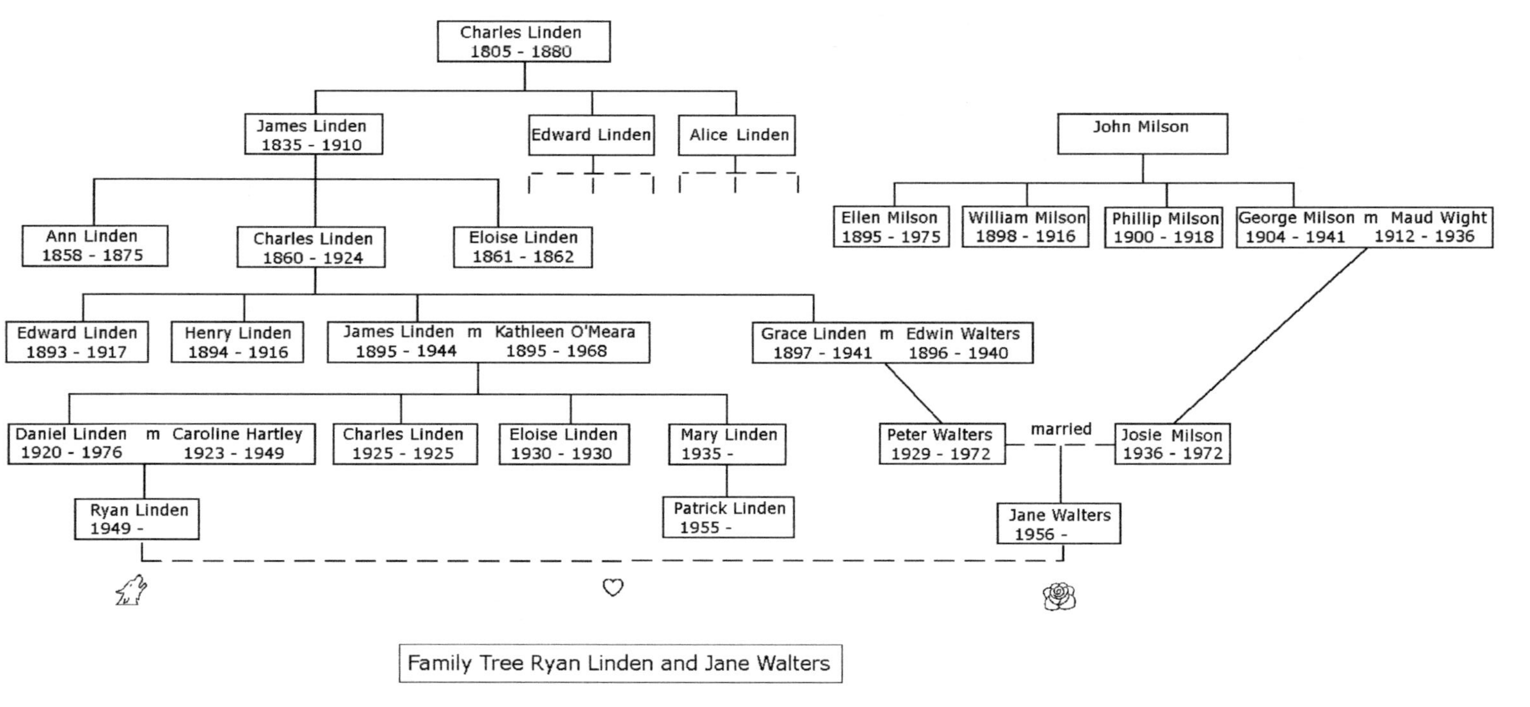

Family Tree Ryan Linden and Jane Walters